Collected Stories

Collected Stories

RUTH RENDELL

Pantheon Books, New York

First American Edition

Copyright © 1987 by Kingsmarkham Enterprises Ltd.

All rights reserved under International and Pan-American Copyright Conventions. Published in the United States by Pantheon Books, a division of Random House, Inc., New York. Originally published in Great Britain as *Collected Short Stories* by Hutchinson Ltd.

"Means of Evil" ("The Case of the Shaggy Caps") © Kingsmarkham Enterprises Ltd 1977; "Achilles Heel" ("Inspector Wexford on Holiday") © Kingsmarkham Enterprises Ltd 1978; "Old Wives' Tales," "When the Wedding Was Over" and "Ginger and the Kingsmarkham Chalk Circle" © Kingsmarkham Enterprises Ltd 1979

The Fever Tree and Other Stories © Kingsmarkham Enterprises Ltd 1982

The New Girl Friend and Other Stories © Kingsmarkham Enterprises Ltd 1985

"The Fallen Curtain" and "The Clinging Woman" © Ruth Rendell 1974; "The Venus Fly Trap" ("Venus's Flytrap") © Ruth Rendell 1973; "A Bad Heart" ("Trapped") © Ruth Rendell 1973; "The Double" ("Meeting in the Park"), "The Fall of a Coin" and "Almost Human" © Ruth Rendell 1975; "You Can't Be Too Careful," "People Don't Do Such Things," "The Vinegar Mother" and "Divided We Stand" © Ruth Rendell 1976

Stories from *Means of Evil* and *The Fallen Curtain* used by arrangement with Doubleday, a division of Bantam/Doubleday/Dell group.

Library of Congress Cataloging-in-Publication Data

Rendell, Ruth, 1930–Collected stories.
Collected stories from the author's early career.
Contents: The fallen curtain—Means of evil—The fever tree—[etc.]
1. Detective and mystery stories, English. I. Title.
PR6068.E63A6   1988   823'.914   87-35949
ISBN 0-394-56942-3

Manufactured in the United States of America

Contents

The Fallen Curtain

The Fallen Curtain

The incident happened in the spring after his sixth birthday. His mother always referred to it as 'that dreadful evening', and always is no exaggeration. She talked about it a lot, especially when he did well at anything, which was often as he was good at school and at passing exams.

Showing her friends his swimming certificate or the prize he won for being top at geography: 'When I think we might have lost Richard that dreadful evening! You have to believe there's Someone watching over us, don't you?' Clasping him in her arms: 'He might have been killed – or worse.' (A remarkable statement, this one.) 'It doesn't bear thinking about.'

Apparently, it bore talking about. 'If I'd told him once, I'd told him fifty times never to talk to strangers or get into cars. But boys will be boys, and he forgot all that when the time came. He was given sweets, of course, and *lured* into this car.' Whispers at this point, meaning glances in his direction. 'Threats and suggestions – persuaded into goodness knows what – I'll never know how we got him back alive.'

What Richard couldn't understand was how his mother knew so much about it. She hadn't been there. Only he and the Man had been there, and he couldn't remember a thing about it. A curtain had fallen over that bit of his memory that held the details of that dreadful evening. He remembered only what had come immediately before it and immediately after.

They were living then in the South London suburb of Upfield, in a little terraced house in Petunia Street, he and his mother and his father. His mother had been over forty when he was born and he had no brothers or sisters. ('That's why we love you so much, Richard.') He wasn't allowed to play in the street with the other kids. ('You want to keep yourself to yourself, dear.') Round the corner in Lupin Street lived his gran, his father's mother. Gran never came to their house, though he thought his father would have liked it if she had.

'I wish you'd have my mother to tea on Sunday,' he once heard his father say.

'If that woman sets foot in this house, Stan, I go out of it.'

So gran never came to tea.

'I hope I know what's right, Stan, and I know better than to keep the boy away from his grandmother. You can have him round there once a week with you, so long as I don't have to come in contact with her.'

That made three houses Richard was allowed into, his own, his gran's, and the house next door in Petunia Street where the Wilsons lived with their Brenda and their John. Sometimes he played in their garden with John, though it wasn't much fun as Brenda, who was much older, nearly sixteen, was always bullying them and stopping them getting dirty. He and John were in the same class at school, but his mother wouldn't let him go to school alone with John, although it was only three streets away. She was very careful and nervous about him, was his mother, waiting outside the gates before school ended to walk him home with his hand tightly clasped in hers.

But once a week he didn't go straight home. He looked forward to Wednesdays because Wednesday evening was the one he spent at gran's, and because the time between his mother's leaving him and his arrival at gran's house was the only time he was ever free and by himself.

This was the way it was. His mother would meet him from school and they'd walk down Plumtree Grove to where Petunia Street started. Lupin Street turned off the Grove a bit further down, so his mother would see him across the road, waving and smiling encouragingly, till she'd seen him turn the corner into Lupin Street. Gran's house was about a hundred yards down. That hundred yards was his free time, his alone time.

'Mind you run all the way,' his mother called after him.

But at the corner he always stopped running and began to dawdle, stopping to play with the cat that roamed about the bit of waste ground, or climbing on the pile of bricks the builders never came to build into anything. Sometimes, if she wasn't too bad with her arthritis, gran would be waiting for him at her gate, and he didn't mind having to forgo the cat and the climbing because it was so nice in gran's house. Gran had a big TV set – unusually big for those days – and he'd watch it, eating chocolate, until his father knocked off at the factory and turned up for tea. Tea was lovely, fish and chips that gran didn't fetch from the shop but cooked herself, cream meringues and chocolate eclairs, tinned peaches with evaporated milk, the lot washed down with fizzy lemonade. ('It's a disgrace the way your mother spoils that boy, Stan.') They were supposed to be home by seven, but every week when it got round to seven, gran would remember there was a cowboy film coming up on TV and there'd be cocoa and biscuits and potato crisps to go with it. They'd be lucky to be home in Petunia Street before nine.

'Don't blame me,' said his mother, 'if his school work suffers next day.'

That dreadful evening his mother left him as usual at the corner and saw him across the road. He could remember that, and remember too how he'd looked to see if gran was at her gate. When he'd made sure she wasn't, he'd wandered on to the building site to cajole the cat out of the nest she'd made for herself among the rubble. It was late March, a fine afternoon and still broad daylight at four. He was stroking the cat, thinking how thin and bony she was and how some of gran's fish and chips would do her good, when – what? What next? At this point the curtain came down. Three hours later it lifted, and he was in Plumtree Grove, walking along quite calmly ('Running in terror with that Man after him'), when whom should he meet but Mrs Wilson's Brenda out for the evening with her boy friend. Brenda had pointed at him, stared and shouted. She ran up to him and clutched him and squeezed him till he could hardly breathe. Was that what had frightened him into losing his memory? They said no. They said he'd been frightened before – ('Terrified out of his life') – and that Brenda's grabbing him and the dreadful shriek his mother gave when she saw him had nothing to do with it.

Petunia Street was full of police cars and there was a crowd outside their house. Brenda hustled him in, shouting, 'I've found him, I've found him!' and there was his father all white in the face, talking to policemen, his mother half-dead on the sofa being given brandy, and – wonder of wonders – his gran there too. That had been one of the strangest things of that whole strange evening, that his gran had set foot in their house and his mother hadn't gone out of it.

They all started asking him questions at once. Had he answered them? All that remained in his memory was his mother's scream. That endured, that shattering sound, and the great open mouth from which it issued as she leapt upon him. Somehow, although he couldn't have explained why, he connected that scream and her seizing him as if to swallow him up, with the descent of the curtain.

He was never allowed to be alone after that, not even to play with

John in the Wilsons' garden, and he was never allowed to forget those events he couldn't remember. There was no question of going to gran's even under supervision, for gran's arthritis had got so bad they'd put her in the old people's ward at Upfield Hospital. The Man was never found. A couple of years later a little girl from Plumtree Grove got taken away and murdered. They never found that Man either, but his mother was sure they were one and the same.

'And it might have been our Richard. It doesn't bear thinking of, that Man roaming the streets like a wild beast.'

'What did he do to me, mum?' asked Richard, trying.

'If you don't remember, so much the better. You want to forget all about it, put it right out of your life.'

If only she'd let him. 'What did he *do*, dad?'

'I don't know, Rich. None of us knows, me nor the police nor your mum, for all she says. Women like to set themselves up as knowing all about things, but it's my belief you never told her no more than you told us.'

She took him to school and fetched him home until he was twelve. The other kids teased him mercilessly. He wasn't allowed to go to their houses or have any of them to his. ('You never know who they know or what sort of connections they've got.') His mother only stopped going everywhere with him when he got taller than she was, and anyone could see he was too big for any Man to attack.

Growing up brought no elucidation of that dreadful evening but it did bring, with adolescence, the knowledge of what might have happened. And as he came to understand that it wasn't only threats and blows and stories of horror which the Man might have inflicted on him, he felt an alien in his own body or as if that body were covered with a slime which nothing could wash away. For there was no way of knowing now, nothing to do about it but wish his mother would leave the subject alone, avoid getting friendly with people and work hard at school.

He did very well there, for he was naturally intelligent and had no outside diversions. No one was surprised when he got to a good university, not Oxford or Cambridge but nearly as good – ('Imagine, all that brainpower might have been wasted if that Man had had his way') – where he began to read for a science degree. He was the first member of his family ever to go to college, and the only cloud in the sky was that his gran, as his father pointed out, wasn't there to see his glory.

She had died in the hospital when he was fourteen and she'd left her house to his parents. They'd sold it and theirs and bought a much nicer, bigger one with a proper garden and a garage in a suburb some five miles further out from Upfield. The little bit of money she'd saved she left to Richard, to come to him when he was eighteen. It was just enough to buy a car, and when he came down from university for the Easter holidays, he bought a two-year-old Ford and took and passed his driving test.

'That boy,' said his mother, 'passes every exam that comes his way. It's like as if he *couldn't* fail if he tried. But he's got a guardian angel watching over him, has had ever since he was six.' Her husband had admonished her for her too-excellent memory and now she referred only obliquely to that dreadful evening. 'When you-know-what happened and he was spared.'

She watched him drive expertly round the block, her only regret that he hadn't got a nice girl beside him, a sensible, hard-working fiancée – not one of your tarty pieces – saving up for the deposit on a house and good furniture. Richard had never had a girl. There was one at college he liked and who, he thought, might like him. But he didn't ask her out. He was never quite sure whether he was fit for any girl to know, let alone love.

The day after he'd passed his test he thought he'd drive over to Upfield and look up John Wilson. There was more in this, he confessed to himself, than a wish to revive old friendship. John was the only friend he'd really ever had, but he'd always felt inferior to him, for John had been (and had had the chance to be) easy and sociable and had had a girl to go out with when he was only fourteen. He rather liked the idea of arriving outside the Wilsons' house, fresh from his first two terms at university and in his own car.

It was a Wednesday in early April, a fine, mild afternoon and still, of course, broad daylight at four. He chose a Wednesday because that was early closing day in Upfield and John wouldn't be in the hardware shop where he'd worked ever since he left school three years before.

But as he approached Petunia Street up Plumtree Grove from the southerly direction, it struck him that he'd quite like to take a look at his gran's old house and see whether they'd ever built anything on that bit of waste ground. For years and years, half his lifetime, those bricks had lain there, though the thin old cat had disappeared or died long before Richard's parents moved. And the bricks were still there, overgrown now by grass and nettles. He drove into Lupin Street, moving slowly along the pavement edge until he was within sight of

7

his gran's house. There was enough of his mother in him to stop him parking directly outside the house – ('Keep yourself to yourself and don't pry into what doesn't concern you') – so he stopped the car some few yards this side of it.

It had been painted a bright pink, the window woodwork picked out in sky-blue. Richard thought he liked it better the way it used to be, cream plaster and brown wood, but he didn't move away. A strange feeling had come over him, stranger than any he could remember having experienced, which kept him where he was, staring at the wilderness of rubble and brick and weeds. Just nostalgia, he thought, just going back to those Wednesdays which had been the high-spots of his weeks.

It was funny the way he kept looking among the rubble for the old cat to appear. If she were alive, she'd be as old as he by now and not many cats live that long. But he kept on looking just the same, and presently, as he was trying to pull himself out of this dreamy, dazed feeling and go off to John's, a living creature did appear behind the shrub-high weeds. A boy, about eight. Richard didn't intend to get out of the car. He found himself out of it, locking the door and then strolling over on to the building site.

You couldn't really see much from a car, not details, that must have been why he'd got out, to examine more closely this scene of his childhood pleasures. It seemed very small, not the wild expanse of brick hills and grassy gullies he remembered, but a scrubby little bit of land twenty feet wide and perhaps twice as long. Of course it had seemed bigger because he had been so much smaller, smaller even than this little boy who now sat on a brick mountain, eyeing him.

He didn't mean to speak to the boy, for he wasn't a child any more but a Man. And if there is an explicit rule that a child mustn't speak to strangers, there is an explicit, unstated one, that a Man doesn't speak to children. If he had *meant* to speak, his words would have been very different, something about having played there himself once perhaps, or having lived nearby. The words he did use came to his lips as if they had been placed there by some external (or deeply internal) ruling authority.

'You're trespassing on private land. Did you know that?'

The boy began to ease himself down. 'All the kids play here, mister.'

'Maybe, but that's no excuse. Where do you live?'

In Petunia Street, but I'm going to my gran's . . . No.

'Upfield High Road.'

'I think you'd better get in my car,' the Man said, 'and I'll take you home.'

Doubtfully, the boy said, 'There won't be no one there. My mum works late Wednesdays and I haven't got no dad. I'm to go straight home from school and have my tea and wait for when my mum comes at seven.'

Straight to my gran's and have my tea and . . .

'But you haven't, have you? You hung about trespassing on other people's property.'

'You a cop, mister?'

'Yes,' said the Man, 'yes, I am.'

The boy got into the car quite willingly. 'Are we going to the cop shop?'

'We may go to the police station later. I want to have a talk to you first. We'll go . . .' Where should they go? South London has many open spaces, commons they're called. Wandsworth Common, Tooting Common, Streatham Common . . . What made him choose Drywood Common, so far away, a place he'd heard of but hadn't visited, so far as he knew, in his life? The Man had known, and he was the Man now, wasn't he? 'We'll go to Drywood and have a talk. There's some chocolate on the dashboard shelf. Have a bit if you like.' He started the car and they drove off past gran's old house. 'Have it all,' he said.

The boy had it all. He introduced himself as Barry. He was eight and he had no brothers or sisters or father, just his mum who worked to keep them both. His mum had told him never to get into strangers' cars, but a cop was different, wasn't it?

'Quite different,' said the Man. 'Different altogether.'

It wasn't easy finding Drywood Common because the signposting was bad around there. But the strange thing was that, once there, the whole lay-out of the common was familiar to him.

'We'll park,' he said, 'down by the lake.'

He found the lake with ease, driving along the main road that bisected the common, then turning left on to a smaller lane. There were ducks on the pond. It was surrounded by trees, but in the distance you could see houses and a little row of shops. He parked the car by the water and switched off the engine.

Barry was very calm and trusting. He listened intelligently to the policeman's lecture on behaving himself and not trespassing, and he didn't fidget or seem bored when the Man stopped talking about that and began to talk about himself. The Man had had a lonely sort of life, a bit like being in prison, and he'd never been allowed out alone. Even when he was in his own room doing his homework, he'd been watched – ('Leave your door open, dear. We don't want any secrets in this house') – and he hadn't had a single real friend. Would Barry be his friend, just for a few hours, just for that evening? Barry would.

'But you're grown up now,' he said.

The Man nodded. Barry said later when he recalled the details of what his mother called that nasty experience – for he was always able to remember every detail – that it was at this point the Man had begun to cry.

A small, rather dirty, hand touched the Man's hand and held it. No one had ever held his hand like that before. Not possessively or commandingly – ('Hold on to me tight, Richard, while we cross the road') – but gently, sympathetically – lovingly? Their hands remained clasped, the small one covering the large, then the large enclosing and gripping the small. A tension, as of time stopped, held the two people in the car still. The boy broke it, and time moved again.

'I'm getting a bit hungry,' he said.

'Are you? It's past your teatime. I'll tell you what, we could have some fish and chips. One of those shops over there is a fish and chip shop.'

Barry started to get out of the car.

'No, not you,' the Man said. 'It's better if I go alone. You wait here. OK?'

'OK,' Barry said.

He was only gone ten minutes – for he knew exactly and from a distance which one of the shops it was – and when he got back Barry was waiting for him. The fish and chips were good, almost as good as those gran used to cook. By the time they had finished eating and had wiped their greasy fingers on his handkerchief, dusk had come. Lights were going up in those far-off shops and houses but here, down by the lake, the trees made it quite dark.

'What's the time?' said Barry.

'A quarter past six.'

'I ought to be getting back now.'

'How about a game of hide and seek first? Your mum won't be home yet. I can get you back to Upfield in ten minutes.'

'I don't know . . . Suppose she gets in early?'

'Please,' the Man said. '*Please*, just for a little while. I used to play hide and seek down here when I was a kid.'

'But you said you never played anywhere. You said . . .'

'Did I? Maybe I didn't. I'm a bit confused.'

Barry looked at him gravely. 'I'll hide first,' he said. He watched Barry disappear among the trees. Grown-ups who play hide and seek don't keep to the rules, they don't bother with that counting to a hundred bit. But the Man did. He counted slowly and seriously, and then he got out of the car and began walking round the pond. It took him a long time to find Barry, who was more proficient at this game than he, a proficiency which showed when it was his turn to do the seeking. The darkness was deepening, and there was no one else on the common. He and the boy were quite alone.

Barry had gone to hide. In the car the Man sat counting – ninety-eight, ninety-nine, one hundred. When he stopped he was aware of the silence of the place, alleviated only by the faint, distant hum of traffic on the South Circular Road, just as the darkness was alleviated by the red blush of the sky, radiating the glow of London. Last time round, it hadn't been this dark. The boy wasn't behind any of the trees or in the bushes by the waterside or covered by the brambles in the ditch that ran parallel to the road.

Where the hell had the stupid kid got to? His anger was irrational, for he had suggested the game himself. Was he angry because the boy had proved better at it than he? Or was it something deeper and fiercer than that, rage at rejection by this puny and ignorant little savage?

'Where are you, Barry? Come on out. I've had about enough of this.'

There was no answer. The wind rustled, and a tiny twig scuttered down out of a treetop to his feet. God, that little devil! What'll I do if I can't find him? What the hell's he playing at?

When I find him I'll – I'll kill him.

He shivered. The blood was throbbing in his head. He broke a stick off a bush and began thrashing about with it, enraged, shouting into the dark silence, 'Barry Barry, come out! Come out at once, d'you hear me?' He doesn't want me, he doesn't care about me, no one will ever want me . . .

Then he heard a giggle from a treetop above him, and suddenly there was a crackling of twigs, a slithering sound. Not quite above him – over there. In the giggle, he thought, there was a note of jeering. But where, where? Down by the water's edge. He'd been up in the tree that almost overhung the pond. There was a thud as small feet bounced on to the ground, and again that maddening, gleeful giggle. For a moment the Man stood still. His hands clenched as on a frail neck, and he held them pressed together, crushing out life. Run, Barry, run . . . Run, Richard, to Plumtree Grove and Brenda, to home and mother who knows what dreadful evenings are.

The Man thrust his way through the bushes, making for the pond. The boy would be away by now, but not far away. And his legs were long enough and strong enough to outrun him, his hands strong enough to ensure there would be no future of doubt and fear and curtained memory.

But he was nowhere, nowhere. And yet . . . What was that sound, as of stealthy, fearful feet creeping away? He wheeled round, and there was the boy coming towards him, walking a little timidly between the straight, grey tree trunks *towards* him. A thick constriction gripped his throat. There must have been something in his face, some threatening gravity made more intense by the half-dark that stopped the boy in his tracks. Run, Barry, run, run fast away . . .

They stared at each other for a moment, for a lifetime, for twelve long years. Then the boy gave a merry laugh, fearless and innocent. He ran forward and flung himself into the Man's arms, and the Man, in a great release of pain and anguish, lifted the boy up, lifted him laughing into his own laughing face. They laughed with a kind of rapture at finding each other at last, and in the dark, under the whispering trees, each held the other close in an embrace of warmth and friendship.

'Come on,' Richard said. 'I'll take you home. I don't know what I was doing, bringing you here in the first place.'

'To play hide and seek,' said Barry. 'We had a nice time.'

They got back into the car. It was after seven when they got to Upfield High Road, but not much after.

'I don't reckon my mum's got in yet.'

'I'll drop you here. I won't go up to your place.' Richard opened the car door to let him out. 'Barry?'

'What is it, Mister?'

'Don't ever take a lift from a Man again, will you? Promise me?'
Barry nodded. 'OK.'

'I once took a lift from a stranger, and for years I couldn't remember what had happened. It sort of came back to me tonight, meeting you. I remember it all now. He was all right, just a bit lonely like me. We had fish and chips on Drywood Common and played hide and seek like you and me, and he brought me back nearly to my house – like I've brought you. But it wouldn't always be like that.'

'How do you know?'

Richard looked at his strong young man's hands. 'I just know,' he said. 'Good-bye, Barry, and – thanks.'

He drove away, turning once to see that the boy was safely in his house. Barry told his mother all about it, but she insisted it must have been a nasty experience and called the police. Since Barry couldn't remember the number of the car and had no idea of the stranger's name, there was little they could do. They never found the Man.

People Don't Do Such Things

Peple don't do such things.

That's the last line of *Hedda Gabler*, and Ibsen makes this chap say it out of a sort of bewilderment at finding truth stranger than fiction. I know just how he felt. I say it myself every time I come up against the hard reality that Reeve Baker is serving fifteen years in prison for murdering my wife, and that I played my part in it, and that it happened to us three. People don't do such things. But they do.

Real life had never been stranger than fiction for me. It had always been beautifully pedestrian and calm and pleasant, and all the people I knew jogged along in the same sort of way. Except Reeve, that is. I suppose I made a friend of Reeve and enjoyed his company so much because of the contrast between his manner of living and my own, and so that when he had gone home I could say comfortably to Gwendolen:

'How dull our lives must seem to Reeve!'

An acquaintance of mine had given him my name when he had got into a mess with his finances and was having trouble with the Inland Revenue. As an accountant with a good many writers among my clients, I was used to their irresponsible attitude to money – the way they fall back on the excuse of artistic temperament for what is, in fact, calculated tax evasion – and I was able to sort things out for Reeve and show him how to keep more or less solvent. As a way, I suppose of showing his gratitude, Reeve took Gwendolen and me out to dinner, then we had him over at our place, and after that we became close friends.

Writers and the way they work hold a fascination for ordinary chaps like me. It's a mystery to me where they get their ideas from, apart from constructing the thing and creating characters and making their characters talk and so on. But Reeve could do it all right, and set the whole lot at the court of Louis Quinze or in medieval Italy or what not. I've read all nine of his historical novels and admired what you might call his virtuosity. But I only read them to please him really. Detective stories were what I preferred and I seldom bothered with any other form of fiction.

Gwendolen once said to me it was amazing Reeve could fill his books with so much drama when he was living drama all the time. You'd imagine he'd have got rid of it all on paper. I think the truth was that every one of his heroes was himself, only transformed into Cesare Borgia or Casanova. You could see Reeve in them all, tall, handsome and dashing as they were, and each a devil with the women. Reeve had got divorced from his wife a year or so before I'd met him, and since then he'd had a string of girl friends, models, actresses, girls in the fashion trade, secretaries, journalists, schoolteachers, high-powered lady executives and even a dentist. Once when we were over at his place he played us a record of an aria from *Don Giovanni* – another character Reeve identified with and wrote about. It was called the 'Catalogue Song' and it listed all the types of girls the Don had made love to, blonde, brunette, redhead, young, old, rich, poor, ending up with something about as long as she wears a petticoat you know what he does. Funny, I even remember the Italian for that bit, though it's the only Italian I know. *Purche porti la gonnella voi sapete quel che fa.* Then the singer laughed in an unpleasant way, laughed to music with a seducer's sneer, and Reeve laughed too, saying it gave him a fellow-feeling.

I'm old-fashioned, I know that. I'm conventional. Sex is for marriage, as far as I'm concerned, and what sex you have before marriage – I never had much – I can't help thinking of as a shameful secret thing. I never even believed that people did have much of it outside marriage. All talk and boasting, I thought. I really did think that. And I kidded myself that when Reeve talked of going out with a new girl he meant going out with. Taking out for a meal, I thought, and dancing with and taking home in a taxi and then maybe a good-night kiss on the doorstep. Until one Sunday morning, when Reeve was coming over for lunch, I phoned him to ask if he'd meet us in the pub for a pre-lunch drink. He sounded half-asleep and I could hear a girl giggling in the background. Then I heard him say:

'Get some clothes on, lovey, and make us a cup of tea, will you? My head's splitting.'

I told Gwendolen.

'What did you expect?' she said.

'I don't know,' I said. 'I thought you'd be shocked.'

'He's very good-looking and he's only thirty-seven. It's natural.'

15

But she had blushed a little. 'I am rather shocked,' she said. 'We don't belong in his sort of life, do we?'

And yet we remained in it, on the edge of it. As we got to know Reeve better, he put aside those small prevarications he had employed to save our feelings. And he would tell us, without shyness, anecdotes of his amorous past and present. The one about the girl who was so possessive that even though he had broken with her, she had got into his flat in his absence and been lying naked in his bed when he brought his new girl home that night; the one about the married woman who had hidden him for two hours in her wardrobe until her husband had gone out; the girl who had come to borrow a pound of sugar and had stayed all night; fair girls, dark girls, plump, thin, rich, poor . . . *Purche porti la gonnella voi sapete quel che fa.*

'It's another world,' said Gwendolen.

And I said, 'How the other half lives.'

We were given to clichés of this sort. Our life was a cliché, the commonest sort of life led by middle-class people in the Western world. We had a nice detached house in one of the right suburbs, solid furniture and lifetime-lasting carpets. I had my car and she hers. I left for the office at half-past eight and returned at six. Gwendolen cleaned the house and went shopping and gave coffee mornings. In the evenings we liked to sit at home and watch television, generally going to bed at eleven. I think I was a good husband. I never forgot my wife's birthday or failed to send her roses on our anniversary or omitted to do my share of the dishwashing. And she was an excellent wife, romantically-inclined, not sensual. At any rate, she was never sensual with me.

She kept every birthday card I ever sent her, and the Valentines I sent her while we were engaged. Gwendolen was one of those women who hoard and cherish small mementoes. In a drawer of her dressing table she kept the menu card from the restaurant where we celebrated our engagement, a picture postcard of the hotel where we spent our honeymoon, every photograph of us that had ever been taken, our wedding pictures in a leather-bound album. Yes, she was an arch-romantic, and in her diffident way, with an air of daring, she would sometimes reproach Reeve for his callousness.

'But you can't do that to someone who loves you,' she said when he had announced his brutal intention of going off on holiday without telling his latest girl friend where he was going or even that he was going at all. 'You'll break her heart.'

'Gwendolen, my love, she hasn't got a heart. Women don't have them. She has another sort of machine, a combination of telescope, lie detector, scalpel and castrating device.'

'You're too cynical,' said my wife. 'You may fall in love yourself one day and then you'll know how it feels.'

'Not necessarily. As Shaw said –' Reeve was always quoting what other writers had said '– "Don't do unto others as you would have others do unto you, as we don't all have the same tastes."'

'We all have the same taste about not wanting to be ill-treated.'

'She should have thought of that before she tried to control my life. No, I shall quietly disappear for a while. I mightn't go away, in fact. I might just say I'm going away and lie low at home for a fortnight. Fill up the deep freeze, you know, and lay in a stock of liquor. I've done it before in this sort of situation. It's rather pleasant and I get a hell of a lot of work done.'

Gwendolen was silenced by this and, I must say, so was I. You may wonder, after these examples of his morality, just what it was I saw in Reeve. It's hard now for me to remember. Charm, perhaps, and a never-failing hospitality; a rueful way of talking about his own life as if it was all he could hope for, while mine was the ideal all men would aspire to; a helplessness about his financial affairs combined with an admiration for my grasp of them; a manner of talking to me as if we were equally men of the world, only I had chosen the better part. When invited to one of our dull modest gatherings, he would always be the exciting friend with the witty small talk, the reviver of a failing party, the industrious barman; above all, the one among our friends who wasn't an accountant, a bank manager, a solicitor, a general practitioner or a company executive. We had his books on our shelves. Our friends borrowed them and told their friends they'd met Reeve Baker at our house. He gave us a *cachet* that raised us enough centimetres above the level of the bourgeoisie to make us interesting.

Perhaps, in those days, I should have asked myself what it was he saw in us.

It was about a year ago that I first noticed a coolness between Gwendolen and Reeve. The banter they had gone in for, which had consisted in wry confessions or flirtatious compliments from him, and shy, somewhat maternal reproofs from her, stopped almost entirely. When we all three were together they talked to each other through me, as if I were their interpreter. I asked Gwendolen if he'd done something to upset her.

She looked extremely taken aback. 'What makes you ask?'

'You always seem a bit peeved with him.'

'I'm sorry,' she said. 'I'll try to be nicer. I didn't know I'd changed.'

She had changed to me too. She flinched sometimes when I touched her, and although she never refused me, there was an apathy about her love-making.

'What's the matter?' I asked her after a failure which disturbed me because it was so unprecedented.

She said it was nothing, and then, 'We're getting older. You can't expect things to be the same as when we were first married.'

'For God's sake,' I said. 'You're thirty-five and I'm thirty-nine. We're not in our dotage.'

She sighed and looked unhappy. She had become moody and difficult. Although she hardly opened her mouth in Reeve's presence, she talked about him a lot when he wasn't there, seizing upon almost any excuse to discuss him and speculate about his character. And she seemed inexplicably annoyed when, on our tenth wedding anniversary, a greetings card arrived addressed to us both from him. I, of course, had sent her roses. At the end of the week I missed a receipt for a bill I'd paid – as an accountant I'm naturally circumspect about these things – and I searched through our wastepaper basket, thinking I might have thrown it away. I found it, and I also found the anniversary card I'd sent Gwendolen to accompany the roses.

All these things I noticed. That was the trouble with me – I noticed things but I lacked the experience of life to add them up and make a significant total. I didn't have the worldly wisdom to guess why my wife was always out when I phoned her in the afternoons, or why she was for ever buying new clothes. I noticed, I wondered, that was all.

I noticed things about Reeve too. For one thing, that he'd stopped talking about his girl friends.

'He's growing up at last,' I said to Gwendolen.

She reacted with warmth, with enthusiasm. 'I really think he is.'

But she was wrong. He had only three months of what I thought of as celibacy. And then when he talked of a new girl friend, it was to me alone. Confidentially, over a Friday night drink in the pub, he told me of this 'marvellous chick', twenty years old, he had met at a party the week before.

'It won't last, Reeve,' I said.

'I sincerely hope not. Who wants it to *last*?'

Not Gwendolen, certainly. When I told her she was incredulous, then aghast. And when I said I was sorry I'd told her since Reeve's backsliding upset her so much, she snapped at me that she didn't want to discuss him. She became even more snappy and nervous and depressed too. Whenever the phone rang she jumped. Once or twice I came home to find no wife, no dinner prepared; then she'd come in, looking haggard, to say she'd been out for a walk. I got her to see our doctor and he put her on tranquillizers which just made her more depressed.

I hadn't seen Reeve for ages. Then, out of the blue he phoned me at work to say he was off to the South of France for three weeks.

'In your state of financial health?' I said. I'd had a struggle getting him to pay the January instalment of his twice-yearly income tax, and I knew he was practically broke till he got the advance on his new book in May. 'The South of France is a bit pricey, isn't it?'

'I'll manage,' he said. 'My bank manager's one of my fans and he's let me have an overdraft.'

Gwendolen didn't seem very surprised to hear about Reeve's holiday. He'd told me he was going on his own – the 'marvellous chick' had long disappeared – and she said she thought he needed the rest, especially as there wouldn't be any of those girls to bother him, as she put it.

When I first met Reeve he'd been renting a flat but I persuaded him to buy one, for security and as an investment. The place was known euphemistically as a garden flat but it was in fact a basement, the lower ground floor of a big Victorian house in Bayswater. My usual route to work didn't take me along his street, but sometimes when the traffic was heavy I'd go through the back doubles and past his house. After he'd been away for about two weeks I happened to do this one morning and, of course, I glanced at Reeve's window. One always does glance at a friend's house, I think, when one is passing even if one knows that friend isn't at home. His bedroom was at the front, the top half of the window visible, the lower half concealed by the rise of lawn. I noticed that the curtains were drawn. Not particularly wise, I thought, an invitation to burglars, and then I forgot about it. But two mornings later I passed that way again, passed very slowly this time as there was a traffic hold-up, and again I glanced at Reeve's window. The curtains were no longer quite drawn. There was a gap about six inches wide between them. Now whatever a burglar may do, it's very unlikely he'll pull back drawn curtains. I didn't consider burglars this time. I thought Reeve must have come back early.

Telling myself I should be late for work anyway if I struggled along in this traffic jam, I parked the car as soon as I could at a meter. I'll knock on old Reeve's door, I thought, and get him to make me a cup of coffee. There was no answer. But as I looked once more at that window I was almost certain those curtains had been moved again, and in the past ten minutes. I rang the doorbell of the woman in the flat upstairs. She came down in her dressing gown.

'Sorry to disturb you,' I said. 'But do you happen to know if Mr Baker's come back?'

'He's not coming back till Saturday,' she said.

'Sure of that?'

'Of course I'm sure,' she said rather huffily. 'I put a note through his door Monday, and if he was back he'd have come straight up for this parcel I took in for him.'

'Did he take his car, d'you know?' I said, feeling like a detective in one of my favourite crime novels.

'Of course he did. What is this? What's he done?'

I said he'd done nothing, as far as I knew, and she banged the door in my face. So I went down the road to the row of lock-up garages. I couldn't see much through the little panes of frosted glass in the door of Reeve's garage, just enough to be certain the interior wasn't empty but that that greenish blur was the body of Reeve's Fiat. And then I knew for sure. He hadn't gone away at all. I chuckled to myself as I imagined him lying low for these three weeks in his flat, living off food from the deep freeze and spending most of his time in the back regions where, enclosed as those rooms were by a courtyard with high walls, he could show lights day and night with impunity. Just wait till Saturday, I thought, and I pictured myself asking him for details of his holiday, laying little traps for him, until even he with his writer's powers of invention would have to admit he'd never been away at all.

Gwendolen was laying the table for our evening meal when I got in. She, I'd decided, was the only person with whom I'd share this joke. I got all her attention the minute I mentioned Reeve's name, but when I reached the bit about his car being in the garage she stared at me and all the colour went out of her face. She sat down, letting the bunch of knives and forks she was holding fall into her lap.

'What on earth's the matter?' I said.

'How could he be so cruel? How could he do that to anyone?'

'Oh, my dear, Reeve's quite ruthless where women are concerned. You remember, he told us he'd done it before.'

'I'm going to phone him,' she said, and I saw that she was shivering. She dialled his number and I heard the ringing tone start.

'He won't answer,' I said. 'I wouldn't have told you if I'd thought it was going to upset you.'

She didn't say any more. There were things cooking on the stove and the table was half-laid, but she left all that and went into the hall. Almost immediately afterwards I heard the front door close.

I know I'm slow on the uptake in some ways but I'm not stupid. Even a husband who trusts his wife like I trusted mine – or, rather, never considered there was any need for trust – would know, after that, that something had been going on. Nothing much, though, I told myself. A crush perhaps on her part, hero-worship which his flattery and his confidences had fanned. Naturally, she'd feel let down, betrayed, when she discovered he'd deceived her as to his whereabouts when he'd led her to believe she was a special friend and privy to all his secrets. But I went upstairs just the same to reassure myself by looking in that dressing table drawer where she kept her souvenirs. Dishonourable? I don't think so. She had never locked it or tried to keep its contents private from me.

And all those little mementoes of our first meeting, our courtship, our marriage, were still there. Between a birthday card and a Valentine I saw a pressed rose. But there too, alone in a nest made out of a lace handkerchief I had given her, were a locket and a button. The locket was one her mother had left to her, but the photograph in it, that of some long-dead unidentifiable relative, had been replaced by a cut-out of Reeve from a snapshot. On the reverse side was a lock of hair. The button I recognized as coming from Reeve's blazer, though it hadn't, I noticed, been cut off. He must have lost it in our house and she'd picked it up. The hair was Reeve's, black, wavy, here and there with a thread of grey, but again it hadn't been cut off. On one of our visits to his flat she must have combed it out of his hairbrush and twisted it into a lock. Poor little Gwendolen . . . Briefly, I'd suspected Reeve. For one dreadful moment, sitting down there after she'd gone out, I'd asked myself, could he have . . . ? Could my best friend have . . . ? But, no. He hadn't even sent her a letter or a flower. It had been all on her side, and for that reason – I knew where she was bound for – I must stop her reaching him and humiliating herself.

I slipped the things into my pocket with some vague idea of using them to show her how childish she was being. She hadn't taken her car. Gwendolen always disliked driving in central London. I took mine and drove to the tube station I knew she'd go to.

She came out a quarter of an hour after I got there, walking fast and glancing nervously to the right and left of her. When she saw me she gave a little gasp and stood stock-still.

'Get in, darling,' I said gently. 'I want to talk to you.'

She got in but she didn't speak. I drove down to the Bayswater Road and into the Park. There, on the Ring, I parked under the plane trees, and because she still didn't utter a word, I said:

'You mustn't think I don't understand. We've been married ten years and I daresay I'm a dull sort of chap. Reeve's exciting and different and – well, maybe it's only natural for you to think you've fallen for him.'

She stared at me stonily. 'I love him and he loves me.'

'That's nonsense,' I said, but it wasn't the chill of the spring evening that made me shiver. 'Just because he's used that charm of his on you . . .'

She interrupted me. 'I want a divorce.'

'For heaven's sake,' I said. 'You hardly know Reeve. You've never been alone with him, have you?'

'Never been alone with him?' She gave a brittle, desperate laugh. 'He's been my lover for six months. And now I'm going to him. I'm going to tell him he doesn't have to hide from women any more because I'll be with him all the time.'

In the half-dark I gaped at her. 'I don't believe you,' I said, but I did. I did. 'You mean you along with all the rest . . . ? My wife?'

'I'm going to be Reeve's wife. I'm the only one that understands him, the only one he can talk to. He told me that just before – before he went away.'

'Only he didn't go away.' There was a great redness in front of my eyes like a lake of blood. 'You fool,' I shouted at her. 'Don't you see it's you he's hiding from, *you*? He's done this to get away from you like he's got away from all the others. Love you? He never even gave you a present, not even a photograph. If you go there, he won't let you in. You're the last person he'd let in.'

'I'm going to him,' she cried, and she began to struggle with the car door. 'I'm going to him, to live with him, and I never want to see you again!'

In the end I drove home alone. Her wish came true and she never did see me again.

When she wasn't back by eleven I called the police. They asked me to go down to the police station and fill out a Missing Persons form, but they didn't take my fear very seriously. Apparently, when a woman of Gwendolen's age disappears they take it for granted she's gone off with a man. They took it seriously all right when a park keeper found her strangled body among some bushes in the morning.

That was on the Thursday. The police wanted to know where Gwendolen could have been going so far from her home. They wanted the names and addresses of all our friends. Was there anyone we knew in Kensington or Paddington or Bayswater, anywhere in the vicinity of the Park? I said there was no one. The next day they asked me again and I said, as if I'd just remembered:

'Only Reeve Baker. The novelist, you know.' I gave them his address. 'But he's away on holiday, has been for three weeks. He's not coming home till tomorrow.'

What happened after that I know from the evidence given at Reeve's trial, his trial for the murder of my wife. The police called on him on Saturday morning. I don't think they suspected him at all at first. My reading of crime fiction has taught me they would have asked him for any information he could give about our private life.

Unfortunately for him, they had already talked to some of his neighbours. Reeve had led all these people to think he had really gone away. The milkman and the paper boy were both certain he had been away. So when the police questioned him about that, and he knew just why they were questioning him, he got into a panic. He didn't dare say he'd been in France. They could have shown that to be false without the least trouble. Instead, he told the truth and said he'd been lying low to escape the attentions of a woman. Which woman? He wouldn't say, but the woman in the flat upstairs would. Time and time again she had seen Gwendolen visit him in the afternoons, had heard them quarrelling, Gwendolen protesting her love for him and he shouting that he wouldn't be controlled, that he'd do anything to escape her possessiveness.

He had, of course, no alibi for the Wednesday night. But the judge and the jury could see he'd done his best to arrange one. Novelists are apt to let their imaginations run away with them; they don't realize how astute and thorough the police are. And there was firmer evidence of his guilt even than that. Three main exhibits were produced in the court: Reeve's blazer with a button missing from the sleeve; that very button; a cluster of his hairs. The button had been found by Gwendolen's body and the hairs on her coat . . .

My reading of detective stories hadn't been in vain, though I haven't read one since then. People don't, I suppose, after a thing like that.

A Bad Heart

They had been very pressing and at last, on the third time of asking, he had accepted. Resignedly, almost fatalistically, he had agreed to dine with them. But as he began the long drive out of London, he thought petulantly that they ought to have had the tact to drop the acquaintance altogether. No other employee he had sacked had ever made such approaches to him. Threats, yes. Several had threatened him and one had tried blackmail, but no one had ever had the effrontery to invite him to dinner. It wasn't done. A discreet man wouldn't have done it. But of course Hugo Crouch wasn't a discreet man and that, among other things, was why he had been sacked.

He knew why they had asked him. They wanted to hold a court of enquiry, to have the whole thing out. Knowing this, he had suggested they meet in a restaurant and at his expense. They couldn't harangue a man in a public restaurant and he wouldn't be at their mercy. But they had insisted he come to their house and in the end he had given way. He was an elderly man with a heart condition; it was sixteen miles slow driving from his flat to their house – monstrous on a filthy February night – but he would show them he could take it, he would be one too many for them. The chairman of Frasers would show them he wasn't to be intimidated by a bumptious do-gooder like Hugo Crouch, and he would cope with the situation just as he had coped in the past with the blackmailer.

By the time he reached the outskirts of the Forest the rain was coming down so hard that he had to put his windscreen wipers on at full speed, and he felt more than ever thankful that he had got his new car with all its efficient gadgets. Certainly, the firm wouldn't have been able to run to it if he had kept Hugo Crouch on a day longer. If he had agreed to all Hugo's demands, he would still be stuck with that old Daimler and he would never have managed that winter cruise. Hugo had been a real thorn in his flesh what with his extravagance and his choosing to live in a house in the middle of

Epping Forest. And it was in the middle, totally isolated, not even on the edge of one of the Forest villages. The general manager of Frasers had to be within reach, on call. Burying oneself out here was ridiculous.

The car's powerful headlights showed a dark winding lane ahead, the grey tree trunks making it appear like some sombre pillared corridor. And this picture was cut off every few seconds by a curtain of rain, to reappear with the sweep of the wipers. Fortunately, he had been there once before, otherwise he might have passed the high brick wall and the wooden gates behind which stood the Crouch house, the peak-roofed Victorian villa, drab, shabby, and to his eyes quite hideous. Anyone who put a demolition order on that would be doing a service to the environment, he thought, and then he drove in through the gates.

There wasn't a single light showing. He remembered that they lived in the back, but they might have put a light on to greet him. But for his car headlamps, he wouldn't have been able to see his way at all. Clutching the box of peppermint creams he had bought for Elizabeth Crouch, he splashed across the almost flooded paving, under eaves from which water poured as from a row of taps, and made for the front door which happened to be – which *would* be – at the far side of the house. It was hard to tell where their garden ended and the Forest began, for no demarcation was visible. Nothing was visible but black rain-lashed branches faintly illuminated by a dim glow showing through the fanlight over the door.

He rang the bell hard, keeping his finger on the push, hoping the rain hadn't got through his coat to his hundred-guinea suit. A jet of water struck the back of his neck, sending a shiver right through him, and then the door was opened.

'Duncan! You must be soaked. Have you had a dreadful journey?'

He gasped out, 'Awful, awful!' and ducked into the dry sanctuary of the hall. 'What a night!' He thrust the chocolates at her, gave her his hand. Then he remembered that in the old days they always used to kiss. Well, he never minded kissing a pretty woman and it hadn't been her fault. 'How are you, Elizabeth?' he said after their cheeks had touched.

'I'm fine. Let me take your coat. I'll take it into the kitchen and dry it. Hugo's in the sitting room. You know your way, don't you?'

Down a long passage, he remembered, that was never properly lighted and wasn't heated at all. The whole place cried out for central heating. He was by now extremely cold and he couldn't help thinking of his flat where the radiators got so hot that you had to open the windows even in February and where, had he been at home, his housekeeper would at this moment be placing before him a portion of hot pâté to be followed by *Poulet San Josef*. Elizabeth Crouch, he recalled, was rather a poor cook.

Outside the sitting room door he paused, girding himself for the encounter. He hadn't set eyes on Hugo Crouch since the man had marched out of the office in a huff because he, Duncan Fraser, chairman of Frasers, had tentatively suggested he might be happier in another job. Well, the sooner the first words were over the better. Very few men in his position, he thought, would let the matter weigh on their minds at all or have his sensitivity. Very few, for that matter, would have come.

He would be genial, casual, perhaps a little avuncular. Above all, he would avoid at any cost the subject of Hugo's dismissal. They wouldn't be able to make him talk about it if he was determined not to; ultimately, the politeness of hosts to guest would put up a barrier to stop them. He opened the door, smiling pleasantly, achieving a merry twinkle in his eye. 'Well, here I am, Hugo! I've made it.'

Hugo wore a very sour look, the kind of look Duncan had often seen on his face when some more than usually extravagant order or request of his had been countermanded. He didn't smile. He gave Duncan his hand gravely and asked him what he would like to drink.

Duncan looked quickly around the room, which hadn't changed and was still furnished with rather grim Victorian pieces. There was, at any rate, a huge fire of logs burning in the grate. 'Ah, yes, a drink,' he said, rubbing his hands together. He didn't dare ask for whisky, which he would have liked best, because his doctor had forbidden it. 'A little dry Vermouth?'

'I'm afraid I don't have any Vermouth.'

This rejoinder, though spoken quite lightly, though he had even expected something of the sort, gave Duncan a slight shock. It put him on his mettle and yet it jolted him. He had known, of course, that they would start on him, but he hadn't anticipated the first move coming so promptly. All right, let the man remind him he couldn't afford fancy drinks because he had lost his job. He, Duncan, wouldn't be drawn. 'Sherry, then,' he said. 'You do have sherry?'

'Oh, yes, we have sherry.' Hugo said. 'Come and sit by the fire.'

As soon as he was seated in front of those blazing logs and had begun to thaw out, he decided to pursue the conversation along the lines of the weather. It was the only subject he could think of to break the ice until Elizabeth came in, and they were doing quite well at it, moving into such sidelines as floods in East Anglia and crashes in motorway fog, when she appeared and sat next to him.

'We haven't asked anyone else, Duncan. We wanted to have you to ourselves.'

A pointless remark, he thought, under the circumstances. Naturally, they hadn't asked anyone else. The presence of other guests would have defeated the exercise. But perhaps it hadn't been so pointless, after all. It could be an opening gambit.

'Delightful,' he said.

'We've got such a lot to talk about. I thought it would be nicer this way.'

'Much nicer.' Such a lot to talk about? There was only one thing she could mean by that. But she needn't think – silent Hugo sitting there with his grim moody face needn't think – that he would help them along an inch of the way. If they were going to get on to the subject they would have to do all the spadework themselves. 'We were just saying,' he said, 'how tragic all these motorway crashes are. Now I feel all this could be stopped by a very simple method.' He outlined the simple method, but he could tell they weren't really interested and he wasn't surprised when Elizabeth said:

'That's fascinating, Duncan, but let's talk about you. What have you been doing lately?'

Controlling the business your husband nearly ruined.

'Oh, this and that,' he said. 'Nothing much.'

'Did you go on a cruise this winter?'

'Er – yes, yes, I did. The Caribbean, as a matter of fact.'

'That's nice. I'm sure the change did you good.'

Implying he needed having good done to him, of course. She had only got on to cruises so that she could point out that some people couldn't afford them. 'I had a real rest,' he said heartily. 'I must just tell you about a most amusing thing that happened to me on the way home.' He told them, but it didn't sound very amusing and although Elizabeth smiled half-heartedly, Hugo didn't. 'Well, it seemed funny at the time,' he said.

'We can eat in five minutes,' said Elizabeth. 'Tell me, Duncan, did you buy that villa you were so keen on in the South of France?'

'Oh, yes, I bought it.' She was looking at him very curiously, very impertinently really – waiting for him to apologize for spending his own money, he supposed. 'Listen to that rain,' he said. 'It hasn't let up at all.'

28

They agreed that it hadn't and silence fell. He could tell from the glance they exchanged – he was very astute in these matters – that they knew they had been baulked for the time being. And they both looked pretty fed-up, he thought triumphantly. But the woman was weighing in again, and a bit nearer the bone this time.

'Who do you think we ran into last week, Duncan? John Churchouse.'

The man who had done that printing for Frasers a couple of years back. He had got the order, Duncan remembered, just about the time of Hugo's promotion. He sat tight, drank the last of his sherry.

'He told us he'd been in hospital for months and lost quite a lot of business. I felt so . . .'

'I wonder if I might wash my hands?' Duncan asked firmly. 'If you could just tell me where the bathroom is?'

'Of course.' She looked disappointed, as well she might. 'It's the door facing you at the top of the stairs.'

Duncan made his way to the bathroom. He mustn't think he was going to get off the hook as easily as that. They would be bound to start on him again during the meal. Very likely they thought a dinner table a good place to hold an inquest. Still, he'd be ready for them, he'd done rather well up to now.

They were both waiting for him at the foot of the stairs to lead him into the dining room, and again he saw the woman give her husband one of those looks that are the equivalent of prompting nudges. Hugo was probably getting cold feet. In these cases, of course, it was always the women who were more aggressive. Duncan gave a swift glance at the table and the plate of *hors d'oeuvres*, sardines and anchovies and artichoke hearts, most unsuitable for the time of year.

'I'm afraid you've been to a great deal of trouble, Elizabeth,' he said graciously.

She gave him a dazzling smile. He had forgotten that smile of hers, how it lit her whole face, her eyes as flashing blue as a kingfisher's plumage. '"The labour we delight in,"' she said, '"physics pain."'

'Ah, Macbeth.' Good, an excellent topic to get them through the first course. 'Do you know, the only time we three ever went to the theatre together was to see Macbeth?'

'I remember,' she said. 'Bread, Duncan?'

'Thank you. I saw a splendid performance of Macbeth by that Polish company last week. Perhaps you've seen it?'

'We haven't been to the theatre at all this winter,' said Hugo.

She must have kicked him under the table to prompt that one.

Duncan took no notice. He told them in detail about the Polish Macbeth, although such was his mounting tenseness that he couldn't remember the names of half the characters or, for that matter, the names of the actors.

'I wish Keith could have seen it,' she said. 'It's his set play for his exam.'

She was going to force him to ask after her sons and be told they'd had to take them away from that absurdly expensive boarding school. Well, he wouldn't. Rude it might be, but he wouldn't ask.

'I don't think you ever met our children, Duncan?'

'No, I didn't.'

'They'll be home on half-term next week. I'm so delighted that their half-term happens to coincide with mine.'

'Yours?' he said suspiciously.

'Elizabeth has gone back to teaching.'

'Really?' said Duncan. 'No, I won't have any more, thank you. That was delicious. Let me give you a hand. If I could carry something . . . ?'

'Please don't trouble. I can manage.' She looked rather offended. 'If you two will excuse me I'll see to our main course.'

He was left alone with Hugo in the chilly dining room. He shifted his legs from under the cloth to bring them closer to the one-bar electric heater. Hugo began to struggle with the cork of a wine bottle. Unable to extract it, he cursed under his breath.

'Let me try.'

'I'll be able to cope quite well, thanks, if you don't watch me,' said Hugo sharply, and then, irrelevantly, if you didn't know nothing those two said was irrelevant, 'I'm doing a course in accountancy.'

'As a wine waiter, Hugo,' said Duncan, 'you make a very good accountant, ha ha!'

Hugo didn't laugh. He got the cork out at last. 'I think I'll do all right. I was always reasonably good at figures.'

'So you were, so you were. And more than reasonably good.' That was true. It had been with personnel that the man was so abysmally bad, giving junior executives and little typists ideas above their station. 'I'm sure you'll do well.'

Why didn't the woman come back? It must have been ten minutes since she had gone off to that kitchen, down those miles of passages. His own wife, long dead, would have got that main course into serving dishes before they had sat down to the *hors d'oeuvres*.

'Get a qualification, that's the thing,' he said. In the distance he

30

heard the wheels of a trolley coming. It was a more welcome sound than that of the wheels of the train one has awaited for an hour on a cold platform. He didn't like the woman, but anything was better than being alone with Hugo. Why not get it over now, he thought, before they began on the amazingly small roasted chicken which had appeared? He managed a smile. He said, 'I can tell you've both fallen on your feet. I'm quite sure, Hugo, you'll look back on all this when you're a successful accountant and thank God you and Frasers parted company.'

And that ought to be that. They had put him through their inquisition and now perhaps they would let him eat this overcooked mess that passed for dinner in peace. At last they would talk of something else, not leave it to him who had been making the running all the evening.

But instead of conversation, there was a deep silence. No-one seemed to have anything to say. And although Duncan, working manfully at his chicken wing, racked his brains for a topic, he could think of nothing. Their house, his flat, the workpeople at Frasers, his car, the cost of living, her job, Hugo's course, Christmas past, summer to come, all these subjects must inevitably lead by a direct route back to Hugo's dismissal. And Duncan saw with irritable despair that *all* subjects would lead to it because he was he and they were they, and the dismissal lay between them like an unavoidable spectre at their dismal feast. From time to time he lifted his eyes from his plate, hoping she would respond to that famous smile of his, that smile that was growing stiff with insincere use, but each time he looked at her he saw that she was staring fixedly at him, eating hardly anything, her expression concentrated, dispassionate and somehow dogged. And her eyes had lost their kingfisher flash. They were dull and dead like smoky glass.

So they hadn't had enough then, she and her subdued morose husband? They wanted to see him abject, not merely referring with open frankness to the dismissal as he had done, but explaining it, apologizing. Well, they should have his explanation. There was no escape. Carefully, he placed his knife and fork side by side on his empty plate. Precisely, but very politely, he refused his hostess's offer of more. He took a deep breath as he often did at the beginning of a board meeting, as he had so very often done at those board meetings when Hugo Crouch pressed insistently for staff rises.

'My dear Elizabeth,' he began, 'my dear Hugo, I know why you asked me here tonight and what you've been hinting at ever since I arrived. And because I want to enjoy your very delightful company without any more awkwardness, I'm going to do here and now what you very obviously want me to do – that is, explain just how it happened that I suggested Hugo would be happier away from Frasers.'

Elizabeth said, 'Now, Duncan, listen . . .'

'You can say your piece in a moment, Elizabeth. Perhaps you'll be surprised when I say *I am entirely to blame* for what happened. Yes, I admit it, the fault was mine.' He lifted one hand to silence Hugo. 'No, Hugo, let me finish. As I said, the fault was mine. I made an error of judgement. Oh, yes, I did. I should have been a better judge of men. I should have been able to see when I promoted you that you weren't up to the job. I blame myself for not understanding – well, your limitations.'

They were silent. They didn't look at him or at each other.

'We men in responsible positions,' he said, 'are to blame when the men we appoint can't rise to the heights we envisage for them. We lack vision, that's all. I take the whole burden of it on my shoulders. So shall we forgive and forget?'

He had seldom seen people look so embarrassed, so shamefaced. It just went to show that they were no match for him. His statement had been the last thing they had expected and it was unanswerable. He handed her his plate with its little graveyard of chicken bones among the potato skins, and as she took it he saw a look of baulked fury cross her face.

'Well, Elizabeth,' he said, unable to resist, 'am I forgiven?'

'It's too late now. It's past,' she said in a very cold stony voice. 'It's too late for any of this.'

'I'm sorry if I haven't given you the explanation you wanted, my dear. I've simply told you the truth.'

She didn't say any more. Hugo didn't say anything. And suddenly Duncan felt most uncomfortable. Their condemnatory faces, the way they both seemed to shrink away from him – it was almost too much. His heart began to pound and he had to tell himself that a racing heart meant nothing, that it was pain and not palpitations he must fear. He reached for one of his little white pills ostentatiously, hoping they would notice what they had done to him.

When still they didn't speak, he said, 'I think perhaps I should go now.'

'But you haven't had coffee,' said Elizabeth.

'Just the same, it might be better . . .'

'Please stay and have coffee,' she said firmly, almost sternly, and then she forced a smile. 'I insist.'

Back in the sitting room they offered him brandy. He refused it because he had to drive home, and the sooner he could begin that drive the happier he would be. Hugo had a large brandy which he drank at a gulp, the way brandy should never be drunk unless one has had a shock or is steeling oneself for something. Elizabeth had picked up the evening paper and was talking in a very artificial way about a murder case which appeared on the front page.

'I really must go,' said Duncan.

'Have some more coffee. It's not ten yet.'

Why did they want him to stay? Or, rather, why did she? Hugo was once more busy with the brandy bottle. Duncan thought his company must be as tiresome to them as theirs was to him. They had got what they wanted, hadn't they? He drank his second cup of coffee so quickly that it scalded his mouth and then he got up.

'I'll get an umbrella. I'll come out with you,' said Hugo.

'Thank you.' It was over. He was going to make his escape and he need never see them again. And suddenly he felt that he wouldn't be able to get out of that house fast enough. Really, since he had made his little speech, the atmosphere had been thoroughly disagreeable. 'Good night, Elizabeth,' he said. What platitudes could he think of that weren't too ludicrous? 'Thank you for the meal. Perhaps we may meet again some day.'

'I hope we shall and soon, Duncan,' she said, but she didn't give him her cheek. Through the open door the rain was driving in against her long skirt. She stood there, watching him go out with Hugo, letting the light pour out to guide them round the corner of the house.

As soon as he was round that corner, Duncan felt an unpleasant jerk of shock. His car lights were dimly on, headlights on but with the feeble glow of sidelights.

'How did I come to do a thing like that?'

'I suppose you left them on to see your way to the door,' said Hugo, 'and then forgot them.'

'I'm sure I did *not*.'

'You must have. Hold the umbrella and I'll try the ignition.' Leaving Duncan on the flooded path under the inadequate umbrella, Hugo got into the driving seat and inserted the ignition key. The lights gave a flash and went out. Nothing else happened at all. It was now pitch dark. 'Not a spark,' said Hugo. 'Your battery's flat.'

'It *can't* be.'

'I'm afraid it is. Try for yourself.'

Duncan tried, getting very wet in the process.

'We'd better go back in the house. We'll get soaked out here.'

'What's the matter?' said Elizabeth, who was still standing in the doorway.

'His battery's flat. The car won't start.'

Of course it wasn't their fault, but somehow Duncan felt it was. It had happened, after all, at their house to which they had fetched him for a disgraceful purpose. He didn't bother to soften his annoyance.

'I'm afraid I'll just have to borrow your car, Hugo.'

Elizabeth closed the door. 'We don't have a car any more. We couldn't afford to run it. It was either keeping a car or taking the boys away from school, so we sold it.'

'I see. Then if I might just use your phone, I'll ring for a hire car. I've a mini-cab number in my wallet.' One look at her face told him that wasn't going to be possible either. 'Now you'll say you've had the phone cut off.' Damn her! Damn them both!

'We could have afforded it, of course. We just didn't need it any more. I'm sorry, Duncan. I just don't know what you can do. But we may as well all go and sit down where it's warmer.'

'I don't want to sit down,' Duncan almost shouted. 'I have to get home.' He shook off the hand she had laid on his arm and which seemed to be forcibly detaining him. 'I must just walk to the nearest house *with* a phone.'

Hugo opened the door. The rain was more like a wall of water than a series of falling drops. 'In this?'

'Then what am I supposed to do?' Duncan cried fretfully.

'Stay the night,' said Elizabeth calmly. 'I really don't know what you can do but stay the night.'

The bed was just what he would have expected a bed in the Crouch ménage to be, hard, narrow and cold. She had given him a hot water bottle which was an object he hadn't set eyes on in ten years. And Hugo had lent him a pair of pyjamas. All the time this was going on he had protested that he couldn't stay, that there must be some other way, but in the end he had yielded. Not that they had been welcoming. They had treated the whole thing rather as if — well, how had they treated it? Duncan lay in the dark, clutching the bottle between his knees, and tried to assess just what their attitude had been. Fatalistic, he thought, that was it. They had behaved as if this were inevitable, that there was no escape for him and here, like it or not, he must stay.

Escape was a ridiculous word, of course, but it was the sort of word you used when you were trapped somewhere for a whole night in the home of people who were obviously antagonistic, if not hostile. Why had he been such a fool as to leave those car lights on? He couldn't remember that he had done and yet he must have. Nobody else would have turned them on. Why should they?

He wished they would go to bed too. That they hadn't he could tell by the light, the rectangular outline of dazzlement that showed round the frame of his bedroom door. And he could hear them talking, not the words but the buzz of conversation. These late-Victorian houses were atrociously built, you could hear every sound. The rain drumming on the roof sounded as if it were pounding on cardboard rather than on slates. He didn't think there was much prospect of sleep. How could he sleep with the noise and all that on his mind, the worry of getting the car moved, of finding some way of getting to the office? And it made him feel very uneasy, their staying up like that, particularly as she had said, 'If you'll go into the bathroom first, Duncan, we'll follow you.' Follow him! That must have been all of half an hour ago. He pressed the switch of his bedlamp and saw that it was eleven thirty. Time they were in bed if she had to get to her school in the morning and he to his accountancy course.

Once more in the dark, but for that gold-edged rectangle, he considered the car lights question again. He was certain he had turned them out. Of course it was hard to be certain of anything when you were as upset as he. The pressure they had put on him had been simply horrible, and the worst moments those when he had been alone with Hugo while that woman was fishing out of her oven the ancient pullet she'd dished up to him. Really, she'd been a hell of a time getting that main course when you considered what it had amounted to. Could she . . . ? Only a madwoman would do such a thing, and what possible motive could she have had? But if you lived in a remote place and you wanted someone to stay in your house overnight, if you wanted to *keep* them there, how better than to immobilize their car? He shivered, even while he told himself such fancies were absurd.

At any rate, they were coming up now. Every board in the house creaked and the stairs played a tune like a broken old violin. He heard Hugo mumble something – the man had drunk far too much brandy – and then she said, 'Leave all the rest to me.'

Another shiver, that hadn't very much to do with the cold, ran through him. He couldn't think why he had shivered. Surely that was quite a natural thing for a woman to say on going to bed? She only meant, You go to bed and I'll lock up and turn off the lights. And yet it was a phrase that was familiar to him in quite another context. Turning on his side away from the light and into fresh caverns of icy sheet, he tried to think where he had heard it. A quotation? Yes – it came from *Macbeth*. Lady Macbeth said it when she and her husband were plotting the old king's murder. And what was the old king's name? Douglas? Donal?

Someone had come out of the bathroom and someone else gone in. Did they always take such ages getting to bed? The lavatory flush roared and a torrent rushed through pipes that seemed to pass under his bed. He heard footsteps cross the landing and a door close. Apparently, they slept in the room next to his. He turned over, longing for the light to go out. It was a pity there was no key in that lock so that he could have locked his door.

As soon as the thought had formed and been uttered in his brain, he thought how fantastic it was. What, lock one's bedroom door in a private house? Suppose his hostess came in the morning with a cup of tea? She would think it very odd. And she might come. She had put this bottle in his bed and had placed a glass of water on the table. Of course he couldn't dream of locking the door, and why should he want to? One of them was in the bathroom *again*.

Suddenly he found himself thinking about one of the men he had sacked and who had threatened him. The man had said, 'Don't think you'll get away with this, and if you show your ugly face within a mile of my place you may not live to regret it.' Of course he had got away with it and had nothing to regret. On the other hand, he hadn't shown himself within a mile of the man's place ... The light had gone out at last. Sleep now, he told himself. Empty your mind or think of something nice. Your summer holiday in the villa, for instance, think about that.

The gardens would be wonderful with the oleanders and the bougainvillea. And the sun would warm his old bones as he sat on his terrace, looking down through the cleft in the pines at the blue triangle of Mediterranean which was brighter and gentler than that woman's eyes ... Never mind the woman, forget her. Perhaps he should have the terrace raised and extended and set up on it that piece of statuary – surely Roman – which he had found in the pinewoods. It would cost a great deal of money, but it was his money. Why shouldn't he spend his own? He must try to be less sensitive, he thought, less troubled by this absurd social conscience which for some reason he had lately developed. Not, he reflected with a faint chuckle, that it actually stopped him spending his money or enjoying himself. It was a nuisance, that was all.

He would have the terrace extended and maybe a black marble floor laid in the *salon*. Fraser's profits looked as if they would hit a new high this year. Why not get that fellow Churchouse to do all their printing for them? If he was really down on his luck and desperate he'd be bound to work for a cut rate, jump at the chance, no doubt . . .

God damn it, it was too much! They were talking in there. He could hear their whisperings, rapid, emotional almost, through the wall. They were an absurd couple, no sense of humour between the pair of them. Intense, like characters out of some tragedy.

'The labour we delight in physics pain' – Macbeth had said that, Macbeth who killed the old king. And she had said it to him, Duncan, when he had apologized for the trouble he was causing. The king was called Duncan too. Of course he was. He was called Duncan and so was the old king and he too, in a way, was an old king, the monarch of the Fraser empire. Whisper, whisper, breathed the walls.

He sat up and put on the light. With the light on he felt better. He was sure, though, that he hadn't left those car lights on. 'Leave all the rest to me . . .' Why say that? Why not say what everyone said, 'I'll see to everything'? Macbeth and his wife had entertained the old king in their house and murdered him in his bed, although he had done them no harm, done nothing but be king. So it wasn't a parallel, was it? For he, Duncan Fraser, had done something, something which might merit vengeance. He had sacked Hugo Crouch and taken away his livelihood. It wasn't a parallel.

He turned off the light, sighed and lay down again. They were still whispering. He heard the floor creak as one of them came out of the bedroom. It wasn't a parallel – it was worse. Why hadn't he seen that? Lady Macbeth and her husband had no cause, no cause . . . A sweat broke out on his face and he reached for the glass of water. But he didn't drink. It was stupid not to but . . . The morning would soon come. 'O, never shall sun that morrow see . . . !' Where did that come from? Need he ask?

Whoever it was in the bathroom had left it and gone back to the

37

other one. But only for a moment. Again he heard the boards creak, again someone was moving about on that dark landing. Dark, yes, pitch-dark, for they hadn't switched the light on this time. And Duncan felt then the first thrill of real fear, the like of which he hadn't known since he was a little boy and had been shut up in the nursery cupboard of his father's manse. He mustn't be afraid, he mustn't. He must think of his heart. Why should they want vengeance? He'd explained. He'd told them the truth, taking the full burden of blame on himself.

The room was so dark that he didn't see the door handle turn. He heard it. It creaked very softly. His heart began a slow steady pounding and he contracted his body, forcing it back against the wall. Whoever it was had come into the room. He could see the shape of him – or her – as a denser blackness in the dark.

'What . . . ? Who . . . ?' he said, quavering, his throat dry.

The shape grew fluid, glided away, and the door closed softly. They wanted to see if he was asleep. They would kill him when he was asleep. He sat up, switched on the light and put his face in his hands. 'O, never shall sun that morrow see!' He'd put all that furniture against the door, that chest of drawers, his bed, the chair. His throat was parched now and he reached for the water, taking a long draught. It was icy cold.

They weren't whispering any more. They were waiting in silence. He got up and put his coat round him. In the bitter cold he began lugging the furniture away from the walls, lifting the iron bedstead that felt so small and narrow when he was in it but was so hideously weighty.

Straightening up from his second attempt, he felt it, the pain in his chest and down his left arm. It came like a clamp, a clamp being screwed and at the same time slowly heated red-hot. It took his body in hot iron fingers and squeezed his ribs. And sweat began to pour from him as if the temperature in the room had suddenly risen tremendously. O God, O God, the water in the glass! They would have to get him a doctor, they would have to, they couldn't be so pitiless. He was old and tired and his heart was bad.

He pulled the coat round the pain and staggered out into the black passage. Their door – where was their door? He found it by fumbling at the walls, scrabbling like an imprisoned animal, and when he found it he kicked it open and swayed on the threshold, holding the pain in both his hands.

They were sitting on their bed with their backs to him, not in bed but sitting there, the shapes of them silhouetted against the light of a small low-bulbed bedlamp.

'Oh, please,' he said, 'please help me. Don't kill me, I beg you not to kill me. I'll go on my knees to you. I know I've done wrong, I did a terrible thing. I didn't make an error of judgement. I sacked Hugo because he wanted too much for the staff, he wanted more money for everyone and I couldn't let them have it. I wanted my new car and my holidays. I had to have my villa – so beautiful, my villa and my gardens. Ah, God, I know I was greedy, but I've borne the guilt of it for months, every day on my conscience, the guilt of it . . .' They turned two white faces, implacable, merciless. They rose and came scrambling across their bed. 'Have pity on me,' he screamed. 'Don't kill me. I'll give you everything I've got, I'll give you a million . . .'

But they had seized him with their hands and it was too late. She had told him it was too late.

'In our house!' she said.

'Don't,' said Hugo. 'That's what Lady Macbeth said. What does it matter whether it was in our house or not?'

'I wish I'd never invited him.'

'Well, it was your idea. You said let's have him here because he's a widower and lonely. I didn't want him. It was ghastly the way he insisted on talking about firing me when we wanted to keep off the subject at any price. I was utterly fed-up when he had to stay the night.'

'What do we do now?' said Elizabeth.

'Get the police, I should think, or a doctor. It's stopped raining. I'll get dressed and go.'

'But you're not well! You kept throwing up.'

'I'm OK now. I drank too much brandy. It was such a strain, all of it, nobody knowing what to talk about. God, what a business! He was all right when you went into his room just now, wasn't he?'

'Half-asleep. I thought. I was going to apologize for all the racket you were making but he seemed nearly asleep. Did you get any of that he was trying to say when he came in here? I didn't.'

'No, it was just gibberish. We couldn't have done anything for him darling. We did try to catch him before he fell.'

'I know.'

'He had a bad heart.'

'In more ways than one, poor old man,' said Elizabeth, and she laid a blanket gently over Duncan, though he was past feeling heat or cold or guilt or fear or anything any more.

You Can't Be Too Careful

Della Galway went out with a man for the first (and almost the last) time on her nineteenth birthday. He parked his car, and as they were going into the restaurant she asked him if he had locked all the doors and the boot. When he turned back and said, yes, he'd better do that, she asked him why he didn't have a burglar-proof locking device on the steering wheel.

Her parents had brought her up to be cautious. When she left that happy home in that safe little provincial town, she took her parents' notions with her to London. At first she could only afford the rent of a single room. It upset her that the other tenants often came in late at night and left the front door on the latch. Although her room was at the top of the house and she had nothing worth stealing, she lay in bed sweating with fear. At work it was just the same. Nobody bothered about security measures. Della was always the last to leave, and sometimes she went back two or three times to check that all the office doors and the outer door were shut.

The personnel officer suggested she see a psychiatrist.

Della was very ambitious. She had an economics degree, a business studies diploma, and had come out top at the end of her secretarial course. She knew a psychiatrist would find something wrong with her – they had to earn their money like everyone else – and long sessions of treatment would follow which wouldn't help her towards her goal, that of becoming the company's first woman director. They always held that sort of thing against you.

'That won't be necessary,' she said in her brisk way. 'It was the firm's property I was worried about. If they like to risk losing their valuable equipment, that's their look-out.'

She stopped going back to check the doors – it didn't prey on her mind much as her own safety wasn't involved – and three weeks later two men broke in, stole all the electric typewriters and damaged the computer beyond repair. It proved her right, but she didn't say so.

41

The threat of the psychiatrist had frightened her so much that she never again aired her burglar obsession at work.

When she got promotion and a salary rise, she decided to get a flat of her own. The landlady was a woman after her own heart. Mrs Swanson liked Della from the first and explained to her, as to a kindred spirit, the security arrangements.

'This is a very nice neighbourhood, Miss Galway, but the crime rate in London is rising all the time, and I always say you can't be too careful.'

Della said she couldn't agree more.

'So I always keep this side gate bolted on the inside. The back door into this little yard must also be kept locked and bolted. The bathroom window looks out into the garden, you see, so I like the garden door and the bathroom door to be locked at night too.'

'Very wise,' said Della, noting that the window in the bed-sitting room had screws fixed to its sashes which prevented its being opened more than six inches. 'What did you say the rent was?'

'Twenty pounds a week.' Mrs Swanson was a landlady first, and a kindred spirit secondly, so when Della hesitated, she said, 'It's a garden flat, completely self-contained and you've got your own phone. I shan't have any trouble in letting it. I've got someone else coming to view it at two.'

Della stopped hesitating. She moved in at the end of the week, having supplied Mrs Swanson with references and assured her she was quiet, prudent as to locks and bolts, and not inclined to have 'unauthorized' people to stay overnight. By unauthorized people Mrs Swanson meant men. Since the episode over the car on her nineteenth birthday, Della had entered tentatively upon friendships with men, but no man had ever taken her out more than twice and none had ever got as far as to kiss her. She didn't know why this was, as she had always been polite and pleasant, insisting on paying her share, careful to carry her own coat, handbag and parcels so as to give her escort no trouble, ever watchful of his wallet and keys, offering to have the theatre tickets in her own safe keeping, and anxious not to keep him out too late. That one after another men dropped her worried her very little. No spark of sexual feeling had ever troubled her, and the idea of sharing her orderly, routine-driven life with a man – untidy, feckless, casual creatures as they all, with the exception of her father, seemed to be – was a daunting one. She meant to get to the top on her own. One day perhaps, when she was about thirty-five and with a high-powered lady executive's salary, then if some like-minded, quiet and prudent man came along ... In the meantime, Mrs Swanson had no need to worry.

Della was very happy with her flat. It was utterly quiet, a little sanctum tucked at the back of the house. She never heard a sound from her neighbours in the other parts of the house and they, of course, never heard a sound from her. She encountered them occasionally when crossing from her own front door to the front door of the house. They were mouselike people who scuttled off to their holes with no more than a nod and a 'good evening.' This was as it should be. The flat, too, was entirely as it should be.

The bed-sitter looked just like a living-room by day, for the bed was let down from a curtained recess in the wall only at night. Its window overlooked the yard which Della never used. She never unbolted the side gate or the back door or, needless to say, attempted to undo the screws and open the window more than six inches.

Every evening, when she had washed the dishes and wiped down every surface in the immaculate well-fitted kitchen, had her bath, made her bedtime drink, and let the bed down from the wall, she went on her security rounds just as her father did at home. First she unlocked and unbolted the back door and crossed the yard to check that the side gate was securely fastened. It always was as no one ever touched it, but Della liked to make absolutely sure, and sometimes went back several times in case her eyes had deceived her. Then she bolted and locked the back door, the garden door and the bathroom door. All these doors opened out of a small room, about ten feet square – Mrs Swanson called it the garden room – which in its turn could be locked off by yet another door from the kitchen. Della locked it. She rather regretted she couldn't lock the door that led from the kitchen into the bed-sitting room but, owing to some oversight on Mrs Swanson's part, there was no lock on it. However, her own front door in the bed-sitter itself was locked, of course, on the Yale. Finally, before getting into bed, she bolted the front door.

Then she was safe. Though she sometimes got up once or twice more to make assurance trebly sure, she generally settled down at this point into blissful sleep, certain that even the most accomplished of burglars couldn't break in.

There was only one drawback – the rent.

'That flat,' said Mrs Swanson, 'is really intended for two people. A married couple had it before you, and before that two ladies shared it.'

'I couldn't share my bed,' said Della with a shudder, 'or, come to that, my room.'

'If you found a nice friend to share I wouldn't object to putting up a single bed in the garden room. Then your friend could come and go by the side gate, provided you were prepared to *promise* me it would always be bolted at night.'

Della wasn't going to advertise for a flatmate. You couldn't be too careful. Yet she had to find someone if she was going to afford any new winter clothes, not to mention heating the place. It would have to be the right person, someone to fill all her own exacting requirements as well as satisfy Mrs Swanson . . .

'Ooh, it's lovely!' said Rosamund Vine. 'It's so quiet and clean. And you've got a garden! You should see the dump I've been living in. It was over-run with mice.'

'You don't get mice,' said Della repressively, 'unless you leave food about.'

'I won't do that. I'll be ever so careful. I'll go halves with the rent and I'll have the key to the back door, shall I? That way I won't disturb you if I come in late at night.'

'I hope you won't come in late at night,' said Della. 'Mrs Swanson's very particular about that sort of thing.'

'Don't worry.' Rosamund sounded rather bitter. 'I've nothing and no one to keep me out late. Anyway, the last bus passes the end of the road at a quarter to twelve.'

Della pushed aside her misgivings, and Mrs Swanson, interviewing Rosamund, appeared to have none. She made a point of explaining the safety precautions, to which Rosamund listened meekly and with earnest nods of her head. Della was glad this duty hadn't fallen to her, as she didn't want Rosamund to tell exaggerated tales about her at work. So much the better if she could put it all on Mrs Swanson.

Rosamund Vine had been chosen with the care Della devoted to every choice she made. It had taken three weeks of observation and keeping her ears open to select her. It wouldn't do to find someone on too low a salary or, on the other hand, someone with too lofty a position in the company. She didn't like the idea of a spectacularly good-looking girl, for such led hectic lives, or too clever a girl, for such might involve her in tiresome arguments. An elegant girl would fill the cupboards with clothes and the bathroom with cosmetics. A gifted girl would bring in musical instruments or looms or paints or trunks full of books. Only Rosamund, of all the candidates, qualified. She was small and quiet and prettyish, a secretary (though not Della's secretary), the daughter of a clergyman who, by coincidence, had been at the same university at the same time as Della's father. Della, who had much the same attitude as Victorian employers had to their maids' 'followers', noted that she had never heard her speak of a boy friend or overheard any cloakroom gossip as to Rosamund's love life.

The two girls settled down happily together. They seldom went out in the evenings. Della always went to bed at eleven sharp and would have relegated Rosamund to her own room at this point but for one small difficulty. With Rosamund in the garden room – necessarily sitting on her bed as there was nowhere else to sit – it wasn't possible for Della to make her security rounds. Only once had she tried doing it with Rosamund looking on.

'Goodness,' Rosamund had said, 'this place is like Fort Knox. All those keys and bolts! What are you so scared of?'

'Mrs Swanson likes to have the place locked up,' said Della, but the next night she made hot drinks for the two of them and sent Rosamund to wait for her in the bed-sitter before creeping out into the yard for a secret check-up.

When she came back Rosamund was examining her bedside table. 'Why do you put everything in order like that, Della? Your book at right angles to the table and your cigarette packet at right angles to your book, and, look, your ashtray's exactly an inch from the lamp as if you'd measured it out.'

'Because I'm a naturally tidy person.'

'I do think it's funny your smoking. I never would have guessed you smoked till I came to live here. It doesn't sort of seem in character. And your glass of water. Do you want to drink water in the night?'

'Not always,' Della said patiently. 'But I might want to, and I shouldn't want to have to get up and fetch it, should I?'

Rosamund's questions didn't displease her. It showed that the girl wanted to learn the right way to do things. Della taught her that a room must be dusted every day, the fridge de-frosted once a week, the table laid for breakfast before they went to bed, all the windows closed and the catches fastened. She drew Rosamund out as to the places she had previously lived in with a view to contrasting past squalor with present comfort, and she received a shock when Rosamund made it plain that in some of those rooms, attics, converted garages, she had lived with a man. Della made no comment but froze slightly. And Rosamund, thank goodness, seemed to understand her disapproval and didn't go into details. But soon after that she began going out in the evenings.

Della didn't want to know where she was going or with whom. She had plenty to occupy her own evenings, what with the work she brought home, her housework, washing and ironing, her twice-weekly letter to her mother and father, and the commercial Spanish she was teaching herself from gramophone records. It was rather a relief not to have Rosamund fluttering about. Besides, she could do her security rounds in peace. Not, of course, that she could check up on the side gate till Rosamund came in. Necessarily, it had to remain unbolted, and the back door to which Rosamund had the key, unlocked. But always by ten to twelve at the latest she'd hear the side gate open and close and hear Rosamund pause to draw the bolts. Then her feet tip-toeing across the yard, then the back door unlocked, shut, locked. After that, Della could sleep in peace.

The first problem arose when Rosamund came in one night and didn't bolt the gate after her. Della listened carefully in the dark, but she was positive those bolts had not been drawn. Even if the back door was locked, it was unthinkable to leave that side gate on nothing all night but its flimsy latch. She put on her dressing gown and went through the kitchen into the garden room. Rosamund was already in bed, her clothes flung about on the coverlet. Della picked them up and folded them. She was coming back from the yard, having fastened those bolts, when Rosamund sat up and said:

'What's the matter? Can't you sleep?'

'Mrs Swanson,' said Della with a light indulgent laugh, 'wouldn't be able to sleep if she knew you'd left that side gate unbolted.'

'Did I? Honestly, Della, I don't know what I'm doing half the time. I can't think of anyone but Chris. He's the most marvellous person and I do think he's just as mad about me as I am about him. I feel as if he's changed my whole life.'

Della let her spend nearly all the following evening describing the marvellous Chris, how brilliant he was – though at present unable to get a job fitting his talents – how amusing, how highly educated – though so poor as to be reduced to borrowing a friend's room while that friend was away. She listened and smiled and made appropriate remarks, but she wondered when she had last been so bored. Every time she got up to try and play one of her Spanish records, Rosamund was off again on another facet of Chris's dazzling personality, until at last Della had to say she had a headache and would Rosamund mind leaving her on her own for a bit?

'Anyway, you'll see him tomorrow. I've asked him for a meal.'

Unluckily, this happened to be the evening Della was going to supper with her aunt on the other side of London. They had evidently enjoyed themselves, judging by the mess in the kitchen, Della thought when she got home. There were few things she disliked more than wet dishes left to drain. Rosamund was asleep. Della crept out into the yard and checked that the bolts were fastened.

'I heard you wandering about ever so late,' said Rosamund in the morning. 'Were you upset about anything?'

'Certainly not. I simply found it rather hard to get to sleep because it was past my normal time.'

'Aren't you funny?' said Rosamund, and she giggled.

The next night she missed the last bus.

Della had passed a pleasant evening, studying firstly the firm's annual report, then doing a Spanish exercise. By eleven she was in bed, reading the memoirs of a woman company chairman. Her bedside light went off at half-past and she lay in the dark waiting for the sound of the side gate.

Her clock had luminous hands, and when they passed ten to twelve she began to feel a nasty tingly jumping sensation all over her body. She put on the light, switched it off immediately. She didn't want Rosamund bursting in with all her silly questions and comments. But Rosamund didn't burst in, and the hands of the clock closed together on midnight. There was no doubt about it. The last bus had gone and Rosamund hadn't been on it.

Well, the silly girl needn't think she was going to stand this sort of thing. She'd bolt that side gate herself and Rosamund could stay out in the street all night. Of course she might ring the front door bell, she was silly and inconsiderate enough to do that, but it couldn't be helped. Della would far rather be awakened at one or two o'clock than lie there knowing that side gate was open for anyone to come in. She put on her dressing gown and made her way through the spotless kitchen to the garden room. Rosamund had hung a silly sort of curtain over the back door, not a curtain really but a rather dirty Indian bedspread. Della lifted it distastefully – and then she realized. She couldn't bolt the side gate because the back door into the yard was locked and Rosamund had the key.

A practical person like herself wasn't going to be done that way. She'd go out by the front door, walk round to the side entrance and – but, no, that wouldn't work either. If she opened the gate and bolted it on the inside, she'd simply find herself bolted inside the yard. The only thing was to climb out of the window. She tried desperately to undo the window screws, but they had seized up from years of

47

disuse and she couldn't shift them. Trembling now, she sat down on the edge of her bed and lit a cigarette. For the first time in her life she was in an insecure place by night, alone in a London flat, with nothing to separate her from hordes of rapacious burglars but a feeble back door lock which any type of a thief could pick open in five minutes.

How criminally careless of Mrs Swanson not to have provided the door between the bed-sitter and the kitchen with a lock! There was no heavy piece of furniture she could place against the door. The phone was by her bed, of course. But if she heard a sound and dialled for the police was there a chance of their getting there before she was murdered and the place ransacked?

What Mrs Swanson had provided was one of the most fearsome-looking breadknives Della had ever seen. She fetched it from the kitchen and put it under her pillow. Its presence made her feel slightly safer, but suppose she didn't wake up when the man came in, suppose . . . ? That was ridiculous, she wouldn't sleep at all. Exhausted, shaken, feeling physically sick, she crawled under the bedclothes and, after concentrated thought, put the light out. Perhaps, if there was no light on, he would go past her, not know she was there, make his way into the main part of the house, and if by then she hadn't actually died of fright . . .

At twenty minutes past one, when she had reached the point of deciding to phone for a car to take her to an hotel, the side gate clicked and Rosamund entered the yard. Della fell back against the pillows with a relief so tremendous that she couldn't even bother to go out and check the bolts. So what if it wasn't bolted? The man would have to pass Rosamund first, kill her first. Della found she didn't care at all about what might happen to Rosamund, only about her own safety.

She sneaked out at half-past six to put the knife back, and she was sullenly eating her breakfast, the flat immaculate, when Rosamund appeared at eight.

'I missed the last bus. I had to get a taxi.'

'You could have phoned.'

'Goodness, you sound just like my mother. It was bad enough having to get up and . . .' Rosamund blushed and put her hand over her mouth. 'I mean, go *out* and get that taxi and . . . Well, I wasn't all that late,' she muttered.

Her little slip of the tongue hadn't been lost on Della. But she was too tired to make any rejoinder beyond saying that Mrs Swanson would be very annoyed if she knew, and would Rosamund give her fair warning next time she intended to be late? Rosamund said when they met again that evening that she couldn't give her fair warning, as she could never be sure herself. Della said no more. What, anyway, would be the use of knowing what time Rosamund was coming in when she couldn't bolt the gate?

Three mornings later her temper flared.

On two of the intervening nights Rosamund had missed the last bus. The funny thing was that she didn't look at all tired or jaded, while Della was worn-out. For three hours on the previous night she had lain stiffly clutching the breadknife while the old house creaked about her and the side gate rattled in the wind.

'I don't know why you bother to come home at all.'

'Won't you mind if I don't?'

'Not a bit. Do as you like.'

Stealthily, before Rosamund left the flat by the front door, Della slipped out and bolted the gate. Rosamund, of course (being utterly imprudent), didn't check the gate before she locked the back door. Della fell into a heavy sleep at ten o'clock to be awakened just after two by a thudding on the side gate followed by a frenzied ringing of the front door bell.

'You locked me out!' Rosamund sobbed. 'Even my mother never did that. I was locked out in the street and I'm frozen. What have I done to you that you treat me like that?'

'You said you weren't coming home.'

'I wasn't going to, but we went out and Chris forgot his key. He's had to sleep at a friend's place. I wish I'd gone there too!'

They were evidently two of a kind. Well-suited, Della thought. Although it was nearly half-past two in the morning, this seemed the best moment to have things out. She addressed Rosamund in her precise schoolmistressy voice.

'I think we'll have to make other arrangements, Rosamund. Your ways aren't my ways, and we don't really get on, do we? You can stay here till you find somewhere else, but I'd like you to start looking round straightaway.'

'But what have I *done*? I haven't made a noise or had my friends here. I haven't even used your phone, not once. Honestly, Della, I've done my best to keep the place clean and tidy, and it's nearly killed me.'

'I've explained what I mean. We're not the same kind of people.'

'I'll go on Saturday. I'll go to my mother — it won't be any worse. God knows — and then maybe Chris and I . . .'

'You'd better go to bed now,' Della said coldly, but she couldn't get any sleep herself. She was wondering how she had been such a bad judge of character, and wondering too what she was going to do about the rent. Find someone else, of course. An older woman perhaps, a widow or a middle-aged spinster . . .

What she was determined not to do was reveal to Rosamund, at this late stage, her anxiety about the side gate. If anything remained to comfort her, it was the knowledge that Rosamund thought her strong, mature and sensible. But not revealing it brought her an almost unbearable agony. For Rosamund seemed to think the very sight of her would be an embarrassment to Della. Each evening she was gone from the flat before Della got home, and each time she had gone out leaving the side gate unbolted and the back door locked. Della had no way of knowing whether she would come in on the last bus or get a taxi or be seen home in the small hours by Chris. She didn't know whether Chris lived near or far away, and now she wished she had listened more closely to Rosamund's confidences and asked a few questions of her own. Instead, she had only thought with a shudder how nasty it must be to have to sleep with a man, and had wondered if she would ever bring herself to face the prospect.

Each night she took the breadknife to bed with her, confirmed in her conviction that she wasn't being unreasonable when one of the mouselike people whom she met in the hall told her the house next door had been broken into and its old woman occupant knocked on the head. Rosamund came in once at one, once at half-past two, and once she didn't come in at all. Della got great bags under her eyes and her skin looked grey. She fell asleep over her desk at work, while a bright-eyed vivacious Rosamund regaled her friends in the cloakroom about the joys of her relationship with Chris.

But now there was only one more night to go . . .

Rosamund had left a note to say she wouldn't be home. She'd see Della on the following evening when she collected her cases to take them to her mother. But she'd left the side gate unbolted. Della seriously considered bolting it and then climbing back over it into the side entrance, but it was too high and smooth for her to climb and there wasn't a ladder. Nothing for it but to begin her vigil with the cigarettes, the glass of water, the phone and the breadknife. It ought to have been easier, this last night, just because it was the last. Instead it was worse than any of the others. She lay in the dark, thinking of the old woman next door, of the house that was precisely the same as the one next door, and of the intruder who now knew

50

the best and simplest way in. She tried to think of something else, anything else, but the strongest instinct of all over-rode all her feeble attempts to concentrate on tomorrow, on work, on ambition, on the freedom and peace of tomorrow when that gate would be fastened for good, never again to be opened.

Rosamund had said she wouldn't be in. But you couldn't rely on a word she said. Della wasn't, therefore, surprised (though she was overwhelmingly relieved) to hear the gate click just before two. Sighing with a kind of ecstasy – for tomorrow had come – she listened for the sound of the bolts being drawn across. The sound didn't come. Well, that was a small thing. She'd fasten the bolts herself when Rosamund was in bed. She heard footsteps moving very softly, and then the back door was unlocked. Rosamund took a longer time than usual about unlocking it, but maybe she was tired or drunk or heaven knew what.

Silence.

Then the back door creaked and made rattling sounds as if Rosamund hadn't bothered to re-lock it. Wearily, Della hoisted herself out of bed and slipped her dressing gown round her. As she did so, the kitchen light came on. The light showed round the edges of the old door in a brilliant phosphorescent rectangle. That wasn't like Rosamund who never went into the kitchen, who fell immediately into bed without even bothering to wash her face. A long shiver ran through Della. Her body taut but trembling, she listened. Footsteps were crossing the kitchen floor and the fridge door was opened. She heard the sounds of fumbling in cupboards, a drawer was opened and silver rattled. She wanted to call out, 'Rosamund, Rosamund, is that you?' but she had no voice. Her mouth was dry and her voice had gone. Something occurred to her that had never struck her before. It struck her with a great thrust of terror. How would she know, how had she ever known, whether it was Rosamund or another who entered the flat by the side gate and the frail back door?

Then there came a cough.

It was a slight cough, the sound of someone clearing his throat, but it was unmistakably *his* throat. There was a man in the kitchen.

Della forgot the phone. She remembered – though she had scarcely for a moment forgotten her – the old woman next door. Blind terror thrust her to her feet, plunged her hand under the pillow for the knife. She opened the kitchen door, and he was there, a tall man, young and strong, standing right there on the threshold with Mrs Swanson's silver in one hand and Mrs Swanson's heavy iron pan in the other. Della didn't hesitate. She struck hard with the knife, struck again and again until the bright blood flew across the white walls and the clean ironing and the table neatly laid for breakfast.

The policeman was very nice to Rosamund Vine. He called her by her Christian name and gave her a cup of coffee. She drank the coffee, though she didn't really want it as she had had a cup at the hospital when they told her Chris was dead.

'Tell me about last night, will you, Rosamund?'

'I'd been out with my boy friend – Chris – Chris Maitland. He'd forgotten his key and he hadn't anywhere to sleep, so I said to come back with me. He was going to leave early in the morning before she – before Della was up. We were going to be very careful about that. And we were terribly quiet. We crept in at about two.'

'You didn't call out?'

'No, we thought she was asleep. That's why we didn't speak to each other, not even in whispers. But she must have heard us.' Her voice broke a little. 'I went straight to bed. Chris was hungry. I said if he was as quiet as a mouse he could get himself something from the fridge, and I told him where the knives and forks and plates were. The next thing I heard this ghastly scream and I ran out and – and Chris was . . . There was blood everywhere . . .'

The policeman waited until she was calmer.

'Why do you think she attacked him with a knife?' he asked.

'I don't know.'

'I think you do, Rosamund.'

'Perhaps I do.' Rosamund looked down. 'She didn't like me going out.'

'Because she was afraid of being there alone?'

'Della Galway,' said Rosamund, 'wasn't afraid of anything. Mrs Swanson was nervous about burglars, but Della wasn't. Everyone in the house knew about the woman next door getting coshed, and they were all nervous. Except Della. She didn't even mention it to me, and she must have known.'

'So she didn't think Chris was a burglar?'

'Of course she didn't.' Rosamund started to cry. 'She saw a man – my man. She couldn't get one of her own. Every time I tried to talk about him she went all cold and stand-offish. She heard us come in last night and she understood and – and it sent her over the edge. It

52

drove her crazy. I'd heard they wanted her to see a psychiatrist at work, and now I know why.'

The policeman shivered a little in spite of his long experience. Fear of burglars he could understand, but this . . . 'She'll see one now,' he said, and then he sent the weeping girl home to her mother.

The Double

Strange dishevelled women who had the air of witches sat round the table in Mrs Cleasant's drawing room. One of them, a notable medium, seemed to be making some sort of divination with a pack of Tarot cards. Later on, when it got dark, they would go on to table-turning. The aim was to raise up the spirit of Mr Cleasant, one year dead, and also perhaps, Peter thought with anger and disgust, to frighten Lisa out of her wits.

'Where are you going?' said Mrs Cleasant when Lisa came back with her coat on.

Peter answered for her. 'I'm taking her for a walk in Holland Park, and then we'll have a meal somewhere.'

'Holland Park?' said the medium. If a corpse could have spoken it would have had a voice like hers. 'Take care, be watchful. That place has a reputation.'

The witch women looked at her expectantly, but the medium had returned to her Tarot and was eyeing the Empress which she had brought within an inch or two of her long nose. Peter was sickened by the lot of them. Six months to go, he thought, and he'd take her out of this – this coven.

It was a Sunday afternoon in spring, and the air in the park was fresh and clean, almost like country air. Peter drew in great gulps of it, cleansing himself of the atmosphere of that drawing room. He wished Lisa would unwind, be less nervous and strung-up. The hand he wasn't holding kept going up to the charm she wore on a chain round her neck or straying out to knock on wood as they passed a fence.

Suddenly she said, 'What did that woman mean about the park's reputation?'

'Some occult rubbish. How should I know? I hate that sort of thing.'

'So do I,' she said, 'but I'm afraid of it.'

'When we're married you'll never have to have any more to do with it. I'll see to that. God, I wish we could get married now or you'd come and live with me till we can.'

'I can't marry you till I'm eighteen without Mummy's permission, and if I go and live with you they'll make me a ward of court.'

'Surely not, Lisa.'

'Anyway, there's only six months to wait. It's hard for me too. Don't you think I'd rather live with you than with Mummy?'

The childish rejoinder made him smile. 'Come on, try and look a bit more cheerful. I want to take your photograph. If I can't have you, I'll have your picture.' They had reached a sunny open space where he sat her on a log and told her to smile. He got the camera out of its case. 'Don't look at those people, darling. Look at me.'

It was a pity the man and the girl had chosen that moment to sit down on the wooden seat.

'Lisa!' he said sharply, and then he wished he hadn't, for her face crumpled with distress. He went up to her. 'What's the matter now, Lisa?'

'Look at that girl,' she said.

'All right. What about her?'

'She's exactly like me. She's my double.'

'Nonsense. What makes you say that? Her hair's the same colour and you're about the same build, but apart from that, there's no resemblance. She's years older than you and she's . . .'

'Peter, you must see it! She might be my twin. Look, the man with her has noticed. He looked at me and said something to her and then they both looked.'

He couldn't see more than a superficial similarity. 'Well, supposing she were your double, which I don't for a moment admit, so what? Why get in such a state about it?'

'Don't you know about doubles? Don't you know that if you see your double, you're seeing your own death, you die within the year?'

'Oh, Lisa, come *on*. I never heard anything so stupid. This is more rubbish you've picked up from those crazy old witches. It's just sick superstition.' But nothing he could say calmed her. Her face had grown white and her eyes troubled. Worried for her rather than angry, he put out his hand and helped her to her feet. She leant against him, trembling, and he saw she was clutching her amulet. 'Let's go,' he said. 'We'll find another place to take your picture. Don't look at her if it upsets you. Forget her.'

When they had gone off along the path, the man on the seat said to his companion, 'Couldn't you really see that girl was the image of you?'

'I've already told you, no.'

'Of course you look a good deal older and harder, I'll give you that.'

'Thank you.'

'But you're almost her double. Take away a dozen years and a dozen love affairs, and you'd *be* her double.'

'Stephen, if you're trying to start another row, just say so and I'll go home.'

'I'm not starting anything. I'm fascinated by an extraordinary phenomenon. Holland Park's known to be a strange place. There's a legend you can see your own double there.'

'I never heard that.'

'Nevertheless, my dear Zoe, it is so.

'"The Magus Zoroaster, my dead child,
Met his own image walking in the garden."'

'Who said that?'

'Shelley. Superstition has it that if you see your own image you die within the year.'

She turned slowly to look at him. 'Do you want me to die within the year, Stephen?'

He laughed. 'Oh, you won't die. You didn't see her, she saw you. And it frightened her. He was taking her photograph, did you see? I wish I'd asked him to take one of you two together. Why don't we see if we can catch them up?'

'You know, you have a sick imagination.'

'No, only a healthy curiosity. Come along now, if we walk fast we'll catch them up by the gate.'

'If it amuses you,' said Zoe.

Peter and Lisa didn't see the other couple approaching. They were walking with their arms round each other, and Peter had managed to distract her from the subject of her double by talking of their wedding plans. At the northern gate someone behind him called out, 'Excuse me!' and he turned to see the man who had been sitting on the seat.

'Yes?' he said rather stiffly.

'I expect you'll think this is frightful cheek, but I saw you back there and I was absolutely – well, struck by the likeness between my girl friend and the young lady with you. There is a terrific likeness, isn't there?'

'I don't see it,' said Peter, not daring to look at Lisa. What a beastly thing to happen! He felt dismay. 'Frankly, I don't see any resemblance at all.'

'Oh, but you must. Look, what I want is for you to do me an enormous favour and take a picture of them together. Will you? Do say you will.'

Peter was about to refuse, and not politely, when Lisa said, 'Why not? Of course he will. It's such a funny coincidence, we ought to have a record of it.'

'Good girl! We'd better introduce ourselves then, hadn't we? I'm Stephen Davidson and this is Zoe Conti.'

'Lisa Cleasant and Peter Milton,' said Peter, still half-stunned by Lisa's warm response.

'Hallo, Lisa and Peter. Lovely to know you. Now you two girls go and stand over there in that spot of sunshine . . .'

So Peter took the photograph and said he'd send Stephen and Zoe a copy when the film was developed. She gave him the address of the flat she and Stephen shared and he noted it was in the next street but one to his. They might have walked there together, which was what Stephen, remarking on this second coincidence, seemed to want. But seeing the tense, strained look in Lisa's eyes, Peter refused, and they separated in Holland Park Avenue.

'You didn't mind about not going with them, did you?' said Lisa.

'Of course not. I'd rather be alone with you.'

'I'm glad,' she said, and then, 'I did it for you.'

He understood. She had done it for him, to prove to him she could conquer those superstitious terrors. For his sake, because he wanted it, she would try. He took her in his arms and kissed her.

She leant against him. He could feel her heart beating. 'I shan't tell anyone else about it,' she said, and he knew she meant her mother and the witch women.

When the film was developed he didn't show it to her. Zoe and Stephen should have their copy and that would be an end of the whole incident. But when he was putting it into an envelope, he realized he would have to write a covering note, which was a bore as he didn't like writing letters. Besides, if he was going to take it to the post, he might as well take it to their home. This, one evening, he did.

He had no intention of going in. But as he was slipping the envelope into the letter box, Zoe appeared behind him on the steps.

'Come in and have a drink.'

He couldn't think of an excuse, so he accepted. She led him up two flights of stairs, looking at the photograph as she went.

'So much for this fantastic likeness,' she said. 'Could you ever see it?'

Peter said he couldn't, wondering how Lisa could have been so silly as to fancy she had seen her double in this woman of thirty, who tonight had a drawn and haggard look. 'It was mostly in your friend's imagination,' he said as they entered the flat. 'We'll see what he says about it now.'

For a moment she didn't answer. When her reply came it was brusque. 'He's left me.'

Peter was embarrassed. 'I'm sorry.' He looked into her face, at the eyes whose dark sockets were like bruises. 'Are you very unhappy?'

'I shan't take an overdose, if that's what you mean. We'd been together for four years. It's hard to take. But I won't bore you with it. Let's talk about something else.'

Peter had only meant to stay half an hour, but the half-hour grew into an hour, and when Zoe said she was going to cook her dinner and would he stay and have it with her, he agreed. She was interesting to talk to. She was a music therapist, and she talked about her work and played records. When they had finished their meal, a simple but excellent one, she reverted to her own private life and told him something of her long and fraught relationship with Stephen. But she spoke without self-pity. And she could listen as well as talk. It meant something to him to be able to confide in a mature well-balanced woman who heard him out without interruption while he spoke of himself and Lisa, how they were going to be married when she was eighteen and when she would inherit half her dead father's fortune. Not, he said, that the money had anything to do with it. He'd have preferred her to be penniless. All he wanted was to get her away from that unhealthy atmosphere of dabbling with the occult, from that cloistral home where she was sheltered yet corrupted.

'What is she afraid of?' asked Zoe when he told her about the wood-touching and the indispensable amulet.

He shrugged. 'Of fate? Of some avenging fury that resents her happiness?'

'Or of loss,' said Zoe. 'She lost her father. Perhaps she's afraid of losing you.'

'That's the last thing she need be afraid of,' he said.

It was midnight before he left. The next day he meant to tell Lisa where he had been. There were no secrets between them. But Lisa was nervous and uneasy – she and Mrs Cleasant had been to a spiritualist meeting – and he thought it unwise to raise once more a subject that was better forgotten. So he said nothing. After all, he would never see Zoe again.

But a month or so later, a month in which he and Lisa had been happy and tranquil together, he met the older girl by chance in the Portobello Road. While they talked, it occurred to him that he had eaten a meal in her flat and that he owed her dinner. He and Lisa would take her out to dinner. In her present mood, Lisa would like that, and it would be good for her to see, after the lapse of time, how her superstitiousness had led her into error. He put the invitation to Zoe who hesitated, then accepted when he explained it would be a threesome. Dinner, then, in a fortnight's time, and he and Lisa would call for her.

'I met that girl Zoe and asked her to have dinner with us. All right with you?'

The frightened child look came back into Lisa's face.

'Oh, no, Peter! I thought you understood, I don't ever want to see her again.'

'But why not? You've seen the photograph, you've seen how silly those ideas of yours were. And Stephen won't be there. I know you didn't like him and neither did I. But they're not together any more. He's left her.'

She shivered. 'Let's not get to know her, Peter.'

'I've invited her,' he said. 'I can't go back on that now.'

When the evening came, Zoe appeared at her door in a long gown, her hair dressed on top of her head. She looked majestic, mysteriously changed.

'Where's Lisa?' she asked.

'She couldn't come. She and her mother are going on holiday to Greece at the end of the week and she's busy packing.' Part of this was true. He said it confidently, as if it were wholly true. He couldn't take his eyes off the new transformed Zoe, and he was glad he had booked a table in an exclusive restaurant.

In the soft lamplight her youth had come back to her. And for the first time he was aware of the likeness between her and Lisa. The older and the younger sister, by a trickery of light and cosmetics and maybe of his own wistful imagination, had met in years and become twins. It might have been his Lisa who spoke to him across the table, across the silver and glass and the single rose in a vase, but a Lisa

59

whom life and experience had matured. Never could Lisa have talked like this of books and music and travel, or listened to him so responsively or advised with such wisdom. He was sorry when the evening came to an end and he left her at her door.

Lisa seemed to have forgotten his engagement to dine with Zoe. She didn't mention it, so he didn't either. On the following morning she was to leave with her mother for the month's holiday the doctor had recommended for Mrs Cleasant's health.

'I wish I wasn't going,' she said to Peter. 'You don't know how I'll miss you.'

'Shan't I miss you?'

'Take care of yourself. I'll worry in case anything happens to you. You mustn't laugh, but when my father was alive and went away from us, I used to listen to the news four or five times a day in case there was a plane crash or a disaster.'

'You're the one that's going away, Lisa.'

'It comes to the same thing.' She put up her hand to the charm she wore. 'I've got this, but you . . . Would you take my four-leaved clover if I gave it to you?'

'I thought you'd given up all that nonsense,' he said, and his disappointment in her soured their farewells. She kissed him good-bye with a kind of passionate sadness.

'Write to me,' she said. 'I'll write every day.'

Her letters started coming at the end of the first week. They were the first he had ever had from her and they were like school essays written by a geography student, with love messages for the class teacher inserted here and there. They left him unsatisfied, a little peevish. He was lonely without her, but frightened of the image of her he carried with him. He needed someone with whom to talk it over and, after a few days of indecision, he telephoned Zoe. Ten minutes later he was in her flat, drinking her coffee and listening to her music. To be with her was a greater comfort than he had thought possible, for in the turn of her head, a certain way of hers of smiling, the way her hair grew from a widow's peak on her forehead, he caught glimpses of Lisa.

And yet on that occasion he said nothing of his fears but 'I can't understand why I thought you and Lisa weren't alike.'

'I didn't see it.'

'It's almost overpowering, it's uncanny.'

She smiled. 'If it helps you to come and see me to get through the time while she's away, that's all right with me, Peter. I can understand that I remind you of her and that makes things easier for you.'

'It isn't only that,' he said. 'You mustn't think it's only that.'

She said no more. It wasn't her way to probe, to hold inquisitions, or to set an egotistical value on herself. But the next time they were together, he explained without being asked, and his explanation was appalling to him, the words more powerful and revealing than the thoughts from which they had sprung.

'It isn't true you remind me of Lisa. That's not it. It's that I see in you what she might become, only she never will.'

'Who would want to be like me?'

'Everyone. Every young girl. Because you're what a woman should be, Zoe, clever and sane and kind and self-reliant and – beautiful.'

'And if that's true,' she said lightly, 'though I disagree, why shouldn't Lisa become like that?'

'Because when she's eighteen she'll be rich, an heiress. She'll never have to work for her living or struggle or learn. We'll live in a house near her mother and she'll get like her mother, vain and neurotic, living on sleeping pills, spending all her time with spiritualists and getting involved in sick cults. When I look at you I don't see Lisa's double. I see her, an alternative she, if you like, thirteen years ahead in time if another path had been marked out for her in life. And at the same time I see you as you'd be if you'd led the sort of life she must and will lead.'

'You can help her not to lead that life if you love her,' said Zoe.

And then Lisa's letters stopped coming. A week went by without a letter. He had resolved, because of what was happening to him, not to see Zoe again. But she lived so near and he thought of her so often that he was unable to resist. He went to her and told a lie that he convinced himself might be the truth. Lisa was too young to have a firm and faithful love for anyone. Her letters had grown cold and had finally ceased to come. Zoe listened to him, to his urgent persuasions, his comparison of his forsaken state with her own, and when he kissed her, she responded at first with doubts, then with an ardour born of her own loneliness. They made love. When, later, he asked her if he might stay the night, she said he could and he did.

After that, he spent every night with her. He hardly went home. When he did he found ten letters waiting for him on the doormat. Lisa and her mother had gone on to some Aegean island – the home of a mystic Mrs Cleasant longed to meet – where the posts were hazardous. He read the childish letters, the 'darling Peter, I miss you,

I'll never go away again' with impatience and with guilt, and then he went back to Zoe.

Why did he have to mention those letters to her? He wished he hadn't. It was for her wisdom and her honesty that he had wanted her, and now those very qualities were striking back at him.

'When is she coming home?'

'Next Saturday,' he said.

'Peter, I don't know what you mean to do, leave me and marry her, or leave her and stay with me. But you must tell her about us, whatever you decide.'

'I can't do that!'

'You must. Either way, you must. And if you mean to stay with me, what alternative have you?'

Stay with them both until he was sure, until he knew for certain. 'You know I can't be without you, Zoe. But I can't tell her, not yet. She's such a child.'

'You're going to marry that child. You love her.'

'Do I?' he said. 'I thought I did.'

'I won't be a party to deceiving her, Peter. You must understand that. If you won't promise to tell her, I can't see you again.'

Perhaps when he saw Lisa . . . He went across the park to her mother's house on the Sunday evening. The medium was there and another woman who looked like a participant in a Black Mass, earnestly listening to Mrs Cleasant's account of the mystic and his investigations into the mysteries of the Great Pyramid. Lisa rushed into his arms, actually crying with happiness.

'This child has dreamed about you every night, Peter,' said Mrs Cleasant with one of her weird faraway looks. 'Such dreams she has had! Of course she's psychic like me. When we knew the posts were delayed I wanted her to get a message through to you by the Power of Thought, but she was unwilling.'

'I knew you wouldn't like it,' said Lisa. She sat on his knee, in his arms. Of course he couldn't tell her. In time, maybe, if he got their wedding postponed and cooled things and . . . But it was out of the question to tell her now.

He told Zoe he had. In order to see her again, he had to do that.

'How did she take it?'

'Oh, quite well,' he lied. 'A lot of men have been paying her attention on holiday. I think she's just beginning to realize I'm not the only man in the world.'

'And she accepts – us?'

Why did she have to persist, why make it so painful for him? He spoke boldly but with an inner self-disgust.

'I daresay she sees it as a let-out for her own freedom.'

She was convinced. The habitual truth-teller is reluctant to detect falsehood in others. 'Of course I've only met her once, and then only for a few minutes. But I wonder if you weren't deceiving yourself, Peter, when you said she loved you so much. You aren't going to see her again?'

He said he wasn't. He said it was all over, they had parted. But the enormity of what he had done appalled him. And when next he was with Lisa he found himself telling her all over again, and meaning it, how much he loved her and longed to take her away. Was he going to sacrifice that childish passionate love for a woman five years older than himself? They were, in many ways, so alike. Suppose, in time to come, he grew tired of the one and regretted the other? Yet, that night, he went back to Zoe.

With a skilful but frightening intrigue, he divided his time between the one and the other. It wasn't too difficult. Social – and occult – demands were always being made on Lisa. Zoe believed him when he said he had been kept late at work. Autumn came, and it was still going on, this double life. His need for, his dependence on, Zoe intensified and he had begun to resent every moment he spent away from her. But Lisa and her mother had fixed his wedding date and with fatality he accepted its inexorable approach.

On an afternoon in October he was to meet Zoe in Holland Park, by the northern gate. Lisa was going for a fitting of her wedding dress and afterwards to dine with her mother in what he called the medium's lair. So that was all right. He waited by the gate for nearly an hour. When Zoe didn't come, he went to her flat but received no answer to his ring. From his own home he telephoned her five times during the evening, but each time the bell rang into emptiness. He passed a sleepless night, the first night he had been on his own for four months.

All the next day, from work, he kept trying to call her, and for the first time since he had known her he made no call to Lisa. But his own phone was ringing when he got home at six. Of course it was Zoe, it must be. He took up the receiver and heard the fraught voice of Mrs Cleasant.

'Peter?'

Disappointment hurt him like pain. 'Yes,' he said. 'How are you? How's Lisa?'

'Peter, I have very bad news. I think you had better come here. Yes, now. At once.'

'What is it? Has anything happened to Lisa?'

'Lisa has – has passed over. Last night she took an overdose of my pills. I found her dead this morning.'

He went out again at once. In the park, at dusk, the leaves were dying and livid, some already fallen. At this point, when they had been showing their first green of spring, he had taken the photograph, at this, he had seated her in a sunny open space and she had seen Zoe.

Mrs Cleasant wasn't alone. Some of the members of her magic circle were with her, but she was calmer than he had ever seen her and he guessed she was drugged.

'How did it happen?' he said.

'I told you. She took an overdose.'

'But – why?' He shrank away from the medium's eyes which, staring, seemed to see ghosts behind him.

'Nothing to do with you, Peter,' said Mrs Cleasant. 'She loved you, you know that. And she was so happy yesterday. Her fitting was cancelled. She said she wanted fresh air because it was such a lovely day, and then she'd walk over to you. She'd thrown away her charm – that amulet she wore – because she said you didn't like it. I told her not to, as it was a harmless thing and might do good. Who knows? If she had been wearing it . . .'

'Ah, if she had been under the Protection!' said the medium.

Mrs Cleasant went on, 'We were going out to dinner. I waited and waited for her. When she didn't come I went alone. I thought she was with you, safe with you. But I came back early and there she was, looking so tired and afraid. She said she was going to bed. I asked her if there was anything wrong and she said . . .' But Mrs Cleasant's voice quavered into sobs and the witch women fluttered about her, touching her and murmuring.

It was the medium who explained in her corpse voice. 'She said she had seen her own double in the park.'

'But that was six months ago,' he burst out. 'That was in April!'

'No, she saw her own double yesterday afternoon, her image walking in the garden. And she dared to speak to it. Who can tell what your own death will tell you when you dare to address it?'

He ran away from them then, out of the house. He hailed a taxi and in a shaking whisper asked the driver to take him to where Zoe lived. All the lights were on in her windows. He rang the bell, rang it again and again. Then, while the lights still blazed but she didn't come down, he hammered on the door with his fists, calling her name. When he knew she wasn't going to come, that he had lost her and her image, her double and her, for ever, he sank down on the doorstep and wept.

The taxi driver, returning along the street in search of a fare, supposed him to be drunk, and learning his address from the broken mutterings, took him home.

The Venus Fly Trap

As soon as Daphne had taken off her hat and put it on Merle's bed, Merle picked it up and rammed it on her own yellow curls. It was a red felt hat and by chance it matched Merle's red dress.

'It's a funny thing, dear,' said Merle, looking at herself in the dressing-table mirror, 'but anyone seeing us two – any outsider, I mean – would never think that I was the single one and you'd had all those husbands and children.'

'I only had two husbands and three children,' said Daphne.

'You know what I mean,' said Merle, and Daphne, standing beside her friend, had to admit that she did. Merle was so big, so pink and overflowing and female, while she – well, she had given up pretending she was anything but a little dried-up widow, seventy years old and looking every day of it.

Merle took off the hat and placed it beside the doll whose yellow satin skirts concealed her nightdress and her bag of hair rollers. 'I'll show you the flat and then we'll have a sherry and put our feet up. I got some of that walnut brown in. You see I haven't forgotten your tastes even after forty years.'

Daphne didn't say it was dry sherry she had then, and still, preferred. She trotted meekly after Merle. She was just beginning to be aware of the intense heat. Clouds of warmth seemed to breathe out of the embossed wallpaper and up through the lush furry carpets.

'I really am thrilled about you coming to live in this block, dear. This is my little spare room. I like to think I can put up a friend if I want. Not that many of them come. Between you and me, dear, people rather resent my having done so well for myself and all on my own initiative. People are so mean-spirited, I've noticed that as I've got older. That's why I was so thrilled when you agreed to come here. I mean, when *someone* took my advice.'

'You've made it all very nice,' said Daphne.

'Well, I always say the flat had the potential and I had the taste. Of course, yours is much smaller and, frankly, I wouldn't say it lends itself to a very ambitious décor. In your place, the first thing I'd do is have central heating put in.'

'I expect I will if I can afford it.'

'You know, Daphne, there are some things we owe it to ourselves to afford. But you know your own business best and I wouldn't dream of interfering. If the cold gets you down you're welcome up here at any time. *Any* time, I mean that. Now this is my drawing room, my *pièce de résistance*.'

Merle opened the door with the air of a girl lifting the lid of a jewel case that holds a lover's gift.

'What a lot of plants,' said Daphne faintly.

'I was always mad about plants. My first business venture was a florist's. I could have made a little goldmine out of that if my partner hadn't been so wickedly vindictive. She was determined to oust me from the first. D'you like my suite? I had it completely re-done in oyster satin last year and I do think it's a success.'

The atmosphere was that of a hothouse. The chairs, the sofa, the lamps, the little piecrust tables with their load of bibelots, were islanded in the centre of the large room. No, not an island perhaps, Daphne thought, but a clearing in a tropical jungle. Shelves, window sills, white troughs on white wrought iron legs, were burgeoned with lush trailing growth, green, glossy, frondy, all quite immobile and all giving forth a strange green scent.

'They take up all my time. It's not just the watering and watching the temperature and so on. Plants know when you love them. They only flourish in an atmosphere of love. I honestly don't believe you'd find a better specimen of an *opuntia* in London than mine. I'm particularly proud of the *peperomias* and the *xygocacti* too of course, I expect you've seen them growing in their natural habitat with all your mad rushing around those foreign places.'

'We were mostly in Stockholm and New York, Merle.'

'Oh, were you? So many years went by when you never bothered to write to me that I really can't keep pace. I thought about you a lot, of course. I want you to know you really had my sympathy, moving house all the time and that awful divorce from what's-his-name, and babies to cope with and then getting married again and everything. I used to feel how sad it was that I'd made so much of my life while you . . . What's the matter?'

'That plant, Merle, it moved.'

67

'That's because you touched it. When you touch one of its mouths it closes up. It's called *Dionaea Muscipula.*'

The plant stood alone in a majolica pot contained in an elaborate white stand. It looked very healthy. It had delicate shiny leaves and from its heart grew five red-gold blossoms. As Daphne peered more closely she saw that these resembled mouths, as Merle had put it, far more than flowers, whiskery mouths, soft and ripe and luscious. One of these was now closed.

'Doesn't it have a common name?'

'Of course it does. The Venus Fly Trap. *Muscipula* means fly-eater, dear.'

'Whatever *do* you mean?'

'It eats flies. I've been trying to grow one for years. I was absolutely thrilled when I succeeded.'

'Yes, but what d'you mean, it eats flies? It's not an animal.'

'It is in a way, dear. The trouble is there aren't many flies here. I feed it on little bits of meat. You've gone rather pale, Daphne. Have you got a headache? We'll have our sherry now and then I'll see if I can catch a fly and you can see it eat it up.'

'I'd really much rather not, Merle,' said Daphne, backing away from the plant. 'I don't want to hurt your feelings but I don't – well, I hate the idea of catching free live things and feeding them to – to that.'

'*Free live things?* We're talking about flies.' Merle large and per-fumed, grabbed Daphne's arm and pulled her away. Her dress was of red chiffon with trailing sleeves and her fingernails matched it. 'The trouble with you,' said Merle, 'is that you're a mass of nerves and you're much worse now than you were when we were girls. I thank God every day of my life I don't know what it is to be neurotic. Here you are, your sherry. I've put it in a big glass to buck you up. I'm going to make it my business to look after you, Daphne. You don't know anybody else in London, do you?'

'Hardly anybody,' said Daphne, sitting down where she couldn't see the Venus Fly Trap. 'My boys are in the States and my daughter's in Scotland.'

'Well, you must come up here every day. No, you won't be intruding. When I first knew you were definitely coming I said to myself, I'm going to see to it Daphne isn't lonely. But don't imagine you'll get on with the other tenants in this block. Those of them who aren't standoffish snobs are – well, not the sort of people you'd want to know. But we won't talk about them. We'll talk about us. Unless, of course, you feel your past has been too painful to talk about?'

'I wouldn't quite say . . .'

'No, you wouldn't care to rake up unpleasant memories. I'll just put a drop more sherry in your glass and then I'll tell you all about my last venture, my agency.'

Daphne rested her head against a cushion, brushed away an ivy frond, and prepared to listen.

From a piece of fillet steak Merle was scraping slivers of meat. She was all in diaphanous gold today, an amber chain around her neck, the finery half-covered by a frilly apron.

'I used to do that for my babies when they first went on solids,' said Daphne.

'Babies, babies. You're always on about your babies. You've been up here every day for three weeks now and I don't think you've once missed an opportunity to talk about your babies and your men. Oh, I'm sorry, dear, I don't mean to upset you, but one really does get so weary of women like you talking about that side of life as if one had actually *missed* something.'

'Why are you scraping that meat, Merle?'

'To feed my little Venus. That's her breakfast. Come along. I've got a fly I caught under a sherry glass but I couldn't catch more than one.'

The fly was very small. It was crawling up the inside of the glass, but when Merle approached it, it began to fly and buzz frenziedly against the transparent dome of its prison. Daphne turned her back. She went to the window, the huge plant-filled bay window, and looked out, pretending to be interested in the view. She heard the scrape of glass and from Merle a triumphant gasp. Merle trod very heavily. Under the thick carpet the boards creaked. Merle began talking to the plant in a very gentle maternal voice.

'This really is a wonderful outlook,' said Daphne brightly. 'You can see for miles.'

Merle said, '*C'est Vénus toute entière à sa proie attachée.*'

'I beg your pardon?'

'You never were any good at languages, dear. Oh, don't pretend you're so mad about that view. You're just being absurdly sensitive about what really amounts to *gardening*. I can't bear that sort of dishonesty. I've finished now, anyway. She's had her breakfast and all her mouths are shut up. Who are you waving to?'

'A rather nice young couple who live in the flat next to me.'

'Well, please don't.' Merle looked down and then drew herself up, all golden pleats and stiff gold curls. 'You couldn't know, dear, but those two people are the very end. For one thing, they're not a couple, they're not married, I'm sure of that. Of course, that's no business of mine. What is my business is that they've been keeping a dog here – look, that spaniel thing – and it's strictly against the rules to keep animals in these flats.'

'What about your Fly Trap?'

'Oh, don't be so silly! As I was saying, they keep that dog and let it foul the garden. I wrote to the managing agents, but those agents are so lax – they've no respect for me because I'm a single woman, I suppose. But I wrote again the day before yesterday and now I understand they're definitely going to be turned out.'

Forty feet below the window, on the parking space between the block and the garden, the boy who wore jeans and a leather jacket picked up his dog and placed it on the back seat of a battered car. His companion, who had waist-length hair much the colour of Merle's dress, got into the passenger seat, but the boy hesitated. As Merle brought her face close to the glass, he looked up and raised two wide-splayed fingers.

'Oaf!' said Merle. 'The only thing to do with people like that is to ignore them. Can you imagine it, he lets that dog of his relieve itself up against a really beautiful specimen of *Cryptomeria japonica*. Let's forget him and have a nice cup of coffee.'

'Merle, how long will those flowers last on that Venus thing of yours? I mean, they'll soon die away, won't they?'

'No, they won't. They'll last for ages. You know Daphne, fond as I am of you, I wouldn't leave you alone in this flat for anything. You've a personal hatred of my *muscipula*. You'd like to destroy it.'

'I'll put the coffee on,' said Daphne.

Merle phoned for a taxi. Then she put her little red address book with all the phone numbers in it into her scarlet patent leather handbag along with her lipstick and her gold compact and her keys, her cheque book and four five-pound notes.

'We could have walked,' said Daphne.

'No, we couldn't, dear. When I have a day at the shops I like to feel fresh. I don't want to half-kill myself walking there. It's not the cost that's worrying you, is it? Because you know I'll pay. I appreciate the difference between our incomes, Daphne, and if I don't harp on it it's only because I try to be tactful. I want to buy you something, something really nice to wear. It seems such a wicked shame to me those men of yours didn't see to it you were well-provided for.'

'I've got quite enough clothes, Merle.'

'Yes, but all grey and black. The only bright thing you've got is that red hat and you've stopped wearing that.'

'I'm old, Merle dear. I don't want to get myself up in bright colours. I've had my life.'

'Well, I haven't had mine! I mean, I . . .' Merle bit her lip, getting scarlet lipstick on her teeth. She walked across the room, picked her ocelot coat off the back of the sofa, and paused in front of the Fly Trap. It's soft flame-coloured mouths were open. She tickled them with her fingertips and they snapped shut. Merle giggled. 'You know what you remind me of, Daphne? A fly. That's just what you look like in your grey coat and that funny bit of veil on your hat. A fly.'

'There's the taxi,' said Daphne.

It deposited them outside a large overheated store. Merle dragged Daphne through the jewellery department, the perfumery, past rotary stands with belts on them, plastic models in lingerie. They went up in the lift. Merle bought a model dress, orange chiffon with sequins on the skirt. They went down in the lift and into the next store. Merle bought face bracer and cologne and a gilt choker. They went up the escalator. Merle bought a brass link belt and tried to buy Daphne a green and blue silk scarf. Daphne consented at last to be presented with a pair of stockings, power elastic ones for her veins.

'Now we'll have lunch on the roof garden,' said Merle.

'I should like a cup of tea.'

'And I'll have a large sherry. But first I must freshen up. I'm dying to spend a penny and do my face.'

They queued with their pennies. The ladies' cloakroom had green marble dressing tables with mirrors all down one side and green washbasins all down the other. Daphne sat down. Her feet had begun to swell. There were twenty or thirty other women in the cloakroom, doing their faces, re-sticking false eyelashes. One girl, whose face seemed vaguely familiar, was actually brushing her long golden hair. Merle put her handbag down on a free bit of green marble. She washed her hands, helped herself to a gush of *Calèche* from the scent-squirting machine, came back, opening and shutting her coat to fan herself. It was even hotter than in her flat.

She sat down, drew her chair to the mirror.

71

'Where's my handbag?' Merle screamed. 'I left my handbag here! Someone's stolen my handbag. Daphne, Daphne, someone's stolen my handbag!'

The oyster satin sofa sagged under Merle's weight. Daphne smoothed back the golden curls and put another pad of cottonwool soaked in cologne on the red corrugated forehead.

'Bit better now?'

'I'm quite all right. I'm not one of your neurotic women to get into a state over a thing like that. Thank God I'd left my spare key with the porter and I hadn't locked the mortice.'

'You'll have to have both locks changed, Merle.'

'Of course I will, eventually. I'll see to it next week. Nobody can get in here, can they? They don't know who I am. I mean, they don't know whose keys they've got.'

'They've got your handbag.'

'Daphne dear, I do wish you wouldn't keep stating the obvious. *I know they have got my handbag.* The point is, there was nothing in my handbag to show who I am.'

'There was your cheque book with your name on it.'

'My name, dear, in case it's escaped your notice, is M Smith. I haven't gone about changing it all my life like you.' Merle sat up and took a gulp of walnut brown sherry. 'The store manager was charming, wasn't he, and the police? I daresay they'll find it, you know. It's a most distinctive handbag, not like that great black thing you cart about with you. My little red one could have gone inside yours. I wish I'd thought to put it there.'

'I wish you had,' said Daphne.

Daphne's phone rang. It was half-past nine and she was finishing her breakfast, sitting in front of her little electric fire.

Merle sounded very excited. 'What do you think? Isn't it marvellous? The store manager's just phoned to say they've found my bag. Well, it wasn't him, it was his secretary, stupid-sounding woman with one of those put-on accents. However, that's no concern of mine. They found my bag fallen down behind a radiator in that cloakroom. Isn't it an absolute miracle? Of course the money had gone, but my cheque book was there and the keys. I'm very glad I didn't take your advice and change those locks yesterday. It never does to act on impulse, Daphne.'

'No, I suppose not.'

'I've arranged to go down and collect my bag at eleven. As soon as I ring off, I'm going to phone for a taxi and I want you to come with me, dear. I'll have a bath and see to my plants – I've managed to catch a bluebottle for Venus – and then the taxi will be here.'

'I'm afraid I can't come,' said Daphne.

'Why on earth not?'

Daphne hesitated. Then she said, 'I said I hardly know anybody in London but I do know this one man, this – well, he was a friend of my second husband, and he's a widower now and he's coming to lunch with me, Merle. He's coming at twelve and I must be here to see to things.'

'A *man*?' said Merle. '*Another* man?'

'I'll look out for your taxi and when I see you come in I'll just pop up and hear all about it, shall I? I'm sorry I can't . . .'

'Sorry? Sorry for what? I can collect my handbag by myself. I'm quite used to standing on my own feet.' The receiver went down with a crash.

Merle had a bath and put on the orange dress. It was rather showy for day wear with its sequins and its fringes, but she could never bear to have a new dress and not wear it at once. The ocelot coat would cover most of it. She watered the *peperomias* and painted a little leaf gloss on the ivy. The bluebottle had died in the night, but *dionaea muscipula* didn't seem to mind. She opened her orange strandy mouths for Merle and devoured the dead bluebottle along with the shreds of fillet steak.

Merle put on her cream silk turban and a long scarf of flame-coloured silk. Her spare mortice key was where she always kept it, underneath the *sanseveria* pot. She locked the Yale and the mortice and then the taxi took her to the store. Merle sailed into the manager's office, and when the manager told her he had no secretary, had never phoned her flat and had certainly not found her handbag, she deflated like a fat orange balloon into which someone has stuck a pin.

'You've been the victim of a hoax, Miss Smith.'

Merle pulled herself together. She could always do that, she had superb control. She didn't want aspirins or brandy or policemen or any of the other aids to quietude offered by the manager. When she had told him he didn't know his job, that if there was a conspiracy against her – as she was sure there must be – he was in it, she floundered down the stairs and flapped her mouth and her arms for a taxi.

When she got home the first thing that struck her as strange was that the door was only locked on the Yale. She could have sworn she had locked it on the mortice too, but no doubt her memory was playing her tricks – and no wonder, the shock she had had. There was a little bit of earth on the hall carpet. Merle didn't like that, earth on her gold Wilton. Inside her ocelot she was sweating. She took off her coat and opened the drawing room door.

Daphne saw the taxi come and Merle bounce out of it, an orange orchid springing from a black bandbox. Merle looked wild with excitement, her turban all askew. Daphne smiled to herself and shook her head. She laid the table and finished making the salad she knew her friend would like with his lunch, and then she went upstairs to see Merle.

There was a mirror on each landing. Daphne was so small and thin that she didn't puff much when she had to climb stairs. As she came to the top of each flight she saw a little grey woman trotting to meet her, a woman with smooth white hair and large, rather diffident, grey eyes, who wore a grey wool dress partly covered by a cloudy stole of lace. She smiled at her reflection. She was old now but she had had her moments, her joy, her gratification, her intense pleasures. And soon there was to be a new pleasure, a confrontation she had looked forward to for weeks. Who could tell what would come of it? With a last smile at her grey and fluttery image, Daphne pushed open the unlatched door of Merle's flat.

In the Garden of Eden, the green paradisal bower, someone had dropped a bomb. No, they couldn't have done that, for the ceiling was still there and the carpet and the oyster satin furniture, torn now and plastered all over with earth. Every plant had been broken and torn apart. Leaves lay scattered in heaps like the leaves of autumn, only these were green, succulent, bruised. In the rape of the room, in the midst of ripped foliage, stems bleeding sap, shards of china, lay the Venus Fly Trap, its roots wrenched from their pot and its mouths closed for ever.

Merle tried to scream but the noise came out only as a gurgle, the glug-glug agonized gasp of a scream in a nightmare. She fell on her knees and crawled about. Choking and muttering, she scrabbled among the earth and, picking up torn leaves, tried to piece them together like bits of a jigsaw puzzle. She crouched over the Fly Trap and nursed it in her hands, keening and swaying to and fro.

She didn't hear the door click shut. It was a long time before she realized Daphne was standing over her, silent, looking down. Merle lifted her red streaming face. Daphne had her hand over her mouth, the hand with the two wedding rings on it. Merle thought Daphne must be covering her mouth to stop herself from laughing out loud.

Slowly, heavily, she got up. Her long orange scarf was in her hands, stretched taut, twisting, twisting. She was surprised how steady her voice was, how level and sane.

'You did it,' she said. 'You did it. You stole my handbag and took my keys and got me out of here and came in and did it.'

Daphne quivered and shook her head. Her whole body shook and her hand flapped against her mouth. Quite whom Merle began to talk to then she didn't know, to herself or to Daphne, but she knew that what she said was true.

'You were so jealous! You'd had nothing, but I'd had success and happiness and love.' Her voice went up and the scarf with it. 'How you hated me, hated, hated . . . !' Merle screamed. 'Hate, hate, poisonous jealous hate!' Huge and red and frondy, she descended on Daphne, engulfing her with musky orange petals, twisting the scarf round the frail insect neck, devouring the fly until the fly quivered into stillness.

An elderly man in a black homburg hat crossed the forecourt and went up the steps, a bunch of flowers in his hand. The boy in the leather jacket took no notice of him. He brushed earth and bits of leaf off his hands and said to the girl with the long hair, 'Revenge is sweet.' Then he tossed the scarlet handbag into the back of his car and he and the girl and the dog got in and drove away.

The Clinging Woman

The girl was hanging by her hands from the railings of a balcony. The balcony was on the twelfth floor of the high-rise block next to his. His flat was on the ninth floor and he had to look up to see her. It was half-past six in the morning. He had been awakened by the sound of an aircraft flying dangerously low overhead, and had got out of bed to look. His sleepy gaze, descending from the blue sky which was empty of clouds, empty of anything but the bright vanishing arrow of the aircraft, alighted – at first with disbelief – on the hanging figure.

He really thought he must be dreaming, for this sunrise time was the hour for dreams. Then, when he knew he wasn't, he decided it must be a stunt. This was to be a scene in a film. There were cameramen down there, a whole film unit, and all the correct safety precautions had been taken. Probably the girl wasn't even a real girl, but a dummy. He opened the window and looked down. The car park, paved courts, grass spaces between the blocks, all were deserted. On the balcony rail one of the dummy's hands moved, clutching its anchorage more tightly, more desperately. He had to believe then what was obviously happening – unbelievable only because melodrama, though a frequent constituent of real life, always is. The girl was trying to kill herself. She had lost her nerve and now was trying to stay alive. All these thoughts and conclusions of his occupied about thirty seconds. Then he acted. He picked up the phone and dialled the emergency number for the police.

The arrival of the police cars and the ultimate rescue of the girl became the focus of gossip and speculation for the tenants of the two blocks. Someone found out that it was he who had alerted the police and he became an unwilling hero. He was a modest, quiet young man, and, disliking this limelight, was relieved when the talk began to die away, when the novelty of it wore off, and he was able to enter and leave his flat without being pointed at as a kind of St George and sometimes even congratulated.

About a fortnight after that morning of melodrama, he was getting ready to go to the theatre, just putting on his overcoat, when the doorbell rang. He didn't recognize the girl who stood outside. He had never seen her face.

She said, 'I'm Lydia Simpson. You saved my life. I've come to thank you.'

His embarrassment was acute. 'You shouldn't have,' he said with a nervous smile. 'You really shouldn't. That's not necessary. I only did what anyone would have done.'

She was calm and tranquil, not at all his idea of a failed suicide. 'But no one else did,' she said.

'Won't you come in? Have a drink or something?'

'Oh, no, I couldn't think of it. I can see you're just going out. I only wanted to say thank you very, very much.'

'It was nothing.'

'Nothing to save someone's life? I'll always be grateful to you.'

He wished she would either come in or go away. If this went on much longer the people in the other two flats on his floor would hear, would come out, and another of those bravest-deeds-of-the-year committee meetings would be convened. 'Nothing at all,' he said desperately. 'Really, I've almost forgotten it.'

'I shall never forget, never.'

Her manner, calm yet intense, made him feel uncomfortable and he watched her retreat into the lift – smiling pensively – with profound relief. Luckily, they weren't likely to meet again. The curious thing was that they did, the next morning at the bus stop. She didn't refer again to his saving of her life, but talked instead about her new job, the reason for her being at this bus stop, at this hour. It appeared that her employers had offices in the City street next to his own and were clients of his own firm. They travelled to work together. He left her with very different feelings from those of the evening before. It was hard to believe she was thirty – his neighbours had given him this information – for she looked much younger, small and fragile as she was, her skin very white and her hair very fair.

They got into the habit of travelling on that bus together in the mornings, and sometimes she waved to him from her balcony. One evening they met by chance outside her office. She was carrying an armful of files to work on at home and confessed she wouldn't have brought them if she had known how heavy they were. Of course he carried them for her all the way up to her flat and stayed for a drink. She said she was going to cook dinner and would he stay for that too? He stayed. While she was out in the kitchen he took his drink out on to the balcony. It gave him a strange feeling, imagining her coming out here in her despair at dawn, lowering herself from those railings, then losing her nerve, beneath her a great space with death at the bottom of it. When she came back into the room, he noticed afresh how slight and frail she was, how in need of protection.

The flat was neat and spotlessly clean. Most of the girls he knew lived in semi-squalor. Liberated, independent creatures, holding down men's jobs, they scorned womanly skills as debasing. He had been carefully brought up by a houseproud mother and he liked a clean home. Lydia's furniture was beautifully polished. He thought that if he were ever asked again he would remember to bring her flowers to go in those sparkling glass vases.

After dinner, an excellent, even elaborate meal, he said suddenly, the food and drink lowering his inhibitions:

'Why did you do it?'

'Try to kill myself?' She spoke softly and evenly, as serenely as if he had asked why she changed her job. 'I was engaged and he left me for someone else. There didn't seem much to live for.'

'Are you over that now?'

'Oh, yes. I'm glad I didn't succced. Or – should I say? – that you didn't let me succeed.'

'Don't ever try that again, will you?'

'No, why should I? What a question!'

He felt strangely happy that she had promised never to try that again. 'You must come and have a meal with me,' he said as he was leaving. 'Let's see. Not Monday. How about . . . ?'

'We don't have to arrange it now, do we? We'll see each other in the morning.'

She had a very sweet smile. He didn't like aggressive, self-reliant women. Lydia never wore trousers or mini-dresses, but long flowing skirts, flower-patterned. When he put his hand under her elbow to shepherd her across the street, she clutched his arm and kept hold of it.

'You choose for me', she said when the menu was given to her in the restaurant.

She didn't smoke or drink anything stronger than sweet white wine. She couldn't drive a car. He wondered sometimes how she managed to hold down an exacting job, pay her rent, live alone. She was so exquisitely feminine, clinging and gentle. And he was flattered when because of the firm's business he was unable to see her one night, tears appeared in her large grey eyes. That was the first night they hadn't met for three weeks and he missed her so much he knew he must be in love with her.

She accepted his proposal, made formally and accompanied by a huge bunch of red roses. 'Of course I'll marry you. My life has been yours ever since you saved it. I've always felt I belonged to you.'

They were married very quietly. Lydia didn't like the idea of a big wedding. He and she were ideally suited, they had so many tastes in common: a love of quietness and order, rather old-fashioned ways, steadiness, regular habits. They had the same aims: a house in a north-western suburb, two children. But for the time being she would continue to work.

It amazed and delighted him that she managed to keep the new house so well, to provide him every morning with freshly laundered underwear and shirt, every night with a perfectly cooked meal. He hadn't been so well looked after since he had left his mother's house. That, he thought, was how a woman should be, unobtrusively efficient, gentle yet expert, feminine and sweet, yet accomplished. The house was run as smoothly as if a couple of silent invisible maids were at work in it all day.

To perform these chores, she got up each morning at six. He suggested they get a cleaner but she wouldn't have one, resisting him without defiance but in a way which was bound to appeal to him.

'I couldn't bear to let any other woman look after your things, darling.'

She was quite perfect.

They went to work together, lunched together, came home together, ate together, watched television or listened to music or read in companionable silence together, slept together. At the weekends they were together all the time. Both had decided their home must be fully equipped with washers and driers and freezers and mixers and cleaners and polishers, beautifully furnished with the brand-new or the extreme antique, so on Saturdays they shopped together.

He adored it. This was what marriage should be, this was what the church service meant – one flesh, forsaking all other. He had, in fact, forsaken most of the people he had once known. Lydia wasn't a very sociable woman and had no women friends. He asked her why not.

'Women,' she said, 'only want to know other women to gossip about their men. I haven't any complaints against my man, darling.'

His own friends seemed a little over-awed by the grandeur and pomp with which she entertained them, by the finger bowls and fruit knives. Or perhaps they were put off by her long silences and the way she kept glancing at her watch. It was only natural, of course, that she didn't want people staying half the night. She wanted to be alone with him. They might have understood that and made allowances. His clients and their wives weren't over-awed. They must have been gratified. Where else, in a private house with no help, would they have been given a five-course dinner, exquisitely cooked and served? Naturally, Lydia had to spend all the pre-dinner time in the kitchen and, naturally too, she was exhausted after dinner, a little snappy with the man who spilt coffee on their new carpet, and the other one, a pleasant if tactless stockbroker, who tried to persuade him to go away on a stag, golfing weekend.

'Why did they get married,' she asked, with some reason, 'if all they want to do is get away from their wives?'

By this time, at the age of thirty-four, he ought to have had promotion at work. He'd been with the firm five years and expected to be made director. Neither he nor Lydia could understand why this directorship was so slow in coming.

'I wonder,' he said, 'if it's because I don't hang around in the office drinking after work?'

'Surely they understand a married man wants to be with his wife?'

'God knows. Maybe I ought to have gone on that river-boat party, only wives weren't invited, if you remember. I could tell you were unhappy at the idea of my going alone.'

In any case, he'd probably been quite wrong about the reason for his lack of promotion because, just as he was growing really worried about it, he got his directorship. An increase in salary, an office and a secretary of his own. He was a little concerned about other perquisites of the job, particularly about the possibility of foreign trips. But there was no need to mention these to Lydia yet. Instead he mentioned the secretary he must engage.

'That's marvellous, darling.' They were dining out, tête-à-tête, to celebrate. Lydia hadn't cared for his idea of a party. 'I'll have to give a fortnight's notice, but you can wait a fortnight, can't you? It'll be lovely being together all day long.'

'I don't quite follow,' he said, though he did.

'Darling, you are slow tonight. Where could you find a better secretary than me?'

They had been married for four years. 'You're going to give up work and have a baby.'

She took his hand, smiling into his face. 'That can wait. We don't need children to bring us together. You're my husband and my child and my friend all in one, and that's enough for me.'

He had to tell her why it wouldn't do for her to be his secretary. It was all true, that stuff about office politics and favouritism and the awkwardness of his position if his wife worked for him, but he made a poor show of explaining.

She said in her small, soft voice, 'Please can we go? Could you ask them for the bill? I'd like to leave now.'

As soon as they were in the house she began to cry. He advanced afresh his explanation. She cried. He said she could ask other people. Everyone would tell her the same. A director of a small firm like his couldn't have his wife working for him. She could phone his chairman if she didn't believe him.

She didn't raise her voice. She was never wild or hysterical. 'You don't want me,' she said like a rejected child.

'I do want you. I love you. But – can't you see? – this is for work, this is different.' He knew, before he said it, that he shouldn't have gone on. 'You don't like my friends and I've given them up. I don't have my clients here any more. I'm only away from you about six hours out of every day. Isn't all that enough for you?'

There was no argument. She simply reiterated that he didn't want her. She cried for most of the night and in the morning she was too tired to go to work. During the day he phoned her twice. She sounded tearful but calm, apparently resigned now. The first thing he noticed when he let himself in at his front door at six was the stench of gas.

She was lying on the kitchen floor, a cushion at the edge of the open oven to support her delicate blonde head. Her face was flushed a warm pink.

He flung open the window and carried her to it, holding her head in the fresh air. She was alive, she would be all right. As her pulse steadied and she began to breathe more evenly, he found himself kissing her passionately, begging her aloud not to die, to live for him. When he thought it was safe to leave her for a moment, he laid her on the sofa and dialled the emergency number for an ambulance.

They kept her in hospital for a few days and there was talk of mental treatment. She refused to undergo it.

'I've never done it except when I've known I'm not loved,' she said.

'What do you mean, "never", darling?'

'When I was seventeen I took an overdose of pills because a boy let me down.'

'You never told me,' he said.

'I didn't want to upset you. I'd rather die than make you unhappy. My life belongs to you and I only want to make yours happy.'

Suppose he hadn't got there in time? He shuddered when he thought of that possibility. The house was horrible without her. He missed her painfully, and he resolved to devote more of his time and his attention to her in future.

She didn't like going away on holiday. Because they never took holidays and seldom entertained and had no children, they had been able to save. They sold the house and bought a bigger, newer one. His firm wanted him to go to Canada for three weeks and he didn't hesitate. He refused immediately.

An up-and-coming junior got the Canada trip. It irritated him when he learned of a rumour that was going about the office to the effect that his wife was some sort of invalid, just because she had given up work since they bought the new house. Lydia, an invalid? She was happier than she had ever been, filling the house with new things, redecorating rooms herself, having the garden landscaped. If either of them was sick, it was he. He hadn't been sleeping well lately and he became subject to fits of depression. The doctor gave him pills for the sleeplessness and advised a change of air. Perhaps he was working too hard. Couldn't he manage to do some of his work at home?

'I took it upon myself,' Lydia said gently, 'to phone the doctor and suggest that. You could have two or three days a week at home and I'd do the secretarial work for you.'

His chairman agreed to it. There was a hint of scorn in the man's smile, he thought. But he was allowed to work at home and sometimes, for four or five days at a stretch, although he talked to people on the phone, he saw no one at all but his wife. She was, he found, as perfect a secretary as a wife. There was scarcely anything for him to do. She composed his press releases for him, wrote his letters without his having to dictate them, answered the phone with efficiency and charm, arranged his appointments. And she waited on him unflaggingly when work was done. No meals on trays for them. Every lunchtime and every evening the dining table was exquisitely laid, and if it occurred to him that in the past two years only six other people had handled this glass, this cutlery, these luxurious appointments, he didn't say so.

His depression wouldn't go away, even though he had tranquillizers now as well as sleeping pills. They never spoke of her suicide attempts, but he often thought of them and wondered if he had somehow been infected by this tendency of hers. When, before settling down for the night, he dropped one pill from the bottle into the palm of his hand, the temptation to let them all trickle out, to swallow them all down with a draught of fresh cold water, was sometimes great. He didn't know why, for he had everything a man could want, a perfect marriage, a beautiful house, a good job, excellent physical health and no ties or restrictions.

As Lydia had pointed out, 'Children would have been such a tie, darling,' or, when he suggested they might buy a dog, 'Pets are an awful tie, and they ruin one's home.' He agreed that this home and these comforts were what he had always wanted. Yet, as he approached forty, he began having bad dreams, and the dreams were of prisons.

One day he said to her, 'I can understand now why you tried to kill yourself. I mean, I can understand that anyone might want to.'

'I think we understand each other perfectly in every way,' she said. 'But don't let's talk about it. I'll never attempt it again.'

'And I'm not the suicidal type, am I?'

'*You?*' She wasn't alarmed, she didn't take him seriously, never thought of him at all as a person except in relation to herself. At once he reproached himself. *Lydia?* Lydia, who had given over her whole life to him, who put his every need and wish before her own? 'You wouldn't have any reason to,' she said gaily. 'You know you're loved. Besides, I should rescue you in time, just like you rescued me.'

His company had expanded and they were planning to open an office in Melbourne. After he had denied hotly that his wife was an invalid, that there was 'some little trouble' with his wife, the chairman offered him the chance of going to Australia for three months to get the new branch on its feet. Again he didn't hesitate. He accepted. The firm would, of course, pay for his trip. He was working out, as he entered his house, how much Lydia's air fare to Melbourne, her board in an hotel, her expenses, would amount to. Suicidal thoughts retreated. He could do it, he could just do it. Three months away, he thought, in a new country, meeting new people, and at the end of it, praise for his work and maybe an increase in salary.

She came out into the hall and embraced him. Her embraces at parting and greeting (though these occasions were no longer frequent) were as passionate now as when they first got engaged. He anticipated a small difficulty in that she wouldn't much want to leave her home, but that could be got over. She would go, as she had often said, anywhere with him.

He walked into their huge living room. It was as immaculate as ever, but something was different, something had undergone a great change. Their red carpet had been replaced by a new one of a delicate creamy velvety pile.

'Do you like it?' she asked, smiling. 'I bought it and had it laid secretly as a surprise for you. Oh, darling, you don't like it?'

'I like it,' he said, and then, 'How much did it cost?'

This was a question he hardly ever asked, but now he had cause to. She named a sum, much about the figure her trip to Australia would have cost.

'We said we were saving it to get something for the house,' she said, putting her arm round him. 'It's not really an extravagance. It'll last for ever. And what else have we got to spend the money on but our own home?'

He kissed her and said it didn't matter. It wasn't really an extravagance and it would last for ever, for ever . . . They dined off Copenhagen china and Georgian silver and Waterford glass. On the table flowers were arranged, wasting their sweetness on the desert air. He must go to Australia, but she couldn't come with him. He was afraid to tell her, gripped by a craven fear.

For weeks he put off telling her, and treacherously the idea came to him – why tell her at all? He longed to go, he must go. Couldn't he simply escape, phone from the aircraft's first stop, somewhere in Europe, and say he had been sent without notice, urgently? He had tried to phone her before but he couldn't get through. She wouldn't attempt suicide, he was sure, if she knew he was too far away to save her. And she'd forgive him, she loved him. But there were too many practical difficulties in the way of that, clothes, for instance, luggage. He must have been losing his mind even to think of it. Do that to *Lydia*? He wouldn't do that to his worst enemy, still less to his beloved wife.

As it turned out, he didn't get the chance. She was his secretary from whom a man, however many he keeps from his wife, can have no secrets. The airline phoned with a query and she found out.

'How long,' she asked dully, 'will you be gone?'

'Three months.'

She paled. She fell back as if physically ill.

'I'll write every day. I'll phone.'

'Three months,' she said.

84

'I was scared stiff of telling you. I have to go. Darling, don't you see I have to? It would cost hundreds and hundreds to take you with me, and we don't have the money.'

'No,' she said. 'No, of course not.'

She cried bitterly that night but on the following morning she didn't refer to his departure. They worked together as efficiently and companionably as ever, but her face was paper-white. Work finished, she began to talk of the clothes he would need, the new suitcases to be bought. In a sad, monotonous voice, she said that she would do everything, he mustn't worry his head at all about preparations.

'And you won't worry about *me* on the flight?'

There was something about the way she said she wouldn't, shaking her head and smiling as if his question had been preposterous, unreal, that told him. The dead cannot worry. She intended to be dead. And he understood that he had been absurdly optimistic in reassuring himself she wouldn't attempt suicide when he was far away.

The days went by. Only one more before he was due to leave. But he wouldn't leave. He knew that. He had known it for more than a week, and he was afraid of telling his chairman he wouldn't as he had been afraid of telling her he would. Again he dreamed of prisons. He awoke to see his life as alternating between fear and captivity, fear and imprisonment . . .

The escape route from both was available. It was on the afternoon of the last day that he decided to take it. He had told neither his wife nor his chairman that he wasn't going to Australia, and everything was packed, his luggage arranged in the hall with a precision of which only Lydia was capable. She had told him she was going out to fetch his best lightweight suit from the cleaners, the suit he was to wear on the following day, and he had heard the front door close.

That had been half an hour before. While she was out he was to go upstairs, she had instructed him sadly and tenderly, and check that there was no vital item she had left unpacked. And at last he went, but for another purpose. A lethal, not a vital, item was what he wanted – the bottle of sleeping pills.

The bedroom door was closed. He opened it and saw her lying on their bed. She hadn't gone out. For half an hour she had been lying there, the empty bottle of pills still clutched feebly in her hand. He felt her pulse, and a firm but unsteady flicker passed into his fingers. She was alive. Another quarter of an hour, say, and the ambulance would have her in hospital. He reached for the phone extension and put his finger to the slot to dial the emergency number. She'd be saved. Thank God, once again, he wasn't too late.

He looked down at her peaceful, tranquil face. She looked no older than on that day when she had come to him to thank him for saving her life. Gradually, almost involuntarily, he withdrew his finger from the dial. A heavy sob almost choked him and he heard himself give a whimpering cry. He lifted her in his arms, kissing her passionately and speaking her name aloud over and over again.

Then he walked quickly out of that room and out of the house. A bus came. He got on it and bought a ticket to some distant, outlying suburb. There in a park he didn't know and had never visited, he lay on the grass and fell into a deep sleep.

When he awoke it was nearly dark. He looked at his watch and saw that more than enough time had passed. Wiping his eyes, for he had apparently cried in his sleep, he got up and went home.

The Vinegar Mother

All this happened when I was eleven.

Mop Felton was at school with me and she was supposed to be my friend. I say 'supposed to be' because she was one of those close friends all little girls seem to have yet don't very much like. I had never liked Mop. I knew it then just as I know it now, but she was my friend because she lived in the next street, was the same age, in the same form, and because my parents, though not particularly intimate with the Feltons, would have it so.

Mop was a nervous, strained, dramatic creature, in some ways old for her age and in others very young. Hindsight tells me that she had no self-confidence but much self-esteem. She was an only child who flew into noisy rages or silent huffs when teased. She was tall and very skinny and dark, and it wasn't her hair, thin and lank, which accounted for her nickname. Her proper name was Alicia. I don't know why we called her Mop, and if now I see in it some obscure allusion to mopping and mowing (a Shakespearean description which might have been associated with her) or in the monosyllable the hint of a witch's familiar (again, not inept) I am attributing to us an intellectual sophistication which we didn't possess.

We were gluttons for nicknames. Perhaps all schoolgirls are. But there was neither subtlety nor finesse in our selection. Margaret myself, I was dubbed Margarine. Rhoda Joseph, owing to some gagging and embarrassment during a public recitation of Wordsworth, was for ever after Lucy; Elizabeth Goodwin Goat because this epithet had once been applied to her by higher authority on the hockey field. Our nicknames were not exclusive, being readily interchangeable with our true Christian names at will. We never used them in the presence of parent or teacher and they, if they had known of them, would not have deigned use them to us. It was, therefore, all the more astonishing to hear them from the lips of Mr Felton, the oldest and richest of any of our fathers.

Coming home from work into a room where Mop and I were:

'How's my old Mopsy, then?' he would say, and to me, 'Well, it's jolly old Margarine!'

I used to giggle, as I always did when confronted by something mildly embarrassing that I didn't understand. I was an observant child but not sensitive. Children, in any case, are little given to empathy. I can't recall that I ever pitied Mop for having a father who, though over fifty, pretended too often to be her contemporary. But I found it satisfactory that my own father, at her entry, would look up vaguely from his book and mutter, 'Hallo – er, Alicia, isn't it?'

The Feltons were on a slightly higher social plane than we, a fact I did know and accepted without question and without resentment. Their house was bigger, each parent possessed a car, they ate dinner in the evenings. Mr Felton used to give Mop half a glass of sherry to drink.

'I don't want you growing up ignorant of wine,' he would say.

And if I were present I would get the sherry too. I suppose it was Manzanilla, for it was very dry and pale yellow, the colour of the stone in a ring Mrs Felton wore and which entirely hid her wedding ring.

They had a cottage in the country where they went at the weekends and sometimes for the summer holidays. Once they took me there for a day. And the summer after my eleventh birthday, Mr Felton said:

'Why don't you take old Margarine with you for the holidays?'

It seems strange now that I should have wanted to go. I had a very happy childhood, a calm, unthinking, unchanging relationship with my parents and my brothers. I liked Rhoda and Elizabeth far more than I liked Mop, whose rages and fantasies and sulks annoyed me, and I disliked Mrs Felton more than any grown-up I knew. Yet I did want to go very much. The truth was that even then I had begun to develop my passion for houses, the passion that has led me to become a designer of them, and one day in that cottage had been enough to make me love it. All my life had been spent in a semi-detached villa, circa 1935, in a London suburb. The Feltons' cottage, which had the pretentious (not to me, then) name of Sanctuary, was four hundred years old, thatched, half-timbered, of wattle and daub construction, a calendar-maker's dream, a chocolate box artist's ideal. I wanted to sleep within those ancient walls, tread upon floors that had been there before the Armada came, press my face against glass panes that had reflected a ruff or a Puritan's starched collar.

My mother put up a little opposition. She liked me to know Mop, she also perhaps liked me to be associated with the Feltons' social *cachet*, but I had noticed before that she didn't much like me to be in the care of Mrs Felton.

'And Mr Felton will only be there at the weekends,' she said.

'If Margaret doesn't like it,' said my father, 'she can write home and get us to send her a telegram saying you've broken your leg.'

'Thanks very much,' said my mother. 'I wish you wouldn't teach the children habits of deception.'

But in the end she agreed. If I were unhappy, I was to phone from the call-box in the village and then they would write and say my grandmother wanted me to go and stay with her. Which, apparently, was not teaching me habits of deception.

In the event, I wasn't at all unhappy, and it was to be a while before I was even disquieted. There was plenty to do. It was fruit-growing country, and Mop and I picked fruit for Mr Gould, the farmer. We got paid for this, which Mrs Felton seemed to think *infra dig*. She didn't associate with the farmers or the agricultural workers. Her greatest friend was a certain Lady Elsworthy, an old woman whose title (I later learned she was the widow of a Civil Service knight) placed her in my estimation in the forefront of the aristocracy. I was stricken dumb whenever she and her son were at Sanctuary and much preferred the company of our nearest neighbour, a Mrs Potter, who was perhaps gratified to meet a juvenile enthusiast of architecture. Anyway, she secured for me the *entrée* to the Hall, a William and Mary mansion, through whose vast chambers I walked hand in hand with her, awed and wondering and very well content.

Sanctuary had a small parlour, a large dining-living room, a kitchen and a bathroom on the ground floor and two bedrooms upstairs. The ceilings were low and sloping and so excessively beamed, some of the beams being carved, that were I to see it now I would probably think it vulgar, though knowing it authentic. I am sure that nowadays I would think the Feltons' furniture vulgar, for their wealth, such as it was, didn't run to the purchasing of true antiques. Instead, they had those piecrust tables and rent tables and little escritoires which, cunningly chipped and scratched in the right places, inlaid with convincingly scuffed and dimly gilded leather, maroon, olive or amber, had been manufactured at a factory in Romford.

I knew this because Mr Felton, down for the weekend, would announce it to whomsoever might be present.

'And how old do you suppose that is, Lady Elsworthy?' he would say, fingering one of those deceitful little tables as he placed on it her glass of citrine-coloured sherry. 'A hundred and fifty years? Two hundred?'

Of course she didn't know or was too well-bred to say. 'One year's your answer! Factory-made last year and I defy anyone but an expert to tell the difference.'

Then Mop would have her half-glass of sherry and I mine while the adults watched us for the signs of intoxication they seemed to find so amusing in the young and so disgraceful in the old. And then dinner with red or white wine, but none for us this time. They always had wine, even when, as was often the case, the meal was only sandwiches or bits of cold stuff on toast. Mr Felton used to bring it down with him on Saturdays, a dozen bottles sometimes in a cardboard case. I wonder if it was good French wine or sour cheap stuff from Algeria that my father called plonk. Whatever Mr Felton's indulgence with the sherry had taught me, it was not to lose my ignorance of wine.

But wine plays a part in this story, an important part. For as she sipped the dark red stuff in her glass, blood-black with – or am I imagining this? – a blacker scaling of lees in its depths, Lady Elsworthy said:

'Even if you're only a moderate wine-drinker, my dear, you ought, you really ought, to have a vinegar mother.'

On this occasion I wasn't the only person present to giggle. There were cries of 'A *what*?' and some laughter, and then Lady Elsworthy began an explanation of what a vinegar mother was, a culture of acetobacter that would convert wine into vinegar. Her son, whom the adults called Peter, supplied the technical details and the Potters asked questions and from time to time someone would say, 'A vinegar mother! What a name!' I wasn't much interested and I wandered off into the garden where, after a few minutes, Mop joined me. She was, as usual, carrying a book but instead of sitting down, opening the book and excluding me, which was her custom, she stood staring into the distance of the Stour Valley and the Weeping Hills – I think she leant against a tree – and her face had on it that protuberant-featured expression which heralded one of her rages. I asked her what was the matter.

'I've been sick.'

I knew she hadn't been, but I asked her why.

'That horrible old woman and that horrible thing she was talking about, like a bit of liver in a bottle, she said.' Her mouth trembled. 'Why does she call it a vinegar *mother*?'

'I don't know,' I said. 'Perhaps because mothers make children and it makes vinegar.'

That only seemed to make her angrier and she kicked at the tree.

'Shall we go down to the pond or are you going to read?' I said.

But Mop didn't answer me so I went down to the pond alone and watched the bats that flitted against a pale green sky. Mop had gone up to our bedroom. She was in bed reading when I got back. No reader myself, I remember the books she liked and remember too that my mother thought she ought not to be allowed to read them. That night it was Lefanu's *Uncle Silas* which engrossed her. She had just finished Dr James's *Ghost Stories of an Antiquary*. I don't believe, at that time, I saw any connection between her literary tastes and her reaction to the vinegar mother, nor did I attribute this latter to anything lacking in her relationship with her own mother. I couldn't have done so, I was much too young. I hadn't, anyway, been affected by the conversation at supper and I went to bed with no uneasy forebodings about what was to come.

In the morning when Mop and I came back from church – we were sent there, I now think, from a desire on the part of Mr and Mrs Felton to impress the neighbours rather than out of vicarious piety – we found the Elsworthys once more at Sanctuary. Lady Elsworthy and her son and Mrs Felton were all peering into a round glass vessel with a stoppered mouth in which was some brown liquid with a curd floating on it. This curd did look quite a lot like a slice of liver.

'It's alive,' said Mop. 'It's a sort of animal.'

Lady Elsworthy told her not to be a little fool and Mrs Felton laughed. I thought my mother would have been angry if a visitor to our house had told me not to be a fool, and I also thought Mop was really going to be sick this time.

'We don't have to have it, do we?' she said.

'Of course we're going to have it,' said Mrs Felton. 'How dare you speak like that when Lady Elsworthy has been kind enough to give it to me! Now we shall never have to buy nasty shop vinegar again.'

'Vinegar doesn't cost much,' said Mop.

'Isn't that just like a child! Money grows on trees as far as she's concerned.'

Then Lady Elsworthy started giving instructions for the maintenance of the thing. It must be kept in a warm atmosphere. 'Not out in your chilly kitchen, my dear.' It was to be fed with wine, the dregs of each bottle they consumed. 'But not white wine. You tell her why not, Peter, you know I'm no good at the scientific stuff. It must never be touched with a knife or metal spoon.'

'If metal touches it,' said Peter Elsworthy, 'it will shrivel and die. In some ways, you see, it's a tender plant.'

Mop had banged out of the room. Lady Elsworthy was once more bent over her gift, holding the vessel and placing it in a suitable position where it was neither too light nor too cold. From the garden I could hear the drone of the lawn mower, plied by Mr Felton. Those other two had moved a little away from the window, away from the broad shaft of sunshine in which we had found them bathed. As Peter Elsworthy spoke of the tender plant, I saw his eyes meet Mrs Felton's and there passed between them a glance, mysterious, beyond my comprehension, years away from anything I knew. His face became soft and strange. I wanted to giggle as I sometimes giggled in the cinema, but I knew better than to do so there, and I went away and giggled by myself in the garden, saying, 'Soppy, soppy!' and kicking at a stone.

But I wasn't alone. Mr Felton came pushing the lawn mower up behind me. He used to sweat in the heat and his face was red and wet like the middle of a joint of beef when the brown part had been carved off. A grandfather rather than a father, I thought him.

'What's soppy, my old Margarine? Mind out of my way or I'll cut your tail off.'

It was August and the season had begun, so on Sunday afternoons he would take the shotgun he kept hanging in the kitchen and go out after rabbits. I believe he did this less from a desire to eat rabbit flesh than from a need to keep in with the Elsworthys who shot every unprotected thing that flew or scuttled. But he was a poor shot and I used to feel relieved when he came back empty-handed. On Sunday evenings he drove away to London.

'Poor old Daddy back to the grindstone,' he would say. 'Take care of yourself, my old Mop.' And to me, with wit, 'Don't melt away in all this sunshine, Margarine.'

That Sunday Mrs Felton made him promise to bring a dozen more bottles of wine when he returned the following weekend.

'Reinforcements for my vinegar mother.'

'It's stupid wasting wine to make it into vinegar,' said Mop. I wondered why she used to hover so nervously about her parents at this leave-taking time, watching them both, her fists clenched. Now I know it was because, although she was rude to them and seemed not to care for them, she longed desperately to see them exchange some demonstration of affection greater than Mrs Felton's apathetic lifting of her cheek and the hungry peck Mr Felton deposited upon it. But she waited in vain, and when the car had gone would burst into a seemingly inexplicable display of ill temper or sulks.

So another week began, a week in which our habits, until then routine and placid, were to change.

Like a proper writer, a professional, I have hinted at Mrs Felton and, I hope, whetted appetites, but I have delayed till now giving any description of her. But having announced her entry through the mouths of my characters (as in all the best plays) I shall delay no more. The stage is ready for her and she shall enter it, in her robes and with her trumpets.

She was a tall thin woman and her skin was as brown as a pale Indian's. I thought her old and very ugly, and I couldn't understand a remark of my mother's that I had overheard to the effect that Mrs Felton was 'quite beautiful if you liked that gypsy look'. I suppose she was about thirty-seven or thirty-eight. Her hair was black and frizzy, like a bush of heather singed by fire, and it grew so low on her forehead that her black brows sprang up to meet it, leaving only an inch or so of skin between. She had a big mouth with brown thick lips she never painted and enormous eyes whose whites were like wet eggshells.

In the country she wore slacks and a shirt. She made some of her own clothes and those she made were dramatic. I remember a hooded cloak she had of brown hessian and a long evening gown of embroidered linen. At that time women seldom wore cloaks or long dresses, either for evening or day. She chain-smoked and her fingers were yellow with nicotine.

Me she almost entirely ignored. I was fed and made to wash properly and told to change my clothes and not allowed to be out after dark. But apart from this she hardly spoke to me. I think she had a ferocious dislike of children, for Mop fared very little better than I did. Mrs Felton was one of those women who fall into the habit of only addressing their children to scold them. However presentable Mop might make herself, however concentratedly good on occasion her behaviour — for I believe she made great efforts —

Mrs Felton couldn't bring herself to praise. Or if she could, there would always be the sting in the tail, the 'Well, but look at your nails!' or 'It's very nice but do you have to pick this moment?' And Mop's name on her tongue – as if specifically chosen to this end – rang with a sour slither, a little green snake slipping from its hole, as the liquid and the sibilant scathed out, 'Alicia!'

But at the beginning of that third week a slight change came upon her. She was not so much nicer or kinder as more vague, more nervously abstracted. Mop's peccadilloes passed unnoticed and I, if late for a meal, received no venomous glance. It was on the Tuesday evening that the first wine bottle appeared at our supper table.

We ate this meal, cold usually but more than a bread and butter tea, at half-past seven or eight in the evening and after it we were sent to bed. There had never before been the suggestion that we should take wine with it. Even at the weekends we were never given wine, apart from our tiny glasses of educative sherry. But that night at sunset – I remember the room all orange and quiet and warm – Mrs Felton brought to the table a bottle of red wine instead of the teapot and the lemon barley water, and set out three glasses.

'I don't like wine,' said Mop.

'Yes, you do. You like sherry.'

'I don't like that dark red stuff. It tastes bitter. Daddy won't let me have wine.'

'Then we won't tell Daddy. If it's bitter you can put sugar in it. My God, any other child would think it was in heaven getting wine for supper. You don't know when you're well off and you never have. You've no appreciation.'

'I suppose you want us to drink it so you can have the leftovers for your horrible vinegar thing,' said Mop.

'It's not horrible and don't you dare to speak to me like that,' said Mrs Felton, but there was something like relief in her voice. Can I remember that? Did I truly observe *that*? No. It is now that I know it, now when all the years have passed, and year by year has come more understanding. Then, I heard no relief. I saw no baser motive in Mrs Felton's insistence. I took it for granted, absurd and somehow an inversion of the proper course of things though it seemed, that we were to drink an expensive substance in order that the remains of it might be converted into a cheap substance. But childhood is a looking-glass country where so often one is obliged to believe six impossible things before breakfast.

I drank my wine and, grudgingly, Mop drank two full glasses into

94

which she had stirred sugar. Most of the rest was consumed by Mrs Felton who then poured the dregs into the glass vessel for the refreshment of the vinegar mother. I don't think I had ever drunk or even tasted table wine before. It went to my head, and as soon as I was in bed at nine o'clock I fell into a profound thick sleep.

But Mop was asleep before me. She had lurched into bed without washing and I heard her heavy breathing while I was pulling on my nightdress. This was unusual. Mop wasn't exactly an insomniac but, for a child, she was a bad sleeper. Most evenings as I was passing into those soft clouds of sleep, into a delightful drowsiness that at any moment would be closed off by total oblivion, I would hear her toss and turn in bed or even get up and move about the room. I knew, too, that sometimes she went downstairs for a glass of water or perhaps just for her mother's company, for on the mornings after such excursions Mrs Felton would take her to task over breakfast, scathingly demanding of invisible hearers why she should have been cursed with such a restless nervy child who, even as a baby, had never slept a peaceful night through.

On the Tuesday night, however, she had no difficulty in falling asleep. It was later, in the depths of the night (as she told me in the morning) that she had awakened and lain wakeful for hours, or so she said. She had heard the church clock chime two and three; her head had ached and she had had a curious trembling in her limbs. But, as far as I know, she said nothing of this to her mother, and her headache must have passed by the middle of the morning. For, when I left the house at ten to go with Mrs Potter to an auction that was being held in some neighbouring mansion, she was lying on a blanket on the front lawn, reading the book Mr Felton had brought down for her at the weekend: *Fifty Haunted Houses*. And she was still reading it, was deep in *The Mezzotint* or some horror of Blackwood's, when I got back at one.

It must have been that day, too, when she began to get what I should now call obsessional about the vinegar mother. Several times, three or four times certainly, when I went into the dining room, I found her standing by the Romford factory antique on which Lady Elsworthy's present stood gazing, with the fascination of someone who views an encapsulated reptile, at the culture within. It was not to me in any way noisome or sinister, nor was it even particularly novel. I had seen a dish of stewed fruit forgotten and allowed to ferment in my grandmother's larder, and apart from the fungus on that being pale green, there was little difference between it and this crust of bacteria. Mop's face, so repelled yet so compelled, made me giggle. A mistake, this, for she turned on me, lashing out with a thin wiry arm.

'Shut up, shut up! I hate you.'

But she had calmed and was speaking to me again by suppertime. We sat on the wall above the road and watched Mr Gould's Herefords driven from their pasture up the lane home to the farm. Swallows perched on the telephone wires like taut strings of black and white beads. The sky was lemony-green and greater birds flew homeward across it.

'I'd like to put a spoon in it,' said Mop, 'and then I'd see it shrivel up and die.'

'She'd know,' I said.

'Who's she?'

'Your mother, of course.' I was surprised at the question when the answer was so obvious. 'Who else?'

'I don't know.'

'It's only an old fungus,' I said. 'It isn't hurting you.'

'Alicia! Aleeciah!' A sharp liquid cry, the sound of a sight, and the sight wine or vinegar flung in a curving jet.

'Come on, Margarine,' said Mop. 'Supper's ready.'

We were given no wine that night, but on the next a bottle and the glasses once more appeared. The meal was a heavier one than usual, meat pie with potatoes as well as salad. Perhaps the wine was sweet this time or of a finer vintage, for it tasted good to me and I drank two glasses. It never occurred to me to wonder what my parents, moderate and very nearly abstemious, would have thought of this corruption of their daughter. Of course it didn't. To a child grown-ups are omniscient and all-wise. Much as I disliked Mrs Felton, I never supposed she could wish to harm me or be indifferent as to whether or not I were harmed.

Mop, too, obeyed and drank. This time there was no demur from her. Probably she was once again trying methods of ingratiation. We went to bed at nine and I think Mop went to sleep before me. I slept heavily as usual, but I was aware of some disturbance in the night, of having been briefly awakened and spoken to. I remembered this, though not much more for a while, when I finally woke in the morning. It was about seven, a pearly morning of bird-song, and Mop was sitting on the window seat in her nightdress.

She looked awful, as if she had got a bad cold coming or had just been sick.

'I tried to wake you up in the night,' she said.

'I thought you had,' I said. 'Did you have a dream?'

She shook her head. 'I woke up and I heard the clock strike one and then I heard footsteps on the path down there.'

'In this garden, d'you mean?' I said. 'Going or coming?'

'I don't know,' she said oddly. 'They must have been coming.'

'It was a burglar,' I said. 'We ought to go down and see if things have been stolen.'

'It wasn't a burglar.' Mop was getting angry with me and her face was blotchy. 'I did go down. I lay awake for a bit and I didn't hear any more, but I couldn't go back to sleep and I wanted a drink of water. So I went down.'

'Well, go on,' I said.

But Mop couldn't go on. And even I, insensitive and unsympathetic to her as I was, could see she had been badly frightened, was still frightened, and then I remembered what had wakened me in the night, exactly what had happened. I remembered being brought to brief consciousness by the choking gasps of someone who is screaming in her sleep. Mop had screamed herself awake and the words she had spoken to me had been, 'The vinegar mother! The vinegar mother!'

'You had a nightmare,' I said.

'Oh, shut up,' said Mop. 'You never listen. I shan't ever tell you anything again.'

But later in the day she did tell me. I think that by this time she had got it into some sort of proportion, although she was still very frightened when she got to the climax of what she insisted couldn't have been a dream. She had, she said, gone downstairs about half an hour after she heard the footsteps in the garden. She hadn't put a light on as the moon was bright. The dining room door was partly open, and when she looked inside she saw a hooded figure crouched in a chair by the window. The figure was all in brown, and Mop said she saw the hood slide back and disclose its face. The thing that had made her scream and scream was this face which wasn't a face at all, but a shapeless mass of liver.

'You dreamed it,' I said. 'You must have. You were in bed when you screamed, so you must have been dreaming.'

'I did go down,' Mop insisted.

'Maybe you did,' I said, 'but the other bit was a dream. Your mother would have come if she'd heard you screaming downstairs.'

No more was said about the dream or whatever it was after that, and on Saturday Mr Felton arrived and took us to the Young Farmers'

Show at Marks Tey. He brought me my parents' love and the news that my eldest brother had passed his exams and got seven O Levels, and I was happy. He went shooting with Peter Elsworthy on Sunday afternoon, and Peter came back with him and promised to drive me and Mop and Mrs Felton to the seaside for the day on Tuesday.

It was a beautiful day that Tuesday, perhaps the best of all the days at Sanctuary, and I who, on the morning after Mop's dream, had begun to wonder about making that deceitful phone call from the village, felt I could happily remain till term began. We took a picnic lunch and swam in the wide shallow sea. Mrs Felton wore a proper dress of blue and white cotton which made her brown skin look like a tan, and had smoothed down her hair, and smiled and was gracious and once called Mop dear. Suddenly I liked Peter Elsworthy. I suppose I had one of those infatuations for him that are fused in young girls by a kind smile, one sentence spoken as to a contemporary, one casual touch of the hand. On that sunny beach I was moved towards him by inexplicable feelings, moved into a passion the sight of him had never before inspired, and which was to die as quickly as it had been born when the sun had gone, the sea was left behind, and he was once more Mrs Felton's friend in the front seats of the car.

I had followed him about that day like a little dog, and perhaps it was my unconcealed devotion that drove him to leave us at our gate and refuse even to come in and view the progress of the vinegar mother. His excuse was that he had to accompany his mother to an aunt's for dinner. Mrs Felton sulked ferociously after he had gone and we got a supper of runny scrambled eggs and lemon barley water.

On the following night there appeared on our table a bottle of claret. The phone rang while we were eating, and while Mrs Felton was away answering it I took the daring step of pouring my wine into the vinegar mother.

'I shall tell her,' said Mop.

'I don't care,' I said. 'I can't drink it, nasty, sour, horrible stuff.'

'You shouldn't call my father's wine horrible when you're a guest,' said Mop, but she didn't tell Mrs Felton. I think she would have poured her own to follow mine except that she was afraid the level in the vessel would rise too much, or was it that by then nothing would have induced her to come within feet of the culture?

I didn't need wine to make me sleep, but if I had taken it I might have slept more heavily. A thin moonlight was in the room when I woke up to see Mop's bed empty. Mop was standing by the door, holding it half-open, and she was trembling. It was a bit eerie in there with Mop's long shadow jumping about against the zig-zag beams on the wall. But I couldn't hear a sound.

'What's the matter now?' I said.

'There's someone down there.'

'How d'you know? Is there a light on?'

'I heard glass,' she said.

How can you hear glass? But I knew what she meant and I didn't much like it. I got up and went over to the doorway and looked down the stairs. There was light coming from under the dining room door, a white glow that could have been from the moon or from the oil lamp they sometimes used. Then I too heard glass, a chatter of glass against glass and a thin trickling sound.

Mop said in a breathy hysterical voice, 'Suppose she goes about in the night to every place where they've got one? She goes about and watches over them and makes it happen. She's down there now doing it. Listen!'

Glass against glass . . .

'That's crazy,' I said. 'It's those books you read.'

She didn't say anything. We closed the door and lay in our beds with the bedlamp on. The light made it better. We heard the clock strike twelve. I said 'Can we go to sleep now?' And when Mop nodded I put out the light.

The moon had gone away, covered perhaps by clouds. Into the black silence came a curious drawn-out cry. I know now what it was, but no child of eleven could know. I was only aware then that it was no cry of grief or pain or terror, but of triumph, of something at last attained; yet it was at the same time unhuman, utterly outside the bounds of human restraint.

Mop began to scream.

I had the light on and was jumping up and down on my bed, shouting to her to stop, when the door was flung open and Mrs Felton came in, her hair a wild heathery mass, a dressing gown of quilted silk, black-blood colour, wrapped round her and tied at the waist with savagery. Rage and violence were what I expected. But Mrs Felton said nothing. She did what I had never seen her do, had never supposed anything would make her do. She caught Mop in an embrace and hugged her, rocking her back and forth. They were both crying, swaying on the bed and crying. I heard footsteps on the garden path, soft, stealthy, finally fading away.

Mop said nothing at all about it to me the next day. She withdrew into her books and sulks. I believe now that the isolated demonstration of affection she had received from her mother in the night led her to hope more might follow. But Mrs Felton had become weirdly reserved, as if in some sort of long dream. I noticed with giggly embarrassment that she hardly seemed to see Mop hanging about her, looking into her face, trying to get her attention. When Mop gave up at last and took refuge in the garden with Dr James on demons, Mrs Felton lay on the dining room sofa, smoking and staring at the ceiling. I went in once to fetch my cardigan – for Mrs Potter was taking me to the medieval town at Lavenham for the afternoon – and she was still lying there, smiling strangely to herself, her long brown hands playing with her necklace of reddish-brown beads.

She went off for a walk by herself on Friday afternoon and she was gone for hours. It was very hot, too hot to be in a garden with only thin apple tree shade. I was sitting at the dining room table, working on a scrapbook of country house pictures Mrs Potter had got me to make, and Mop was reading, when the phone rang. Mop answered it, but from the room where I was, across the passage, I could hear Mr Felton's hearty bray.

'How's life treating you, my old Mop?'

I heard it all, how he was coming down that night instead of in the morning and would be here by midnight. She might pass the message on to her mother, but not to worry as he had his own key. And his kind regards to jolly old Margarine if she hadn't, by this time, melted away into a little puddle!

Mrs Felton came back at five in Peter Elsworthy's car. There were leaves in her hair and bits of grass on the back of her skirt. They pored over the vinegar mother, moving it back into a cool dark corner, and enthusing over the colour of the liquor under the floating liver-like mass.

'A tender plant that mustn't get overheated,' said Peter Elsworthy, picking a leaf out of Mrs Felton's hair and laughing. I wondered why I had ever liked him or thought him kind.

Mop and I were given *rosé* with our supper out of a dumpy little bottle with a picture of cloisters on its label. By now Mrs Felton must have learned that I didn't need wine to make me sleep, so she didn't insist on my having more than one glass. The vinegar mother's vessel was three-quarters full.

I was in bed and Mop nearly undressed when I remembered about her father's message.

'I forgot to tell her,' said Mop, yawning and heavy-eyed.

'You could go down and tell her now.'

'She'd be cross. Besides, he's got his key.'

'You don't like going down in the dark by yourself,' I said. Mop didn't answer. She got into bed and pulled the sheet over her head.

We never spoke to each other again.

She didn't return to school that term, and at the end of it my mother told me she wasn't coming back. I never learned what happened to her. The last — almost the last — I remember of her was her thin sallow face that lately had always looked bewildered, and the dark circles round her old woman's eyes. I remember the books on the bedside table: *Fifty Haunted Houses*, the *Works of Sheridan Lefanu*, *The Best of Montague Rhodes James*. The pale lacquering of moonlight in that room with its beams and its slanted ceiling. The silence of night in an old and haunted countryside. Wine breath in my throat and wine weariness bringing heavy sleep . . .

Out of that thick slumber I was awakened by two sharp explosions and the sound of breaking glass. Mop had gone from the bedroom before I was out of bed, scarcely aware of where I was, my head swimming. Somewhere downstairs Mop was screaming. I went down. The whole house, the house called Sanctuary, was bright with lights. I opened the dining room door.

Mr Felton was leaning against the table, the shotgun still in his hand. I think he was crying. I don't remember much blood, only the brown dead nakedness of Mrs Felton spread on the floor with Peter Elsworthy bent over her, holding his wounded arm. And the smell of gunpowder like fireworks and the stronger sickening stench of vinegar everywhere, and broken glass in shards, and Mop screaming, plunging a knife again and again into a thick slimy liver mass on the carpet.

The Fall of a Coin

The manageress of the hotel took them up two flights of stairs to their room. There was no lift. There was no central heating either and, though April, it was very cold.

'A bit small, isn't it?' said Nina Armadale.

'It's a double room and I'm afraid it's all we had left.'

'I suppose I'll have to be thankful it hasn't got a double bed,' said Nina.

Her husband winced at that, which pleased her. She went over to the window and looked down into a narrow alley bounded by brick walls. The cathedral clock struck five. Nina imagined what that would be like chiming every hour throughout the night, and maybe every quarter as well, and was glad she had brought her sleeping pills.

The manageress was still making excuses for the lack of accommodation. 'You see, there's this big wedding in the cathedral tomorrow. Sir William Tarrant's daughter. There'll be five hundred guests and most of them are putting up in the town.'

'We're going to it,' said James Armadale. 'That's why we're here.'

'Then you'll appreciate the problem. Now the bathroom's just down the passage, turn right and it's the third door on the left. Dinner at seven thirty and breakfast from eight till nine. Oh, and I'd better show Mrs Armadale how to work the gas fire.'

'Don't bother,' said Nina, enraged. 'I can work a gas fire.' She was struggling with the wardrobe door which at first wouldn't open, and when opened refused to close.

The manageress watched her, apparently decided it was hopeless to assist, and said to James, 'I really meant about working the gas *meter*. There's a coin-in-the-slot meter – it takes five pence pieces – and we really find it the best way for guests to manage.'

James squatted on the floor beside her and studied the grey metal box. It was an old-fashioned gas meter with brass fittings of the kind he hadn't seen since he had been a student living in a furnished room.

A gauge with a red arrow marker indicated the amount of gas paid for, and at present it showed empty.

'You turn this handle to the left, insert your coin in the slot, and then turn to the right . . .' Nina had stopped listening, James was glad to see. Perhaps when the inevitable quarrel started – as it would as soon as the woman had gone – it would turn upon the awfulness of going to this wedding for which he could hardly be blamed, instead of the squalid arrangements of the hotel for which he could. '. . . turn it to the right and wait until you hear the coin fall. Is that clear?' James said it was quite clear, thanks very much, and immediately the manageress had left the room Nina, who wasted no time, said:

'Can you tell me one good reason why we couldn't have come here tomorrow?'

'I could tell you several,' said James, resigning himself, 'but the principal one is that I didn't fancy driving a hundred and fifty miles in a morning coat and top hat.'

'Didn't fancy driving with your usual Saturday morning hangover, you mean.'

'Let's not start a row, Nina. Let's have a bit of peace for just one evening. Sir William is my company chairman. I have to take it as an honour that we were asked to this wedding, and if we have an uncomfortable evening and night because of it, that can't be helped. It's part of the job.'

'Just how pompous can you get?' said Nina with what in a less attractive woman would have been a called a snarl. 'I wonder what Sir William-Bloody-Tarrant would say if he could see his sales director after he's got a bottle of whisky inside him.'

'He doesn't see me,' said James, lighting a cigarette, and adding because she hadn't yet broken his spirit, 'That's your privilege.'

'*Privilege!*' Nina, who had been furiously unpacking her case and throwing clothes on to one of the beds, now stopped doing this because it sapped some of the energy she needed for quarrelling. She sat down on the bed and snapped, 'Give me a cigarette. You've no manners, have you? Do you know how uncouth you are? This place'll suit you fine, it's just up to your mark, gas meters and a loo about five hundred yards away. That won't bother you as long as there's a bar. I'll be able to have the *privilege* of sharing my bedroom with a disgusting soak.' She drew breath like a swimmer and plunged on. 'Do you realize we haven't slept in the same room for two years? Didn't think of that, did you, when you left booking up till the last minute? Or maybe – yes, that was it, my God! – maybe you did think of it. Oh, I know you so well, James Armadale. You thought being in here with me, undressing with me, would work the miracle. I'd come round. I'd – what's the expression? – *resume marital relations*. You got them to give us this – this cell on purpose. You bloody fixed it!'

'No,' said James. He said it quietly and rather feebly because he had experienced such a strong inner recoil that he could hardly speak at all.

'You liar! D'you think I've forgotten the fuss you made when I got you to sleep in the spare room? D'you think I've forgotten about that woman, that Frances? I'll never forget and I'll never forgive you. So don't think I'm going to let bygones be bygones when you try pawing me about when the bar closes.'

'I shan't do that,' said James, reflecting that in a quarter of an hour the bar would be opening. 'I shall never again try what you so charmingly describe as pawing you about.'

'No, because you know you wouldn't get anywhere. You know you'd get a slap round the face you wouldn't forget in a hurry.'

'Nina,' he said, 'let's stop this. It's hypothetical, it won't happen. If we are going to go on living together – and I suppose we are, though God knows why – can't we try to live in peace?'

She flushed and said in a thick sullen voice, 'You should have thought of that before you were unfaithful to me with that woman.'

'That,' he said, 'was three years ago, *three years*. I don't want to provoke you and we've been into this enough times, but you know very well why I was unfaithful to you. I'm only thirty-five, I'm still young. I couldn't stand being permitted *marital relations*, pawing you about, if you like that better, about six times a year. Do I have to go over it all again?'

'Not on my account. It won't make any difference to me what excuses you make.' The smoke in the tiny room made her cough and, opening the window, she inhaled the damp cold air. 'You asked me,' she said, turning round, 'why we have to go on living together. I'll tell you why. Because you married me. I've got a right to you and I'll never divorce you. You've got me till death parts us. Till death, James. Right?'

He didn't answer. An icy blast had come into the room when she had opened the window, and he felt in his pocket. 'If you're going to stay in here till dinner,' he said, 'you'll want the gas fire on. Have you got any five pence pieces? I haven't, unless I can get some change.'

'Oh, you'll get some all right. In the bar. And just for your information, I haven't brought any money with me. That's *your* privilege.'

When he had left her alone, she sat in the cold room for some minutes, staring at the brick wall. Till death parts us, she had told him, and she meant it. She would never leave him and he must never be allowed to leave her, but she hoped he would die. It wasn't her fault she was frigid. She had always supposed he understood. She had supposed her good looks and her capacity as housewife and hostess compensated for a revulsion she couldn't help. And it wasn't just against him, but against all men, any man. He had seemed to accept it and to be happy with her. In her sexless way, she had loved him. And then, when he had seemed happier and more at ease than at any time in their marriage, when he had ceased to make those painful demands and had become so sweet to her, so generous with presents, he had suddenly and without shame confessed it. She wouldn't mind, he had told her, he knew that. She wouldn't resent his finding elsewhere what she so evidently disliked giving him. While he provided for her and spent nearly all his leisure with her and respected her as his wife, she should be relieved, disliking sex as she did, that he had found someone else.

He had said it was the pent-up energy caused by her repressions that made her fly at him, beat at him with her hands, scream at him words he didn't know she knew. To her dying day she would remember his astonishment. He had genuinely thought she wouldn't mind. And it had taken weeks of nagging and screaming and threats to make him agree to give Frances up. She had driven him out of her bedroom and settled into the bitter unremitting vendetta she would keep up till death parted them. Even now, he didn't understand how agonisingly he had hurt her. But there were no more women and he had begun to drink. He was drinking now, she thought, and by nine o'clock he would be stretched out, dead drunk on that bed separated by only eighteen inches from her own.

The room was too cold to sit in any longer. She tried the gas fire, turned on the switch to 'full', but the match she held to it refused to ignite it, and presently she made her way downstairs and into a little lounge where there was a coal fire and people were watching television.

They met again at the dinner table.

James Armadale had drunk getting on for half a pint of whisky, and now, to go with the brown Windsor soup and hotted-up roast lamb, he ordered a bottle of burgundy.

'Just as a matter of idle curiosity,' said Nina, 'why do you drink so much?'

'To drown my sorrows,' said James. 'The classic reason. Happens to be true in my case. Would you like some wine?'

'I'd better have a glass, hadn't I, otherwise you'll drink the whole bottle.'

The dining room was full and most of the other diners were middle-aged or elderly. Many of them, he supposed, would be wedding guests like themselves. He could see that their arrival had been noted and that at the surrounding tables their appearance was being favourably commented upon. It afforded him a thin wry amusement to think that they would be judged a handsome, well-suited and perhaps happy couple.

'Nina,' he said, 'we can't go on like this. It's not fair on either of us. We're destroying ourselves and each other. We have to talk about what we're going to do.'

'Pick your moments, don't you? I'm not going to talk about it in a public place.'

She had spoken in a low subdued voice, quite different from her hectoring tone in their bedroom, and she shot quick nervous glances at the neighbouring tables.

'It's because this is a public place that I think we stand a better chance of talking about it reasonably. When we're alone you get hysterical and then neither of us can be rational. If we talk about it now, I think I know you well enough to say you won't scream at me.'

'I could walk out though, couldn't I? Besides, you're drunk.'

'I am not drunk. Frankly, I probably shall be in an hour's time and that's another reason why we ought to talk here and now. Look, Nina, you don't love me, you've said so often enough, and whatever crazy ideas you have about my having designs on you, I don't love you either. We've been into the reasons for that so many times that I don't need to go into them now, but can't we come to some sort of amicable arrangement to split up?'

'So that you can have all the women you want? So that you can bring that bitch into my house?'

'No,' he said, 'you can have the house. The court would probably award you a third of my income, but I'll give you more if you want. I'd give you half.' He had nearly added, 'to be rid of you,' but he bit off the words as being too provocative. His speech was already thickening and slurring.

It was disconcerting – though this was what he had wanted – to hear how inhibition made her voice soft and kept her face controlled. The words she used were the same, though. He had heard them a thousand times before. 'If you leave me, I'll follow you. I'll go to your office and tell them all about it. I'll sit on your doorstep. I won't be abandoned. I'd rather die. I won't be a divorced woman just because you've got tired of me.'

'If you go on like this,' he said thickly, 'you'll find yourself a widow. Will you like that?'

Had they been alone, she would have screamed the affirmative at him. Because they weren't, she gave him a thin, sharp and concentrated smile, a smile which an observer might have taken for amusement at some married couple's private joke. 'Yes,' she said, 'I'd like to be a widow, *your* widow. Drink yourself to death, why don't you? That's what you have to do if you want to be rid of me.'

The waitress came to their table. James ordered a double brandy and 'coffee for my wife.' He knew he would never be rid of her. He wasn't the sort of man who can stand public disruption of his life, scenes at work, molestation, the involvement of friends and employers. It must be, he knew, an amicable split or none at all. And since she would never see reason, never understand or forgive, he must soldier on. With the help of this, he thought, as the brandy spread its dim cloudy euphoria through his brain. He drained his glass quickly, muttered an 'excuse me' to her for the benefit of listeners, and left the dining room.

Nina returned to the television lounge. There was a play on whose theme was a marital situation that almost paralleled her own. The old ladies with their knitting and the old men with their after-dinner cigars watched it apathetically. She thought she might take the car and go somewhere for a drive. It didn't much matter where, anywhere would do that was far enough from this hotel and James and that cathedral clock whose chimes split the hours into fifteen minute segments with long brazen peals. There must be somewhere in this town where one could get a decent cup of coffee, some cinema maybe where they weren't showing a film about marriage or what people, she thought shudderingly, called sexual relationships. She went upstairs to get the car keys and some money.

James was fast asleep. He had taken off his tie and his shoes, but otherwise he was fully dressed, lying on his back and snoring. Stupid of him not to get under the covers. He'd freeze. Maybe he'd die of exposure. Well, she wasn't going to cover him up, but she'd close the window for when she came in. The car keys were in his jacket pocket, mixed up with a lot of loose change. The feel of his warm body through the material made her shiver. His breath smelt of spirits and he was sweating in spite of the cold. Among the change were two five pence pieces. She'd take one of those and keep it till the morning to feed that gas meter. It would be horrible dressing for that wedding in here at zero temperature. Why not feed it now so that it would be ready for the morning, ready to turn the gas fire on and give her some heat when she came in at midnight, come to that?

The room was faintly illuminated by the yellow light from the street lamp in the alley. She crouched down in front of the gas fire and noticed she hadn't turned the tap off after her match had failed to ignite the jets. It wouldn't do to feed that meter now with the tap turned on full and have five pence worth of gas flood the room. Not with the window tight shut and not a crack round that heavy old door. Slowly she put her hand out to turn off the tap.

Her fingers touched it. Her hand remained still, poised. She heard her heart begin to thud softly in the silence as the idea in all its brilliant awfulness took hold of her. Wouldn't do . . . ? Was she mad? It wouldn't do to feed that meter now with the tap turned on? What would do as well, as efficiently, as finally? She withdrew her hand and clasped it in the other to steady it. Rising to her feet, she contemplated her sleeping husband. The sweat was standing on his pale forehead now. He snored as rhythmically, as stertorously, as her own heart beat. A widow, she thought, alone and free in her own unshared house. Not divorced, despised, disowned, laughed at by judges and solicitors for her crippling frigidity, not mocked by that Frances and her successors, but a widow whom all the world would pity and respect. Comfortably-off too, if not rich, with an income from James's life assurance and very likely a pension from Sir William Tarrant.

James wouldn't wake up till midnight. No, that was wrong. He wouldn't *have* wakened up till midnight. What she meant was he wouldn't wake up at all.

The gas tap was still on, full on. She took the five pence coin and tip-toed over to the meter. Nothing would wake him, but still she tip-toed. The window was tight shut with nothing beyond it but that alley, that glistening lamp and the towering wall of the cathedral. She studied the meter, kneeling down. It was the first time in her sheltered, cosseted, snug life that she had ever actually seen a coin-in-the-slot gas meter. But if morons like hotel servants and the sort of people who would stay in a place like this could work it, she could. It wouldn't matter that she hadn't attended closely to the manageress's instructions. What had she said? Turn the handle to the left, insert the coin, turn it to the right. Nina hesitated for a moment, just long enough for brief fractured memories to cross her mind, James when they were first married, James patient and kind and self-denying on their honeymoon, James promising that her coldness didn't matter, that with time and love . . . James confessing with a defiant smirk, throwing Frances's name at her, James going on a three-day bender because she couldn't pretend the wound he'd given her was just a surface scratch, James drunk night after night after night . . . She didn't hesitate for long. She got her coat, put the car keys in her handbag. Then she knelt down again, turned the handle to the left, inserted the five pence coin, turned it to the right and, without looking back, walked out of the room, closing the door behind her.

The cathedral clock chimed the last quarter before nine.

When the bar closed at eleven thirty, a crowd of people coming upstairs and chattering in loud voices would have awakened even the deepest sleeper. They woke James. He didn't move for some time but lay there with his eyes open till he heard the clock chime midnight. When the last stroke died away he reached out and turned on the bedside lamp. The light was like knives going into his head, and he groaned. But he felt like this most nights at midnight and there was no use making a fuss. Who would hear or care if he did? Nina was evidently still downstairs in that lounge. It was too much to hope she might stay there all night out of fear of being alone with him. No, she'd be up now the television had closed down and she'd start berating him for his drunkenness and his infidelity – not that there had been any since Frances – and they would lie there bickering and smarting until grey light mingled with that yellow light, and the cathedral clock told them it was dawn.

And yet she had been so sweet once, so pathetic and desperate in her sad failure. It had never occurred to him to blame her, though his body suffered. And his own solution, honestly confessed, might have worked so well for all three of them if she had been rational. He wondered vaguely, for the thousandth time, why he had been such a fool as to confess when, with a little deception, he might be happier now than at any time in his marriage. But he was in no fit state to think. Where had that woman said the bathroom was? Turn right down the passage and the third door on the left. He lay there till the clock struck the quarter before he felt he couldn't last out any longer and he'd have to find it.

The cold air in the passage – God, it was more like January than April – steadied him a little and made his head bang and throb. He must be crazy to go on like this. What the hell was he doing, turning himself into an alcoholic at thirty-five? Because there were no two ways about it, he was an alcoholic all right, a drunk. And if he stayed with Nina he'd be a dead alcoholic by forty. But how can you leave a woman who won't leave you? Give up his job, run away, go to the ends of the earth . . . It wasn't unusual for him to have wild thoughts like this at midnight, but when the morning came he knew he would just soldier on.

He stayed in the bathroom for about ten minutes. Coming back along the passage, he heard footsteps on the stairs, and knowing he must look horrible and smell horribly of liquor, he retreated behind the open door of what proved to be a broom cupboard. But it was only his wife. She approached their room door slowly as if she were bracing herself to face something – himself, probably, he thought. Had she really that much loathing of him that she had to draw in her breath and clench her hands before confronting him? She was very pale. She looked ill and frightened, and when she had opened the door and gone inside he heard her give a kind of shrill gasp that was almost a shriek.

He followed her into the room, and when she turned and saw him he thought she was going to faint. She had been pale before, but now she turned paper white. Once, when he had still loved her and had hoped he might teach her to love him, he would have been concerned. But now he didn't care, and all he said was:

'Been watching something nasty on the TV?'

She didn't answer him. She sat down on her bed and put her head into her hands. James undressed and got into bed. Presently Nina got up and began taking her clothes off slowly and mechanically. His head and body had begun to twitch as they did when he was recovering from the effects of a drinking bout. It left him wide awake. He wouldn't sleep again for hours. He watched her curiously but dispassionately, for he had long ago ceased to derive the slightest pleasure or excitement from seeing her undress. What intrigued him now was that, though she was evidently in some sort of state of shock, her hands shaking, she still couldn't discard those modest subterfuges of hers, her way of turning her back when she stepped out of her dress, of pulling her nightgown over her head before she took off her underclothes.

She put on her dressing gown and went to the bathroom. When she came back her face was greasy where she had cleaned off the make-up and she was shivering.

'You'd better take a sleeping tablet,' he said.

'I've already taken one in the bathroom. I wanted a bath but there wasn't any hot water.' Getting into bed, she exclaimed in her normal fierce way, 'Nothing works in this damned place! Nothing goes right!'

'Put out the light and go to sleep. Anyone would think you'd got to spend the rest of your life here instead of just one night.'

She made no reply. They never said good night to each other. When she had put her light out the room wasn't really dark because a street lamp was still lit in the alley outside. He had seldom felt less like sleep, and now he was aware of a sensation he hadn't expected because he hadn't thought about it. He didn't want to share a bedroom with her.

That cold modesty, which had once been enticing, now repelled him. He raised himself on one elbow and peered at her. She lay in the defensive attitude of a woman who fears assault, flat on her stomach, her arms folded under her head. Although the sleeping pill had taken effect and she was deeply asleep, her body seemed stiff, prepared to galvanize into violence at a touch. She smelt cold. A sour saltiness emanated from her as if there were sea water in her veins instead of blood. He thought of real women with warm blood, women who awoke from sleep when their husband's faces neared theirs, who never recoiled but smiled and put out their arms. For ever she would keep him from them until the drink or time made him as frozen as she.

Suddenly he knew he couldn't stay in that room. He might do something dreadful, beat her up perhaps or even kill her. And much as he wanted to be rid of her, spend no more time with her, no more money on her, the notion of killing her was as absurd as it was grotesque. It was unthinkable. But he couldn't stay here.

He got up and put on his dressing gown. He'd go to that lounge where she'd watched television, take a blanket and spend the rest of the night there. She wouldn't wake till nine and by then he'd be back, ready to dress for that wedding. Funny, really, their going to a wedding, to watch someone else getting into the same boat. But it wouldn't be the same boat, for if office gossip was to be relied on,

III

Sir William's daughter had already opened her warm arms to many men . . .

The cathedral clock struck one. By nine the room would be icy and they'd need that gas fire. Why not put a five pence piece in the meter now, so that the fire would work when he wanted it?

The fire itself lay in shadow, but the meter was clearly illuminated by the street lamp. James knelt down, recalling the instructions of the manageress. Better try it out first before he put his coin in, his only five pence coin. Strange, that. He could have sworn he'd had two when he first went to bed. What had she said? Turn the lever to the left, insert the coin, turn it to the right *until you hear the coin fall.* Keeping hold of his coin – he didn't want to waste it if what Nina said was true and nothing worked in this place – he turned the lever to the left, then to the right as far as it would go.

A coin fell with a small dull clang and the red marker moved along the gauge to register payment. Good. He was glad he hadn't wasted his money. The previous guest must have put one in and failed to turn the lever far enough.

James checked that the window was shut to keep out the cold, gave a last look at the sleeping woman and went out of the room, closing the door behind him.

Almost Human

The Chief was stretched out on the settee, half-asleep. Monty sat opposite him, bolt upright in his chair. Neither of them moved as Dick helped himself to gin and water. They didn't care for strong drink, the Chief not even for the smell of it, though it wasn't his way to show his feelings. Monty would sometimes drink beer in the George Tavern with Dick. It was cigarette smoke that upset him, and now as he caught a whiff from Dick's Capstan, he sneezed.

'Bless you,' said Dick.

Better smoke the rest of it in the kitchen while he was getting their supper. It wasn't fair on Monty to start him coughing at his age, bring on his bronchitis maybe. There was nothing Dick wouldn't have done for Monty's comfort, but when he had taken the steak out of the fridge and gone once more into the sitting room for his drink, it was the Chief he addressed. Monty was his friend and the best company in the world. You couldn't look on the Chief in that light, but more as a boss to be respected and deferred to.

'Hungry, Chief?' he said.

The Chief got off the settee and walked into the kitchen. Dick went after him. It was almost dark outside now but enough light remained to show Dick Monty's coat, the old check one, still hanging on the clothesline. Better take it in in case it rained in the night. Dick went out into the yard, hoping against hope old Tom, his next-door neighbour, wouldn't see the kitchen light and come out. Such hope was always vain. He'd got the first of the pegs out when he heard the door open and the cracked whining voice.

'Going to be a cold night.'

'Mmm,' said Dick.

'Shouldn't be surprised if there was to be a frost.'

Who cared? Dick saw the great angular shadow of the Chief appear in the rectangle of light. Good, that would fix him. Standing erect, as he now was against the fence, the Chief was a good head taller than old Tom, who backed away, grinning nervously.

'Come on, Chief,' said Dick. 'Suppertime.'

'Just like children, aren't they?' old Tom whined. 'Almost human. It's uncanny. Look at him. He understands every word you say.'

Dick didn't answer. He followed the Chief into the kitchen and slammed the door. Nothing angered him more than the way people thought they were paying compliments to animals by comparing them with people. As if the Chief and Monty weren't in every way, mentally, physically, morally, a hundred times better than any human being he'd ever known. Just like children – what a load of crap. Children wanting their supper would be crying, making a nuisance of themselves, getting under his feet. His dogs, patient, stoical, single-minded, sat still and silent, watching while he filled the earthenware bowls with steak and meal and vitamin supplement. And when the bowls were placed side by side on the floor, they moved towards them with placid dignity.

Dick watched them feed. Monty's appetite, at fourteen, was as good as ever, though he took longer about it than the Chief. His teeth weren't what they had been. When the old dog had cleared his plate he did what he'd always done ever since he was a pup, came over to Dick and laid his grey muzzle in the palm of the outstretched hand. Dick fondled his ears.

'Good old dog,' Dick said. He scorned the popular way of calling dogs boy. They weren't boys. Boys were dirty and smelly and noisy and uncontrolled. 'You're a cracker, you are. You're a fine old dog.'

The Chief behaved in a grander manner. Such signs of affection and gratitude would have been inconsistent with his pedigree and his dignified presence. Dick and Monty knew their place and they both stepped aside to allow the Chief to pass majestically through the doorway and resume his position on the settee. Dick pushed Monty's chair nearer to the radiator. Half-past six. He finished his gin.

'I have to go out now,' he said, 'but I'll be back by ten at the latest, so you get a bit of shut-eye and when I come back we'll all have a good walk. OK?'

Monty came to the front door with him. He always had and always would, though his hind legs were stiff with rheumatism. We all have to get old, Dick thought, I'll have to face up to it, I'm going to lose him this year or next . . . he knelt down by the door and did what he'd never done to a man, woman or child, performed that disgusting act which sickened him when he saw it done by human beings to human beings. Holding Monty's head in his hands, he pressed his lips to the wrinkled forehead. Monty wagged his tail and emitted little grunts of happiness. Dick closed the door and got his car out of the garage.

He drove it two or three hundred yards down the street to the phone box. For business he never used his own phone, but one or other of the call boxes between his house and the George Tavern. Five minutes to go and the bell inside it would begin to ring. Unless something went wrong again, of course. Unless, once more, things weren't working out the way she'd planned them. The stupid – what? Dick hated the habit of using the names of female animals – bitch, cow, mare – as insulting epithets for women. When he wanted to express his loathing for the sex he chose one of the succinct four-letter words or the five-letter one that was the worst he could think of – woman. He used it now, rolling it on his tongue. Stupid, bloody, greedy, Goddamned *woman*!

When his watch showed nearly a quarter to seven, he went into the box. He only had to wait sixty seconds. The bell began to ring on the dot of a quarter to. Dick lifted the receiver and spoke the password that would tell her it was he and not some interfering busybody answering phones for the hell of it.

He'd never heard her voice before. It was nervous, upper-class, a thousand miles from any world in which he'd ever move. 'It's going to be all right tonight,' she said.

'About time.' All their previous transactions had been arranged through his contact and every plan had come to grief through a hold-up at her end. It was six weeks since he'd had the tip-off and the first instalment. 'Let's have it then.'

She cleared her throat. 'Listen. I don't want you to know anything about us – who we are, I mean. Agreed?'

As if he cared who they were or what dirty passions had brought her to this telephone, this conspiracy. But he said contemptuously:

'It'll be in the papers, won't it?'

Fear thinned her voice. 'You could blackmail me!'

'And you could blackmail me, come to that. It's a risk we have to take. Now get on with it, will you?'

'All right. He's not been well but he's better now and started taking his usual walk again. He'll leave this house at half-past eight and walk through the West Heath path towards the Finchley Road. You don't have to know why or where he's going. That's not your business.'

'I couldn't care less,' said Dick.

'It'll be best for you to wait in one of the lonelier bits of the path, as far from the houses as you can.'

'You can leave all that to me. I know the area. How'll I know it's him?'

'He's fifty, well-built, middle height, silver hair, small moustache. He won't be wearing a hat. He'll have on a black overcoat with a black fur collar over a grey tweed suit. He ought to get to the middle of the West Heath path by ten to nine.' The voice wavered slightly. 'It won't be too messy, will it? How will you do it?'

'D'you expect me to tell you that on the phone?'

'No, perhaps not. You've had the first thousand?'

'For six weeks,' said Dick.

'I couldn't help the delay. It wasn't my fault. You'll get the rest within a week, in the way you got the first . . .'

'Through the usual channel. Is that all? Is that all I have to know?'

'I think so,' she said. 'There's one other thing – no it doesn't matter.' She hesitated. 'You won't fail me, will you? Tonight's the last chance. If it doesn't happen tonight there's no point in its happening at all. The whole situation changes tomorrow and I shan't . . .'

'Good-bye,' said Dick, slamming down the receiver to cut short the voice that was growing hysterical. He didn't want to know any of the circumstances or be involved in her sick emotions. Bloody – *woman*. Not that he had any qualms. He'd have killed a hundred men for what she was paying him to kill one, and he was interested only in the money. What did it matter to him who he was or she was or why she wanted him out of the way? She might be his wife or his mistress. So what? Such relationships were alien to Dick and the thought of what they implied nauseated him, kissing, embracing, the filthy act they did like – no, not like animals. Animals were decent, decorous – like people. He spat into the corner of the kiosk and came out into the cold evening air.

As he drove up towards Hampstead, he thought of the money. It would be just enough to bring his accumulated savings to his target. For years, ever since he'd got Monty from the pet shop, he'd been working to this end. Confidence tricks, a couple of revenge killings, the odd beating up, casing places for robbery, they'd all been lucrative, and by living modestly – the dog's food was his biggest expense – he'd got nearly enough to buy the house he'd got his eye on. It was to be in Scotland, on the north-west coast and miles from a village, a granite croft with enough grounds round it for Monty and the Chief to run free all day. He liked to think of the way they'd look when they saw their own bit of moorland, their own rabbits to chase. He'd have sufficient left over to live on without working for the rest of his life, and maybe he'd get more animals, a horse perhaps, a couple of goats. But no more dogs while Monty was alive. That wouldn't be fair, and it seemed wrong, the height of treachery, to make plans for after Monty was dead . . .

What there wouldn't be anywhere in the vicinity of his home were people. With luck he wouldn't hear a human voice from one month's end to another. The human race, its ugly face, would be excluded for ever. In those hills with Monty and the Chief he'd forget how for forty years they'd pressed around him with their cruelty and their baseness, his drunken savage father, his mother who'd cared only for men and having a good time. Then, later, the foster home, the reform school, the factory girls sniggering at his shyness and his pimply face, the employers who wouldn't take him because he had a record instead of an education. At last he'd have peace.

So he had to kill a man to get it? It wouldn't be the first time. He would kill him without passion or interest, as easily as the slaughterer kills the lamb and with as little mercy. A light blow to the head first, just enough to stun him – Dick wasn't worried about giving pain but about getting blood on his clothes – and then that decisive pressure just here, on the hyoid . . .

Fingering his own neck to site the spot, Dick parked the car and went into a pub for another small gin and water and a sandwich. The licensee's cat came and sat on his knee. Animals were drawn to him as by a magnet. They knew who their friends were. Pity really that the Chief had such a hatred of cats, otherwise he might have thought of adding a couple to his Scottish menagerie. Half-past seven. Dick always allowed himself plenty of time to do a job, take it slowly, that was the way. He put the cat gently on the floor.

By eight he'd driven up through Hampstead village, along Branch Hill by the Whitestone Pond, and parked the car in West Heath Road. A fine starry night, frosty too, like that old fool had said it would be. For a few minutes he sat in the car, turning over in his mind whether there was anything at all to connect him with the woman he'd spoken to. No, there was nothing. His contact was as reliable and trustworthy as any human being could be and the method of handing over the money was foolproof. As for associating him with the man he was going to kill – Dick knew well that the only safe murder is the murder of a complete stranger. Fortunately for him and his clients, he was a stranger to the whole world of men.

Better go up and look at the path now. He put the car in Templewood Avenue as near as he could to the point where the path left it to wind across West Heath. This was to be on the safe side. There weren't any real risks, but it was always as well to ensure a quick getaway. He strolled into the path. It led between the fences of gardens, a steep lane about five feet wide, with steps here and there where the incline grew too sharp. At the summit was a street lamp and another about fifty yards further on where the path became walled. Between the lights was a broader sandy space, dotted about with trees and shrubs. He'd do it here, Dick decided. He'd stand among the trees until the man appeared from the walled end, wait until he left the first pool of light but hadn't yet reached the second, and catch him in the darkest part. No roofs were visible, only the backs of vast gardens, jungly and black, and though the stars were bright, the moon was a thin white curve that gave little light.

Luckily, the bitter cold was keeping most people indoors. As soon as this thought had passed through his mind, he heard footsteps in the distance and his hand tightened on the padded metal bar in his pocket. But not yet, surely? Not at twenty-five past eight? Or had that fool woman made another of her mistakes? No, this was a girl. The click of her heels told him that, and then he saw her emerge into the lamplight. With a kind of sick curiosity he watched her approach, a tall slim girl yet with those nauseating repulsive bulges under her coat. She walked swiftly and nervously in this lonely place, looking with swift birdlike glances to the right and the left, her whole body deformed by the tight stupid clothes she wore and the stiff stance her heels gave her. No animal grace, no assurance. Dick would dearly have loved to give her a scare, jump on her and shake her till her teeth chattered, or chase her down those steps. But the idea of unnecessary contact with human flesh repelled him. Besides, she'd see his face and know him again when they found the body and raised the hue and cry. What would happen to Monty and the Chief if they caught him and put him inside? The thought made him shudder.

He let the girl pass by and settled down to wait again. A thin wrack of cloud passed across the stars. All to the good if it got a bit darker . . . Twenty to nine. He'd have left by now and be coming up to the Whitestone Pond.

Dick would have liked a cigarette but decided it wasn't worth the risk. The smell might linger and alert the man. Again he fingered the metal bar and the thin coil of picture cord. In a quarter of an hour, with luck, it would all be over. Then back home to the Chief and Monty for their evening walk, and tomorrow he'd get on to that house agent he'd seen advertising in the Sunday paper. Completely isolated, he'd say. It must be completely isolated and with plenty of land, maybe near the sea. The Chief would enjoy a swim, though he'd probably never had one in his life, spent as it had been in the dirty back street of a city. But all dogs could swim by the light of nature. Different from human beings who had to be taught like they had to be taught every damn-fool stupid thing they undertook . . .

Footsteps. Yes, it was time. Ten to nine, and evidently he was of a punctual habit. So much the worse for him. Dick kept perfectly still, staring at the dark hole between the walls, until the vague shape of his quarry appeared at the end of the tunnel. As the man came towards the light, he tensed, closing his hand over the bar. Her description had been precise. It was a stoutish figure that the lamplight showed him, its gleam falling on thick silver hair and the glossy black fur of a coat collar. If Dick had ever felt the slightest doubt as to the ethics of what he was about to do, that sight would have dispelled it. Did scum like that ever pause to think of the sufferings of trapped animals, left to die in agony just to have their pelts stuck on some rich bastard's coat? Dick gathered saliva in his mouth and spat silently but viciously into the undergrowth.

The man advanced casually and confidently and the dark space received him. Dick stepped out from among the trees, raised his arm and struck. The man gave a grunt, not much louder than a hiccup, and fell heavily. There was no blood, not a spot. Bracing himself to withstand the disgust contact with a warm heavily-fleshed body would bring, Dick thrust his arms under the sagging shoulders and dragged him under the lamp. He was unconscious and would be for five minutes – except that in five minutes or less he'd be dead.

Dick didn't waste time examining the face. He had no interest in it. He put his cosh back in his pocket and brought out the cord. A slip knot here, slide it round here, then a quick tightening of pressure on the hyoid . . .

A soft sound stayed him, the cord still slack in his hands. It wasn't a footstep he'd heard but a light padding. He turned sharply. Out of the tunnel, tail erect, nose to ground, came a hound dog, a black and tan and white basset. It was one of the handsomest dogs Dick had ever seen, but he didn't want to see it now. Christ, he thought, it'd be bound to come up to him. They always did.

And sure enough the hound hesitated as it left the darkness and entered the patch of light where Dick was. It lifted its head and advanced on him, waving its tail. Dick cursed fate, not the dog, and held out his hand.

'Good dog,' he whispered. 'You're a cracker. You're a fine dog, you are. But get out of it now, go off home.'

The hound resisted his hand with an aloof politeness and, by-passing him, thrust its nose against the unconscious man's face. Dick didn't like that much. The guy might wake up.

'Come on now,' he said, laying his hands firmly on the glossy tricolour coat. 'This is no place for you. You get on with your hunting or whatever.'

But the basset wouldn't go. Its tail trembled and it whined. It looked at Dick and back at the man and began to make those soft hound cries that are half-way between a whimper and a whistle. And then Dick loosened his hold on the thick warm pelt. A terrible feeling had come over him, dread coupled with nausea. He felt in the pocket of the black fur-collared coat and brought out what he was afraid to find there – a plaited leather dog leash.

That God-damned woman! Was that what she'd meant about one other thing but it didn't matter? That this guy would be coming along here because he was taking his dog for a walk? Didn't matter – Christ! It didn't matter the poor little devil seeing its owner murdered and then having to make its own way home across one of the busiest main roads out of London. Or maybe she'd thought he'd kill the dog too. The sheer inhumanity of it made his blood boil. He wanted to kick the man's face as he lay there, but didn't like to, couldn't somehow, with the dog looking on.

He wouldn't be done, though. His house in Scotland was waiting for him. He owed it to the Chief and Monty to get that house. All that money wasn't going to be given up just because she'd gone and got things wrong again. There were ways. Like putting the dog on the leash and taking him back across the road by the Whitestone Pond. He'd be safe then. And so by that time, thought Dick, would his owner who was already stirring and moaning. Or he could put him in the car. God knew, he was gentle enough, utterly trusting, not suspecting what Dick had done, was going to do . . . And then? Kill the man and take the dead man's dog home? Be seen with the dog in his car? That was a laugh. Tie him up to a lamp-post? He'd never in his life tied up a dog and he wasn't going to start now.

A cold despair took hold of him. He bore the dog no malice, felt for him no anger, nothing more than the helpless resignation of a father whose child has come into a room and interrupted his love-making. The child comes first – inevitably.

Slowly he put away the cord. He lifted the silver head roughly and the man groaned. There had been a hard metal object in the pocket where the leash was, a brandy flask. Dick uncapped it and poured some of the liquid down the man's throat. The hound watched, thumping its tail.

'Where – where am I? Wha – what happened?'

Dick didn't bother to answer him.

'I had a – a bang on the head. God, my head's sore. I was mugged, was I?' He felt in his pocket and scrabbled with a wallet. 'Not touched, thank God. I'll – I'll try to sit up. God, that's better. Where's Bruce? Oh, there he is. Good boy, Bruce. I'm glad he's all right.'

'He's a fine dog,' Dick said remotely, and then, 'Come on, you'd better hang on to me. I've got a car.'

'You're most kind, most kind. What a blessing for me you came along when you did.'

Dick said nothing. He almost heaved when the man clung to his arm and leant on him. Bruce anchored to his leash, they set off down the steps to the car. It was a relief to be free of that touch, that solid weight that smelt of the sweat of terror. Dick got Bruce on to the back seat and stroked him, murmuring reassuring words.

The house he was directed to was a big one, almost a mansion on the East Heath. Lights blazed in its windows. Dick hauled the man out and propelled him up to the front door, leaving Bruce to follow. He rang the bell and a uniformed maid answered it. Behind her, in the hall, stood a tall young woman in evening dress.

She spoke the one word 'Father!' and her voice was sick with dismay. But it was the same voice. He recognized it just as she recognized his when, turning away from the glimpse of wealth in that hall, he said, 'I'll be off now.'

Their eyes met. Her face was chalk-white, made distorted and ugly by the destruction of her hopes. She let her father take her arm and then she snapped, 'What happened?'

'I was mugged, dear, but I'm all right now. This gentleman happened to come along at the opportune moment. I haven't thanked him properly yet.' He put out his hand to Dick. 'You must come in. You must let us have your name. No, I insist. You probably saved my life. I could have died of exposure out there.'

'Not you,' said Dick. 'Not with that dog of yours.'

'A lot of use he was! Not much of a bodyguard, are you, Bruce?'

Dick bent down and patted the dog. He shook off the detaining hand and said as he turned away, 'You'll never know how much use he was.'

He got into the car without looking back. In the mirror, as he drove away, he saw the woman retreat into the house while her father stood dizzily on the path, making absurd gestures of gratitude after his rescuer.

Dick got home by a quarter to ten. Monty was waiting for him in the hall, but the Chief was still in the sitting room on the settee. Dick put on their leashes and his best coat on Monty and opened the front door.

'Time for a beer before the pub closes, Mont,' he said, 'and then we'll go on the common.' He and the dogs sniffed the diesel-laden air and Monty sneezed. 'Bless you,' said Dick. 'Lousy hole, this, isn't it? It's a bloody shame but you're going to have to wait a bit longer for our place in Scotland.'

Slowly, because Monty couldn't make it fast any more, the three of them walked up towards the George Tavern.

Divided We Stand

I t was Mother who told Marjorie about Pauline's friend, not Pauline herself. Pauline never said much. She had always been a sulky girl, though hardly a girl any more, Marjorie thought. Mother waited until she had gone out of the room to get the tea and then, leaning forward in her chair, whispering, closing both her hands over the top of her walking stick, she said:

'Pauline's got a gentleman friend.'

'How do you know?' asked Marjorie – a stupid question as there was only one way Mother could know seeing that she and Pauline were always together.

'He was here last night. He came after I'd gone to bed but I could hear them talking down here. He didn't stay long and when he was going I heard him say, "Speaking as a doctor, Pauline..." so I reckon she met him when she was in *that place*.'

Marjorie didn't like to hear 'that place' spoken of. It was foolish – narrow-minded, George said – but a lunatic asylum is a lunatic asylum even if they do call them mental hospitals these days, and she didn't care to think of her sister having been in one. A mental breakdown – why couldn't the specialist have called it a *nervous* breakdown? – was such an awful thing to have in the family.

'Maybe he came – well, professionally,' she said. 'Didn't you ask her?'

'I didn't like to, dear. You know what Pauline is.'

Marjorie did. And now they had to stop talking about it, for Pauline had come in with the tea things. She buttered a scone for Mother, cut it into small pieces, tucked a napkin round Mother's neck, and all this she did in silence.

'Why are you using the best china?' Mother said.

'What d'you mean, dear?' said Marjorie. 'This is the old blue china you always use.'

'No, it isn't.'

Marjorie started once more to protest, but Pauline interrupted her.

'Leave it. She can't see. You know how bad her sight is.' She gave mother one of her bright nurse's smiles. 'OK, so we're using the best china,' she said, and she wiped the corners of Mother's mouth with a tissue.

Not long after they had finished Marjorie left. She had the perfectly valid excuse of George and the children. It wasn't possible for her to stay long, Mother understood that. And she had, after all, washed the dishes before she went, with Pauline's eye on her and Pauline's silence more difficult to bear than any noise. On Saturday afternoon she was back again, 'just looking in' as she put it, on her way to the shops.

'He was here again last night,' Mother whispered.

'Who was?'

'That doctor friend of Pauline's. He was here ever so late. I rang my bell for Pauline because I wanted to go to the toilet. It was gone eleven and I could hear him talking after I'd gone back to bed.'

Pauline had been in the garden, getting the clean linen, drawsheets and towels and napkins and Mother's nightgowns, in from the line. When she re-entered the room Marjorie studied her appearance uneasily. Her sister looked exhausted. She was a tall gaunt woman, dark and swarthy, and now she was so thin that the shapeless old trousers she wore hung loose against her hips. Dark shadows ringed her eyes, and those eyes had a glazed look, due perhaps to the drugs she had been on ever since she came out of 'that place'.

'Have I got a spot?' said Pauline. 'Or am I so lovely you can't take your eyes off me?'

'Sorry, I was off in a dream.' Marjorie said she had better get away before the shops shut, and Mother thanked her for coming 'to see an old nuisance like me'. After that one, Marjorie didn't dare look at Pauline again. She did her shopping and went home in a troubled frame of mind, but she waited until the children had gone out before opening her heart to her husband. Seventeen-year-old Brian and sixteen-year-old Susan were apt, with the ignorance of youth, to remark when their grandmother was mentioned that Nanna was 'a dear old love'; that they wouldn't mind at all if she came to live with them; and that it was 'a drag for Auntie Pauline' never being able to go out.

'Pauline's got a boy friend, George.'

'You're joking.'

'No, I'm not. He's a doctor she met when she was in that Hightrees place, and he's called round twice in the evenings and stopped ever so late. Mother told me.'

'Well, good old Pauline,' said George. 'She's forty if she's a day.'

'She's forty-two,' said Marjorie. 'You know very well she's seven years younger than I am.'

'Doesn't look it though, does she? People always take you for the younger one.' George smiled affectionately at his wife and took up the evening paper.

'You're to listen to me, George. Don't read that now. I haven't finished. George, suppose – suppose she was to get married?' The words came out in a breathless, almost hysterical rush. 'Suppose she was to marry this doctor?'

'What, old Pauline?'

'Well, why not? I know she's not young and she's nothing to look at, but when you think of the women who do get married . . . I mean, looks don't seem to have much to do with it. I don't care what these young people say nowadays, *all* women want to get married. So why not Pauline?'

'A man's got to want to marry them.'

'Yes, but look at it this way. He's a doctor, and Pauline always wanted to be a doctor, only Mother wouldn't have it so she had to settle for nursing instead. And she's got a masculine sort of mind. She can talk way above my head when she wants. They might have a lot in common.'

'Good luck to her then, is what I say. She's never so much as been out with a man all the time I've known her, and if she can get herself one now and get married – well, like I said, the best of luck.'

'But, George, don't you see? What about Mother? A doctor's bound to have a practice and be overworked and everything. He wouldn't want Mother. You don't know how awful Mother is. She gets Pauline up five or six times some nights. She rings that bell by her bedside for the least little thing. And when she's up she keeps Pauline on the trot, wanting her glasses or her knitting or her pills. Pauline never complains but sometimes I reckon she'd do anything to get away. I know I shouldn't say it, and yet I wonder if she didn't stage that breakdown when Mother had her first stroke in the hope she'd never have to go back and . . .'

'Aren't you getting steamed up about nothing?' George said placidly. 'As far as we know, the bloke's only been there twice and maybe he'll never go there again.'

But this was the major worry of Marjorie's life: that the time

125

might come when Mother would have to live with her. She hardly understood how she had managed to escape it so long. From the onset of Mother's illness, she had been the obvious person to care for her. For one thing, she was and always had been Mother's favourite daughter. Pauline was to have been a boy. Even now Marjorie could remember, as a child of seven, Mother saying to her friends, 'I'm carrying forward, so it'll be a boy this time.' Paul. The name was ready, the blue baby clothes. Mother had never really got over having a second daughter. There had been, Marjorie recalled, some neglect, some degree of cruelty. Scathing words for Pauline when she wanted to take up medicine, cruel words when she had never married. Marjorie had quite a big house, big enough for Mother to have a bedsitting room of her own; she had no job; her children fended for themselves. How lucky it was for her Pauline hadn't been Paul, for no man would have given up his job, his flat, his whole way of life, to care for an unloved, unloving mother . . .

While Mother lived, though, it would never be too late for a change. And Marjorie knew she couldn't depend on George and the children for support. Even George would surrender quietly to the invasion of his home by a mother-in-law, for it wouldn't be he Mother would get up in the night to or nag about draughts and rheumatism and eyedrops and hot milk. He wouldn't be expected to listen to interminable stories about what things were like in nineteen-ten, or be asked daily in a mournful tone:

'D'you think I'll see another winter out, dear?'

She had always, in spite of her seniority, been a little afraid of Pauline. As a child, her sister had been a very withdrawn person, spending long hours shut up in her bedroom. She had had an imaginary friend in those days, one of those not uncommon childhood creations – Marjorie's own Susan had behaved in much the same way – but Pauline's Pablo had persisted almost into her teens, and had always been put forward as the mouthpiece of Pauline's own feelings. 'Pablo says he doesn't want to go,' when some outing had been proposed on which Pauline herself didn't want to go; 'Pablo hates you,' when there was a need to express Pauline's own hatred. He had disappeared at Pauline's puberty, and since then Marjorie couldn't remember her sister once showing her feelings. No, not when Father died or Marjorie's first baby was born dead. And when she had been told that the only alternative to Mother's going into a sixty-pound a week nursing home was her abandoning her job and her home, she had said merely, with a blank face:

'I suppose I've got no choice, then.'

Never once had she suggested Marjorie as an alternative. But the first time Marjorie called at the new Pauline-Mother ménage Pauline, who in the past had always kissed her when they met and parted, made a quiet but marked point of not doing so. And since that day they had never exchanged a kiss. Not when Mother had her second stroke; not when Mother was temporarily in hospital and Marjorie visited Pauline in Hightrees. No complaints about the arduousness of her duties ever escaped Pauline's narrow set lips, nor would she ever protest to Mother herself, however exigent she might be. Instead, she would sometimes enumerate in a cold monotonous voice the tasks she had accomplished since the night before.

'Mother got me up at midnight and again at four and five. But she still had a wet bed. I got everything washed out by eight and then I turned out the living room. I went down to the shops but I forgot Mother's prescription, so I had to go back for it.'

Marjorie would cringe with guilt and shame during this catalogue and actually shiver when, at the end of it, Pauline turned upon her large glazed eyes in which seemed to lurk a spark of bitter irony. Those eyes said, though the lips never did, 'To her that has shall be given, but from her that has not shall be taken away, even that which she has.' Marjorie could have borne it better, have worried less and agonized less, if they could have had a real ding-dong battle. But that was impossible with Pauline. Apologize to Pauline for a missed visit and all she said was 'That's OK. Suit yourself.' Tell her to cheer up and you got 'I'm all right. Leave me alone.' Offer sympathy combined with excuses about having your own family to attend to, and you got no answer at all, unless a stare of profound contempt is an answer. So Marjorie felt she couldn't, as yet at any rate, tackle Pauline about her doctor friend.

But she was driven to do so a week later. She could see something had happened to upset Mother the minute she walked into the room. Mother's mouth was turned down and she kept looking at Pauline in a truculent injured kind of way. And Pauline just sat there, determined not to leave Mother and Marjorie alone for a moment, although she must have been able to see Mother was dying to get Marjorie on her own. But at three the laundryman called, and luckily for Mother, there seemed to be some problem about a missing pillowcase which kept Pauline arguing on the step for nearly five minutes.

'That man was here again last night, Marjorie,' Mother said, 'and he came into my room and spoke to me. He bullied me, Marjorie, he said awful things to me.'

'What on earth d'you mean, Mother?'

'Oh, dear, I hope she won't come back for a minute. I heard him talking down here last night. About ten, it was. I'd drunk my water and Pauline had brought me another glass, but I couldn't sleep, I was so hot. I rang the bell for Pauline to take the eiderdown off me. I had to ring and ring before she came and of course I couldn't help – well, I was feeling a bit weepy by then, Marjorie.' Mother sniffed and gave a sort of gulp. 'The next thing I knew that man, that doctor, had marched right into my room and started bullying me.'

'But what did he say?'

'He was very rude. He was very impertinent, Marjorie. I wish you'd heard him, I wish you'd been there to stand up for me. Pauline wasn't there, just him shouting at me.'

Marjorie was aghast. 'What did he *say*?'

'Just because he's a doctor . . . Doctors don't have the right to say what they like if you're not their patient, do they?'

'Mother, please tell me before Pauline gets back.'

'He said I was a very lucky woman and I ought to understand that, and I was selfish and demanding and I'd driven my daughter into a breakdown, and if I didn't stop her getting up in the night she'd have another one and . . . Oh, Marjorie, it was awful. He went on and on in a very deep bossy sort of voice. I started crying and then I thought he was going to get hold of me and shake me. He just stood there in the doorway against the light, shaking his finger at me and – and *booming* at me and . . .'

'Oh, dear God,' said Marjorie. Now she *would* have to speak to Pauline. She sighed wretchedly. Why did this have to happen? Not that she cared very much about what anyone said to Mother – do her good, it was all true, anyway – but that someone should point out to Pauline facts which Pauline herself had possibly never realized! Much more of that and . . . She went out into the hall and intercepted Pauline parting from the laundryman.

'Mother's been on about nothing else since first thing this morning,' said Pauline.

'Well, I don't wonder. You know I don't like to criticize you, but you really shouldn't let people – I mean, strangers – upset Mother.'

Pauline dumped the heavy laundry box on the kitchen table. She looked even more tired than usual. Her skin had a battered appearance as if lack of sleep and peace and recreation had actually dented and bruised it. She shrugged.

'You believe her? You take all that rubbish for gospel?'

'You mean you don't have a friend who's a doctor? He didn't go into Mother's room and boss her about last night? It's all her imagination?'

'That's right,' said Pauline laconically, and she filled the kettle. 'She imagined it, she's getting senile.'

'But Mother never had any imagination. She heard him. She *saw* him.'

'She can't see,' said Pauline. 'Or not much. It was a dream.'

For a moment Marjorie was certain that she was lying. But you could never tell with Pauline. And what was more likely, after all? That Pauline who had everything to gain in esteem and interest by having a man friend should deny his existence, or that Mother who was eighty and half-blind and maybe senile like Pauline said, should magnify a nightmare into reality? Could it be, Marjorie wondered, that it had been Mother's conscience talking? That was very far-fetched, of course, what her son and daughter would call way-out — but if only it were true! The alternative was almost too unpleasant to face. It took George to put it into words.

'Old Pauline's always been a dark horse. I can see what game she's playing. She's keeping him in the background till he's popped the question.'

'Oh, George, no! But she did look very funny when I spoke about him. And, George, the awful thing is, if he does marry Pauline he'll never have Mother to live with them when he feels like that about her, never.'

Worrying about it brought on such a headache that when the time came for her next duty visit, Marjorie had to phone Mother's house and say she couldn't come over. A man's voice answered.

'Hallo?'

'I'm sorry, I think I've got a wrong number. I want to speak to Miss Needham.'

'Miss Needham is lying down, having a well-earned rest.' The voice was deep, cultured, authoritative. 'Is that by any chance Mrs Crossley?'

Marjorie said breathlessly that it was. But she was too taken aback to ask if her mother was all right, and who was he, anyway? She cared very little about the answer to the first question and she knew the answer to the second. Besides, he had interrupted her reply by launching into a flood of hectoring.

'Mrs Crossley, as a doctor I don't think I'm overstepping the bounds of decorum by telling you that I think you personally take a very irresponsible attitude to the situation here. I've hoped for an opportunity to tell you so. There seems to me, from what your sister tells me, no reason at all why you shouldn't share some of the burden of caring for Mrs Needham.'

'I don't, I . . .' Marjorie stammered, thunderstruck.

'No, you don't realize, do you? Perhaps you haven't cared to think about it too deeply. Your mother is a very demanding woman, a very selfish woman. I have spoken to her myself, though I know from experience that it is almost useless telling home truths to someone of her age and in her condition.'

So it was true, after all. Marjorie felt a spurt of real rage against Pauline. 'I should have thought it was for my mother's own doctor,' she blustered. 'I don't know what an outsider . . .'

'An *outsider*?' She might have levelled at him some outrageous insult. 'I am a close friend of your sister, Mrs Crossley, perhaps the only true friend she has. Please don't speak of *outsiders*. Now if you have any feeling for your sister, I'm sure you'll appreciate . . .'

'I don't want to talk about it,' Marjorie almost shouted. Her head was splitting now. 'It's no business of yours and I don't want to discuss it.'

She told George.

'He said he was a close friend, her only true friend. They're cooking this up together, George. He means to marry her, but he'll get Mother out of the way first. He'll foist Mother on to me and then they'll get married and . . . Oh, George, what am I going to do?'

Not see Mother or Pauline, at any rate. Marjorie extended her headache over the next two visiting times, and after that she half-invented, half-suffered, a virus infection. Of course, she had to phone and explain, and it was with a trembling hand that she dialled the number in case that awful man should answer. He didn't. Pauline was more abrupt than ever. Marjorie didn't mention her doctor friend, though she fancied, just as she was replacing the receiver, that she heard the murmur of his voice in the background talking to Mother.

It was George and Brian together who at last paid a visit to Mother's house. Marjorie was in bed when they came back, cowering under the sheets and trying to make the mercury in her thermometer go above ninety-eight by burying it in her electric blanket.

They hadn't, they said, seen Pauline's friend, but Nanna had been full of him, now entirely won over to him as a charming man, while Pauline, as she talked, had sat looking very close with an occasional flash of impatience in her eyes.

'He's got some Russian name,' said George, though he couldn't remember what it was, and Brian kept talking nonsense about dogs and reactions and other things Marjorie couldn't follow. 'He lives in Kensington, got a big practice. One of those big houses on Campden Hill. You know where I mean. Pauline did a private nursing job in one of them years ago. Quite a coincidence.'

Marjorie didn't want to hear about coincidences.

'Is he going to marry her?'

'I reckon,' said Brian, 'going from the way Nanna talks about what he says.'

'What *do* you mean?'

'Well, Auntie Pauline went off to get us coffee and while she was outside Nanna said he's always telling her how lovely her daughter is and what a fine mind and how she's wasted and all that.'

'Nanna must have changed. She's never had a good word to say for your auntie.'

'She *is* changed,' said George. 'She's all for Pauline going off and leading her own life and her coming here to live with us. Dr Whatsit's told her it would be a good idea, you see. And I must say, Marje, it might be the best thing in the long run. If Nanna sold her house and let us have some of the money and we had an extension built on . . .'

'And I'll be off to university in the autumn,' put in Brian.

'I never did think it quite fair,' said George, 'poor old Pauline having to bear the whole burden of Nanna on her own. It's not as if they ever really got on and . . .'

'Nanna's an old love with people she gets on with,' said Brian.

'I won't do it, I won't!' Marjorie screamed. 'And no one's going to make me!'

For a little while no one attempted to. Marjorie prolonged her illness, augmenting it with back pains and vague menopausal symptoms, for as long as she could. Mother never used the telephone, and Marjorie could have counted on the fingers of one hand the number of times Pauline had phoned her in the past two years. Now there was no communication between the two houses. Marjorie began to go out again but she avoided going near Mother's, and her own family, George and Brian and Susan, wishing perhaps to prevent a

131

further outburst of hysterics, kept off the subject of her mother. Until one day George said:

'I had a call at work from that doctor friend of Pauline's.'

'I don't want to know, George,' said Marjorie. 'It's no business of his. I've told you I won't have Mother here and I won't.'

'As a matter of fact,' her husband admitted, 'he's phoned me a couple of times before, only I didn't tell you, seeing how upset it makes you.'

'Of course it upsets me. I'm ill.'

'No, you're not,' said George with unexpected firmness. 'You're as right as rain. A sick woman couldn't eat a meal like the one you've just eaten. It's Pauline who's ill. Marje. She's cracking up. He told me in the nicest possible way, he's a very decent chap. But we have to do something about it.'

'Any other man,' said Marjorie tearfully, 'would be thankful to have a wife who stopped her mother coming to live with them.'

'Well, I'm not any other man. I don't mind the upheaval and the extra expense. We'll all do our bit, Brian and Sue too. Don't you see, it's our *turn*. Pauline's had two years of it. The doctor says she'll have another breakdown if we don't, and God knows what might be the outcome.'

'You're all against me,' Marjorie sobbed, and because he was her husband and she didn't much care what she said in front of him. 'Pauline's got pills from her nursing days, morphine and I don't know what. There ought to be – what's it called? – euthanasia. There ought to be a way of putting people like Mother out of their misery.'

He looked at her, his eyes narrowing. 'There isn't. Maybe dogs are luckier than people. There isn't a geriatric hospital that'll take her either. There's no one but us, Marge, so you'd better turn off the waterworks and make up your mind to it.'

She saw how it would be. It would take months for Mother to sell her house and get the money for an extension to theirs, a year perhaps before that extension was built. Even when it was built and Mother was installed, things would be bad enough. But before that . . . ! Her dining room turned into a bedroom, every evening spoiled by the business of getting Mother to bed, nights that would be even worse than when Brian and Susan were babies. And she wasn't thirty any more. The television turned down to a murmur once Mother was in bed, her shopping times curtailed, her little afternoon visits to the cinema over for good. Marjorie wondered if she would have the courage to throw herself downstairs, break a leg, so that they would understand having Mother was out of the question. But she might break her neck . . .

And all the while this was going on, Pauline would be living in the splendour of Campden Hill, Mrs Something Russian, with a new husband, an educated, important, rich man. Giving parties. Entertaining eminent surgeons and professors and whatnot. Going abroad. It was unbearable. She might lack the courage to throw herself downstairs, but she thought she could be brave enough to confront Pauline here and now and tell her No. No, I won't. You took it on, you must go through with it. Crack up, break down, go crazy, die. Yes, die before I'll ruin my life for you.

Of course, she wouldn't put it like that. She would be firm and kind. She would even offer to sit with Mother sometimes so that Pauline could go out. Anything, anything, except that permanency which would trap her as Pauline had been trapped.

Things are never as we imagine they will be. No situation ever parallels our prevision of it. Marjorie, when she at last called, expected an irate resentful Pauline, perhaps even a Pauline harassed by wedding plans. She expected Mother to be bewildered by the proposed changes in her life. And both, she thought, would be bitter against her for her long absence. But Mother was just the same, pleased to see her, anxious to get her alone for those little whispered confidences, even more anxious to know if she was better. Her purblind eyes searched Marjorie's face for signs of debility, held her hand, pressed her to wrap up warm.

Anyone less like a potential bride than Pauline Marjorie couldn't have imagined. She seemed thinner than ever, and her face, bruise-dark, patchily shadowed, lined like raisin skin, reminded her of pictures she had seen of Indian beggars. Marjorie followed her into the kitchen when she went to make tea and gathered up her courage.

'How have you been keeping, Pauline?'

'All right. Just the same.' And although she hadn't been asked, Pauline said, 'Mother had me up four times in the night. She fell over in the passage and I had to drag her back to bed. The laundry didn't come, so I did the sheets myself. It's a job getting them dry when it's raining like today.'

'I was thinking, I could come in two evenings a week and sit with her so that you could go out. There's no reason why I shouldn't take some of the washing and do it in my machine. Come to that, I could take it all. Every week.'

Pauline shrugged. 'Suit yourself.'

'Yes, well, it's all very well saying that,' said Marjorie, working herself up to the required pitch, 'but if you keep on complaining like this, what am I to say?'

'I don't complain.'

'Maybe not. But everyone else does. You know very well who I mean. I can't take all this outside interference and just pretend it's not happening.'

'I shouldn't call a husband outside interference.'

For a moment Marjorie thought she was referring to George. Realization of what she actually meant gave her the impetus she needed. 'I may as well tell you straight out, Pauline, I'm not having Mother to live with us and that's flat. I'll do anything else in my power, but not that. No one can make me and I shan't.'

Pauline made no answer. They ate their tea in almost total silence. Marjorie couldn't remember ever having felt so uncomfortable in the whole of her life. On the doorstep, as she was leaving, she said, 'You'd better tell me which evenings you want me, and you can let me know when you want George to come round in the car for the washing.'

'It makes no difference to me,' said Pauline. 'I'm always here.'

Of course, she didn't phone. Marjorie knew she wouldn't. And what was the point of going round in the evening when Pauline didn't want to go out, when she was snug at home with her doctor?

'We're not having Mother,' she said to George. 'That's definite. I've cleared it all up with Pauline. She's quite capable of carrying on if I help out a bit.'

'That's not what I was told.'

'It's what I'm telling you.' Marjorie hated the way he looked at her these days, with a kind of dull distasteful reproach. 'She's done the washing for this week, and next week the laundry'll do the sheets and the heavy stuff. I thought we might go over on Friday and collect their bits and pieces, put them in my machine.'

So on Thursday Marjorie phoned. She chose the morning just in case that man might answer. Doctors are never free to make social calls in the morning. Pauline answered.

'OK. Tomorrow, if you like.'

'It's what *you* like, Pauline,' said Marjorie, feeling that her sister might at least have said thank you.

She added that they would be there at seven. But by seven George hadn't yet got home, so Marjorie dialled her mother's number. It didn't matter if *he* answered. Show him she wasn't the indifferent creature he took her for. He did. And he was quite polite. Mr and Mrs Crossley couldn't get there till eight thirty? Never mind. He would still be there and would be delighted to meet them at last.

'We're going to get a look at him at last,' said Marjorie to George as he came in at the door. 'Now don't you forget, I expect you to back me up if we have any more nonsense about us having Mother and all that. United we stand, divided we fall.'

Mother's house was in darkness and the hall light didn't come on when Marjorie rang the bell. She rang it again, and then George rang it.

'Have you got a key?' said George.

'In my bag. Oh, George, you don't think . . . ? I mean . . . ?'

'I don't know, do I? Let's get this door open.'

No one in the hall or in any of the downstairs rooms. Marjorie, who had turned on lights, began to climb the stairs with George behind her. Half-way up, she heard a man's voice, speaking soothingly but with authority. It came from Mother's room, the door of which was ajar.

'It was the best thing, Pauline. I gave her two hundred milligrammes crushed in her milk drink. She didn't suffer. She just fell asleep, Pauline.'

Marjorie gave a little gasping whimper. She clutched George, clawing at his shoulder. As he pushed past her, she heard the voice come again, the same words repeated in the same lulling hypnotic tone.

'I gave her two hundred milligrammes crushed in her milk drink. She didn't suffer. It was the only thing. I did it for you, Pauline, for us . . .'

George threw open the bedroom door. Mother lay on her back, her face waxen and slack in death, her now totally sightless eyes wide open. There was no one else in the room but Pauline.

Pauline got up as they entered, and giving them a nod of quiet dignity, she placed her fingers on Mother's eyes, closing the lids. Marjorie stared in frozen, paralysed terror, like one in the presence of the supernatural. And then Pauline turned from the bed, came forward with her right hand outstretched.

In a deep, cultured and authoritative voice, a voice whose hectoring manner on the telephone was softened now by sympathy for the bereaved, she said:

'How do you do? I am Dr Pavlov. It's unfortunate we should meet under such sad circumstances but . . .'

Marjorie began to scream.

135

Means of Evil

Means of Evil

'**B**lewits,' said Inspector Burden, 'parasols, horns of plenty, morels and boletus. Mean anything to you?'

Chief Inspector Wexford shrugged. 'Sounds like one of those magazine quizzes. What have these in common? I'll make a guess and say they're crustacea. Or sea anemones. How about that?'

'They are edible fungi,' said Burden.

'Are they now? And what have edible fungi to do with Mrs Hannah Kingman throwing herself off, or being pushed off, a balcony?'

The two men were sitting in Wexford's office at the police station, Kingsmarkham, in the County of Sussex. The month was November, but Wexford had only just returned from his holiday. And while he had been away, enjoying in Cornwall an end of October that had been more summery than the summer, Hannah Kingman had committed suicide. Or so Burden had thought at first. Now he was in a dilemma, and as soon as Wexford had walked in that Monday morning, Burden had begun to tell the whole story to his chief.

Wexford, getting on for sixty, was a tall, ungainly, rather ugly man who had once been fat to the point of obesity but had slimmed to gauntness for reasons of health. Nearly twenty years his junior, Burden had the slenderness of a man who has always been thin. His face was ascetic, handsome in a frosty way. The older man, who had a good wife who looked after him devotedly, nevertheless always looked as if his clothes came off the peg from the War on Want Shop, while the younger, a widower, was sartorially immaculate. A tramp and a Beau Brummell, they seemed to be, but the dandy relied on the tramp, trusted him, understood his powers and his perception. In secret he almost worshipped him.

Without his chief he had felt a little at sea in this case. Everything had pointed at first to Hannah Kingman's having killed herself. She had been a manic-depressive, with a strong sense of her own inadequacy; apparently her marriage, though not of long duration, had been unhappy, and her previous marriage had failed. Even in the absence of a suicide note or suicide threats, Burden would have taken her death for self-destruction – if her brother hadn't come along and told him about the edible fungi. And Wexford hadn't been there to do what he always could do, sort out sheep from goats and wheat from chaff.

'The thing is,' Burden said across the desk, 'we're not looking for proof of murder so much as proof of *attempted* murder. Axel Kingman could have pushed his wife off that balcony – he has no alibi for the time in question – but I had no reason to think he had done so until I was told of an attempt to murder her some two weeks before.'

'Which attempt has something to do with edible fungi?'

Burden nodded. 'Say with administering to her some noxious substance in a stew made from edible fungi. Though if he did it, God knows how he did it, because three other people, including himself, ate the stew without ill effects. I think I'd better tell you about it from the beginning.'

'I think you had,' said Wexford.

'The facts,' Burden began, very like a Prosecuting Counsel, 'are as follows. Axel Kingman is thirty-five years old and he keeps a health-food shop here in the High Street called Harvest Home. Know it?' When Wexford signified by a nod that he did, Burden went on, 'He used to be a teacher in Myringham, and for about seven years before he came here he'd been living with a woman named Corinne Last. He left her, gave up his job, put all the capital he had into this shop, and married a Mrs Hannah Nicholson.'

'He's some sort of food freak, I take it,' said Wexford.

Burden wrinkled his nose. 'Lot of affected nonsense,' he said. 'Have you ever noticed what thin pale weeds these health-food people are? While the folks who live on roast beef and suet and whisky and plum cake are full of beans and rarin' to go.'

'Is Kingman a thin pale weed?'

'A feeble – what's the word? – aesthete, if you ask me. Anyway, he and Hannah opened this shop and took a flat in the high-rise tower our planning geniuses have been pleased to raise over the top of it. The fifth floor. Corinne Last, according to her and according to Kingman, accepted the situation after a while and they all remained friends.'

'Tell me about them,' Wexford said. 'Leave the facts for a bit and tell me about them.'

Burden never found this easy. He was inclined to describe people as 'just ordinary' or 'just like anyone else', a negative attitude which exasperated Wexford. So he made an effort. 'Kingman looks the sort who wouldn't hurt a fly. The fact is, I'd apply the word gentle to him if I wasn't coming round to thinking he's a cold-blooded wife-killer. He's a total abstainer with a bee in his bonnet about drink. His father went bankrupt and finally died of alcoholism, and our Kingman is an anti-booze fanatic.

'The dead woman was twenty-nine. Her first husband left her after six months of marriage and went off with some girl friend of hers. Hannah went back to live with her parents and had a part-time job helping with the meals at the school where Kingman was a teacher. That was where they met.'

'And the other woman?' said Wexford.

Burden's face took on a repressive expression. Sex outside marriage, however sanctioned by custom and general approval, was always distasteful to him. That, in the course of his work, he almost daily came across illicit sex had done nothing to mitigate his disapproval. As Wexford sometimes derisively put it, you would think that in Burden's eyes all the suffering in the world, and certainly all the crime, somehow derived from men and women going to bed together outside the bonds of wedlock. 'God knows why he didn't marry her,' Burden now said. 'Personally I think things were a lot better in the days when education authorities put their foot down about immorality among teachers.'

'Let's not have your views on that now, Mike,' said Wexford. 'Presumably Hannah Kingman didn't die because her husband didn't come to her a pure virgin.'

Burden flushed slightly. 'I'll tell you about this Corinne Last. She's very good-looking, if you like the dark sort of intense type. Her father left her some money and the house where she and Kingman lived, and she still lives in it. She's one of those women who seem to be good at everything they put their hands to. She paints and sells her paintings. She makes her own clothes, she's more or less the star in the local dramatic society, she's a violinist and plays in some string trio. Also she writes for health magazines and she's the author of a cookery book.'

'It would look then,' Wexford put in, 'as if Kingman split up with her because all this was more than he could take. And hence he took up with the dull little school-meals lady. No competition from her, I fancy.'

'I daresay you're right. As a matter of fact, that theory has already been put to me.'

'By whom?' said Wexford. 'Just where did you get all this information, Mike?'

'From an angry young man, the fourth member of the quartet, who happens to be Hannah's brother. His name is John Hood and I think he's got a lot more to tell. But it's time I left off describing the people and got on with the story.

'No one saw Hannah fall from the balcony. It happened last Thursday afternoon at about four. According to her husband, he was in a sort of office behind the shop doing what he always did on early-closing day – stock-taking and sticking labels on various bottles and packets.

'She fell on to a hard-top parking area at the back of the flats, and her body was found by a neighbour a couple of hours later between two parked cars. We were sent for, and Kingman seemed to be distraught. I asked him if he had had any idea that his wife might have wished to take her own life and he said she had never threatened to do so but had lately been very depressed and there had been quarrels, principally about money. Her doctor had put her on tranquillizers – of which, by the way, Kingman disapproved – and the doctor himself, old Dr Castle, told me Mrs Kingman had been to him for depression and because she felt her life wasn't worth living and she was a drag on her husband. He wasn't surprised that she had killed herself and neither, by that time, was I. We were all set for an inquest verdict of suicide while the balance of the mind was disturbed when John Hood walked in here and told me Kingman had attempted to murder his wife on a previous occasion.'

'He told you just like that?'

'Pretty well. It's plain he doesn't like Kingman, and no doubt he was fond of his sister. He also seems to like and admire Corinne Last. He told me that on a Saturday night at the end of October the four of them had a meal together in the Kingmans' flat. It was a lot of vegetarian stuff cooked by Kingman – he always did the cooking – and one of the dishes was made out of what I'm old-fashioned enough, or narrow-minded enough, to call toadstools. They all ate it and they were all OK but for Hannah who got up from the table, vomited for hours, and apparently was quite seriously ill.'

Wexford's eyebrows went up. 'Elucidate, please,' he said.

Burden sat back, put his elbows on the arms of the chair, and pressed the tips of his fingers together. 'A few days before this meal was eaten, Kingman and Hood met at the squash club of which they are both members. Kingman told Hood that Corinne Last had promised to get him some edible fungi called shaggy caps from her own garden, the garden of the house which they had at one time shared. A crop of these things show themselves every autumn under a tree in this garden. I've seen them myself, but we'll come to that in a minute.

'Kingman's got a thing about using weeds and whatnot for cooking, makes salads out of dandelion and sorrel, and he swears by this fungi rubbish, says they've got far more flavour than mushrooms. Give me something that comes in a plastic bag from the supermarket every time, but no doubt it takes all sorts to make a world. By the way, this cookbook of Corinne Last's is called *Cooking for Nothing*, and all the recipes are for making dishes out of stuff you pull up by the wayside or pluck from the hedgerow.'

'These warty blobs or spotted puffets or whatever, had he cooked them before?'

'Shaggy caps,' said Burden, grinning, 'or *coprinus comatus*. Oh, yes, every year, and every year he and Corinne had eaten the resulting stew. He told Hood he was going to cook them again this time, and Hood says he seemed very grateful to Corinne for being so – well, magnanimous.'

'Yes, I can see it would have been a wrench for her. Like hearing "our tune" in the company of your ex-lover and your supplanter.' Wexford put on a vibrant growl. '"Can you bear the sight of me eating our toadstools with another?"'

'As a matter of fact,' said Burden seriously, 'it could have been just like that. Anyway, the upshot of it was that Hood was invited round for the following Saturday to taste these delicacies and was told that Corinne would be there. Perhaps it was that fact which made him accept. Well, the day came. Hood looked in on his sister at lunchtime. She showed him the pot containing the stew which Kingman had already made and she said *she had tasted it* and it was delicious. She also showed Hood half a dozen specimens of shaggy caps which she said Kingman hadn't needed and which they would fry for their breakfast. This is what she showed him.'

Burden opened a drawer in the desk and produced one of those plastic bags which he had said so inspired him with confidence. But the contents of this one hadn't come from a supermarket. He removed the wire fastener and tipped out four whitish scaly objects. They were egg-shaped, or rather elongated ovals, each with a short fleshy stalk.

'I picked them myself this morning,' he said, 'from Corinne Last's garden. When they get bigger, the egg-shaped bit opens like an umbrella, or a pagoda really, and there are sort of black gills underneath. You're supposed to eat them when they're in the stage these are.'

'I suppose you've got a book on fungi?' said Wexford.

'Here.' This also was produced from the drawer. *British Fungi, Edible and Poisonous.* 'And here we are – shaggy caps.'

Burden had opened it at the *Edible* section and at a line and wash drawing of the species he held in his hand. He passed it to the chief inspector.

'*Coprinus comatus*,' Wexford read aloud, '*a common species, attaining when full-grown a height of nine inches. The fungus is frequently to be found, during late summer and autumn, growing in fields, hedgerows and often in gardens. It should be eaten before the cap opens and disgorges its inky fluid, but is at all times quite harmless.*' He put the book down but didn't close it. 'Go on, please, Mike,' he said.

'Hood called for Corinne and they arrived together. They got there just after eight. At about eight-fifteen they all sat down to table and began the meal with avocado *vinaigrette*. The next course was to be the stew, followed by nut cutlets with a salad and then an apple-cake. Very obviously, there was no wine or liquor of any sort on account of Kingman's prejudice. They drank grape juice from the shop.

'The kitchen opens directly out of the living-dining room. Kingman brought in the stew in a large tureen and served it himself at the table, beginning, of course, with Corinne. Each one of those shaggy caps had been sliced in half lengthwise and the pieces were floating in a thickish gravy to which carrots, onions and other vegetables had been added. Now, ever since he had been invited to this meal, Hood had been feeling uneasy about eating fungi, but Corinne had reassured him, and once he began to eat it and saw the others were eating it quite happily, he stopped worrying for the time being. In fact, he had a second helping.

'Kingman took the plates out and the tureen and immediately *rinsed them under the tap*. Both Hood and Corinne Last have told me this, though Kingman says it was something he always did, being fastidious about things of that sort.'

'Surely his ex-girl friend could confirm or deny that,' Wexford put in, 'since they lived together for so long.'

'We must ask her. All traces of the stew were rinsed away. Kingman then brought in the nut concoction and the salad, but before he could begin to serve them Hannah jumped up, covered her mouth with her napkin, and rushed to the bathroom.

'After a while Corinne went to her. Hood could hear a violent vomiting from the bathroom. He remained in the living room while Kingman and Corinne were both in the bathroom with Hannah. No one ate any more. Kingman eventually came back, said that Hannah must have picked up some "bug" and that he had put her to bed. Hood went into the bedroom where Hannah was lying on the bed with Corinne beside her. Hannah's face was greenish and covered with sweat and she was evidently in great pain because while he was there she doubled up and groaned. She had to go to the bathroom again and that time Kingman had to carry her back.

'Hood suggested Dr Castle should be sent for, but this was strenuously opposed by Kingman who dislikes doctors and is one of those people who go in for herbal remedies — raspberry leaf tablets and camomile tea and that sort of thing. Also he told Hood rather absurdly that Hannah had had quite enough to do with doctors and that if this wasn't some gastric germ it was the result of her taking "dangerous" tranquillizers.

'Hood thought Hannah was seriously ill and the argument got heated, with Hood trying to make Kingman either call a doctor or take her to a hospital. Kingman wouldn't and Corinne took his part. Hood is one of those angry but weak people who are all bluster, and although he might have called a doctor himself, he didn't. The effect on him of Corinne again, I suppose. What he did do was tell Kingman he was a fool to mess about cooking things everyone knew weren't safe, to which Kingman replied that if the shaggy caps were dangerous, how was it they weren't all ill? Eventually, at about midnight, Hannah stopped retching, seemed to have no more pain, and fell asleep. Hood drove Corinne home, returned to the Kingmans' and remained there for the rest of the night, sleeping on their sofa.

'In the morning Hannah seemed perfectly well, though weak, which rather upset Kingman's theory about the gastric bug. Relations between the brothers-in-law were strained. Kingman said he hadn't liked Hood's suggestions and that when he wanted to see his sister he, Kingman, would rather he came there when he was out or in the shop. Hood went off home, and since that day he hasn't seen Kingman.

'The day after his sister's death he stormed in here, told me what

I've told you, and accused Kingman of trying to poison Hannah. He was wild and nearly hysterical, but I felt I couldn't dismiss this allegation as – well, the ravings of a bereaved person. There were too many peculiar circumstances, the unhappiness of the marriage, the fact of Kingman rinsing those plates, his refusal to call a doctor. Was I right?'

Burden stopped and sat waiting for approval. It came in the form of a not very enthusiastic nod.

After a moment Wexford spoke. 'Could Kingman have pushed her off that balcony, Mike?'

'She was a small fragile woman. It was physically possible. The back of the flats isn't overlooked. There's nothing behind but the parking area and then open fields. Kingman could have gone up by the stairs instead of using the lift and come down by the stairs. Two of the flats on the lower floors are empty. Below the Kingmans lives a bedridden woman whose husband was at work. Below that the tenant, a young married woman, was in but she saw and heard nothing. The invalid says she thinks she heard a scream during the afternoon but she did nothing about it, and if she did hear it, so what? It seems to me that a suicide, in those circumstances, is as likely to cry out as a murder victim.'

'OK,' said Wexford. 'Now to return to the curious business of this meal. The idea would presumably be that Kingman intended to kill her that night but that his plan misfired because whatever he gave her wasn't toxic enough. She was very ill but she didn't die. He chose those means and that company so that he would have witnesses to his innocence. They all ate the stew out of the same tureen, but only Hannah was affected by it. How then are you suggesting he gave her whatever poison he did give her?'

'I'm not,' said Burden frankly, 'but others are making suggestions. Hood's a bit of a fool, and first of all he would only keep on about all fungi being dangerous and the whole dish being poisonous. When I pointed out that this was obviously not so, he said Kingman must have slipped something into Hannah's plate, or else it was the salt.'

'What salt?'

'He remembered that no one but Hannah took salt with the stew. But that's absurd because Kingman couldn't have known that would happen. And, incidentally, to another point we may as well clear up now – the avocados were quite innocuous. Kingman halved them *at the table* and the *vinaigrette* sauce was served in a jug. The bread was not in the form of rolls but a home-made wholemeal loaf. If there was anything there which shouldn't have been it was in the stew all right.

'Corinne Last refuses to consider the possibility that Kingman might be guilty. But when I pressed her she said she was not actually sitting at the table while the stew was served. She had got up and gone into the hall to fetch her handbag. So she didn't see Kingman serve Hannah.' Burden reached across and picked up the book Wexford had left open at the description and drawing of the shaggy caps. He flicked over to the *Poisonous* section and pushed the book back to Wexford. 'Have a look at some of these.'

'Ah, yes,' said Wexford. 'Our old friend, the fly agaric. A nice-looking little red job with white spots, much favoured by illustrators of children's books. They usually stick a frog on top of it and a gnome underneath. I see that when ingested it causes nausea, vomiting, tetanic convulsions, coma and death. Lots of these agarics, aren't there? Purple, crested, warty, verdigris – all more or less lethal. Aha! The death cap, *amanita phalloides*. How very unpleasant. The most dangerous fungus known, it says here. Very small quantities will cause intense suffering and often death. So where does all that get us?'

'The death cap, according to Corinne Last, is quite common round here. What she doesn't say, but what I infer, is that Kingman could have got hold of it easily. Now suppose he cooked just one specimen separately and dropped it into the stew just before he brought it in from the kitchen? When he comes to serve Hannah he spoons up for her this specimen, or the pieces of it, in the same way as someone might select a special piece of chicken for someone out of a casserole. The gravy was thick, it wasn't like thin soup.'

Wexford looked dubious. 'Well, we won't dismiss it as a theory. If he had contaminated the rest of the stew and others had been ill, that would have made it look even more like an accident, which was presumably what he wanted. But there's one drawback to that, Mike. If he meant Hannah to die, and was unscrupulous enough not to mind about Corinne and Hood being made ill, why did he rinse the plates? To *prove* that it was an accident, he would have wanted above all to keep some of that stew for analysis when the time came, for analysis would have shown the presence of poisonous as well as non-poisonous fungi, and it would have seemed that he had merely been careless.

'But let's go and talk to these people, shall we?'

*

147

The shop called Harvest Home was closed. Wexford and Burden went down an alley at the side of the block, passed the glass-doored main entrance, and went to the back to a door that was labelled *Stairs and Emergency Exit*. They entered a small tiled vestibule and began to mount a steepish flight of stairs.

On each floor was a front door and a door to the lift. There was no one about. If there had been and they had had no wish to be seen, it would only have been necessary to wait behind the bend in the stairs until whoever it was had got into the lift. The bell by the front door on the fifth floor was marked *A. and H. Kingman*. Wexford rang it.

The man who admitted them was smallish and mild-looking and he looked sad. He showed Wexford the balcony from which his wife had fallen. It was one of two in the flat, the other being larger and extending outside the living-room windows. This one was outside a glazed kitchen door, a place for hanging washing or for gardening of the window-box variety. Herbs grew in pots, and in a long trough there still remained frost-bitten tomato vines. The wall surrounding the balcony was about three feet high, the drop sheer to the hard-top below.

'Were you surprised that your wife committed suicide, Mr Kingman?' said Wexford.

Kingman didn't answer directly. 'My wife set a very low valuation on herself. When we got married I thought she was like me, a simple sort of person who doesn't ask much from life but has quite a capacity for contentment. It wasn't like that. She expected more support and more comfort and encouragement than I could give. That was especially so for the first three months of our marriage. Then she seemed to turn against me. She was very moody, always up and down. My business isn't doing very well and she was spending more money than we could afford. I don't know where all the money was going and we quarrelled about it. Then she'd become depressed and say she was no use to me, she'd be better dead.'

He had given, Wexford thought, rather a long explanation for which he hadn't been asked. But it could be that these thoughts, defensive yet self-reproachful, were at the moment uppermost in his mind. 'Mr Kingman,' he said, 'we have reason to believe, as you know, that foul play may have been involved here. I should like to ask you a few questions about a meal you cooked on October 29th, after which your wife was ill.'

'I can guess who's been telling you about that.'

Wexford took no notice. 'When did Miss Last bring you these — er, shaggy caps?'

'On the evening of the 28th. I made the stew from them in the morning, according to Miss Last's own recipe.'

'Was there any other type of fungus in the flat at the time?'

'Mushrooms, probably.'

'Did you at any time add any noxious object or substance to that stew, Mr Kingman?'

Kingman said quietly, wearily. 'Of course not. My brother-in-law has a lot of ignorant prejudices. He refuses to understand that that stew, which I have made dozens of times before in exactly the same way, was as wholesome as, say, a chicken casserole. More wholesome, in my view.'

'Very well. Nevertheless, your wife was very ill. Why didn't you call a doctor?'

'Because my wife was not "very" ill. She had pains and diarrhoea, that's all. Perhaps you aren't aware of what the symptoms of fungus poisoning are. The victim doesn't just have pain and sickness. His vision is impaired, he very likely blacks out or has convulsions of the kind associated with tetanus. There was nothing like that with Hannah.'

'It was unfortunate that you rinsed those plates. Had you not done so and called a doctor, the remains of that stew would almost certainly have been sent for analysis, and if it was harmless as you say, all this investigation could have been avoided.'

'It was harmless,' Kingman said stonily.

Out in the car Wexford said, 'I'm inclined to believe him, Mike. And unless Hood or Corinne Last has something really positive to tell us, I'd let it rest. Shall we go and see her next?'

The cottage Corinne had shared with Axel Kingman was on a lonely stretch of road outside the village of Myfleet. It was a stone cottage with a slate roof, surrounded by a well-tended pretty garden. A green Ford Escort stood on the drive in front of a weatherboard garage. Under a big old apple tree, from which the yellow leaves were falling, the shaggy caps, immediately recognisable, grew in three thick clumps.

She was a tall woman, the owner of this house, with a beautiful, square-jawed, high-cheekboned face and a mass of dark hair. Wexford was at once reminded of the Klimt painting of a languorous red-lipped woman, gold-neckleted, half covered in gold draperies, though Corinne Last wore a sweater and a denim smock. Her voice was low and measured. He had the impression she could never be flustered or caught off her guard.

'You're the author of a cookery book, I believe?' he said.

She made no answer but handed him a paperback which she took down from a bookshelf. *Cooking for Nothing, Dishes from Hedgerow and Pasture* by Corinne Last. He looked through the index and found the recipe he wanted. Opposite it was a coloured photograph of six people eating what looked like brown soup. The recipe included carrots, onions, herbs, cream, and a number of other harmless ingredients. The last lines read: *Stewed shaggy caps are best served piping hot with wholewheat bread. For drinkables, see page 171.* He glanced at page 171, then handed the book to Burden.

'This was the dish Mr Kingman made that night?'

'Yes.' She had a way of leaning back when she spoke and of half lowering her heavy glossy eyelids. It was serpentine and a little repellent. 'I picked the shaggy caps myself out of this garden. I don't understand how they could have made Hannah ill, but they must have done because she was fine when we first arrived. She hadn't got any sort of gastric infection, that's nonsense.'

Burden put the book aside. 'But you were all served stew out of the same tureen.'

'I didn't see Axel actually serve Hannah. I was out of the room.' The eyelids flickered and almost closed.

'Was it usual for Mr Kingman to rinse plates as soon as they were removed?'

'Don't ask me.' She moved her shoulders. 'I don't know. I do know that Hannah was very ill just after eating that stew. Axel doesn't like doctors, of course, and perhaps it would have – well, embarrassed him to call Dr Castle in the circumstances. Hannah had black spots in front of her eyes, she was getting double vision. I was extremely concerned for her.'

'But you didn't take it on yourself to get a doctor, Miss Last? Or even support Mr Hood in his allegations?'

'Whatever John Hood said, I knew it couldn't be the shaggy caps.' There was a note of scorn when she spoke Hood's name. 'And I was rather frightened. I couldn't help thinking it would be terrible if Axel got into some sort of trouble, if there was an inquiry or something.'

'There's an inquiry now, Miss Last.'

'Well, it's different now, isn't it? Hannah's dead. I mean, it's not just suspicion or conjecture any more.'

She saw them out and closed the front door before they had reached the garden gate. Farther along the roadside and under the hedges more shaggy caps could be seen as well as other kinds of fungi Wexford couldn't identify – little mushroom-like things with pinkish gills, a cluster of small yellow umbrellas, and on the trunk of an oak tree, bulbous smoke-coloured swellings that Burden said were oyster mushrooms.

'That woman,' said Wexford, 'is a mistress of the artless insinuation. She damned Kingman with almost every word, but she never came out with anything like an accusation.' He shook his head. 'I suppose Kingman's brother-in-law will be at work?'

'Presumably,' said Burden, but John Hood was not at work. He was waiting for them at the police station, fuming at the delay, and threatening 'if something wasn't done at once' to take his grievances to the Chief Constable, even to the Home Office.

'Something is being done,' said Wexford quietly. 'I'm glad you've come here, Mr Hood. But try to keep calm, will you, please?'

It was apparent to Wexford from the first that John Hood was in a different category of intelligence from that of Kingman and Corinne Last. He was a thick-set man of perhaps no more than twenty-seven or twenty-eight, with bewildered, resentful blue eyes in a puffy flushed face. A man, Wexford thought, who would fling out rash accusations he couldn't substantiate, who would be driven to bombast and bluster in the company of the ex-teacher and that clever subtle woman.

He began to talk now, not wildly, but still without restraint, repeating what he had said to Burden, reiterating, without putting forward any real evidence, that his brother-in-law had meant to kill his sister that night. It was only by luck that she had survived. Kingman was a ruthless man who would have stopped at nothing to be rid of her. He, Hood, would never forgive himself that he hadn't made a stand and called the doctor.

'Yes, yes, Mr Hood, but what exactly were your sister's symptoms?'

'Vomiting and stomach pains, violent pains,' said Hood.

'She complained of nothing else?'

'Wasn't that enough? That's what you get when someone feeds you poisonous rubbish.'

Wexford merely raised his eyebrows. Abruptly, he left the events of that evening and said, 'What had gone wrong with your sister's marriage?'

Before Hood replied, Wexford could sense he was keeping something back. A wariness came into his eyes and then was gone. 'Axel wasn't the right person for her,' he began. 'She had problems, she needed understanding, she wasn't . . .' His voice trailed away.

'Wasn't what, Mr Hood? What problems?'

'It's got nothing to do with all this,' Hood muttered.

'I'll be the judge of that. You made this accusation, you started this business off. It's not for you now to keep anything back.' On a sudden inspiration, Wexford said, 'Had these problems anything to do with the money she was spending?'

Hood was silent and sullen. Wexford thought rapidly over the things he had been told – Axel Kingman's fanaticism on one particular subject, Hannah's desperate need of an unspecified kind of support during the early days of her marriage. Later on, her alternating moods, and then the money, the weekly sums of money spent and unaccounted for.

He looked up and said baldly, 'Was your sister an alcoholic, Mr Hood?'

Hood hadn't liked this directness. He flushed and looked affronted. He skirted round a frank answer. Well, yes, she drank. She was at pains to conceal her drinking. It had been going on more or less consistently since her first marriage broke up.

'In fact, she was an alcoholic,' said Wexford.

'I suppose so.'

'Your brother-in-law didn't know?'

'Good God, no. Axel would have killed her!' He realized what he had said. 'Maybe that's why. Maybe he found out.'

'I don't think so, Mr Hood. Now I imagine that in the first few months of her marriage she made an effort to give up drinking. She needed a good deal of support during this time but she couldn't, or wouldn't, tell Mr Kingman why she needed it. Her efforts failed, and slowly, because she couldn't manage without it, she began drinking again.'

'She wasn't as bad as she used to be,' Hood said with pathetic eagerness. 'And only in the evenings. She told me she never had a drink before six, and after that she'd have a few more, gulping them down on the quiet so Axel wouldn't know.'

Burden said suddenly, 'Had your sister been drinking that evening?'

'I expect so. She wouldn't have been able to face company, not even just Corinne and me, without a drink.'

'Did anyone besides yourself know that your sister drank?'

'My mother did. My mother and I had a sort of pact to keep it dark from everyone so that Axel wouldn't find out.' He hesitated and then said rather defiantly, 'I did tell Corinne. She's a wonderful person, she's very clever. I was worried about it and I didn't know what to do. She promised she wouldn't tell Axel.'

'I see.' Wexford had his own reasons for thinking she hadn't done so. Deep in thought, he got up and walked to the other end of the room where he stood gazing out of the window. Burden's continuing questions, Hood's answers, reached him only as a confused murmur of voices. Then he heard Burden say more loudly, 'That's all for now, Mr Hood, unless the chief inspector has anything more to ask you.'

'No, no,' said Wexford abstractedly, and when Hood had somewhat truculently departed, 'Time for lunch. It's past two. Personally, I shall avoid any dish containing fungi, even *psalliota campestris*.'

After Burden had looked that one up and identified it as the common mushroom, they lunched and then made a round of such wineshops in Kingsmarkham as were open at that hour. At the Wine Basket they drew a blank, but the assistant in the Vineyard told them that a woman answering Hannah Kingman's description had been a regular customer, and that on the previous Wednesday, the day before her death, she had called in and bought a bottle of Courvoisier Cognac.

'There was no liquor of any kind in Kingman's flat,' said Burden. 'Might have been an empty bottle in the rubbish, I suppose.' He made a rueful face. 'We didn't look, didn't think we had any reason to. But she couldn't have drunk a whole bottleful on the Wednesday, could she?'

'Why are you so interested in this drinking business, Mike? You don't seriously see it as a motive for murder, do you? That Kingman killed her because he'd found out, or been told, that she was a secret drinker?'

'It was a means, not a motive,' said Burden. 'I know how it was done. I know how Kingman tried to kill her that first time.' He grinned. 'Makes a change for me to find the answer before you, doesn't it? I'm going to follow in your footsteps and make a mystery of it for the time being, if you don't mind. With your permission we'll go back to the station, pick up those shaggy caps and conduct a little experiment.'

*

Michael Burden lived in a neat bungalow in Tabard Road. He had lived there with his wife until her untimely death and continued to live there with his sixteen-year-old daughter, his son being away at university. But that evening Pat Burden was out with her boy friend, and there was a note left for her father on the refrigerator. *Dad, I ate the cold beef from yesterday. Can you open a tin for yourself? Back by 10.30. Love, P.*

Burden read this note several times, his expression of consternation deepening with each perusal. And Wexford could precisely have defined the separate causes which brought that look of weariness into Burden's eyes, that frown, that drooping of the mouth. Because she was motherless his daughter had to eat not only cold but leftover food, she who should be carefree was obliged to worry about her father, loneliness drove her out of her home until the appallingly late hour of half-past ten. It was all nonsense, of course, the Burden children were happy and recovered from their loss, but how to make Burden see it that way? Widowhood was something he dragged about with him like a physical infirmity. He looked up from the note, screwed it up and eyed his surroundings vaguely and with a kind of despair. Wexford knew that look of desolation. He saw it on Burden's face each time he accompanied him home.

It evoked exasperation as well as pity. He wanted to tell Burden — once or twice he had done so — to stop treating John and Pat like re-tarded paranoiacs, but instead he said lightly, 'I read somewhere the other day that it wouldn't do us a scrap of harm if we never ate another hot meal as long as we lived. In fact, the colder and rawer the better.'

'You sound like the Axel Kingman brigade,' said Burden, rallying and laughing which was what Wexford had meant him to do. 'Anyway, I'm glad she didn't cook anything. I shouldn't have been able to eat it and I'd hate her to take it as criticism.'

Wexford decided to ignore that one. 'While you're deciding just how much I'm to be told about this experiment of yours, d'you mind if I phone my wife?'

'Be my guest.'

It was nearly six. Wexford came back to find Burden peeling carrots and onions. The four specimens of *coprinus comatus*, beginning to look a little wizened, lay on a chopping board. On the stove a saucepanful of bone stock was heating up.

'What the hell are you doing?'

'Making shaggy cap stew. My theory is that the stew is harmless when eaten by non-drinkers, and toxic, or toxic to some extent, when taken by those with alcohol in the stomach. How about that? In a minute, when this lot's cooking, I'm going to take a moderate quantity of alcohol, then I'm going to eat the stew. Now say I'm a damned fool if you like.'

Wexford shrugged. He grinned. 'I'm overcome by so much courage and selfless devotion to the duty you owe the taxpayers. But wait a minute. Are you sure only Hannah had been drinking that night? We know Kingman hadn't. What about the other two?'

'I asked Hood that when you were off in your daydream. He called for Corinne Last at six, at her request. They picked some apples for his mother, then she made him coffee. He did suggest they call in at a pub for a drink on their way to the Kingmans', but apparently she took so long getting ready that they didn't have time.'

'OK. Go ahead then. But wouldn't it be easier to call in an expert? There must be such people. Very likely someone holds a chair of fungology or whatever it's called at the University of the South.'

'Very likely. We can do that after I've tried it. I want to know for sure *now*. Are you willing too?'

'Certainly not. I'm not your guest to that extent. Since I've told my wife I won't be home for dinner, I'll take it as a kindness if you'll make me some innocent scrambled eggs.'

He followed Burden into the living room where the inspector opened a door in the sideboard. 'What'll you drink?'

'White wine, if you've got any, or vermouth if you haven't. You know how abstemious I have to be.'

Burden poured vermouth and soda. 'Ice?'

'No, thanks. What are you going to have? Brandy? That was Hannah Kingman's favourite tipple apparently.'

'Haven't got any,' said Burden. 'It'll have to be whisky. I think we can reckon she had two double brandies before that meal, don't you? I'm not so brave I want to be as ill as she was.' He caught Wexford's eye. 'You don't think some people could be more sensitive to it than others, do you?'

'Bound to be,' said Wexford breezily. 'Cheers!'

Burden sipped his heavily watered whisky, then tossed it down. 'I'll just have a look at my stew. You sit down. Put the television on.'

Wexford obeyed him. The big coloured picture was of a wood in autumn, pale blue sky, golden beech leaves. Then the camera closed in on a cluster of red-and-white-spotted fly agaric. Chuckling, Wexford turned it off as Burden put his head round the door.

'I think it's more or less ready.'

155

'Better have another whisky.'

'I suppose I had.' Burden came in and re-filled his glass. 'That ought to do it.'

'What about my eggs?'

'Oh, God, I forgot. I'm not much of a cook, you know. Don't know how women manage to get a whole lot of different things brewing and make them synchronize.'

'It is a mystery, isn't it? I'll get myself some bread and cheese, if I may.'

The brownish mixture was in a soup bowl. In the gravy floated four shaggy caps, cut lengthwise. Burden finished his whisky at a gulp.

'What was it the Christians in the arena used to say to the Roman Emperor before they went to the lions?'

'*Morituri, te salutamus*,' said Wexford. '"We who are about to die salute thee."'

'Well . . .' Burden made an effort with the Latin he had culled from his son's homework. '*Moriturus, te saluto*. Would that be right?'

'I daresay. You won't die, though.'

Burden made no answer. He picked up his spoon and began to eat. 'Can I have some more soda?' said Wexford.

There are perhaps few stabs harder to bear than derision directed at one's heroism. Burden gave him a sour look. 'Help yourself. I'm busy.'

Wexford did so. 'What's it like?' he said.

'All right. It's quite nice, like mushrooms.'

Doggedly he ate. He didn't once gag on it. He finished the lot and wiped the bowl round with a piece of bread. Then he sat up, holding himself rather tensely.

'May as well have your telly on now,' said Wexford. 'Pass the time.' He switched it on again. No fly agaric this time, but a dog fox moving across a meadow with Vivaldi playing. 'How d'you feel?'

'Fine,' said Burden gloomily.

'Cheer up. It may not last.'

But it did. After fifteen minutes had passed, Burden still felt perfectly well. He looked bewildered. 'I was so damned positive. I *knew* I was going to be retching and vomiting by now. I didn't put the car away because I was certain you'd have to run me down to the hospital.'

Wexford only raised his eyebrows.

'You were pretty casual about it, I must say. Didn't say a word to stop me, did you? Didn't it occur to you it might have been a bit awkward for you if anything had happened to me?'

'I knew it wouldn't. I said to get a fungologist.' And then Wexford, faced by Burden's aggrieved stare, burst out laughing. 'Dear old Mike, you'll have to forgive me. But you know me, d'you honestly think I'd have let you risk your life eating that stuff? I knew you were safe.'

'May one ask how?'

'One may. And you'd have known too if you'd bothered to take a proper look at that book of Corinne Last's. Under the recipe for shaggy cap stew it said, *"For drinkables, see page 171."* Well, I looked at page 171, and there Miss Last gave a recipe for cowslip wine and another for sloe gin, both highly intoxicating drinks. Would she have recommended a wine and a spirit to drink with those fungi if there'd been the slightest risk? Not if she wanted to sell her book she wouldn't. Not unless she was risking hundreds of furious letters and expensive lawsuits.'

Burden had flushed a little. Then he too began to laugh.

After a little while they had coffee.

'A little logical thinking would be in order, I fancy,' said Wexford. 'You said this morning that we were not so much seeking to prove murder as attempted murder. Axel Kingman could have pushed her off that balcony, but no one saw her fall and no one heard him or anybody else go up to that flat during the afternoon. If, however, an attempt to murder her was made two weeks before, the presumption that she was eventually murdered is enormously strengthened.'

Burden said impatiently, 'We've been through all that. We know that.'

'Wait a minute. The attempt failed. Now just how seriously ill was she? According to Kingman and Hood, she had severe stomach pains and she vomited. By midnight she was peacefully sleeping and by the following day she was all right.'

'I don't see where all this is getting us.'

'To a point which is very important and which may be the crux of the whole case. You say that Axel Kingman attempted to murder her. In order to do so he must have made very elaborate plans – the arranging of the meal, the inviting of the two witnesses, the ensuring that his wife tasted the stew earlier in the same day, and the preparation for some very nifty sleight of hand at the time the meal was served. Isn't it odd that the actual method used should so signally have failed? That Hannah's *life* never seems to have been in danger? And what if the method had succeeded? At post-mortem some noxious agent would have been found in her body or the effects of such. How could he have hoped to get away with that since, as we know, neither of his witnesses actually watched him serve Hannah and one of them was even out of the room?

'So what I am postulating is that no one attempted to murder her, but someone *attempted* to make her ill so that, taken in conjunction with the sinister reputation of non-mushroom fungi and Hood's admitted suspicion of them, taken in conjunction with the known unhappiness of the marriage, *it would look as if there had been a murder attempt.*'

Burden stared at him. 'Kingman would never have done that. He would either have wanted his attempt to succeed or not to have looked like an attempt at all.'

'Exactly. And where does that get us?'

Instead of answering him, Burden said on a note of triumph, his humiliation still rankling, 'You're wrong about one thing. She *was* seriously ill, she didn't just have nausea and vomiting. Kingman and Hood may not have mentioned it, but Corinne Last said she had double vision and black spots before her eyes and . . .' His voice faltered. 'My God, you mean . . . ?'

Wexford nodded. 'Corinne Last only of the three says she had those symptoms. Only Corinne Last is in a position to say, because she lived with him, if Kingman was in the habit of rinsing plates as soon as he removed them from the table. What does she say? That she doesn't know. Isn't that rather odd? Isn't it rather odd too that she chose that precise moment to leave the table and go out into the hall for her handbag?

'She knew that Hannah drank because Hood had told her so. On the evening that meal was eaten you say Hood called for her at her own request. Why? She has her own car, and I don't for a moment believe that a woman like her would feel anything much but contempt for Hood.'

'She told him there was something wrong with the car.'

'She asked him to come at six, although they were not due at the Kingmans' till eight. She gave him *coffee.* A funny thing to drink at that hour, wasn't it, and before a meal? So what happens when he suggests calling in at a pub on the way? She doesn't say no or say it isn't a good idea to drink and drive. She takes so long getting ready that they don't have time.

'She didn't want Hood to drink any alcohol, Mike, and she was determined to prevent it. She, of course, would take no alcohol and she knew Kingman never drank. But she also knew Hannah's habit of having her first drink of the day at about six.

'Now look at her motive, far stronger than Kingman's. She strikes me as a violent, passionate and determined woman. Hannah had taken Kingman away from her. Kingman had rejected her. Why not revenge herself on both of them by killing Hannah and seeing to it that Kingman was convicted of the crime? If she simply killed Hannah, she had no way of ensuring that Kingman would come under suspicion. But if she made it look as if he had previously attempted her life, the case against him would become very strong indeed.

'Where was she last Thursday afternoon? She could just as easily have gone up those stairs as Kingman could. Hannah would have admitted her to the flat. If she, known to be interested in gardening, had suggested that Hannah take her on to that balcony and show her the pot herbs, Hannah would willingly have done so. And then we have the mystery of the missing brandy bottle with some of its contents surely remaining. If Kingman had killed her, he would have left that there as it would greatly have strengthened the case for suicide. Imagine how he might have used it. "Heavy drinking made my wife ill that night. She knew I had lost respect for her because of her drinking. She killed herself because her mind was unbalanced by drink."

'Corinne Last took that bottle away because she didn't want it known that Hannah drank, and she was banking on Hood's keeping it dark from us just as he had kept it from so many people in the past. And she didn't want it known because the fake murder attempt that *she* staged depended on her victim having alcohol present in her body.'

Burden sighed, poured the last dregs of coffee into Wexford's cup. 'But we tried that out,' he said. 'Or I tried it out, and it doesn't work. You knew it wouldn't work from her book. True, she brought the shaggy caps from her own garden, but she couldn't have mixed up poisonous fungi with them because Axel Kingman would have realized at once. Or if he hadn't, they'd all have been ill, alcohol or no alcohol. She was never alone with Hannah before the meal, and while the stew was served she was out of the room.'

'I know. But we'll see her in the morning and ask her a few more questions.' Wexford hesitated, then quoted softly, '"Out of good still to find means of evil."'

'What?'

'That's what she did, isn't it? It was good for everyone but Hannah, you look as if it's done you a power of good, but it was evil for Hannah. I'm off now, Mike, it's been a long day. Don't forget to put your car away. You won't be making any emergency trips to hospital tonight.'

They were unable to puncture her self-possession. The languorous Klimt face was carefully painted this morning, and she was dressed as befitted the violinist or the actress or the author. She had been forewarned of their coming and the gardener image had been laid aside. Her long smooth hands looked as if they had never touched the earth or pulled up a weed.

Where had she been on the afternoon of Hannah Kingman's death? Her thick shapely eyebrows went up. At home, indoors, painting. Alone?

'Painters don't work with an audience,' she said rather insolently, and she leaned back, dropping her eyelids in that way of hers. She lit a cigarette and flicked her fingers at Burden for an ashtray as if he were a waiter.

Wexford said, 'On Saturday, October 29th, Miss Last, I believe you had something wrong with your car?'

She nodded lazily.

In asking what was wrong with it, he thought he might catch her. He didn't.

'The glass in the offside front headlight was broken while the car was parked,' she said, and although he thought how easily she could have broken that glass herself, he could hardly say so. In the same smooth voice she added, 'Would you like to see the bill I had from the garage for repairing it?'

'That won't be necessary.' She wouldn't have offered to show it to him if she hadn't possessed it. 'You asked Mr Hood to call for you here at six, I understand.'

'Yes. He's not my idea of the best company in the world, but I'd promised him some apples for his mother and we had to pick them before it got dark.'

'You gave him coffee but had no alcohol. You had no drinks on the way to Mr and Mrs Kingman's flat. Weren't you a little disconcerted at the idea of going out to dinner at a place where there wouldn't even be a glass of wine?'

'I was used to Mr Kingman's ways.' But not so used, thought Wexford, that you can tell me whether it was normal or abnormal for him to have rinsed those plates. Her mouth curled, betraying her a little. 'It didn't bother me, I'm not a slave to liquor.'

'I should like to return to these shaggy caps. You picked them from here on October 28th and took them to Mr Kingman that evening. I think you said that?'

'I did. I picked them from this garden.'

She enunciated the words precisely, her eyes wide open and gazing sincerely at him. The words, or perhaps her unusual straightforwardness, stirred in him the glimmer of an idea. But if she had said nothing more, that idea might have died as quickly as it had been born.

'If you want to have them analysed or examined or whatever, you're getting a bit late. Their season's practically over.' She looked at Burden and gave him a gracious smile. 'But you took the last of them yesterday, didn't you? So that's all right.'

Wexford, of course, said nothing about Burden's experiment. 'We'll have a look in your garden, if you don't mind.'

She didn't seem to mind, but she had been wrong. Most of the fungi had grown into black-gilled pagodas in the twenty-four hours that had elapsed. Two new ones, however, had thrust their white oval caps up through the wet grass. Wexford picked them, and still she didn't seem to mind. Why, then, had she appeared to want their season to be over? He thanked her and she went back into the cottage. The door closed. Wexford and Burden walked out into the road.

The fungus season was far from over. From the abundant array by the roadside it looked as if the season would last weeks longer. Shaggy caps were everywhere, some of them smaller and greyer than the clump that grew out of Corinne Last's well-fed lawn. There were green and purple agarics, horn-shaped toadstools, and tiny mushrooms growing in fairy rings.

'She doesn't exactly mind our having them analysed,' Wexford said thoughtfully, 'but it seems she'd prefer the analysis to be done on the ones you picked yesterday than on those I picked today. Can that be so or am I just imagining it?'

'If you're imagining it, I'm imagining it too. But it's no good, that line of reasoning. We know they're not potentiated – or whatever the word is – by alcohol.'

'I shall pick some more all the same,' said Wexford. 'Haven't got a paper bag, have you?'

'I've got a clean handkerchief. Will that do?'

'Have to,' said Wexford who never had a clean one. He picked a dozen more young shaggy caps, big and small, white and grey, immature and fully grown. They got back into the car and Wexford told the driver to stop at the public library. He went in and emerged a few minutes later with three books under his arm.

'When we get back,' he said to Burden, 'I want you to get on to the university and see what they can offer us in the way of an expert in fungilogy.'

He closeted himself in his office with the three books and a pot of coffee. When it was nearly lunchtime, Burden knocked on the door.

'Come in,' said Wexford. 'How did you get on?'

'It's not fungologist or fungilogist,' said Burden with triumphant severity. 'It's *mycologist* and they don't have one. But there's a man on the faculty who's a toxicologist and who's just published one of those popular science books. This one's about poisoning by wild plants and fungi.'

Wexford grinned. 'What's it called? *Killing for Nothing*? He sounds as if he'd do fine.'

'I said we'd see him at six. Let's hope something will come of it.'

'No doubt it will.' Wexford slammed shut the thickest of his books. 'We need confirmation,' he said, 'but I've found the answer.'

'For God's sake! Why didn't you say?'

'You didn't ask. Sit down.' Wexford motioned him to the chair on the other side of the desk. 'I said you'd done your homework, Mike, and so you had, only your textbook wasn't quite comprehensive enough. It's got a section on edible fungi and a section on poisonous fungi – *but nothing in between*. What I mean by that is, there's nothing in your book about fungi which aren't wholesome yet don't cause death or intense suffering. There's nothing about the kind that can make people ill in certain circumstances.'

'But we know they ate shaggy caps,' Burden protested. 'And if by "circumstances" you mean the intake of alcohol, we know shaggy caps aren't affected by alcohol.'

'Mike,' said Wexford quietly, '*do* we know they ate shaggy caps?' He spread out on the desk the haul he had made from the roadside and from Corinne Last's garden. 'Look closely at these, will you?'

Quite bewildered now, Burden looked at and fingered the dozen or so specimens of fungi. 'What am I to look *for*?'

'Differences,' said Wexford laconically.

'Some of them are smaller than the others, and the smaller ones are greyish. Is that what you mean? But, look here, think of the differences between mushrooms. You get big flat ones and small button ones and . . .'

'Nevertheless, in this case it is that small difference that makes all the difference.' Wexford sorted the fungi into two groups. 'All the small greyer ones,' he said, 'came from the roadside. Some of the larger whiter ones came from Corinne Last's garden and some from the roadside.'

He picked up between forefinger and thumb a specimen of the former. 'This isn't a shaggy cap, it's an ink cap. Now listen.' The thick book fell open where he had placed a marker. Slowly and clearly he read: '*The ink cap*, coprinus atramentarius, *is not to be confused with the shaggy cap*, coprinus comatus. *It is smaller and greyer in colour, but otherwise the resemblance between them is strong. While* coprinus atramentarius *is usually harmless when cooked, it contains, however, a chemical similar to the active principle in* Antabuse, *a drug used in the treatment of alcoholics, and if eaten in conjunction with alcohol will cause nausea and vomiting.'*

'We'll never prove it.'

'I don't know about that,' said Wexford. 'We can begin by concentrating on the one lie we know Corinne Last told when she said she picked the fungi she gave Axel Kingman *from her own garden.*'

163

Old Wives' Tales

They looked shocked and affronted and somehow ashamed. Above all, they looked old. Wexford thought that in the nature of things a woman of seventy ought to be an orphan, ought to have been an orphan for twenty years. This one had been an orphan for scarcely twenty days. Her husband, sitting opposite her, pulling his wispy moustache, slowly and mechanically shaking his head, seemed older than she, perhaps not so many years the junior of his late mother-in-law. He wore a brown cardigan with a small neat darn at one elbow and sheepskin slippers, and when he spoke he snuffled. His wife kept saying she couldn't believe her ears, she couldn't believe it, why were people so wicked? Wexford didn't answer that. He couldn't, though he had often wondered himself.

'My mother died of a stroke,' Mrs Betts said tremulously. 'It was on the death certificate, Dr Moss put it on the death certificate.'

Betts snuffled and wheezed. He reminded Wexford of an aged rabbit, a rabbit with myxomatosis perhaps. It was partly the effect of the brown woolly cardigan and the furry slippers, and partly the moustache and the unshaven bristly chin. 'She was ninety-two,' Betts said in his thick catarrhal voice. '*Ninety-two.* I reckon you lot must have got bats in the belfry.'

'I mean,' said Mrs Betts, 'are you saying Dr Moss was telling untruths? A doctor?'

'Why don't you ask him? We're only ordinary people, the wife and me, we're not educated. Doctor said a cerebral haemorrhage,' Betts stumbled a little over the words, 'and in plain language that's a stroke. That's what he said. Are you saying me or the wife gave Mother a stroke? Are you saying that?'

'I'm making no allegations, Mr Betts.' Wexford felt uncomfortable, wished himself anywhere but in this newly decorated, paint-smartened house. 'I am merely making enquiries which information received obliges me to do.'

'Gossip,' said Mrs Betts bitterly. 'This street's a hotbed of gossip. Pity they've nothing better to do. Oh, I know what they're saying. Half of them turn up their noses and look the other way when I pass them. All except Elsie Parrish, and that goes without saying.'

'She's been a brick,' said her husband. 'A real brick is Elsie.' He stared at Wexford with a kind of timid outrage. 'Haven't you folk got nothing better to do than listen to a bunch of old hens? What about the real crime? What about the muggings and the break-ins?'

Wexford sighed. But he went on doggedly questioning, remembering what the nurse had said, what Dr Moss had said, keeping in the forefront of his mind that motive which was so much more than merely wanting an aged parent out of the way. If he hadn't been a policeman with a profound respect for the law and for human life, he might have felt that these two, or one of them, had been provoked beyond bearing to do murder.

One of them? Or both? Or neither? Ivy Wrangton had either died an unnatural death or else there had been a series of coincidences and unexplained contingencies which were nothing short of incredible.

It was the nurse who had started it, coming to him three days before. Sergeant Martin brought her to him because what she alleged was so serious. Wexford knew her by sight, had seen her making her calls, and had sometimes wondered how district nurses could endure their jobs, the unremitting daily toil, the poor pay, the unsavoury tasks. Perhaps she felt the same about his. She was a fair, pretty woman, about thirty-five, overweight, with big red hands, who always looked tired. She looked tired now, though she hadn't long been back from two weeks' holiday. She was in her summer uniform, blue and white print dress, white apron, dark cardigan, small round hat and the stout shoes that served for summer and winter alike. Nurse Radcliffe. Judith Radcliffe.

'Mr Wexford?' she said. 'Chief Inspector Wexford? Yes. I believe I used to look in on your daughter after she'd had a baby. I was doing my midwifery then. I can't remember her name but the baby was Benjamin.'

Wexford smiled and told her his daughter's name and wondered, looking at the bland faded blue eyes and the stolid set of the neck and shoulders, just how intelligent this woman was, how perceptive and how truthful. He pulled up one of the little yellow chairs for her.

His office was cheerful and sunny-looking even when the sun wasn't shining, not much like a police station.

'Please sit down, Nurse Radcliffe,' he said. 'Sergeant Martin's given me some idea what you've come about.'

'I feel rather awful. You may think I'm making a mountain out of a molehill.'

'I shouldn't worry about that. If I do I'll tell you so and we'll forget it. No one else will know of it, it'll be between us and these four walls.'

At that she gave a short laugh. 'Oh, dear, I'm afraid it's gone *much* further than that already. I've three patients in Castle Road and each one of them mentioned it to me. That's what Castle Road gossip is at the moment, poor old Mrs Wrangton's death. And I just thought – well, you can't have that much smoke without fire, can you?'

Mountains and molehills, Wexford thought, smoke and fire. This promised to be a real volcano. He said firmly, 'I think you'd better tell me all about it.'

She was rather pathetic. 'It's best you hear it from someone *professional*.' She planted her feet rather wide apart in front of her and leant forward, her hands on her knees. 'Mrs Wrangton was a very old woman. She was ninety-two. But allowing for her age, she was as fit as a fiddle, thin, strong, continent, her heart as sound as a bell. The day she died was the day I went away on holiday, but I was in there the day before to give her her bath – I did that once a week, she couldn't get in and out of the bath on her own – and I remember thinking she was fitter than I'd seen her for months. You could have knocked me down with a feather when I came back from holiday and heard she'd had a stroke the next day.'

'When did you come back, Nurse Radcliffe?'

'Last Friday, Friday the 16th. Well, it's Thursday now and I was back on my district on Monday and the first thing I heard was that Mrs Wrangton was dead and suggestions she'd been – well, helped on her way.' She paused, worked something out on her fingers. 'I went away June 2nd, that was the day she died, and the funeral was June 7th.'

'Funeral?'

'Well, cremation,' said Nurse Radcliffe, glancing up as Wexford sighed. 'Dr Moss attended Mrs Wrangton. She was really Dr Crocker's patient, but he was on holiday too like me. Look, Mr Wexford, I don't know the details of what happened that day, June

2nd, not first-hand, only what the Castle Road ladies say. D'you want to hear that?'

'You haven't yet told me what she died of.'

'A stroke – according to Dr Moss.'

'I'm not at all sure,' said Wexford dryly, 'how one sets about giving someone a stroke. Would you give them a bad fright or push an empty hypodermic into them or get them into a rage or what?'

'I really don't know.' Nurse Radcliffe looked a little put out and as if she would like to say, had she dared, that to find this out was Wexford's job, not hers. She veered away from the actual death. 'Mrs Wrangton and her daughter – that's Mrs Betts, Mrs Doreen Betts – they hated each other, they were cat and dog. And I don't think Mr Betts had spoken to Mrs Wrangton for a year or more. Considering the house was Mrs Wrangton's and every stick of furniture in it belonged to her, I used to think they were very ungrateful. I never liked the way Mrs Betts spoke about her mother, let alone the way she spoke *to* her, but I couldn't say a word. Mr Betts is retired now but he only had a very ordinary sort of job in the Post Office and they lived rent-free in Mrs Wrangton's home. It's a nice house, you know, late Victorian, and they built to last in those days. I used to think it badly needed doing up and it was a pity Mr Betts couldn't get down to a bit of painting, when Mrs Wrangton said to me she was having decorators in, having the whole house done up inside and out . . .'

Wexford cut short the flow of what seemed like irrelevancies. 'Why were the Bettses and Mrs Wrangton on such bad terms?'

The look he got implied that seldom had Nurse Radcliffe come across such depths of naivety. 'It's a sad fact, Mr Wexford, that people can outstay their welcome in this world. To put it bluntly, Mr and Mrs Betts couldn't wait for something to happen to Mrs Wrangton.' Her voice lingered over the euphemism. 'They hadn't been married all that long, you know,' she said surprisingly. 'Only five or six years. Mrs Betts was just a spinster before that, living at home with Mother. Mr Betts was a widower that she met at the Over-Sixties Club. Mrs Wrangton used to say she could have done better for herself – seems funny to say that about a woman of her age, doesn't it? – and that Mr Betts was only after the house and her money.'

'You mean she said it to you?'

'Well, not just to me, to anybody,' said Nurse Radcliffe, unconsciously blackening the dead woman to whom she showed such conscious bias. 'She really felt it. I think she bitterly resented having him in the house.'

Wexford moved a little impatiently in his chair. 'If we were to investigate every death just because the victim happened to be on bad terms with his or her relations . . .'

'Oh, no, no, it's not just that, not at all. Mrs Betts sent for Dr Moss on May 23rd, just four days after Dr Crocker went away. Why did she? There wasn't anything wrong with Mrs Wrangton. I was getting her dressed after her bath and I was amazed to see Dr Moss. Mrs Wrangton said, I don't know what you're doing here, I never asked my daughter to send for you. Just because I overslept a bit this morning, she said. She was so proud of her good health, poor dear, never had an illness in her long life but the once and that was more an allergy than an illness. I can tell you why he was sent for, Mr Wexford. So that *when Mrs Wrangton died* he'd be within his rights signing the death certificate. He wasn't her doctor, you see, but it'd be all right if he'd attended her within the past two weeks, that's the law. They're all saying Mrs Betts waited for Dr Crocker to go away, she knew he'd never have just accepted her mother's death like that. He'd have asked for a post-mortem and then the fat would have been in the fire.' Nurse Radcliffe didn't specify how, and Wexford thought better of interrupting her again. 'The last time I saw Mrs Wrangton,' she went on, 'was on June 1st. I had a word with the painter as I was going out. There were two of them but this was a young boy, about twenty. I asked him when they expected to finish, and he said, sooner than they thought, next week, because Mrs Betts had told them just to finish the kitchen and the outside and then to leave it. I thought it was funny at the time, Mrs Wrangton hadn't said a word to me about it. In fact, what she'd said was, wouldn't it be nice when the bathroom walls were all tiled and I wouldn't have to worry about splashing when I bathed her.

'Mr Wexford, it's possible Mrs Betts stopped that work because she knew her mother was going to die the next day. She personally didn't want the whole house re-decorated and she didn't want to have to pay for it out of the money her mother left her.'

'Was there much money?' Wexford asked.

'I'd guess a few thousands in the bank, maybe three or four, and there was the house, wasn't there? I know she'd made a will, I witnessed it. I and Dr Crocker. In the presence,' said Nurse Radcliffe sententiously, 'of the legatee and of each other, which is the law. But naturally I didn't see what its *provisions* were. Mrs Wrangton did tell me the house was to go to Mrs Betts and there was a little something for her friend Elsie Parrish. Beyond that, I couldn't tell you. Mind you, Mrs Parrish won't have it that there could have been foul play. I met her in Castle Road and she said, wasn't it wicked the things people were saying?'

'Who is Elsie Parrish?'

'A very nice old friend of Mrs Wrangton's. Nearly eighty but as spry as a cricket. And that brings me to the worst thing. June 2nd, that Friday afternoon, Mr and Mrs Betts went off to a whist drive. Mrs Parrish knew they were going. Mrs Betts had promised to knock on her door before they went so that she could come round and sit with Mrs Wrangton. She sometimes did that. It wasn't right to leave her alone, not at her age. Well, Mrs Parrish waited in and Mrs Betts never came, so naturally she thought the Bettses had changed their minds and hadn't gone out. But they had. They deliberately didn't call to fetch Mrs Parrish. They left Mrs Wrangton all alone but for that young boy painter, and they'd never done such a thing before, not once.'

Wexford digested all this in silence, not liking it but not really seeing it as a possible murder case. Nurse Radcliffe seemed to have dried up. She slackened back in the chair with a sigh.

'You mentioned an allergy . . . ?'

'Oh, my goodness, that was about fifty years ago! Only some kind of hay fever, I think. There's asthma in the family. Mrs Betts's brother had asthma all his life, and Mrs Betts gets *urticaria* – nettle rash, that is. They're all connected, you know.'

He nodded. He had the impression she had a bombshell yet to explode, or that the volcano was about to erupt. 'If they weren't there,' he said, 'how could either of them possibly have hastened Mrs Wrangton's end?'

'They'd been back two hours before she died. When they came back she was in a coma, and they waited *one hour and twenty minutes* before they phoned Dr Moss.'

'Would you have signed that death certificate, Len?' said Wexford to Dr Crocker. They were in the purpose-built bungalow that housed two consulting rooms and a waiting room. Dr Crocker's evening surgery was over, the last patient packed off with reassurance and a prescription. Crocker gave Wexford rather a defiant look.

'Of course I would. Why not? Mrs Wrangton was ninety-two. It's

169

ridiculous of Radcliffe to say she didn't expect her to die. You expect everyone of ninety-two to die and pretty soon. I hope nobody's casting any aspersions on my extremely able partner.'

'I'm not,' said Wexford. 'There's nothing I'd like more than for this to turn out a lot of hot air. But I do have to ask you, don't I? I do have to ask Jim Moss.'

Dr Crocker looked a little mollified. He and the chief inspector were lifelong friends, they had been at school together, had lived most of their lives in Kingsmarkham where Crocker had his practice and Wexford was head of the CID. But for a medical practitioner, no amount of friendship will excuse hints that he or one of his fellows have been negligent. And he prickled up again when Wexford said:

'How could he *know* it was a stroke without a post-mortem?'

'God give me patience! He saw her before she was dead, didn't he? He got there about half an hour before she died. There are unmistakable signs of stroke, Reg. An experienced medical man couldn't fail to recognize them. The patient is unconscious, the face flushed, the pulse slow, the breathing stertorous with a puffing of the cheeks during expiration. The only possible confusion is with alcoholic poisoning, but in alcoholic poisoning the pupils of the eyes are widely dilated whereas in apoplexy or stroke they're contracted. Does that satisfy you?'

'Well, OK, it was a stroke, but aren't I right in thinking a stroke can be the consequence of something else, of an operation, for instance, or in the case of a young woman, of childbirth, or in an old person even of bedsores?'

'Old Ivy Wrangton didn't have bedsores and she hadn't had a baby for seventy years. She had a stroke because she was ninety-two and her arteries were worn out. "The days of our age",' quoted the doctor solemnly, '"are threescore years and ten, and though men be so strong that they come to fourscore years, yet is their strength then but labour and sorrow." She'd reached fourscore years and twelve and she was worn out.' He had been pacing up and down, getting heated, but now came to sit on the edge of his desk, a favourite perch of his. 'A damn good thing she was cremated,' he said. 'That puts out of court all the ghastliness of exhumation and cutting her up. She was a remarkable old woman, you know, Reg. Tough as old boots. She told me once about having her first baby. She was eighteen, out scrubbing the doorstep when she had a labour pain. Indoors she went, called her mother to fetch the midwife and lay down on her bed. The baby was born after two more pains, and the daughter came even easier.'

'Yes, I heard there'd been another child.' Wexford saw the absurdity of referring to someone who must necessarily be in his seventies as a child. 'Mrs Betts has a brother?' he corrected himself.

'*Had*. He died last winter. He was an old man, Reg, and he'd been bronchial all his life. Seventy-four *is* old till you start comparing it with Mrs Wrangton's age. She was so proud of her good health, boasted about never being ill. I used to drop in every three months or so as a matter of routine, and when I'd ask her how she was she'd say, I'm fine, Doctor, I'm in the pink.'

'But I understand she'd had some illness connected with an allergy?' Wexford was clutching at straws. 'Nurse Radcliffe told me about it. I've been wondering if anything to do with that could have contributed to . . . ?'

'Of course not,' the doctor cut in. 'How could it? That was when she was middle-aged and the so-called illness was an asthmatic attack with some swelling of the eyes and a bit of gastric trouble. I fancy she used to exaggerate it the way healthy people do when they're talking about the one little bit of illness they've ever had . . . Oh, here's Jim. I thought I'd heard his last patient leave.'

Dr Moss, small, dark and trim, came in from the corridor between the consulting rooms. He gave Wexford the very wide smile that showed thirty-two large white teeth which the chief inspector had never been able to precisely define as false, as crowns or simply as his own. The teeth were rather too big for Dr Moss's face which was small and smooth and lightly tanned. His small black eyes didn't smile at all.

'Enter the villainous medico,' he said, 'who is notoriously in cahoots with greedy legatees and paranoid Post Office clerks. What evidence can I show you? The number of my Swiss bank account? Or shall I produce the hammer, a crafty tap from which ensured an immediate subarachnoid haemorrhage?'

It is very difficult to counter this kind of facetiousness. Wexford knew he would only get more fatuous pleasantries, heavy irony, outrageous confessions, if he attempted to rebut any of it or if he were to assure Moss that this wasn't what he had meant at all. He smiled stiffly, tapping his feet against the leg of Crocker's desk, while Dr Moss elaborated on his fantasy of himself as corrupt, a kind of latter-day William Palmer, poison-bottle-happy and ever-ready with his hypodermic to gratify the impatient next-of-kin. At length, unable to bear any more of it, Wexford cut across the seemingly interminable harangue and said to Crocker:

'You witnessed her will, I understand?'

'I and that busybody Radcliffe, that's right. If you want to know what's in it, the house and three thousand pounds go to Doreen Betts, and the residue to another patient of mine, a Mrs Parrish. Residue would have been about fifteen hundred at that time, Mrs Wrangton told me, but considering her money was in a building society and she managed to save out of her pension and her annuity, I imagine it'll be a good deal more by now.'

Wexford nodded. By now Dr Moss had dried up, having run out, presumably, of subject matter and witticisms. His teeth irradiated his face like lamps, and when his mouth was closed he looked rather ill-tempered and sinister. Wexford decided to try the direct and simple approach. He apologized.

'I'd no intention of suggesting you'd been negligent, Dr Moss. But put yourself in my position . . .'

'Impossible!'

'Very well. Let me put it this way. Try to understand that in my position I had no choice but to make enquiries.'

'Mrs Betts might try an action for slander. She can count on my support. The Bettses had neither the opportunity nor the motive to do violence to Mrs Wrangton, but a bunch of tongue-clacking old witches are allowed to take their characters away just the same.'

'Motive,' said Wexford gently, 'I'm afraid they did have, the straightforward one of getting rid of Mrs Wrangton who had become an encumbrance to them, and of inheriting her house.'

'Nonsense.' Momentarily the teeth showed in a white blaze. 'They were going to get rid of her in any case. They would have had the house to themselves in any case. Mrs Wrangton was going into a nursing home.' He paused, enjoying the effect of what he had said. 'For the rest of her days,' he added with a touch of drama.

Crocker shifted off the edge of the desk. 'I never knew that.'

'No? Well, it was you who told her about a new nursing home opening in Stowerton, or so she said. She told me all about it that day Mrs Betts called me when you'd gone away. Sometime at the end of May it was. She was having the house decorated for her daughter and son-in-law prior to her leaving.'

'Did she tell you that too?' asked Wexford.

'No, but it was obvious. I can tell you exactly what happened during that visit if it makes you happy. That interfering harpy,

Radcliffe, had just been bathing her, and when she'd dressed her she left. Thank God. I'd never met Mrs Wrangton before. There was nothing wrong with her, bar extreme old age and her blood pressure up a bit, and I was rather narked that Mrs Betts had called me out. Mrs Wrangton said her daughter got nervous when she slept late in the mornings as she'd done that day and the day before. Wasn't to be wondered at, she said, considering she'd been sitting up in bed watching the World Cup on television till all hours. Only Mrs Betts and her husband didn't know that and I wasn't to tell them. Well, we had a conspiratorial laugh over that, I liked her, she was a game old dear, and then she started talking about the nursing home — what's it called? Springfield? Sunnyside?'

'Summerland,' said Dr Crocker.

'Cost you a lot, that will, I said, and she said she'd got a good bit coming in which would die with her anyway. I assumed she meant an annuity. We talked for about five minutes and I got the impression she'd been tossing around this nursing home idea for months. I asked her what her daughter thought and she said . . .'

'Yes?' prompted Wexford.

'Oh, my God, people like you make one see sinister nuances in the most innocent remarks. It's just that she said, You'd reckon Doreen'd be only too glad to see the back of me, wouldn't you? I mean, it rather implied she wouldn't be glad. I don't know what she was inferring and I didn't ask. But you can rest assured Mrs Betts had no motive for killing her mother. Leaving sentiment apart, it was all the same to her whether her mother was alive or dead. The Bettses would still have got the house and after her death Mrs Wrangton's capital. The next time I saw her she was unconscious, she was dying. She did die, at seven-thirty, on June 2nd.'

Both Wexford's parents had died before he was forty. His wife's mother had been dead twenty years, her father fifteen. None of these people had been beyond their seventies, so therefore Wexford had no personal experience of the geriatric problem. It seemed to him that for a woman like Mrs Wrangton, to end one's days in a nursing home with companionship and good nursing and in pleasant surroundings was not so bad a fate. And an obvious blessing to the daughter and son-in-law whose affection for a parent might be renewed when they only encountered her for an hour or so a week. No, Doreen Betts and her husband had no motive for helping Mrs Wrangton out of this world, for by retiring to Summerland she wouldn't even make inroads into that three or four thousand pounds of capital. Her pension and her annuity would cover the fees. Wexford wondered what those fees would be, and remembered vaguely from a few years back hearing a figure of twenty pounds a week mentioned in a similar connection. Somebody's old aunt, some friend of his wife. You'd have to allow for inflation, of course, but surely it would cost no more than thirty pounds a week now. With the Retirement Pension at eighteen pounds and the annuity worth, say, another twenty, Mrs Wrangton could amply have afforded Summerland.

But she had died first – of natural causes. It no longer mattered that she and Harry Betts hadn't been on speaking terms, that no one had fetched Elsie Parrish, that Dr Moss had been called out to visit a healthy woman, that Mrs Betts had given orders to stop the painting. There was no motive. Eventually the tongues would cease to wag, Mrs Wrangton's will would be proved, and the Bettses settle down to enjoy the rest of their lives in their newly decorated home.

Wexford put it out of his head, apart from wondering whether he should visit Castle Road and drop a word of warning to the gossips. Immediately he saw how impossible this would be. The slander would be denied, and besides he hardly saw his function as extending so far. No, let it die a natural death – as Mrs Wrangton had.

On Monday morning he was having breakfast, his wife reading a letter just come from her sister in Wales.

'Frances says Bill's mother has got to go into a nursing home at last.' Bill was Wexford's brother-in-law. 'It's either that or Fran having her, which really isn't on.'

Wexford, from behind his newspaper, made noises indicative of sympathy with and support for Frances. He was reading a verbatim report of the trial of some bank robbers.

'Ninety pounds a week,' said Dora.

'What did you say?'

'I was talking to myself, dear. You read your paper.'

'Did you say ninety pounds a week?'

'That's right. For the nursing home. I shouldn't think Bill and Fran could stand that for long. It's getting on for five thousand a year.'

'But . . .' Wexford almost stammered, '. . . I thought a couple of years ago you said it was twenty a week for what's-her-name, Rosemary's aunt, wherever they put her?'

'Darling,' said Dora gently, 'first of all, that wasn't a couple of years ago, it was at least *twelve* years ago. And secondly, haven't you heard of the rising cost of living?'

An hour later he was in the matron's office at Summerland, having made no attempt to disguise who he was, but presenting himself as there to enquire about a prospective home for an aged relative of his wife. Aunt Lilian. Such a woman had actually existed, perhaps still did exist in the remote Westmorland village from which the Wexfords had last heard of her in a letter dated 1959.

The matron was an Irishwoman, Mrs Corrigan. She seemed about the same age as Nurse Radcliffe. At her knee stood a boy of perhaps six, at her feet, playing with a toy tractor, was another of three. Outside the window three little girls were trying to coax a black cat from its refuge under a car. You might have thought this was a children's home but for the presence of half a dozen old women sitting on the lawn in a half circle, dozing, muttering to themselves or just staring. The grounds were full of flowers, mauve and white lilac everywhere, roses coming out. From behind a hedge came the sound of a lawn mower, plied perhaps by the philoprogenitive Mr Corrigan.

'Our fees are ninety-*five* pounds a week, Mr Wexford,' said the matron. 'And with the extra for laundry and dry-cleaning, sure and you might say five thousand a year for a good round figure.'

'I see.'

'The ladies only have to share a room with one other lady. We bath them once a week and change their clothes once a week. And if you could please see to it your aunt only has synthetic fabrics, if you know what I mean, for the lot's popped in the washing machine all together. We like the fees a month in advance and paid on a banker's order, if you please.'

'I'm afraid I don't please,' said Wexford. 'Your charges are more than I expected. I shall have to make other arrangements.'

'Then there's no more to be said,' said Mrs Corrigan with a smile nearly equalling the candlepower of Dr Moss's.

'Just out of curiosity, Mrs Corrigan, how do your – er, guests meet your fees? Five thousand a year is more than most incomes would be equal to.'

'Sure and aren't they widows, Mr Wexford, and didn't their husbands leave them their houses? Mostly the ladies sell their houses, and with prices the way they are today that's enough to keep them in Summerland for four years or five.'

*

Mrs Wrangton had intended to sell her house, and she was having it re-decorated inside and out in order to get a better price. She had intended to sell the roof over the Bettses' heads – no wonder she had implied to Dr Moss that Doreen Betts would be sorry to see the back of her. What a woman! What malevolence at ninety-two! And who could have said she wouldn't have been within her moral as well as her legal rights to sell? It was her house. Doreen Wrangton might long ago have found a home of her own, ought perhaps to have done so, and as Doreen Betts might have expected her husband to provide one for her. It is universally admitted to be wrong to anticipate stepping into dead men's shoes. And yet what a monstrous revenge to have on an uncongenial son-in-law, a not always co-operative daughter. There was a subtlety about it that evoked Wexford's admiration nearly as much as its cruelty aroused his disgust. It was a motive all right, and a strong one.

So at last he had found himself in Castle Road, in the Bettses' living room, confronting an elderly orphan and her husband. The room was papered in a silvery oyster colour, the woodwork ivory. He was sure that that door had never previously sported a shade lighter than chocolate brown, just as the hall walls had, until their recent coat of magnolia, been gloomily clothed in dark Lincrusta.

When the two of them had protested bitterly about the gossip and the apparent inability of the police to get their priorities right, Doreen Betts agreed without too much mutiny to answer Wexford's questions. To the first one she reacted passionately.

'Mother would never have done it. I know she wouldn't, it was all bluff with her. Even Mother wouldn't have been that cruel.'

Her husband pulled his moustache, slowly shuffling his slippered feet back and forth. His angry excitement had resulted in a drop of water appearing on the end of his nose. It hung there, trembling.

Doreen Betts said, 'I knew she didn't meant to go ahead with it when I said, Can I tell the builders to leave the upstairs? And she said, I daresay. That's what she said. I daresay, she said, I'm not bothered either way. Of course she wouldn't have gone ahead with it. You don't even get a room to yourself in that place. Ninety-five pounds a week! They'll put you to bed at eight o'clock, Mother, I said, so don't think they'll let you sit up till all hours watching TV.'

'Quite right,' said Harry Betts ambiguously.

'Why, if we'd known Mother meant to do a thing like that, we could have lived in Harry's flat when we got married. He had a nice little flat over the freezer centre in the High Street. It wasn't just one room like Mother went about saying, it was a proper flat, wasn't it, Harry? What'd wc have done if Mother'd done a thing like that? We'd have had nowhere.' Her husband's head-shaking, the trembling droplet, the fidgety feet, seemed suddenly to unnerve her. She said to him, distress in her voice, 'I'm going to have a little talk to the officer on my own, dear.'

Wexford followed her into the room where Mrs Wrangton had slept for the last years of her life. It was on the ground floor at the back, presumably originally designated as a dining room, with a pair of windows looking out on to a long narrow concrete terrace and a very long, very narrow garden. No re-decorations had been carried out here. The walls were papered in a pattern of faded nasturtiums, the woodwork grained to look like walnut. Mrs Wrangton's double bed was still there, the mattress uncovered, a pile of folded blankets on top of it. There was a television set in this room as well as in the front room, and it had been placed so that the occupant of the bed could watch it.

'Mother came to sleep down here a few years back,' said Mrs Betts. 'There's a toilet just down the passage. She couldn't manage the stairs any more except when nurse helped her.' She sat on the edge of the mattress, nervously fingering a cage-like object of metal bars. 'I'll have to see about her walking frame going back, I'll have to get on to the welfare people.' Her hands resting on it, she said dolefully, 'Mother hated Harry. She always said he wasn't good enough for me. She did everything she could to stop me marrying him.' Mrs Betts's voice took on a rebellious girlish note. 'I think it's awful having to ask your mother's consent to marry when you're sixty-five, don't you?'

At any rate, he thought, she had gone ahead without receiving it. He looked wonderingly at this grey wisp of a woman, seventy years old, who talked as if she were a fairy princess.

'You see, she talked for years of changing her will and leaving the house to my brother. It was after he died that the nursing home business started. She quarrelled outright with Harry. Elsie Parrish was in here and Mother accused Harry in front of her of only marrying me to get this place. Harry never spoke a word to Mother again, and quite right too. I said to Mother, You're a wicked woman, you promised me years ago I'd have this house and now you're going back on your word. Cheats never prosper, I said.'

The daughter had inherited the mother's tongue. Wexford could imagine the altercations, overheard by visitors, by neighbours, which had contributed to the gossip. He turned to look at the framed photograph on a mahogany tallboy. A wedding picture, *circa* 1903. The bride was seated, lilies in her lap under a bolster of a bosom hung with lace and pearls. The bridegroom stood behind her, frock coat, black handlebar moustache. Ivy Wrangton must have been seventeen, Wexford calculated, her face plain, puffy, young, her figure modishly pouter-pigeon-like, her hair in that most unflattering of fashions, the cottage loaf. She had been rather plump then, but thin, according to Nurse Radcliffe in old age. Wexford said quietly, apparently idly:

'Mrs Betts, why did you send for Dr Moss on May 23rd? Your mother wasn't ill. She hadn't complained of feeling ill.'

She held the walking frame, pushing it backwards and forwards. 'Why shouldn't I? Dr Crocker was away. Elsie came in at nine and Mother was still asleep, and Elsie said it wasn't right the amount she slept. We couldn't wake her, though we shook her, we were so worried. I wasn't to know she'd get up as fit as a flea ten minutes after I'd phoned for him, was I?'

'Tell me about the day your mother died, Mrs Betts, Friday, June 2nd,' he said, and it occurred to him that no one had yet told him anything much about that day.

'Well . . .' Her mouth trembled and she said quickly, 'You don't think Harry did anything to Mother, do you? He wouldn't, I swear he wouldn't.'

'Tell me about that Friday.'

She made an effort to control herself, clenching her hands on the metal bar. 'We wanted to go to a whist drive. Elsie came round in the morning and I said, if we went out would she sit with Mother, and she said, OK, of course she would if I'd just give her a knock before we left.' Mrs Betts sighed and her voice steadied. 'Elsie lives two doors down. She and Mother'd been pals for years and she always came to sit with her when we went out. Though it's a lie,' her old eyes flashing like young ones, 'to say we were always out. Once in a blue moon we went out.'

Wexford's eyes went from the pudding-faced girl in the photograph, her mouth smug and proud even then, to the long strip of turfed-over garden — why did he feel Betts had done that turfing, had uprooted flowers? — and back to the nervous little woman on the mattress edge.

'I gave Mother her lunch and she was sitting in the front room, doing a bit of knitting. I popped down to Elsie's and rang her bell but she can't have heard it, she didn't come. I rang and rang and I thought, well, she's gone out, she's forgotten and that's that. But Harry said, Why not go out just the same? The painter was there, he was only a bit of a boy, twenty, twenty-two, but he and Mother got on a treat, a sight better than her and I ever did, I can tell you. So the upshot was, we went off and left her there with the painter – what was he called? Ray? Rafe? No, Roy, that was it, Roy – with Roy doing the hall walls. She was OK, fit as a flea. It was a nice day so I left all the windows open because that paint did smell. I'll never forget the way she spoke to me before I left. That was the last thing she ever said to me. Doreen, she said, you ought to be lucky at cards. You haven't been very lucky in love. And she laughed and I'll swear Roy was laughing too.'

You're building an edifice of motives for yourself, Mrs Betts, reflected Wexford. 'Go on,' was all he said.

She moved directly into hearsay evidence, but Wexford didn't stop her. 'That Roy closed the door to keep the smell out, but he popped in a few times to see if Mother was all right. They had a bit of a chat, he said, and he offered to make her a cup of tea but she didn't want any. Then about half-past three Mother said she'd got a headache – that was the onset of the stroke but she didn't know that, she put it down to the paint – and would he fetch her a couple of her paracetamols from the bathroom. So he did and he got her a glass of water and she said she'd try and have a sleep in her chair. Anyway, the next thing he knew she was out in the hall walking with her walking frame, going to have a lay-down on her bed, she said.

'Well, Harry and me came in at five-thirty and Roy was just packing up. He said Mother was asleep on her bed, and I just put my head round the door to check. She'd drawn the curtains.' Mrs Betts paused, burst out, 'To tell you the honest truth, I didn't look too closely. I thought, well, thank God for half an hour's peace to have a cup of tea in before she starts picking on Harry. It was just about a quarter to seven, ten to seven, before I went in again. I could tell there was something going on, the way she was breathing, sort of puffing out her cheeks, and red in the face. There was blood on her lips.' She looked fearfully at Wexford, looked him in the eye for the first time. 'I wiped that clean before I called the doctor, I didn't want him seeing that.

'He came straightaway. I thought maybe he'd call an ambulance but he didn't. He said she'd had a stroke and when people had strokes they shouldn't be moved. We stayed with her – well, doctor and I stayed with her – but she passed away just before half-past.'

Wexford nodded. Something about what she had said was wrong. He felt it. It wasn't that she had told a lie, though she might well have done, but something else, something that rang incongruously in that otherwise commonplace narrative, some esoteric term in place of a household word . . . He was checking back, almost there, when a footstep sounded in the hall, the door opened and a face appeared round it.

'There you are, Doreen!' said the face which was very pretty considering its age. 'I was just on my way to – Oh, I beg your pardon, I'm intruding.'

'That's all right,' said Mrs Betts. 'You can come in, Elsie.' She looked blankly at Wexford, her eyes once more old and tired. 'This is Mrs Parrish.'

Elsie Parrish, Wexford decided, looked exactly as an old lady should. She had a powdery, violet cashew, creamy smell, which might equally well have been associated with a very clean baby. Her legs were neat and shapely in grey stockings, her hands in white gloves with tiny darns at the fingertips, her coat silky navy-blue over blue flowery pleats, and her face withered rose leaves with rouge on. The bouffant mass of silvery hair was so profuse that from a distance it might have been taken for a white silk turban. She and Wexford walked down the street together towards the shops, Elsie Parrish swinging a pink nylon string bag.

'It's wicked the way they gossip. You can't understand how people can be so evil-minded. You'll notice how none of them are able to say how Doreen gave Ivy a stroke when she wasn't even there.' Mrs Parrish gave a dry satirical laugh. 'Perhaps they think she bribed that poor young man, the painter, to give Ivy a fright. I remember my mother saying that fright could give you a stroke – an apoplexy, she called it – or too much excitement or drinking too much or over-eating even.'

To his surprise, because this isn't what old ladies of elegant appearance usually do or perhaps should do, she opened her handbag, took out a packet of cigarettes and put one between her lips. He shook his head when the packet was offered to him, watched her light the cigarette with a match from a matchbook with a black shiny cover.

She puffed delicately. He didn't think he had ever before seen someone smoke a cigarette while wearing white gloves. He said:

'Why didn't you go round and sit with Mrs Wrangton, that afternoon, Mrs Parrish?'

'The day she died, you mean?'

'Yes.' Wexford had the impression she didn't want to answer, she didn't want to infer anything against Doreen Betts. She spoke with care.

'It's quite true I'm getting rather deaf.' He hadn't noticed it. She had heard everything he said, in the open noisy street, and he hadn't raised his voice. 'I don't always hear the bell. Doreen must have rung and I didn't hear. That's the only explanation.'

Was it?

'I thought she and Harry had changed their minds about going out.' Elsie Parrish put the cigarette to her lips between thumb and forefinger. 'I'd give a lot,' she said, 'to be able to go back in time. I wouldn't hesitate this time, I'd go round and check on Ivy whether Doreen had asked me or not.'

'Probably your presence would have made no difference,' he said, and then, 'Mrs Betts had told the builders not to do any work upstairs . . .'

She interrupted him. 'Maybe it didn't need it. I've never been upstairs in Ivy's house, so I couldn't say. Besides, when she'd sold it the new people might have had their own ideas, mightn't they? They might have wanted to do their own decorating.'

They were standing still now on the street corner, he about to go in one direction, she in the other. She dropped the cigarette end, stamped it out over-thoroughly with a high heel. From her handbag she took a small lacy handkerchief and dabbed her nostrils with it. The impression was that the tears, though near, would be restrained. 'She left me two thousand pounds. Dear Ivy, she was so kind and generous. I knew I was to have something, I didn't dream as much as that.' Elsie Parrish smiled, a watery, girlish, rueful smile, but still he was totally unprepared for what she said next. 'I'm going to buy a car.'

His eyebrows went up.

'I've kept my licence going. I haven't driven since my husband died and that's twenty-two years ago. I had to sell our car and I've always longed and longed for another.' She really looked as if she had, a yearning expression crumpling the roses still further. 'I'm going to have my own dear little car!' She was on the verge of executing a dance on the pavement. 'And dear Ivy made that possible!' Anxiously: 'You don't think I'm too old to drive?'

Wexford did, but he only said that this kind of judgement wasn't really within his province. She nodded, smiled again, whisked off surprisingly fast into the corner supermarket. Wexford moved more slowly and thoughtfully away, his eyes down. It was because he was looking down that he saw the matchbook, and then he remembered fancying he had seen her drop something when she got out that handkerchief.

She wasn't in the shop. She must have left by the other exit into the High Street and now she was nowhere to be seen. Deciding that matchbooks were in the category of objects which no one much minds losing, Wexford dropped it into his pocket and forgot it.

'You want Roy?'

'That's right,' said Wexford.

The foreman, storekeeper, proprietor, whatever he was, didn't ask why. 'You'll find him,' he said, 'doing the Snowcem on them flats up the Sewingbury Road.'

Wexford drove up there. Roy was a gigantic youth, broad-shouldered, heavily muscled, with an aureole of thick curly fair hair. He came down the ladder and said he'd just been about to knock off for his tea break, anyway. There was a carmen's café conveniently near. Roy lit a cigarette, put his elbows on the table.

'I never knew a thing about it till I turned up there the next day.'

'But surely when Mrs Betts came in the afternoon before she asked you how her mother had been?'

'Sure she did. And I said the truth, that the old lady'd got a headache and asked for something for it and I'd given it her, and then she'd felt tired and gone in for a lay-down. But there was no sign she was *dying*. My God, that'd never have crossed my mind.'

A headache, Wexford reflected, was often one of the premonitory signs of a cerebral haemorrhage. Roy seemed to read his thoughts, for he said quickly:

'She'd had a good many headaches while I was in the place working. Them non-drip plastic-based paints have got a bit of a smell to them, used to turn *me* up at first. I mean, you don't want to get thinking there was anything out of the way in her having an aspirin and laying down, guv. That'd happened two or three times while I was there. And she'd shovel them aspirins down, swallow four as soon as look at you.'

Wexford said, 'Tell me about that afternoon. Did anyone come into the house between the time Mr and Mrs Betts went out and the time they got back?'

Roy shook his head. 'Definitely not, and I'd have known. I was working on the hall, see? The front door was wide open on account of the smell. Nobody could have come in there without my seeing, could they? The other old girl – Mrs Betts, that is – she locked the back door before she went out and I hadn't no call to unlock it. What else d'you want to know, guv?'

'Exactly what happened, what you and Mrs Wrangton talked about, the lot.'

Roy swigged his tea, lit a fresh cigarette from the stub of the last. 'I got on OK with her, you know. I reckon she reminded me of my gran. It's a funny thing, but everyone got on OK with her bar her own daughter and the old man. Funny old git, isn't he? Gave me the creeps. Well, to what you're asking, I don't know that we talked much. I was painting, you see, and the door to the front room was shut. I looked in a couple of times. She was sitting there knitting, watching cricket on the TV. I do remember she said I was making a nice job of the house and it was a pity she wouldn't be there to enjoy it. Well, I thought she meant she'd be dead, you know the way they talk, and I said, Now come on, Mrs Wrangton, you mustn't talk like that. That made her laugh. She said, I don't mean that, you naughty boy, I mean I'm going into a nursing home and I've got to sell the place, didn't you know? No, I said, I didn't, but I reckoned it'd fetch a packet, big old house like that, twenty thousand at least, I said, and she said she hoped so.'

Wexford nodded. So Mrs Wrangton had intended to go ahead with her plans, and Doreen Betts's denial had either been purposeful lying to demolish her motive or a post-mortem white-washing of her mother's character. For it had certainly been black-hearted enough, he thought, quite an act it had been, that of deliberately turning your own daughter and her husband out of their home. He looked back to Roy.

'You offered to make her tea?'

'Yeah, well, the daughter, Mrs Betts, said to make myself and her a cup of tea if she wanted, but she didn't want. She asked me to turn off the TV and then she said she'd got a headache and would I go to the bathroom cupboard and get her aspirins? Well, I'd seen Mrs Betts do it often enough, though I'd never actually . . .'

'You're sure she said aspirins?' Quite suddenly Wexford knew what it was that had seemed incongruous to him in Mrs Betts's description of her mother's last afternoon of life. Doreen Betts had specified paracetamol instead of the common household remedy. 'You're sure she used that word?' he said.

Roy pursed his mouth. 'Well, now you mention it, I'm not sure. I reckon what she said was, my tablets or the tablets for my head, something like that. You just do say aspirins, don't you, like naturally? I mean, that's what everybody takes. Anyway, I brought them down, the bottle and gave them to her with a glass of water, and she says she's going to have a bit of shut-eye in her chair. But the next thing I knew she was coming out, leaning on that walking frame the welfare people give her. I took four, Roy, she says, but my head's that bad, I reckon it's worse, and I'm ever so giddy. Well, I didn't think much of that, they're all giddy at that age, aren't they? I remember my gran. She says she's got ringing in her ears, so I said, I'll help you into your room, shall I? And I sort of give her my arm and helped her in and she lay down on the bed with all her things on and shut her eyes. The light was glaring so I pulled the curtains over and then I went back to my painting. I never heard another thing till Mrs Betts and the old boy come in at half five . . .'

Wexford closed *Practical Forensic Medicine* by Francis E. Camps and J. M. Cameron and made his way back to Castle Road. He had decided to discuss the matter no further with Mrs Betts. The presence of her husband, shuffling about almost silently in his furry slippers, his feet like the paws of an old hibernating animal, rather unnerved him. She made no demur at his proposal to remove from the bathroom cabinet the prescription bottle of pain-killing tablets, labelled: Mrs I. Wrangton, Paracetamol.

Evening surgery had only just begun. Wexford went home for his dinner, having sent two items away for fingerprint analysis. By eight-thirty he was back in the surgery building and again Dr Crocker had finished first. He groaned when he saw Wexford.

'What is it now, Reg?'

'Why did you prescribe paracetamol for Mrs Wrangton?'

'Because I thought it suitable for her, of course. She was allergic to aspirin.'

Wexford looked despairingly at his friend. 'Now he tells me. I'd rather gathered it. I mean, today I caught on, but you might have told me.'

'For God's sake! You *knew*. You said to me, Nurse Radcliffe told me all about it. Those were your words. You said . . .'

'I thought it was asthma.'

Crocker sat on the edge of his desk. 'Look, Reg, we've both been barking up the wrong trees. There was asthma in Mrs Wrangton's family. Mrs Betts has nettle rash, her brother was a chronic asthmatic. People with asthma or a family history of asthma are sometimes allergic to acetylsalicylic acid or aspirin. In fact, about ten per cent of such people are thought to have the allergy. One of the reactions of the hypersensitive person to aspirin is an asthmatic attack. That's what Mrs Wrangton had when she was in her forties, that and haematemesis. Which means,' he added kindly for the layman, 'bringing up blood from an internal haemorrhage.'

'OK, I'm not bone ignorant,' Wexford snapped, 'and I've been reading up hypersensitivity to acetylsalicylic acid . . .'

'Mrs Wrangton couldn't have had aspirin poisoning,' said the doctor quickly. 'There were never any aspirins in the house. Mrs Betts was strict about that.'

They were interrupted by the arrival of smiling Dr Moss. Wexford wheeled round on him.

'What would you expect to be the result of – let me see – one point two grammes of acetylsalicylic acid on a woman of ninety-two who was hypersensitive to the drug?'

Moss looked at him warily. 'I take it this is academic?' Wexford didn't answer. 'Well, it'd depend on the degree of hypersensitivity. Nausea, maybe, diarrhoea, dizziness, tinnitus – that's ringing in the ears – breathing difficulties, gastric haemorrhages, oedema of gastric mucosa, possible rupture of the oesophagus. In a person of that age, consequent upon such a shock and localized haemorrhages, I suppose a brain haemorrhage . . .' He stopped, realizing what he had said.

'Thanks very much,' said Wexford. 'I think you've more or less described what happened to Mrs Wrangton on June 2nd after she'd taken four three hundred milligram tablets of aspirin.'

Dr Moss was looking stunned. He looked as if he would never smile again. Wexford passed an envelope to Crocker.

'Those are aspirins?'

Crocker looked at them, touched one to his tongue. 'I suppose so, but . . .'

'I've sent the rest away to be analysed. To be certain. There were fifty-six in the bottle.'

'Reg, it's unthinkable there could have been a mistake on the part of the pharmacist, but just supposing by a one in a million chance there was, she couldn't have taken forty-four tablets of aspirin. Not even over the months she couldn't.'

'You're being a bit slow,' said Wexford. 'You prescribed one hundred paracetamol, and one hundred paracetamol were put into that bottle at Fraser's, the chemist's. Between the time the prescription was made up and the day before, or a few days before, or a week before, she died, she took forty tablets of paracetamol, leaving sixty in the bottle. But on June 2nd she took four tablets of aspirin. Or, to put it bluntly, some time before June 2nd someone removed those sixty tablets of paracetamol and substituted sixty tablets of aspirin.'

Dr Moss found his voice. 'That would be murder.'

'Well . . .' Wexford spoke hesitantly. 'The hypersensitivity might not have resulted in a stroke. The intent may only have been to cause illness of a more or less severe kind. Ulceration of the stomach, say. That would have meant hospitalization for Mrs Wrangton. On the Welfare State. No exorbitant nursing home fees to be paid there, no swallowing up of capital or selling of property. Later on, if she survived, she would probably have been transferred, again for free, to a geriatric ward in the same hospital. It's well-known that no private nursing home will take the chronically sick.'

'You think Mrs Betts . . . ?' Dr Moss began.

'No, I don't. For two good reasons, Mrs Betts is the one person who wouldn't have done it this way. If she had wanted to kill her mother or to make her seriously ill, why go to all the trouble of changing over sixty tablets in a bottle, when she had only to give Mrs Wrangton the aspirins in her hand? And if she had changed them, wouldn't she, immediately her mother was dead, have changed them back again?'

'Then who was it?'

'I shall know tomorrow,' said Wexford.

Crocker came to him at his office in the police station.

'Sorry I'm late. I just lost a patient.'

Wexford made sympathetic noises. Having walked round the room, eyed the two available chairs, the doctor settled for the edge of Wexford's desk.

'Yesterday,' Wexford began, 'I had a talk with Mrs Elsie Parrish.' He checked the doctor's exclamation and sudden start forward. 'Wait a minute, Len. She dropped a matchbook before we parted. It was one of those with a glossy surface that very easily take prints. I had the prints on it and those on the paracetamol bottle compared. There were Mrs Betts's prints on the bottle, and a set that were presumably Mrs Wrangton's, and a man's that were presumably the painter's. And there was also a very clear set identical to those on the matchbook.

'It was Elsie Parrish who changed those tablets, Len. She did it because she knew that Mrs Wrangton fully intended to retire to Summerland and that the first money to go, perhaps before the house was sold, would be the few thousands of capital she and Doreen Betts were to share. Elsie Parrish had waited for years for that money, she wanted to buy a car. A few more years and if she herself survived it would be too late for driving cars. Besides, by then her legacy would have been swallowed up in nursing home fees.'

'A nice old creature like that?' Crocker said. 'That's no proof, her prints on the bottle. She'll have fetched that bottle often enough for old Ivy.'

'No. She told me she had never been upstairs in Ivy Wrangton's house.'

'Oh, God.'

'I don't suppose she saw it as murder. It wouldn't seem like murder, or manslaughter, or grievous bodily harm, changing tablets over in a bottle.' Wexford sat down, wrinkled up his face. He said crossly, dispiritedly, 'I don't know what to do, Len. We've no way of proving Mrs Wrangton died of aspirin poisoning. We can't exhume her, we can't analyse "two handfuls of white dust shut in an urn of brass". And even if we could, would we be so inhumane as to have a woman of – how old is Elsie Parrish?'

'Seventy-eight.'

'Seventy-eight up in court on a murder charge. On the other hand, should she be allowed to profit from her crime? Should she be permitted to terrorize pedestrians in a smart little Ford Fiesta?'

'She won't,' said Crocker.

Something in his voice brought Wexford to his feet. 'Why? What d'you mean?'

The doctor slid lightly off the edge of the desk. 'I told you I'd lost

187

a patient. Elsie Parrish died last night. A neighbour found her and called me.'

'Maybe that's for the best. What did she die of?'

'A stroke,' said Crocker, and went.

Ginger and the Kingsmarkham
Chalk Circle

'There's a girl downstairs, sir,' said Polly Davies, 'and she says someone's taken her baby out of its pram.'

Chief Inspector Wexford had been contemplating a sheet of foolscap. On it, written by himself in the cause of crime prevention, was a politely worded request to the local authority, asking them to refrain from erecting scaffolding around their rented property a full nine months before building work was due to commence. Because of the scaffolding there had already been two burglaries and an assault on a young woman. He looked up from the paper, adjusted his thoughts and sighed.

'They will do it,' he said. 'Leave their babies about I mean. You'd never find them leaving their handbags outside shops.'

'It was outside her flat, sir, not a shop, and the thing is, whoever took the baby left another one in its place.'

Slowly Wexford got up. He came round the desk and looked narrowly at Polly.

'Constable Davies, you have to be pulling my leg.'

'No, sir, you know I wouldn't. She's a Mrs Bond and she says that when she went downstairs to fetch in her pram, her baby had gone and another one been put there.'

Wexford followed Polly down to the ground floor. In one of the interview rooms a girl was sitting at the bleak, rectangular, plastic-topped table, drinking tea and crying. She looked about nineteen. She had long straw-coloured hair and a small childish face, naive and innocent and frightened, and she was wearing blue denims and a tee-shirt with apples and oranges and cherries printed all over the front. From her appearance one would not have supposed her to be a mother. But also in the room was a baby. The baby, in short white frock and woolly coat and napkin and cotton socks, slept in the uneasy arms of Detective Constable Loring.

It had occurred to Wexford on the way down that women who have recently had babies are, or are said to be, prone to various kinds of mental disturbance, and his first thought was that Mrs Bond might only think or only be saying that this child was not hers.

'Now, Mrs Bond,' he began, 'this is a strange business. Do you feel like telling me about it?'

'I've told it all,' she said.

'Well, yes, but not to me. Why not start by telling me where you live and where your baby was?'

She gulped. She pushed the teacup away. 'Greenhill Court. We're on the fifth floor. We haven't got a balcony or anything. I have to go all the way down in the lift to put Karen out in her pram. She's got to have fresh air. And when she's there I can't watch her all the time. I can't even see her from my lounge on account of it looks out over the car park.'

'So you put her out in the pram this afternoon,' said Wexford. 'What time would that have been?'

'It was just on two. I put the pram on the grass with the cat net on it, and when I went to fetch it in at half-past four the cat net was still on it and the baby was asleep but it – it wasn't Karen!' She made little whimpering noises that exploded in a sob. 'It wasn't Karen, it was that baby he's holding!'

The baby woke up and also began to cry. Loring wrinkled up his nose and shifted his left hand from under its buttocks. His eyes appealed to Polly who nodded and left the room.

'So what did you do?' said Wexford.

'I didn't even go back upstairs. I got hold of the pram and I pushed it and I started to run and I ran all the way down here to you.'

He was touched by her childish faith. In real or imaginary trouble, at time of fear, she ran to those whom her sheltered small-town upbringing had taught her to trust, the kindly helmeted man in blue, the strong arm of the law. Not for her the grosser cynical image her city-bred contemporaries held of brutal and bribable policemen.

'Mrs Bond,' he said, and then, 'What's your first name?'

'Philippa. I'm called Pippa.'

'Then I'll call you that if you don't mind. Describe your baby to me, will you, Pippa? Is she dark or fair? How old is she?'

'She's two months old — well, nine weeks. She's got blue eyes, she's wearing a white frock.' The voice broke and trembled again. 'And she's got the most beautiful red-gold hair you've ever seen!'

Inevitably, Wexford's eyes went to the child in Loring's arms whom this description seemed perfectly to fit. He said gently to Pippa Bond, 'Now you're quite sure you aren't imagining all this? No one will be angry if you are, we shall understand. Perhaps you worried or felt a bit guilty about leaving Karen out of your sight for so long, and then when you came down you got a feeling she looked rather different from usual and . . .'

A wail of indignation and misery cut across the rest of what he had to say. The girl began to cry with long tearing sobs. Polly Davies came back, carrying a small square hand towel from the women's lavatory. She took the baby from Loring, laid it on its back on the table and undid the big safety pin above its navel. Pippa Bond flinched away from the baby as if it were carrying a disease.

'I'm not imagining it,' she shouted at Wexford. 'I'm not! D'you think I wouldn't know my own baby? D'you think I wouldn't know my Karen from *that*?'

Polly had folded the towel cornerwise. She moved a little so that Wexford could see the baby's waving legs and bare crotch. 'Whoever this baby is, sir, it isn't Karen. Look for yourself — it's a boy.'

Trevor Bond was fetched from the Stowerton estate agent's where he worked. He looked very little older than his wife. Pippa clung to him, crying and inarticulate, and over her bent head he cast despairing eyes at the policemen.

He had arrived in a car driven by a young woman he said was his sister-in-law, Pippa's sister, who also lived at Greenhill Court with her husband. She sat stiffly at the wheel, giving Pippa no more than a nod and what seemed like a shrug of exasperation when she came out of the police station with Trevor's arm round her. Susan Rains, her name was, and a quarter of an hour later it was she who was showing Loring and Sergeant Martin just where the pram had stood on the lawn between the block of flats and the main road from Kingsmarkham to Stowerton. While this thin red-haired girl castigated her sister's negligence and put forward her own theories as to where Karen might be, Dr Moss arrived with sedation for Pippa, though she had become calmer once she understood no one would expect her to have charge of the changeling boy.

His fate was removal to a Kingsmarkham Borough nursery for infants in the care of the local authority.

'Poor lamb,' said the children's officer Wexford spoke to. 'I expect Kay will be able to take him in Bystall Lane. There's no one to fetch him, though, they've got ten to bath and get to bed down there.'

Young Ginger, Wexford had begun to call him. He was a fine-looking baby with large eyes, strong pudgy features, and hair of a curious pale red, the colour of a new raw carrot. To Wexford's not inexperienced eye, he looked older than the missing Karen, nearer four months than two. His eyes were able to focus firmly, and now they focused on the chief inspector, a scrutiny which moved the baby to yell miserably. Young Ginger buried his face in Polly's boyish bosom, crying and searching for sustenance.

'You don't know what they're thinking, do you, sir?' Polly said. 'Just because we can't remember anything about when we were his age we sort of think babies don't feel much or notice things. But suppose what they feel is so awful they sort of block it off just so as they won't be able to remember? Suppose it's dreadful pain being separated from your mother and not being able to say and – Oh, I don't know, but does anyone think of these things, sir?'

'Well, psychiatrists do,' said Wexford, 'and philosophers, I expect, but not many ordinary people like us. You'll have to remember it when you have babies of your own. Now take him down to Bystall Lane, will you?'

A few minutes after she had gone Inspector Burden came in. He had heard the story downstairs but had not entirely believed it. It was the part about putting another baby in Karen's place that he couldn't believe, he told Wexford. He hadn't either, said Wexford, but it was true.

'You can't think of a reason why anyone would do such a thing,' said Burden. 'You can't think of a single reason why even a mentally disturbed person would do such a thing.'

'I suppose,' said Wexford, 'that by "you" you mean yourself or "one" because *I* can think of several reasons for doing it. First of all, you've got to take some degree of mental disturbance for granted here. Well-adjusted normal people don't steal other people's babies, let alone exchange them. It's going to be a woman. It's a woman who's done it because she wants to be rid of that particular child, yet she must have a child. Agreed?'

'Right,' said Burden. 'Why?'

'She has to show it to someone else,' Wexford said slowly, as if thinking aloud, 'someone who expects to see a baby nearer in age and appearance to Karen Bond than to young Ginger, or who expects a baby of Karen's sex. She may be a woman who has several sons and whose husband was away when the last one was born. She has told him he has a daughter, and to bear this out because she's afraid of him, she has to have a girl to produce for him. On the other hand, she may not be married. She may have told a boy friend or ex-boy friend the child is younger than it is in order to convince him of his paternity.'

'I'm glad you mentioned mental disturbance,' said Burden sarcastically.

'She may simply be exhausted by looking after a child who screams incessantly – young Ginger's got a good pair of lungs – so she exchanges him for a baby she believes won't scream. Or she may have been told that Ginger has some illness or even hereditary defect which frightened her so she wanted to be rid of him, but she still has to have a baby for her husband or mother or whoever to see.'

Burden seemed to be considering this inventiveness with reluctant admiration but not much conviction. He said, 'So what are we going to do about it?'

'I've taken everyone in the place off what they were doing and put them on to this. We're getting on to all the hospitals and GPs, the Registrar of births, and the post-natal and baby clinics. I think it has to be someone local, maybe even someone who knew the pram would be there because she'd seen it there before.'

'And seen the baby who was in it before?' asked Burden, quirking up an eyebrow.

'Not necessarily. A pram with a cat net over and whose occupant can't be seen implies a very young baby.' Wexford hesitated. 'This is a hell of a lot more worrying,' he said, 'than a run-of-the-mill baby-snatching.'

'Because Karen Bond's so young?' Burden hazarded.

'No, not that. Look, Mike, your typical baby-snatcher loves babies, she yearns for one of her own, and that's why she takes someone else's. But this one's *got* a baby of her own and one she dislikes enough to hand him over to a stranger. You can pretty well take it for granted the ordinary baby-snatcher will care for a child almost extravagantly well, but will this one? If she doesn't care for her own child, will she care for a substitute? I say it's worrying because we can be certain this woman's taken Karen for a purpose, a use, and what happens when that use is over?'

*

The block of flats in which the Bonds lived was not one of those concerning whose vulnerability to break-ins Wexford had been drafting his letter, but a privately owned five-storeyed building standing on what not long ago had been open green meadows. There were three such blocks, Greenhill, Fairlawn and Hillside Courts, interspersed with rows of weatherboarded town houses, and each block was separated from the main road to Stowerton only by a strip of lawn thirty feet deep. On this turf, a little way in from the narrow service road, Karen Bond's pram had stood.

Wexford and Burden talked to the porter who had charge of the three blocks. He had been cleaning a car in the car park at the relevant time and had noticed nothing. Wexford, going up in the Greenhill lift, commented to Burden that it was unfortunate children were forbidden to play on the lawns. They would have served as protection for Karen or at least as witnesses. There were a good many children on this new estate which was mainly occupied by young couples. Between two and four-thirty that afternoon the little ones had been cooped up in small rooms or out for walks with their mothers, the older ones at school.

Mrs Louise Pelham had fetched her son and her next-door neighbour's two sons home from school, passing within a few feet of Karen's pram. That was at a quarter to four. She had glanced into the pram, as she always did, and now she said she remembered thinking Karen looked 'funny'. The baby in the pram had seemed to have a bigger face and redder hair than the one she had looked at when she passed on her way to the children's school half an hour before. Wexford felt that there was a real lead here, a pinpointing of the time of the substitution, until he learned that Susan Rains had been with Mrs Pelham before him and told her the whole story in detail.

Susan Rains and her sister Pippa had each been married at the age of eighteen, but Pippa at twenty already had a baby while Susan, seven years older, was childless. She was without a job too, it appeared, and at three years short of thirty was leading the life of a middle-aged houseproud gossip. She seemed very anxious to tell Wexford and Burden that, in her opinion, her sister was far too young to have a child, her brother-in-law too young to be a father, and that they were both too irresponsible to look after a baby. Pippa, she said, was always bringing Karen round for her to mind, and now Wexford, who had been wondering about the two folded napkins, the plastic spoon and bottle of concentrated orange juice on Mrs Rains's spotless kitchen counter, understood why they were there.

'Are you fond of babies, Mrs Rains?' Wexford asked, and got an almost frightening response.

Hard lines bit into Mrs Rains's face and her redhead's pale eyes flashed. 'I'd be an unnatural woman if I wasn't, wouldn't I?' What else she might have said – a defence? An explanation? – was cut off by the arrival of a woman in her late forties whom she introduced in a mutter as her mother. It was left to Wexford to find out that this was Mrs Leighton who had left Pippa in a drugged sleep and Trevor trying to answer Sergeant Martin's second spate of questions.

Mrs Leighton was sprightly and not too concerned. 'Well, babies that get taken out of prams, they always turn up safe and sound, don't they?' Her hair was dyed to a more glorious red than her daughter's natural shade. She was on her way to babysit for her son and daughter-in-law who had a six-month-old son, and she had just looked in on Pippa to collect the one pound twenty she owed her for dry-cleaning. Imagine what she'd felt, the whole place full of police-men and Karen gone. She really thought Trevor or Susan might have phoned her, and now she was in two minds whether to go and babysit for Mark or not. 'But she's bound to turn up OK, isn't she?' she said to Wexford.

Wexford said they must hope so, and then he and Burden left the two women to argue between themselves as to which was the more important, keeping a promise to the son or commiserating with the daughter.

The world, or this small corner of it, suddenly seemed full of babies. From behind two doors on the ground floor came the whimpers and low peevish grizzlings of infants put unwillingly in their cots for the night. As they left by the glass double doors, they passed on the step an athletic-looking girl in sweater and denims with a very small baby clamped to her chest in a canvas baby carrier. The car park was filling as men returned home from work, some of them commuters from London, and among them, walking from a jaunty red sports car, a couple swinging between them a baby in a shallow rush basket. Wexford wondered just how many children under the age of two lived in those flats and small neat houses. Nearly as many as there were adults, he thought, and he stood aside to let pass a girl pushing twins in a wide push-chair.

There was very little more that he could do that night beyond embroiling himself in another discussion with Burden as to the reason why. Burden put forward several strange suggestions. Having previously declared that he couldn't think of a single motive, he now posited that the baby-snatcher was due to have her own baby immunized against whooping cough on the following day. She had read in the newspaper that this could cause brain damage but was too diffident to refuse the immunization, so planned to substitute someone else's baby for her own.

'The trouble with you unimaginative people,' said Wexford, 'is that when you do fantasize you really go crazy. She wants to protect her child from what's something like a one in a million chance of brain damage, but she doesn't mind entrusting him to the care of strangers who might do him far more harm.'

'But the point is she knew they wouldn't do him harm. She'd know that what's happened is exactly what must happen, that he'd be brought to us and then put in the care of the local authority.' Burden waited for some show of enthusiasm and when he didn't get it he went home. For three hours. At eleven that night he was destined to be called out again.

But not on account of Karen Bond.

In normal circumstances Sergeant Willoughby, going off duty, wouldn't have given a second glance at the Ford Transit parked under some overhanging bushes at the foot of Ploughman's Lane. But the sergeant's head, like those of most members of the Mid-Sussex Constabulary, was full of thoughts of missing children. He saw the van as a possible caravan substitute, and his mind went vaguely back to old tales of infants stolen by gypsies. He parked his scooter and went over to investigate.

The young man sitting in the driving seat switched on the ignition, put the van into gear and moved off as fast as he could on a roar of the engine. There was no real danger of his hitting Sergeant Willoughby, nor did that seem to have been his intention, but he passed within a yard or so of him and swung down the lane towards the town.

The nearest phone was in the sergeant's own home in Queen Street, and he went quickly to it.

But the Ford Transit turned out to have had nothing to do with Karen Bond. It was the getaway car for two men who were taking advantage of the absence of a Kingsmarkham stockbroker and his wife to remove a safe from their home.

Ploughman's Lane was Kingsmarkham's millionaire's row, and Stephen Pollard's house, pretentiously named Baron's Keep, by no means the smallest or most modest house in it. It was a nineteen-thirties palace of red brick and leaded lattices and neo-Tudor twisty chimneys. All the windows on the ground floor had stout bars to them, but there were no bars on the french window which led from the largest of the rear bedrooms on to a spacious balcony. When Burden and Loring got there they found signs that two men had climbed up to this balcony, ignored the thief-proof locks on the french window, and cut the glass neatly out of its frame with a glass cutter.

Where the safe had been in the study on the ground floor was now a gaping cavity. This room was said to be a precise replica of some writing room or den or hidey-hole of Mary Queen of Scots in Holyrood Palace, and the safe had been concealed behind a sliding door in the linenfold panelling. The thieves had chipped it out of its niche with a cold chisel and removed it bodily. Burden thought it must have been immensely heavy, which explained the need for having the van nearby.

Although the weather was dry, a long wet spell had only just ended. Deeply indented footprints, one set of a size eight shoe, the other of a size twelve, had ground into the flowerbed under the balcony. These same prints crossed the rear lawn to where there was a gate in the tall wattle fence, and alongside them went parallel grooves about two inches apart.

'I reckon,' said Burden, 'they had a set of those wheels people have for pushing heavy luggage along. That's what they used. The sheer cheek of it!'

Loring shone his torch. 'They rested it down here, sir, in front of the gate. Must have been a bit of a blow when they found their motor gone and they had to keep on wheeling.'

In vain they searched the lane, the ditches and the copse which bordered the lane on one side. They didn't find the safe and no fingerprints were found on the window ledges or in the study at Baron's Keep. The thieves had worn gloves.

'And Big Feet,' said Burden in the morning, 'should have worn snow shoes. There aren't going to be many villains about with great plates of meat like that.'

'I'd think of Lofty Peters first thing,' said Wexford, 'only he's inside.'

'Well, he's not actually. He came out last week. But we were round at his place, knocking him up at midnight and waking all the neighbours, and there was no doubt where he'd been all evening. He was blind drunk, smashed out of his mind. I reckon this lot came down from London. Old Pollard's been shooting his mouth off around the City about his missus's diamonds and this is the outcome.'

'The van was nicked,' said Wexford. 'I've just had a call from the super at Myringham. They found it ditched on the edge of a wood with the licence plates missing.'

'What a lively time we are having,' said Burden, and he looked out of the window at the geraniums on the forecourt and the shops opening, striped awnings gradually being unfurled, shoppers' cars moving in, the July sun spreading a great sheet of light and warmth across the Pomfret Road – and a little figure walking through it in unseasonable black. 'My God,' he said, 'I don't believe it, not another one!'

Wexford got up and came over to the window. The small stout man in the black cassock was now on the forecourt, walking between the geranium tubs. In his arms was a bundle that was undoubtedly a baby. He was carrying the baby very confidently and securely as might be expected in one who so often performed the sacrament of baptism. Wexford watched him in silence, craning out to follow the priest's progress under the overhanging canopy and through the swing doors into the police station.

He said in a distant speculative voice, 'You don't suppose, do you, Mike, that this is the latest craze? I mean, we've had wife-swapping, are we going to have baby-swapping? Maybe it's something that bored young housewives are going to take up instead of going to evening classes or playing with their deep freezes.'

'Or maybe there's a maniac on the rampage who gets his kicks from changing them all round and confusing their mums.'

'Musical babes,' said Wexford. 'Come on, let's go down and see.' They descended to the foyer in the lift. 'Good morning, Father. And who might this be?'

The priest in charge of the Catholic church of Our Lady of Loretto was leaning against the long parabola-shaped counter behind which the station sergeant, Sergeant Camb, presided. The sleeping baby in his arms was swathed, indeed tightly cocooned, in a clean pale blue cellular blanket. Only its face, fragile yet healthy-looking, and one hand were exposed. Thick dark lashes rested on the rose-leaf skin, but otherwise the child was fair, eyebrow-less and with fine downy hair as bright as a new copper coin. Holding it with tender firmness, Father Glanville looked round from his conversation with the sergeant to give Wexford a mystified grin, while Polly Davies stroked the baby's tiny fingers with her own forefinger.

'Your guess is as good as mine, Mr Wexford. I went over to the church just before nine and when I came back this little one was on the front steps of the presbytery. My lady help, Mrs Bream, had come in by the back door and hadn't even noticed him.'

'You found him just like that?' said Wexford. 'Just wrapped in that blanket and lying on the doorstep.'

'No indeed. He was wrapped in this blanket inside a cardboard box. The cardboard box,' said Father Glanville, smiling, 'is of the kind one sees in grocery supermarkets. This particular one has printed on it: Smith's Ready Salted Crisps, Ten Family Packs.' He added rather anxiously, 'I'm afraid I haven't brought it with me.'

Wexford couldn't help laughing. 'Well, don't throw it away. It's very likely a vital piece of evidence.' He came closer to the child who slept on regardless of the talk and the four large alien presences. 'You brought it straight here?'

'I brought *him* straight here,' said Father Glanville with the faintest note of reproof in his voice. Wexford reflected that he ought to have known the priest would never refer to any human soul, however youthful, however unknown and unidentified, as 'it', and then he said:

'I suppose he is a he? Blue blankets don't necessarily denote maleness, do they?'

The three men, for some obscure reason known to none of them, turned their eyes simultaneously on Polly Davies. And she, somehow recognizing that to ascertain gender was her peculiar function, gently took the baby out of Father Glanville's arms, turned away and began unwrapping the blue blanket. The baby woke up and at once began a strenuous crying. Polly re-wrapped the blanket, set the child against her shoulder, her hand pressed against the four-inch wide back.

'This is a little girl, sir.' She put the baby's cheek against her own. 'Sir, don't you think it's Karen Bond? I'm sure it is, it must be.' Her voice had a catch in it. To her own evident horror, there were tears coming into her eyes. 'To think someone just dumped her, someone else's child, on a doorstep, in a cardboard box!'

'Well, the someone couldn't have left her in a better place, could she?' said Wexford with a grin at the priest. 'Come now, Constable Davies, this is no way for a liberated woman to go on. Let us pull ourselves together and go and phone Mrs Bond.'

Trevor and Pippa Bond arrived together, having again been brought to the police station in Susan Rains's car. The young husband was plainly terrified that the child would turn out not to be theirs, that their journey would prove to have been a cruel and vain awakening of hope, and for this reason he had tried to persuade his wife not to come. But she had come. Nothing could have kept her away, though she was fuddled and dazed still from Dr Moss's sedatives.

But once she saw the baby the muzziness left her and the glazed look went out of her eyes. She seized her in her arms, crushing her until Karen cried out and struggled with all her nine-week-old energy. Inscrutably, Susan Rains watched the little drama, watched her sister throw the blue blanket on to the floor, shuddering as she did so, watched the tears run down her cheeks on to the baby's head. Pippa began frenetically examining the white frock, the matinée jacket, the minute socks, as if hunting for visible germs.

'Why don't you burn the lot?' said Susan very coolly. 'Then you won't have to worry.'

Trevor Bond said quickly and awkwardly, 'Well, thanks very much, thanks a lot. I'll just see these girls of mine home and then I'll get off to the office. We've got a lot on our plates, always have this time of the year.'

'I'll take them back, Trev,' said Susan. 'You get off to work. And I'll phone Mother.'

'I'd let Dr Moss have a look at Karen if I were you,' said Wexford. 'She seems fine and I'm sure she is, but better be on the safe side.'

They went on their way. Susan Rains walked a little behind the others, already marked for her role as the eternal aunt. Wexford's thoughts went to her nephew, her brother Mark's child, though he didn't know why he should think of him just then, and then to young Ginger, that grass orphan, down in Bystall Lane. He picked up the blanket – young Ginger's blanket? – and examined it, coming to the conclusion at the end of a few minutes' scrutiny of its texture and its label, that it was made of pure wool, had been manufactured in Wales, was old but clean and had been mended in one corner by someone who was no tyro when it came to handling a darning needle. From its honeycombing he picked a quantity of hairs. Most of these were baby hair, very fine red-gold filaments that might (or then again might not) all have come from the same child's scalp, but among them were a few coarser longer hairs that were clearly from a woman's head. A red-headed woman. He was thinking about the two red-headed women he had encountered during the time Karen was missing, when there came a knock at the door.

Wexford called, 'Come in,' and Sergeant Willoughby first put his head round the door, then advanced a little sheepishly into the office. Behind him came Burden.

'The young chap I saw driving that van last night, sir,' said Willoughby, 'I knew his face was familiar, I knew I'd seen him before. Anyway, I've remembered who he is. Tony Jasper, sir. I'm certain of it.'

'And am I supposed to know who Tony Jasper is?'

Burden said quickly, 'You know his brother. His brother's Paddy Jasper.'

'Paddy Jasper went up north.'

'That's what they said,' said Burden, 'and maybe he did, but his girl friend's back living round here. You know Leilie Somers, he's lived with her on and off for years, ever since she left Stowerton Secondary Modern when she was sixteen.'

'D'you know where she's living?'

'In one of those flats over the shops in Roland Road,' said Burden.

Roland Road was in Stowerton, running behind and parallel to the High Street. Wexford's driver took him and Burden along the High Street to reach it and, looking out of the window, Wexford saw Pippa Bond's mother walking along, shop-window-gazing and pushing a pram that was higher and grander than her daughter's and of a rich dark green colour. Its occupant was presumably her grandson. Mrs Leighton was also dressed in dark green and her dyed hair looked redder than ever.

The car turned left, then right into Roland Road. The row of shops, eight of them, was surmounted by a squat upper floor of aimlessly peaked roofs and, on its façade, a useless adornment of green-painted studs and beams. The block had been put up at approximately the same period as Baron's Keep, the time which Wexford called the Great Tudor Revival. He remarked to Burden that the whole face of urban and semi-rural Britain would have been changed immeasurably for the better if architects in the third and fourth decades of the century had revived the Georgian instead of the Elizabethan. Think of it, he said, long elegant sash windows instead of poky casements, columns instead of half-timbering and pediments instead of gables. Burden didn't answer him. He had given a push to the door between the newsagent's and the pet food shop, and it gave under his hand and swung inwards.

The passage was rather dark. At the foot of the stairs was a pram from which a young woman was lifting a baby. She turned round as the light fell on her and said·

'Oh, hallo, I was just coming back to shut that. Were you wanting something?'

Burden was inspired. He said, remembering Leilie Somers's character, guessing at her hopes and fears, 'We're looking for Mrs Jasper.'

The girl knew at once whom he meant. 'Leilie's door's the one on the right at the top of the stairs.' The baby on her hip, she parked the pram a little way down the passage, pulled and fastened the cover up over it.

'Do you know if her husband's at home?'

Her reply came guilelessly up to them as they mounted the steep stairs: 'Not unless he's come back. I heard him go out at just after eight this morning.'

At the top there was a door to the left and a door to the right. Burden knocked on the right one, and it was so rapidly opened that it was apparent Leilie Somers had been listening behind it. And she wanted them inside the flat just as fast. Her neighbour was steadily coming up the stairs and Leilie knew better than to let her hear the law introducing itself or see warrant cards flashed. She was a thin little person of twenty-eight or nine with a pinched face and hennaed hair. Throughout her whole youth she had been the mistress of a man who lived by robbery and occasionally by violent crime, and she had herself been in the dock. But she had never come to adopt, as other such women adopt, an attitude of insolence or truculence towards the police. She was always polite, she was always timid, and now as Wexford said, 'So you've moved back to your old stamping ground, Leilie,' she only nodded and smiled nervously and said yes, that was right, she'd moved back, managed to get this flat which was a piece of luck.

'And Paddy with you, I gather.'

'Sometimes,' she said. 'On and off. He's not what you'd call *living* here.'

'What would I call it then? Staying here for his holidays?' Leilie made no answer. The flat seemed to consist of a living room, a bedroom, a lavatory and a kitchen with covered bath in it. They went through to the living room. The furniture in it was ugly and cheap and old but it was very clean and the woodwork and walls were fresh white. The room had been re-decorated perhaps only the week before. There was still a lingering smell of paint. 'He was here last night,' said Wexford. 'He went out around eight this morning. When's he coming back?'

She would be rid of the man if she could be. Wexford had that impression now as he had received it from her once before, years before. Some bond she couldn't break bound her to Paddy Jasper, love or merely habit, but she would be relieved if external circumstances could sever it. Meanwhile, she would be unremittingly loyal.

'What did you want to see him for?'

Two can play at that game, thought Wexford, answering questions with another question. 'Where was he last evening?'

'He was here. He had a couple of pals in playing cards and for a beer.'

'I don't suppose,' said Burden, 'that one of these pals was by any chance his little brother Tony?'

Leilie looked at the rug on the floor, up at the ceiling, then out of the window so intently that it seemed there must be at least Concorde manifesting itself up in the sky if not a flying saucer.

'Come on, Leilie, you know Tony. That nice clean-living young Englishman who did two years for mugging an old lady up in the Smoke.'

She said very quietly, now staring down at her fingers, ''Course I know Tony. I reckon he was here too, I don't know, I was out at my job.' Her voice went up a bit and her chin went up. 'I've got an evening job down the Andromeda. Cloakroom attendant, eight till midnight.'

A sign of the times, was what Wexford called the Andromeda. It was Kingsmarkham's casino, a gambling club in a spruced-up Victorian house out on the Sewingbury Road. He was going to ask why an evening job, what had happened to her full-time work — for at the time of his last encounter with Leilie she had been a stylist at Mr Nicholas, the hairdresser's — when his eye fixed itself on an object which stood on one end of the mantelpiece. It was a baby's feeding bottle with dregs of milk still in it.

'I didn't know you had a baby, Leilie,' he said.

'He's in the bedroom,' she said, and as if to confirm her words there sounded through the wall a reedy wail which quickly gained in volume. She listened. As the cries grew shrill she smiled and the smile became a laugh, a burst of laughter. Then she bit her lip and said in her usual monotone, 'Paddy and them were here babysitting for me. They were here all evening.'

'I see,' said Wexford. He knew then beyond a doubt that Paddy Jasper had not been there, that his friends had not been there, but that on the other hand they, or some of them including Jasper and his brother, had been up in Ploughman's Lane robbing Baron's

Keep. 'I see,' he said again. The baby went on crying, working itself up into a passion of rage or misery. 'Is Paddy the child's father?'

She came the nearest to rudeness she ever had. 'You've no right to ask me that, Mr Wexford. What's it to you?'

No, maybe he had no right, he thought. That ninety-nine out of a hundred policemen would have asked it was no reason why he should. 'It's nothing to me,' he said. 'I'm sorry, Leilie. You'd better go and see to him, hadn't you?'

But at that moment the crying stopped. Leilie Somers sighed. In the flat next door footsteps sounded and a door slammed. Wexford said, 'We'll be back,' and followed Leilie out into the passage. She went into the bedroom and shut herself in.

Burden let them out and closed the front door. 'That's her second child, you know,' he said as they went down the stairs. 'She had a kid by Jasper years ago.'

'Yes, I remember.' Wexford recalled Father Glanville's implied admonition and said carefully, 'Where is he or she now?'

'She's a baby batterer, is Leilie Somers. Didn't you know? No, you wouldn't. The case came up when you were ill and had all that time off.' Wexford didn't much like hearing his month's convalescence after a thrombosis described as 'all that time off' but he said nothing. 'I was amazed,' said Burden severely, 'to hear you apologizing to her as if she were a decent respectable sort of woman. She's a woman who's capable of giving a helpless baby a fractured skull and a broken arm. Those were her kid's injuries. And what did Leilie get? A suspended sentence, a recommendation for psychiatric treatment, all the nonsense.'

'What happened to the little boy?'

'He was adopted,' said Burden. 'He was quite a long time in hospital and then I heard that Leilie had agreed to have him adopted. Best thing for him.'

Wexford nodded. 'Strange, though,' he said. 'She always seems such a gentle meek creature. I can imagine her not knowing how to cope with a child or being a bit too easy-going or not noticing it was ill, say, but baby-battering – it seems so out of character.'

'You're always saying how inconsistent people are. You're always saying people are peculiar and you never can tell what they'll do next.'

'I suppose I am,' said Wexford.

He sent Loring to keep the Roland Road flat under observation, and then he and Burden went to lunch in the police station canteen. Polly Davies came up to Wexford while he was eating his dessert.

'I looked in at Bystall Lane, sir, and saw young Ginger. They said, did we think of making other arrangements for him or were they to keep him for a bit?'

'My God, they haven't had him twenty-four hours yet.'

'That's what I said, sir. Well, I sort of said that. I think they're short-staffed.'

'So are we,' said Wexford. 'Now then, I don't suppose anyone saw Karen Bond being put on that doorstep?'

'I'm afraid not, sir. No one I've spoken to, anyway, and no one's come forward. Mrs Bream who housekeeps for the priest, she says the cardboard box – the Smith's Crisps box, you know – was there when she came at nine only she didn't look at it. She thought it was something someone had left for the father and she was going to take it in once she'd got the kitchen cleared up and his bed made. Father Glanville says he went out at ten to nine and he's positive the box wasn't there then, so someone must have put it there in those ten minutes. It looks like someone who knows their habits, the father's and Mrs Bream's, doesn't it, sir?'

'One of his flock, d'you mean?'

'It could be. Why not?'

'If you're right,' said Wexford dryly, 'whoever it was is probably confessing it at this moment and Father Glanville will, of course, have to keep her identity locked in his bosom.'

He went off up to his office to await word from Loring. There, sitting at his desk, thinking, he remembered noticing in Susan Rains's flat, honoured on a little shelf fixed there for the purpose, a plaster statuette of the Virgin with lilies in her arms. The Leightons were perhaps a Catholic family. He was on the point of deciding to go back to Greenhill Court for a further talk with Susan Rains when a phone call from Sergeant Camb announced the arrival of Stephen Pollard.

The stockbroker and his wife had been on holiday in Scotland and had driven all the way back, non-stop, all five hundred and forty miles, starting at six that morning. Wexford had met Pollard once before and remembered him as a choleric person. Now he was tired from the long drive but he still rampaged and shouted with as much misery as Pippa Bond had shown over the loss of her baby. The safe, it appeared, had contained a sapphire and platinum necklace and bracelet, four rings, three cameos and a diamond cross which Pollard said were worth thirty thousand pounds. No, of course no one knew he had a safe in which he kept valuables. Well, he supposed the cleaning woman did and the cleaning woman before her and all of the series of *au pair* girls, and maybe the builders who had painted the outside of the house, and the firm who had put up the bars.

'It's ludicrous,' said Burden when he had gone. 'All that carry-on when it's a dead cert his insurance company'll fork out. He might as well go straight back to Scotland. We're the people who've got the slog and we'll get stick if those villains aren't caught, while it won't make a scrap of difference to him one way or the other. And I'll tell you another thing that's ludicrous,' he said, warming to a resentful theme. 'The ratepayers of Sussex could have the expense of young Ginger's upbringing for eighteen years because his mother's too scared to come and claim him.'

'What shall I do about it? Hold a young wives' meeting and draw them a chalk circle?'

Burden looked bewildered.

'Haven't you ever heard of the Chinese chalk circle and Brecht's *Caucasian Chalk Circle*? You have to draw a circle in chalk on the ground and put the child in it, and of the mothers who claim him the one who can pull him out of the circle is his true mother and may have him.'

'That's all very well,' said Burden after a pause, 'but in this case, it's not mothers who want him, it's he who wants a mother. No one seems to want him.'

'Poor Ginger,' said Wexford, and then the phone rang. It was Loring on his radio to say Paddy Jasper had come into Roland Road and gone up the stairs to Leilie Somers's flat.

By the time Wexford and Burden got there Tony Jasper had arrived as well. The brothers were both tall, heavily built men but Tony's figure still had a youthfully athletic look about it while Paddy had the beginnings of a paunch. Tony's otherwise handsome appearance was ruined by a broken nose which had never been put right and through which he had difficulty in breathing. The repulsive and even sinister air he had was partly due to his always breathing through his mouth. Paddy and he were sitting facing each other at Leilie's living-room table. They were both smoking, the air in the room was thick with smoke, and Tony was dealing a pack of cards. Wexford thought the cards were the inspiration of the moment, hastily fetched out when they heard the knock at the downstairs door.

'Put the cards away, Tone,' said Paddy. 'It's rude to play when we've got company.' He was always polite in a thoroughly offensive way. 'Leilie here,' he said, 'has got something in her head about you wanting to know where I was last evening. Like what sort of time did you have in mind?'

Wexford told him. Paddy smiled. Somehow he managed to make it a paternal smile. He was stopping a few days with Leilie, he said, and his son. He hadn't seen much of his son since the child was born on account of having this good job up north but not a chance of accommodation for a woman and a kid, no way. So he'd come down for his holidays the previous Saturday and what does he hear but that Leilie's got this evening job up the Andromeda. Well, she'd taken Monday night off to be with him and done an exchange with another girl for Tuesday, but when it got to last night she couldn't very well skive off again so he said not to worry, he'd babysit, him and Tony here, and they'd have some of their old mates round. Johnny Farrow and Pip Monkton, for a beer and a hand of solo.

'Which is what we did, Mr Wexford.'

'Right,' said Tony.

'Leilie put Matthew in his cot and then the boys came round and she got us a bite to eat. She's a good girl is Leilie. She went off to work about half seven, didn't you, love? Then we did the dishes and had our game. Oh, and the lady next door came round to check up if four grown men could look after baby OK, very kind of her, I'm sure. And then at half eleven Pip went off home on account of his missus being the boss round his place, and at quarter past twelve Leilie came back. She got a lift so she was early. That's right, isn't it, love?'

Leilie nodded. 'Except you never did no dishes.'

Wexford kept looking at the man's huge feet which were no longer under the table but splayed out across the cheap bright bit of carpet. He wondered where the shoes were that had made those prints. Burnt, probably. The remains of the safe, once they had blown it open, might be in any pond or river in the Home Counties. Johnny Farrow was a notorious peterman or expert with explosives. He turned to Leilie and asked a question perhaps none of them had expected.

'Who usually looks after the baby when you're working?'

'Julie next door. That girl you were talking to when you came earlier. I used to take him to my mum, my mum lives up Charteris

207

Road, it's not very far, but he started getting funny in the evenings, crying and screaming, and he got worse if I took him out and left him in a strange place.' Wexford wondered if she was giving him such a detailed answer to his question because she sometimes left the baby unattended and thought she might be breaking the law. He remembered the other boy, the one with the fractured skull and broken arm, and he hardened towards her. 'Then Mum had to go into hospital, anyway, she only came out yesterday. So Julie said to leave him here and she'd pop in every half hour, and she'd hear him anyway if he cried. You can hear a pin drop through these walls. And Julie never goes out on account of she's got a baby of her own. She's been very good has Julie because I reckon Matthew does cry most evenings, and you can't just leave them to cry, can you?'

'I'm glad to inform you, my dear,' said Paddy with outrageous pomposity, 'that my son did not utter a squeak last evening but was as good as gold,' and on the last word he looked hard at Wexford and stretched his lips into a huge humourless smile.

Julie Lang confirmed that Paddy Jasper, Tony Jasper, Pip Monkton and Johnny Farrow had all been in the flat next door when she called to check on the safety and comfort of Matthew at eight-thirty. She had a key to Leilie's flat but she hadn't used it, knowing Mr Jasper to be there. She wouldn't have dreamt of doing that because it was Mr Jasper's home really, wasn't it? So she had knocked at the door and Mr Jasper had let her in and not been very nice about it actually, and she had felt very awkward especially when he'd said, go in and see for yourself if I'm not to be trusted to look after my own child. He had opened the bedroom door and made her look and she had just glanced at the cot and seen Matthew was all right and sleeping.

'Well, I felt so bad about it,' said Julie Lang, 'that I said to him, perhaps he'd like the key back, and he said, yes, he'd been going to ask me for it as they wouldn't be needing my services any longer, thanks very much. He was quite rude really but I did feel bad about it.'

She had given Paddy Jasper the key. As far as she knew, the four men had remained in the flat with Matthew till Leilie got back at twelve-fifteen. By then, anyway, her husband had come home and they were both in bed asleep. No, she had heard no footsteps on the stairs, not even those of Pip Monkton going home at eleven-thirty. Of course she had had the television on so maybe she wouldn't have heard, but she was positive there hadn't been a sound out of Matthew.

Wexford and Burden went next to the home of Pip Monkton. Johnny Farrow's confirmation of the alibi would amount to very little, for he had a long criminal record for safebreaking, but Monkton had never been convicted of anything, had never even been charged with anything. He was an ex-publican, apparently perfectly respectable, and the only blot on his white innocent life was his known friendship with Farrow with whom he had been at school and whom he had supported and stuck to during Farrow's long prison sentences and periods of poverty-stricken idleness. If Monkton said that the four of them had been together all that evening babysitting in Leilie Somers's flat, Wexford knew he might as well throw up the sponge. The judge, the jury, the court, would believe Pip Monkton just as they would believe Julie Lang.

And Monkton did say it. Looking Wexford straight in the eye (so that the chief inspector knew he must be lying) he declared boldly that he and the Jaspers and Johnny had been in Roland Road, playing solo and drinking beer, until he left for home at half-past eleven. Wexford had him down to the police station and went on asking him about it, but he couldn't break him down. Monkton sounded as if he had learnt by heart what he had to say, and he went on saying it over and over again like a talking bird or a record on which the needle has got stuck.

When it got to six Wexford had himself driven to the Andromeda where the manager, who had an interest in keeping on the right side of the police, answered his questions very promptly. He got back to the station to find Burden and Polly discussing the one relevant piece of information Burden had succeeded in finding out about Monkton – that he had recently had an extension built on to his house. To cover the cost of this he had taken out a second mortgage, but the costs had come to three thousand pounds more than the builder's estimate.

'That'll be about what Monkton's getting for perjury,' said Burden. 'That'll be his share. Tony drove the van, Paddy and Johnny did the job while Monkton covers for them. I imagine they left Leilie's place around nine and got to Ploughman's Lane by a quarter past. They'll have got the safe out in an hour and got to the gate in the fence with it by ten-thirty, which was just about the time Willoughby spotted the van. Tony drove off, ditched the van in Myringham, came back to Stowerton on the last bus, the one that leaves Myringham at ten past eleven and which would have got him to Stowerton High Street by ten to twelve. God knows how the others got that safe back. My guess is that they didn't. They hid it in one of the meadows at the back of Ploughman's Lane and went back for it this morning – with Johnny Farrow's car. Then Johnny blew it. They used the wheels again and Johnny blew it somewhere up on the downs.'

Wexford hadn't spoken for some minutes. Now he said, 'When Leilie Somers was charged with this baby-battering thing, did she plead guilty or not guilty?'

Rather surprised by the apparent irrelevance of this question, Burden said. 'Guilty. There wasn't much evidence offered apart from the doctor's. Leilie pleaded guilty and said something about being tired and strained and not being able to stand it when the baby cried. Damned disgraceful nonsense.'

'Yes, it was damned disgraceful nonsense,' said Wexford quietly, and then he said, 'The walls in those flats are very thin, aren't they? So thin that from one side you can hear a pin drop on the other.' He was silent and meditative for a moment. 'What was Leilie Somers's mother's maiden name?'

'*What?*' said Burden. 'How on earth do you expect me to know a thing like that?'

'I just thought you might. I thought it might be an Irish name, you see. Because Leilie is probably short for Eileen, which is an Irish name. I expect she called herself Leilie when she was too young to pronounce her name properly.'

Burden said with an edge of impatience to his voice, 'Look, do I get to know what all this is leading up to?'

'Sure you do. The arrest of Paddy and Tony Jasper and Johnny Farrow. You can get down to Roland Road and see to it as soon as you like.'

'For God's sake, you know as well as I do we'll never make it stick. We couldn't break Monkton and he'll alibi the lot of them.'

'That'll be OK,' said Wexford laconically. 'Trust me. Believe me, there is no alibi. And now, Polly, you and I will turn our attention to the matter of young Ginger and the Kingsmarkham Chalk Circle.'

Wexford left Polly sitting outside in the car. It was eight o'clock and still light. He rang the bell that had fetched Leilie down that afternoon, and when she didn't come he rang the other. Julie Lang appeared.

'She's upset. I've got her in with me having a cup of tea.'

'I'd like to see her, Mrs Lang, and I'll need to see her alone. I'll go and sit in my car for five minutes and then if she'll . . .'

Leilie Somers's voice from the top of the stairs cut off the end of his sentence. 'You can come up. I'm OK now.'

Wexford climbed the stairs towards her, Julie Lang following him. Leilie stood back to let him pass. She seemed smaller than ever, thinner, meeker, her hennaed hair showing a paler red at the roots, her face white and deeply sad. Julie Lang put her hand on her arm, squeezed it, went off quickly into her own flat. Leilie put the key into the lock of her front door and opened the door and stood looking at the empty neat place, the passage, the open doors into the other rooms, now all made more melancholy by the encroaching twilight. Tears stood in her eyes and she turned her face so that Wexford should not see them fall.

'He's not worth it, Leilie,' said Wexford.

'I know *that*, I know what he's worth. But you won't get me being disloyal to him, Mr Wexford, I shan't say a word.'

'Let's go in and sit down.' He made his way to the table where it was lightest and sat down in the chair Tony Jasper had sat in. 'Where's the baby?'

'With my mum.'

'Rather much for someone who's just come out of hospital, isn't it?' Wexford looked at his watch. 'You're going to be late for work. What time is it you start? Eight-thirty?'

'Eight,' she said. 'I'm not going. I couldn't, not after what's happened to Paddy. Mr Wexford, you might as well go. I'm not going to say anything. If I was Paddy's wife you couldn't make me say anything, and I'm as good as his wife, I've been more to him than most wives'd have been.'

'I know that, Leilie,' said Wexford, 'I know all about that,' and his voice was so loaded with meaning that she stared at him with frightened eyes whose whites shone in the dusk. 'Leilie,' he said, 'when they drew the chalk circle and put the child in it the girl who had brought him up refused to pull him out because she knew she would hurt him. Rather than hurt him she preferred that someone else should have him.'

'I don't know what you're talking about,' she said.

'I think you do. It's not so different from Solomon's judgement of cutting the baby in half. The child's mother wouldn't have that happen, better let the other woman have him. You pleaded guilty in court to crimes against your first son you had never committed. It was Jasper who injured that child, and it was Jasper who got you to take the blame because he knew you would get a light sentence whereas he would get a heavy one. And afterwards you had the baby adopted – not because you didn't love him but because like the chalk circle woman you would rather lose him than have him hurt again. Isn't it true?'

She stared at him. Her head moved, a tiny affirmative bob. Wexford leaned across to the window and opened it. He waved his hand out of the window, withdrew it and closed the casement again. Leilie was crying, making no attempt to dry her tears.

'Were you brought up as a Catholic?' he said.

'I was baptized,' she said in a voice not much above a whisper. 'Mum's a Catholic. Her and Dad, they got married in Galway where Mum comes from, and Dad had to promise to bring the kids up Catholic.' A sob caught her throat. 'I haven't been to mass for years. Mr Wexford, please go away now and leave me alone. I just want to be left alone.'

He said, 'I'm sorry to hear you say that because I've got a visitor for you, and he'll certainly be staying the night.' He switched on lights, the living-room light, the light in the hall and one over the top of the door, and then he opened the door and Polly Davies walked in with young Ginger in her arms.

Leilie blinked at the light. She closed her eyes and lowered her head, and then she lifted it and opened her eyes and made a sort of bound for Polly, nearly knocking Wexford over. But she didn't snatch Ginger. She stood trembling, looking at Polly, her hands moving slowly forward until, with an extreme gentle tenderness, they closed over and caressed the baby's downy red-gold head.

'Matthew,' she said. 'Matthew.'

The baby lay in Leilie's lap. He had whimpered a little at first, but now he lay quiet and relaxed, gripping one of her fingers, and for the first time in their acquaintance Wexford saw him smile. It was a beautiful spontaneous smile of happiness at being home again with Mother.

'You're going to tell me all about it, aren't you, Leilie?' said Wexford.

She was transformed. He had never seen her so animated, so high-spirited. She was giggly with joy so that Matthew, sensing her mood, gurgled in response, and she hugged him again, calling him her lovely lovely sweetheart, her precious boy.

'Come on now, Leilie,' said Wexford, 'you've got him back without the least trouble to yourself which is more than you damn' well deserve. Now you can give an account of yourself.'

'I don't know where to start,' said Leilie, giggling.

'At the beginning, whenever that is.'

'Well, the beginning,' said Leilic, 'I reckon was when Patrick, my first boy, was adopted.' She had stopped laughing and a little of the old melancholy had come back into her face. 'That was four years ago. Paddy went off up north and after a bit he wrote and said would I join him, and I don't know why I said yes, I reckon I always do say yes to Paddy, and there didn't seem anything else, there didn't seem any future. It was all right with Paddy for a bit, and then a couple of years back he got this other girl. I sort of pretended I didn't know about it, I thought he'd get tired of her, but he didn't and I was lonely, I was so lonely. I didn't know a soul up there but Paddy, not like I could talk to, and he'd go away for weeks on end. I sort of took to going out with other fellas, anyone, I didn't care, just for the company.' She paused, shifted Matthew on her knees. 'When I knew I was pregnant I told Paddy I wasn't having the baby up there, I was going home to Mum. But he said to stay and he wouldn't see the other girl, and I did stay till after Matthew was born, and then I knew he was carrying on again so I came back here and Mum got me this flat. I know what you're going to say, Mr Wexford!'

'I wasn't going to say a word.'

'You were thinking it. So what? It's true. I couldn't tell you who Matthew's father is, I don't know. It might be Paddy, it might be one of half a dozen.' Her expression had grown fierce. She almost glared at him. 'And I'm glad I don't know, I'm glad. It makes him more mine. I never went out with any other fella but Paddy till he drove me to it.'

'All right,' said Wexford, 'all right. So you lived here with Matthew and you had your job at the Andromeda and then Paddy wrote to say he was coming down, and on Saturday he did come. And you took Monday evening off work to be with him and exchanged your Tuesday turn with another girl — and so we come to Wednesday, yesterday.'

Leilie sighed. She didn't seem unhappy, only rueful. 'Paddy said he'd babysit. He said he'd asked Tony over and Johnny and a fella called Pip Monkton, and they'd be in all evening. I said he wasn't to bother, I could take Matthew next door into Julie's, and Paddy got mad at me and said Julie was an interfering bitch and didn't I trust him to look after his own child? Well, that was it, I didn't, I kept remembering what he'd done to Patrick, and that was because Patrick cried. Paddy used to go crazy when he cried, I used to think he'd kill

213

him, and when I tried to stop him he nearly killed me. And, you see, Mr Wexford, Matthew'd got into this way of crying in the evenings. They said at the clinic some babies cry at night and some in the evenings and it's hard to know why, but they all grow out of it. I knew Matthew'd start screaming about eight and I thought, my God, what'll Paddy do? He gets in a rage, he doesn't know what he's doing, and Tony wouldn't stop him, he's scared of him like they all are, Paddy's so big. Well, I got in a real state. Mum'd come out of hospital that morning, she'd had a major op, so I couldn't take him there and go back there myself and hide from Paddy, and I couldn't take him to work. I did once and they made a hell of a fuss. I just couldn't see any way out of it.

'Paddy went out about eleven. He never said where he was going and I didn't ask. Anyway, I went out too, carrying Matthew in the baby carrier, and I just walked about thinking. I reckon I must have walked miles, worrying about it and wondering what to do and imagining all sorts of things, you know how you do. I'd been feeding Matthew myself and I'm still giving him one feed a day, so I took him into a field and fed him under a hedge, and after that I walked a bit more.

'Well, I was coming back along the Stowerton Road. I knew I'd have to go home on account of Matthew was wet and he'd soon be hungry again, and then I saw this pram. I knew who it belonged to, I'd seen it there before and I'd seen this girl lift her baby out of it. I mean, I didn't know her name or anything but I'd talked to her once queuing for the check-out in the Tesco, and we'd got talking about our babies and she said hers never cried except sometimes for a feed in the night. She was such a good baby, they never got a peep out of her all day and all evening. She was a bit younger than Matthew but it was funny, they looked a bit alike and they'd got just the same colour hair.

'That was what gave me the idea, them having the same colour hair. I know I was mad, Mr Wexford, I know that now. I was crazy, but you don't know how scared of Paddy I was. I went over to that pram and I bent over it. I unhooked the cat net and took the other baby out and put Matthew in.'

Until now quite silent in her corner, Polly Davies gave a suppressed exclamation. Wexford drew in his breath, shaking his head.

'It's interesting,' he said, and his voice was frosty, 'how I supposed at first that whoever had taken Karen Bond wanted her and wished to be rid of her own child. Now it looks as if the reverse was true. It looks as if she didn't at all mind sacrificing Karen for her own child's safety.'

Leilie said passionately, 'That's not true!'

'No, perhaps it isn't, I believe you did have second thoughts. Go on.'

'I put Matthew in the pram. I knew he'd be all right, I knew no one'd hurt him, but it went to my heart when he started to cry.'

'Weren't you afraid someone would see you?' asked Polly.

'I wouldn't have cared if they had. Don't you see? I was past caring for any of that. If I'd been seen I wouldn't have had to go home, I'd have lost my job, but they wouldn't have taken Matthew from me, would they? No one saw me. Did you say her name was Karen? Well, I took Karen home and I fed her and bathed her. No one can say I didn't look after her like she was my own.'

'Except for delivering her into the hands of that ravening wolf, Paddy Jasper,' said Wexford unpleasantly.

She shivered a little but otherwise she took no notice. 'Paddy came in at six with Tony. The baby was in Matthew's cot by then. All you could see was its red hair like Matthew's. I remembered what that girl had said about her never crying in the evenings, and I thought, I prayed, don't cry tonight, don't cry because you're in a strange place.' Leilie lifted her head and began to speak more rapidly. 'I cooked egg and chips for the lot of them and I went out at half seven. I got back at a quarter past twelve and she was OK, she was fast asleep and she hadn't cried at all.'

Wexford said softly, 'Haven't you forgotten something, Leilie?'

Her eyes darted over him. He fancied she had grown a little paler. She picked up Matthew and held him closely against her. 'Well, the next day,' she said. 'Today. Paddy went off out early so I thought about getting the baby back. I thought of taking her to the priest. I knew about the priest, when he went out and when the lady cleaner came, I knew about it from Mum. So I got on the bus to Kingsmarkham and just by the bus stop's a shop where they'd put all their boxes out on the pavement for the dustmen. I took a box and put the baby in and left her on the doorstep of the priest's house. But I didn't know how I was going to get Matthew back, I thought I'd never get him back.

'And then you came. I said Matthew was in the bedroom and just then Julie's baby started crying and you thought it was Matthew. I couldn't help laughing, though I felt I was going to pieces, I was being torn apart. And that's all, that's everything, and now you can charge me with whatever it is I've done.'

'But you've forgotten something, Leilie.'

'I don't know what you mean,' she said.

'Of course you do. Why d'you think I had Paddy and Tony and Johnny Farrow arrested even though Pip Monkton had given them all a cast-iron alibi? How do you think I know Pip will break down and tell me that tale of his was all moonshine and tell me as well just where the contents of that safe are now? I had a little talk with the management of the Andromeda this afternoon, Leilie.'

She gave him a stony stare.

'You've got the sack, haven't you?' he said. 'Work out your notice till the end of next week or go now. They were bound to catch you out.'

'If you know all about it, Mr Wexford, why ask?'

'Because I want you to say yes.'

She whispered something to the baby, but the baby had fallen asleep.

'If you won't tell me, I shall tell you,' said Wexford, 'and if I get it wrong you can stop me. I'm going to tell you about those second thoughts you had, Leilie. You went off to work like you said but you weren't easy in your mind. You kept thinking about that baby, that other baby, that good baby that never cried in the evenings. But maybe the reason she didn't cry was that she was usually in her own bed, safe and secure in her own home with her own mother, maybe it'd be different if she woke up to find herself in a strange place. So you started worrying. You ran around that glorified ladies' loo where you work, wiping the basins and filling the towel machines and taking your ten pence tips, but you were going off your head with worry about that other baby. You kept thinking of her crying and what that animal Paddy Jasper might do to her if she cried, punch her with his great fists perhaps or bash her head against the wall. And then you knew you hadn't done anything so clever after all in swapping Matthew for her, because you're a kind loving woman at heart, Leilie, though you're a fool, and you were as worried about her as you'd have been about him.'

'And you're a devil,' whispered Leilie, staring at him as if he had supernatural powers. 'How d'you know what I thought?'

'I just know,' said Wexford. 'I know what you thought and I know what you did. When it got to half-past nine you couldn't stand it any longer. You put on your coat and ran out to catch the nine-thirty-five bus and you were home, walking up those stairs, by five to ten. There were lights on in the flat. You let yourself in and went straight into the bedroom, and Karen was in there, safe and sound and fast asleep.'

Leilie smiled a little. A ghost of a smile of happy recollection crossed her face and was gone. 'I don't know how you know,' she said, 'but yes, she was OK and asleep, and oh God, the relief of it. I'd been picturing her lying there with blood on her and I don't know what.'

'So all you had to do then was explain to Paddy why you'd come home.'

'I told him I felt ill,' said Leilie carefully. 'I said I felt rotten and I'd got one of my migraines coming.'

'No, you didn't. He wasn't there.'

'What d'you mean, wasn't there? He was there! Him and Tony and Pip and Johnny, they were in here playing cards. I said to Paddy, I feel rotten, I had to come home. I'm going to have a lay-down, I said, and I went into the bedroom and laid down.'

'Leilie, when you came in the flat was empty. You know it was empty. You know Pip Monkton's lying and you know his story won't stand up for two seconds once you tell the truth that at *five to ten this flat was empty*. Listen to me, Leilie. Paddy will go away for quite a long time over this business. It'll be a chance for you and young Ginge – er, Matthew, to make a new life. You don't want him round you for ever, do you? Ruining your life, beating up your kids? Do you, Leilie?'

She lifted the baby in her arms. She walked the length of the room and half back again as if he were restless and needed soothing instead of peacefully asleep. In front of Wexford she stood still, looking at him, and he got to his feet.

'We'll come and fetch you in the morning, Leilie,' he said, 'and take you to the police station where I'll want you to make a statement. Maybe two statements. One about taking Karen and one about Paddy not being here when you came back last night.'

'I won't say a thing about that,' she said.

'It might be that we wouldn't proceed with any charge against you for taking Karen.'

'I don't care about that!'

He hated doing it. He knew he had to. 'A woman who knew what you knew about Paddy and who still exposed a child to him, someone else's child – how'll that sound in court, Leilie? When they know you're living with Paddy again? And when they hear your record?'

Her face had gone white and she clasped Matthew against her. 'They wouldn't take him away from me? They wouldn't make a what-d'you-call-it?'

'A care order? They might.'

'Oh God, oh God. I promised myself I'd stick by Paddy all my life . . .'

'Romantic promises, Leilie, they haven't much to do with real life.' Wexford moved a little away from her. He went to the window. It was quite dark outside now. 'They told me at the Andromeda that you came back at half-past ten. You'd been away an hour and there had been complaints so they sacked you.'

She said feverishly, 'I did go back. I told Paddy I felt better, I . . .'

'All in the space of five minutes? Or ten at the most? You were quickly ill and well, Leilie. Shall I tell you why you went back, shall I tell you the only circumstances in which you'd have dared go back? You didn't want to lose your job but you were more afraid of what Paddy might do to the baby. If Paddy had been there the one thing you wouldn't have done is go back. Because he wasn't there you went back with a light heart. You believed he could only get in again when you were there to let him in. You didn't know then that he had a key, the key he had taken from Julie Lang.'

She spoke at last the word he had been waiting for. 'Yes.' She nodded. 'Yes, it's true. If I'd known he had that key,' she said, and she shivered, 'I'd no more have gone and left that baby there than I'd have left it in the lion house at the zoo.'

'We'll be on our way,' he said. 'Come along, Constable Davies. See you in the morning, Leilie.'

Still holding Matthew, she came up to him just as he reached the door and laid a hand on his sleeve. 'I've been thinking about what you said, Mr Wexford,' she said, 'and I don't think I'd be able to pull anybody's baby, *any* baby, out of that circle.'

Achilles Heel

The walls of the city afforded on one side a view of the blue Adriatic, on the other, massed roofs, tiled in weathered terracotta, and cataracts of stone streets descending to the cathedral and the Stradun Placa. It was very hot on the walls, the sun hard and the air dry and clear. Among the red-brown roofs and the complexities of ramparts and stairs, different colours shimmered, the purple of the bougainvillaea, the sky blue of the plumbago, and the flame flash of the orange trumpet flower.

'Lovely,' said Dora Wexford. 'Breathtaking. Aren't you glad now I made you come up here?'

'It's all right for you dark-skinned people,' grumbled her husband. 'My nose is beginning to feel like a fried egg.'

'We'll go down at the next lot of steps and you can administer some more sun cream over a glass of beer.'

It was noon, the date Saturday, 18 June. The full heat of the day had kept the Yugoslavs, but not the tourists, off the walls. Germans went by with cameras or stood murmuring, *'Wunderschön!'* Vivacious Italians chattered, unaffected by the midsummer sun. But some of the snatches of talk which reached Wexford were in languages not only incomprehensible but unidentifiable. It was a surprise to hear English spoken.

'Don't keep on about it, Iris!'

At first they couldn't see the speaker. But now, as they came out of the narrow defile and emerged on to one of the broad jutting courts made by a buttress top, they came face to face with the Englishman. A tall, fair young man, he was standing in the furthest angle of the court, and with him was a dark-haired girl. Her back was to the Wexfords. She was staring out to sea. From her clothes, she looked as if she would have been more at home in the South of France than on the walls of Dubrovnik. She wore a jade-green halter top that left her deeply tanned midriff bare, and a calf-length silk skirt in green and blue with parabolas on it of flamingo pink. Her sandals were pink, the strings criss-crossed up her legs, the wedge heels high. But perhaps the most striking thing about her was her hair. Raven black and very short, it was cut at the nape in three sharp Vs.

She must have replied to her companion, though Wexford hadn't heard the words. But now, without turning round, she stamped her foot and the man said:

'How can you go to the bloody place, Iris, when we can't find anyone to take us? There's nowhere to land. I wish to God you'd give it a rest.'

Dora took her husband's arm, hastening him along. He could read her thoughts, not to eavesdrop on someone else's quarrel.

'You're so nosy, darling,' she said when they had reached the steps and were out of earshot. 'I suppose it's what comes of being a policeman.'

Wexford laughed. 'I'm glad you realize that's the reason. Any other man's wife would accuse him of looking at that girl.'

'She *was* beautiful, wasn't she?' said Dora wistfully, conscious of her age. 'Of course we couldn't see her face, but you could tell she had a perfect figure.'

'Except for the legs. Pity she hasn't got the sense to wear trousers.'

'Oh, Reg, what was wrong with her legs? And she was so beautifully tanned. When I see a girl like that it makes me feel such an old has-been.'

'Don't be so daft,' said Wexford crossly. 'You look fine.' He meant it. He was proud of his handsome wife, so young-looking for her late fifties, elegant and decorous in navy skid and crisp white blouse, her skin already golden after only two days of holiday. 'And I'll tell you one thing,' he added. 'You'd beat her hollow in any ankle competition.'

Dora smiled at him, comforted. They sat down at a table in a pavement café where the shade was deep and a cool breeze blew. Just time for a beer and an orange juice, and then to catch the water taxi back down the coast to Mirna.

In Serbo-Croat *mirna* means peaceful. And so Wexford found the resort after a gruelling winter and spring in Kingsmarkham, after petty crime and serious crime, and finally a squalid murder case which had been solved, not by him in spite of his work and research, but by a young expert from Scotland Yard. It was Mike Burden who had advised him to get right away for his holiday. Not Wales or Cornwall this time, but the Dalmatian coast of Yugoslavia where he, Burden, had taken his children the previous year.

'Mirna,' said Burden. 'There are three good hotels but the village is quite unspoilt. You can go everywhere by water. Two or three old chaps run taxi boats. It never rained once while we were there. And you're into all this nature stuff, this ecology. The marine life's amazing and so are the flowers and butterflies.'

It was the marine life with which Wexford was getting acquainted two mornings after the trip to Dubrovnik. He had left Dora prone on an air bed by the hotel swimming pool, knowing full well that sunbathing was impossible for his Anglo-Saxon skin. Already his nose was peeling. So he had anointed his face, put on a long-sleeved shirt, and walked round the wooded point to Mirna harbour. The little port had a harbour wall built of the same stone as the city of Dubrovnik, and kneeling down to peer over, he saw that beneath the water line the rocks and masonry were thickly covered by a tapestry of sea anemones and tiny shells and flowering weed and starfishes. The water was perfectly clear and unpolluted. He could clearly see the bottom, fifteen feet down, and now a shoal of silvery-brown fish glided out from a sea-bed bush. Fascinated, he leaned over, understanding why so many swimmers out there were equipped with goggles and schnorkels. A scarlet fish darted out from a rock, then a broad silver one, banded with black.

Behind him, a voice said, 'You like it?'

Wexford got up on to his haunches. The man who had spoken was older than he, skinny and wrinkled and tough-looking. He had a walnut face, a dry smile and surprisingly good teeth. He wore a sailor's cap and a blue and white striped tee-shirt, and Wexford recognized him as one of the taxi boatmen.

He replied slowly and carefully, 'I like it very much. It is pretty, beautiful.'

'The shores of your country were like this once. But in the nineteenth century a man called Gosse, a marine biologist, wrote a book about them and within a few years collectors had come and divested the rocks of everything.'

Wexford couldn't help laughing. 'Good God,' he said. 'I beg your pardon, but I thought . . .'

'That an old boatman can say "please" and "zank you" and "ten dinara"?'

'Something like that.' Wexford got up to stand inches taller than the other man. 'You speak remarkable English.'

A broad smile. 'No, it is too pedantic. I have only once been to England and that many years ago.' He put out his hand. 'How do you do, *gospodine*? Ivo Racic at your service.'

'Reginald Wexford.'

The hand was iron hard but the grip gentle. Racic said, 'I do not wish to intrude. I spoke to you because it is rare to find a tourist interested in nature. With most it is only the sunbathing and the food and drink, eh? Or to catch the fish and take the shells.'

'Come and have a drink,' said Wexford, 'or are you working?'

'Josip and Mirko and I, we have a little syndicate, and they will not mind if I have a half an hour off. But I buy the drinks. This is my country and you are my guest.'

They walked towards the avenue of stout palm trees. 'I was born here in Mirna,' said Racic. 'At eighteen I left for the university and when I retired and came back here after forty years and more, those palm trees were just the same, no bigger, no different. Nothing was changed till they built the hotels.'

'What did you do in those forty years? Not run a boat service?'

'I was professor of Anglo-Saxon studies at the University of Beograd, Gospodin Wexford.'

'Ah,' said Wexford, 'all is made plain. And when you retired you took up with Josip and Mirko to run the water taxis. Perhaps they were childhood friends?'

'They were. I see you have perspicacity. And may I enquire in return what is your occupation?'

Wexford said what he always said on holiday, 'I'm a civil servant.'

Racic smiled. 'Here in Yugoslavia we are all civil servants. But let us go for our drinks. *Hajdemo, drug!*'

They chose a cluster of tables set under a vine-covered canopy, through which the sun made a gentle dappling on cobbles. Racic drank *slivovic*. The fiery brandy with its hinted undertaste of plums was forbidden to Wexford who had to watch his blood pressure. He even felt guilty when the white wine called Posip which Racic ordered for him arrived in a tumbler filled to the brim.

'You live here in Mirna?'

'Here alone in my *kucica* that was once my father's house. My wife died in Beograd. But it is a good and pleasant life. I have my pension and my boat and the grapes I grow and the figs, and sometimes a guest like yourself, Gospodin Wexford, on whom to practise my English.'

Wexford would have liked to question him about the political regime, but he felt that this might be unwise and perhaps discourteous. So instead he remarked on the stately appearance of a woman in national costume, white coif, heavily embroidered stiff black dress, who had emerged with a full basket from the grocer's shop. Racic nodded, then pointed a brown thumb to a table outside the shadow of the vines.

'That is better, I think. Healthier, eh? And freer.'

She was sitting in the full sun, a young woman with short black hair geometrically cut, who wore only a pair of white shorts and jade-green halter top. A man came out of the currency exchange bureau, she got up to meet him, and Wexford recognized them as the couple he had seen on the walls of Dubrovnik. They went off hand in hand and got into a white Lancia Gamma parked under the palms.

'Last time I saw them they were quarrelling.'

'They are staying at the Hotel Bosnia,' said Racic. 'On Sunday evening they drove here from Dubrovnik and they are going to remain for a week. Her name I cannot tell you, but his is Philip.'

'May I ask how you come to be such a mine of information, Mr Racic?'

'They came out in my boat this morning.' Racic's dark bright eyes twinkled. 'Just the two of them, to be ferried across to Vrt and back. But let me tell you a little story. Once, about a year ago, a young English couple hired my boat. They were, I think, on their wedding journey, their honeymoon, as you say, and it was evident they were much in love. They had no eyes but for each other and certainly no inclination to speak to the boatman. We were coming into the shore here, perhaps a hundred metres out, when the young husband began telling his wife how much he loved her and how he could hardly wait to get back to the hotel to make love to her. Oh, very frank and explicit he was – and why not with only the old Yugoslav there who speaks nothing but his own outlandish tongue?

'I said nothing. I betrayed nothing in my face. We pulled in, he paid me twenty dinars and they walked off up the quay. Then I saw the young lady had left her bag behind and I called to her. She came back, took it and thanked me. Gospodin Wexford, I could not resist it. "You have a charming husband, madame," I said, "but no more than you deserve." Oh, how she blushed, but I think she was not displeased, though they never came in my boat again.'

Laughing, Wexford said, 'It was hardly a similar conversation you overheard between Philip and his wife, though?'

'No.' Racic looked thoughtful. 'I think I will not tell you what I overheard. It is no business of ours. And now I must make my excuses, but we shall meet again.'

'In your boat, certainly. I must take my wife over to Vrt for the bathing.'

'Better than that. Bring your wife and I will take you for a trip round the islands. On Wednesday? No, I'm not touting for custom. This will be a trip — now for a good colloquial expression — on the house! You and me and Gospoda Wexford.'

'Those very nice Germans,' said Dora, 'have asked us to go with them in their car to Cetinje on Wednesday.'

'Mm,' said Wexford absently. 'Good idea.' It was nine o'clock but very dark beyond the range of the waterside lights. They had walked into Mirna after dinner, it being too late for the taxi boats, and were having coffee on the terrace of a restaurant at the harbour edge. The nearly tideless Adriatic lapped the stones at their feet with soft gulping sounds.

Suddenly he remembered. 'Oh, God, I can't. I promised that Yugoslav I told you about to go on a trip round the islands with him. It'd look discourteous to let him down. But you go to Cetinje.'

'Well, I should like to. I may never get another chance to see Montenegro. Oh, look, darling, there are those people we saw in Dubrovnik!'

For the first time Wexford saw the girl full-face. Her haircut from the front was as spectacular as from the back, a fringe having been cut into a sharp peak in the centre of her forehead. It looked less like hair, he thought, than a black cap painted on. In spite of the hour, she wore large tinted glasses. Her coloured skirt was the same one she had been wearing that first time.

She and her companion had come on to the terrace from the harbour walk. They walked slowly, she somehow reluctantly, the man called Philip looking about him as if for friends they had arranged to meet here. It couldn't have been for a vacant table, for the terrace was half-empty. Dora kicked her husband's foot under the table, a warning against overt curiosity, and started to talk about her German friends, Werner and Trudi. Out of the corner of his eye, Wexford saw the man and the girl hesitate, then sit down at a neighbouring table. He made some sort of reply to Dora, conscious that it was he now who was being stared at. A voice he had heard once before said:

'Excuse me, we don't seem to have an ashtray. Would you mind if we had yours?'

Dora handed it to him. 'Please do.' She hardly looked up.

He insisted, smiling. 'You're sure you won't need it?'

'Quite sure. We don't smoke.'

He wasn't the kind to give up easily, thought Wexford, and now, very intrigued by something he had noticed, he didn't want to. Another prod from Dora's foot merely made him withdraw his own under his chair. He turned towards the other table, and to the next question, 'Are you staying long in Mirna?' replied pleasantly, 'A fortnight. We've been here four days.'

The effect of this simple rejoinder was startling. The man couldn't have expressed more satisfaction – and, yes, relief – if Wexford had brought him news of some great inheritance or that a close friend, presumed in danger, was safe.

'Oh, fantastic! That's really great. It's such a change to meet some English people. We must try and get together. This is my wife. We're called Philip and Iris Nyman. Are you Londoners too?'

Wexford introduced himself and Dora and said that they were from Kingsmarkham in Sussex. It was lovely to meet them, said Philip Nyman. They must let him buy them a drink. No? More coffee, then? At last Wexford accepted a cup of coffee, wondering what was so upsetting Iris Nyman that she had responded to the introduction only with a nod and now seemed almost paralysed. Her husband's extrovert behaviour? Certainly his effusive manner would have embarrassed all but the most insensitive. As soon as they had settled the question of the drinks, he launched into a long account of their trip from England, how they had come down through France and Italy, the people they had met, the weather, their delight at their first sight of the Dalmatian coast which they had never previously visited. Iris Nyman showed no delight. She simply stared out to sea, gulping down *slivovic* as if it were lemonade.

'We absolutely adored it. They say it's the least spoilt of the Mediterranean resorts, and that I can believe. We all loved Dubrovnik. That is, I mean, we brought a cousin of my wife's along with us. She was going on to holiday with some people she knows in Greece, so she flew to Athens from Dubrovnik on Sunday and left us to come on here.'

Dora said, 'We saw you in Dubrovnik. On the walls.'

Iris Nyman's glass made a little clinking sound against her teeth. Her husband said, 'You saw us on the walls? D'you know, I think I remember that.' He seemed just slightly taken aback. But not deterred. 'In fact, I seem to remember we were having a bit of a row at the time.'

Dora made a deprecating movement with her hands. 'We just walked past you. It was terribly hot, wasn't it?'

'You're being very charmingly discreet, Mrs Wexford – or may I call you Dora? The point was, Dora, my wife wanted to climb one of the local mountains and I was telling her just how impractical this was. I mean, in that heat, and for what? To get the same view you get from the walls.'

'So you managed to dissuade her?' Wexford said quietly.

'Indeed I did, but you came along rather at the height of the ding-dong. Another drink, darling? And how about you, Dora? Won't you change your mind?'

They replied simultaneously, 'Another *slivovic*,' and 'Thank you so much, but we must go.' It was a long time since Wexford had seen his wife so huffy and so thoroughly out of countenance. He marvelled at Nyman's continuing efforts, his fixed smile.

'Let me guess, you're staying at the Adriatic?' He took silence for assent. 'We're at the Bosnia. Wait a minute, how about making a date for, say, Wednesday? We could all have a trip somewhere in my car.'

The Wexfords, having previous engagements, were able to refuse with clear consciences. They said good night, Wexford nodding non-committally at Nyman's insistence that they must meet again, mustn't lose touch after having been so lucky as to encounter each other. His eyes followed them. Wexford looked back once to see.

'Well!' said Dora when they were out of earshot, 'what an insufferably rude woman!'

'Just very nervous, I think,' said Wexford thoughtfully. He gave her his arm and they began the walk back along the waterside path. It was very dark, the sea inky and calm, the island invisible. 'When you come to think of it, that was all very odd.'

'Was it? She was rude and he was effusive to the point of impertinence, if you call that odd. He forced himself on us, got us to tell him our names – you could see she just didn't want to know. I was amazed when he called me Dora.'

'That part wasn't so odd. After all, that's how one does make holiday acquaintances. Presumably it was much the same with Werner and Trudi.'

'No, it wasn't, Reg, not at all. For one thing, we're much of an age

226

and we're staying at the same hotel. Trudi speaks quite good English, and we were watching the children in the paddling pool and she happened to mention her grandsons who are just the same age as ours, and that started it. You must see that's quite different from a man of thirty walking into a café and latching on to a couple old enough to be his parents. I call it pushy.'

Wexford reacted impatiently. 'That's as may be. Perhaps you didn't notice there was a perfectly clean ashtray in the middle of that table before they sat down at it.'

'*What?*' Dora halted, staring at him in the dark.

'There was. He must have put it in his pocket to give him an excuse for speaking to us. Now that was odd. And giving us all that gratuitous information was odd. And telling a deliberate lie was very odd indeed. Come along, my dear. Don't stand there gawping at me.'

'What do you mean, a deliberate lie?'

'When you told them we'd seen them on the walls, he said he remembered it and we must have overheard the quarrel between himself and his wife. Now that was odd in itself. Why mention it at all? Why should we care about his domestic – or maybe I should say mural – rows? He said the quarrel had been over climbing a mountain, but no one climbs the mountains here in summer. Besides, I remember precisely what he did say up on the walls. He said, "We can't find anyone to take us." OK, so he might have meant they couldn't get a guide. But "there's nowhere to land"? That's what he said, no doubt about it. You don't land on mountains, Dora, unless you assault them by helicopter.'

'I wonder why, though? I wonder what he's up to?'

'So do I,' said Wexford, 'but I'm pretty sure it's not pinching ashtrays from waterside cafés.'

They rounded the point and came within sight of the lights of the Hotel Adriatic. A little further and they could see each other's faces. Dora saw his and read there much to disquiet her.

'You're not going to start detecting, Reg!'

'Can't help it, it's in my bones. But I won't let it interfere with your holiday, that's a promise.'

On Tuesday morning Racic's taxi boat was waiting at the landing stage outside the hotel.

'Gospoda Wexford, it is a great pleasure to meet you.'

Courteously he handed Dora into the boat. Its awning of green canvas, now furled, gave it somewhat the look of a gondola. As the engines started, Dora made her excuses for the following day.

'You will like Cetinje,' said Racic. 'Have a good time. Gospodin Wexford and I will have a bachelor day out. All boys together, eh? Are you quite comfortable? A little more suitable than that one for a lady, I hope.'

He pointed across the bay to where a man was paddling a yellow and blue inflatable dinghy. The girl with him wore a very brief bikini. The Nymans.

'If you could manage to avoid passing those people, Mr Racic,' said Dora, 'that would make me very comfortable indeed.'

Racic glanced at Wexford. 'You have met them? They have annoyed you?'

'Not that. They spoke to us last night in Mirna and the man was rather pushing.'

'I will keep close to the shore and cross to Vrt from the small peninsula there.'

For most of the morning there was no one else on the little shingly beach of Vrt, which Racic had told them meant a garden. The huddle of cottages behind were overhung with the blue trumpet flowers of the morning glory, and among the walls rose the slender spires of cypress trees. Wexford sat in the shade reading while Dora sunbathed. The dinghy came close only once, but the Wexfords went unrecognized, perhaps because they were in swimming costumes. Iris Nyman stood up briefly before jumping with an explosive splash into the deep water.

'Rude she may be,' said Dora, 'but I'll grant she's got a lovely figure. And you were wrong about her legs, Reg. Her legs are perfect.'

'Didn't notice,' said Wexford.

Josip took them back. He was a thin smiling brown man, not unlike Racic, but he had no English beyond 'thank you' and 'good-bye'. They hired him again in the afternoon to take them into Mirna, and they spent a quiet, pleasant evening drinking coffee with Werner and Trudi Muller on the Germans' balcony.

Wednesday came in with a storm at sunrise, and Wexford, watching the lightning and the choppy sea, wondered if Burden had been over-optimistic with his guarantee of fine weather. But by nine the sun was out and the sky clear. He saw Dora off in the Mullers' Mercedes, then walked down to the landing stage. Racic's boat glided in.

'I have brought bread and sausage for our lunch, and Posip in a flask to keep it cool.'

'Then we must eat it for our elevenses because I'm taking you out to lunch.'

This they ate in Dubrovnik after Racic had taken him to the island of Lokrum. Wexford listened with deepening interest to the boatman-professor's stories. How the ease and wealth of the city merchants had led to a literary renascence, how Dubrovnik-built ships had taken part in the Spanish Armada, how an earthquake had devastated the city and almost destroyed the state. They set off again for Lopud, Sipan and Kolocep, returning across the broad calm waters as the sun began to dip towards the sea.

'Does that little island have a name?' Wexford asked.

'It is called Vrapci, which is to say "sparrows". There are thousands of sparrows, so they say, and only sparrows, for no one goes there. One cannot land a boat.'

'You mean you can't get off a boat because the rocks are too sheer? What about the other side?'

'I will pull in close and you shall see. There is a beach but no one would wish to use it. Wait.'

The island was very small, perhaps no more than half a mile in circumference, and totally overgrown with stunted pines. At their roots the grey rock fell sheer to the water from a height of about ten feet. Racic brought the boat about and they came to the Adriatic side of Vrapci. No sparrows were to be seen, no life of any kind. Between ramparts of rock was a small and forbidding beach of shingle over which an overhanging pine cast deep shade. Looking up at the sky and then down at this dark and stony cove, Wexford could see that, no matter what its altitude, the sun would never penetrate to this beach. Where the shingle narrowed, at the apex, was a cleft in the rock just wide enough to allow the passage of a man's body.

'Not very attractive,' he said. 'Why should people want to come here?'

'They don't, as far as I know. Except perhaps – well, there is a new fashion, Gospodin Wexford, or Mister as I should call you.'

'Call me Reg.'

Racic inclined his head. 'Reg, yes, thank you. I like the name, though I have not previously encountered it. There is a fashion, as I mentioned, for nude bathing. Here in Yugoslavia we do not allow it, for it is not proper, not decorous. No doubt you have seen painted on some of the rocks the words – in, I fear, lamentable English –

"No Nudist". But there are some who would defy this rule, especially on the small islands. Vrapci might take their fancy if they could find a boat and a boatman to bring them.'

'A boat could land on the beach and its occupants swim off the rocks on the other side in the sun.'

'If they were good swimmers. But we will not try it, Reg, not at our age being inclined to strip ourselves naked and risk our necks, eh?'

Once more they were off across the wide sea. Wexford looked back to the city walls, those man-made defensive cliffs, and brought himself hesitantly to ask:

'Would you tell me what you overheard of the conversation between that English couple, Philip and Iris Nyman, when you took them out in your boat?'

'So that is their name? Nyman?' He was stalling.

'I have a good reason for asking.'

'May I know it?'

Wexford sighed. 'I'm a policeman.'

Racic's face went very still and tight. 'I don't much like that. You were sent here to watch these people? You should have told me before.'

'No, Ivo, no.' Wexford brought out the unfamiliar name a little self-consciously. 'No, you've got me wrong. I never saw or heard of them till last Saturday. But now I've seen them and spoken to them I believe they're doing something illegal. If that's so it's my duty to do something about it. They're my countrymen.'

'Reg,' said Racic more gently, 'what I overheard can have nothing to do with this matter of an illegality. It was personal and private.'

'You won't tell me?'

'No. We are not old housewives to spend our time in gossip over the garden walls of our *kucice*, eh?'

Wexford grinned. 'Then will you *do* something for me? Will you contrive to let these people know — subtly, of course — that you understand the English language?'

'You are sure that what they are doing is against the law?'

'I am sure. It's drugs or some kind of confidence trick.'

There was silence, during which Racic seemed to commune with his sea. Then he said quietly, 'I trust you, Reg. Yes, I will do this if I can.'

'Then go into Mirna. They're very likely having a drink on the waterfront.'

Mirko's boat passed them as they came in and Mirko waved, calling, '*Dobro vece!*'

On the jetty stood a queue of tourists, waiting to be ferried back to the Adriatic or to the hotel at Vrt. There were perhaps a dozen people, and Philip and Iris Nyman brought up the end of the line. It worked out better than Wexford could have hoped. The first four got into Josip's boat, bound for Vrt, the next group into Mirko's which, with its capacity of only eight, was inadequate to take the Nymans.

'Hotel Adriatic,' said Philip Nyman. Then he recognized Wexford. 'Well, well, we meet again. Had a good day?'

Wexford replied that he had been to Dubrovnik. He helped the girl into the boat. She thanked him, seeming less nervous and even gave him a diffident smile. The motor started and they were off, Racic the anonymous taxi-man, the piece of equipment without which the vehicle won't go.

'I saw you out in your dinghy yesterday,' said Wexford.

'Did you?' Philip Nyman seemed gratified. 'We can't use it tonight, though. It's not safe after dark and you've really got to be in swimming costumes. We're dining at your hotel with another English couple that we met yesterday and we thought we'd have a romantic walk back along the path.'

They were rather more dressed up than usual. Nyman wore a cream-coloured safari suit, his wife a yellow and black dress and high-heeled black sandals. Wexford was on the alert for an invitation to join them for dinner and was surprised when none came.

Both the Nymans lit cigarettes. Wexford noticed Racic stiffen. He had learned enough about the man's principles and shibboleths to be aware of his feelings on pollution. Those cigarette butts would certainly end up in the sea. Anger with his passengers might make him all the more willing to fulfil his promise. But for the moment he remained silent. They rounded the point on to a sea where the sun seemed to have laid a skin of gold.

'So beautiful!' said Iris Nyman.

'A pity you have to go so soon.'

'We're staying till Saturday,' said Nyman, though without renewing his suggestion that they and the Wexfords should meet again. The girl took a last draw on her cigarette and threw it overboard.

'Oh, well,' said Nyman, 'there's so much muck in there already, a bit more won't do any harm,' and he cast his still-lighted butt into the ripples of melted gold.

They were approaching the hotel landing stage and Racic cut the motor. Nyman felt in his pocket for change. It was Wexford who got up first. He said to Racic as the Yugoslav made the boat fast:

'I've had a splendid day. Thanks very much indeed.'

He wasn't looking at them but he fancied the amused glance Nyman would have given his wife at this display of the Englishman's well-known assumption that all but cretins speak his language. Racic drew himself up to his not very great height. What accent he had, what stiltedness and syntactical awkwardness, seemed to be lost. He spoke as if he had been born in Kensington and educated at Oxford.

'I'm glad you enjoyed it, I certainly did. Give my regards to your wife and tell her I hope to see her soon.'

There was no sound from the Nymans. They got out of the boat, Racic saying, 'Let me give you a hand, madame.' Nyman's voice sounded stifled when he produced his twenty dinars and muttered his thanks. Neither said a word to Wexford. They didn't look back. They walked away and his eyes followed them.

'Did I do all right, Reg? I was moved by the foul contamination of my sea.'

Absently, still staring, Wexford said, 'You did fine.'

'What do you look at with such concentration?'

'Legs,' said Wexford. 'Thanks again. I'll see you tomorrow.'

He walked up towards the hotel, looking for them, but they were nowhere in sight. On the terrace he turned and looked back and there they were, walking hurriedly along the waterfront path back to Mirna, their new friends and their dinner engagement forgotten. Wexford went into the hotel and took the lift up to his room. Dora wasn't back yet. Feeling rather shaken, he lay down on one of the twin beds. This latest development or discovery was, at any rate, far from what he had expected. And what now? Somehow get hold of the Dubrovnik police? He reached for the phone to call reception but dropped it again when Dora walked in.

She came up to him in consternation. 'Are you all right, darling?'

His blood pressure, his heart, too much sun – he could tell what she was thinking. It was rare for him to take a rest in the daytime. 'Of course I am. I'm fine.' He sat up. 'Dora, something most peculiar . . .'

'You're detecting again! I knew it.' She kicked off her shoes and threw open the doors to the balcony. 'You haven't even asked me if I've had a nice day.'

'I can see you have. Come in, my dear, don't be difficult. I always like to think you're the only woman I know who isn't difficult.' She looked at him warily. 'Listen,' he said. 'Do something for me. Describe the woman we saw on the walls.'

'Iris Nyman? What do you mean?'

'Just do as I ask, there's a good girl.'

'You're mad. You *have* had a touch of the sun. Well, I suppose if it humours you . . . Medium height, good figure, very tanned, about thirty, geometric haircut. She was wearing a jade green halter top and a blue and green and pink skirt.'

'Now describe the woman we saw with Nyman on Monday.'

'There's no difference except for a black top and a stole.'

Wexford nodded. He got off the bed, walked past her on to the balcony and said:

'They're not the same woman.'

'What on earth are you suggesting?'

'I wish I knew,' said Wexford, 'but I do know the Iris Nyman we saw on the walls is not the Iris Nyman I saw in Mirna on Monday morning and we saw that night and we saw yesterday and I saw this evening.'

'You're letting your imagination run away with you. You are, Reg. That hair, for instance, it was striking, and those clothes, and being with Philip Nyman.'

'Don't you see you've named the very things that would be used to make anyone think they're the same woman? Neither of us saw her face that first time. Neither of us heard her voice. We only noticed the striking things about her.'

'What makes you think they're not the same?'

'Her legs. The legs are different. You drew my attention to them. One might say you set me off on this.'

Dora leaned over the balcony rail. Her shoulders sagged. 'Then I wish I hadn't. Reg, you never discuss cases with me at home. Why do it here?'

'There's no one else.'

'Thanks very much. All this about their not being the same woman, it's nonsense, you've dreamed it up. Why would anyone try and fake a thing like that? Come to that, *how* could anyone?'

'Easily. All you need is a female accomplice of similar build and age. On Saturday or Sunday this accomplice had her hair cut and dyed and assumed Iris Nyman's clothes. I mean to find out why.'

Dora turned her back on the sunset and fixed him with a cold and stony look. 'No, Reg, no. I'm not being difficult. I'm just behaving like any normal woman would when she goes on holiday and finds her husband can't leave his job at home for just two weeks. This is the first foreign holiday I've had in ten years. If you'd been sent here to watch these people, if it was work, I wouldn't say a word. But it's just something you've dreamed up because you can't relax and enjoy the sun and the sea like other people.'

'OK,' said her husband, 'look at it that way.' He was very fond of his wife, he valued her and quickly felt guilt over his frequent enforced neglect of her. This time any neglect would be as if by design, the result of that bone-deep need of his to unravel mysteries. 'Don't give me that Gorgon face. I've said I won't let this spoil your holiday and I won't.' He touched her cheek, gently rubbing it. 'And now I'm going to have my bath.'

Not much more than twelve hours later he was walking the path to Mirna. The sun was already hot and there was a speedboat out in the bay. Carpet sellers had spread their wares in the market place, and the cafés were open for those who wanted coffee or – even at this hour – plum brandy.

The Bosnia, most of it mercifully concealed by pines and ranks of cypresses, looked from close to, with its floors in plate-like layers and its concrete flying buttresses, more like an Unidentified Flying Object come to rest in the woods than a holiday hotel. Wexford crossed a forecourt as big as a football pitch and entered a foyer that wouldn't have disgraced some capital city's palace of justice.

The receptionist spoke good English.

'Mr and Mrs Nyman checked out last evening, sir.'

'Surely they expected to stay another three days?'

'I cannot tell you, sir. They left last evening before dinner. I cannot help you more.'

So that was that.

'What are you going to do now?' said Dora over a late breakfast. 'Have a hilarious cops and robbers car chase up the Dalmatian coast?'

'I'm going to wait and see. And in the meantime I'm going to enjoy my holiday and see that you enjoy yours.' He watched her relax and smile for the first time since the previous evening.

The Nymans were at the back of his mind all the time, but he did manage to enjoy the rest of his holiday. Werner and Trudi took them to Mostar to see the Turkish bridge. They went on a coach to Budva, and the members of the taxi boat syndicate ferried them from Mirna to Vrt and out to Lokrum. It was in secret that Wexford daily bought a London newspaper, a day old and three times its normal price. He wasn't sure why he did so, what he hoped or feared. On their last morning he nearly didn't bother. After all, he would be home in not much more than twenty-four hours and then he would have to take some action. But as he passed the reception desk, Dora having already entered the dining room for breakfast, the clerk held out the newspaper to him as a matter of course.

Wexford thanked him – and there it was on the front page.

Disappearance of Tycoon's Daughter, said the headline. *Beachwear King Fears Kidnap Plot.*

The text beneath read: 'Mrs Iris Nyman, 32, failed to return to her North London home from a shopping expedition yesterday. Her father, Mr James Woodhouse, Chairman of Sunsports Ltd, a leading manufacturer of beachwear, fears his daughter may have been kidnapped and expects a ransom demand. Police are taking a serious view.

'Mrs Nyman's husband, 33-year-old Philip Nyman, said at the couple's home in Flask Walk, Hampstead, today, "My wife and I had just got back from a motoring holiday in Italy and Yugoslavia. On the following morning Iris went out shopping and never returned. I am frantic with worry. She seemed to be happy and relaxed."

'Mr Woodhouse's company, of which Mrs Nyman is a director, was this year involved in a vast takeover bid as a result of which two other major clothing firms were absorbed into Sunsports Ltd. The company's turnover last year was in the region of £100,000,000.'

There was a photograph of Iris Nyman in black glasses. Wexford would have been hard put to it to say whether this was of the woman on the walls or the woman in Mirna.

That night they gave Racic a farewell dinner at the Dubrovacka restaurant.

'Don't say what they all say, Reg, that you will come back next year. Dalmatia is beautiful to you and Gospoda Wexford now, but a few days and the memory will fade. Someone will say, San Marino for you next time, or Ibiza, and there you will go. Is it not so?'

'I said I shall be back,' said Wexford, 'and I meant it.' He raised his glass of Posip. 'But not in a year's time. It'll be sooner than that.'

Three hundred and sixty-two days sooner, as Racic pointed out.

'And here I am, sitting in the *vrt* of your *kucica*!'

'Reg, we shall have you fluent in Serbo-Croat yet.'

'Alas, no. I must be back in London again tomorrow night.'

They were in Racic's garden, halfway up the terraced hill behind Mirna, sitting in wicker chairs under his vine and his fig tree. Pink and white and red oleanders shimmered in the dusk, and above their heads bunches of small green grapes hung between the slats of a canopy. On the table was a bottle of Posip and the remains of a dinner of king prawns and Dalmatian buttered potatoes, salad and bread and big ripe peaches.

'And now we have eaten,' said Racic, 'you will please tell me the tale of the important business that brought you back to Mirna so pleasantly soon. It concerns Mr and Mrs Nyman?'

'Ivo, we shall have you a policeman yet.'

Racic laughed and re-filled Wexford's glass. Then he looked serious. 'Not a laughing matter, I think, not pleasant.'

'Far from it. Iris Nyman is dead, murdered, unless I am much mistaken. This afternoon I accompanied the Dubrovnik police out into the bay and we took her body out of the cave on Vrapci.'

'*Zaboga!* You cannot mean it! That girl who was at the Bosnia and who came out with her husband in my boat?'

'Well, no, not that one. She's alive and in Athens from where, I imagine, she'll be extradited.'

'I don't understand. Tell me the tale from the beginning.'

Wexford leaned back in his chair and looked up through the vines at the violet sky where the first stars had begun to show. 'I'll have to start with the background,' he said, and after a pause, 'Iris Nyman was the daughter and only child of James Woodhouse, the chairman of a company called Sunsports Ltd which makes sports- and beachwear and has a large export trade. She married when she was very young, less than twenty, a junior salesman in her father's firm. After the marriage Woodhouse made a director of her, settled a lot of money on her, bought her a house and gave her a company car. To justify her company fees and expenses, she was in the habit of annually making a trip to holiday resorts in Europe with her husband, ostensibly to wear Sunsports clothes and note who else was wearing them, and also to study the success of rival markets. Probably, she simply holidayed.

'The marriage was not a happy one. At any rate, Philip Nyman wasn't happy. Iris was a typically arrogant rich girl who expected always to have her own way. Besides, the money and the house and the car were all hers. He remained a salesman. Then, a year or so ago, he fell in love with a cousin of Iris, a girl called Anna Ashby.

Apparently, Iris knew nothing about this, and her father certainly didn't.'

'Then how can you . . . ?' Racic interrupted.

'These affairs are always known to someone, Ivo. One of Anna's friends has made a statement to Scotland Yard.' Wexford paused and drank some of his wine. 'That's the background,' he said. 'Now for what happened a month or so ago.

'The Nymans had arranged to motor down as usual to the south of France, but this time to cross northern Italy and spend a week or ten days here on the Dalmatian coast. Anna Ashby had planned to spend part of the summer with friends in Greece so, *at Iris's invitation*, she was to accompany the Nymans as far as Dubrovnik where she would stay a few days with them, then go on by air to Athens.

'In Dubrovnik, after the three of them had been there a few days, Iris got hold of the idea of bathing off Vrapci. Perhaps she wanted to bathe in the nude, perhaps she had already been on the "topless" beach at St Tropez. I don't know. Philip Nyman has admitted nothing of this. Up until the time I left, he was still insisting that his wife had returned to England with him.'

'It was your idea, then,' put in Racic, 'that this poor woman's body was concealed on the isle of sparrows?'

'It was a guess,' said Wexford. 'I overheard some words, I was later told a lie. I'm a policeman. Whether they went to Vrapci on Saturday, June 18th, or Sunday, June 19th, I can't tell you. Suffice that they did go – in that inflatable dinghy of theirs. The three of them went but only two came back, Nyman and Anna Ashby.'

'They killed Mrs Nyman?'

Wexford looked thoughtful. 'I think so, certainly. Of course there's a possibility that she drowned, that it was an accident. But in that case wouldn't any normal husband have immediately informed the proper authority? If he had recovered the body, wouldn't he have brought it back with him? We're awaiting the results of the post-mortem, but even if that shows no wounds or bruises on the body, even if the lungs are full of water, I should be very surprised to learn that Nyman and, or, Anna hadn't hastened her death or watched her drown.'

Both were silent for a moment, Racic nodding slowly as he digested what Wexford had told him. Then he got up and fetched from the house a candelabrum, but thinking better of it, switched on an electric lamp attached to the wall.

'Any light will attract the insects, but there at least they will not trouble us. So it was this Anna Ashby who came to Mirna, posing as Mrs Nyman?'

'According to the manager of the hotel in Dubrovnik where the three of them had been staying, Nyman checked out and paid his bill early on the evening of the 19th. Neither of the women was with him. Iris was dead and Anna was at the hairdresser's, having her hair cut and dyed to the same style and colour as her cousin's. The police have already found the hairdresser who did the job.'

'They came here next,' said Racic. 'Why didn't they go straight back to England? And now I must ask, surely they did not intend to play this game in England? Even if the two women, as cousins, to a degree resembled each other, this Anna could not hope to deceive a father, close friends, Mrs Nyman's neighbours.'

'The answer to your first question is that to have returned to England a week earlier than expected would have looked odd. Why go back? The weather was perfect. Nyman wanted to give the impression they had both been well and happy during their holiday. No, his idea was to make sufficient people here in Yugoslavia believe that Iris was alive after June 19th. That's why he latched on to us and got our name and home town out of us. He wanted to be sure of witnesses if need be. Anna was less bold, she was frightened to death. But Philip actually found himself two more English witnesses, though, thanks to your intervention, he never kept the appointment to dine with them.'

'My intervention?'

'Your excellent English. And now perhaps you'll tell me what you overheard in the boat.'

Racic laughed. His strong white teeth gleamed in the lamplight. 'I knew she was not Mrs Nyman, Reg, but that knowledge would not have helped you then, eh? You had seen the lady on the walls but not, I presume, her marriage document. I thought to myself, why should I tell this busybody of a policeman the secrets of my passengers? But now, to use an idiom, here goes. Reg, the lady said, "I feel so guilty, it is terrible what we have done," and he replied, "Everyone here thinks you are my wife, and no one at home will suspect a thing. One day you will be and we shall forget all this." Now, would you have supposed they were talking of murder or of illicit passion?'

Wexford smiled. 'Nyman must have thought we'd confer, you and I, and jump to the former conclusion. Or else he'd forgotten what he'd said. He has rather a way of doing that.'

'And after they left?'

'Anna was to travel on Iris's passport in the hope it would be stamped at at least one frontier. In fact, it was stamped at two, between Yugoslavia and Italy and again at Calais. At Dover Anna presumably left him and caught the first plane to Athens she could get. Nyman went home, reaching there in the night of the 28th, the precise date on which he and Iris had planned to return. On the following afternoon he told his father-in-law and the police that Iris was missing.'

'He hoped the search for her or her body,' said Racic, 'would be confined to England because he had incontrovertible proof she had stayed with him in Mirna and had travelled back with him to England. No one would think of looking for her here, for it was known to many witnesses that she left here alive. But what did he hope to gain? Surely, if your laws are like ours, and I believe all laws are alike in this, without her body it would be years before he could inherit her money or marry again?'

'You have to remember this wasn't a premeditated murder. It must have happened on the spur of the moment. So conceal the body where it may never be found or not found until it's beyond identification, announce that his wife has gone missing in England, and he gets the sympathy of his powerful father-in-law and certainly Iris's house to live in and Iris's car to drive. He keeps his job which he would have lost had he divorced Iris, and very likely gets all or some of her allowance transferred to him. Anna gets her hair back to its natural colour – brown, incidentally – lets it grow out, returns home and they resume their friendship. One day Iris will be presumed dead and they can marry.'

Racic cut himself a slice of bread and nibbled at an olive. 'I see it all or nearly all. I see that, but for your presence here in Mirna, the conspiracy had every chance of success. What I don't see is, if this woman made herself look so much like this woman you saw on the walls, if she had the same hair and clothes – but I am a fool! You saw her face.'

'I didn't see her face and I didn't hear her voice. Dora and I saw her very briefly and then only from the back.'

'It is beyond my comprehension.'

'The legs,' said Wexford. 'The legs were different.'

'But, my dear Reg, my dear policeman, surely the leg of one brown-skinned slender young woman is much like the leg of such another? Or was there a mole perhaps or a protruding vein?'

'Not as far as I know. The only time I saw the true Iris Nyman she wore a skirt that covered her legs to mid-calf. In fact, I could see very little of her legs.'

'Then I am flummoxed.'

'Ankles,' said Wexford. 'There are two types of normal ankle in this world, and the difference between them can only be seen from the back. In one type the calf seems to join the heel with a narrowing but no distinct shaft. In the other, the type of beauty, the Achilles tendon makes a long slender shaft with deep indentations on either side of it beneath the ankle bones. I saw Iris Nyman's legs only from behind and in her the Achilles tendon was not apparent. It was a flaw in her appearance. When I first noticed Anna Ashby's legs from behind as she was getting off your boat, I observed the long shaft of the tendon leading up into the muscle of a shapely calf. She had no flaw in her legs, but you might call that perfection her Achilles Heel.'

'*Zaboga!* Beauty, eh? Only two types in the world?' Racic extended one foot and rolled up his trouser leg. Wexford's was already rucked up. In the lamplight they peered down at each other's calves from behind. 'Yours are all right,' said Racic. 'In fact, they are fine. In the beauty class.'

'So are yours, you old professor and boatman.'

Racic burst out laughing. '*Tesko meni!* Two elderly gentlemen who should know better, airing their limbs in an ankle competition! Whatever next?'

'Well, I shouldn't,' said Wexford, 'but next let's finish up the Posip.'

When the Wedding Was Over

'Matrimony,' said Chief Inspector Wexford, 'begins with dearly beloved and ends with amazement.'

His wife, sitting beside him on the bridegroom's side of the church, whispered, 'What did you say?'

He repeated it. She steadied the large floral hat which her husband had called becoming but not exactly conducive to *sotto voce* intimacies. 'What on earth makes you say that?'

'Thomas Hardy. He said it first. But look in your Prayer Book.'

The bridegroom waited, hang-dog, with his best man. Michael Burden was very much in love, was entering this second marriage with someone admirably suited to him, had agreed with his fiancée that nothing but a religious ceremony would do for them, yet at forty-four was a little superannuated for what Wexford called 'all this white wedding gubbins'. There were two hundred people in the church. Burden, his best man and his ushers were in morning dress. Madonna lilies and stephanotis and syringa decorated the pews, the pulpit and the chancel steps. It was the kind of thing that is properly designed for someone twenty years younger. Burden had been through it before when he *was* twenty years younger. Wexford chuckled silently, looking at the anxious face above the high white collar. And then as Dora, leafing through the marriage service, said, 'Oh, I *see*,' the organist went from voluntaries into the opening bars of the Lohengrin march and Jenny Ireland appeared at the church door on her father's arm.

A beautiful bride, of course. Seven years younger than Burden, blonde, gentle, low-voiced, and given to radiant smiles. Jenny's father gave her hand into Burden's and the Rector of St Peter's began:

'Dearly beloved, we are gathered together . . .'

While bride and groom were being informed that marriage was not for the satisfaction of their carnal lusts, and that they must bring up their children in a Christian manner, Wexford studied the congregation. In front of himself and Dora sat Burden's sister-in-law,

241

Grace, whom everyone had thought he would marry after the death of his first wife. But Burden had found consolation with a red-headed woman, wild and sweet and strange, gone now God knew where, and Grace had married someone else. Two little boys now sat between Grace and that someone else, giving their parents a full-time job keeping them quiet.

Burden's mother and father were both dead. Wexford thought he recognized, from one meeting a dozen years before, an aged aunt. Beside her sat Dr Crocker and his wife, beyond them and behind were a crowd whose individual members he knew either only by sight or not at all. Sylvia, his elder daughter, was sitting on his other side, his grandsons between her and their father, and at the central aisle end of the pew, Sheila Wexford of the Royal Shakespeare Company. Wexford's actress daughter, who on her entry had commanded nudges, whispers, every gaze, sat looking with unaccustomed wistfulness at Jenny Ireland in her clouds of white and wreath of pearls.

'I, Michael George, take thee, Janina, to my wedded wife, to have and to hold from this day forward . . .'

Janina. *Janina?* Wexford had supposed her name was Jennifer. What sort of parents called a daughter Janina? Turks? Fans of Dumas? He leaned forward to get a good look at these philonomatous progenitors. They looked ordinary enough, Mr Ireland apparently exhausted by the effort of giving the bride away, Jenny's mother making use of the lace handkerchief provided for the specific purpose of crying into it those tears of joy and loss. What romantic streak had led them to dismiss Elizabeth and Susan and Anne in favour of – Janina?

'Those whom God hath joined together, let no man put asunder. Forasmuch as Michael George and Janina have consented together in holy wedlock . . .'

Had they been as adventurous in the naming of their son? All Wexford could see of him was a broad back, a bit of profile, and now a hand. The hand was passing a large white handkerchief to his mother. Wexford found himself being suddenly yanked to his feet to sing a hymn.

> 'O, Perfect Love, all human thought transcending,
> Lowly we kneel in prayer before Thy throne . . .'

These words had the effect of evoking from Mrs Ireland audible sobs. Her son – hadn't Burden said he was in publishing? – looked embarrassed, turning his head. A young woman, strangely dressed in black with an orange hat, edged past the publisher to put a consoling arm round his mother.

'O Lord, save Thy servant and Thy handmaid.'

'Who put their trust in Thee,' said Dora and most of the rest of the congregation.

'O Lord, send them help from Thy holy place.'

Wexford, to show team spirit, said, 'Amen,' and when everyone else said, 'And evermore defend them,' decided to keep quiet in future.

Mrs Ireland had stopped crying. Wexford's gaze drifted to his own daughters, Sheila singing lustily, Sylvia, the Women's Liberationist, with less assurance as if she doubted the ethics of lending her support to so archaic and sexist a ceremony. His grandsons were beginning to fidget.

'Almighty God, who at the beginning did create our first parents, Adam and Eve . . .'

Dear Mike, thought Wexford with a flash of sentimentality that came to him perhaps once every ten years, you'll be OK now. No more carnal lusts conflicting with a puritan conscience, no more loneliness, no more worrying about those selfish kids of yours, no more temptation-of-St-Anthony stuff. For is it not ordained as a remedy against sin, and to avoid fornication, that such persons as have not the gift of continency may marry and keep themselves undefiled?

'For after this manner in the old time the holy women who trusted in God . . .'

He was quite surprised that they were using the ancient form. Still, the bride had promised to obey. He couldn't resist glancing at Sylvia.

'. . . being in subjection to their own husbands . . .'

Her face was a study in incredulous dismay as she mouthed at her sister 'unbelievable' and 'antique'.

'. . . Even as Sarah obeyed Abraham, calling him Lord, whose daughters ye are as long as ye do well, and are not afraid with any amazement.'

At the Olive and Dove hotel there was a reception line to greet guests, Mrs Ireland smiling, re-rouged and restored, Burden looking like someone who has had an operation and been told the prognosis is excellent, Jenny serene as a bride should be.

Dry sherry and white wine on trays. No champagne. Wexford

remembered that there was a younger Ireland daughter, absent with her husband in some dreadful place – Botswana? Lesotho? No doubt all the champagne funds had been expended on her. It was a buffet lunch, but a good one. Smoked salmon and duck and strawberries. Nobody, he said to himself, has ever really thought of anything better to eat than smoked salmon and duck and strawberries unless it might be caviare and grouse and syllabub. He was weighing the two menus against one another, must without knowing it have been thinking aloud, for a voice said:

'Asparagus, trout, apple pie.'

'Well, maybe,' said Wexford, 'but I do like meat. Trout's a bit insipid. You're Jenny's brother, I'm sorry I don't remember your name. How d'you do?'

'How d'you do? I know who you are. Mike told me. I'm Amyas Ireland.'

So that funny old pair hadn't had a one-off indulgence when they had named Janina. Again Wexford's thoughts seemed revealed to this intuitive person.

'Oh, I know,' said Ireland, 'but how about my other sister? She's called Cunegonde. Her husband calls her Queenie. Look, I'd like to talk to you. Could we get together a minute away from all this crush? Mike was going to help me out, but I can't ask him now, not when he's off on his honeymoon. It's about a book we're publishing.'

The girl in black and orange, Burden's nephews, Sheila Wexford, Burden's best man and a gaggle of children, all carrying plates, passed between them at this point. It was at least a minute before Wexford could ask, 'Who's we?' and another half-minute before Amyas Ireland understood what he meant.

'Carlyon Brent,' he said, his mouth full of duck. 'I'm with Carlyon Brent.'

One of the largest and most distinguished of publishing houses. Wexford was impressed. 'You published the Vandrian, didn't you, and the de Coverley books?'

Ireland nodded. 'Mike said you were a great reader. That's good. Can I get you some more duck? No? I'm going to. I won't be a minute.' Enviously Wexford watched him shovel fat-rimmed slices of duck breast on to his plate, take a brioche, have second thoughts and take another. The man was as thin as a rail too, positively emaciated.

'I look after the crime list,' he said as he sat down again. 'As I said, Mike half-promised . . . This isn't fiction, it's fact. The Winchurch case?'

'Ah.'

'I know it's a bit of a nerve asking, but would you read a manuscript for me?'

Wexford took a cup of coffee from a passing tray. 'What for?'

'Well, in the interests of truth. Mike was going to tell me what he thought.' Wexford looked at him dubiously. He had the highest respect and the deepest affection for Inspector Burden but he was one of the last people he would have considered as a literary critic. 'To tell me what he thought,' the publisher said once again. 'You see, it's worrying me. The author has discovered some new facts and they more or less prove Mrs Winchurch's innocence.' He hesitated. 'Have you ever heard of a writer called Kenneth Gandolph?'

Wexford was saved from answering by the pounding of a gavel on the top table and the beginning of the speeches. A great many toasts had been drunk, several dozen telegrams read out, and the bride and groom departed to change their clothes before he had an opportunity to reply to Ireland's question. And he was glad of the respite, for what he knew of Gandolph, though based on hearsay, was not prepossessing.

'Doesn't he write crime novels?' he said when the enquiry was repeated. 'And the occasional examination of a real-life crime?'

Nodding, Ireland said, 'It's good, this script of his. We want to do it for next spring's list. It's an eighty-year-old murder, sure, but people are still fascinated by it. I think this new version could cause quite a sensation.'

'Florence Winchurch was hanged,' said Wexford, 'yet there was always some margin of doubt about her guilt. Where does Gandolph get his fresh facts from?'

'May I send you a copy of the script? You'll find all that in the introduction.'

Wexford shrugged, then smiled. 'I suppose so. You do realize I can't do more than maybe spot mistakes in forensics? I did say maybe, mind.' But his interest had already been caught. It made him say, 'Florence was married at St Peter's, you know, and she also had her wedding reception here.'

'And spent part of her honeymoon in Greece.'

'No doubt the parallels end there,' said Wexford as Burden and Jenny came back into the room.

Burden was in a grey lounge suit, she in pale blue sprigged muslin. Wexford felt an absurd impulse of tenderness towards him. It was partly caused by Jenny's hat which she would never wear again, would never have occasion to wear, would remove the minute they got into the car. But Burden was the sort of man who could never be happy with a woman who didn't have a hat as part of her 'going-away' costume. His own clothes were eminently unsuitable for flying to Crete in June. They both looked very happy and embarrassed.

Mrs Ireland seized her daughter in a crushing embrace.

'It's not for ever, Mother,' said Jenny. 'It's only for two weeks.'

'Well, in a way,' said Burden. He shook hands gravely with his own son, down from university for the weekend, and planted a kiss on his daughter's forehead. Must have been reading novels, Wexford thought, grinning to himself.

'Good luck, Mike,' he said.

The bride took his hand, put a soft cool kiss on to the corner of his mouth. Say I'm growing old but add, Jenny kissed me. He didn't say that aloud. He nodded and smiled and took his wife's arm and frowned at Sylvia's naughty boys like the patriarch he was. Burden and Jenny went out to the car which had Just Married written in lipstick on the rear window and a shoe tied on the back bumper.

There was a clicking of handbag clasps, a flurry of hands, and then a tempest of confetti broke over them.

It was an isolated house, standing some twenty yards back from the Myringham road. Plumb in the centre of the façade was a plaque bearing the date 1896. Wexford had often thought that there seemed to have been positive intent on the part of late-Victorian builders to design and erect houses that were not only ugly, complex and inconvenient, but also distinctly sinister in appearance. The Limes, though well-maintained and set in a garden as multi-coloured, cushiony and floral as a quilt, nevertheless kept this sinister quality. Khaki-coloured brick and grey slate had been the principal materials used in its construction. Without being able to define exactly how, Wexford could see that, in relation to the walls, the proportions of the sash windows were wrong. A turret grew out of each of the front corners and each of these turrets was topped by a conical roof, giving the place the look of a cross between Balmoral castle and a hotel in Kitzbuehl. The lime trees which gave it its name had been lopped so many times since their planting at the turn of the century that now they were squat and misshapen.

In the days of the Winchurches it had been called Paraleash House. But this name, of historical significance on account of its connection with the ancient manor of Paraleash, had been changed specifically as a result of the murder of Edward Winchurch. Even so, it had stood empty for ten years. Then it had found a buyer a year or so before the First World War, a man who was killed in that war. Its present owner had occupied it for half a dozen years, and in the time intervening between his purchase of it and 1918 it had been variously a nursing home, the annexe of an agricultural college and a private school. The owner was a retired brigadier. As he emerged from the front door with two Sealyhams on a lead, Wexford retreated to his car and drove home.

It was Monday evening and Burden's marriage was two days old. Monday was the evening of Dora's pottery class, the fruits of which, bruised-looking and not invariably symmetrical, were scattered haphazardly about the room like windfalls. Hunting along the shelves for G. Hallam Saul's *When the Summer is Shed* and *The Trial of Florence Winchurch* from the Notable British Trials series, he nearly knocked over one of those rotund yet lop-sided objects. With a sigh of relief that it was unharmed, he set about refreshing his memory of the Winchurch case with the help of Miss Saul's classic.

Florence May Anstruther had been nineteen at the time of her marriage to Edward Winchurch and he forty-seven. She was a good-looking fair-haired girl, rather tall and Junoesque, the daughter of a Kingsmarkham chemist — that is, a pharmacist, for her father had kept a shop in the High Street. In 1895 this damned her as of no account in the social hierarchy, and few people would have bet much on her chances of marrying well. But she did. Winchurch was a barrister who, at this stage of his life, practised law from inclination rather than from need. His father, a Sussex landowner, had died some three years before and had left him what for the last decade of the nineteenth century was an enormous fortune, two hundred thousand pounds. Presumably, he had been attracted to Florence by her youth, her looks and her ladylike ways. She had been given the best education, including six months at a finishing school, that the chemist could afford. Winchurch's attraction for Florence was generally supposed to have been solely his money.

They were married in June 1895 at the parish church of St Peter's, Kingsmarkham, and went on a six-months honeymoon, touring Italy, Greece and the Swiss Alps. When they returned home Winchurch took a lease of Sewingbury Priory while building began on Paraleash

House, and it may have been that the conical roofs on those turrets were inspired directly by what Florence had seen on her alpine travels. They moved into the lavishly furnished new house in May 1896, and Florence settled down to the life of a Victorian lady with a wealthy husband and a staff of indoor and outdoor servants. A vapid life at best, even if alleviated by a brood of children. But Florence had no children and was to have none.

Once or twice a week Edward Winchurch went up to London by the train from Kingsmarkham, as commuters had done before and have been doing ever since. Florence gave orders to her cook, arranged the flowers, paid and received calls, read novels and devoted a good many hours a day to her face, her hair and her dress. Local opinion of the couple at that time seemed to have been that they were as happy as most people, that Florence had done very well for herself and knew it, and Edward not so badly as had been predicted.

In the autumn of 1896 a young doctor of medicine bought a practice in Kingsmarkham and came to live there with his unmarried sister. Their name was Fenton. Frank Fenton was an extremely handsome man, twenty-six years old, six feet tall, with jet black hair, a Byronic eye and an arrogant lift to his chin. The sister was called Ada, and she was neither good-looking nor arrogant, being partly crippled by poliomyelitis which had left her with one leg badly twisted and paralysed.

It was ostensibly to befriend Ada Fenton that Florence first began calling at the Fentons' house in Queen Street. Florence professed great affection for Ada, took her about in her carriage and offered her the use of it whenever she had to go any distance. From this it was an obvious step to persuade Edward that Frank Fenton should become the Winchurches' doctor. Within another few months young Mrs Winchurch had become the doctor's mistress.

It was probable that Ada knew nothing, or next to nothing, about it. In the eighteen-nineties a young girl could be, and usually was, very innocent. At the trial it was stated by Florence's coachman that he would be sent to the Fentons' house several times a week to take Miss Fenton driving, while Ada's housemaid said that Mrs Winchurch would arrive on foot soon after Miss Fenton had gone out and be admitted rapidly through a french window by the doctor himself. During the winter of 1898 it seemed likely that Frank Fenton had performed an abortion on Mrs Winchurch, and for some months afterwards they met only at social gatherings and occasionally when Florence was visiting Ada. But their feelings for each other were too strong for them to bear separation and by the following summer they were again meeting at Fenton's house while Ada was out, and now also at Paraleash House on the days when Edward had departed for the law courts.

Divorce was difficult but by no means impossible or unheard-of in 1899. At the trial Frank Fenton said he had wanted Mrs Winchurch to ask her husband for a divorce. He would have married her in spite of the disastrous effect on his career. It was she, he said, who refused to consider it on the grounds that she did not think she could bear the disgrace.

In January 1900 Florence went to London for the day and, among other purchases, bought at a grocer's two cans of herring fillets marinaded in a white wine sauce. It was rare for canned food to appear in the Winchurch household, and when Florence suggested that these herring fillets should be used in the preparation of a dish called *Filets de hareng marinés à la Rosette*, the recipe for which she had been given by Ada Fenton, the cook, Mrs Eliza Holmes, protested that she could prepare it from fresh fish. Florence, however, insisted, one of the cans was used, and the dish was made and served to Florence and Edward at dinner. It was brought in by the parlourmaid, Alice Evans, as a savoury or final course to a four-course meal. Although Florence had shown so much enthusiasm about the dish, she took none of it. Edward ate a moderate amount and the rest was removed to the kitchen where it was shared between Mrs Holmes, Alice Evans and the housemaid, Violet Stedman. No one suffered any ill-effects. The date was 30 January 1900.

Five weeks later on 5 March Florence asked Mrs Holmes to make the dish again, using the remaining can, as her husband had liked it so much. This time Florence too partook of the marinaded herrings, but when the remains of it were about to be removed by Alice to the kitchen, she advised her to tell the others not to eat it as she 'thought it had a strange taste and was perhaps not quite fresh'. However, although Mrs Holmes and Alice abstained, Violet Stedman ate a larger quantity of the dish than had either Florence or Edward.

Florence, as was her habit, left Edward to drink his port alone. Within a few minutes a strangled shout was heard from the dining room and a sound as of furniture breaking. Florence and Alice Evans and Mrs Holmes went into the room and found Edward Winchurch lying on the floor, a chair with one leg wrenched from its socket tipped over beside him and an overturned glass of port on the table. Florence approached him and he went into a violent convulsion, arching his back and baring his teeth, his hands grasping the chair in apparent agony.

John Barstow, the coachman, was sent to fetch Dr Fenton. By this time Florence was complaining of stomach pains and seemed unable to stand. Fenton arrived, had Edward and Florence removed upstairs and asked Mrs Holmes what they had eaten. She showed him the empty herring fillets can, and he recognized the brand as that by which a patient of a colleague of his had recently been infected with botulism, a virulent and usually fatal form of food poisoning. Fenton immediately assumed that it was *bacillus botulinus* which had attacked the Winchurches, and such is the power of suggestion that Violet Stedman now said she felt sick and faint.

Botulism causes paralysis, difficulty in breathing and a disturbance of the vision. Florence appeared to be partly paralysed and said she had double vision. Edward's symptoms were different. He continued to have spasms, was totally relaxed between spasms, and although he had difficulty in breathing and other symptoms of botulism, the onset had been exceptionally rapid for any form of food poisoning. Fenton, however, had never seen a case of botulism, which is extremely rare, and he supposed that the symptoms would vary greatly from person to person. He gave jalap and cream of tartar as a purgative and, in the absence of any known relatives of Edward Winchurch, he sent for Florence's father, Thomas Anstruther.

If Fenton was less innocent than was supposed, he had made a mistake in sending for Anstruther, for Florence's father insisted on a second opinion, and at ten o'clock went himself to the home of that very colleague of Fenton's who had recently witnessed a known case of botulism. This was Dr Maurice Waterfield, twice Fenton's age, a popular man with a large practice in Stowerton. He looked at Edward Winchurch, at the agonized grin which overspread his features, and as Edward went into his last convulsive seizure, pronounced that he had been poisoned not by *bacillus botulinus* but by strychnine.

Edward died a few minutes afterwards. Dr Waterfield told Fenton that there was nothing physically wrong with either Florence or Violet Stedman. The former was suffering from shock or 'neurasthenia', the latter from indigestion brought on by over-eating. The police were informed, an inquest took place, and after it Florence was immediately arrested and charged with murdering her husband by administering to him a noxious substance, to wit *strychnos nux vomica*, in a decanter of port wine.

Her trial took place in London at the Central Criminal Court. She was twenty-four years old, a beautiful woman, and was by then known to have been having a love affair with the young and handsome Dr Fenton. As such, she and her case attracted national attention. Fenton had by then lost his practice, lost all hope of succeeding with another in the British Isles, and even before the trial his name had become a by-word, scurrilous doggerel being sung about him and Florence in the music halls. But far from increasing his loyalty to Florence, this seemed to make him the more determined to dissociate himself from her. He appeared as the prosecution's principal witness, and it was his evidence which sent Florence to the gallows.

Fenton admitted his relationship with Florence but said that he had told her it must end. The only possible alternative was divorce and ultimately marriage to himself. In early January 1900 Florence had been calling on his sister Ada, and he had come in to find them looking through a book of recipes. One of the recipes called for the use of herring fillets marinaded in white wine sauce, the mention of which had caused him to tell them about a case of botulism which a patient of Dr Waterfield was believed to have contracted from eating the contents of a can of just such fillets. He had named the brand and advised his sister not to buy any of that kind. When, some seven weeks later, he was called to the dying Edward Winchurch, the cook had shown him an empty can of that very brand. In his opinion, Mrs Winchurch herself was not ill at all, was not even ill from 'nerves' but was shamming. The judge said that he was not there to give his opinion, but the warning came too late. To the jury the point had already been made.

Asked if he was aware that strychnine had therapeutic uses in small quantities, Fenton said he was but that he kept none in his dispensary. In any case, his dispensary was kept locked and the cupboards inside it locked, so it would have been impossible for Florence to have entered it or to have appropriated anything while on a visit to Ada. Ada Fenton was not called as a witness. She was ill, suffering from what her doctor, Dr Waterfield, called 'brain fever'.

The prosecution's case was that, in order to inherit his fortune and marry Dr Fenton, Florence Winchurch had attempted to poison her husband with infected fish, or fish she had good reason to suppose might be infected. When this failed she saw to it that the dish was provided again, and herself added strychnine to the port decanter. It was postulated that she obtained the strychnine from her father's shop, without his knowledge, where it was kept in stock for the destruction of rats and moles. After her husband was taken ill, she herself simulated symptoms of botulism in the hope that the convulsions of strychnine poisoning would be confused with the paralysis and impeded breathing caused by the bacillus.

The defence tried to shift the blame to Frank Fenton, at least to suggest a conspiracy with Florence, but it was no use. The jury were out for only forty minutes. They pronounced her guilty, the judge sentenced her to death, and she was hanged just twenty-three days later, this being some twenty years before the institution of a Court of Appeal.

After the execution Frank and Ada Fenton emigrated to the United States and settled in New England. Fenton's reputation had gone before him. He was never again able to practise as a doctor but worked as the travelling representative of a firm of pharmaceutical manufacturers until his death in 1932. He never married. Ada, on the other hand, surprisingly enough, did. Ephraim Hurst fell in love with her in spite of her sickly constitution and withered leg. They were married in the summer of 1902 and by the spring of 1903 Ada Hurst was dead in childbirth.

By then Paraleash House had been re-named The Limes and lime trees planted to conceal its forbidding yet fascinating façade from the curious passer-by.

The parcel from Carlyon Brent arrived in the morning with a very polite covering letter from Amyas Ireland, grateful in anticipation. Wexford had never before seen a book in this embryo stage. The script, a hundred thousand words long, was bound in red, and through a window in its cover appeared the provisional title and the author's name: *Poison at Paraleash, A Reappraisal of the Winchurch Case* by Kenneth Gandolph.

'Remember all that fuss about Gandolph?' Wexford said to Dora across the coffee pot. 'About four years ago?'

'Somebody confessed a murder to him, didn't they?'

'Well, maybe. While a prison visitor, he spent some time talking to Paxton, the bank robber, in Wormwood Scrubs. Paxton died of cancer a few months later, and Gandolph then published an article in a newspaper in which he said that during the course of their conversations, Paxton had confessed to him that he was the per- petrator of the Conyngford murder in 1962. Paxton's widow pro- tested, there was a heated correspondence, MPs wanting the libel laws extended to libelling the dead, Gandolph shouting about the power of truth. Finally, the by then retired Detective Superintendent Warren of Scotland Yard put an end to all further controversy by issuing a statement to the press. He said Paxton couldn't have killed James Conyngford because on the day of Conyngford's death in Brighton Warren's sergeant and a constable had had Paxton under constant surveillance in London. In other words, he was never out of their sight.'

'Why would Gandolph invent such a thing, Reg?' said Dora.

'Perhaps he didn't. Paxton may have spun him all sorts of tales as a way of passing a boring afternoon. Who knows? On the other hand, Gandolph does rather set himself up as the elucidator of unsolved crimes. Years ago, I believe, he did find a satisfactory and quite reasonable solution to some murder in Scotland, and maybe it went to his head. Marshall, Groves, Folliott used to be his publishers. I wonder if they've refused this one because of the Paxton business, if it was offered to them and they turned it down?'

'But Mr Ireland's people have taken it,' Dora pointed out.

'Mm-hm. But they're not falling over themselves with enthusiasm, are they? They're scared. Ireland hasn't sent me this so that I can check up on the police procedural part. What do I know about police procedure in 1900? He's sent it to me in the hope that if Gandolph's been up to his old tricks I'll spot what they are.'

The working day presented no opportunity for a look at *Poison at Paraleash*, but at eight o'clock that night Wexford opened it and read Gandolph's long introduction.

Gandolph began by saying that as a criminologist he had always been aware of the Winchurch case and of the doubt which many felt about Florence Winchurch's guilt. Therefore, when he was staying with friends in Boston, Massachusetts, some two years before and they spoke to him of an acquaintance of theirs who was the niece of one of the principals in the case, he had asked to be introduced to her. The niece was Ada Hurst's daughter, Lina, still Miss Hurst, seventy-four years old and suffering from a terminal illness.

Miss Hurst showed no particular interest in the events of March 1900. She had been brought up by her father and his second wife and had hardly known her uncle. All her mother's property had come into her possession, including the diary which Ada Fenton Hurst had kept for three years prior to Edward Winchurch's death. Lina Hurst told Gandolph she had kept the diary for sentimental reasons but that he might borrow it and after her death she would see that it passed to him.

253

Within weeks Lina Hurst did die and her stepbrother, who was her executor, had the diary sent to Gandolph. Gandolph had read it and had been enormously excited by certain entries because in his view they incriminated Frank Fenton and exonerated Florence Winchurch. Here Wexford turned back a few pages and noted the author's dedication: *In memory of Miss Lina Hurst, of Cambridge, Massachusetts, without whose help this reappraisal would have been impossible.*

More than this Wexford had no time to read that evening, but he returned to it on the following day. The diary, it appeared, was a five-year one. At the top of each page was the date, as it might be 1 April, and beneath that five spaces each headed 18 . . . There was room for the diarist to write perhaps forty or fifty words in each space, no more. On the 1 January page in the third heading down, the number of the year, the eight had been crossed out and a nine substituted, and so it went on for every subsequent entry until March 6, after which no more entries were made until the diarist resumed in December 1900, by which time she and her brother were in Boston.

Wexford proceeded to Gandolph's first chapters. The story he had to tell was substantially the same as Hallam Saul's, and it was not until he came to chapter five and the weeks preceding the crime that he began to concentrate on the character of Frank Fenton. Fenton, he suggested, wanted Mrs Winchurch for the money and property she would inherit on her husband's death. Far from encouraging Florence to seek a divorce, he urged her never to let her husband suspect her preference for another man. Divorce would have left Florence penniless and homeless and have ruined his career. Fenton had known that it was only by making away with Winchurch and so arranging things that the death appeared natural, that he could have money, his profession and Florence.

There was only his word for it, said Gandolph, that he had spoken to Florence of botulism and had warned her against these particular canned herrings. Of course he had never seriously expected those cans to infect Winchurch, but that the fish should be eaten by him was necessary for his strategy. On the night before Winchurch's death, after dining with his sister at Paraleash House, he had introduced strychnine into the port decanter. He had also, Gandolph suggested, contrived to bring the conversation round to a discussion of food and to fish dishes. From that it would have been a short step to get Winchurch to admit how much he had enjoyed *Filets de hareng marinés à la Rosette* and to ask Florence to have them served again on the following day. Edward, apparently would have been highly likely to take his doctor's advice, even when in health, even on such a matter as what he should eat for the fourth course of his dinner, while Edward's wife did everything her lover, if not her husband, told her to do.

It was no surprise to Frank Fenton to be called out on the following evening to a man whose spasms only he would recognize as symptomatic of having swallowed strychnine. The arrival of Dr Waterfield was an unlooked-for circumstance. Once Winchurch's symptoms had been defined as arising from strychnine poisoning there was nothing left for Fenton to do but shift the blame on to his mistress. Gandolph suggested that Fenton attributed the source of the strychnine to Anstruther's chemist's shop out of revenge on Anstruther for calling in Waterfield and thus frustrating his hopes.

And what grounds had Gandolph for believing all this? Certain entries in Ada Hurst's diary. Wexford read them slowly and carefully.

For 27 February 1900, she had written, filling the entire small space: *Very cold. Leg painful again today. FW sent round the carriage and had John drive me to Pomfret. Compton says rats in the cellars and the old stables. Dined at home with F who says rats carry leptospiral jaundice, must be got rid of.* 28 February: *Drove in FW's carriage to call on old Mrs Paget. FW still here, having tea with F when I returned. I hope there is no harm in it. Dare I warn F?* 29 February: *F destroyed twenty rats with strychnine from his dispensary. What a relief!* 1 March: *Poor old Mrs Paget passed away in the night. A merciful release. Compton complained about the rats again. Warmer this evening and raining.* There was no entry for 2 March. 3 March: *Annie gave notice, she is getting married. Shall be sorry to lose her. Would not go out in carriage for fear of leaving FW too much alone with F. To bed early as leg most painful.* 4 March: *My birthday. 26 today and an old maid now, I think. FW drove over, brought me beautiful Indian shawl. She is always kind. Invited F and me to dinner tomorrow.* There was no entry for 5 March, and the last entry for nine months was the one for 6 March: *Dined last night at Paraleash House, six guests besides ourselves and the Ws. F left cigar case in the dining room, went back after seeing me home. I hope and pray there is no harm.*

Gandolph was evidently basing his case on the entries for 29 February and 6 March. In telling the court he had no strychnine in his dispensary, Fenton had lied. He had had an obvious opportunity for the introduction of strychnine into the decanter when he returned to Paraleash House in pursuit of his mislaid cigar case, and when he no doubt took care that he entered the dining room alone.

The next day Wexford re-read the chapters in which the new information was contained and he studied with concentration the section concerning the diary. But unless Gandolph were simply lying about the existence of the diary or of those two entries – things which he would hardly dare to do – there seemed no reason to differ from his inference. Florence was innocent, Frank Fenton the murderer of Edward Winchurch. But still Wexford wished Burden were there so that they might have one of their often acrimonious but always fruitful discussions. Somehow, with old Mike to argue against him and put up opposition, he felt things might have been better clarified.

And the morning brought news of Burden, if not the inspector himself, in the form of a postcard from Agios Nikolaios. The blue Aegean, a rocky escarpment, green pines. Who but Burden, as Wexford remarked to Dora, would send postcards while on his honeymoon? The post also brought a parcel from Carlyon Brent. It contained books, a selection from the publishing house's current list as a present for Wexford, and on the compliments slip accompanying them, a note from Amyas Ireland. *I shall be in Kingsmarkham with my people at the weekend. Can we meet? AI.* The books were the latest novel about Regency London by Camilla Barnet; *Put Money in Thy Purse*, the biography of Vassili Vandrian, the financier; the memoirs of Sofya Bolkinska, Bolshoi ballerina; an omnibus version of three novels of farming life by Giles de Coverley; the *Cosmos Book of Stars and Calendars*; and Vernon Trevor's short stories, *Raise me up Samuel*. Wexford wondered if he would ever have time to read them, but he enjoyed looking at them, their handsome glossy jackets, and smelling the civilized, aromatic, slightly acrid print smell of them. At ten he phoned Amyas Ireland, thanked him for the present and said he had read *Poison at Paraleash*.

'We can talk about it?'

'Sure. I'll be at home all Saturday and Sunday.'

'Let me take you and Mrs Wexford out to dinner on Saturday night,' said Ireland.

But Dora refused. She would be an embarrassment to both of them, she said, they would have their talk much better without her, and she would spend the evening at home having a shot at making a coil pot on her own. So Wexford went alone to meet Ireland in the bar of the Olive and Dove.

'I suppose,' he said, accepting a glass of Moselle, 'that we can dispense with the fiction that you wanted me to read this book to check on police methods and court procedure? Not to put too fine a point on it, you were apprehensive Gandolph might have been up to his old tricks again?'

'Oh, well now, come,' said Ireland. He seemed thinner than ever. He looked about him, he looked at Wexford, made a face, wrinkling up nose and mouth. 'Well, if you must put it like that – yes.'

'There may not have been any tricks, though, may there? Paxton couldn't have murdered James Conyngford, but that doesn't mean he didn't tell Gandolph he did murder him. Certainly the people who give Gandolph information seem to die very conveniently soon afterwards. He picks on the dying, first Paxton, then Lina Hurst. I suppose you've seen this diary?'

'Oh, yes. We shall be using prints of the two relevant pages among the illustrations.'

'No possibility of forgery?'

Ireland looked unhappy. 'Ada Hurst wrote a very stylized hand, what's called a *ronde* hand, which she had obviously taught herself. It would be easy to forge. I can't submit it to handwriting experts, can I? I'm not a policeman. I'm just a poor publisher who very much wants to publish this reappraisal of the Winchurch case if it's genuine – and shun it like the plague if it's not.'

'I think it's genuine.' Wexford smiled at the slight lightening in Ireland's face. 'I take it that it was usual for Ada Hurst to leave blanks as she did for March 2nd and March 5th?'

Ireland nodded. 'Quite usual. Every month there'd have been half a dozen days on which she made no entries.' A waiter came up to them with two large menus. 'I'll have the *bouillabaisse* and the lamb *en croûte* and the *médaillon* potatoes and french beans.'

'Consommé and then the parma ham,' said Wexford austerely. When the waiter had gone he grinned at Ireland. 'Pity they don't do *Filets de hareng marinés à la Rosette*. It might have provided us with the authentic atmosphere.' He was silent for a moment, savouring the delicate tangy wine. 'I'm assuming you've checked that 1900 genuinely was a Leap Year?'

'All first years of a century are.'

Wexford thought about it. 'Yes, of course, all years divisible by four are Leap Years.'

'I must say it's a great relief to me you're so happy about it.'

'I wouldn't quite say that,' said Wexford.

They went into the dining room and were shown, at Ireland's request, to a sheltered corner table. A waiter brought a bottle of Château de Portets 1973. Wexford looked at the basket of rolls, croissants, little plump brioches, miniature wholemeal loaves, Italian sticks, swallowed his desire and refused with an abrupt shake of the head. Ireland took two croissants.

'What exactly do you mean?' he said.

'It strikes me as being odd,' said the chief inspector, 'that in the entry for February 29th Ada Hurst says that her brother destroyed twenty rats with strychnine, yet in the entry for March 1st that Compton, whom I take to be the gardener, is still complaining about the rats. Why wasn't he told how effective the strychnine had been? Hadn't he been taken into Fenton's confidence about the poisoning? Or was twenty only a very small percentage of the hordes of rats which infested the place?'

'Right. It is odd. What else?'

'I don't know why, on March 6th, she mentions Fenton's returning for the cigar case. It wasn't interesting and she was limited for space. She doesn't record the name of a single guest at the dinner party, doesn't say what any of the women wore, but she carefully notes that her brother had left his cigar case in the Paraleash House dining room and had to go back for it. Why does she?'

'Oh, surely because by now she's nervous whenever Frank is alone with Florence.'

'But he wouldn't have been alone with Florence, Winchurch would have been there.'

They discussed the script throughout the meal, and later pored over it, Ireland with his brandy, Wexford with coffee. Dora had been wise not to come. But the outcome was that the new facts were really new and sound and that Carlyon Brent could safely publish the book in the spring. Wexford got home to find Dora sitting with a wobbly looking halffinished coil pot beside her and deep in the *Cosmos Book of Stars and Calendars*.

'Reg, did you know that for the Greeks the year began on Midsummer Day? And that the Chinese and Jewish calendars have twelve months in some years and thirteen in others?'

'I can't say I did.'

'We avoid that, you see, by using the Gregorian Calendar and correct the error by making every fourth year a Leap Year. You really must read this book, it's fascinating.'

But Wexford's preference was for the Vassili Vandrian and the farming trilogy, though with little time to read he hadn't completed a single one of these works by the time Burden returned on the following Monday week. Burden had a fine even tan but for his nose which had peeled.

'Have a good time?' asked Wexford with automatic politeness.

'What a question,' said the inspector, 'to ask a man who has just come back from his honeymoon. Of course I had a good time.' He cautiously scratched his nose. 'What have you been up to?'

'Seeing something of your brother-in-law. He got me to read a manuscript.'

'Ha!' said Burden. 'I know what that was. He said something about it but he knew Gandolph'd get short shrift from me. A devious liar if ever there was one. It beats me what sort of satisfaction a man can get out of the kind of fame that comes from foisting on the public stories he *knows* aren't true. All that about Paxton was a pack of lies, and I've no doubt he bases this new version of the Winchurch case on another pack of lies. He's not interested in the truth. He's only interested in being known as the great criminologist and the man who shows the police up for fools.'

'Come on, Mike, that's a bit sweeping. I told Ireland I thought it would be OK to go ahead and publish.'

Burden's face wore an expression that was almost a caricature of sophisticated scathing knowingness. 'Well, of course, I haven't seen it, I can't say. I'm basing my objection to Gandolph on the Paxton affair. Paxton never confessed to any murder and Gandolph knows it.'

'You can't say that for sure.'

Burden sat down. He tapped his fist lightly on the corner of the desk. 'I *can* say. I knew Paxton, I knew him well.'

'I didn't know that.'

'No, it was years back, before I came here. In Eastbourne, it was, when Paxton was with the Garfield gang. In the force down there we knew it was useless ever trying to get Paxton to talk. He *never* talked. I don't mean he just didn't give away any info, I mean he didn't answer when you spoke to him. Various times we tried to interrogate him he just maintained this total silence. A mate of his told me he'd made it a rule not to talk to policemen or social workers or lawyers or any what you might call establishment people, and he never had. He talked to his wife and his kids and his mates all right. But I remember once he was in the dock at Lewes Assizes and the judge addressed him. He just didn't answer – he wouldn't – and the judge, it was old Clydesdale, sent him down for contempt. So don't tell me Paxton made any sort of confession to Kenneth Gandolph, not *Paxton*.'

The effect of this was to reawaken all Wexford's former doubts. He trusted Burden, he had a high opinion of his opinion. He began to wish he had advised Ireland to have tests made to determine the age of the ink used in the 29 February and 6 March entries, or to have the writing examined by a handwriting expert. Yet if Ada Hurst had had a stylized hand self-taught in adulthood . . . What good were handwriting experts anyway? Not much, in his experience. And of course Ireland couldn't suggest to Gandolph that the ink should be tested without offending the man to such an extent that he would refuse publication of *Poison at Paraleash* to Carlyon Brent. But Wexford was suddenly certain that those entries were false and that Gandolph had forged them. Very subtly and cunningly he had forged them, having judged that the addition to the diary of just thirty-four words would alter the whole balance of the Winchurch case and shift the culpability from Florence to her lover.

Thirty-four words. Wexford had made a copy of the diary entries and now he looked at them again. 29 February: *F destroyed twenty rats with strychnine from his dispensary. What a relief!* 6 March: *F left cigar case in the dining room, went back after seeing me home. I hope and pray there is no harm.* There were no anachronisms – men certainly used cigar cases in 1900 – no divergence from Ada's usual style. The word 'twenty' was written in letters instead of two figures. The writer, on 6 March, had written not about that day but about the day before. Did that amount to anything? Wexford thought not, though he pondered on it for most of the day.

That evening he was well into the last chapter of *Put Money in Thy Purse* when the phone rang. It was Jenny Burden. Would he and Dora come to dinner on Saturday? Her parents would be there and her brother.

Wexford said Dora was out at her pottery class, but yes, they would love to, and had she had a nice time in Crete?

'How sweet of you to ask,' said the bride. 'No one else has. Thank you, we had a lovely time.'

He had meant it when he said they would love to, but still he didn't feel very happy about meeting Amyas Ireland again. He had a notion that once the book was published some as yet unimagined Warren or Burden would turn up and denounce it, deride it, laugh at the glaring giveaway he and Ireland couldn't see. When he saw Ireland again he ought to say, don't do it, don't take the risk, publish and be damned can have another meaning than the popular one. But how to give such a warning with no sound reason for giving it, with nothing but one of those vague feelings, this time of foreboding, which had so assisted him yet run him into so much trouble in the past? No, there was nothing he could do. He sighed, finished his chapter and moved on to the farmer's fictionalized memoirs.

Afterwards Wexford was in the habit of saying that he got more reading done during that week than he had in years. Perhaps it had been a way of escape from fretful thought. But certainly he had passed a freakishly slack week, getting home most nights by six. He even read Miss Camilla Barnet's *The Golden Reticule*, and by Friday night there was nothing left but the *Cosmos Book of Stars and Calendars*.

It was a large party, Mr and Mrs Ireland and their son, Burden's daughter Pat, Grace and her husband and, of course, the Burdens themselves. Jenny's face glowed with happiness and Aegean sunshine. She welcomed the Wexfords with kisses and brought them drinks served in their own wedding present to her.

The meeting with Amyas Ireland wasn't the embarrassment Wexford had feared it would be – had feared, that is, up till a few minutes before he and Dora had left home. And now he knew that he couldn't contain himself till after dinner, till the morning, or perhaps worse than that – a phone call on Monday morning. He asked his hostess if she would think him very rude if he spoke to her brother alone for five minutes.

She laughed. 'Not rude at all. I think you must have got the world's most wonderful idea for a crime novel and Ammy's going to publish it. But I don't know where to put you unless it's the kitchen. And you,' she said to her brother, 'are not to eat anything, mind.'

'I couldn't wait,' Wexford said as they found themselves stowed away into the kitchen where every surface was necessarily loaded with the constituents of dinner for ten people. 'I only found out this evening at the last minute before we were due to come out.'

'It's something about the Winchurch book?'

Wexford said eagerly, 'It's not too late, is it? I was worried I might be too late.'

'Good God, no. We hadn't planned to start printing before the autumn.' Ireland, who had seemed about to disobey his sister and help himself to a macaroon from a silver dish, suddenly lost his appetite. 'This is serious?'

'Wait till you hear. I was waiting for my wife to finish dressing.' He grinned. 'You should make it a rule to read your own books, you know. That's what I was doing, reading one of those books you sent me and that's where I found it. You won't be able to publish *Poison at Paraleash*.' The smile went and he looked almost fierce. 'I've no hesitation in saying Kenneth Gandolph is a forger and a cheat and you'd be advised to have nothing to do with him in future.'

Ireland's eyes narrowed. 'Better know it now than later. What did he do and how do you know?'

From his jacket pocket Wexford took the copy he had made of the diary entries. 'I can't prove that the last entry, the one for March 6th that says, *F left cigar case in the dining room, went back after seeing me home*, I can't prove that's forged, I only think it is. What I know for certain is a forgery is the entry for February 29th.'

'Isn't that the one about strychnine?'

'*F destroyed twenty rats with strychnine from his dispensary. What a relief!*'

'How do you know it's forged?'

'Because the day itself didn't occur,' said Wexford. 'In 1900 there was no February 29th, it wasn't a Leap Year.'

'Oh, yes, it was. We've been through all that before.' Ireland sounded both relieved and impatient. 'All years divisible by four are Leap Years. All century years are divisible by four and 1900 was a century year. 1897 was the year she began the diary, following 1896 which was a Leap Year. Needless to say, there was no February 29th in 1897, 1898 or 1899 so there must have been one in 1900.'

'It wasn't a Leap Year,' said Wexford. 'Didn't I tell you I found this out through that book of yours, the *Cosmos Book of Stars and Calendars*? There's a lot of useful information in there, and one of the bits of information is about how Pope Gregory composed a new civil calendar to correct the errors of the Julian Calendar. One of his rulings was that every fourth year should be a Leap Year except in certain cases . . .'

Ireland interrupted him. 'I don't believe it!' he said in the voice of someone who knows he believes every word.

Wexford shrugged. He went on, 'Century years were not to be Leap Years unless they were divisible not by four but by four hundred. Therefore, 1600 would have been a Leap Year if the Gregorian Calendar had by then been adopted, and 2000 will be a Leap Year, but 1800 was not and 1900 was not. So in 1900 there was no February 29th and Ada Hurst left the space on that page blank for the very good reason that the day following February 28th was March 1st. Unluckily for him, Gandolph, like you and me and most people, knew nothing of this as otherwise he would surely have inserted his strychnine entry into the blank space of March 2nd and his forgery might never have been discovered.'

Ireland slowly shook his head at man's ingenuity and perhaps his chicanery. 'I'm very grateful to you. We should have looked fools, shouldn't we?'

'I'm glad Florence wasn't hanged in error,' Wexford said as they went back to join the others. 'Her marriage didn't begin with dearly beloved, but if she was afraid at the end it can't have been with any amazement.'

The Fever Tree

The Fever Tree

Where malaria is, there grows the fever tree.

It has the feathery fern-like leaves, fresh green and tender, that are common to so many trees in tropical regions. Its shape is graceful with an air of youth, as if every fever tree is still waiting to grow up. But the most distinctive thing about it is the colour of its bark which is the yellow of an unripe lemon. The fever trees stand out from among the rest because of their slender yellow trunks.

Ford knew what the tree was called and he could recognize it but he didn't know what its botanical name was. Nor had he ever heard why it was called the fever tree, whether the tribesmen used its leaves or bark or fruit as a specific against malaria or if it simply took its name from its warning presence wherever the malaria-carrying mosquito was. The sight of it in Ntsukunyane seemed to promote a fever in his blood.

An African in khaki shorts and shirt lifted up the bar for them so that their car could pass through the opening in the fence. Inside it looked no different from outside, the same bush, still, silent, unstirred by wind stretching away on either side. Ford, driving the two miles along the tarmac road to the reception hut, thought of how it would be if he turned his head and saw Marguerite in the passenger seat beside him. It was an illusion he dared not have but was allowed to keep for only a minute. Tricia shattered it. She began to belabour him with schoolgirl questions, uttered in a bright and desperate voice.

Another African, in a fancier, more decorated, uniform, took their booking voucher and checked it against a ledger. You had to pay weeks in advance for the privilege of staying here. Ford had booked the day after he had said goodbye to Marguerite and returned, for ever, to Tricia.

'My wife wants to know the area of Ntsukunyane,' he said.

'Four million acres.'

Ford gave the appropriate whistle. 'Do we have a chance of seeing a leopard?'

The man shrugged, smiled, 'Who knows? You may be lucky. You're here a whole week so you should see lion, elephant, hippo, cheetah maybe. But the leopard is nocturnal and you must be back in camp by six p.m.' He looked at his watch. 'I advise you to get on now, sir, if you're to make Thaba before they close the gates.'

Ford got back into the car. It was nearly four. The sun of Africa, a living presence, a personal god, burned through a net of haze. There was no wind. Tricia, in a pale yellow sundress with frills, had hung her arm outside the open window and the fair downy skin was glowing red. He told her what the man had said and he told her about the notice pinned inside the hut: *It is strictly forbidden to bring firearms into the game reserve, to feed the animals, to exceed the speed limit, to litter.*

'And most of all you mustn't get out of the car,' said Ford.

'What, not ever?' said Tricia, making her pale blue eyes round and naive and marble-like.

'That's what it says.'

She pulled a face. 'Silly old rules!'

'They have to have them,' he said.

In here as in the outside world. It is strictly forbidden to fall in love, to leave your wife, to try to begin anew. He glanced at Tricia to see if the same thoughts were passing through her mind. Her face wore its arch expression, winsome.

'A prize,' she said, 'for the first one to see an animal.'

'All right.' He had agreed to this reconciliation, to bring her on this holiday, this second honeymoon, and now he must try. He must work at it. It wasn't just going to happen as love had sprung between him and Marguerite, unsought and untried for. 'Who's going to award it?' he said.

'You are if it's me and I am if it's you. And if it's me I'd like a presey from the camp shop. A very nice pricey presey.'

Ford was the winner. He saw a single zebra come out from among the thorn trees on the right-hand side, then a small herd. 'Do I get a present from the shop?'

He could sense rather than see her shake her head with calculated coyness. 'A kiss,' she said and pressed warm dry lips against his cheek.

It made him shiver a little. He slowed down for the zebra to cross the road. The thorn bushes had spines on them two inches long. By the roadside grew a species of wild zinnia with tiny flowers, coral red, and these made red drifts among the coarse pale grass. In the bush were red ant hills with tall peaks like towers on a castle in a fairy story. It was thirty miles to Thaba. He drove on just within the speed limit, ignoring Tricia as far as he could whenever she asked him to slow down. They weren't going to see one of the big predators, anyway not this afternoon, he was certain of that, only impala and zebra and maybe a giraffe. On business trips in the past he'd taken time off to go to Serengeti and Kruger and he knew. He got the binoculars out for Tricia and adjusted them and hooked them round her neck, for he hadn't forgotten the binoculars and cameras she had dropped and smashed in the past through failing to do that, and her tears afterwards. The car wasn't air-conditioned and the heat lay heavy and still between them. Ahead of them, as they drove westwards, the sun was sinking in a dull yellow glare. The sweat flowed out of Ford's armpits and between his shoulder blades, soaking his already wet shirt and laying a cold sticky film on his skin.

A stone pyramid with arrows on it, set in the middle of a junction of roads, pointed the way to Thaba, to the main camp at Waka-suthu and to Hippo Bridge over the Suthu River. On top of it sat a baboon with her grey fluffy infant on her knees. Tricia yearned for it, stretching out her arms. She had never had a child. The baboon began picking fleas out of its baby's scalp. Tricia gave a little nervous scream, half-disgusted, half-joyful. Ford drove down the road to Thaba and in through the entrance to the camp ten minutes before they closed the gates for the night.

The dark comes down fast in Africa. Dusk is of short duration; no sooner have you noticed it than it has gone and night has fallen. In the few moments of dusk, pale things glimmer brightly and birds make a soft murmuring. In the camp at Thaba were a restaurant and a shop, round huts with thatched roofs and wooden chalets with porches. Ford and Tricia had been assigned a chalet on the northern perimeter and from their porch, beyond the high, wire fence, you could see the Suthu River flowing smoothly and silently between banks of tall reeds. Dusk had just come as they walked up the wooden steps, Ford carrying their cases. It was then that he saw the fever trees, two of them, their ferny leaves bleached to grey by the twilight but their trunks a sharper, stronger yellow than in the day.

'Just as well we took our anti-malaria pills,' said Ford as he pushed open the door. When the light was switched on he could see two mosquitoes on the opposite wall. 'Anopheles is the malaria carrier but unfortunately they don't announce whether they're anopheles or not.'

Twin beds, a table, lamps, an air conditioner, a fridge, a door, standing open, to lavatory and shower. Tricia dropped her make-up case, without which she went nowhere, on to the bed by the window. The light wasn't very bright. None of the lights in the camp were because the electricity came from a generator. They were a small colony of humans in a world that belonged to the animals, a reversal of the usual order of things. From the window you could see other chalets, other dim lights, other parked cars. Tricia talked to the two mosquitoes.

'Is your name Anna Phyllis? No. Darling, you're quite safe. She says she's Mary Jane and her husband's John Henry.'

Ford managed to smile. He had accepted and grown used to Tricia's facetiousness until he had encountered Marguerite's wit. He shoved his case, without unpacking it, into the cupboard and went to have a shower. Tricia stood on the porch, listening to the cicadas, thousands of them. It had gone pitch dark while she was hanging up her dresses and the sky was punctured all over with bright stars.

She had got Ford back from that woman and now she had to keep him. She had lost some weight, bought a lot of new clothes and had had highlights put in her hair. Men had always made her feel frightened, starting with her father when she was a child. It was then, when a child, that she had purposely began *playing* the child with its winning little ways. She had noticed that her father was kinder and more forbearing towards little girls than towards her mother. Ford had married a little girl, clinging and winsome, and had liked it well enough till he had met a grown woman. Tricia knew all that, but now she knew no better how to keep him than she did then; the old methods were as weary and stale to her as she guessed they might be to him. Standing there on the porch, she half-wished she were alone and didn't have to have a husband, didn't, for the sake of convention and of pride, for support and society, have to hold tight on to him. She listened wistfully for a lion to roar out there in the bush beyond the fence, but there was no sound except the cicadas.

Ford came out in a towelling robe. 'What did you do with the mosquito stuff? The spray?'

Frightened at once, she said, 'I don't know.'

'What do you mean, you don't know? You must know. I gave you the aerosol at the hotel and said to put it in that make-up case of yours.'

She opened the case, though she knew the mosquito stuff wasn't there. Of course it wasn't. She could see it on the bathroom shelf in the hotel, left behind because it was too bulky. She bit her lip, looked sideways at Ford. 'We can get some more at the shop.'

'Tricia, the shop closes at seven and it's now ten past.'

'We can get some in the morning.'

'Mosquitoes happen to be most active at night.' He rummaged among the bottles and jars in the case. 'Look at all this useless rubbish. "Skin cleanser", "pearlized foundation", "moisturizer" – like some young model girl. I suppose it didn't occur to you to bring the anti-mosquito spray and leave the "pearlized foundation" behind.'

Her lip trembled. She could feel herself, almost involuntarily, rounding her eyes, forming her mouth into the shape for lisping. 'We did 'member to take our pills.'

'That won't stop the damn' things biting.' He went back into the shower and slammed the door.

Marguerite wouldn't have forgotten to bring that aerosol. Tricia knew he was thinking of Marguerite again, that his head was full of her, that she had entered his thoughts powerfully and insistently on the long drive to Thaba. She began to cry. The water went on running out of her eyes and wouldn't stop, so she changed her dress while she cried and the tears came through the powder she put on her face.

They had dinner in the restaurant. Tricia, in pink flowered crepe, was the only dressed-up woman there, and while once she would have fancied the other diners looked at her in admiration now she thought it must be with derision. She ate her small piece of overcooked hake and her large piece of overcooked, breadcrumbed veal, and watched the red weals from mosquito bites coming up on Ford's arms.

There were no lights on in the camp but those which shone from the windows of the main building and from the chalets. Gradually the lights went out and it became very dark. In spite of his mosquito bites, Ford fell asleep at once but the noise of the air-conditioning kept Tricia awake. At eleven she switched it off and opened the window. Then she did sleep but she awoke again at four, lay awake for half an hour, got up and put her clothes on and went out.

It was still dark but the darkness was lifting as if the thickest veil of it had been withdrawn. A heavy dew lay on the grass. As she passed under the merula tree, laden with small green apricot-shaped fruits, a flock of bats flew out from its branches and circled her head. If Ford had been with her she would have screamed and clung to him but because she was alone she kept silent. The camp and the bush beyond the fence were full of sound. The sounds brought to Tricia's mind the paintings of Hieronymus Bosch, imps and demons and dreadful homunculi which, if they had uttered, might have made noises like these, gruntings and soft whistles and chirps and little thin squeals.

She walked about, waiting for the dawn, expecting it to come with drama. But it was only a grey pallor in the sky, a paleness between parting black clouds, and the feeling of let-down frightened her as if it were a symbol or an omen of something more significant in her life than the coming of morning.

Ford woke up, unable at first to open his eyes for the swelling from mosquito bites. There were mosquitoes like threads of thistledown on the walls, all over the walls. He got up and staggered, half-blind, out of the bedroom and let the water from the shower run on his eyes. Tricia came and stared at his face, giggling nervously and biting her lip.

The camp gates opened at five-thirty and the cars began their exodus. Tricia had never passed a driving test and Ford couldn't see, so they went to the restaurant for breakfast instead. When the shop opened Ford bought two kinds of mosquito repellant and, impatiently, because he could no longer bear her apologies and her pleading eyes, a necklace of ivory beads for Tricia and a skirt with giraffes printed on it. At nine o'clock, when the swelling round Ford's eyes had subsided a little, they set off in the car, taking the road for Hippo Bridge.

The day was humid and thickly hot. Ford had counted the number of mosquito bites he had and the total was twenty-four. It was hard to believe that two little tablets of quinine would be proof against twenty-four bites, some of which must certainly have been inflicted by anopheles. Hadn't he seen the two fever trees when they arrived last night? Now he drove the car slowly and doggedly, hardly speaking, his swollen eyes concealed behind sunglasses. By the Suthu River and then by a water hole he stopped and they watched. But they saw nothing come to the water's edge unless you counted the log which at last disappeared, thus proving itself to have been a crocodile. It was too late in the morning to see much apart from the marabou storks which stood one-legged, still and hunched, in a clearing or on the gaunt branch of a tree. Through binoculars Ford stared at the bush which stretched in unbroken, apparently untenanted, sameness to the blue ridge of mountains on the far horizon.

There could be no real fever from the mosquito bites. If malaria were to come it wouldn't be yet. But Ford, sitting in the car beside Tricia, nevertheless felt something like a delirium of fever. It came perhaps from the gross irritation of the whole surface of his body, from the tender burning of his skin and from his inability to move without setting up fresh torment. It affected his mind too, so that each time he looked at Tricia a kind of panic rose in him. Why had he done it? Why had he gone back to her? Was he mad? His eyes and his head throbbed as if his temperature was raised. Tricia's pink jeans were too tight for her and the frills on her white voile blouse ridiculous. With the aid of the binoculars she had found a family of small grey monkeys in the branches of a peepul tree and she was cooing at them out of the window. Presently she opened the car door, held it just open and turned to look at him the way a child looks at her father when he has forbidden something she nevertheless longs and means to do.

They hadn't had sight of a big cat or an elephant, they hadn't even seen a jackal. Ford lifted his shoulders.

'OK. But if a ranger comes along and catches you we'll be in dead trouble.'

She got out of the car, leaving the door open. The grass which began at the roadside and covered the bush as far as the eye could see was long and coarse. It came up above Tricia's knees. A lioness or a cheetah lying in it would have been entirely concealed. Ford picked up the binoculars and looked the other way to avoid watching Tricia who had once again forgotten to put the camera strap round her neck. She was making overtures to the monkeys who shrank away from her, embracing each other and burying heads in shoulders, like menaced refugees in a sentimental painting. He moved the glasses slowly. About a hundred yards from where a small herd of buck grazed uneasily, he saw the two cat faces close together, the bodies nestled together, the spotted backs. Cheetah. It came into his mind how he had heard that they were the fastest animals on earth.

He ought to call to Tricia and get her back at once into the car. He didn't call. Through the glasses he watched the big cats that reclined there so gracefully, satiated, at rest, yet with open eyes. Marguerite would have liked them, she loved cats, she had a Burmese, as lithe and slim and poised as one of these wild creatures. Tricia got back into the car, exclaiming how sweet the monkeys were. He started the car and drove off without saying anything to her about the cheetahs.

Later, at about five in the afternoon, she wanted to get out of the car again and he didn't stop her. She walked up and down the road, talking to mongooses. In something over an hour it would be dark. Ford imagined starting up the car and driving back to the camp without her. Leopards were nocturnal hunters, waiting till dark. The swelling around his eyes had almost subsided now but his neck and arms and hands ached from the stiffness of the bites. The mongooses fled into the grass as Tricia approached, whispering to them, hands outstretched. A car with four men in it was coming along from the Hippo Bridge direction. It slowed down and the driver put his head out. His face was brick-red, thick-featured, his hair corrugated blond, and his voice had the squashed vowels accent of the white man born in Africa.

'The lady shouldn't be out on the road like that.'

'I know,' said Ford. 'I've told her.'

'Excuse me, d'you know you're doing a very dangerous thing, leaving your car?' The voice had a hectoring boom. Tricia blushed. She bridled, smiled, bit her lip, though she was in fact very afraid of this man who was looking at her as if he despised her, as if she disgusted him. When he got back to camp, would he betray her?

'Promise you won't tell on me?' she faltered, her head on one side.

He gave an exclamation of anger and withdrew his head. The car moved forward. Tricia gave a skip and a jump into the passenger seat beside Ford. They had under an hour in which to get back to Thaba. Ford drove back, following the car with the four men in it.

At dinner they sat at adjoining tables. Tricia wondered how many people they had told about her, for she fancied that some of the diners looked at her with curiosity or antagonism. The man with fair curly hair they called Eric boasted loudly of what he and his companions had seen that day, a whole pride of lions, two rhinoceros, hyena and the rare sable antelope.

'You can't expect to see much down that Hippo Bridge road, you know,' he said to Ford. 'All the game's up at Sotingwe. You take the Sotingwe road first thing tomorrow and I'll guarantee you lions.'

He didn't address Tricia, he didn't even look at her. Ten years before, men in restaurants had turned their heads to look at her and though she had feared them, she had basked, trembling, in their gaze. Walking across the grass, back to their chalet, she held on to Ford's arm.

'For God's sake, mind my mosquito bites,' said Ford.

He lay awake a long while in the single bed a foot away from

Tricia's, thinking about the leopard out there beyond the fence that hunted at night. The leopard would move along the branch of a tree and drop upon its prey. Lionesses hunted in the early morning and brought the kill to their mate and the cubs. Ford had seen all that sort of thing on television. How cheetahs hunted he didn't know except that they were very swift. An angry elephant would lean on a car and crush it or smash a windscreen with a blow from its foot. It was too dark for him to see Tricia but he knew she was awake, lying still, sometimes holding her breath. He heard her breath released in an exhalation, a sigh, that was audible above the rattle of the air-conditioner.

Years ago he had tried to teach her to drive. They said a husband should never try to teach his wife, he would have no patience with her and make no allowances. Tricia's progress had never been maintained, she had always been liable to do silly reckless things and then he had shouted at her. She took a driving test and failed and she said this was because the examiner had bullied her. Tricia seemed to think no one should ever raise his voice to her, and at one glance from her all men should fall slaves at her feet.

He would have liked her to be able to take a turn at driving. There was no doubt you missed a lot when you had to concentrate on the road. But it was no use suggesting it. Theirs was one of the first cars in the line to leave the gates at five-thirty, to slip out beyond the fence into the grey dawn, the still bush. At the stone pyramid, on which a family of baboons sat clustered, Ford took the road for Sotingwe.

A couple of miles up they came upon the lions. Eric and his friends were already there, leaning out of the car windows with cameras. The lions, two full-grown lionesses, two lioness cubs and a lion cub with his mane beginning to sprout, were lying on the roadway. Ford stopped and parked the car on the opposite side to Eric.

'Didn't I say you'd be lucky up here?' Eric called to Tricia, 'Not got any ideas about getting out and investigating, I hope.'

Tricia didn't answer him or look at him. She looked at the lions. The sun was coming up, radiating the sky with a pinkish-orange glow and a little breeze fluttered all the pale green, fern-like leaves. The larger of the adult lionesses, bored rather than alarmed by Eric's elaborate photographic equipment, got up slowly and strolled into the bush, in among the long dry grass and the red zinnias. The cubs followed her, the other lioness followed her. Through his binoculars Ford watched them stalk with proud, lifted heads, walking, even the little ones, in a graceful, measured, controlled way. There were no impala anywhere, no giraffe, no wildebeest. The world here belonged to the lions.

All the game was gathered at Sotingwe, near the water hole. An elephant with ears like punkahs was powdering himself with red earth blown out through his trunk. Tricia got out of the car to photograph the elephant and Ford didn't try to stop her. He scratched his mosquito bites which had passed the burning and entered the itchy stage. Once more Tricia had neglected to pass the camera strap round her neck. She made her way down to the water's edge and stood at a safe distance — was it a safe distance? Was any distance safe in here? — looking at a crocodile. Ford thought, without really explaining to himself or even fully understanding what he meant, that it was the wrong time of day, it was too early. They went back to Thaba for breakfast.

At breakfast and again at lunch Eric was very full of what he had seen. He had taken the dirt road that ran down from Sotingwe to Suthu Bridge and there, up in a tree near the water, had been a leopard. Malcolm had spotted it first, stretched out asleep on a branch, a long way off but quite easy to see through field glasses.

'Massive great fella with your authentic square-type spots,' said Eric, smoking a cigar.

Tricia, of course, wanted to go to Suthu Bridge, so Ford took the dirt road after they had had their siesta. Malcolm described exactly where he had seen the leopard which might, for all he knew, still be sleeping on its branch.

'About half a mile up from the bridge. You look over on your left and there's a sort of clearing with one of those trees with yellow trunks in it. This chap was on a branch on the right side of the clearing.'

The dirt road was a track of crimson earth between green verges. Ford found the clearing with the single fever tree but the leopard had gone. He drove slowly down to the bridge that spanned the sluggish green river. When he switched off the engine it was silent and utterly still, the air hot and close, nothing moving but the mosquitoes that danced in their haphazard yet regular measure above the surface of the water.

Tricia was getting out of the car as a matter of course now. This time she didn't even trouble to give him the coy glance that asked permission. She was wearing a red and white striped sundress with straps that were too narrow and a skirt that was too tight. She ran down to the water's edge, took off a sandal and dipped in a daring foot. She laughed and twirled her feet, dabbling the dry round stones with water drops. Ford thought how he had loved this sort of thing when he had first met her, and now he was going to have to bear it for the rest of his life. He broke into a sweat as if his temperature had suddenly risen.

She was prancing about on the stones and in the water holding up her skirt. There were no animals to be seen. All afternoon they had seen nothing but impala, and the sun was moving down now, beginning to colour the hazy, pastel sky. Tricia, on the opposite bank, broke another Ntsukunyane rule and picked daisies, tucking one behind each ear. With a flower between her teeth like a Spanish dancer, she swayed her hips and smiled.

Ford turned the ignition key and started the car. It would be dark in just over an hour and long before that they would have closed the gates at Thaba. He moved the car forward, reversed, making what Tricia, no doubt, would call a three-point turn. Facing towards Thaba now, he put the selector into drive, his foot on the accelerator, he took a deep breath as the sweat trickled between his shoulder blades. The heat made mirages on the road and out of them a car was coming. Ford stopped and switched off the engine. It wasn't Eric's car but one belonging to a couple of young Americans on holiday. The boy raised his hand in a salute at Ford.

Ford called out to Tricia, 'Come on or we'll be late.' She got into the car, dropping her flowers on to the roadway. Ford had been going to leave her there, that was how much he wanted to be rid of her. Her body began to shake and she clasped her hands tightly together so that he shouldn't see. He had been going to drive away and leave her there to the darkness and the lions, the leopard that hunted by night. He had been driving away, only the Americans' car had come along.

She was silent, thinking about it. The Americans turned back soon after they did and followed them up the dirt road. Impala stood around the solitary fever tree, listening perhaps to inaudible sounds or scenting invisible danger. The sky was smoky yellow with sunset. Tricia thought about what Ford must have intended to do, drive back to camp just before they closed the gates, watch the darkness come down, knowing she was out there, say not a word of her absence to anyone – and who would miss her? Eric? Malcolm? Ford wouldn't have gone to the restaurant and in the morning when they opened the gates he would have driven away. No need even to check out at Ntsukunyane where you paid weeks in advance.

The perfect murder. Who would search for her, not knowing there was need for search? And if her bones were found? One set of bones, human, impala, waterbuck, looks very much like another after the jackals have been at them and the vultures. And when he reached home he would have said he had left her for Marguerite . . .

He was nicer to her that evening, gentler. Because he was afraid she had guessed or might guess the truth of what had happened at Sotingwe?

'We said we'd have champagne one night. How about now? No time like the present.'

'If you like,' Tricia said. She felt sick all the time, she had no appetite.

Ford toasted them in champagne. 'To us!'

He ordered the whole gamut of the menu, soup, fish, Wiener schnitzel, *crème brûlée*. She picked at her food, thinking how he had meant to kill her. She would never be safe now, for having failed once he would try again. Not the same method perhaps but some other. How was she to know he hadn't already tried? Maybe, for instance, he had substituted aspirin for those quinine tablets, or when they were back in the hotel in Mombasa he might try to drown her. She would never be safe unless she left him.

Which was what he wanted, which would be the next best thing to her death. Lying awake in the night, she thought of what that would mean, going back to live with her mother while he went to Marguerite. He wasn't asleep either. She could hear the sound of his irregular wakeful breathing. She heard the bed creak as he moved in it restlessly, the air conditioning grinding, the whine of a mosquito. Now, if she hadn't already been killed she might be wandering out there in the bush, in terror in the dark, afraid to take a step but afraid to remain still, fearful of every sound yet not knowing which sound most to fear. There was no moon. She had taken note of that before she came to bed and had seen in her diary that tomorrow the moon would be new. The sky had been overcast at nightfall and now it was pitch dark. The leopard could see, perhaps by the light of the stars or with an inner instinctive eye more sure than simple vision and would drop silently from its branch to sink its teeth into the lifted throat.

The mosquito that had whined bit Ford in several places on his face and neck and on his left foot. He had forgotten to use the repellant the night before. Early in the morning, at dawn, he got up and dressed and went for a walk round the camp. There was no one about but one of the African staff, hosing down a guest's car. Squeaks and shufflings came from the bush beyond the fence.

Had he really meant to rid himself of Tricia by throwing her, as one might say, to the lions? For a mad moment, he supposed, because fever had got into his blood, poison into his veins. She knew, he could tell that. In a way it might be all to the good, her knowing, it would show her how hopeless the marriage was that she was trying to preserve.

The swellings on his foot, though covered by his sock, were making the instep bulge through the sandal. His foot felt stiff and burning and he became aware that he was limping slightly. Supporting himself against the trunk of a fever tree, his skin against its cool, dampish, yellow bark, he took off his sandal and felt his swollen foot tenderly with his fingertips. Mosquitoes never touched Tricia, they seemed to shirk contact with her pale dry flesh.

She was up when he hobbled in, she was sitting on her bed, painting her fingernails. How could he live with a woman who painted her fingernails in a game reserve?

They didn't go out till nine. On the road to Waka-suthu Eric's car met them, coming back.

'There's nothing down there for miles, you're wasting your time.'

'OK,' said Ford. 'Thanks.'

'Sotingwe's the place. Did you see the leopard yesterday?' Ford shook his head. 'Oh, well, we can't all be lucky.'

Elephants were playing in the river at Hippo Bridge, spraying each other with water and nudging heavy shoulders. Ford thought that was going to be the high spot of the morning until they came upon the kill. They didn't actually see it. The kill had taken place some hours before, but the lioness and her cubs were still picking at the carcase, at a blood-blackened rib cage. They sat in the car and watched. After a while the lions left the carcase and walked away in file through the grass, but the little jackals were already gathered, a pack of them, posted behind trees. Ford came back that way again at four and by then the vultures had moved in, picking the bones.

It was a hot day of merciless sunshine, the sky blue and perfectly clear. Ford's foot was swollen to twice its normal size. He noticed that Tricia hadn't once left the car that day, nor had she spoken girlishly to him or giggled or given him a roguish kiss. She thought he had been trying to kill her, a preposterous notion really. The truth was he had only been giving her a fright, teaching her how stupid it was to flout the rules and leave the car. Why should he kill her, anyway? He could leave her, he *would* leave her, and once they were back in Mombasa he would tell her so. The thought of it made him turn to her and smile. He had stopped by the clearing where the fever tree stood, yellow of bark, delicate and fern-like of leaf, in the sunshine like a young sapling in springtime.

'Why don't you get out any more?'

She faltered, 'There's nothing to see.'

'No?'

He had spotted the porcupine with his naked eye but he handed her the binoculars. She looked and laughed with pleasure. That was the way she used to laugh when she was young, not from amusement but delight. He shut his eyes. 'Oh, the sweetie porky-pine!'

She reached onto the back seat for the camera. And then she hesitated. He could see the fear, the caution in her eyes. Silently he took the key out of the ignition and held it out to her on the palm of his hand. She flushed. He stared at her, enjoying her discomfiture, indignant that she should suspect him of such baseness.

She hesitated but she took the key. She picked up the camera and opened the car door, holding the key by its fob in her left hand, the camera in her right. He noticed that she hadn't passed the strap of the camera, his treasured Pentax, round her neck, she never did. For the thousandth time he could have told her but he lacked the heart to speak. His swollen foot throbbed and he thought of the long days at Ntsukunyane that remained to them. Marguerite seemed infinitely far away, further even than at the other side of the world where she was.

He knew Tricia was going to drop the camera some fifteen seconds before she did so. It was because she had the key in her other hand. If the strap had been round her neck it wouldn't have mattered. He knew how it was when you held something in each hand and lost your grip or your footing. You had no sense then, in that instant, of which of the objects was valuable and mattered and which was not and didn't. Tricia held on to the key and dropped the camera. The better to photograph the porcupine, she had mounted on to the twisted roots of a tree, roots that looked as hard as a flight of stone steps.

She gave a little cry. At the sounds of the crash and the cry the porcupine erected its quills. Ford jumped out of the car, wincing when he put his foot to the ground, hobbling through the grass to Tricia who stood as if petrified with fear of him. The camera, the pieces of camera, had fallen among the gnarled, stone-like tree roots. He dropped on to his knees, shouting at her, cursing her.

Tricia began to run. She ran back to the car and pushed the key into the ignition. The car was pointing in the direction of Thaba and the clock on the dashboard shelf said five thirty-five. Ford came limping back, waving his arms at her, his hands full of broken pieces of camera. She looked away and put her foot down hard on the accelerator.

The sky was clear orange with sunset, black bars of the coming night lying on the horizon. She found she could drive when she had to, even though she couldn't pass a test. A mile along the road she met the American couple. The boy put his head out. 'Anything worth going down there for?'

'Not a thing,' said Tricia, 'you'd be wasting your time.'

The boy turned his car and followed her back. It was two minutes past six when they entered Thaba, the last cars to do so. The gates closed behind them.

The Dreadful Day of Judgement

T here were four of them working in the cemetery. They were
employed by the city corporation — to do what? Even the
foreman was vague about their duties which had not been very
precisely specified. Not to clear the central part, certainly, for that
would have been a task not for four but for four hundred. And a
wild life sanctuary, for which purpose it was designated, must be
wild. To tidy it, then, to remove the worst signs of vandalism, to
carry away such gravestones as had fallen, to denude certain of the
many winding paths of the intrusive bramble and ivy and nettle.
When they asked the foreman whether this should be done or that,
he would say to use their own judgement, he couldn't be sure, he
would find out. But he never did. Sometimes an official from the
corporation came and viewed the work and nodded and disappeared
into the hut with the foreman to drink tea. As the winter came on
the official appeared less often, and the foreman said it was a hopeless
task, they needed more men, but the corporation could no longer
afford to spend the money, they must just do the best they could.

The hut was just inside the main gates. The foreman had a plan of
the cemetery pinned to the wall next to Gilly's calendar of the girl in
the transparent nightdress. He had a kettle and a spirit stove, but the
cups and the teapot had been brought by Marlon who got them from
his mother. The hut was always hot and smelly and smoky. The
foreman chain-smoked and so did Marlon, although he was so young,
and everywhere in the hut were saucers full of ash and cigarette stubs.
One day Gilly, who didn't smoke, brought into the hut a tin can he
had found in an open vault. The foreman and Marlon seemed pleased
to have a new, clean ashtray, for they never considered emptying the
others but let them fill up and spill about the floor.

'Marlon'd be scared stiff if he knew where that came from,' said
John. 'He'd die of fright.'

But Gilly only laughed. He found everything about the cemetery
funny, even the soldiers' graves, the only well-tended ones, that the

Imperial War Graves Commission still looked after. In the beginning he had amused himself by jumping out on Marlon from behind a monument or a pillared tomb, but the foreman, lethargic as he was, had stopped that because Marlon was not quite as they were, being backward and not able to read or write much.

The main gates hung between what the foreman called stone posts but which John alone knew were Corinthian columns. A high wall surrounded the cemetery, which was of many acres, and the periphery of it, a wide space just inside the wall, had been cleared long before and turfed and planted with trees that were still tiny. This was to be a public park for the townsfolk. It was the centre, the deep heart of the place, once the necropolis for this mercantile city, that was to be left for the birds and such small animals who would venture in and stay.

Many species of bird already nested in the ilexes and the laurels, the elms and the thin, silver-trunked birch trees. Crows with wings like black fans, woodpeckers whose tap-tap-tapping could be heard from the almost impenetrable depths, little birds which even John couldn't name and which crept rather than hopped over the lichen on the fallen stones. It was silent in there but for the rare rustle of wings or the soft crack of a decayed twig dropping. The city lay below, all round, but in winter it was often masked by fog, and it was hard to believe that thousands lived down there and worked and scurried in glare and noise. Their forbears' tombs stood in rows or gathered in clusters or jostled each other haphazardly: domed follies, marble slabs, granite crosses, broken columns, draped urns, simple stones, all overgrown and shrouded and half-obscured. Not a famous name among them, not a memorable title, only the obscure dead, forgotten, abandoned, capable now of nothing more than to decree a hush.

The silence was violated only by Gilly's talk. He had one topic of conversation, but that one was inexhaustible and everything recalled him to it. A name on a tomb, a scrap of verse on a gravestone, a pair of sparrows, the decorously robed statue of an angel. 'Bit of all right, that one,' he would say, stroking the stone flesh of a weeping muse, his hands so coarse and calloused that John wondered how any real woman could bear them to touch her. Or, lifting the ivy from a grave where lay a matron who had married three times, 'Couldn't get enough of it, could she?' And these reflections led him into endless reminiscences of the women he had had, those he now possessed, and anticipations of those awaiting him in the future.

Nothing stayed him. Not the engraved sorrow of parents mourning a daughter dead at seventeen, not the stone evocations of the sufferings of those dead in childbirth. Some of the vaults had been despoiled and left open, and he would penetrate them, descending subterranean stairs, shouting up to John and Marlon from the depths that here was a good place to bring a girl. 'Be OK in the summer. There's shelves here, make a good bed, they would. Proper little boudoir.'

John often regretted the thing he had done which made Gilly admire him. It had been on his first day there. He knew, even before he had done it, that this was to show them he was different from them, to make it clear from the start that he was a labourer only because there was no other work obtainable for such as he. He wanted them to know he had been to a university and was a qualified teacher. The shame and humiliation of being forced to take this unskilled work ate into his soul. They must understand his education had fitted him for something higher. But it had been a foolish vanity.

There had been nothing in the deep cavity any more but stones and dead leaves. But he had jumped in and held up a big pitted stone and cried ringingly: 'That skull had a tongue in it and could sing once. How the knave jowls it to the ground, as if 'twere Cain's jawbone that did the first murder!'

Gilly stared. 'You make that up yourself?'

'Shakespeare,' he said. 'Hamlet,' and the awe on Gilly's unformed pug-nosed face made him go on, excited with success, a braggart in a squalid pit. 'Prithee, Horatio, tell me one thing. Dost thou think Alexander looked o' this fashion i' the earth? And smelt so? pah!'

Marlon had gone white, his face peaked between the falls of thin yellow hair. He wore a heavy blue garment, a kind of anorak, but it gave him a medieval look standing there against the chapel wall, an El Greco sky flowing above its tower, purple and black and rushing in scuds above this northern Toledo. But Gilly was laughing, begging John to go on, and John went on, playing to the groundlings, holding the stone aloft. 'Alas, poor Yorick . . .' until at last he flung it from him with the ham actor's flourish, and up on the path again was being clapped on the back by Gilly and told what a brain he'd got. And Gilly was showing what he was and what all that had meant to him by demanding to have that bit again, the bit about the lips that I have kissed I know not how oft.

Marlon hadn't laughed or congratulated him. Bewildered, fright-ened by the daring of it and the incomprehensibility, he fumbled to light a fresh cigarette, another of the sixty he would smoke that day. Cigarettes were all he had, a tenuous hold on that real world in which his mother, sixteen years before, had named him after a famous actor. The smoke flowed from his loose lips. In a way, but for that cigarette, he might have been an actor in a miracle play perhaps or in a chorus of madmen. On that day as on all the others that followed, he walked behind them as they made their way back through the shaded aisles, under the leather-leaved ilexes, between the little houses of the dead.

In the hut there was tea to be drunk, and then home, the foreman off to his semidetached and his comfortable wife, Marlon to his mother and stuffy rooms and television commercials, John to his bedsit, Gilly (as John, the favoured, was now privileged to be told) to the arms of a casino owner's wife whose husband lacked a gravedigger's virility.

The chapel was built of yellowish-grey stones. It had an octagonal nave, and on its floor thin, hair-like grass grew up between the flags. To one of its sides was attached a square tower, surmounted at each angle by a thin ornamented spire. The four spires, weather-worn, corroded, stained, were like four needles encrusted with rust. The workmen used the chapel as a repository for pieces of broken stone and iron rails. Even Gilly's bullying could not make Marlon go inside. He was afraid of Gilly and the foreman, but not so afraid as he was of the echoing chapel and of the dust beneath his feet.

Gilly said, 'What'd you do, Marl, if you turned round now and it wasn't me here but a skeleton in a shroud, Marl?'

'Leave him alone,' said John, and when they were alone in the nave, 'You know he's a bit retarded.'

'Big words you use, John. I call him cracked. D'you know what he said to me yesterday? All them graves are going to open up and the dead bodies come out. On some special day that's going to be. What day's that then? I said. But he only wobbled his head.'

'The dreadful Day of Judgement,' said John, 'when the secrets of all hearts shall be revealed.'

'Wouldn't suit me, that. Some of them old skulls'd blush a bit if I told them what I'd been getting up to last night. The secrets of all hearts? Open some of them up and I'd have a good many blokes on my track, not to mention that old git, you-know-who. Break his bloody roulette wheel, he would.'

'Over your head, no doubt,' said John.

'A short life and a randy one, that's what I say.' They came out into the cold, pale sunlight. 'Here, have a shufty at this. Angelina

Clara Bowyer, 1816 to 1839. Same age as what you are, mate, and she'd had five kids! Must have worn her old man out.'

'It wore her out,' said John, and he seemed to see her with her piled plaited hair and her long straight dress and the consumption in her face. He saw the young husband mourning among those five bread-and-butter-fed children, the crepe on his hat, the black coat. Under a sky like this, the sun a white puddle in layered cloud, he came with the clergyman and the mourners and the coffin-bearers to lay her in the earth. The flowers withered in the biting wind – or did they bring flowers to funerals then? He didn't know, and not knowing broke the vision and brought him back to the clink of spade against granite, the smell of Marlon's cigarette, Gilly talking, talking, as boringly as an old woman of her aches and pains only he was talking of sex.

They always stopped work at four now the dusk came early. 'Nights are drawing in,' said the foreman, brewing tea, filling up with dog ends the can Gilly had found in the grave.

'When'll we get it over with?' Marlon faltered, coming close to the stove, coughing a little.

'Depends on what we've got to get over,' said the foreman. 'Digging a bit here, clearing a bit there. My guess is that council fellow'll come round one of these days and say, That's it, lads, now you can leave it to the squirrels.'

Gilly was looking at his calendar, turning over the November nightdress girl to the December Santa Claus girl. 'If I had my way they'd level it all over, the centre bit, and put grass down, make the whole place a park. That's healthy, that is. Somewhere a young kid could take his girl. Lover's Lane Park, that'd be a good name. I'd like to see real birds there, not them bloody crows.'

'You can't do that,' said Marlon. 'There's the dead people in there.'

'So what? There was dead people round the edges, but they took them up. They done something – what they call it, John?'

'They deconsecrated the ground.'

'Hear what John says? He's educated, he knows.'

Marlon got up, the cigarette clinging to his lip. 'You mean they dug them up? There was others and they dug them up?'

''Course they did. You didn't think they was under there, did you?'

'Then where'll they be when the Day comes? How'll they lift up the stones and come out?'

'Here, for Christ's sake,' said the foreman, 'that's enough of that, young Marlon. I don't reckon your mum'd better take you to church no more if that's what you come out with.'

'They must come out, they must come and judge,' Marlon cried, and then the foreman told him sharply to shut up, for even he could be shaken by this sort of thing, with the darkness crowding in on the hut, and the heart of the cemetery a black mound horned by the spires of the chapel.

John wondered what church Marlon went to, that of some strange sect perhaps. Or was it only his incomplete brain that distorted the accepted meaning of the Day of Judgement into this version of his own? The resentful dead, the judging dead, lying censorious in the earth.

For his part, he had at first seen the cemetery as no more than a wooded knoll and the stones no more than granite outcroppings. It was not so now. The names in inscriptions, studied by him quietly or derisively read out by Gilly, evoked images of their bearers. James Calhoun Stokes, 1798–1862, Merchant of this City; 'Upright in all his dealings, he stood firm to meet his Maker'. Gilly had an obscene rendering of that, of course. Thomas Charles Macpherson, 1802–79, Master Builder; 'Blest are the Pure in Heart'. Lucy Matilda Osborne, 1823–96; 'Her submissive duty to her husband and devotion to her sons was exceeded only by her pious adoration of her God'. John saw them in cutaway coats, in bombazine gowns, or night-capped on their deathbeds.

But Marlon saw them as a magisterial procession. Listening, watching, waiting perhaps for the ultimate outrage.

'What a load of old cobblers! You'll be down there yourself soon, all the fags you get through in a day.' Gilly sat on a toppled stone, laughing. He had been telling John more about the casino man's wife, trying to find among the statues they had piled up one whose figure might be comparable to hers. Britannias, muses, embodiments of virtues or arts, they lay prostrate, their blank grey or bronze faces all staring upwards at the clouded sky.

'What are we going to do with them?' Marlon said in the voice that was as desperate when he asked about trivialities as when he gave his prophet-like cries.

'Ask the foreman,' said John.

'He won't bloody know.' And Gilly lifted on to his lap the bronze that was nearly nude, just veiled over her loins with metal drapery. 'Randy old devil, he must have been, that Sidney George Whatsit, having her sitting on top of him when he was dead.'

'He was a historian, the plaque says,' said John. 'She's supposed to be Clio, the Muse of History. That's why she's got a scroll in her hand.' And then, because he was bored with Gilly and afraid for Marlon, 'Let's stick them all in the chapel till the council guy comes.'

But Gilly refused to abandon the huge joke of caressing the bronze. Every reachable inch of her anatomy was examined until, suddenly, he jumped up, leaving her to roll into one of the muddy ruts the truck had made, and ran up to the pillared monument from whose dome she had toppled. He stood inside, a satyr, John thought, in a temple defiled by northern rains. He threw up his arms.

'I said you was a randy old goat, Sidney, and so you was! I had a bird called Clio once myself, real hot stuff.' His shouts punctured the thick greyness, the silence, the fog-textured air. He leapt down the steps, kicking a gravestone here, a marble urn there, and perched on a broken column. 'Come out, all the lot of you, if you want, only you can't because you're bloody dead!'

And then Marlon made a horrible sound, the moan a man makes in sleep, in a nightmare, when he thinks he is screaming. He got into the cab of the truck and hunched there.

'You stupid bastard.' John picked up Marlon's fallen cigarette packet, brushed the grit off it. 'D'you have to act like a kid of ten?'

'Got to get some sort of kick out of this dump,' Gilly said sulkily. 'Dead-end hole.'

'Well, that's what it is, isn't it? What d'you expect? A bar? Booze? Bring on the dancing girls?'

Gilly started to laugh again, picked up his muse again. 'I wouldn't mind this dancing girl. Don't reckon they'd miss her, do you? She'd look OK in my place. I could stand her on the table.'

'What for?'

'People have statues, don't they? They've got them in the town hall. It'd give my place a bit of class.'

'Come on,' said John, 'let's stick the lot of them in the chapel. The foreman'll do his nut if he sees you going off with that. She's too big to go under your jacket.'

So they piled the statues and the urns in the chapel, and Gilly amused himself by shouting insults and obscenities which the lofty walls echoed back at him, black pigeons, white doves flapping from the crannies in fear.

'What d'you do in that room of yours, John? Must be a real drag all on your own night after night. Fancy coming over to my bird's place? She's got a real dishy friend. We could have ourselves a ball, and I don't mean wining and dining.'

No, thanks, John said, and softened his refusal by saying he had to study which impressed Gilly. It wasn't that he was a prude so much as that the idea of association with Gilly's friends offended some snobbish delicacy in his nature, some fastidiousness. Better the speechless company of James Calhoun Stokes and Angelina Bowyer and the historian, better, in the evenings, the dreams of them and the wonderings about their lost lives. Though, in refusing, he thought it likely that brash insensitive Gilly might not take his no for an answer but turn up one night with his girl and that other girl to rout him out. He feared it a little, but not with Marlon's obsessional dread of threats from another world.

When at last Gilly did come, it was on a cold moonlit night, and he came alone.

'I'm going to split,' said Gilly, 'I'm getting the hell out. All good things come to an end. You can tell the foreman in the morning, OK? I'm going south. I've got a girl in London, worships the ground I tread on, poor cow. She'll take me in. But that's between you and I, right?'

'But why?'

'He's found out, her old man, and I reckon he'll have his heavies out gunning for me. He's beat her up – bunch of bloody gangsters that lot are. I'll miss her.' The tears stood in his eyes, and John stared, amazed, confounded. 'Poor cow,' said Gilly, the epithet an endearment, a caress.

'D'you want me to come to the station with you?'

'No need for that. I only come in to tell you to tell the foreman. Anyway, I got something to do first, get that statue, that Clio. The train don't go till eleven, and I want her.' He turned half away. 'For a souvenir like, she's the dead spitting image.'

'You'd go into the cemetery tonight, for *that*?'

'Like I said, I want her.' His eyes, glazed, held a pathetic hunger. Of love, in those bare words, he had expressed all he knew how to. On lechery only he was articulate. 'It's moonlight,' he said. 'I've got a torch. I'll climb the wall.'

'Goodbye, Gilly,' said John. 'Good luck.'

In the morning the sky was coppery, grey above, reddish on the horizon where the sun hung. The Winter Solstice had come.

'It's like the end of the world,' said Marlon.

The foreman came in, rubbing his hands. 'Going to have snow

before the day's over. Gilly's late.' John told him Gilly wasn't coming in. He didn't tell him why not, and he expected an outburst. But the foreman only stuck out his lip and put the kettle on and helped himself to one of Marlon's cigarettes.

'No loss, that,' he said. 'We shan't miss him. And if I'm not much mistaken we'll all be laid off by tonight when this dump's snowed up. You'll be able to get yourselves dug in nice for Christmas, lads.'

Marlon showed no inclination to leave the stuffy warmth of the hut, where the foreman now had a brazier of coke, for the raw air and yellowed dimness of the cemetery. But the foreman wanted to be rid of them, to be on his own, to be idle and warm in peace. He took down Gilly's calendar and pushed it among the glowing coke, and the last John saw of it was the glossy tanned body of a naked girl gyrating in the fire. They moved out into the chill of the shortest day, the foreman hurrying them along by cleaning frost off the truck's windscreen himself.

John expected trouble from the boy, so forbidding was the cemetery in the gloom and under that strange sky. But Marlon, when John had repeated several times that Gilly was not coming, when this had at last sunk in, became more cheerful and more like a normal person than John had ever seen him. He even laughed. He pushed John about in the cab, and when this made the truck swerve, he hooted with laughter.

But when they had come to the centre and were working on clearing the main aisle, he fell silent, though he seemed tranquil enough. All those months John had longed for peace, for a respite from Gilly's ceaseless bragging and innuendo, but now he had it he felt only uneasy. Being alone up here with Marlon had something to do with it. He despised himself for being afraid of a poor retarded boy, yet he was afraid. The thickening atmosphere was part of it, and the windless cold, and the increasing darkness like an eclipse, and the way Marlon would stand for whole minutes on end, staring vacantly, swinging his spade. But what made him long for the snow to begin and drive them back to the hut was Marlon's new habit, now Gilly was not here to deride him, of touching the gravestones and seeming to whisper to them. That he did this reverently and cautiously did nothing to ease John's mind. It was as if he were placating the dead, assuring them that now all would be well. And John had an awareness, growing in intensity as the time slowly passed, that the cemetery had somehow undergone a change. For him it had been just a place to work in, later an abode of sadness and the lost past, never till now macabre. Perhaps much of this feeling was due to the strangeness of the day itself, the permanent twilight, the knowledge that in these hours the earth had turned to its ultimate distance away from the sun.

Yet it was more than that. That might account for the distortions he seemed to see, so that the tombs appeared more closely crowded and the chapel tower taller and darker, but not for his sensation that there had taken place in the cemetery since he had last seen it, some upheaval and some outrage. It was when these fancies grew so strong as to make him imagine some actual physical change, the positions of the slabs and stones altered, that he looked at his watch and told Marlon they could stop now for their midday meal.

The foreman said to bring down one truck-load of rubble from the chapel, and then they could knock off. The sky had lightened a little, becoming uniformly livid, but still they needed the headlights on. The pale misty shafts of light probed the undergrowth and died into blackness. They parked beside the tower.

'Can you make an effort and come in?' said John, 'Or do I have to do it on my own?'

Marlon managed a sheepish, crafty smile. 'You go first.'

The rubble was heaped against the furthest side of the octagon. He saw Gilly before he got there. Gilly was lying on his back among the muses and the virgins, his head, his face, a mass of black clotted blood to which fragments and crumbs of stone adhered. Clio, memento of love, had rolled from his grasp. His eyes still stared, as if they still saw those meters-out of vengeance.

'Gilly, Gilly!' John cried, and the eight walls called back, 'Gilly, Gilly!' – calling them to Marlon as he came through the tower and into the nave.

Marlon did not speak Gilly's name. He gave a great cry.

'The dead people came out! The dead people judged him! The day has come, the end of the world . . . the Day, the Day, the Day!'

From the eaves, out of the broken roof, the birds came, circling, cawing, a great rush of wings. And the echo roared like a knell. John stumbled out after Marlon, after the flying figure that cried like a prophet in the wilderness, into a whiteness that cleaned the world.

In great shaggy flakes, the snow had begun to fall.

A Glowing Future

'S ix should be enough,' he said. 'We'll say six tea chests, then, and one trunk. If you'll deliver them tomorrow, I'll get the stuff all packed and maybe your people could pick them up Wednesday.' He made a note on a bit of paper. 'Fine,' he said. 'Round about lunchtime tomorrow.'

She hadn't moved. She was still sitting in the big oak-armed chair at the far end of the room. He made himself look at her and he managed a kind of grin, pretending all was well.

'No trouble,' he said. 'They're very efficient.'

'I couldn't believe,' she said, 'that you'd really do it. Not until I heard you on the phone. I wouldn't have thought it possible. You'll really pack up all those things and have them sent off to her.'

They were going to have to go over it all again. Of course they were. It wouldn't stop until he'd got the things out and himself out, away from London and her for good. And he wasn't going to argue or make long defensive speeches. He lit a cigarette and waited for her to begin, thinking that the pubs would be opening in an hour's time and he could go out then and get a drink.

'I don't understand why you came here at all,' she said.

He didn't answer. He was still holding the cigarette box, and now he closed its lid, feeling the coolness of the onyx on his fingertips.

She had gone white. 'Just to get your things? Maurice, did you come back just for that?'

'They are my things,' he said evenly.

'You could have sent someone else. Even if you'd written to me and asked me to do it —'

'I never write letters,' he said.

She moved then. She made a little fluttering with her hand in front of her mouth. 'As if I didn't know!' She gasped, and making a great effort she steadied her voice. 'You were in Australia for a year, a whole year, and you never wrote to me once.'

'I phoned.'

'Yes, twice. The first time to say you loved me and missed me and were longing to come back to me and would I wait for you and there wasn't anyone else was there? And the second time, a week ago, to say you'd be here by Saturday and could I – could I put you up. My God, I'd lived with you for two years, we were practically married, and then you phone and ask if I could put you up!'

'Words,' he said. 'How would you have put it?'

'For one thing, I'd have mentioned Patricia. Oh, yes, I'd have mentioned her. I'd have had the decency, the common humanity, for that. D'you know what I thought when you said you were coming? I ought to know by now how peculiar he is, I thought, how detached, not writing or phoning or anything. But that's Maurice, that's the man I love, and he's coming back to me and we'll get married and I'm so happy!'

'I did tell you about Patricia.'

'Not until after you'd made love to me first.'

He winced. It had been a mistake, that. Of course he hadn't meant to touch her beyond the requisite greeting kiss. But she was very attractive and he was used to her and she seemed to expect it – and oh, what the hell. Women never could understand about men and sex. And there was only one bed, wasn't there? A hell of a scene there'd have been that first night if he'd suggested sleeping on the sofa in here.

'You made love to me,' she said. 'You were so passionate, it was just like it used to be, and then the next morning you told me. You'd got a resident's permit to stay in Australia, you'd got a job all fixed up, you'd met a girl you wanted to marry. Just like that you told me, over breakfast. Have you ever been smashed in the face, Maurice? Have you ever had your dreams trodden on?'

'Would you rather I'd waited longer? As for being smashed in the face –' he rubbed his cheekbone '– that's quite a punch you pack.'

She shuddered. She got up and began slowly and stiffly to pace the room. 'I hardly touched you. I wish I'd killed you!' By a small table she stopped. There was a china figurine on it, a bronze paperknife, an onyx pen jar that matched the ashtray. 'All those things,' she said. 'I looked after them for you. I treasured them. And now you're going to have them all shipped out to her. The things we lived with. I used to look at them and think, Maurice bought that when we went to – oh God, I can't believe it. Sent to her!'

He nodded, staring at her. 'You can keep the big stuff,' he said.

'You're specially welcome to the sofa. I've tried sleeping on it for two nights and I never want to see the bloody thing again.'

She picked up the china figurine and hurled it at him. It didn't hit him because he ducked and let it smash against the wall, just missing a framed drawing. 'Mind the Lowry,' he said laconically, 'I paid a lot of money for that.'

She flung herself onto the sofa and burst into sobs. She thrashed about, hammering the cushions with her fists. He wasn't going to be moved by that – he wasn't going to be moved at all. Once he'd packed those things, he'd be off to spend the next three months touring Europe. A free man, free for the sights and the fun and the girls, for a last fling of wild oats. After that, back to Patricia and a home and a job and responsibility. It was a glowing future which this hysterical woman wasn't going to mess up.

'Shut up, Betsy, for God's sake,' he said. He shook her roughly by the shoulder, and then he went out because it was now eleven and he could get a drink.

Betsy made herself some coffee and washed her swollen eyes. She walked about, looking at the ornaments and the books, the glasses and vases and lamps, which he would take from her tomorrow. It wasn't that she much minded losing them, the things themselves, but the barrenness which would be left, and the knowing that they would all be Patricia's.

In the night she had got up, found his wallet, taken out the photographs of Patricia, and torn them up. But she remembered the face, pretty and hard and greedy, and she thought of those bright eyes widening as Patricia unpacked the tea chests, the predatory hands scrabbling for more treasures in the trunk. Doing it all perhaps before Maurice himself got there, arranging the lamps and the glasses and the ornaments in their home for his delight when at last he came.

He would marry her, of course. I suppose she thinks he's faithful to her, Betsy thought, the way I once thought he was faithful to me. I know better now. Poor stupid fool, she doesn't know what he did the first moment he was alone with her, or what he would do in France and Italy. That would be a nice wedding present to give her, wouldn't it, along with all the pretty bric-a-brac in the trunk?

Well, why not? Why not rock their marriage before it had even begun? A letter. A letter to be concealed in, say, that blue-and-white ginger jar. She sat down to write. Dear Patricia – what a stupid way to begin, the way you had to begin a letter even to your enemy.

Dear Patricia: I don't know what Maurice has told you about me, but we have been living here as lovers ever since he arrived. To be more explicit, I mean we have made love, have slept together. Maurice is incapable of being faithful to anyone. If you don't believe me, ask yourself why, if he didn't want me, he didn't stay in a hotel. That's all. Yours — and she signed her name and felt a little better, well enough and steady enough to take a bath and get herself some lunch.

Six tea chests and a trunk arrived on the following day. The chests smelled of tea and had drifts of tea leaves lying in the bottom of them. The trunk was made of silver-coloured metal and had clasps of gold-coloured metal. It was rather a beautiful object, five feet long, three feet high, two feet wide, and the lid fitted so securely it seemed a hermetic sealing.

Maurice began to pack at two o'clock. He used tissue paper and newspapers. He filled the tea chests with kitchen equipment and cups and plates and cutlery, with books, with those clothes of his he had left behind him a year before. Studiously, and with a certain grim pleasure, he avoided everything Betsy might have insisted was hers — the poor cheap things, the stainless steel spoons and forks, the Woolworth pottery, the awful coloured sheets, red and orange and olive, that he had always loathed. He and Patricia would sleep in white linen.

Betsy didn't help him. She watched, chain-smoking. He nailed the lids on the chests and on each lid he wrote in white paint his address in Australia. But he didn't paint in the letters of his own name. He painted Patricia's. This wasn't done to needle Betsy but he was glad to see it was needling her.

He hadn't come back to the flat till one that morning, and of course he didn't have a key. Betsy had refused to let him in, had left him down there in the street, and he had to sit in the car he'd hired till seven. She looked as if she hadn't slept either. Miss Patricia Gordon, he wrote, painting fast and skilfully.

'Don't forget your ginger jar,' said Betsy. 'I don't want it.'

'That's for the trunk.' Miss Patricia Gordon, 23 Burwood Park Avenue, Kew, Victoria, Australia 3101. 'All the pretty things are going in the trunk. I intend it as a special present for Patricia.'

The Lowry came down and was carefully padded and wrapped. He wrapped the onyx ashtray and the pen jar, the alabaster bowl, the bronze paperknife, the tiny Chinese cups, the tall hock glasses. The china figurine, alas . . . he opened the lid of the trunk.

'I hope the customs open it!' Betsy shouted at him. 'I hope they

295

confiscate things and break things! I'll pray every night for it to go to the bottom of the sea before it gets there!'

'The sea,' he said, 'is a risk I must take. As for the customs –' He smiled. 'Patricia works for them, she's a customs officer – didn't I tell you? I very much doubt if they'll even glance inside.' He wrote a label and pasted it on the side of the trunk. Miss Patricia Gordon, 23 Burwood Park Avenue, Kew . . . And now I'll have to go out and get a padlock. Keys, please. If you try to keep me out this time, I'll call the police. I'm still the legal tenant of this flat remember.'

She gave him the keys. When he had gone she put her letter in the ginger jar. She hoped he would close the trunk at once, but he didn't. He left it open, the lid thrown back, the new padlock dangling from the gold-coloured clasp.

'Is there anything to eat?' he said.

'Go and find your own bloody food! Go and find some other woman to feed you!'

He liked her to be angry and fierce; it was her love he feared. He came back at midnight to find the flat in darkness, and he lay down on the sofa with the tea chests standing about him like defences, like barricades, the white paint showing faintly in the dark. Miss Patricia Gordon . . .

Presently Betsy came in. She didn't put on the light. She wound her way between the chests, carrying a candle in a saucer which she set down on the trunk. In the candlelight, wearing a long white nightgown, she looked like a ghost, like some wandering madwoman, a Mrs Rochester, a Woman in White.

'Maurice.'

'Go away, Betsy, I'm tired.'

'Maurice, please. I'm sorry I said all those things. I'm sorry I locked you out.'

'OK, I'm sorry too. It's a mess, and maybe I shouldn't have done it the way I did. But the best way is for me just to go and my things to go and make a clean split. Right? And now will you please be a good girl and go away and let me get some sleep?'

What happened next he hadn't bargained for. It hadn't crossed his mind. Men don't understand about women and sex. She threw herself on him, clumsily, hungrily. She pulled his shirt open and began kissing his neck and his chest, holding his head, crushing her mouth to his mouth, lying on top of him and gripping his legs with her knees.

He gave her a savage push. He kicked her away, and she fell and struck her head on the side of the trunk. The candle fell off, flared and died in a pool of wax. In the darkness he cursed floridly. He put on the light and she got up, holding her head where there was a little blood.

'Oh, get out, for God's sake,' he said, and he manhandled her out, slamming the door after her.

In the morning, when she came into the room, a blue bruise on her forehead, he was asleep, fully clothed, spreadeagled on his back. She shuddered at the sight of him. She began to get breakfast but she couldn't eat anything. The coffee made her gag and a great nauseous shiver went through her. When she went back to him he was sitting up on the sofa, looking at his plane ticket to Paris.

'The men are coming for the stuff at ten,' he said as if nothing had happened, 'and they'd better not be late. I have to be at the airport at noon.'

She shrugged. She had been to the depths and she thought he couldn't hurt her any more.

'You'd better close the trunk,' she said absent-mindedly.

'All in good time.' His eyes gleamed. 'I've got a letter to put in yet.'

Her head bowed, the place where it was bruised sore and swollen, she looked loweringly at him. 'You never write letters.'

'Just a note. One can't send a present without a note to accompany it, can one?'

He pulled the ginger jar out of the trunk, screwed up her letter without even glancing at it, and threw it on the floor. Rapidly yet ostentatiously and making sure that Betsy could see, he scrawled across a sheet of paper: *All this is for you, darling Patricia, for ever and ever.*

'How I hate you,' she said.

'You could have fooled me.' He took a large angle lamp out of the trunk and set it on the floor. He slipped the note into the ginger jar, rewrapped it, tucked the jar in between the towels and cushions which padded the fragile objects. 'Hatred isn't the word I'd use to describe the way you came after me last night.'

She made no answer. Perhaps he should have put a heavy object like that lamp in one of the chests, perhaps he should open up one of the chests now. He turned round for the lamp. It wasn't there. She was holding it in both hands.

'I want that, please.'

'Have you ever been smashed in the face, Maurice?' she said breathlessly, and she raised the lamp and struck him with it full on the forehead. He staggered and she struck him again, and again and again, raining blows on his face and his head. He screamed. He sagged, covering his face with bloody hands. Then with all her strength she gave him a great swinging blow and he fell to his knees, rolled over and at last was stilled and silenced.

There was quite a lot of blood, though it quickly stopped flowing. She stood there looking at him and she was sobbing. Had she been sobbing all the time? She was covered with blood. She tore off her clothes and dropped them in a heap around her. For a moment she knelt beside him, naked and weeping, rocking backwards and forwards, speaking his name, biting her fingers that were sticky with his blood.

But self-preservation is the primal instinct, more powerful than love or sorrow, hatred or regret. The time was nine o'clock, and in an hour those men would come. Betsy fetched water in a bucket, detergent, cloths and a sponge. The hard work, the great cleansing, stopped her tears, quieted her heart and dulled her thoughts. She thought of nothing, working frenziedly, her mind a blank.

When bucket after bucket of reddish water had been poured down the sink and the carpet was soaked but clean, the lamp washed and dried and polished, she threw her clothes into the basket in the bathroom and had a bath. She dressed carefully and brushed her hair. Eight minutes to ten. Everything was clean and she had opened the window, but the dead thing still lay there on a pile of reddened newspapers.

'I loved him,' she said aloud, and she clenched her fists. 'I hated him.'

The men were punctual. They came at ten sharp. They carried the six tea chests and the silver-coloured trunk with the gold-coloured clasps downstairs.

When they had gone and their van had driven away, Betsy sat down on the sofa. She looked at the angle lamp, the onyx pen jar and ashtray, the ginger jar, the alabaster bowls, the hock glasses, the bronze paperknife, the little Chinese cups, and the Lowry that was back on the wall. She was quite calm now and she didn't really need the brandy she had poured for herself.

Of the past she thought not at all and the present seemed to exist only as a palpable nothingness, a thick silence that lay around her. She thought of the future, of three months hence, and into the silence she let forth a steady, rather toneless peal of laughter. Miss Patricia Gordon, 23 Burwood Park Avenue, Kew, Victoria, Australia 3101. The pretty, greedy, hard face, the hands so eager to undo that padlock and prise open those golden clasps to find the treasure within . . .

And how interesting that treasure would be in three months' time, like nothing Miss Patricia Gordon had seen in all her life! It was as well, so that she would recognize it, that it carried on top of it a note in a familiar hand: *All this is for you, darling Patricia, for ever and ever.*

An Outside Interest

Frightening people used to be a hobby of mine. Perhaps I should rather say an obsession and not people but, specifically, women. Making others afraid *is* enjoyable as everyone discovers who has tried it and succeeded. I suppose it has something to do with power. Most people never really try it so they don't know, but look at the ones who do. Judges, policemen, prison warders, customs officers, tax inspectors. They have a great time, don't they? You don't find them giving up or adopting other methods. Frightening people goes to their heads, they're drunk on it, they live by it. So did I. While other men might go down to the pub with the boys or to football, I went off to Epping Forest and frightened women. It was what you might call my outside interest.

Don't get me wrong. There was nothing – well, nasty, about what I did. You know what I mean by that, I'm sure I don't have to go into details. I'm far from being some sort of pervert, I can tell you. In fact, I err rather on the side of too much moral strictness. Nor am I one of those lonely, deprived men. I'm happily married and the father of a little boy, I'm six feet tall, not bad-looking and, I assure you, entirely physically and mentally normal.

Of course I've tried to analyse myself and discover my motives. Was my hobby ever any more than an antidote to boredom? By anyone's standards the life I lead would be classed as pretty dull, selling tickets and answering passengers' queries at Anglo-Mercian Airways terminal, living in a semi in Muswell Hill, going to tea with my mother-in-law on Sundays and having an annual fortnight in a holiday flat in South Devon. I got married very young. Adventure wasn't exactly a conspicuous feature of my existence. The biggest thing that happened to me was when we thought one of our charters had been hi-jacked in Greece, and that turned out to be a false alarm.

My wife is a nervous sort of girl. Mind you, she has cause to be, living where we do close to Highgate Wood and Queens Wood. A woman takes her life in her hands, walking alone in those places. Carol used to regale me with stories – well, she still does.

'At twenty past five in the afternoon! It was still broad daylight. He raped her and cut her in the face, she had to have seventeen stitches in her face and neck.'

She doesn't drive and if she comes home from anywhere after dark I always go down to the bus stop to meet her. She won't even walk along the Muswell Hill Road because of the woods on either side.

'If you see a man on his own in a place like that you naturally ask yourself what he's doing there, don't you? A young man, just walking aimlessly about. It's not as if he had a dog with him. It makes your whole body go tense and you get a sort of awful crawling sensation all over you. If you didn't come and meet me I don't think I'd go out at all.'

Was it that which gave me the idea? At any rate it made me think about women and fear. Things are quite different for a man, he never thinks about being afraid of being in dark or lonely places. I'm sure I never have and therefore, until I got all this from Carol, I never considered how important this business of being scared when out alone might be to them. When I came to understand it gave me a funny feeling of excitement.

And then I actually frightened a woman myself – by chance. My usual way of going to work is to cut through Queens Wood to Highgate tube station and take the Northern Line down into London. When the weather is very bad I go to the station by bus but most of the time I walk there and back and the way through the wood is a considerable short cut. I was coming back through the wood at about six one evening in March. It was dusk, growing dark. The lamps, each a good distance apart from each other, which light the paths, were lit, but I often think these give the place a rather more bleak and sinister appearance than if it were quite dark. You leave a light behind you and walk along a dim shadowy avenue towards the next lamp which gleams faintly some hundred yards ahead. And no sooner is it reached, an acid yellow glow among the bare branches, than you leave it behind again to negotiate the next dark stretch. I thought about how it must be to be a woman walking through the wood and, yes, I gloried in my maleness and my freedom from fear.

Then I saw the girl coming. She was walking along the path from Priory Gardens. It came into my head that she would be less wary of me if I continued as I had been, marching briskly and purposefully towards Wood Vale, swinging along and looking like a man homeward bound to his family and his dinner. There was no definite intent present in my mind when I slackened my pace, then stopped and stood still. But as soon as I'd done that I knew I was going to carry it through. The girl came up to where the paths converged and where the next lamp was. She gave me a quick darting look. I stood there in a very relaxed way and I returned her look with a blank stare. I suppose I consciously, out of some sort of devilment, made my eyes fixed and glazed and let my mouth go loose. Anyway, she turned very quickly away and began to walk much faster.

She had high heels so she couldn't go very fast, not as fast as I could, just strolling along behind her. I gained on her until I was a yard behind.

I could smell her fear. She was wearing a lot of perfume and her sweat seemed to potentiate it so that there came to me a whiff and then a wave of heady, mixed-up animal and floral scent. I breathed it in, I breathed heavily. She began to run and I strode after her. What she did then was unexpected. She stopped, turned round and cried out in a tremulous terrified voice: 'What do you want?'

I stopped too and gave her the same look. She held her handbag out to me. 'Take it!'

The joke had gone far enough. I lived round there anyway, I had my wife and son to think of. I put on a cockney voice. 'Keep your bag, love. You've got me wrong.'

And then, to reassure her, I turned back along the path and let her escape to Wood Vale and the lights and the start of the houses. But I can't describe what a feeling of power and – well, triumphant manhood and what's called machismo the encounter gave me. I felt grand. I swaggered into my house and Carol said had I had a Premium Bond come up?

Since I'm being strictly truthful in this account, I'd better add the other consequence of what happened in the wood, even though it does rather go against the grain with me to mention things like that. I made love to Carol that night and it was a lot better than it had been for a long time, in fact it was sensational for both of us. And I couldn't kid myself that it was due to anything but my adventure with the girl.

Next day I looked at myself in the mirror with all the lights off but the little tubular one over our bed, and I put on the same look I'd given the girl when she turned in my direction under the lamp. I can tell you I nearly frightened myself. I've said I'm not bad looking and that's true but I'm naturally pale and since I'm thin, my face tends to be a bit gaunt. In the dim light my eyes seemed sunk in deep sockets and my mouth hung loose in a vacant mindless way. I stepped back from the glass so that I could see the whole of myself, slouching, staring, my arms hanging. There was no doubt I had the potential of being a woman-frightener of no mean calibre.

They say it's the first step that counts. I had taken the first step but the second was bigger and it was weeks before I took it. I kept telling myself not to be a fool, to forget those mad ideas. Besides, surely I could see I'd soon be in trouble if I made a habit of frightening women in Queens Wood, on my own doorstep. But I couldn't stop thinking about it. I remembered how wonderful I'd felt that evening, how tall I'd walked and what a man I'd been.

The funny thing was what a lot of humiliating things seemed to happen to me at that time, between the Queens Wood incident and the next occasion. A woman at the air terminal actually spat at me. I'm not exaggerating. Of course she was drunk, smashed out of her mind on duty-free Scotch, but she spat at me and I had to stand there in the middle of the ticket hall with all those tourists milling about, and wipe the spittle off my uniform. Then I got a reprimand for being discourteous to a passenger. It was totally unjust and, strictly speaking, I should have resigned on the spot, only I've got a wife and son and jobs aren't easy to come by at present. There was all that and trouble at home as well with Carol nagging me to take her on holiday with this girl friend of hers and her husband to Minorca instead of our usual Salcombe fortnight. I told her straight we couldn't afford it but I didn't like being asked in return why I couldn't earn as much as Sheila's Mike.

My manhood was at a low ebb. Then Sheila and Mike asked us to spend the day with them, Carol, Timothy and me. They had been neighbours of ours but had just moved away to a new house in one of those outer suburbs that are really in Essex. So I drove the three of us out to Theydon Bois and made my acquaintance with Epping Forest.

There are sixty-four square miles of forest, lying on the northeastern borders of London. But when you drive from the Wake Arms to Theydon along a narrow road bordered by woodland, stretches of turf and undergrowth, little coppices of birch trees, you can easily believe yourself in the depths of the country. It seems impossible that London is only fourteen or fifteen miles away. The forest is green and silent and from a car looks unspoilt, though of course it can't be. We passed a woman walking a very unguard-like dog, a tiny Maltese terrier . . . That gave me the idea. Why shouldn't I come out here? Why shouldn't I try my frightening act out here where no one knew me?

Two days after that I did. It was spring and the evenings stayed light till nearly eight. I didn't take the car. Somehow it didn't seem to me as if the sort of person I was going to be, going to *act*, would have a car. The journey was awful, enough to deter anyone less determined than I. I went straight from work, taking the Central Line tube as far as Loughton and then a bus up the hills and into the forest. At the Wake Arms I got off and began to walk down the hill, not on the pavement but a few yards inside the forest itself. I didn't see a woman on her own until I had reached the houses of Theydon and begun the return trip. I had gone about a hundred yards up again when she came out of one of the last houses, a young girl in jeans and a jacket, her hands in her pockets.

It was clear she was going to walk to the Wake Arms. Or so I thought. For a while I walked, keeping step with her, but unseen among the hawthorn and crab apple bushes, the tangle of brambles. I let us get a quarter of a mile away from the houses before I showed myself and then I stepped out on to the pavement ahead of her. I turned round to face her and stood there, staring in the way I'd practised in the mirror.

She wasn't nervous. She was brave. It was only very briefly that she hesitated. But she didn't quite dare walk past me. Instead she crossed the road. There's never much traffic on that road and so far not a single car had passed. She crossed the road, walking faster. I crossed too but behind her and I walked along behind her. Presently she began to run, so of course I ran too, though not fast enough to catch her up, just enough to gain on her a little.

We had been going on like that for some minutes, the Wake Arms still a mile off, when she suddenly doubled back, hared across the road and began running back the way she had come. That finished me for chasing her. I stood there and laughed. I laughed long and loud, I felt so happy and free, I felt so much all-conquering power that I – I alone, humble, ordinary, dull *me* – could inspire such fear.

After that I took to going to Epping Forest as a regular thing. Roughly speaking, I'd say it would have been once a fortnight. Since I do shift work, four till midnight just as often as ten till six, I sometimes managed to go in the daytime. A lot of women are alone at home in the daytime and have no men to escort them when they go out. I never let it go more than two weeks without my going there and occasionally I'd go more often, if I was feeling low in spirits, for instance, or Carol and I had a row or I got depressed over money. It did me so much good, I wish I could make you understand how much. Just think what it is you do that gives you a tremendous lift, driving a car really fast or going disco dancing or getting high on something – well, frightening women did all that for me and then some. Afterwards it was like Christmas, it was almost like being in love.

And there was no harm in it, was there? I didn't hurt them. There's a French saying: it gives me so much pleasure and you so little pain. That was the way it was for me and them, though it wasn't without pleasure for them either. Imagine how they must have enjoyed talking about it afterwards, going into all the details like Carol did, distorting the facts, exaggerating, making themselves for a while the centre of attention.

For all I knew they may have got up search parties, husbands and boy friends and fathers all out in a pack looking for me, all having a great time as people invariably do when they're hunting something or someone. After all, when all was said and done, what did I do? Nothing. I didn't molest them or insult them or try to touch them, I merely stood and looked at them and ran after them – or ran when they ran which isn't necessarily the same thing.

There was no harm in it. Or so I thought. I couldn't see what harm there could ever be, and believe me, I thought about this quite a lot, for I'm just as guilt-ridden as the rest of us. I thought about it, justifying myself, keeping guilt at bay. Young women don't have heart attacks and fall down dead because a man chases them. Young women aren't left with emotional traumas because a man stares at them. The oldest woman I ever frightened was the one with the Maltese terrier and she was no more than forty. I saw her again on my third or fourth visit and followed her for a while, stepping out from behind bushes and standing in her path. She used the same words the girl in Queens Wood had used, uttered in the same strangled voice: 'What is it you want?'

I didn't answer her. I had mercy on her and her little ineffectual dog and I melted away into the woodland shades. The next one who asked me that I answered with professorial gravity: 'Merely collecting lichens, madam.'

It was proof enough of how harmless I was that there was never a sign of a policeman in that area. I'm sure none of them told the police, for they had nothing to tell. They had only what they imagined and what the media had led them to expect. Yet harm did come from it, irrevocable harm and suffering and shame.

No doubt by now you think you've guessed. The inevitable must have happened, the encounter which any man who makes a practice of intimidating women is bound to have sooner or later, when the tables are turned on him. Yes, that did happen but it wasn't what stopped me. Being seized by the arm, hurled in the air and laid out, sprawled and bruised, by a judo black belt, was just an occupational hazard. I've always been glad, though, that I behaved like a gentleman. I didn't curse her or shout abuse. I merely got up, rubbed my legs and my elbows, made her a little bow and walked off in the direction of the Wake. Carol wanted to know how I'd managed to get green stains all over my clothes and I think to this day she believes it was from lying on the grass in a park somewhere with another woman. As if I would!

That attack on me deterred me. It didn't put me off. I let three weeks go by, three miserable yearning weeks, and then I went back to the Wake road one sunny July morning and had one of my most satisfying experiences. A girl walking, not on the road, but taking a short cut through the forest itself. I walked parallel to her, sometimes letting her catch a glimpse of me. I knew she did, for like it had been with the girl in Queens Wood, I could sense and smell her fear.

I strolled out from the bushes at last and stood ahead of her, waiting. She didn't dare approach me, she didn't know what to do. At length she turned back and I followed her, threading my way among the bushes until she must have thought I had gone, then appearing once more on the path ahead. This time she turned off to the left, running, and I let her go. Laughing the way I always did, out loud and irrepressibly, I let her go. I hadn't done her any harm. Think of the relief she must have felt when she knew she'd got away from me and was safe. Think of her going home and telling her mother or her sister or her husband all about it.

You could even say I'd done her a good turn. Most likely I'd warned her off going out in the forest on her own and therefore protected her from some real pervert or molester of women.

It was a point of view, wasn't it? You could make me out a public benefactor. I showed them what could happen. I was like the small electric shock that teaches a child not to play with the wires. Or that's what I believed. Till I learned that even a small shock can kill.

I was out in the forest, on the Wake road, when I had a piece of luck. It was autumn and getting dark at six, the earliest I'd been able to get there, and I didn't have much hope of any woman being silly enough to walk down that road alone in the dark. I had got off the bus at the Wake Arms and was walking slowly down the hill when I saw this car parked ahead of me at the kerb. Even from a distance I could hear the horrible noise it made as the driver tried to start it, that anguished grinding you get when ignition won't take place.

The offside door opened and a woman got out. She was on her own. She reached back into the car and turned the lights off, slammed the door, locked it and began walking down the hill towards Theydon. I had stepped in among the trees and she hadn't yet seen me. I followed her, working out what technique I should use this time. Pursuing her at a run to start with was what I decided on.

I came out on to the pavement about a hundred yards behind her and began running after her, making as much noise with my feet as I could. Of course she stopped and turned round as I knew she would. Probably she thought I was a saviour who was going to do something about her car for her. She looked round, waiting for me, and as soon as I caught her eye I veered off into the forest once more. She gave a sort of shrug, turned and walked on. She wasn't frightened yet.

It was getting dark, though, and there was no moon. I caught her up and walked alongside her, very quietly, only three or four yards away, yet in among the trees of the forest. By then we were out of sight of the parked car and a long way from being in sight of the lights of Theydon. The road was dark, though far from being impenetrably black. I trod on a twig deliberately and made it snap and she turned swiftly and saw me.

She jumped. She looked away immediately and quickened her pace. Of course she didn't have a chance with me, a five-foot woman doesn't with a six-foot man. The fastest she could walk was still only my strolling pace.

There hadn't been a car along the road since I'd been following her. Now one came. I could see its lights welling and dipping a long way off, round the twists in the road. She went to the edge of the pavement and held up her hand the way a hitchhiker does. I stayed where I was to see what would happen. What had I done, after all? Only been there. But the driver didn't stop for her. Of course he didn't, no more than I would have done in his place. We all know the sort of man who stops his car to pick up smartly dressed, pretty hitchhikers at night and we know what he's after.

The next driver didn't stop either. I was a little ahead of her by then, still inside the forest, and in his headlights I saw her face. She *was* pretty, not that that aspect particularly interested me, but I saw that she was pretty and that she belonged to the same type as Carol, a small slender blonde with rather sharp features and curly hair.

The darkness seemed much darker after the car lights had passed. I could tell she was a little less tense now, she probably hadn't seen me for the past five minutes, she might have thought I'd gone. And I was tempted to call it a day, give up after a quarter of an hour, as I usually did when I'd had my fun.

I wish to God I had. I went on with it for the stupidest of reasons. I went on with it because I wanted to go in the same direction as she was going, down into Theydon and catch the tube train from there, rather than go back and hang about waiting for a bus. I could have waited and let her go. I didn't. Out of some sort of perverse need, I kept step with her and then I came out of the forest and got on to the pavement behind her.

I walked along, gaining on her, but quietly. The road dipped, wound a little. I got two or three yards behind her, going very softly, she didn't know I was there, and then I began a soft whistling, a hymn tune it was, the Crimond version of *The Lord is My Shepherd*. What a choice!

She spun round. I thought she was going to say something but I don't think she could. Her voice was strangled by fear. She turned again and began to run. She could run quite fast, that tiny vulnerable blonde girl.

The car lights loomed up over the road ahead. They were full-beam, undipped headlights, blazing blue-white across the surrounding forest, showing up every tree and making long black shadows spring from their trunks. I jumped aside and crouched down in the long grass. She ran into the road, holding up both arms and crying: 'Help me! Help me!'

He stopped. I had a moment's tension when I thought he might get out and come looking for me, but he didn't. He pushed open the passenger door from inside. The girl got in, they waited, sitting there for maybe half a minute, and then the white Ford Capri moved off.

It was a relief to me to see that car disappear over the top of the hill. And I realized, to coin a very appropriate phrase, that I wasn't yet out of the wood. What could be more likely than that girl and the car driver would either phone or call in at Loughton police station? I knew I'd better get myself down to Theydon as fast as possible.

As it happened I did so without meeting or being passed by another vehicle. I was walking along by the village green when the only cars I saw came along. On the station platform I had to wait for nearly half an hour before a train came, but no policeman came either. I had got away with it again.

In a way. There are worse things than being punished for one's crimes. One of those is not being punished for them. I am suffering for what I did of course by not being allowed – that is, by not allowing myself – to do it again. And I shall never forget that girl's face, so pretty and vulnerable and frightened. It comes to me a lot in dreams.

The first time it appeared to me was in a newspaper photograph, two days after I had frightened her on the Wake road. The newspaper was leading on the story of her death and that was why it used the picture. On the previous morning, when she had been dead twelve hours, her body had been found, stabbed and mutilated, in a field between Epping and Harlow. Police were looking for a man, thought to be the driver of a white Ford Capri.

Her rescuer, her murderer. Then what was I?

A Case of Coincidence

Of the several obituaries which appeared on the death of Michael Lestrange not one mentioned his connection with the Wrexlade murders. Memories are short, even journalists' memories, and it may be that the newspapermen who wrote so glowingly and so mournfully about him were mere babes in arms, or not even born, at the time. For the murders, of course, took place in the early fifties, before the abolition of capital punishment.

Murder is the last thing one would associate with the late Sir Michael, eminent cardiac specialist, physician to Her Royal Highness the Duchess of Albany, and author of that classic work, the last word on its subject, so succinctly entitled *The Heart*. Sir Michael did not destroy life, he saved it. He was as far removed from Kenneth Edward Brannel, the Wrexlade Strangler, as he was from the carnivorous spider which crept across his consulting room window. Those who knew him well would say that he had an almost neurotic horror of the idea of taking life. Euthanasia he had refused to discuss, and he had opposed with all his vigour the legalizing of abortion.

Until last March when an air crash over the North Atlantic claimed him among its two hundred fatalities, he had been a man one automatically thought of as life-enhancing, as having on countless occasions defied death on behalf of others. Yet he seemed to have had no private life, no family, no circle to move in, no especially beautiful home. He lived for his work. He was not married and few knew he ever had been, still fewer that his wife had been the last of the Wrexlade victims.

There were four others and all five of them died as a result of being strangled by the outsized, bony hands of Kenneth Edward Brannel. Michael Lestrange, by the way, had exceptionally narrow, well-shaped hands, dextrous and precise. Brannel's have been described as resembling bunches of bananas. In her study of the Wrexlade case, the criminologist Miss Georgina Hallam Saul, relates how Brannel, in the condemned cell, talked about committing these crimes to a prison officer. He had never understood why he killed those women, he didn't dislike women or fear them.

'It's like when I was a kid and in a shop and there was no one about,' he is alleged to have said. 'I had to take something, I couldn't help myself. I didn't even do it sort of of my own will. One minute it'd be on the shelf and the next in my pocket. It was the same with those girls. I had to get my hands on their throats. Everything'd go dark and when it cleared my hands'd be round their throats and the life all squeezed out . . .'

He was twenty-eight, an agricultural labourer, illiterate, classified as educationally subnormal. He lived with his widowed father, also a farm worker, in a cottage on the outskirts of Wrexlade in Essex. During 1953 he strangled Wendy Cutforth, Maureen Hunter, Ann Daly and Mary Trenthyde without the police having the least suspicion of his guilt. Approximately a month elapsed between each of these murders, though there was no question of Brannel killing at the full moon or anything of that sort. Four weeks after Mary Trenthyde's death he was arrested and charged with murder, for the strangled body of Norah Lestrange had been discovered in a ditch less than a hundred yards from his cottage. They found him guilty of murder in November of that same year, twenty-five days later he was executed.

'A terrible example of injustice,' Michael Lestrange used to say. 'If the M'Naughten Rules apply to anybody they surely applied to poor Brannel. With him it wasn't only a matter of not knowing that what he was doing was wrong but of not knowing he was doing it at all till it was over. We have hanged a poor idiot who had no more idea of evil than a stampeding animal has when it tramples on a child.'

People thought it amazingly magnanimous of Michael that he could talk like this when it was his own wife who had been murdered. She was only twenty-five and they had been married less than three years.

It is probably best to draw on Miss Hallam Saul for the most accurate and comprehensive account of the Wrexlade stranglings. She attended the trial, every day of it, which Michael Lestrange did not. When prosecuting counsel, in his opening speech, came to describe Norah Lestrange's reasons for being in the neighbourhood of Wrexlade that night, and to talk of the Dutchman and the hotel at Chelmsford, Michael got up quietly and left the court. Miss Hallam Saul's eyes, and a good many other pairs of eyes, followed him with compassion. Nevertheless, she didn't spare his feelings in her book. Why should she? Like everyone else who wrote about Brannel and Wrexlade, she was appalled by the character of Norah Lestrange.

This was the fifties, remember, and the public were not used to hearing of young wives who admitted shamelessly to their husbands that one man was not enough for them. Michael had been obliged to state the facts to the police and the facts were that he had known for months that his wife spent nights in this Chelmsford hotel with Jan Vandepeer, a businessman on his way from The Hook and Harwich to London. She had told him so quite openly.

'Darling . . .' Taking his arm and leading him to sit close beside her while she fondled his hand. 'Darling, I absolutely have to have Jan, I'm crazy about him. I do have to have other men, I'm made that way. It's nothing to do with the way I feel about you, though, you do see that, don't you?'

These words he didn't, of course, render verbatim. The gist was enough.

'It won't be all that often, Mike darling, once a month at most. Jan can't fix a trip more than once a month. Chelmsford's so convenient for both of us and you'll hardly notice I'm gone, will you, you're so busy at that old hospital.'

But all this came much later, in the trial and in the Hallam Saul book. The first days (and the first chapters) were occupied with the killing of those four other women.

Wendy Cutforth was young, married, a teacher at a school in Ladeley. She went to work by bus from her home in Wrexlade, four miles away. In February, at four o'clock dusk, she got off the bus at Wrexlade Cross to walk to her bungalow a quarter of a mile away. She was never seen alive again, except presumably by Brannel, and her strangled body was found at ten that night in a ditch near the bus stop.

Fear of being out alone which had seized Wrexlade women after Wendy's death died down within three or four weeks. Maureen Hunter, who was only sixteen, quarrelled with her boyfriend after a dance at Wrexlade village hall and set off to walk home to Ingleford on her own. She never reached it. Her body was found in the small hours only a few yards from where Wendy's had been. Mrs Ann Daly, a middle-aged widow, also of Ingleford, had a hairdressing business in Chelmsford and drove herself to work each day via Wrexlade. Her car was found abandoned, all four doors wide open, her body in a small wood between the villages. An unsuccessful attempt had been made to bury it in the leaf mould.

Every man between sixteen and seventy in the whole of that area of Essex was closely examined by the police. Brannel was questioned, as was his father, and was released after ten minutes, having aroused no interest. In May, twenty-seven days after the death of Ann Daly, Mary Trenthyde, thirty-year-old mother of two small daughters and herself the daughter of Brannel's employer, Mark Stokes of Cross Farm, disappeared from her home during the course of a morning. One of her children was with its grandmother, the other in its pram just inside the garden gate. Mary vanished without trace, without announcing to anyone that she was going out or where she was going. A massive hunt was mounted and her strangled body finally found at midnight in a disused well half a mile away.

All these deaths took place in the spring of 1953.

The Lestranges had a flat in London not far from the Royal Free Hospital. They were not well off but Norah had a rich father who was in the habit of giving her handsome presents. One of these, for her twenty-fifth birthday, was a Triumph Alpine sports car. Michael had a car too, the kind of thing that is called an 'old banger'.

As frontispiece to Miss Hallam Saul's book is a portrait photograph of Norah Lestrange as she appeared a few months before her death. The face is oval, the features almost too perfectly symmetrical, the skin flawless and opaque. Her thick dark hair is dressed in the high fashion of the time, in short smooth curls. Her make-up is heavy and the dark, greasy lipstick coats the parted lips in a way that is somehow lascivious. The eyes stare with a humourless complacency.

Michael was furiously, painfully jealous of her. When, after they had been married six months, she began a flirtation with his best friend, a flirtation which soon developed into a love affair, he threatened to leave her, to divorce her, to lock her up, to kill Tony. She was supremely confident he would do none of these things. She talked to him. Reasonably and gently and lovingly she put it to him that it was he whom she loved and Tony with whom she was amusing herself.

'I *love* you, darling, don't you understand? This thing with Tony is just – fun. We have fun and then we say goodbye till next time and I come home to you, where my real happiness is.'

'You promised to be faithful to me,' he said, 'to forsake all others and keep only to me.'

'But I do keep only to you, darling. You have all my trust and my thoughts – Tony just has this tiny share in a very unimportant aspect of me.'

After Tony there was Philip. And after Philip, for a while, there was no one. Michael believed Norah might have tired of the 'fun' and be settling for the real happiness. He was working hard at the time for his Fellowship of the Royal College of Surgeons.

That Fellowship he got, of course, in 1952. He was surgical registrar at a big London hospital, famous for successes in the field of cardiac surgery, when the first of the Wrexlade murders took place. Wendy Cutforth. Round about the time the account of that murder and of the hunt for the Wrexlade strangler appeared in the papers, Norah met Jan Vandepeer.

Michael wasn't a reader of the popular press and the Lestranges had no television. Television wasn't, in those days, the indispensable adjunct to domestic life it has since become. Michael listened sometimes to the radio, he read *The Times*. He knew of the first of the Wrexlade murders but he wasn't much interested in it. He was busy in his job and he had Jan Vandepeer to worry about too.

The nature of the Dutchman's business in London was never clear to Michael, perhaps because it was never clear to Norah. It seemed to have something to do with commodity markets and Michael was convinced it was shady, not quite above board. Norah used to say that he was a smuggler, and she found the possibility he might be a diamond smuggler exciting. She met him on the boat coming from The Hook to Harwich after spending a week in The Hague with her parents, her father having a diplomatic post there.

'Darling, I absolutely have to have Jan, I'm crazy about him. It's nothing to do with us, though, you do see that, don't you? No one could ever take me away from you.'

He used to come over about once a month with his car and drive down to London through Colchester and Chelmsford, spend the night somewhere, carry out his business the following day and get the evening boat back. Whether he stayed in Chelmsford rather than London because it was cheaper or because Chelmsford, in those days, still kept its pleasant rural aspect, does not seem to be known. It hardly matters. Norah Lestrange was more than willing to drive the forty or so miles to Chelmsford in her Alpine and await the arrival of her dashing, blond smuggler at the Murrey Gryphon Hotel.

Chelmsford is the county town of Essex, standing on the banks of the river Chelmer and in the midst of a pleasant, though featureless, arable countryside. The land is rather flat, the fields wide, and there are many trees and numerous small woods. Wrexlade lies some four miles to the north of the town, Ingleford a little way further west. It was some time before the English reader of newspapers began to think of Wrexlade as anywhere near Chelmsford. It was simply

Wrexlade, a place no one had heard of till Wendy Cutforth and then Maureen Hunter died there, a name on a map or maybe a signpost till the stranglings began – and then, gradually, a word synonymous with fascinating horror.

Bismarck Road, Hilldrop Crescent, Rillington Place – who can say now, except the amateur of crime, which of London's murderers lived in those streets? Yet in their day they were names on everyone's lips. Such is the English sense of humour that there were even jokes about them. There were jokes, says Miss Hallam Saul, about Wrexlade, sick jokes for the utterance of one of which a famous comedian was banned by the BBC. Something on the lines of what a good idea it would be to take one's mother-in-law to Wrexlade . . .

Chelmsford, being so close to Wrexlade, became public knowledge when Mrs Daly died. She was last seen locking up her shop in the town centre and getting into her car. It was after this that Norah said to Michael: 'When I'm in Chelmsford, darling, I promise you I won't go out alone after dark.'

It was presumably to be a consolation to him that if she went out after dark it would be in the company of Jan Vandepeer.

Did he passively acquiesce, then, in this infidelity of hers? In not leaving her, in being at the flat when she returned home, in continuing to be seen with her socially, he did acquiesce. In continuing to love her in spite of himself, he acquiesced. But his misery was terrible. He was ill with jealousy. All his time, when he was not at the hospital, when he was not snatching a few hours of sleep, was spent in thrashing out in his mind what he should do. It was impossible to go on like this. If he remained in her company he was afraid he would do her some violence, but the thought of being permanently parted from her was horrible. When he contemplated it he seemed to feel the solid ground sliding away from under his feet, he felt like Othello felt – 'If I love thee not, chaos is come again.'

In June, on Friday, 19 June, Norah went down to Chelmsford, to the Murrey Gryphon Hotel, to spend the night with Jan Vandepeer.

Michael, who had worked every day without a break at the hospital for two weeks, had two days off, the Friday and the Saturday. He was tired almost to the point of sickness, but those two days he was to have off loomed large and glowing and inviting before him at the end of the week. He got them out of proportion. He told himself that if he could have those two days off to spend alone with Norah, to take Norah somewhere into the country and laze those two days away with her, to walk with her hand in hand down country lanes (that he thought with such maudlin romanticism is evidence of his extreme exhaustion), if he could do that, all would miraculously become well. He would explain and she would explain and they would listen to each other and, in the words of the cliché, make a fresh start. Michael was convinced of all this. He was a little mad with tiredness.

After she was dead, and they came in the morning to tell him of her death, he took time off work. Miss Hallam Saul gives the period as three weeks and she is probably correct. Without those weeks of rest Michael Lestrange would very likely have had a mental breakdown or – even worse to his way of thinking – have killed a patient on the operating table. So when it is said that Norah's death, though so terrible to him, saved his sanity and his career, this is not too far from the truth. And then, when he eventually returned to his work, he threw himself into it with total dedication. He had nothing else, you see, nothing at all but his work for the rest of his life that ended in the North Atlantic last March.

Brannel had nothing either. It is very difficult for the educated middle-class person, the kind of person we really mean when we talk about 'the man in the street', to understand the lives of people like Kenneth Edward Brannel and his father. They had no hobbies, no interests, no skill, no knowledge in their heads, virtually no friends. Old Brannel could read. Tracing along the lines with his finger, he could just about make out the words in a newspaper. Kenneth Brannel could not read at all. These days they would have television, not then. Romantic town-dwellers imagine such as the Brannels tending their cottage gardens, growing vegetables, occupying themselves with a little carpentry or shoemaking in the evenings, cooking country stews and baking bread. The Brannels, who worked all day in another man's fields, would not have dreamt of further tilling the soil in the evenings. Neither of them had ever so much as put up a shelf or stuck a sole on a boot. They lived on tinned food and fish and chips, and when the darkness came down they went to bed. There was no electricity in their cottage, anyway, and no running water or indoor sanitation. It would never have occurred to Mr Stokes of Cross Farm to provide these amenities or to the Brannels to demand them.

Downstairs in the cottage was a living room with a fireplace and a kitchen with a range. Upstairs was old Brannel's room into which the stairs went, and through the door from this room was the bedroom and only private place of Kenneth Edward Brannel. There, in a drawer in the old, wooden-knobbed tallboy, unpolished since Ellen Brannel's death, he kept his souvenirs: Wendy Cutforth's bracelet, a lock of Maureen Hunter's red hair, Ann Daly's green silk scarf, Mary Trenthyde's handkerchief with the lipstick stain and the embroidered M. The small, square handbag mirror was always assumed to have been the property of Norah Lestrange, to be a memento of her, but this was never proved. Certainly, there was no mirror in her handbag when her body was found.

In Miss Hallam Saul's *The Wrexlade Monster* there were several pictures of Brannel, a snapshot taken by his aunt when he was ten, a class group at Ingleford Middle School (which he should properly have never, with his limitations, been allowed to attend), a portrait by a Chelmsford photographer that his mother had had taken the year before her death. He was very tall, a gangling, bony man with a bumpy, tortured-looking forehead and thick, pale, curly hair. The eyes seem to say to you: The trouble is that I am puzzled, I am bewildered, I don't understand the world or you or myself and I live always in a dark mist. But when, for a little, that mist clears, look what I do . . .

His hands, hanging limply at his sides, are turned slightly, the palms half-showing, as if in helplessness and despair.

Miss Hallam Saul includes no picture of Sir Michael Lestrange, MD, FRCS, eminent cardiac specialist, author of *The Heart*, Physician to Her Royal Highness the Duchess of Albany, professor of cardiology at St Joachim's Hospital. He was a thin, dark young man in those days, slight of figure and always rather shabbily dressed. One would not have given him a second glance. Very different he was then from the Sir Michael who was mourned by the medical elite of two continents and whose austere yet tranquil face with its sleek silver hair, calm light eyes and aquiline features appeared on the front pages of the world's newspapers. He had changed more than most men in twenty-seven years. It was a total metamorphosis, not merely an ageing.

At the time of the murder of his wife Norah he was twenty-six. He was ambitious but not inordinately so. The ambition, the vocation one might well call it, came later, after she was dead. He was worn out with work on 19 June 1953, and he was longing to get away to the country with his wife and to rest.

'But, darling, I'm sure I told you. I'm going to meet Jan at the Murrey Gryphon. I did tell you, I never have any secrets from you, you know that. *You* didn't tell me you were going to have two days off. How was I to know? You never seem to take time off these days and I do like to have *some* fun *some*times.'

'Don't go,' he said.

'But, darling, I want to see Jan.'

'It's more than I can bear, the way we live,' he said. 'If you won't stop seeing this man I shall stop you.'

He buried his face in his hands and presently she came and laid a hand on his shoulder. He jumped up and struck her a blow across the face. When she left for Chelmsford to meet Jan Vandepeer she had a bruise on her cheek which she did her best to disguise with make-up.

They had a message for her at the hotel when she got there, from her 'husband' in Holland to say he had been delayed at The Hook. Hotels, in those days, were inclined to be particular that couples who shared bedrooms should at least pretend to be husband and wife. It was insinuated at Brannel's trial that Jan Vandepeer failed to arrive on this occasion because he was growing tired of Norah, but there was no evidence to support this. He was genuinely delayed and unable to leave.

Why didn't she go back to London? Perhaps she was afraid to face Michael. Perhaps she hoped Vandepeer would still come, since the phone message had been received at four-thirty. She dined alone and went out for a walk. To pick up a man, insisted prosecuting counsel, though he was not prosecuting *her* and the Old Bailey is not a court of morals. Nobody saw her go and no one seems to have been sure where she went. Eventually, of course, to Wrexlade.

Brannel also went out for a walk. The long light evenings disquieted him because he could not go to bed and he had nothing to do but sit with his father while the old man puzzled out the words in the evening paper. He went first to his bedroom to look at and handle the secret things he kept there, the scarf and the lock of hair and the bracelet and the handkerchief with M on it for Mary Trenthyde, and then he went out for his walk. Along the narrow lanes, to stop sometimes and stand, to lean over a gate, or to kick a pebble aimlessly ahead of him, dribbling it slowly from side to side of the long, straight, lonely road.

Did Norah Lestrange walk all the way to Wrexlade or did someone give her a lift and for reasons unknown abandon her there? She could have walked, it is no more than two miles from the Murrey Gryphon to the spot where her body was found half an hour before midnight. Miss Hallam Saul suggests that she was friendly with a second man in the Chelmsford neighbourhood and, in the absence of Vandepeer, set off to meet him that evening. Unlikely though that seems, similar suggestions were put forward in court. It was as if they all said, a woman like that, a woman so immoral, so promiscuous, so lacking in all proper feeling, a woman like that will do anything.

Her body was found by two young Wrexlade men going home after an evening spent at the White Swan on the Ladeley-Wrexlade road. They phoned the police from the call box on the opposite side of the lane, and the first place the police went to, because it was the nearest habitation, was the Brannels' cottage. Norah Lestrange's body lay half-hidden in long grass on the verge by the bridge over the river Lade, and the Brannels' home, Lade Cottage, was a hundred yards the other side of the bridge. They went there initially only to ask the occupants if they had seen or heard anything untoward that evening.

Old Brannel came down in his nightshirt with a coat over it. He hadn't been asleep when the police came, he said, he had been awakened a few minutes before by his son coming in. The detective superintendent looked at Kenneth Edward Brannel, at his huge dangling hands, as he stood leaning against the wall, his eyes bewildered, his mouth a little open. No, he couldn't say where he had been, round and about, up and down, he couldn't say more.

They searched the house, although they had no warrant. Much was made of this by the defence at the trial. In Kenneth Brannel's bedroom, in the drawer of the tallboy, they found Wendy Cutforth's bracelet, Maureen Hunter's lock of red hair, Ann Daly's green silk scarf, and the handkerchief with M on it for Mary Trenthyde. The Wrexlade Monster had been caught at last. They cautioned Brannel and charged him and he looked at them in a puzzled way and said: 'I don't think I killed the lady. I don't remember. But maybe I did, I forget things and it's like a mist comes up . . .'

Michael Lestrange was told of the death of his wife in the early hours of the morning. Their purpose in coming to him was to tell him the news and ask him if he would later go with them to Chelmsford formally to identify his wife's body. They asked him no questions and would have expressed their sympathy and left him in peace, had he not declared that it was he who had killed Norah and that he wanted to make a full confession.

They had no choice after that but to drive him at once to Chelmsford and take a statement from him. No one believed it. The detective chief superintendent in charge of the case was very kind to him, very gentle but firm.

'But if I tell you I killed her you must believe me. I can prove it.'

'Can you, Dr Lestrange?'

'My wife was constantly unfaithful to me . . .'

'Yes, so you have told me. And you bore with her treatment of you because of your great affection for her. The truth seems to be, doctor, that you were a devoted husband and your wife – well, a less than ideal wife.'

Michael Lestrange insisted that he had driven to Chelmsford in pursuit of Norah, intending to appeal to Jan Vandepeer to leave her alone. He had not gone into the hotel. By chance he had encountered her walking aimlessly along a Chelmsford street as he was on his way to the Murrey Gryphon.

'Mrs Lestrange was still having her dinner at the time you mention,' said Chief Superintendent Masters.

'What does that matter? It was earlier or later, I can't be precise about times. She got into the car beside me. I drove off, I don't know where, I didn't want a scene in the hotel. She told me she had to get back, she was expecting Vandepeer at any moment.'

'Vandepeer had sent her a message he wasn't coming. She didn't tell you that?'

'Is it important?' He was impatient to get his confession over. 'It doesn't matter what she told me. I can't remember what we said.'

'Can you remember where you went?'

'Of course I can't. I don't know the place. I just drove and parked somewhere, I don't know where, and we got out and walked and she drove me mad, the things she said, and I got hold of her throat and . . .' He put his head in his hands. 'I can't remember what happened next. I don't know where it was or when. I was so tired and I was mad, I think.' He looked up. 'But I killed her. If you'd like to charge me now, I'm quite ready.'

The chief superintendent said very calmly and stolidly, 'That won't be necessary, Dr Lestrange.'

Michael Lestrange shut his eyes momentarily and clenched his fists and said, 'You don't believe me.'

'I quite believe you believe it yourself, doctor.'

'Why would I confess it if it wasn't true?'

'People do, sir, it's not uncommon. Especially people like yourself who have been overworking and worrying and not getting enough sleep. You're a doctor, you know what the psychiatrists would say, that you had a reason for doing violence to your wife so that now she's dead your mind has convinced itself you killed her, and you're feeling guilt for something you had nothing to do with.

'You see, doctor, look at it from our point of view. Is it likely that you, an educated man, a surgeon, would murder anyone? Not very. And if you did, would you do it in Wrexlade? Would you do it a hundred yards from the home of a man who has murdered four other women? Would you do it by strangling with the bare hands which is the method that man always used? Would you do it four weeks after the last strangling which itself was four weeks after the previous one? Coincidences like that don't happen, do they, Dr Lestrange? But people do get overtired and suffer from stress so that they confess to crimes they never committed.'

'I bow to your superior judgement,' said Michael Lestrange.

He went to the mortuary and identified Norah's body and then he made a statement to the effect that Norah had gone to Chelmsford to meet her lover. He had last seen her at four on the previous afternoon.

Brannel was found guilty of Norah's murder, for he was specifically charged only with that, after the jury had been out half an hour. And in spite of the medical evidence as to his mental state he was condemned to death and executed a week before Christmas.

For the short time after that execution that capital punishment remained law, Michael Lestrange was bitterly opposed to it. He used to say that Brannel was a prime example of someone who had been unjustly hanged and that this must never be allowed to happen in England again. Of course there was never any doubt that Brannel had strangled Wendy Cutforth, Maureen Hunter, Ann Daly and Mary Trenthyde. The evidence was there and he repeatedly confessed to these murders. But that was not what Michael Lestrange meant. People took him to mean that a man must not be punished for committing a crime whose seriousness he is too feeble-minded to understand. This is the law, and there can be no exceptions to it merely because society wants its revenge. People took Michael Lestrange to mean that when he spoke of injustice being done to this multiple killer.

And perhaps he did.

Thornapple

T he plant, which was growing up against the wall between the gooseberry bushes, stood about two feet high and had pointed, jaggedly toothed, oval leaves of a rich dark green. It bore, at the same time, a flower and a fruit. The trumpet-shaped flower had a fine, delicate texture and was of the purest white, while the green fruit, which rather resembled a chestnut though it was of a darker colour, had spines growing all over it that had a rather threatening or warning look.

According to *Indigenous British Flora*, which James held in his hand, the thornapple or Jimson's Weed or *datura stramonium* also had an unpleasant smell, but he did not find it so. What the book did not say was that *datura* was highly poisonous. James already knew that, for although this was the plant's first appearance in the Fyfields' garden, he had seen it in other parts of the village during the previous summer. And then he had only had to look at it for some adult to come rushing up and warn him of its dangers, as if he were likely at his age to eat a spiky object that looked more like a sea urchin than a seed head. Adults had not only warned him and the other children, but had fallen upon the unfortunate *datura* and tugged it out of the ground with exclamations of triumph as of a dangerous job well done.

James had discovered three specimens in the garden. The thornapple had a way of springing up in unexpected places and the book described it as 'a casual in cultivated ground'. His father would not behave in the way of those village people but he would certainly have it out as soon as he spotted it. James found this understandable. But it meant that if he was going to prepare an infusion or brew of *datura* he had better get on with it. He went back thoughtfully into the house, taking no notice of his sister Rosamund who was sitting at the kitchen table reading a foreign tourists' guide to London, and returned the book to his own room.

James's room was full of interesting things. A real glory-hole, his mother called it. He was a collector and an experimenter, was James, with an enquiring, analytical mind and more than his fair share of curiosity. He had a fish tank, its air pump bubbling away, a glass box containing hawk moth caterpillars, and mice in a cage. On the walls were crustacean charts and life cycle of the frog charts and a map of the heavens. There were several hundred books, shells and dried grasses, a snakeskin and a pair of antlers (both naturally shed) and on the top shelf of the bookcase his bottles of poison. James replaced the wild flower book and, climbing on to a stool, studied these bottles with some satisfaction.

He had prepared their contents himself by boiling leaves, flowers and berries and straining off the resulting liquor. This had mostly turned out to be a dark greenish brown or else a purplish red, which rather disappointed James who had hoped for bright green or saffron yellow, these colours being more readily associated with the sinister or the evil. The bottles were labelled *conium maculatum* and *hyoscyamus niger* rather than with their common English names, for James's mother, when she came in to dust the glory-hole, would know what hemlock and henbane were. Only the one containing his prize solution, that deadly nightshade, was left unlabelled. There would be no concealing, even from those ignorant of Latin, the significance of *atropa belladonna*.

Not that James had the least intention of putting these poisons of his to use. Nothing could have been further from his mind. Indeed, they stood up there on the high shelf precisely to be out of harm's way and, even so, whenever a small child visited the house, he took care to keep his bedroom door locked. He had made the poisons from the pure, scientific motive of *seeing if it could be done*. With caution and in a similar spirit of detachment, he had gone so far as to taste, first a few drops and then half a teaspoonful of the henbane. The result had been to make him very sick and give him painful stomach cramps which necessitated sending for the doctor who diagnosed gastritis. But James had been satisfied. It worked.

In preparing his poisons, he had had to maintain a close secrecy. That is, he made sure his mother was out of the house and Rosamund too. Rosamund would not have been interested, for one plant was much the same as another to her, she shrieked when she saw the hawk moth caterpillars and her pre-eminent wish was to go and live in London. But she was not above tale-bearing. And although neither of his parents would have been cross or have punished him or peremptorily have destroyed his preparations, for they were reasonable, level-headed people, they would certainly have prevailed upon him to throw the bottles away and have lectured him and appealed to his better nature and his common sense. So if he was going to add to his collection with a potion of *datura*, it might be wise to select Wednesday afternoon when his mother was at the meeting of the Women's Institute, and then commandeer the kitchen, the oven, a saucepan and a sieve.

His mind made up, James returned to the garden with a brown paper bag into which he dropped five specimens of thornapple fruits, all he could find, and for good measure two flowers and some leaves as well. He was sealing up the top of the bag with a strip of Scotch tape when Rosamund came up the path.

'I suppose you've forgotten we've got to take those raspberries to Aunt Julie?'

James had. But since the only thing he wanted to do at that moment was boil up the contents of the bag, and that he could not do till Wednesday, he gave Rosamund his absent-minded professor look, shrugged his shoulders and said it was impossible for *him* to forget anything *she* was capable of remembering.

'I'm going to put this upstairs,' he said. 'I'll catch you up.'

The Fyfield family had lived for many years – centuries, some said – in the village of Great Sindon in Suffolk, occupying this cottage or that one, taking over small farmhouses, yeomen all, until in the early nineteen hundreds some of them had climbed up into the middle class. James's father, son of a schoolmaster, himself taught at the University of Essex at Wivenhoe, some twenty miles distant. James was already tipped for Oxford. But they were very much of the village too, were the Fyfields of Ewes Hall Farm, with ancestors lying in the churchyard and ancestors remembered on the war memorial on the village green.

The only other Fyfield at present living in Great Sindon was Aunt Julie who wasn't really an aunt but a connection by marriage, her husband having been a second cousin twice removed or something of that sort. James couldn't recall that he had ever been particularly nice to her or specially polite (as Rosamund was) but for all that Aunt Julie seemed to prefer him over pretty well everyone else. With the exception, perhaps, of Mirabel. And because she preferred him she expected him to pay her visits. Once a week these visits would have taken place if Aunt Julie had had her way, but James was not prepared to fall in with that and his parents had not encouraged it.

'I shouldn't like anyone to think James was after her money,' his mother had said.

'Everyone knows that's to go to Mirabel,' said his father.

'All the more reason. I should hate to have it said James was after Mirabel's rightful inheritance.'

Rosamund was unashamedly after it or part of it, though that seemed to have occurred to no one. She had told James so. A few thousand from Aunt Julie would help enormously in her ambition to buy herself a flat in London, for which she had been saving up since she was seven. But flats were going up in price all the time (she faithfully read the estate agents' pages in the *Observer*), her £28.50 would go nowhere, and without a windfall her situation looked hopeless. She was very single-minded, was Rosamund, and she had a lot of determination. James supposed she had picked the raspberries herself and that her 'we've got to take them' had its origins in her own wishes and was in no way a directive from their mother. But he didn't much mind going. There was a mulberry tree in Aunt Julie's garden and he would be glad of a chance to examine it. He was thinking of keeping silkworms.

It was a warm sultry day in high summer, a day of languid air and half-veiled sun, of bumble bees heavily laden and roses blown but still scented. The woods hung on the hillsides like blue smoky shadows, and the fields where they were beginning to cut the wheat were the same colour as Rosamund's hair. Very long and straight was the village street of Great Sindon, as is often the case in Suffolk. Aunt Julie lived at the very end of it in a plain, solidly built, grey brick, double-fronted house with a shallow slate roof and two tall chimneys. It would never, in the middle of the nineteenth century when it had been built, have been designated a 'gentleman's house', for there were only four bedrooms and a single kitchen, while the ceilings were low and the stairs steep, but nowadays any gentleman might have been happy to live in it and village opinion held that it was worth a very large sum of money. Sindon Lodge stood in about two acres of land which included an apple orchard, a lily pond and a large lawn on which the mulberry tree was.

James and his sister walked along in almost total silence. They had little in common and it was hot, the air full of tiny insects that came off the harvest fields. James knew that he had only been invited to join her because if she had gone alone Aunt Julie would have wanted to know where he was and would have sulked and probably not been at all welcoming. He wondered if she knew that the basket in which she had put the raspberries, having first lined it with a white paper table napkin, was in fact of the kind that is intended for wine, being made with a loop of cane at one end to hold the neck of the bottle. She had changed, he noticed, from her jeans into her new cotton skirt, the Laura Ashley print, and had brushed her wheat-coloured hair and tied a black velvet ribbon round it. Much good it would do her, thought James, but he decided not to tell her the true function of the basket unless she did anything particular to irritate him.

But as they were passing the church Rosamund suddenly turned to face him and asked him if he knew Aunt Julie now had a lady living with her to look after her. A companion, this person was called, said Rosamund. James hadn't known – he had probably been absorbed in his own thoughts when it was discussed – and he was somewhat chagrined.

'So what?'

'So nothing. Only I expect she'll open the door to us. You didn't know, did you? It isn't true you know things I don't. I often know things you don't, I *often* do.'

James did not deign to reply.

'She said that if ever she got so she *had* to have someone living with her, she'd get Mirabel to come. And Mirabel wanted to, she actually liked the idea of living in the country. But Aunt Julie didn't ask her, she got this lady instead, and I heard Mummy say Aunt Julie doesn't want Mirabel in the house any more. I don't know why. Mummy said maybe Mirabel won't get Aunt Julie's money now.'

James whistled a few bars from the overture to the *Barber of Seville*. 'I know why.'

'Bet you don't.'

'OK, so I don't.'

'Why, then?'

'You're not old enough to understand. And, incidentally, you may not know it but that thing you've got the raspberries in is a wine basket.'

The front door of Sindon Lodge was opened to them by a fat woman in a cotton dress with a wrap-around overall on top of it. She seemed to know who they were and said she was Mrs Crowley but they could call her Auntie Elsie if they liked. James and Rosamund were in silent agreement that they did not like. They went down the long passage where it was rather cold even on the hottest day.

Aunt Julie was in the room with the french windows, sitting in a chair looking into the garden, the grey cat Palmerston on her lap.

326

Her hair was exactly the same colour as Palmerston's fur and nearly as fluffy. She was a little wizened woman, very old, who always dressed in jumpers and trousers which, James thought privately, made her look a bit like a monkey. Arthritis twisted and half-crippled her, slowly growing worse, which was probably why she had engaged Mrs Crowley.

Having asked Rosamund why she had put the raspberries in a wine basket – she must be sure to take it straight back to Mummy – Aunt Julie turned her attention to James, demanding of him what he had been collecting lately, how were the hawk moth caterpillars and what sort of a school report had he had at the end of the summer term? A further ten minutes of this made James, though not unusually tender-hearted towards his sister, actually feel sorry for Rosamund, so he brought himself to tell Aunt Julie that she had passed her piano exam with distinction and, if he might be excused, he would like to go out and look at the mulberry tree.

The garden had a neglected look and in the orchard tiny apples, fallen during the 'June drop', lay rotting in the long grass. There were no fish in the pond and had not been for years. The mulberry tree was loaded with sticky-looking squashy red fruit, but James supposed that silkworms fed only on the leaves. Would he be allowed to help himself to mulberry leaves? Deciding that he had a lot to learn about the rearing of silkworms, he walked slowly round the tree, remembering now that it was Mirabel who had first identified the tree for him and had said how wonderful she thought it would be to make one's own silk.

It seemed to him rather dreadful that just because Mirabel had had a baby she might be deprived of all this. For 'all this', the house, the gardens, the vaguely huge sum of money which Uncle Walter had made out of building houses and had left to his widow, was surely essential to poor Mirabel who made very little as a free-lance designer and must have counted on it.

Had he been alone, he might have raised the subject with Aunt Julie who would take almost anything from him even though she called him an *enfant terrible*. She sometimes said he could twist her round his little finger, which augured well for getting the mulberry leaves. But he wasn't going to talk about Mirabel in front of Rosamund. Instead, he mentioned it tentatively to his mother immediately after Rosamund, protesting, had been sent to bed.

'Well, darling, Mirabel did go and have a baby without being married. And when Aunt Julie was young that was a terrible thing to do. We can't imagine, things have changed so much. But Aunt Julie has very strict ideas and she must think of Mirabel as a bad woman.'

'I see,' said James, who didn't quite. 'And when she dies Mirabel won't be in her will, is that right?'

'I don't think we ought to talk about things like that.'

'Certainly we shouldn't,' said James's father.

'No, but I want to know. You're always saying people shouldn't keep things secret from children. Has Aunt Julie made a new will, cutting Mirabel out?'

'She hasn't made a will at all, that's the trouble. According to the law, a great niece doesn't automatically inherit if a person dies intestate – er, that is, dies . . .'

'I know what intestate means,' said James.

'So I suppose Mirabel thought she could get her to make a will. It doesn't sound very nice put like that but, really, why shouldn't poor Mirabel have it? If she doesn't, I don't believe there's anyone else near enough and it will just go to the state.'

'Shall we change the subject now?' said James's father.

'Yes, all right,' said James. 'Will you be going to the Women's Institute the same as usual on Wednesday?'

'Of course I will, darling. Why on earth do you ask?'

'I just wondered,' said James.

James's father was on holiday while the university was down and on the following day he went out into the fruit garden with a basket and his weeder and uprooted the thornapple plant that was growing between the gooseberry bushes. James, sitting in his bedroom, reading *The Natural History of Selborne*, watched him from the window. His father put the thornapple on the compost heap and went hunting for its fellows, all of which he found in the space of five minutes. James sighed but took this destruction philosophically. He had enough in the brown paper bag for his needs.

As it happened, he had the house to himself for the making of his newest brew. His father announced at lunch that he would be taking the car into Bury St Edmunds that afternoon and both children could come with him if they wanted to. Rosamund did. Bury, though not London, was at any rate a sizeable town with plenty of what she liked, shops and restaurants and cinemas and crowds. Once alone, James chose an enamel saucepan of the kind which looked as if all traces of *datura* could easily be removed from it afterwards, put into it about a pint of water and set this to boil. Meanwhile, he cut up the green spiny fruits to reveal the black seeds they contained. When the water boiled he dropped in the fruit pieces and the seeds and leaves and flowers and kept it all simmering for half an hour, occasionally stirring the mixture with a skewer. Very much as he had expected, the bright green colour hadn't been maintained, but the solid matter and the liquid had all turned a dark khaki brown. James didn't dare use a sieve to strain it in case he couldn't get it clean again, so he pressed all the liquor out with his hands until nothing remained but some soggy pulp.

This he got rid of down the waste disposal unit. He poured the liquid, reduced now to not much more than half a pint, into the medicine bottle he had ready for it, screwed on the cap and labelled it: *datura stramonium*. The pan he scoured thoroughly but a few days later, when he saw that his mother had used it for boiling the peas they were about to eat with their fish for supper, he half-expected the whole family to have griping pains and even tetanic convulsions. But nothing happened and no one suffered any ill effects.

By the time the new school term started James had produced a substance he hoped might be muscarine from boiling up the fly agaric fungus and some rather doubtful cyanide from apricot kernels. There were now ten bottles of poison on the top shelf of his bookcase. But no one was in the least danger from them, and even when the Fyfield household was increased by two members there was no need for James to keep his bedroom door locked, for Mirabel's little boy was only six months old and naturally as yet unable to walk.

Mirabel's arrival had been entirely impulsive. A ridiculous way to behave, James's father said. The lease of her flat in Kensington was running out and instead of taking steps to find herself somewhere else to live, she had waited until the lease was within a week of expiry and had turned up in Great Sindon to throw herself on the mercy of Aunt Julie. She came by taxi from Ipswich station, lugging a suitcase and carrying the infant Oliver.

Mrs Crowley had opened the door to her and Mirabel had never got as far as seeing Aunt Julie. A message was brought back to say she was not welcome at Sindon Lodge as her aunt thought she had made clear enough by telephone and letter. Mirabel, who had believed that Aunt Julie would soften at the sight of her, had a choice between going back to London, finding a hotel in Ipswich or taking refuge with the Fyfields. She told the taxi to take her to Ewes Hall Farm.

'How could I turn her away?' James heard his mother say. Mirabel was upstairs putting Oliver to bed. 'There she was on the doorstep with that great heavy case and the baby screaming his head off, poor mite. And she's such a little scrap of a thing.'

James's father had been gloomy ever since he got home. 'Mirabel is exactly the sort of person who would come for the weekend and stay ten years.'

'No one would stay here for ten years if they could live in London,' said Rosamund.

In the event, Mirabel didn't stay ten years, though she was still there after ten weeks. And on almost every day of those ten weeks she tried in vain to get her foot in the door of Sindon Lodge. Whoever happened to be in the living room of Ewes Hall Farm in the evening – and in the depths of winter that was usually everyone – was daily regaled with Mirabel's grievances against life and with denunciations of the people who had injured her, notably Oliver's father and Aunt Julie. James's mother sometimes said that it was sad for Oliver having to grow up without a father, but since Mirabel never mentioned him without saying how selfish he was, the most immature, heartless, mean, lazy and cruel man in London, James thought Oliver would be better off without him. As for Aunt Julie, she must be senile, Mirabel said, she must have lost her wits.

'Can you imagine anyone taking such an attitude, Elizabeth, in this day and age? She literally will not have me in the house because I've got Oliver and I wasn't married to Francis. Thank God I wasn't, that's all I can say. But wouldn't you think that sort of thing went out with the dark ages?'

'She'll come round in time,' said James's mother.

'Yes, but how much time? I mean, she hasn't got that much, has she? And here am I taking shameful advantage of your hospitality. You don't know how guilty it makes me, only I literally have nowhere else to go. And I simply cannot afford to take another flat like the last, frankly, I couldn't raise the cash. I haven't been getting the contracts like I used to before Oliver was born and of course I've never had a penny from that unspeakable, selfish, pig of a man.'

James's mother and father would become very bored with all this but they could hardly walk out of the room. James and Rosamund could, though after a time Mirabel took to following James up to the glory-hole where she would sit on his bed and continue her long, detailed, repetitive complaints just as if he were her own contemporary.

It was a little disconcerting at first, though he got used to it. Mirabel was about thirty but to him and his sister she seemed the same age as their parents, middle-aged, old, much as anyone did who was over, say, twenty-two. And till he got accustomed to her manner he hardly knew what to make of the way she gazed intensely into his eyes or suddenly clutched him by the arm. She described herself (frequently) as passionate, nervous and highly strung.

She was a small woman and James was already taller than she. She had a small, rather pinched face with large prominent dark eyes and she wore her long hair hanging loose like Rosamund's. The Fyfields were big-boned, fair-headed people with ruddy skins but Mirabel was dark and very thin and her wrists and hands and ankles and feet were very slender and narrow. There was, of course, no blood relationship, Mirabel being Aunt Julie's own sister's granddaughter.

Mirabel was not her baptismal name. She had been christened Brenda Margaret but it had to be admitted that the name she had chosen for herself suited her better, suited her feyness, her intense smiles and brooding sadnesses, and the clinging clothes she wore, the muslins and the trailing shawls. She always wore a cloak or a cape to go into the village and James's mother said she couldn't remember Mirabel ever having possessed a coat.

James had always had rather a sneaking liking for her, he hadn't known why. But now that he was older and saw her daily, he understood something he had not known before. He liked Mirabel, he couldn't help himself, because she seemed to like him so much and because she flattered him. It was funny, he could listen to her flattery and distinguish it for what it was, but this knowledge did not detract a particle from the pleasure he felt in hearing it.

'You're absolutely brilliant for your age, aren't you, James?' Mirabel would say. 'I suppose you'll be a professor one day. You'll probably win the Nobel prize.'

She asked him to teach her things: how to apply Pythagoras' Theorem, how to convert Fahrenheit temperatures into Celsius, ounces into grammes, how to change the plug on her hair dryer.

'I'd like to think Oliver might have half your brains, James, and then I'd be quite content. Francis is clever, mind you, though he's so immature and lazy with it. I literally think *you're* more mature than he is.'

Aunt Julie must have known for a long time that Mirabel was staying with the Fyfields, for nothing of that kind could be concealed in a village of the size of Great Sindon, but it was December before she mentioned the matter to James. They were sitting in front of the fire in the front sitting room at Sindon Lodge, eating crumpets

331

toasted by Mrs Crowley and drinking Earl Grey tea, while Palmerston stretched out on the hearth rug. Outside a thin rain was driving against the window panes.

'I hope Elizabeth knows what she's doing, that's all. If you're not careful you'll all be stuck with that girl for life.'

James said nothing.

'Of course you don't understand the ins and outs of it at your age, but in my opinion your parents should have thought twice before they let her come into their home and bring her illegitimate child with her.' Aunt Julie looked at him darkly and perhaps spitefully. 'That could have a very bad effect on Rosamund, you know. Rosamund will think immoral behaviour is quite all right when she sees people like Mirabel getting rewarded for it.'

'She's not exactly *rewarded*,' said James, starting on the tea cakes and the greengage jam. 'We don't give her anything but her food and she has to sleep in the same room as Oliver.' This seemed to him by far the worst aspect of Mirabel's situation.

Aunt Julie made no reply. After a while she said, looking into the fire, 'How d'you think you'd feel if you knew people only came to see you for the sake of getting your money? That's all Madam Mirabel wants. She doesn't care for me, she couldn't care less. She comes here sweet talking to Mrs Crowley because she thinks once she's in here I'll take her back and make a will leaving everything I've got to her and that illegitimate child of hers. How d'you think you'd like it? Maybe you'll come to it yourself one day, your grandchildren sucking up to you for what they can get.'

'You don't *know* people come for that,' said James awkwardly, thinking of Rosamund.

Aunt Julie made a sound of disgust. 'Aaah!' She struck out with her arthritic hand as if pushing something away. 'I'm not green, am I? I'm not daft. I'd despise myself, I can tell you, if I pretended it wasn't as plain as the nose on my face what you all come for.'

The fire crackled and Palmerston twitched in his sleep.

'Well, I don't,' said James.

'Don't you now, Mr Pure-and-holy?'

James grinned. 'There's a way you could find out. You could make a will and leave your money to other people and tell me I wasn't getting any – and then see if I'd still come.'

'I could, could I? You're so sharp, James Fyfield, you'll cut yourself badly one of these fine days.'

Her prophecy had a curious fulfilment that same evening. James, groping about on the top shelf of his bookcase, knocked over the bottle of muscarine and cut his hand on the broken glass. It wasn't much of a cut but the stuff that had been inside the bottle got onto it and gave him a very uncomfortable and anxious hour. Nothing happened, his arm didn't swell up or go black or anything of that sort, but it made him think seriously about the other nine bottles remaining. Wasn't it rather silly to keep them? That particular interest of his, no longer compelling, he was beginning to see as childish. Besides, with Oliver in the house, Oliver who was crawling now and would soon walk, to keep the poisons might be more than dangerous, it might be positively criminal.

His mind made up, he took the bottles down without further vacillation and one by one poured their contents away down his bedroom washbasin. Some of them smelt dreadful. The henbane smelt like the inside of his mouse cage when he hadn't cleaned it out for a day.

He poured them all away with one exception. He couldn't quite bring himself to part with the *datura*. It had always been his pride, better even than the nightshade. Sometimes he had sat there at his desk, doing his homework, and glanced up at the *datura* bottle and wondered what people would think if they had known he had the means in his bedroom to dispose of (probably) half the village. He looked at it now, recalling how he had picked the green spiny thornapples in the nick of time before his father had uprooted all the beautiful and sinister plants — he looked at it and replaced it on the top shelf. Then he sat down at the desk and did his Latin unseen.

Mirabel was still with them at Christmas. On Christmas Eve she carried up to Sindon Lodge the pale blue jumper, wrapped in holly-patterned paper, the two-pound box of chocolates and the poinsettia in a golden pot she had bought for Aunt Julie. And she took Rosamund with her. Rosamund wore her new scarlet coat with the white fur which was a Christmas present in advance, and the scarf with Buckingham Palace and the Tower of London printed on it which was another, and Mirabel wore her dark blue cloak and her angora hat and very high-heeled grey suede boots that skidded dangerously about on the ice. Oliver was left behind in the care of James's mother.

But if Mirabel had thought that the presence of Rosamund would provide her with an entrée to the house she was mistaken. Mrs Crowley, with a sorrowful expression, brought back the message that Aunt Julie could see no one. She had one of her gastric attacks, she was feeling very unwell, and she never accepted presents when she had nothing to give in return. Mirabel read a great deal, perhaps more than had been intended, into this valedictory shot.

'She means she'll never have anything to give me,' she said, sitting on James's bed. 'She means she's made up her mind not to leave me anything.'

It was a bit – James sought for the word and found it – a bit *degrading* to keep hanging on like this for the sake of money you hadn't earned and had no real right to. But he knew better than to say something so unkind and moralistic. He suggested tentatively that Mirabel might feel happier if she went back to her designing of textiles and forgot about Aunt Julie and her will. She turned on him in anger.

'What do you know about it? You're only a child. You don't know what I've suffered with that selfish brute of a man. I was left all alone to have my baby, I might have been literally destitute for all he cared, left to bring Oliver up on my own and without a roof over my head. How can I work? What am I supposed to do with Oliver? Oh, it's so unfair. Why shouldn't I get her money? It's not as if I was depriving anyone else, it's not as if she'd left it to someone and I was trying to get her to change anything. If I don't get it, it'll just go to the government.'

Mirabel was actually crying by now. She wiped her eyes and sniffed. 'I'm sorry, James, I shouldn't take it out on you. I think I'm just getting to the end of my tether.'

James's father had used those very words earlier in the day. He was getting to the end of his tether as far as Mirabel was concerned. Once get Christmas over and then, if James's mother wouldn't tell her she had outstayed her welcome, he would. Let her make things up with that chap of hers, Oliver's father, or get rooms somewhere or move in with one of those arty London friends. She wasn't even a relation, he didn't even like her, and she had now been with them for nearly three months.

'I know I can't go on staying here,' said Mirabel to James when hints had been dropped, 'but where am I to go?' She cast her eyes heavenwards or at least as far as the top shelf of the bookcase where they came to rest on the bottle of greenish-brown liquid labelled: *datura stramonium*.

'What on earth's that?' said Mirabel. 'What's in that bottle? *Datura* whatever-it-is, I can't pronounce it. It isn't cough mixture, is it? It's such a horrible colour.'

Six months before, faced with that question, James would have prevaricated or told a lie. But now he felt differently about those experiments of his, and he also had an obscure feeling that if he told Mirabel the truth and she told his mother, he would be forced to do something his own will refused to compel him to and throw the bottle away.

'Poison,' he said laconically.

'*Poison?*'

'I made it out of something called Jimson's Weed or thornapple. It's quite concentrated. I think a dose of it might be lethal.'

'Were you going to kill mice with it or something?'

James would not have dreamt of killing a mouse or, indeed, any animal. It exasperated him that Mirabel who ought to have known him quite well, who had lived in the same house with him and talked to him every day, should have cared so little about him and been so uninterested in his true nature as not to be aware of this.

'I wasn't going to kill anything with it. It was just an experiment.'

Mirabel gave a hollow ringing laugh. 'Would it kill me? Maybe I'll come up here while you're at school and take that bottle and – and put an end to myself. It would be a merciful release, wouldn't it? Who'd care? Not a soul. Not Francis, not Aunt Julie. They'd be glad. There's not a soul in the world who'd miss me.'

'Well, Oliver would,' said James.

'Yes, my darling little boy would, my Oliver would care. People don't realize I only want Aunt Julie's money for Oliver. It's not for me. I just want it to give Oliver a chance in life.' Mirabel looked at James, her eyes narrowing. 'Sometimes I think you're the only person on earth Aunt Julie cares for. I bet if you said to her to let bygones be bygones and have me back, she'd do it. I bet she would. She'd even make a will if you suggested it. I suppose it's because you're clever. She admires intellectuals.'

'If I suggested she make a will in Oliver's favour, I reckon she just might,' said James. 'He's her great-great-nephew, isn't he? That's quite a good idea, she might do that.'

He couldn't understand why Mirabel had suddenly become so angry, and with a shout of 'Oh, you're impossible, you're as bad as the rest of them!' had banged out of his room. Had she thought he was being sarcastic? It was obvious she wanted him to work on Aunt Julie for her and he wondered if she had flattered him simply towards this end. Perhaps. But however that might be, he could see a kind of

335

justice in her claim. She had been a good niece, or great-niece, to Aunt Julie, a frequent visitor to Sindon Lodge before the episode of Francis, a faithful sender of birthday and Christmas cards, or so his mother said, and attentive when Aunt Julie had been ill. On the practical or selfish side, getting Mirabel accepted at Sindon Lodge would take her away from Ewes Hall Farm where her presence frayed his father's temper, wore his mother out, made Rosamund sulk and was beginning to bore even him. So perhaps he would mention it to Aunt Julie on his next visit. And he began to plan a sort of strategy, how he would suggest a meeting with Oliver, for all old people seemed to like babies, and follow it up with persuasive stuff about Oliver needing a home and money and things to make up for not having had a father. But, in fact, he had to do nothing. For Mrs Crowley had been offered a better job in a more lively place and had suddenly departed, leaving Aunt Julie stiff with arthritis and in the middle of a gastric attack.

She crawled to the door to let James in, a grotesque figure in red corduroy trousers and green jumper, her witch's face framed in a woolly fuzz of grey hair, and behind her, picking his way delicately, Palmerston with tail erect.

'You can tell that girl she can come up here tonight if she likes. She'd better bring her illegitimate child with her, I don't suppose your mother wants him.'

Aunt Julie's bark was worse than her bite. Perhaps, indeed, she had no real bite. When James next went to Sindon Lodge some three weeks later Mirabel was settled in as if she had lived there all her life, Oliver was on the hearthrug where he had usurped Palmerston's place and Aunt Julie was wearing Mirabel's Christmas present.

She hardly spoke to James while her great-niece was in the room. She lay back in her armchair with her eyes closed and though the young woman's clothes she wore gave to her appearance a kind of bizarre mockery of youth, you could see now that she was very old. Recent upheavals had aged her. Her face looked as if it were made of screwed-up brown paper. But when Mirabel went away – was compelled to leave them by Oliver's insistent demands for his tea – Aunt Julie seemed to revive. She opened her eyes and said to James in her sharpest and most offhand tone: 'This is the last time you'll come here, I daresay.'

'Why do you say that?'

'I've made my will, that's why, and you're not in it.'

She cocked a distorted thumb in the direction of the door. 'I've left the house and the furniture and all I've got to *her*. And a bit to someone else we both know.'

'Who?' said James.

'Never you mind. It's not you and it's none of your business.' A curious look came into Aunt Julie's eyes. 'What I've done is leave my money to two people I can't stand and who don't like me. You think that's silly, don't you? They've both sucked up to me and danced attendance on me and told a lot of lies about caring for me. Well, I'm tired, I'm sick of it. They can have what they want and I'll never again have to see that look on their faces.'

'What look?'

'A kind of greedy pleading. The kind of look no one ought to have unless she's starving. You don't know what I'm talking about, do you? You're as clever as they come but you don't know what life is, not yet you don't. How could you?'

The old woman closed her eyes and there was silence in which the topmost log crumpled and sank into the heart of the fire with a rush of sparks, and Palmerston strode out from where he had taken refuge from Oliver, rubbed himself against James's legs and settled down in the red glow to wash himself. Suddenly Aunt Julie spoke.

'I didn't want you corrupted, can you understand that? I didn't want to *spoil* the only one who means more than a row of pins to me. But I don't know . . . If I wasn't too old to stand the fuss there'd be I'd go back on what I've done and leave the house to you. Or your mother, she's a nice woman.'

'She's got a house.'

'Houses can be sold, you silly boy. You don't suppose Madam Mirabel will *live* here, do you?' Mirabel must have heard that, James thought, as the door opened and the tea trolley appeared, but there was no warning Aunt Julie or catching her eye. 'I could make another will yet, I could bring myself to it. They say it's a woman's privilege to change her mind.'

Mirabel looked cross and there was very little chance of conversation after that as Oliver, when he was being fed or bathed or played with, dominated everything. He was a big child with reddish hair, not in the least like Mirabel but resembling, presumably, the mean and heartless Francis. He was now ten months old and walking, 'into everything', as James's mother put it, and it was obvious that he tired Aunt Julie whose expression became quite distressed when screams followed Mirabel's refusal to give him chocolate cake. Oliver's face and hands were wiped clean and he was put on the floor where he tried to eat pieces of coal out of the scuttle and, when prevented, set about tormenting the cat. James got up to go and Aunt Julie clutched his hand as he passed her, whispering with a meaning look that virtue was its own reward.

It was not long before he discovered who the 'someone else we both know' was. Aunt Julie wrote a letter to James's parents in which she told them she was leaving a sum of money to Rosamund in her will. Elizabeth Fyfield said she thought there was something very unpleasant about this letter and that it seemed to imply Rosamund had gone to Sindon Lodge with 'great expectations' in mind. She was upset by it but Rosamund was jubilant. Aunt Julie had not said what the sum was but Rosamund was sure it must be thousands and thousands of pounds – half a million was the highest figure she mentioned – and with her birthday money (she was eleven on 1 March) she bought herself a book of photographs of London architecture, mostly of streets in Mayfair, Belgravia and Knightsbridge, so that she could decide which one to have her flat in.

'I think we made a great mistake in telling her,' said James's father.

For Rosamund had taken to paying weekly visits to Sindon Lodge. She seldom went without some small gift for Aunt Julie, a bunch of snowdrops, a lop-sided pot she had made at school, a packet of peppermints.

'Wills can be changed, you know,' said James.

'That's not why I go. Don't you dare say that! I go because I love her. You're just jealous of me and you haven't been for weeks and weeks.'

It was true. He saw that Rosamund had indeed been corrupted and he, put to the test, had failed it. Yet it was not entirely disillusionment or pique which kept him from Sindon Lodge but rather a feeling that it must be wrong to manipulate people in this way. He had sometimes heard his father use the expression 'playing God' and now he understood what it meant. Aunt Julie had played God with him and with Rosamund and with Mirabel too. Probably she was still doing it, hinting at will-changing each time Mirabel displeased her. So he would go there to defy this manipulating, not to be a puppet moved by her strings, he would go on the following day on his way home from school.

But although he went as he had promised himself he would, to show her his visits were disinterested and that he could stick to his word, he never saw her alive again. The doctor's car was outside when he turned in at the gate. Mirabel let him in after he had rung the bell three times, a harassed, pale Mirabel with Oliver fretful in her arms. Aunt Julie had had one of her gastric attacks, a terrible attack which had gone on all night. Mirabel had not known what to do and Aunt Julie had refused to let her call an ambulance, she wouldn't go into hospital. The doctor had come first thing and had come back later and was with her now.

She had had to scrub out the room and actually *burn* the sheets, Mirabel said darkly. The mess had been frightful, worse than James could possibly imagine, but she couldn't have let the doctor see her like that. Mirabel said she hoped the worst was over but she didn't look very hopeful, she looked unhappy. James went no further inside than the hall. He said to tell Aunt Julie he had been, please not to forget to tell her, and Mirabel said she wouldn't forget. He walked away slowly. Spring was in the air and the neat, symmetrical front garden of Sindon Lodge was full of daffodils, their bent heads bouncing in the breeze. At the gate he met Palmerston coming in with the corpse of a fieldmouse dangling from his mouth. Without dropping his booty, Palmerston rubbed himself against James's legs and James stroked him, feeling rather depressed.

Two days later Aunt Julie had another attack and it killed her. Or the stroke which she had afterwards killed her, the doctor said. The cause of death on the certificate was 'food poisoning and cerebral haemorrhage', according to Mrs Hodges who had been Aunt Julie's cleaner and who met James's mother in the village. Apparently on death certificates the doctor has to put down the main cause and the contributory cause, which was another piece of information for James to add to his increasing store.

James's parents went to the funeral and of course Mirabel went too. James did not want to go and it never crossed his mind that he would be allowed to on a school day, but Rosamund cried when they stopped her. She wanted to have her red and white coat dyed black and to carry a small bouquet of violets. The provisions of the will were made known during the following days, though there was no dramatic will-reading after the funeral as there is in books.

Sindon Lodge was to go to Mirabel and so was all Aunt Julie's money with the exception of Rosamund's 'bit', and bit, relatively speaking, it turned out to be. Five hundred pounds. Rosamund cried (and said she was crying because she missed Aunt Julie) and then she sulked, but when the will was proved and she actually got the money, when she was shown the cheque and it was paid into her Post Office Savings account, she cheered up and became quite sensible. She even confided to James, without tears or flounces, that it would have been a terrible responsibility to have half a million and she would always have been worried that people were only being nice to her for the sake of the money.

James got Palmerston. It was set out in the will, the cat described and mentioned by name, and bequeathed 'if the animal should survive me, to James Alexander Fyfield, of Ewes Hall Farm, Great Sindon, he being the only person I know I can trust . . .'

'What an awful thing to say,' said Mirabel. 'Imagine, literally to have a thing like that written down. I'm sure James is welcome to it. I should certainly have had it destroyed, you can't have a cat about the place with a baby.'

Palmerston had lived so long at Sindon Lodge that he was always going back there, though he kept instinctively out of Mirabel's way. For Mirabel, contrary to what Aunt Julie had predicted, did not sell the house. Nor did she make any of those changes the village had speculated about when it knew she was not going to sell. Sindon Lodge was not painted white with a blue front door or recarpeted or its kitchen fitted out with the latest gadgets. Mirabel did nothing ostentatious, made no splash and bought herself nothing but a small and modest car. For a while it seemed as if she were lying low, keeping herself to herself, mourning in fact, and James's mother said perhaps they had all misjudged her and she had really loved Aunt Julie after all.

Things began to change with the appearance on the scene of Gilbert Coleridge. Where Mirabel had met him no one seemed to know, but one day his big yellow Volvo estate car was seen outside Sindon Lodge, on the next Mirabel was seen in the passenger seat of that car, and within hours it was all over the village that she had a man friend.

'He sounds a nice, suitable sort of person,' said James's mother, whose bush telegraph system was always sound. 'Two or three years older than she and never had a wife – well, you never know these days, do you? – and already a partner in his firm. It would be just the thing for Oliver. He needs a man about the house.'

'Let's hope she has the sense to marry this one,' said James's father.

But on the whole, apart from this, the Fyfield family had lost interest in Mirabel. It had been galling for them that Mirabel, having got what she wanted with their help, first the entrée to Sindon Lodge and then the possession of it, had lost interest in *them*. She was not to be met with in the village because she scarcely walked anywhere if she could help it, and although Rosamund called several times, Mirabel was either not at home or else far too busy to ask anyone in. James overheard his mother saying that it was almost as if Mirabel felt she had said too much while she stayed with them, had shown too openly her desires, and now these were gratified, wanted as little as possible to do with those who had listened to her confidences. But it suited the Fyfields equally, for the arrival of Mirabel was always followed by trouble and by demands.

The summer was hotter and dryer than the previous one had been, and the soft fruit harvest was exceptionally good. But this year there was no Aunt Julie to cast a cynical eye over baskets of raspberries. And Jimson's Weed, *datura*, the thornapple, did not show itself in the Fyfields' garden or, apparently, in any part of Great Sindon. A 'casual', as the wild plant book described it, it had gone in its mysterious way to ground or else wandered to some distant place away over the meadows.

Had it appeared, it would have exercised no fascination over James. He had his thirteenth birthday in June and he felt immeasurably, not just a year, older than he had done the previous summer. For one thing, he was about six inches taller, he had 'shot up' as his mother said, and sometimes the sight in a mirror of this new towering being could almost alarm him. He looked back with incredulous wonder on the child he had been, the child who had boiled noxious fruits and leaves in a pot, who had kept white mice in a cage and caterpillars in a box. He had entered his teens and was a child no more.

Perhaps it was his height that led directly to the drama – 'the absolutely worst day of my life', Rosamund called it – or it might have been Mrs Hodges's operation or even the fact, that, for once in a way, the Women's Institute met on a Tuesday rather than a Wednesday. It might have been any of those factors, though most of all it happened because Mirabel was inevitably and unchangingly Mirabel.

The inhabitants of Ewes Hall Farm knew very little about her life since they hardly ever saw her. It came as a surprise to Elizabeth Fyfield to learn how much time Mrs Hodges had been spending sitting in with Oliver or minding him in her own home. It was Mrs Hodges's daughter who told her, at the same time as she told her that her mother would be three weeks in hospital having her hysterectomy and another goodness knows how many convalescing. Mirabel would have to look elsewhere for a babysitter.

She looked, as they might have known she would, to the Fyfields.

Presenting herself on their doorstep with Oliver on one arm and a heavy shopping basket on the other, she greeted James's mother with a winsome, nervous smile. It might have been last year all over again, except that Oliver was a little boy now and no longer a baby. James, home for the long summer holidays, heard her sigh with despair and break into a long apology for having 'neglected' them for so long. The fact was she was engaged to be married. Did Elizabeth know that?

'I hope you'll be very happy, Mirabel.'

'Gilbert will make a marvellous father,' said Mirabel. 'When I compare him with that stupid, immature oaf, that Francis, it just makes me – oh, well, that's all water under the bridge now. Anyway, Elizabeth dear, what I came to ask you was, do you think James or Rosamund would do some baby-sitting for me? I'd pay them the going rate, I'd pay them what I pay Mrs Hodges. Only it's so awful for me never being able to go out with my fiancé, and actually tomorrow I'm supposed to be meeting his parents for the first time. Well, I can't take a baby of Oliver's age to a dinner party, can I?'

'Rosamund's out of the question,' said James's mother, and she didn't say it very warmly. 'She's only eleven. I couldn't possibly let her have sole charge of Oliver.'

'But James would be all right, wouldn't he? James has got so *tall*, he looks almost a grown man. And James is terribly mature, anyway.'

His mother didn't answer that. She gave one of those sighs of hers that would have effectively prevented James asking further favours. It had no effect on Mirabel.

'Just this once. After tomorrow I'll stay at home like a good little mum and in a month Mrs Hodges will be back. Just from seven till – well, eleven would be the absolute latest.'

'I'll sit with Oliver,' said James's mother.

Mirabel's guarantee came to nothing, however, for far from staying home with Oliver, she turned up at Ewes Hall Farm three days later, this time to leave him with them while she went shopping with Gilbert's mother. She was gone for four hours. Oliver made himself sick from eating toffees he found in Rosamund's room and he had uprooted six houseplants and stripped off their leaves before James caught him at it.

Next time, James's mother said she would put her foot down. She had already promised to sit with Oliver on the coming Saturday night. That she would do and that must be the end of it. And this resolve was strengthened by Mirabel's failure to return home until

342

half-past one on the Sunday morning. She would have told Mirabel so in no uncertain terms, Elizabeth Fyfield told her family at breakfast, but Gilbert Colcridge had been there and she had not wanted to embarrass Mirabel in front of him.

On the Tuesday, the day to which the Women's Institute meeting had been put forward, the fine weather broke with a storm which gave place by the afternoon to steady rain. James was spending the day turning out the glory-hole. He had been told to do it often enough and he had meant to do it, but who would be indoors in a stuffy bedroom when the sun is shining and the temperature in the eighties? That Tuesday was a very suitable sort of day for disposing of books one had outgrown, tanks and cages and jars that were no longer inhabited, for throwing away collections that had become just boxfuls of rubbish, for making a clean sweep on the path to adulthood.

Taking down the books from the top shelf, he came upon an object whose existence he had almost forgotten – the bottle labelled *datura stramonium*. That was something he need not hesitate to throw away. He looked at it curiously, at the clear greenish-brown fluid it contained and which seemed in the past months to have settled and clarified. Why had he made it and what for? In another age, he thought he might have been an alchemist or a warlock, and he shook his head ruefully at the juvenile James who was no more.

So many of these books held no interest for him any longer. They were kids' stuff. He began stacking them in a 'wanted' and an 'unwanted' pile on the floor. Palmerston sat on the window sill and watched him, unblinking golden eyes in a big round grey face. It was a good thing, James thought, that he had ceased keeping mice before Palmerston arrived. Perhaps the mouse cage could be sold. There was someone in his class at school who kept hamsters and had been talking of getting an extra cage. It wouldn't do any harm to give him a ring.

James went down to the living room and picked up the receiver to dial Timothy Gordon's number; the phone was dead. There was no dialling tone but a silence broken by occasional faint clicks and crepitations. He would have to go up the lane to the call box and phone the engineers, but not now, later. It was pouring with rain.

As he was crossing the hall and was almost at the foot of the stairs the doorbell rang. His mother had said something about the laundry coming. James opened the door absent-mindedly, prepared to nod to the man and take in the laundry box, and saw instead Mirabel. Her car was parked on the drive and staring out of its front window was Oliver, chewing something, his fingers plastering the glass with stickiness. Mirabel was dressed up to the nines, as Aunt Julie might have said, and dressed very unsuitably for the weather in a trailing, cream-coloured pleated affair with beads round her neck and two or three chiffon scarves and pale pink stockings and cream shoes that were all straps no thicker than bits of string.

'Oh, James, you are going to be an angel, aren't you, and have Oliver for me just for the afternoon? You won't be on your own, Rosamund's in, I saw her looking out of her bedroom window. I did try to ring you but your phone's out of order.'

Mirabel said this in an accusing tone as if James had purposely broken the phone himself. She was rather breathless and seemed in a hurry.

'Why can't you take him with you?' said James.

'Because, if you must know, Gilbert is going to buy me something rather special and important and I can't take a baby along.'

Rosamund, under the impression that excitement was afoot, appeared at the bend in the staircase.

'It's only Mirabel,' said James.

But Mirabel took the opportunity, while his attention was distracted, of rushing to the car – her finery getting much spotted with rain in the process – and seizing the sticky Oliver.

'You'd like to stay with James and Rosamund, wouldn't you, sweetheart?'

'Do we have to?' said Rosamund, coming downstairs and bestowing on Oliver a look of such unmistakable distaste that even Mirabel flinched. Flinched but didn't give up. Indeed, she thrust Oliver at James, keeping his sticky mouth well clear of her dress, and James had no choice but to grab hold of him. Oliver immediately started to whine and hold out his arms to his mother.

'No, darling, you'll see Mummy later. Now listen, James. Mrs Hodges's daughter is going to come for him at five-thirty. That's when she finishes work. She's going to take him back to her place and I'll pick him up when I get home. And now I must fly, I'm meeting Gilbert at three.'

'Well!' exploded Rosamund as the car disappeared down the drive.

'Isn't she the end? Fancy getting lumbered with *him*. I was going to do my holiday art project.'

'I was going to turn my room out, but it's no good moaning. We've got him and that's that.'

Oliver, once the front door was closed, had begun to whimper.

344

'If it wasn't raining we could go in the garden. We could take him out for a walk.'

'It *is* raining,' said James. 'And what would we take him in? Mum's basket on wheels? The wheelbarrow? In case you hadn't noticed, dear Mirabel didn't think to bring his push chair. Come on, let's take him in the kitchen. The best thing to do with him is to feed him. He shuts up when he's eating.'

In the larder James found a packet of Penguin biscuits, the chocolate-covered kind, and gave one to Oliver. Oliver sat on the floor and ate it, throwing down little bits of red and gold wrapping paper. Then he opened the saucepan cupboard and began taking out all the pots and pans and the colander and the sieves, getting chocolate all over the white Melamine finish on the door. Rosamund wiped the door and then she wiped him which made him grizzle and hit out at her with his fists. When the saucepans were spread about the floor, Oliver opened all the drawers one after the other and took out cutlery and cheese graters and potato peelers and dishcloths and dusters.

James watched him gloomily. 'I read somewhere that a child of two, even a child with a very high IQ, can't ever concentrate on one thing for more than nineteen minutes at a time.'

'And Oliver isn't two yet and I don't think his IQ's all that amazing.'

'Exactly,' said James.

'Ink,' said Oliver. He kicked the knives and forks out of his way and came to James, hitting out with a wooden spoon. 'Ink.'

'Imagine him with ink,' said Rosamund.

'He's probably not saying ink. It's something else he means only we don't know what.'

'Ink, ink, ink!'

'If we lived in London we could take him for a ride on a bus. We could take him to the zoo.'

'If we lived in London,' said James, 'we wouldn't be looking after him. I tell you what, I reckon he'd like television. Mirabel hasn't got television.'

He picked Oliver up and carried him into the living room. The furniture in there was dark brown leather and would not mark so it seemed sensible to give him another Penguin. James switched the television on. At this time of day there wasn't much on of interest to anyone, let alone someone of Oliver's age, only a serial about people working at an airport. Oliver, however, seemed entranced by the colours and the movement, so James shoved him into the back of an armchair and with a considerable feeling of relief, left him.

There was a good deal of clearing up to be done in the kitchen. Oliver had got brown stains on two tablecloths and James had to wash the knives and forks. Rosamund (typically, he thought) had vanished. Back to her art project, presumably, making some sort of collage with dried flowers. He put all the saucepans back and tidied up the drawers so that they looked much as they had done before Oliver's onslaught. Then he thought he had better go back and see how Oliver was getting on.

The living room was empty. James could soon see why. The serial had come to an end and the bright moving figures and voices and music had been replaced by an old man with glasses talking about molecular physics. Oliver wasn't anywhere downstairs. James hadn't really imagined he could climb stairs, but of course he could. He was a big strong boy who had been walking for months and months now.

He went up, calling Oliver's name. It was only a quarter past three and his mother wouldn't be back from the village hall until four-thirty at the earliest. The rain was coming down harder now, making the house rather dark. James realized for the first time that he had left his bedroom door open. He had left it open – because Palmerston was inside – when he went downstairs to phone Timothy Gordon about the mouse cage, and then Mirabel had come. It all seemed hours ago but it was only about forty minutes.

Oliver was in James's bedroom. He was sitting on the floor with the empty *datura* bottle clutched in his hands, and from the side of the mouth trickled a dribble of brown fluid.

James had read in books about people being rooted to the spot and that was exactly what happened at that moment. He seemed anchored where he stood. He stared at Oliver. In his inside there seemed to swell up and throb a large hard lump. It was his own heart beating so heavily that it hurt.

He forced himself to move. He took the bottle away from Oliver and automatically, he didn't know why, rinsed it out at the washbasin. Oliver looked at him in silence. James went down the passage and banged on Rosamund's door.

'Could you come, please? Oliver's drunk a bottle of poison. About half a pint.'

'*What?*'

She came out. She looked at him, her mouth open. He explained to her swiftly, shortly, in two sentences.

'What are we going to do?'

'Phone for an ambulance.'

She stood in the bedroom doorway, watching Oliver. He had put his fists in his eyes, he was rubbing his eyes and making fretful little sounds.

'D'you think we ought to try and make him sick?'

'No. I'll go and phone. It's my fault. I must have been out of my tree making the stuff, let alone keeping it. If he dies . . . Oh, God, Roz, we can't phone! The phone's out of order. I was trying to phone Tim Gordon but it was dead and I was going to go down to the call box and report it.'

'You can go to the call box now.'

'That means you'll have to stay with him.'

Rosamund's lip quivered. She looked at the little boy who was lying on the floor now, his eyes wide open, his thumb in his mouth. 'I don't want to. Suppose he dies?'

'You go,' said James. 'I'll stay with him. Go to the call box and dial nine-nine-nine for an ambulance and then go into the village hall and fetch mum. OK?'

'OK,' said Rosamund, and she went, the tears running down her face.

James picked Oliver up and laid him gently on the bed. There were beads of perspiration on the child's face but that might have been simply because he was hot. Mirabel had wrapped him very warmly for the time of year in a woolly cardigan as well as a jumper and a tee-shirt. He had been thirsty, of course. That was what 'ink' had meant. 'Ink' for 'drink'. Was there the slightest chance that during the year since he had made it the *datura* had lost its toxicity? He did not honestly think so. He could remember reading somewhere that the poison was resistant to drying and to heat, so probably it was also resistant to time.

Oliver's eyes were closed now and some of the bright red colour which had been in his face while he was watching television had faded. His fat cheeks looked waxen. At any rate, he didn't seem to be in pain, though the sweat stood in tiny glistening pinpoints on his forehead. James asked himself again why he had been such a fool as to keep the stuff. An hour before he had been on the point of throwing it away and yet he had not. It was useless to have regrets, to 'job backwards', as his father put it.

But James was looking to the future, not to the past. Suddenly he knew that if Oliver died he would have murdered him as surely, or almost as surely, as if he had fired at him with his father's shotgun. And his whole life, his entire future, would be wrecked. For he would never forgive himself, never recover, never be anything but a broken person. He would have to hide away, live in a distant part of the country, go to a different school, and when he left that school get some obscure job and drag out a frightened, haunted existence. Gone would be his dreams of Oxford, of work in some research establishment, of happiness and fulfilment and success. He was not overdramatizing, he knew it would be so. And Mirabel . . . ? If his life would be in ruins, what of hers?

He heard the front door open and his mother come running up the stairs. He was sitting on the bed, watching Oliver, and he turned round slowly.

'Oh, James . . . !'

And James said like a mature man, like a man three times his age, 'There's nothing you can say to me I haven't already said to myself.'

She touched his shoulder. 'I know that,' she said. 'I know you.' Her face was white, the lips too, and with anger as much as fear. 'How dare she bring him here and leave him with two *children*?'

James hadn't the spirit to feel offended. 'Is he – is he *dying*?'

'He's asleep,' said his mother and she put her hand on Oliver's head. It was quite cool, the sweat had dried. 'At least I suppose he is. He could be in a coma, for all I know.'

'It will be the end of me if he dies.'

'James, oh, James . . .' She did something she had not done for a long time. She put her arms round him and held him close to her, though he was half a head taller than she.

'There's the ambulance,' said James. 'I can hear the bell.'

Two men came up the stairs for Oliver. One of them wrapped him in a blanket and carried him downstairs in his arms. Rosamund was sitting in the hall with Palmerston on her lap and she was crying silently into his fur. It seemed hard to leave her but someone had to wait in for Mrs Hodges's daughter. James and his mother got into the ambulance with Oliver and went with him to the hospital.

They had to sit in a waiting room while the doctors did things to Oliver – pumped his stomach, presumably. Then a young black doctor and an old white doctor came and asked James a whole string of questions. What exactly was the stuff Oliver had drunk? When was it made? How much of it had been in the bottle? And a host of others. They were not very pleasant to him and he wanted to prevaricate. It would be so easy to say he hadn't known what the stuff really was, that he had boiled the thornapples up to make a green dye, or something like that. But when it came to it he couldn't. He had to tell the bald truth, he had to say he had made poison, knowing it might kill.

After they had gone away there was a long wait in which nothing happened. Mrs Hodges's daughter would have come by now and James's father would be home from where he was teaching at a summer seminar. It got to five-thirty, to six, when a nurse brought them a cup of tea, and then there was another long wait. James thought that no matter what happened to him in years to come, nothing could actually be worse than those hours in the waiting room had been. Just before seven the young doctor came back. He seemed to think James's mother was Oliver's mother and when he realized she was not he just shrugged and said as if they couldn't be all that anxious, as if it wouldn't be a matter of great importance to them:

'He'll be OK. No need for you to hang about any longer.'

James's mother jumped to her feet with a little cry. 'He's all right? He's really all right?'

'Perfectly, as far as we can tell. The stomach contents are being analysed. We'll keep him in for tonight, though, just to be on the safe side.'

The Fyfield family all sat up to wait for Mirabel. They were going to wait up, no matter what time she came, even if she didn't come till two in the morning. A note, put into the letter box of Sindon Lodge, warned her what had happened and told her to phone the hospital.

James was bracing himself for a scene. On the way back from the hospital his mother had told him he must be prepared for Mirabel to say some very unpleasant things to him. Women who would foist their children on to anyone and often seemed indifferent to them were usually most likely to become hysterical when those children were in danger. It was guilt, she supposed. But James thought that if Mirabel raved she had a right to, for although Oliver had not died and would not, he might easily have done. He was only alive because they had been very quick about getting that deadly stuff out of him. Mirabel wouldn't be able to phone Ewes Hall Farm, for the phone was still out of order. They all had coffee at about ten and James's father, who had gone all over his room to make sure there were no more killing bottles and had given James a stern but just lecture on responsibility, poured himself a large whisky.

The yellow Volvo came up the drive at twenty to twelve. James sat tight and kept calm the way he had resolved to do while his father went to answer the door. He waited to hear a shriek or a sob. Rosamund had put her fingers in her ears.

The front door closed and there were footsteps. Mirabel walked in, smiling. She had a big diamond on the third finger of her left hand. James's mother got up and went to her, holding out her hands, looking into Mirabel's face.

'You found our note? Of course you must have. Mirabel, I hardly know what to say to you . . .'

Before Mirabel could say anything James's father came in with the man she was going to marry, a big teddy bear of a man with a handlebar moustache. James found himself shaking hands. It was all very different from what he had expected. And Mirabel was all smiles, vague and happy, showing off her engagement ring on her thin little hand.

'What did they say when you phoned the hospital?'

'I didn't.'

'You didn't phone? But surely you . . . ?'

'I knew he was all right, Elizabeth. I didn't want to make a fool of myself telling them he'd drunk half a pint of coloured water, did I?'

James stared at her. And suddenly her gaiety fell from her as she realized what she had said. Her hand went up to cover her mouth and a dark flush mottled her face. She stepped back and took Gilbert Coleridge's arm.

'I'm afraid you underrate my son's abilities as a toxicologist,' said James's father, and Mirabel took her hand down and made a serious face and said that of course they must get back so that she could phone at once.

James knew then. He understood. The room seemed to move round him in a slow circle and to rock up and down. He knew what Mirabel had done, and although it would not be the end of him or ruin things for him or spoil his future, it would be with him all his life. And in Mirabel's eyes he saw that she knew he knew.

But they were moving back towards the hall now in a flurry of excuses and thank yous and good nights, and the room had settled back into its normal shape and equilibrium. James said to Mirabel, and his voice had a break in it for the first time: 'Good night. I'm sorry I was so stupid.'

She would understand what he meant.

May and June

Their parents named them May and June because their birthdays occurred in those months. A third sister, an April child, had been christened Avril but she had died. May was like the time of year in which she had been born, changeable, chilly and warm by turns, sullen yet able to know and show a loveliness that couldn't last.

In the nineteen thirties, when May was in her twenties, it was still important to get one's daughters well married, and though Mrs Thrace had no anxieties on that head for sunny June, she was less sanguine with regard to May. Her elder daughter was neither pretty nor graceful nor clever, and no man had ever looked at her twice. June, of course, had a string of admirers. Then May met a young lawyer at a *thé dansant*. His name was Walter Symonds, he was extremely good looking, his father was wealthy and made him a generous allowance, and there was no doubt he belonged in a higher social class than that of the Thraces. May fell passionately in love with him, but no one was more surprised than she when he asked her to marry him.

The intensity of her passion frightened Mrs Thrace. It wasn't quite nice. The expression on her face while she awaited the coming of her fiancé, her ardour when she greeted him, the hunger in her eyes — that sort of thing was all very well in the cinema, but unsuitable for a civil servant's daughter in a genteel suburb.

Briefly, she had become almost beautiful. 'I'm going to marry him,' she said when warned. 'He wants me to love him, doesn't he? He loves me. Why shouldn't I show my love?'

June, who was clever as well as pretty, was away at college training to be a schoolteacher. It had been considered wiser, long before Walter Symonds was thought of, to keep May at home. She had no particular aptitude for anything and she was useful to her mother about the house. Now, of course, it turned out that she had an aptitude for catching a rich, handsome and successful husband. Then, a month before the wedding, June came home for the summer holidays.

It was all very unfortunate, Mrs Thrace said over and over again. If Walter Symonds had jilted May for some unknown girl, they would have been bitterly indignant, enraged even, and Mr Thrace would have felt old-fashioned longings to apply a horsewhip. But what could anyone say or do when he transferred his affections from the elder daughter to the younger?

May screamed and sobbed and tried to attack June with a knife. 'We're all terribly sorry for you, my darling,' said Mrs Thrace, 'but what can anyone do? You wouldn't marry a man who doesn't love you, would you?'

'He does love me, he does! It's just because she's pretty. She's cast a spell on him. I wish she was dead and then he'd love me again.'

'You mustn't say that, May. It's all very cruel, but you have to face the fact that he's changed his mind. Isn't it better to find out now than later?'

'I would have had him,' said May.

Mrs Thrace blushed. She was shocked to the core.

'I shall never marry now,' said May. 'She's ruined my life and I shall never have anything ever again.'

Walter and June were married, and Walter's father bought them a big house in Surrey. May stayed at home, being useful to her mother. The war came. Walter went straight into the army, became a captain, a major, finally a colonel. May also went into the army, where she remained a private for five years, working in some catering department. After that, there was nothing for it but to go home to her parents once more.

She never forgave her sister.

'She stole my husband,' she said to her mother.

'He wasn't your husband, May.'

'As good as. You wouldn't forgive a thief who came into your house and stole the most precious thing you had or were likely to have.'

'We're told to forgive those who trespass against us, as we hope to be forgiven.'

'I'm not religious,' said May, and on those occasions when the Symondses came to the Thrace home she took care to be out of it. But she knew all about them – all, that is, except one thing.

Mr and Mrs Thrace were most careful never to speak of June in her presence, so May listened outside the door, and she secretly read all June's letters to her mother. Whenever Walter's name was spoken or mentioned in a letter, she winced and shivered with the pain of it. She knew that they had moved to a much larger house, that they were building up a collection of furniture and pictures. She knew where they went for their holidays and what friends they entertained. But what she was never able to discover was how Walter felt about June. Had he ever really loved her? Had he repented of his choice? May thought that perhaps, after the first flush of infatuation was over, he had come to long for his former love as much as she longed for him. Since she never saw them she could never know, for, however he might feel, Walter couldn't leave June. When you have done what he had done you can't change again. You have to stick it out till death.

It comforted her, it was perhaps the only thing that kept her going, to convince herself that Walter regretted his bargain. If there had been children, what the Victorians called pledges of love . . .

Sometimes, after a letter had come from June, May would see her mother looked particularly pleased and satisfied. And then, shaking with dread, she would read the letter, terrified to find that June was pregnant. But Mrs Thrace's pleasure and satisfaction must have come from some other source, from some account of Walter's latest coup in court or June's latest party, for no children came and now June was past forty.

Trained for nothing, May worked as canteen supervisor in a women's hostel. She continued to live at home until her parents died. Their deaths took place within six months, Mrs Thrace dying in March and her widower in August. And that was how it happened that May saw Walter again.

At the time of her mother's cremation, May was ill with a virus infection and unable to attend. But she had no way of avoiding her father's funeral. When she saw Walter come into the church a faintness seized her and she huddled against the pew rail, trembling. She covered her face with her hands to make it seem as if she were praying, and when at last she took them away he was beside her. He took her hand and looked into her face. May's eyes met his which were as blue and compelling as ever, and she saw with anguish that he had lost none of his looks but that they had become only more distinguished. She would have liked to die then, holding his hand and gazing into his face.

'Won't you come and speak to your sister, May?' said Walter in the rich deep voice which charmed juries, struck terror into the hearts of witnesses and won women. 'Shall we let bygones be bygones on this very sad day?'

May shivered. She withdrew her hand and marched to the back of the church. She placed herself as far away from June as she could get, but not too far to observe that it was June who took Walter's arm as they left and not Walter June's, June who looked up to Walter for comfort while his face remained grave and still, June who clung to him while he merely permitted the clinging. It couldn't be that he was behaving like that because she, May, was there. He must hate and despise June as she, with all her heart, hated and despised her still.

But it was at a funeral that they were reconciled. May learnt of Walter's death through reading an announcement of it in a newspaper. And the pain of it was as great as that she had suffered when her mother had told her he wanted to marry June. She sent flowers, an enormous wreath of snow-white roses that cost her half a week's wages. And of course she would go to the funeral, whether June wanted her there or not.

Apparently June did want her. Perhaps she thought the roses were for the living bereaved and not for the dead. She came up to May and put her arms round her, laying her head against her sister's shoulder in misery and despair. May broke their long silence.

'Now you know what it's like to lose him,' she said.

'Oh, May, May, don't be cruel to me now! Don't hold that against me now. Be kind to me now, I've nothing left.'

So May sat beside June, and after the funeral she went back to the house where June had lived with Walter. In saying she had nothing left, June had presumably been referring to emotional rather than material goods. Apart from certain stately homes she had visited on tours, May had never seen anything like the interior of that house.

'I'm going to retire next month,' she said, 'and then I'll be living in what they call a flatlet – one room and a kitchen.'

Two days later there came a letter from June.

'Dearest May, Don't be angry with me for calling you that. You have always been one of my dearest, in spite of what I did and in spite of your hatred of me. I can't be sorry for what I did because so much happiness came of it for me, but I am truly, deeply, sorry that you were the one to suffer. And now, dear May, I want to try to make up to you for what I did, though I know I can never really do that, not now, not after so long. You said you were going to retire and wouldn't be living very comfortably. Will you come and live with me? You can have as many rooms in this house as you want, you are

354

welcome to share everything with me. You will know what I mean when I say I feel that would be just. Please make me happy by saying you forgive me and will come. Always your loving sister, June.'

What did the trick was June saying it would be just. Yes, it would be justice if May could now have some of those good things which were hers by right and which June had stolen from her along with her man. She waited a week before replying and then she wrote: 'Dear June, What you suggest seems a good idea. I have thought about it and I will make my home with you. I have very little personal property, so moving will not be a great headache. Let me know when you want me to come. It is raining again here and very cold. Yours, May.' There was nothing, however, in the letter about forgiveness.

And yet May, sharing June's house, was almost prepared to forgive. For she was learning at last what June's married life had been.

'You can talk about him if you want to,' she had said hungrily on their first evening together. 'If it's going to relieve your feelings, I don't mind.'

'What is there to say except that we were married for forty years and now he's dead?'

'You could show me some of the things he gave you.' May picked up ornaments, gazed at pictures. 'Did he give you that? What about this?'

'They weren't presents. I bought them or he did.'

May couldn't help getting excited. 'I wonder you're not afraid of burglars. This is a proper Aladdin's Cave. Have you got lots of jewellery too?'

'Not much,' said June uncomfortably.

May's eyes were on June's engagement ring, a poor thing of diamond chips in nine carat gold, far less expensive than the ring Walter had given his first love. Of course she had kept hers and Walter, though well off even then, hadn't been rich enough to buy a second magnificent ring within six months of the first. But later, surely . . . ?

'I should have thought you'd have an eternity ring.'

'Marriage doesn't last for eternity,' said June. 'Let's not talk about it any more.'

May could tell she didn't like talking about it. Soon she shied at mentioning Walter's name and she put away the photographs of him which had stood on the piano and the drawing room mantelpiece. May wondered if Walter had ever written any letters to his wife. They had seldom been parted, of course, but it would be strange if

355

June had received no letter from him in forty years. The first time June went out alone, May tried to open her desk. It was locked. The drawers of June's dressing table disclosed a couple of birthday cards with 'Love from Walter' scrawled hastily on them, and the only other written message from her husband June had considered worth keeping May found tucked into a cookery book in the kitchen. It was a note written on the back of a bill, and it read: 'Baker called. I ordered large white for Saturday.'

That night May reread the two letters she had received from Walter during their engagement. Each began, 'Dearest May.' She hadn't looked at them for forty years – she hadn't dared – but now she read them with calm satisfaction. 'Dearest May, This is the first love letter I have ever written. If it isn't much good you must put it down to lack of practice. I miss you a lot and rather wish I hadn't told my parents I would come on this holiday with them . . .' 'Dearest May, Thanks for both your letters. Sorry I've taken so long to reply but I feel a bit nervous that my letters don't match up to yours. Still, with luck, we soon shan't have to write to each other because we shan't be separated. I wish you were here with me . . .' Poor Walter had been reticent and shy, unable to express his feelings on paper or by word of mouth. But at least he had written love letters to her and not notes about loaves of bread. May decided to start wearing her engagement ring again – on her little finger of course because she could no longer get it over the knuckle of her ring finger. If June noticed she didn't remark on it.

'Was it you or Walter who didn't want children?' May asked.

'Children just didn't come.'

'Walter *must* have wanted them. When he was engaged to me we talked of having three.'

June looked upset but May could have talked of Walter all day long.

'He was only sixty-five,' she said. 'That's young to die these days. You never told me what he died of.'

'Cancer,' said June. 'They operated but he never regained consciousness.'

'Just like mother,' said May. Suppose June had had cancer and had died, what would have happened then? Remembering Walter's tender look and strong handclasp at her father's funeral, May thought he would have married her. She twisted the ring on her little finger. 'You were almost like a second wife, weren't you? It must be a difficult position.'

356

'I'd much rather not talk about it,' said June, and with her handkerchief to her eyes she left the room.

May was happy. For the first time in forty years she was happy. She busied herself about the house, caring for June's things, dusting and polishing, pausing to look at a picture and reflecting that Walter must often have looked at it. Sometimes she imagined him sitting in this chair or standing by that window, his heart full of regret for what he might have had. And she thought now, while he had been longing for her she, far away, had been crying for him. She never cried now, though June did.

'I'm an old fool, I can't help giving way. You're strong, May, but I'm weak and I miss him so.'

'Didn't I miss him?'

'He was always fond of you. It upset him a lot to think you were unhappy. He often talked about you.' June looked at her piteously. 'You have forgiven me, haven't you, May?'

'As a matter of fact, I have,' said May. She was a little surprised at herself but, yes, she had forgiven June. 'I think you've been punished for what you did.' A loveless marriage, a husband who talked constantly of another woman . . .

'I've been punished,' said June and she put her arms round May's neck.

The strong and the weak. May remembered those words when a movement downstairs woke her in the night. She heard footsteps and the sound of a door being forced. It was the burglar she feared and had warned June about, but June would be cowering in her room now, incapable of taking any action.

May put on her dressing gown and went stealthily along the passage to June's room. The bed was empty. She looked out of the window, and the moonlight showed her a car parked on the gravel drive that led down to the lane. A yellower, stronger light streamed from the drawing room window. A shiver of fear went through her, but she knew she must be strong.

Before she reached the head of the stairs she heard a violent crash as of something heavy yet brittle hurled against a wall. There was a cry from below, footsteps running. May got to the stairs in time to see a slight figure rush across the hall and slam the front door behind him. The car started up.

In his wake he had left a thin trail of blood. May followed the blood trail into the drawing room. June stood by her desk which had been torn open and all its contents scattered on to the table. She was

357

trembling, tearful and laughing with shaky hysteria, pointing to the shards of cut glass that lay everywhere.

'I threw the decanter at him. I hit him and it cut his head and he ran.'

May went up to her. 'Are you all right?'

'He didn't touch me. He pointed that gun at me when I came in, but I didn't care. I couldn't bear to see him searching my desk, getting at all my private things. Wasn't I brave? He didn't get away with anything but a few bits of silver. I hit him and he heard you coming and he panicked. Wasn't I brave, May?'

But May wasn't listening. She was reading the letter which lay open and exposed on top of the paper the burglar had pulled out of the desk. Walter's bold handwriting leapt at her, weakened though it was, enfeebled by his last illness. 'My darling love, It is only a moment since you walked out of the ward, but nevertheless I must write to you. I can't resist an impulse to write now and tell you how happy you have made me in all the years we have been together. If the worst comes to the worst, my darling, and I don't survive the operation, I want you to know you are the only woman I have ever loved . . .'

'I wouldn't have thought I'd have had the courage,' said June, 'but perhaps the gun wasn't loaded. He was only a boy. Would you call the police, please, May?'

'Yes,' said May. She picked up the gun.

The police arrived within fifteen minutes. They brought a doctor with them, but June was already dead, shot through the heart at close range.

'We'll get him, Miss Thrace, don't you worry,' said the inspector.

'It was a pity you touched the gun, though. Did it without thinking, I suppose?'

'It was the shock,' said May. 'I've never had a shock like that, not since I was a girl.'

358

A Needle for the Devil

The devil finds work for idle hands to do, as Mrs Gibson used to say to her daughter, and Alice had found that in her case the devil (or her own mysterious inner compulsions) led her to violence. As a child she would strike people who annoyed her and when she was fourteen she attacked her sister with a knife, though no harm was done. But if her hands itched to injure, they were also gifted hands and as she was taught to occupy them with handicrafts, the impulse to violence grew less. Or was sublimated, as she learned to say when she began training to be a nurse.

Only her mother had opposed Alice's choice of a career. Perhaps it was only her mother who understood her. But her objections were overruled by Alice's father, her headmistress, the school careers officer and Alice herself. And certainly Alice did well. There were no unfortunate incidents of the kind Mrs Gibson had feared.

Naturally, in her new life, she had had to abandon her handicrafts. One cannot keep a loom or a potter's wheel in one's room in the nurses' residence. And there were many occasions when Alice would come off duty worn-out, not so much from lifting patients, making beds and running to and fro, as from the exercise of an iron self-control. The impulse to hit, pinch or otherwise manhandle a patient who had angered her had to be constantly suppressed.

Then the girl who shared her room came back from two days off duty wearing a knee-length white wool coat.

'I love your coat,' said Alice. 'It's gorgeous. It must have cost the earth.'

'I made it,' said Pamela.

'You *made* it? You mean you knitted it?'

'It wasn't very difficult and it only took three weeks.'

Alice had never thought of knitting. Knitting was something one's grandmother did or one's aunts or pregnant women making layettes. But if Pamela could make the coat, which neither savoured of aunts nor was layette-like, she was very sure she could. And it might solve that problem of hers which had lately become so pressing that she was afraid she might have to leave without finishing her training.

Knitting has the advantage over sewing or weaving that it requires basically only a ball of wool and a pair of needles. It can be done in one's lunch break, in a train, during night duty. It calms the nerves, occupies the hands, provides therapy – and supplies a wardrobe. Alice began knitting with enthusiasm and found that, because of its ubiquity and the way it can be taken up at any free moment, it answered her purpose better than any of her other crafts had done.

She progressed in her career, became a staff nurse, a sister, and by the time she was thirty had full charge of the men's medical ward at St Gregory's Hospital for Officers. It was there, three or four years later, that she first set eyes on Rupert Clarigate who had been brought in after having a heart attack.

Rupert Clarigate was fifty-two at the time of his coronary. He was a bachelor who had retired from the army two years before with the rank of Lieutenant Colonel and had since been living very comfortably – too comfortably perhaps – on his handsome pension. Had he smoked less and walked more, eaten less lavishly of roast pheasant at his club and drunk less old Napoleon brandy afterwards he might not, according to his doctor, have been seized one night by a fierce pain down his left arm and up his left side and found himself a moment later lying on the floor, fighting for breath. His doctor was one of those who believe that a coronary patient should never be left unattended for the first few days after an attack. Hence, St Gregory's and Sister Gibson. On his first morning in hospital he awoke to look into the sea-blue eyes of a slim young woman in a trim uniform whose blonde hair was half-covered by a starched white coif.

'Good morning, Colonel Clarigate,' said Alice. 'My goodness, but aren't you looking better this morning! It just shows what a good night's sleep can do.'

Alice said this sort of thing to all her new patients but Rupert, who had never been in hospital before and had in fact been riotously healthy all his life till now, thought it was specially designed for him and that her tone was exceptionally sweet. He did not hear her, five minutes later, telling one of her students who had dropped a kidney dish that she was not only hopelessly unfitted to be a nurse but mentally retarded as well, because this diatribe was delivered in the cleansing department off the ward known as the sluice. He thought Alice must have a delightful disposition, always cheerful, always

360

encouraging, endlessly patient, as well as being the sort of girl who looked as if she knew how to have a good time.

'Who's the lucky chap that's taking you out tonight, sister?' Rupert said as Alice put her head round the door before going off duty. 'I envy him, I don't mind telling you.'

'No chap, Colonel,' said Alice. 'I'm going to have a quiet evening doing my knitting in front of the TV.'

Those statements were quite true. There was no chap. There had been in days gone by, several in fact, including one whom Alice would probably have married had she not once slapped his face (and thereby dislodged a filling from a molar) for teasing her. But she had been very young then and without her prop and resort. Since those days she had put her career before a possible husband and had become so used to the overtures and the flirtatious remarks of patients that she hardly took in what they said and scarcely thought of them as men.

Rupert Clarigate, however, was different. He was one of the handsomest men she had ever seen and he had such a wonderful head of hair. For although his face was still youthful and unlined, his hair was snow-white; white and thick and ever so slightly wavy, and since he had left the army it had been allowed to grow just long enough to cover the tops of his ears. It was the first thing Alice had noticed about him. She had always felt a peculiar antipathy to baldness, and though accustomed to the most repulsive sights and to washing a wound or cleaning an abscess without a flicker of distaste, it was still as much as she could do to wash a man's bald pate or comb the hair which surrounded it. Rupert Clarigate looked as if he would never be bald, for not even a coin-sized bare spot showed amid the lush snowy mass.

Besides that, she liked his hearty jovial manner, the public school accent, the Sandhurst voice. The slightly lecherous admiration in his eyes, kept well under control, excited her. By the end of the first week of his stay she was in love, or would have said she was in love, having no criterion to judge by.

As for Colonel Clarigate, he had always intended to get married one day. A long-standing affair with another officer's wife had kept him single till he was thirty-five and after that was over he felt too set in his ways to embark on matrimony. Too selfish, the other officer's wife said. And it was true that Rupert could see no point in having a wife when he didn't want to stay in in the evenings, had no desire for children, disliked the idea of sharing his income and in any case had his officer's servant to wait on him and clean his quarters.

361

But he would marry one day – when he retired. Now retirement had come and he was living in the big inconvenient old house his parents had left him. There was no one to keep it clean. He ate rich food in expensive restaurants because there was no one at home to cook for him and he told himself he smoked too much because he was lonely. In fact, he had had his heart attack because he had no wife. Why should not pretty, efficient, kindly Sister Gibson be his wife?

Why not retire from nursing? thought Alice. Why should she not marry Colonel Clarigate and have a home of her own instead of a two-room flat that went with the job? Besides, she was in love with him and he had such beautiful thick hair.

He must be in love with Sister Gibson, thought Rupert, otherwise he would surely not feel so uneasy about her in the evenings when he was certain she must be out with some chap. This, he knew from his experience with the other officer's wife, was jealousy and a proof of love.

He left the hospital after three weeks and went to convalesce in the country. From there he wrote to Alice nearly every day. When he came home again he took her to the theatre to see a slapstick sexy comedy at which they both laughed very much, and then to the cinema to see a reissue of *Carry On Nurse* which had them equally convulsed. On their third evening out together they became engaged.

'People may say it was sudden,' said Alice, 'but I feel we know each other through and through. After all there's no more intimate situation, is there, than that of nurse and patient?'

'I can think of one,' said Rupert with a wink, and they both fell about laughing.

His fifty-third birthday occurred about a month after their engagement and Alice knitted him a pullover. It was rust red, bordered at the welt and on the neckline with fine stripes of cream and dark green and it suited him well, for Rupert, in spite of his high living, had never become fat. Alice insisted on looking after him. She took him out for sensible walks and gently discouraged him from smoking. The Clarigate house was not to her taste so he set about selling it and buying another. The prospect of furnishing this house which was in a seaside resort on the south coast – they could live anywhere they chose, Rupert said, there was no need to stay in London – filled Alice with excited anticipation, especially as Rupert was giving her a free hand with his savings.

362

The marriage took place in May, three months after their first meeting.

It was a quiet wedding, followed by a small luncheon party. Mrs Gibson, now a widow, was present and so was Alice's sister and that friend Pamela who had introduced her to the charms of knitting, and Pamela's husband Guy, a freelance writer and author of mystery novels. On Rupert's side were a cousin of his and his former commanding officer and Dr Nicholson, that conscientious medical man who had been responsible for sending him to St Gregory's. The newly married couple left at three to catch the plane that was to take them to Barbados for their honeymoon.

Alice had never before been away on a holiday without taking her knitting with her. In Palma de Mallorca she had knitted a Fair Isle cap and gloves for her niece, in Innsbruck she had begun an Aran for her brother-in-law and in the Isles of Greece she had finished a slipover for herself. But some instinct as to the rightness or suitability of certain actions told her that one does not take knitting on one's honeymoon, and indeed she found there would scarcely have been the opportunity to knit. One can hardly knit on a beach and they were mostly on the beach when they were not dining and dancing, for Rupert had been right when he assessed his wife as a girl who knew how to have a good time. Alice would have danced harder, eaten more heartily and stayed up even later were it not for her prudent care of her husband's health. While Rupert, vigorous and virile as he was, might in some ways seem as young as she, there was no getting away from the fact that he had had one coronary and might have another. She was glad to see that he had given up smoking and if, towards the end of their stay, she noticed an edge to his temper, she put this down to the heat.

Furnishing the new house took up all her time once they were returned. There were carpets to choose and order, plumbing and heating and electrical engineers to call, upholsterers and curtain makers to be urged on. Alice worked briskly, refusing to allow Rupert to help, but taking him out each evening with her for a therapeutic stroll along the sea front. He looked fitter than he had in all the five months she had known him and he could run upstairs now without shortness of breath.

It was on the morning after the day when the new carpets were fitted, after Alice had rearranged and polished the furniture, that she felt she could at last begin to relax. Rupert had gone to Dr Nicholson's for his monthly check-up. She set out for the shopping centre to buy herself some wool. On the previous evening, while they were out for their walk, Rupert had pointed out a man leaning over the sea wall who was wearing just the kind of sleeveless pullover he would fancy for himself. Alice had said nothing but had smiled and squeezed his arm.

During the years that had passed since Pamela walked in wearing that white coat, Alice had become an expert at her craft. She knew all there was to be known about it. She understood the finer points of grafting, of invisible casting off, of the weaving in of contrasts. She knew every kind of yarn available from top heavyweight natural wool to two-ply cotton and exactly which needles to use with each. Without reference to charts she could tell you that an English size fourteen needle is equivalent to the European two millimetre and the American double O. She could with ease adapt a pattern to a different size or, if necessary, work without a pattern at all. Once she had seen a jumper or cardigan she could copy it and turn out a precisely identical garment. And besides all this, the whole area of knitting was an emotive one to her. She could not help regarding it as having been a life saver and therefore it had become far more to her than some other woman's embroidery or crochet work. So it was natural that on entering a wool shop she should have a sensation of sick excitement as well as experiencing the deep pleasure felt, for example, by a scholar going into a library.

Woolcraft Limited she quickly judged a good shop of its kind and she spent a happy half-hour inside before finally choosing a pattern for a sleeveless pullover and six twenty-five gramme balls of a fine saxe blue wool and acrylic mixture.

There was no opportunity to begin that day. Rupert must have his lunch and then there would be an afternoon's gardening for both of them and in the evening they were going to a dinner-dance in the Pump Room. But on the following afternoon, while Rupert was down the garden trimming the privet hedge, Alice drew out her first ball of blue wool and began.

On moving into the house, she had appropriated the large bottom drawer of a chest in their living room for her knitting materials. In it were all her many leftover balls of wool and ends of wool from a multiplicity of garments made over the years, her gauge, her tape measure, her bodkins for sewing up and her sewing-up skeins and, ranged in front, all her pairs of needles, a pair of every possible size and each pair in its long plastic envelope. Alice had selected a pair of number fourteens, the very finest size for beginning on the welt of Rupert's pullover.

As she cast on the required number of one hundred and fifty stitches and felt the familiar thin metal pins against her hands and the soft, faintly fluffy yarn slip rhythmically between her fingers, a great calm descended upon Alice. It was like coming home after a long absence. It was like having a cigarette (she supposed) or a drink after a month's abstention. It was wonderful. It seemed to set the seal on her happiness. Here she was married, with a charming husband whom she loved, very well off, living in the home of her dreams, and now she was settled in her new life, once more taking up the hobby that afforded her so much pleasure. She had knitted about half an inch, for the work was slow with such fine materials, when she heard Rupert come in from the garden and rinse his hands under the kitchen tap. Presently he walked into the room where she was.

He stood a yard or two in from the doorway and stared at her. 'What are you doing, sweetie?'

'Knitting,' said Alice, smiling at him.

Rupert came and sat opposite her. He was fascinated. He knew there was such a thing as hand-knitting, or that there used to be, for he seemed to remember his mother mentioning it about forty years before, but he had never actually seen it being done. Alice's fingers flicked up and down, making precisely the same movement about a hundred times a minute. And they seemed to move independently of the rest of Alice, of her body which was gracefully relaxed, of her eyes which occasionally met his, and of her mind too, he suspected, which might be wandering off anywhere.

'I didn't know you knitted,' he said after a while.

'Darling! Where do you think your red sweater came from? I told you I made it.'

Rupert had not given much thought to the provenance of the red sweater. 'I suppose I thought you must have done it on a machine,' he said.

Alice laughed heartily at this. She continued to knit. Rupert read the evening paper which had just been delivered. After a time he said, 'Can I talk to you while you're doing that?'

He sounded so like a little boy whose mother cannot be bothered with him that Alice's heart was touched. 'Darling, of course you can. Talk away! I'm a very practised knitter, you know. I can not only talk while I'm knitting, I can read, watch television – my goodness,

I could knit in the dark!' And she fixed her eyes on him, smiling tenderly, while her fingers jerked up and down like pistons.

But Rupert didn't talk. He hardly said a word until they were out for their evening walk, and next day when she again took up the blue pullover she was once more conscious of his stare. After a while he lit a cigarette, his first for several weeks. Without a word he left the room and when she went into the kitchen to prepare their evening meal she found him sitting at the table, reading one of his favourite war memoirs.

It was not until Alice had had four sessions of work on the pullover and had completed six inches of the back, having changed by now to the slightly coarser needle, number twelve and made of red plastic, that Rupert made any further reference to her occupation.

'You know, sweetie,' he said, 'there's absolutely no reason why we shouldn't buy our clothes ready-made. We're not poor. I hope I haven't given you the impression that I'm a tight-fisted sort of chap. Any time you want the money to buy yourself a blouse or a dress or whatever that is, you've only to say the word.'

'This isn't for me, Rupert, it's for you. You said you wanted a pullover like the one we saw on that man on the sea front.'

'Did I? I suppose I must have if you say so but I don't recall it. Anyway, I can pop down to the men's outfitters and buy one if I feel inclined, can't I, eh? There's no need for you to wear yourself out making something I can buy in ten minutes.'

'But I *like* knitting, darling. I love it. And I think home-knitted garments are much nicer than bought ones.'

'Must make your fingers ache, I should think,' said Rupert. 'Talk about wearing one's fingers to the bone. I know the meaning of that phrase all right now, eh?'

'Don't be so silly,' snapped Alice. 'Of course it doesn't make my fingers ache. I enjoy it. And I think it's a great pity you've started smoking again.'

Rupert smoked five cigarettes that day and ten the next and the day after that Pamela and Guy came to stay for a fortnight's holiday.

Rupert thought, and Alice agreed with him, that if you lived by the sea it was positively your duty to invite close friends for their summer holidays. Besides, Guy and Pamela, who hadn't a large income, had two children at expensive boarding schools and probably would otherwise have had no holiday at all. They arrived, while their children were away camping, for the middle two weeks of August.

Pamela had not knitted a row since her daughter was two but she liked to watch Alice at work. She said she found it soothing. And when she looked inside the knitting drawer in the chest and saw the leftover hanks of yarn in such delectable shades, pinks and lilacs and subtle greens and honey yellows and chocolate browns, she said it made her feel she must take it up again, for clothes cost so much and it would be a great saving.

Guy was not one of those writers who never speak of their work. He was always entertaining on the subject of the intricate and complex detective stories he yearly produced and would weave plots out of all kinds of common household incidents or create them from things he observed while they were out for a drive. Alice enjoyed hearing him evolve new murder methods and he played up to her with more and more ingenious and bizarre devices.

'Now take warfarin,' he would say. 'They use it to kill rats. It inhibits the clotting of the blood, so that when the rats fight among themselves and receive even a small wound they bleed to death.'

'They give it to human beings too,' said Alice, the nurse. 'Or something very close to it. It stops clots forming in people who've had a thrombosis.'

'Do they now? That's very interesting. If I were going to use that method in a book I'd have the murderer give his victim warfarin plus a strong sedative. Then a small cut, say to the wrist . . .'

Another time he was much intrigued by a book of Alice's on plants inadvisable for use in winemaking. Most illuminating for the thriller writer, he said.

'It says here that the skunk cabbage, whatever that may be, contains irritant crystals of calcium oxalate. If you eat the stuff the inside of your mouth swells up and you die because you can't breathe. Now your average pathologist might notice the swellings but I'd be willing to bet you anything he'd never suppose them the result of eating *lysichiton symplocarpus*. There's another undetectable murder method for you.'

Alice was excited by his ingenuity and Pamela was used to it. Only Rupert, who had perhaps been nearer actual death than any of them, grew squeamish and was not sorry when the two weeks came to an end and Guy and Pamela were gone. Alice too felt a certain relief. It troubled her that her latent sadism, which she recognized for what it was, should be titillated by Guy's inventions. With thankfulness she returned to the gentle placebo of her knitting and took up the blue pullover again, all eight inches of it.

Rupert lit a cigarette.

'I say, I've been thinking, why don't I buy you a knitting machine?'

'I don't want a knitting machine, darling,' said Alice.

'Had a look at one actually while I was out with old Guy one day. A bit pricey but I don't mind that, sweetie, if it makes you happy.'

'I said I don't want a knitting machine. The point is that I like knitting by hand. I've already told you, it's my hobby, it's a great interest of mine. Why do I want a big cumbersome machine that takes up space and makes a noise when I've got my own two hands?'

He was silent. He watched her fingers working.

'As a matter of fact, it's the noise I don't like,' he said.

'What noise?' said Alice, exasperated.

'That everlasting click-click-click.'

'Oh, nonsense! You can't possibly hear anything right across the room.'

'I can.'

'You'll get used to it,' said Alice.

But Rupert did not get used to it, and the next time Alice began her knitting he said: 'It's not just the clicking, sweetie, it's the sight of your hands jerking about mechanically all the time. To be perfectly honest with you it gets on my nerves.'

'Don't look then.'

'I can't help it. There's an awful sort of fascination that draws my eyes.'

Alice was beginning to feel nervous herself. A good deal of her pleasure was spoilt by those staring eyes and the knowledge of his dislike of what she did. It began to affect the texture of her work, making her take uneven stitches. She went on rather more slowly and after half an hour she let the nine-inch-long piece of blue fabric and the needles fall into her lap.

'Let's go out to dinner,' said Rupert eagerly. 'We'll go and have a couple of drinks down on the front and then we'll drive over to the Queen's for dinner.'

'If you like,' said Alice.

'And, sweetie, give up that silly old knitting, eh? For my sake? You wouldn't think twice about doing a little thing like that for me, would you?'

A little thing, he called it. Alice thought of it not twice but many times. She hardly thought of anything else and she lay awake for a large part of the night. But next day she did no knitting and she laid away what she had done in the drawer. Rupert was her husband, and marriage, as she had often heard people say, was a matter of give and take. This she would give to him, remembering all he had given her.

She missed her knitting bitterly. Those years of doing an active job, literally on her feet all day, and those leisure times when her hands had always been occupied, had unfitted her for reading or listening to music or watching television. With idle hands, it was hard for her to keep still. Incessantly, she fidgeted. And when Rupert, who had not once mentioned the sacrifice she had made for him, did at last refer to her knitting, she had an only just controllable urge to hit him.

They were passing, on an evening walk, that men's outfitters of which he had spoken when first he saw knitting in her hands, and there in the window was a heavyweight wool sweater in creamy white with on it an intricate Fair Isle pattern in red and grey.

'Bet you couldn't do that, eh, sweetie? It takes a machine to make a garment like that. I call that a grand job.'

Alice's hands itched to slap his face. She not make that! Why, give her half a chance and she could make it in a week and turn out a far more beautiful piece of work than that object in the window. But her heart yearned after it, for all that. How easily, when she had been allowed to knit, could she have copied it! How marvellously would it have occupied her, working out those checks and chevrons on squared paper, weaving in the various threads with the yarn skilfully hooked round three fingers! She turned away. Was she never to be allowed to knit again? Must she wait until Rupert died before she could take up her needles?

It began to seem to Alice a monstrous cruelty, this thing which her husband had done to her. Why had she been so stupid as to marry someone she had known only three months? She thought she would enjoy punching him with her fists, pummelling his head, until he cried to her to stop and begged her to knit all she liked.

The change Rupert noticed in his wife he did not attribute to the loss of her hobby. He had forgotten about her knitting. He thought she had become irritable and nervous because she was anxious about his smoking – after all, none knew better than she that he shouldn't smoke – and he made a determined effort, his second since his marriage, to give it up.

After five days of total abstention it seemed to him as if every fibre of his body cried out for, yearned for, put out straining anguished stalks for, a cigarette. It was worst of all in the pub on the sea front where the atmosphere was laden with aromatic cigarette smoke, and there, while Alice was sitting at their table, he bought a surreptitious packet of twenty at the bar.

Back home, he took one out and lit it. His need for nicotine was so great that he had forgotten everything else. He had even forgotten that Alice was sitting opposite him. He took a wonderful long inhalation, the kind that makes the room rock and waves roar in one's head, a cool, aromatic, heady, glorious draw.

The next thing he knew the cigarette had been pulled out of his mouth and hurled into the fireplace and Alice was belabouring him with her fists while stamping on the remaining nineteen cigarettes in the packet.

'You mean selfish cruel beast! You can keep on with your filthy evil-smelling addiction that makes me sick to my stomach, you can keep that up, killing yourself, while I'm not allowed to do my poor harmless useful work. You selfish insensitive pig!'

It was their first quarrel and it went on for hours.

Next morning Rupert went into town and bought a hundred cigarettes and Alice locked herself in her bedroom and knitted. They were reconciled after two or three days. Rupert promised to undergo hypnosis for his smoking. Nothing was said at the time about Alice's knitting, but soon afterwards she explained quite calmly and rationally to Rupert that she needed to knit for her 'nerves' and would have to devote specific time to it, such as an hour every evening during which she would go and sit in their little-used dining room.

Rupert said he would miss her. He hadn't got married for his wife to be in one room and he in another. But all right, he hadn't much option, he supposed, so long as it was only an hour.

It began as an hour. Alice found she didn't miss Rupert's company. It seemed to her that they had said to each other all they had to say and all they ever would have. If there had been any excitement in their marriage, there was none left now. Knitting itself was more interesting, though when this garment was completed she would make no more for Rupert. Let him go to his men's outfitters if that was what he wanted. She thought she might make herself a burgundy wool suit. And as she envisaged it, longing to begin, the allotted hour lengthened into an hour and a half, into two.

She had almost completed the back of the pullover after two and a half hours concentrated work, when Rupert burst into the room, a cigarette in his mouth and his breath smelling of whisky. He snatched the knitting out of her hands and pulled it off the red plastic needles and snapped each needle in half.

Alice screamed at him and seized his collar and began shaking him, but Rupert tore the pattern across and unravelled stitches as fast as he could go. Alice struck him repeatedly across the face. He dodged and hit her such a blow that she fell to the floor, and then he pulled out every one of those two or three hundred rows of knitting until all that remained was a loose and tangled pile of crinkled blue yarn.

Three days later she told him she wanted a divorce. Rupert said she couldn't want one as much as he did. In that case, said Alice, perhaps he would like to pack his things and leave the house as soon as possible.

'Me? Leave this house? You must be joking.'

'Indeed I'm not joking. That's what a decent man would do.'

'What, just walk out of a house I bought with my inheritance from my parents? Walk out on the furniture you bought with my life savings? You're not only a hysterical bitch, you're out of your mind. *You* can go. I'll pay my maintenance, the law forces me to do that, though it'll be the minimum I can get away with, I promise you.'

'And you call yourself an officer and a gentleman!' said Alice. 'What am I supposed to do? Go back to nursing? Go back to a poky flat? I'd rather die. Certainly I'm staying in this house.'

They argued about it bitterly day after day. Rupert's need overcame the hypnosis and he chain-smoked. Alice was now afraid to knit in his presence, for he was physically stronger than she, even if she had had the heart to start the blue pullover once again. And whom would she give it to? She would not get out of the house, *her* house which Rupert had given her for which, in exchange, she had given him the most important thing she had.

'I gave up my knitting for you,' she screamed at him, 'and you can't even give me a house and a few sticks of furniture.'

'You're mad,' said Rupert. 'You ought to be locked up.'

Alice rushed at him and smacked his face. He caught her hands and threw her into a chair and slammed out of the room. He went down to the pub on the sea front and had two double whiskies and smoked a packet of cigarettes. When he got back Alice was in bed in the spare room. Just as he refused to leave the house, so Rupert had refused to get out of his own bedroom. He took two sleeping tablets and went to bed.

In the morning Alice went into the room where Rupert was and washed his scalp and combed his beautiful thick white hair. She changed the pillowcases, wiped a spot off Rupert's pyjama jacket and then she phoned the doctor to say Rupert was dead. He must have passed away in his sleep. She had awakened to find him dead beside her.

'His heart, of course,' said the doctor, and because Alice had been a nurse, 'a massive myocardial infarction.'

She nodded. 'I suppose I should have expected it.'

'Well, in these cases . . .'

'You never know, do you? I must be grateful for the few happy months we had together.'

The doctor signed the death certificate. There was no question of an autopsy. Pamela and Guy came to the cremation and took Alice back home with them for four weeks. When Alice left to return to the house that was now entirely hers they promised to take her at her word and come to stay once again in the summer. Alice was very comfortably off, for by no means all Rupert's savings had been spent on the furniture, his life assurance had been considerable, and there was his army pension, reduced but still generous.

It was an amazingly young-looking Alice, her hair rinsed primrose, her figure the trimmest it had been in ten years, who met Guy and Pamela at the station. She was driving a new white Lancia coupé and wearing a very smart knitted suit in a subtle shade of burgundy.

'I love your suit,' said Pamela.

'I made it.'

'I really must take up knitting again. I used to be so good at it, didn't I? And think of the money one saves.'

On the following evening, a Sunday, after they had spent most of the day on the beach, Pamela again reverted to the subject of knitting and said her fingers itched to start on something straightaway. Alice looked thoughtful. Then she opened the bottom drawer of the chest and took out the saxe blue wool.

'You could have this if you like, and this pattern. You could make it for Guy.'

Pamela took the pattern which had apparently been torn in half and mended with sticking tape. She looked at the hanks of wool. 'Has some of it been used?'

'I didn't like what I'd done so I undid it. The wool's been washed and carded to get the crinkles out.'

'If you're thinking of making that for me,' said Guy, 'I'm all for it. Splendid idea.'

'All right. Why not? Very fine needles it takes, doesn't it? Have you got a pair of fourteens, Alice?'

A shadow passed across Alice's face. She hesitated. Then she picked up the plastic envelopes one by one, but desultorily, until Pamela, fired now with enthusiasm, dropped on her knees beside her and began hunting through the drawer.

'Here we are. Number fourteen, two millimetres, US double O . . . There's only one needle here, Alice.'

'Sorry about that, it must be lost.' Alice took the single needle from her almost roughly and made as if to close the drawer.

'No, wait a minute, it's bound to be loose in there somewhere.'

'I'm sure it isn't, it's lost. You won't have time to start tonight, anyway.'

Guy said, 'I don't see how you could lose one knitting needle.'

'In a train,' said Pamela, peering into each needle packet. 'It could fall down the side of the seat and before you could get it out you'd be at your station.'

'Alice never goes in trains.'

'I suppose you could use it to unblock a drainpipe?'

'You'd use a big fat one for that. Now if this situation happened in one of my books I'd have it that the needle was a murder weapon. Inserted into the scalp of a person who was, say drugged or drunk, it would penetrate the covering of the brain and the brain itself, causing a subdural haemorrhage. You'd have to sharpen the point a bit, file it maybe, and then of course you'd throw it away afterwards. Hence, you see, only one number fourteen needle in the drawer.'

'And immediately they examined the body they'd find out,' said his wife.

'Well, you know, I don't think they would. Did you know that almost all men over middle age have enough signs of coronary disease for a pathologist, unless he was exceptionally thorough, to assume that as the cause of death? Of course your victim would have to have a good head of hair to cover up the mark of entry . . .'

'For heaven's sake, let's change the subject,' said Pamela, closing the drawer, for she had noticed that Alice, perhaps because of that tactless reference to coronaries, had gone very white and that the hands which held the wool were trembling.

But she managed a smile, 'We'll buy you a pair of number fourteens tomorrow,' she said, 'and perhaps I'll start on something new as well. My mother always used to say that the devil finds work for idle hands to do.'

Front Seat

Along the sea front, between the pier and the old town, was a row of wooden seats. There were six of them, regularly spaced on the grass, and they faced the dunes, the sea wall, and the sea. To some people, including Mrs Jones, they were known by name as Fisher, Jackson, Teague, Prendergast, Lubbock and Rupert Moore. It was on this last, the one that was curiously known by the Christian as well as the family name of the man it commemorated, that Mrs Jones invariably chose to sit.

She sat there every day, enjoying the peace and quiet, looking at the sea and thinking about the past. It was most pleasant on mild winter days or on those days of summer when the sky was overcast, for then the holiday visitors stayed in their cars or went off to buy prawns and crabs and expensive knick-knacks. Mrs Jones thought how glad she was that last year, when Mr Jones had been taken from her, she had bought the house in the old town, even though this had meant separating herself from her daughter. She thought about her son in London and her daughter in Ipswich, good loving children that they were, and about her grandchildren, and sometimes about her good fortune in having a comfortable annuity as well as her pension.

But mostly, sitting on Rupert Moore, between Fisher and Teague, she thought about the first man in her life to whom even now, after so long, she always referred to as her darling. She had so accustomed herself to calling him this that to her the endearment had become his name. My darling, thought Mrs Jones, as some other old woman might have thought of John or Charlie or Tom.

She felt closer to him here than anywhere, which was why she chose to rest on this seat and not on one of the others.

On 15 July, St Swithin's Day, Hugh and Cecily Branksome sat in their car, which was parked on the promenade, and looked at the grey choppy sea. Or, rather, Hugh looked at the sea while Cecily looked at Mrs Jones. The temperature was around ten degrees, according to Cecily who moved with the times, or fifty, according to Hugh who did not. It was not yet raining, though the indications were that it soon would be. Hugh was wishing they had gone to the Costa Brava where there would have been high-rise blocks and fish and chips and bull fights, but at least the sun would have shone. Cecily had got it into her head that it was bourgeois and unpatriotic to go abroad for one's holidays.

'I wonder why she always sits there,' said Cecily.

'Who sits where?'

'That old woman. She always sits on that particular seat. She was there yesterday and the day before.'

'Didn't notice,' said Hugh.

'You never notice anything. While you were in the pub yesterday,' said Cecily with emphasis, 'I waited till she'd gone and then I read the inscription on that seat. On the metal plate on the back. D'you know what it says?'

'Of course I don't,' said Hugh, opening the window to let out cigarette smoke. An icy breeze hit him in the face.

'Do close the window. It says: "Rupert Moore gave this seat to Northwold in thanks for his deliverance. I was in prison and ye came unto me, Matthew, chapter twenty-five, verse thirty-five." How about that?'

'Remarkable.' Hugh thought he knew all about being in prison. He looked at his watch. 'Opening time,' he said. 'We can go and get a drink, thank God.'

On the following morning he went out fishing without her. They met in their room before dinner, Hugh bracing himself to face certain sarcastic questions, not without precedent, as to whether he had had a nice day. Forestalling them by telling her they had caught only one small mackerel, for the censure would be greater if he had enjoyed himself, he was soon interrupted.

'I've got the whole story about the seat out of that nice man with the beard.'

Hugh's memory was poor and for a moment he didn't know which seat she was talking about, but he recognized the nice man from her description. A busybody know-all who lived in Northwold and hung about the hotel bar.

'He insisted on buying me a drink. Well, two, as a matter of fact.' She smiled archly and patted her hair as if the bearded know-all had, at the very least, invited her to Aldeburgh for the weekend. 'He's called Arnold Cottle and he said this Rupert Moore put that seat there because he'd murdered his wife. He was put on trial and he was acquitted and that's what it means about "deliverance" and being in prison.'

'You can't say he murdered his wife if he was acquitted.'

'You know what I mean,' said Cecily. 'It was ages ago, in 1930. I mean, I was only a baby.' Hugh thought it wiser not to point out that at ten one is hardly a baby. 'They acquitted him, or he got off on appeal, something like that, and he came back here to live and had that seat put there. Only the local people didn't want a murderer and they broke his windows and called after him in the street and he had to go.'

'Poor devil,' said Hugh.

'Well, I don't know about that, Hugh. From what Arnold said, the case was very unsavoury. Moore was quite young and very good looking and he was a painter, though he had a private income. His poor wife was much older and an invalid. He gave her cyanide they'd got for killing wasps. He gave it to her in a cup of coffee.'

'I thought you said he didn't do it.'

'Everyone *knew* he'd done it. He only got off because the judge misdirected the jury. You can't imagine how anyone would have the nerve to put up a sort of monument, can you, after a thing like that?'

Hugh started to run his bath. Resignedly, he accepted the fact, from past experience, that part of the evening would be spent in the company of Arnold Cottle. Cecily was not, and never had been, particularly flirtatious except in her own imagination. It was not that. Rather it was that she liked to get hold of causes or what she called examples of injustice or outrage and worry at them, roping in to assist her any helper who might be on hand. There had been the banning of the proposed motorway, the petition against the children's playground, the eviction of the squatters down the road. She was not always reactionary, for she worshipped free speech and racial equality and health foods and clean air. She was a woman of principle who threw herself whole-heartedly into upheaval and change and battles that right might be done, and sometimes into cults for the improvement of her soul. The unfortunate part of all this, or one of the unfortunate parts, was that it brought her so often into the company of bores or rogues. Hugh wondered what she was up to now, and why, and hoped it might be, though it seldom was, a flash in the pan.

Two hours later he found himself with his wife and Arnold Cottle, standing on the wet grass and examining the inscription on the Rupert Moore seat. It wasn't yet dark and wouldn't be for an hour. The sky was heavily overcast and the sea the colour of a recently scoured aluminium pot. No one would have supposed, thought Hugh, that somewhere up there in the west was the sun which, contrary to all present evidence, science told him was throwing off light at the rate of two hundred and fifty million tons a minute.

The others were too rapt to be distracted. He had a look at Fisher ('In memory of Colonel Marius Fisher, VC, DSO, 1874–1951') and at Teague ('William James Teague, of this Town, lost at the Battle of Jutland') and then he prodded Rupert Moore and announced, for something to say, 'That's oak.'

'It is indeed, my dear old chap.' Arnold Cottle spoke to Hugh very warmly and kindly, as if he had decided a priori that he was a harmless lunatic. 'You could get oak in those days. This one was made by a chap called Sarafin, Arthur Sarafin. Curious name, eh? Corruption of Seraphim, I daresay. Fine craftsman, lived up the coast at Lowestoft, but he died quite young, more's the pity. My father knew him, had some of the furniture he made. You can see his initials up there where the crossbar at the top joins the post. AS in a little circle, see?'

Hugh thought this most interesting. He had done a bit of carpentry himself until Cecily had stopped it on the ground that she needed his workshop for her groups. That had been in the days when she was into Gestalt. Hugh preferred not to think about them. He had a look at Prendergast ('This seat was placed here by the Hon. Clara Prendergast that the weary might find rest') and was about to ask Cottle if this one was oak or teak, when Cecily said: 'Where did he get the cyanide?'

'Moore?' said Cottle. 'It was never actually proved that he did get it. He said they kept some in their garden shed for killing wasps and his wife had taken it herself. In point of fact, Mrs Moore had written to her sister, saying her life wasn't worth living and she wanted to put an end to it. But this gardener chappie said he'd thrown the wasp killing stuff away a year before.'

'It must have come from somewhere,' said Cecily in such a hectoring tone and looking so belligerent that Hugh felt even more sympathy for Rupert Moore.

Cottle didn't seem to mind the tone or the look. 'Moore had been to several chemists' shops in the area, though not actually in Northwold, and tried to buy cyanide, ostensibly for killing wasps. No chemist admitted to having let him have it. There was one in Tarrington, up the coast here, who sold him another kind of vespicide that contained no cyanide and got him to sign the poison book. Dear Cecily, since you're so interested, why don't you read up the case in the library? Perhaps I might have the pleasure of taking you there tomorrow?'

The offer was accepted with enthusiasm. They all went into the Cross Keys where Hugh bought three rounds of drinks and Arnold Cottle bought none, having failed to bring his wallet with him. Cecily fastened on to the barman and elicited from him that the old woman who always sat on the Rupert Moore seat was called Mrs Jones, that she had come to Northwold the year before from Ipswich and was of Suffolk, though not Northwold, origins.

'Why does she always sit there?'

'Ask me another,' said the barman, presumably meaning this rejoinder rhetorically, which was not the way Cecily took it.

'What's so fascinating about that seat?'

'It seems to fascinate you,' said Hugh. 'Can't you give it a rest? The whole thing's been over and done with for going on fifty years.'

Cecily said, 'There's nothing else to do in this damned place,' which displeased the barman so much that he moved off in a huff. 'I've got a very active brain, Hugh. You ought to know that by now. I'm afraid I'm not content to fuddle it with drink or spend ten hours pulling one poor little fish out of the sea.'

The library visit, from which Hugh was excused, took place. But books having been secured, a journey had to be made to the house in which Rupert Moore had lived with his wife and painted his pictures and where the crime had been committed. Arnold Cottle seemed delighted at the prospect, especially as the excursion, at Cecily's suggestion, was to include lunch. Hugh had to go because Cecily couldn't drive and he wasn't going to lend his car to Cottle.

The house was a dull and ugly mansion, now used as a children's home. The superintendent (quite reasonably, Hugh thought) refused to let them tour the interior, but he had no objection to their walking round the grounds. It was bitterly cold for the time of year, but not cold enough to keep the children indoors. They tagged around behind Arnold Cottle and the Branksomes, making unfriendly or impertinent remarks. One of them, a boy with red curly hair and a cast in his eye, threw an apple core at Cecily and when reproved, used a word which, though familiar, is still unexpected on the lips of a five-year-old.

They had lunch, and throughout the meal Cecily read aloud extracts from the trial of Rupert Moore. The medical evidence was so unpleasant that Hugh was unable to finish his steak *au poivre*. Cottle drank nearly a whole bottle of Nuits St Georges and had a double brandy with his coffee. Hugh thought about men who had murdered their wives, and how much easier it must have been when you could get wasp killer made out of cyanide and weed killer made of arsenic. But even if he could have got those things, or have pushed Cecily downstairs, or fixed it for the electric wall heater to fall into the bath while she also was in it, he knew he never would. Even if he got away with it, as poor Rupert Moore had done, he would have the shame and the fear and the guilt for the rest of his life, again as had been the case with Rupert Moore.

Not that he had lived for long. 'He died of some kidney disease just twelve months after they let him out,' said Cecily, 'and by then he'd been hounded out of this place. He had Sarafin make that seat and that was about the last thing he ever did in Northwold.' She scanned through the last chapter of her book. 'There doesn't seem to have been any real motive for the murder, Arnold.'

'I suppose he wanted to marry someone else,' said Cottle, swigging brandy. 'I remember my father saying there were rumours he'd had a girlfriend but nobody seemed to know her name and she wasn't mentioned at the trial.'

'She certainly wasn't,' said Cecily, flicking back in her book so rapidly that she nearly knocked Hugh's coffee cup over. 'You mean there was no clue as to who she was? How did the rumours start, then?'

'Dear Cecily, how do rumours ever start? In point of fact, Moore was known often to have been absent from home in the evenings. There was gossip he'd been seen in Clacton with a girl.'

'Fascinating,' said Cecily. 'I shall spend the rest of the day thoroughly studying all this literature. You and Hugh must amuse yourselves on your own.'

After a dreadful afternoon spent listening to Cottle's troubles, how enemies had prevented him making a success at any career, how his two attempts at getting married had been scotched by his mother, and how his neighbours had a vendetta against him, Hugh finally escaped. Though not before he had lent Cottle ten pounds, this being the lowest of the sums his guest had suggested as appropriate. Cecily had a wonderful time, making herself conversant with the Moore case and now she was in the bath. Hugh wondered if a mighty thump on the bedroom side of the bathroom wall would dislodge the heater and make it fall into the water, but this was merely academic speculation.

After dinner he went for a walk on his own in the rain while Cecily made notes — for what purpose Hugh neither knew nor cared. He poked about in the ruins of the castle; he bought two tickets for the repertory theatre on the following night, hoping that the play, though it was called *Murder-on-Sea*, might distract Cecily; he wandered about the streets of the old town and he had a drink in the Oyster Catcher's Arms. On the whole, he didn't have a bad time.

The morning being better — a pale, sickly sun was shining and making quite attractive tints on the undersides of black clouds — he thought they might go on the beach. But Cecily had other plans. She got him to take her to Tarrington, and in the little shopping centre she left him to his own devices which included buying two pairs of thicker socks. After that, because it was raining again, there was nothing to do but sit in the car park. She kept him waiting two hours.

'What d'you think?' she said. 'I found that chemist, the one that sold Rupert Moore the wasp killer that hadn't got cyanide in it. And, would you believe it, it's still the same firm. The original pharmacist's grandson is the manager.'

'I suppose,' said Hugh, 'that he told you his grandfather had made a deathbed confession he did give Moore the cyanide after all.'

'Do try not to be so silly. I already knew they had cyanide wasp killer in the shop. It said so in the library book. This young man, the grandson, couldn't tell me much, but he did say his grandfather had had a very pretty young girl assistant. How about that?'

'I've noticed that very pretty young girls often do work in chemist's shops.'

'I'm glad you notice something, at any rate. However, she is not the one. The grandson knows her present whereabouts, and she is a Mrs Lewis. So I shall have to look elsewhere.'

'What d'you mean, the one?' said Hugh dismally.

'My next task,' said Cecily, taking no notice, 'will be to hunt for persons in this case of the name of Jones. Young women, that is. I know where to begin now. Sooner or later I shall root out a girl who was an assistant in a chemist's shop at the time and who married a Jones.'

'What for?'

'That right may be done,' said Cecily solemnly. 'That the truth may at last come out. I see it as my mission. You know I always have a mission, Hugh. It was the merest chance we happened to come to Northwold because Diana Richards recommended it. You wanted to go to Lloret de Mar. I feel it was meant we should come here because there was work for me to do. I am convinced Moore was guilty of this crime, but not alone in his guilt. He had a helper who, I believe, is alive at this moment. I'd like you to drive me to Clacton now. I shall begin by interviewing some of the oldest inhabitants.'

So Hugh drove to Clacton where he lost a pound on the fruit machines. Indefatigably, Cecily pursued her investigations.

Mrs Jones came back from morning service at St Mary's and although she was a good walker and not at all tired, for she had slept well ever since she came to Northwold, she sat down for half an hour on her favourite seat. Two other elderly people who had also been in church were sitting on Jackson ('In memory of Bertrand Jackson, 1859–1924, Philanthropist and Lover of the Arts'). Mrs Jones nodded pleasantly at them; but she didn't speak. It wasn't her way to waste in chat time that was more satisfactorily spent in reminiscence.

A pale grey mackerel sky, a fitful sun. Perhaps it would brighten up later. She thought about her daughter who was coming to lunch. Brenda would be tired after the drive, for the children, dears though they were, would no doubt be troublesome in the car. They would all enjoy that nice piece of sirloin and the Yorkshire pudding and the fresh peas and the chocolate ice cream. She had got in a bottle of sherry so that she and Brenda and Brenda's husband could have a glass each before the meal.

Her son and daughter had been very good to her. They knew she had been a devoted wife to their father, and they didn't resent the place in her love she kept for her darling. Not that she had ever spoken of him in front of their father or of them when they were small. That would have been unkind and in bad taste. But later she had told them about him and told Brenda, in expansive moments, about the long-past happiness and the tragedy of her darling's death, he so young and handsome and gifted. Perhaps, this afternoon when the rest of them were on the beach, she might allow herself the luxury of mentioning him again. Discreetly, of course, because she had always respected Mr Jones and loved him after a fashion, even though he had taken her away to Ipswich and never attained those heights of talent and success her darling would have enjoyed had he lived. Tranquilly, not unhappily, she recalled to her mind his face, his voice, and some of their conversations.

Mrs Jones was disturbed in her reverie by the presence of that tiresome woman. She had seen her before, hanging about on the promenade and once examining the seat Mrs Jones thought of as her own. An ugly, thin, neurotic-looking woman who was sometimes in the company of a sensible elderly man and sometimes with that shameless scrounger, old Cottle's boy, whom Mrs Jones in her old-fashioned way called a barfly. Today, however, she was alone and to Mrs Jones's dismay was approaching her with intent to speak.

'Do excuse me for speaking to you but I've seen you here so often.'

'Oh, yes?' said Mrs Jones. 'I've seen you too. I'm afraid I have to go now. I've guests for lunch.'

'Please don't go. I won't keep you more than a moment. But I must tell you I'm terribly interested in the Moore case. I can't help wondering if you knew him, you're here so much.'

'I knew him,' said Mrs Jones distantly.

'That's terribly exciting.' And the woman did look very excited. 'I suppose you first met him when he came into the shop?'

'That's right,' said Mrs Jones and she got up. 'But I don't care to talk about it. It's a very long time ago and it's best forgotten. Good morning.'

'Oh, but please . . . !'

Mrs Jones ignored her. She walked far more rapidly than usual, breathing heavily, along the path towards the old town. She was flustered and upset and very put out. To rake up all that now just when she was thinking of the lovely events of that time! For that day, though not, she hoped, for the future, the encounter had spoiled the seat for her.

'Had a good day with Cottle?' said Hugh.

'Don't speak to me about that man. Can you imagine it, I gave him a ring and a woman answered! She turned out to be some creature on holiday like us who was taking him to Lowestoft in her car. I could come too if I liked. No, thank you very much, I said. What about my finding the girl called Jones? I said. And he was pleased to tell me I was getting *obsessional*. So I gave him a piece of my mind, and that's the last of Arnold Cottle.'

And the last of his ten pounds, thought Hugh. 'So you went on the beach instead?'

'I did not. While you were out in that boat I researched on my own. And most successfully, I may add. You remember that old man in Clacton, the one in the old folks' home? Well, he was quite fit enough to see me today, and I questioned him exhaustively.'

Hugh said nothing. He could guess which of them had been exhausted.

'Ultimately,' said Cecily, 'I was able to prod him into remembering. I asked him to try and recall everyone he had ever known called

Jones. And at last he remembered a local policeman, Constable Jones, who got married in or around 1930. And the girl he married worked in *a local chemist's shop*. How about that?'

'You mean she was Moore's girlfriend?'

'Isn't it obvious? Her name was Gladys Palmer. She is now Mrs Jones. Moore was seen about with a girl in Clacton. This girl lived in Clacton and worked in a Clacton chemist's shop. Now it's quite evident that Moore was having a love affair with Gladys Palmer and that he persuaded her to give him the cyanide from the shop where she worked. The *real* evidence is that, according to all the books, that was one of the few chemist's shops from which Moore *never tried to obtain cyanide*!'

'That's real evidence?' said Hugh.

'Of course it is, to anyone with any deductive powers. Gladys Palmer took fright when Moore was found guilty, so she married a policeman for protection, and the policeman's name was Jones. Isn't that proof?'

'Proof of what?'

'Don't you ever remember anything? The barman in that Cross Keys place told us the old woman who sits on the Rupert Moore seat was a Mrs Jones.' Cecily smiled triumphantly. 'They are one and the same.'

'But it's a very common name.'

'Maybe. But Mrs Jones had admitted it. I spoke to her this morning before I went to Clacton. She has admitted knowing Moore and that she first met him when he came into the shop. How about that? And she was very nervous and upset, I can tell you, as well she might be.'

Hugh stared at his wife. He didn't at all like the turn things were taking. 'Cecily, it may be so. It looks like it, but it's no business of ours. I wish you'd leave it.'

'Leave it! For nearly fifty years this woman had got off scot-free when she was as much guilty of the murder of Mrs Moore as Moore was, and you say leave it! It's her guilt brings her to that seat day after day, isn't it? Any psychologist would tell you that.'

'She must be at least seventy. Surely she can be left in peace now?'

'I'm afraid it's much too late for that, Hugh. There must be an inquiry, all the facts must come out. I have written three letters, one to the Home Secretary, one to the Chief Commissioner at Scotland Yard, and a third to the author of this very incomplete book. There they are on the dressing table. Perhaps you'd like to look at them while I have my bath.'

Hugh looked at them. If he were to tear them up she would only write them again. If he walked into the bathroom now and dislodged the heater from the wall and it fell into the water, and she died and it was called an accident . . . The letters would never be sent, he could have his workshop back, he could chat up pretty girls who worked in chemist's shops and go on holiday to the Costa Brava and be free. He sighed heavily and went down to the bar to get a drink.

Thank goodness, thought Mrs Jones, that woman wasn't anywhere to be seen this morning. The intrusion of yesterday had upset her for hours, even after Brenda arrived, but she was getting over it now. Unfortunately in a way, the weather had taken a turn for the better, and several of the seats were occupied. But not Rupert Moore. Mrs Jones sat down on it and put her shopping bag on the ground at her feet.

She was aware of the proximity of the barfly who was sitting on Lubbock ('Elizabeth Anne Lubbock, for many years Headmistress of Northwold Girls' High School') and with him was a different woman, much younger than the other and very well dressed. With an effort, Mrs Jones expelled them from her mind. She looked at the calm blue sea and felt the warm and firm pressure of the oak against her back and thought about her darling. How sweet their love and companionship had been! It had endured for such a short time, and then separation and the unbearable loneliness. But she had been right to marry Mr Jones, for he had been a good husband and she the wife he wanted, and without him there would have been no Brian and no Brenda and no money to buy the house and come here every day to remember. If her darling had lived, though, and the children had been his, and if she had had him to sit beside her on his seat and be the joy of her old age . . .

'Do forgive me,' said a voice, 'but I'm a local man myself, and I happened to be in Lowestoft yesterday and someone told me they'd heard you'd come back to this part of the world to live.'

Mrs Jones looked at the barfly. Was there to be no end to this kind of thing?

'I've seen you on this seat and I did wonder, and when this friend in Lowestoft told me your present name, all was made plain.'

'I see,' said Mrs Jones, gathering up her shopping bag.

'I want you to know how greatly I admire his work. My father had some charming examples of it – all sold now, alas – and anyone can see that this seat was made by a craftsman compared with the others.'

Her stony face, her hostility, made him hesitate. 'You are,' he said, 'who I think you are, aren't you?'

'Of course I am,' said Mrs Jones crossly, another morning spoilt. 'Arthur Sarafin was my first husband. And now I really must be on my way.'

Paintbox Place

Elderly ladies as detectives are not unknown in fiction. Avice Julian could think of two or three, the creations of celebrated authors, and no doubt there were more. It would seem that the quiet routine of an old woman's life, her penchant for gossip and knitting and her curiosity, born of boredom, provide a suitable climate for the consideration of motive and the assessment of clues. In fiction, that is. Would it, Mrs Julian sometimes wondered, also be true in reality?

She took a personal interest. She was eighty-four years old, thin, sharp-witted, arthritic, cantankerous and intolerant. Most of her time she spent sitting in an upright chair in the bay window of her drawing room in her very large house, observing what her neighbours got up to. From the elderly ladies of mystery fiction, though, she differed in one important respect. They were spinsters, she was a widow. In fact, she had been twice married and twice widowed. Could that, she asked herself after reading a particularly apposite detective novel, be of significance? Could it affect the deductive powers and it be her spinsterhood which made Miss Marple, say, a detective of genius? Perhaps. Anthropologists say (Mrs Julian was an erudite person) that in ancient societies maidenhood was revered as having awesome and unique powers. It might be that this was true and that prolonged virginity, though in many respects disagreeable, only serves to enhance them. Possibly, one day, she would have an opportunity to put to the test the Aged Female Sleuth Theory. She saw enough from her window, sitting there knitting herself a twinset in dark blue two-ply. Mostly she eyed the block of houses opposite, on the other side of broad, tree-lined Abelard Avenue.

There were six of them, all joined together, all exactly the same. They all had three storeys, plate-glass windows, a bit of concrete to put the car on, a flowerbed, an outside cupboard to put parcels in and an outside cupboard to put the rubbish sack in. Mrs Julian thought that unhygienic. She had an old-fashioned dustbin, though she had to keep a black plastic bag inside it if she wanted Northway Borough Council to collect her rubbish.

The houses had been built on the site of an old mansion. There had been several such in Abelard Avenue, as well as big houses like Mrs Julian's which were not quite mansions. Most of these had been pulled down and those which remained converted into flats. They would do that to hers when she was gone, thought Mrs Julian, those nephews and nieces and great nephews and great nieces of hers would do that. She had watched the houses opposite being built. About ten years ago it had been. She called them the paintbox houses because there was something about them that reminded her of a child's drawing and because each had its front door painted a different colour, yellow, red, blue, lime, orange and chocolate.

'It's called Paragon Place,' said Mrs Upton, her cleaner and general help, when the building was completed.

'What a ridiculous name! Paintbox Place would be far more suitable.'

Mrs Upton ignored this as she ignored all of Avice Julian's remarks which she regarded as 'showing off', affected or just plain senile. 'They do say,' she said, 'that the next thing'll be they'll start building on that bit of waste ground next door.'

'Waste ground?' said Mrs Julian distantly. 'Can you possibly mean the wood?'

'Waste ground' had certainly been a misnomer, though 'wood' was an exaggeration. It was a couple of rustic acres, more or less covered with trees of which part of one side bordered Mrs Julian's garden, part the Great North Road, and which had its narrow frontage on Abelard Avenue. People used the path through it as a short cut from the station. At Mrs Upton's unwelcome forebodings, Avice Julian had got up and gone to the right hand side of the bay window which overlooked the 'wood' and thought how disagreeable it would be to have another Paintbox Place on her back doorstep. In these days when society seemed to have gone mad, when the cost of living was frightening, when there were endless strikes and she was asked to pay 98 per cent income tax on the interest on some of her investments, it was quite possible, anything could happen.

However, no houses were built next door to Mrs Julian. It appeared that the 'wood', though hardly National Trust or an Area of Outstanding Natural Beauty, was nevertheless scheduled as 'not for residential development'. For her lifetime, it seemed, she would look out on birch trees and green turf and small hawthorn bushes – when she was not, that is, looking out on the inhabitants of Paintbox Place, on Mr and Mrs Arnold and Mr Laindon and the Nicholsons, all young people, none of them much over forty. Their activities were of absorbing interest to Mrs Julian as she knitted away in dark blue two-ply, and a source too of disapproval and sometimes outright condemnation.

After Christmas, in the depths of the winter, when Mrs Julian was in the kitchen watching Mrs Upton peeling potatoes for lunch, Mrs Upton said: 'You're lucky I'm private, have you thought of that?'

This was beyond Mrs Julian's understanding. 'I beg your pardon?'

'I mean it's lucky for you I'm not one of those council home helps. They're all coming out on strike, the lot of them coming out. They're NUPE, see? Don't you read your paper?'

Mrs Julian certainly did read her paper, the *Daily Telegraph*, which was delivered to her door each morning. She read it from cover to cover after she had had her breakfast, and she was well aware that the National Union of Public Employees was making rumbling noises and threatening to bring its members out over a pay increase. It was typical, in her view, of the age in which she found herself living. Someone or other was always on strike. But she had very little idea of how to identify the Public Employee and had hoped the threatened action would not affect her. To Mrs Upton she said as much.

'Not affect you?' said Mrs Upton, furiously scalping brussels sprouts. She seemed to find Mrs Julian's innocence uproariously funny. 'Well, there'll be no gritters on the roads for a start and maybe you've noticed it's snowing again. Gritters are NUPE. They'll have to close the schools so there'll be kids all over the streets. School caretakers are NUPE. No ambulances if you fall on the ice and break your leg, no hospital porters, and what's more, no dustmen. We won't none of us get our rubbish collected on account of dustmen are NUPE. So how about that for not affecting you?'

Mrs Julian's dustbin, kept just inside the front gate on a concrete slab and concealed from view by a laurel bush and a cotoneaster, was not emptied that week. On the following Monday she looked out of the right hand side of the bay window and saw under the birch trees, on the frosty ground, a dozen or so black plastic sacks, apparently filled with rubbish, their tops secured with wire fasteners. There was no end to the propensities of some people for making disgusting litter, thought Mrs Julian, give them half a chance. She would telephone Northway Council, she would telephone the police. But first she would put on her squirrel coat and take her stick and go out and have a good look.

The snow had melted, the pavement was wet. A car had pulled up and a young woman in jeans and a pair of those silly boots that came up to the thighs like in a pantomime was taking two more black plastic sacks out of the back of it. Mrs Julian was on the point of telling her in no uncertain terms to remove her rubbish at once, when she caught sight of a notice stuck up under the trees. The notice was of plywood with printing on it in red chalk: *Northway Council Refuse Tip. Bags This Way.*

Mrs Julian went back into her house. She told Mrs Upton about the refuse tip and Mrs Upton said she already knew but hadn't told Mrs Julian because it would only upset her.

'You don't know what the world's coming to, do you?' said Mrs Upton, opening a tin of peaches for lunch.

'I most certainly do know,' said Mrs Julian. 'Anarchy. Anarchy is what it is coming to.'

Throughout the week the refuse on the tip mounted. Fortunately, the weather was very cold; as yet there was no smell. In Paintbox Place black plastic sacks of rubbish began to appear outside the cupboard doors, on the steps beside the coloured front doors, overflowing into the narrow flowerbeds. Mrs Upton came five days a week but not on Saturdays or Sundays. When the doorbell rang at ten on Saturday morning Mrs Julian answered it herself and there outside was Mr Arnold from the house with the red front door, behind him on the gravel drive a wheelbarrow containing five black plastic sacks of rubbish.

He was a good-looking, cheerful, polite man was Mr Arnold. Forty-two or three, she supposed. Sometimes she fancied she had seen a melancholy look in his eyes. No wonder, she could well understand if he was melancholic. He said good morning, and he was on his way to the tip with his rubbish and Mr Laindon's and could he take hers too?

'That's very kind and thoughtful of you, Mr Arnold,' said Mrs Julian. 'You'll find my bag inside the dustbin at the gate. I do appreciate it.'

'No trouble,' said Mr Arnold. 'I'll make a point of collecting your bag, shall I, while the strike lasts?'

Mrs Julian thought. A plan was forming in her mind. 'That won't be necessary, Mr Arnold. I shall be disposing of my waste by other means. Composting, burning,' she said, 'beating tins flat, that kind of thing. Now if everyone were to do the same . . .'

'Ah, life's too short for that, Mrs Julian,' said Mr Arnold and he smiled and went off with his wheelbarrow before she could say what was on the tip of her tongue, that it was shorter for her than for most people.

She watched him take her sack out of the dustbin and trundle his barrow up the slope and along the path between the wet black mounds. Poor man. Many an evening, when Mr Arnold was working late, she had seen the chocolate front door open and young Mr Laindon, divorced, they said, just before he came there, emerge and tap at the red front door and be admitted. Once she had seen Mrs Arnold and Mr Laindon coming back from the station together, taking the short cut through the 'wood'. They had been enjoying each other's company and laughing, though it had been cold and quite late, all of ten at night. And here was Mr Arnold performing kindly little services for Mr Laindon, all innocent of how he was deceived. Or perhaps he was not quite innocent, not ignorant and that accounted for his sad eyes. Perhaps he was like Othello who doted yet doubted, suspected yet strongly loved. It was all very disagreeable, thought Avice Julian, employing one of her favourite words.

She went back into the kitchen and examined the boiler, a small coke-burning furnace disused since 1963 when the late Alexander Julian had installed central heating. The chimney, she was sure, was swept, the boiler could be used again. Tins could be hammered flat and stacked temporarily in the garden shed. And – why not? – she would start a compost heap. No one should be without a compost heap at the best of times, any alternative was most wasteful.

Her neighbours might contribute to the squalor; she would not. Presently she wrapped herself up in her late husband's Burberry and made her way down to the end of the garden. On the 'wood' side, in the far corner, that would be the place. Up against the fence, thought Mrs Julian. She found a bundle of stout sticks in the shed – Alexander had once grown runner beans up them – and selecting four of these, managed to drive them into the soft earth, one at each of the angles of a roughly conceived square. Next, a strip of chicken wire went round the posts to form an enclosure. She would get Mrs Upton to buy her some garotta next time she went shopping. Avice Julian knew all about making compost heaps, she and her first husband had been experts during the war.

In the afternoon, refreshed by a nap, she emptied the vegetable cupboard and found some strange potatoes growing stems and leaves and some carrots covered in blue fur. Mrs Upton was not a hygienic housekeeper. The potatoes and carrots formed the foundation of the new compost heap. Mrs Julian pulled up a handful of weeds and scattered them on the top.

'I shall have my work cut out, I can see that,' said Mrs Upton on Monday morning. She laughed unpleasantly. 'I'm sure I don't know when the cleaning'll get done if I'm traipsing up and down the garden path all day long.'

Between them they got the boiler alight and fed it Saturday's *Daily Telegraph* and Sunday's *Observer*. Mrs Upton hammered out a can that had contained baked beans and banged her thumb. She made a tremendous fuss about it which Mrs Julian tried to ignore. Mrs Julian went back to her window, cast on for the second sleeve of the dark blue two-ply jumper, and watched women coming in cars with their rubbish sacks for the tip. Some of them hardly bothered to set foot on the pavement but opened the boots of their cars and hurled the sacks from where they stood. With extreme distaste, Mrs Julian watched one of these sacks strike the trunk of a tree and burst open, scattering tins and glass and peelings and leavings and dregs and grounds in all directions.

During the last week of January, Mrs Julian always made her marmalade. She saw no reason to discontinue this custom because she was eighty-four. Grumbling and moaning about her back and varicose veins, Mrs Upton went out to buy preserving sugar and Seville oranges. Mrs Julian peeled potatoes and prepared a cabbage for lunch, carrying the peelings and the outer leaves down the garden to the compost heap herself. Most of the orange peel would go on there in due course. Mrs Julian's marmalade was the clear jelly kind with only strands of rind in it, pared hair-thin.

They made the first batch in the afternoon. Mr Arnold called on the following morning with his barrow. 'Your private refuse operative, Mrs Julian, at your service.'

'Ah, but I've done what I told you I should do,' she said and insisted on his coming down the garden with her to see the compost heap.

'You eat a lot of oranges,' said Mr Arnold.

Then she told him about the marmalade and Mr Arnold said he had never tasted home-made marmalade, he didn't know people made it any more. This shocked Mrs Julian and rather confirmed her opinion of Mrs Arnold. She gave him a jar of marmalade and he was profuse in his thanks.

She was glad to get indoors again. The meteorological people had been right when they said there was another cold spell coming. Mrs Julian knitted and looked out of the window and saw Mrs Arnold brought back from somewhere or other by Mr Laindon in his car. By lunchtime it had begun to snow. The heavy, grey, louring sky looked full of snow.

This did not deter Mrs Julian's great-niece from dropping in unexpectedly with her boyfriend. They said frankly that they had come to look at the rubbish tip which was said to be the biggest in London apart from the one which filled the whole of Leicester Square. They stood in the window staring at it and giggling each time anyone arrived with fresh offerings.

'It's surrealistic!' shrieked the great-niece as a sack, weighted down with snow, rolled slowly out of the branches of a tree where it had been suspended for some days. 'It's fantastic! I could stand here all day just watching it.'

Mrs Julian was very glad that she did not but departed after about an hour (with a jar of marmalade) to something called the Screen on the Hill which turned out to be a cinema in Hampstead. After they had gone it snowed harder than ever. There was a heavy frost that night and the next.

'You don't want to set foot outside,' said Mrs Upton on Monday morning. 'The pavements are like glass.' And she went off into a long tale about her son Stewart who was a police constable finding an old lady who had slipped over and was lying helpless on the ice.

Mrs Julian nodded impatiently. 'I have no intention whatsoever of going outside. And you must be very careful when you go down that path to the compost heap.'

They made a second batch of marmalade. The boiler refused to light so Mrs Julian said to leave it but try it again tomorrow, for there was quite an accumulation of newspapers to be burnt. Mrs Julian sat in the window, sewing together the sections of the dark blue two-ply jumper and watching the people coming through the snow to the refuse tip. Capped with snow, the mounds on the tip resembled a mountain range. In the Arctic perhaps, thought Mrs Julian fancifully, or on some planet where the temperature was always sub-zero.

All the week it snowed and froze and snowed and melted and froze again. Mrs Julian stayed indoors. Her nephew, the one who wrote science fiction, phoned to ask if she was all right, and her other nephew, the one who was a commercial photographer, came round to sweep her drive clear of snow. By the time he arrived Mr Laindon had already done it, but Mrs Julian gave him a jar of marmalade just the same. She had resisted giving one to Mr Laindon because of the way he carried on with Mrs Arnold.

It started thawing on Saturday. Mrs Julian sat in the window, casting on for the left front of her cardigan and watching the snow and ice drip away and flow down the gutters. She left the curtains undrawn, as she often did, when it got dark.

At about eight Mrs Arnold came out of the red front door and Mr Laindon came out of the chocolate front door and they stood chatting and laughing together until Mr Arnold came out. Mr Arnold unlocked the doors of his car and said something to Mr Laindon. How Mrs Julian wished she could have heard what it was! Mr Laindon only shook his head. She saw Mrs Arnold get quickly into the car and shut the door. Very cowardly, not wanting to get involved, thought Mrs Julian. Mr Arnold was arguing now with Mr Laindon, trying to persuade him to something, apparently. Perhaps to leave Mrs Arnold alone. But all Mr Laindon did was give a silly sort of laugh and retreat into the house with the chocolate door. The Arnolds went off, Mr Arnold driving quite recklessly fast in this sort of weather, as if he were fearfully late for wherever they were going or, more likely, in a great rage.

Mrs Julian saw nothing of Mr Laindon on the following day, the Sunday, but in the afternoon she saw Mrs Arnold go out on her own. She crossed the road from Paintbox Place and took the path, still mercifully clear of rubbish sacks, through the 'wood' towards the station. Off to a secret assignation, Mrs Julian supposed. The weather was drier and less cold but she felt no inclination to go out. She sat in the window, doing the ribbing part of the left front of her cardigan and noting that the rubbish sacks were mounting again in Paintbox Place. For some reason, laziness perhaps, Mr Arnold had failed to clear them away on Saturday morning. Mrs Julian had a nap and a cup of tea and read the *Observer*.

It pleased her that Mrs Upton had burnt up all the old newspapers. At any rate, there were none to be seen. But what had she done with the empty tins? Mrs Julian looked everywhere for the hammered-out, empty tins. She looked in the kitchen cupboards and the cupboards under the stairs and even in the dining room and the morning room. You never knew with people like Mrs Upton. Perhaps she had put them in the shed, perhaps she had actually done what her employer suggested and put them in the shed.

Mrs Julian went back to the living room, back to her window, and got there just in time to see Mr Arnold letting himself into his house. Time tended to pass slowly for her at weekends and she was surprised to find it was as late as nine o'clock. It had begun to rain. She could see the slanting rain shining gold in the light from the lamps in Paintbox Place.

She sat in the window and picked up her knitting. After a little while the red front door opened and Mr Arnold came out. He had changed out of his wet clothes, changed grey trousers for dark brown, blue jacket for sweater and anorak. He took hold of the nearest rubbish sack and dragged it just inside the door. Within a minute or two he had come out again, carrying the sack, which he loaded onto the barrow he fetched from the parking area.

It was at this point that Mrs Julian's telephone rang. The phone was at the other end of the room. Her caller was the elder of her nephews, the commercial photographer, wanting to know if he might borrow pieces from her Second Empire bedroom furniture for some set or background. They had all enjoyed the marmalade, it was nearly gone. Mrs Julian said he should have another jar of marmalade next year but he certainly could not borrow her furniture. She didn't want pictures of her wardrobe and dressing table all over those vulgar magazines, thank you very much. When she returned to her point of vantage at the window Mr Arnold had disappeared.

Disappeared, that is, from the forecourt of Paintbox Place. Mrs Julian crossed to the right hand side of the bay to draw the curtains and shut out the rain, and there he was scaling the wet slippery black mountains, clutching a rubbish sack in his hand. The sack looked none too secure, for its side had been punctured by the neck of a bottle and its top was fastened not with a wire fastener but wound round and round with blue string. Finally, he dropped it at the side of one of the high mounds round the birch tree. Mrs Julian drew the curtains.

Mrs Upton arrived punctually in the morning, agog with her news. It was a blessing she had such a strong constitution, Mrs Julian thought. Many a woman of her advanced years would have been made ill – or worse – by hearing a thing like that.

'How can you possibly know?' she said. 'There's nothing in this morning's paper.'

Stewart, of course. Stewart, the policeman.

'She was coming home from the station,' said Mrs Upton, 'through that bit of waste ground.' She cocked a thumb in the direction of the 'wood'. 'Asking for trouble, wasn't she? Nasty dark lonely place. This chap, whoever he was, he clouted her over the head with what they call a blunt instrument. That was about half-past eight, though they never found her till ten. Stewart says there was blood all over, turned him up proper it did, and him used to it.'

'What a shocking thing,' said Mrs Julian. 'What a dreadful thing. Poor Mrs Arnold.'

'Murdered for the cash in her handbag, though there wasn't all that much. No one's safe these days.'

When such an event takes place it is almost impossible for some hours to deflect one's thoughts onto any other subject. Her knitting lying in her lap, Mrs Julian sat in the window, contemplating the paintbox houses. A vehicle that was certainly a police car, though it had no blue lamp, arrived in the course of the morning and two policemen in plain clothes were admitted to the house with the red front door. Presumably by Mr Arnold who was not, however, visible to Mrs Julian.

What must it be like to lose, in so violent a manner, one's marriage partner? Even so unsatisfactory a marriage partner as poor Mrs Arnold had been. Did Mr Laindon know? Mrs Julian wondered. She found herself incapable of imagining what his feelings must be. No one came out of or went into any of the houses in Paintbox Place and at one o'clock Mrs Julian had to leave her window and go into the dining room for lunch.

'Of course you know what the police always say, don't you?' said Mrs Upton, sticking a rather underdone lamb chop down in front of her. 'The husband's always the first to be suspected. Shows marriage up in a shocking light, don't you reckon?'

Mrs Julian made no reply but merely lifted her shoulders. Both her husbands had been devoted to her and she told herself that she had no personal experience of the kind of uncivilized relationship Mrs Upton was talking about. But could she say the same for Mrs Arnold? Had she not, in fact, for weeks, for months, now been deploring the state of the Arnolds' marriage and even awaiting some fearful climax?

It was at this point, or soon after when she was back in her window, that Avice Julian began to see herself as a possible Miss Marple or Miss Silver, though she had not recently been reading the works of either of those ladies' creators. Rather it was that she saw the sound common-sense which lay behind the notion of elderly women as detectives. Who else has the leisure to be so observant? Who else had behind them a lifetime of knowledge of human nature? Who else has suffered sufficient disillusionment to be able to face so squarely such unpalatable facts?

Beyond a doubt, the facts Mrs Julian was facing were unpalatable. Nevertheless, she marshalled them. Mrs Arnold had been an unfaithful wife. She had been conducting some sort of love affair with Mr Laindon. That Mr Arnold had not known of it was evident from her conduct of this extra-marital adventure in his absence. That he was beginning to be aware of it was apparent from his behaviour of Saturday evening. What more probable than that he had set off to meet his wife at the station on Sunday evening, had quarrelled with her about this very matter, and had struck her down in a jealous rage? When Mrs Julian had seen him first he had been running home from the scene of the crime, clutching to him under his jacket the weapon for which Mrs Upton said the police were now searching.

The morning had been dull and damp but after lunch it had dried up and a weak, watery sun came out. Mrs Julian put on her squirrel coat and went out into the garden, the first time she had been out for nine days.

The compost heap had not increased much in size. Perhaps the weight of snow had flattened it down or, more likely, Mrs Upton had failed in her duty. Displeased, Mrs Julian went back into the front garden and down to the gate where she lifted the lid of her dustbin, confident of what she would find inside. But, no, she had done Mrs Upton an injustice. The dustbin was empty and quite clean. She stood by the fence and viewed the tip.

What an eyesore it was! A considerable amount of leakage, due to careless packing and fastening, had taken place, and the wet, fetid, black hillocks were strewn all over with torn and soggy paper, cartons and packages, while in the valleys between clustered, like some evil growth, a conglomeration of decaying fruit and vegetable parings, mildewed bread, tea leaves, coffee grounds and broken glass. In one hollow there was movement. Maggots or the twitching nose of a rat? Mrs Julian shuddered and looked hastily away. She raised her eyes to take in the continued presence under the birch tree of the sack Mr Arnold had deposited there on the previous evening, the sack that was punctured by the neck of a bottle and bound with blue string.

She returned to the house. Was she justified in keeping this knowledge of hers to herself? There was by then no doubt in her mind as to what Mr Arnold had done. After killing his wife he had run home, changed his bloodstained clothes for clean ones and, fetching in the rubbish sack from outside, inserted into it the garments he had just removed and the blunt instrument, so-called, he had used. An iron bar perhaps or a length of metal piping he had picked up in the 'wood'. In so doing he had mislaid the wire fastener and could find no other, so he had been obliged to fasten the sack with the nearest thing to hand, a piece of string. Then across the road with it as he had been on several previous occasions, this time to deposit there a sack containing evidence that would incriminate him if found on his property. But what could be more anonymous than a black plastic sack on a council refuse tip? There it would be only one among a thousand and, he must have supposed, impossible to identify.

Mrs Julian disliked the idea of harming her kind and thoughtful neighbour. But justice must be done. If she was in possession of knowledge the police could not otherwise acquire, it was plainly her duty to reveal it. And the more she thought of it the more convinced she was that there was the correct solution to the crime against Mrs Arnold. Would not Miss Seaton have thought so? Would not Miss Marple, having found parallels between Mr Arnold's behaviour and that of some St Mary Mead husband, having considered and weighed the awful significance of the quarrel on Saturday night and the extraordinary circumstance of taking rubbish to a tip at nine-thirty on a wet Sunday evening, would she not have laid the whole matter before the CID?

She hesitated for only a few minutes before fetching the telephone directory and looking up the number. By three o'clock in the afternoon she was making a call to her local police station.

The detective sergeant and constable who came to see Mrs Julian half an hour later showed no surprise at being supplied with information by such as she. Perhaps they too read the works of the inventors of elderly lady sleuths. They treated Mrs Julian with great courtesy and after she had told them what she suspected they suggested she accompany them to the vicinity of the tip and point out the incriminating sack.

However, it was quite possible for her to do this from the right-hand side of the bay window. The detectives nodded and wrote things in notebooks and thanked her and went away, and after a little while a van arrived and a policeman in uniform got out and removed the sack. Mrs Julian sat in the window, working away at the lacy pattern on the front of her dark blue cardigan and watching for the arrest of Mr Arnold. She watched with trepidation and fear for him and a reluctant sympathy. There were policemen about the area all day, tramping around among the rubbish sacks, investigating gardens and ringing doorbells, but none of them went to arrest Mr Arnold.

Nothing happened at all apart from Mr Laindon calling at eight in the evening. He seemed very upset and his face looked white and drawn. He had come, he said, to ask Mrs Julian if she would care to contribute to the cost of a wreath for Mrs Arnold or would she be sending flowers personally?

'I should prefer to see to my own little floral tribute,' said Mrs Julian rather frostily.

'Just as you like, of course. I'm really going round asking people to give myself something to do. I feel absolutely bowled over by this business. They were wonderful to me, the Arnolds, you know. You couldn't have better friends. I was feeling pretty grim when I first came here – my divorce and all that – and the Arnolds, well, they looked after me like a brother, never let me be on my own, even insisted I go out with them. And now a terrible thing like this has to happen and to a wonderful person like that . . .'

Mrs Julian had no wish to listen to this sort of thing. No doubt, there were some gullible enough to believe it. She went to bed wondering if the arrest would take place during the night, discreetly, so that the neighbours should not witness it.

The paintbox houses looked just the same in the morning. But of course they would. The arrest of Mr Arnold would hardly affect their appearance. The phone rang at 9.30 and Mrs Upton took the call. She came into the morning room where Mrs Julian was finishing her breakfast.

'The police want to come round and see you again. I said I'd ask. I said you mightn't be up to it, not being so young as you used to be.'

'Neither are you or they,' said Mrs Julian and then she spoke to the police herself and told them to come whenever it suited them.

During the next half hour some not disagreeable fantasies went round in Mrs Julian's head. Such is often the outcome of identifying with characters in fiction. She imagined herself congratulated on her acumen and even, on a future occasion when some other baffling crime had taken place, consulted by policemen of high rank. Mrs Upton had served her well on the whole, as well as could be expected in these trying times. Perhaps one day, when it came to the question of Stewart's promotion, a word from her in the right place . . .

The doorbell rang. It was the same detective sergeant and detective constable. Mrs Julian was a little disappointed, she thought she rated an inspector now. They greeted her with jovial smiles and invited her into her own kitchen where they said they had something to show her. Between them they were lugging a large canvas bag.

The sergeant asked Mrs Upton if she could find them a sheet of newspaper, and before Mrs Julian could say that they had burnt all the newspapers, Saturday's *Daily Telegraph* was produced from where it had been secreted. Then, to Mrs Julian's amazement, he pulled out of the canvas bag the black plastic rubbish sack, punctured on one side and secured at the top with blue string, which she had seen Mr Arnold deposit on the tip on Sunday evening.

'I hope you won't find it too distasteful, madam,' he said, 'just to cast your eyes over some of the contents of this bag.'

Mrs Julian was astounded that he should ask such a thing of someone of her age. But she indicated with a faint nod and wave of her hand that she would comply, while inwardly she braced herself for the sight of some hideous bludgeon, perhaps encrusted with blood and hair, and for the emergence from the depths of the sack of a bloodstained jacket and pair of trousers. She would not faint or cry out, she was determined on that, whatever she might see.

It was the constable who untied the string and spread open the neck of the sack. With care, the sergeant began to remove its contents and to drop them on the newspaper Mrs Upton had laid on the floor. He dropped them, in so far as he could, in small separate heaps: a quantity of orange peel, a few lengths of dark blue two-ply knitting wool, innumerable Earl Grey tea bags, potato peelings, cabbage leaves, a lamb chop bone, the sherry bottle whose neck had pierced the side of the sack, and seven copies of the *Daily Telegraph* with one of the *Observer*, all with 'Julian, 1 Abelard Avenue' scrawled above the masthead ...

Mrs Julian surveyed her kitchen floor. She looked at the sergeant and the constable and at the yard or so of dark blue two-ply knitting wool which he still held in his hand and which he had unwound from the neck of the sack.

'I fail to understand,' she said.

'I'm afraid this sack would appear to contain waste from your own household, Mrs Julian,' said the sergeant. 'In other words to have been yours and been disposed of from your premises.'

Mrs Julian sat down. She sat down rather heavily on one of the bentwood chairs and fixed her eyes on the opposite wall and felt a strange tingling hot sensation in her face that she hadn't experienced for some sixty years. She was blushing.

'I see,' she said.

The constable began stuffing the garbage back into the sack. Mrs Upton watched him, giggling.

'If you haven't consumed all our stock of sherry, Mrs Upton,' said Mrs Julian, 'perhaps we might offer these two gentlemen a glass.'

The policemen, though on duty – which Mrs Julian had formerly supposed put the consumption of alcohol out of the question – took two glasses apiece. They were not at a loss for words and chatted away with Mrs Upton, possibly on the subject of the past and future exploits of Stewart. Mrs Julian scarcely listened and said nothing. She understood perfectly what had happened, Mr Arnold changing his clothes because they were wet, deciding to empty his rubbish that night because he had forgotten or failed to do so on the Saturday morning, gathering up his own and very likely Mr Laindon's too. At that point she had left the window to go to the telephone. In the few minutes during which she had been talking to her nephew, Mr Arnold had passed her gate with his barrow, lifted the lid of her dustbin and, finding a full sack within, taken it with him. It was this sack, her own, that she had seen him disposing of on the tip when she had next looked out.

No wonder the boiler had hardly ever been alight, no wonder the compost heap had scarcely grown. Once the snow and frost began and she knew her employer meant to remain indoors, Mrs Upton had abandoned the hygiene regimen and reverted to sack and dustbin. And this was what it had led to.

The two policemen left, obligingly discarding the sack on to the tip as they passed it. Mrs Upton looked at Mrs Julian and Mrs Julian looked at Mrs Upton and Mrs Upton said very brightly: 'Well, I wonder what all that was about then?'

Mrs Julian longed and longed for the old days when she would have given her notice on the spot, but that was impossible now. Where would she find a replacement? So all she said was, knowing it to be incomprehensible: 'A faux pas, Mrs Upton, that's what it was,' and walked slowly off and into the living room where she picked up her knitting from the chair by the window and carried it into the furthest corner of the room.

As a detective she was a failure. Yet, ironically, it was directly due to her efforts that Mrs Arnold's murderer was brought to justice. Mrs Julian could not long keep away from her window and when she returned to it the next day it was to see the council men dismantling the tip and removing the sacks to some distant disposal unit or incinerator. As her newspaper had told her, the strike was over. But the hunt for the murder weapon was not. There was more room to manoeuvre and investigate now the rubbish was gone. By nightfall the weapon had been found and twenty-four hours later the young out-of-work mechanic who had struck Mrs Arnold down for the contents of her handbag had been arrested and charged.

They traced him through the spanner with which he had killed her and which, passing Mrs Julian's garden fence, he had thrust into the depths of her compost heap.

The Wrong Category

There hadn't been a killing now for a week. The evening paper's front page was devoted instead to the economic situation and an earthquake in Turkey. But page three kept up the interest in this series of murders. On it were photographs of the six victims all recognizably belonging to the same type. There, in every case although details of feature naturally varied, were the same large liquid eyes, full soft mouth, and long dark hair.

Barry's mother looked up from the paper. 'I don't like you going out at night.'

'What, me?' said Barry.

'Yes, you. All these murders happened round here. I don't like you going out after dark. It's not as if you had to, it's not as if it was for work.' She got up and began to clear the table but continued to speak in a low whining tone. 'I wouldn't say a word if you were a big chap. If you were the size of your cousin Ronnie I wouldn't say a word. A fellow your size doesn't stand a chance against that maniac.'

'I see,' said Barry. 'And whose fault is it I'm only five feet two? I might just point out that a woman of five feet that marries a bloke only two inches more can't expect to have giants for kids. Right?'

'I sometimes think you only go roving about at night, doing what you want, to prove you're as big a man as your cousin Ronnie.'

Barry thrust his face close up to hers. 'Look, leave off, will you?' He waved the paper at her. 'I may not have the height but I'm not in the right category. Has that occurred to you? Has it?'

'All right, all right. I wish you wouldn't be always shouting.'

In his bedroom Barry put on his new velvet jacket and dabbed cologne on his wrists and neck. He looked spruce and dapper. His mother gave him an apprehensive glance as he passed her on his way to the back door, and returned to her contemplation of the pictures in the newspaper. Six of them in two months. The girlish faces, doe-eyed, diffident, looked back at her or looked aside or stared at distant unknown objects. After a while she folded the paper and switched on the television. Barry, after all, was not in the right category, and that must be her comfort.

He liked to go and look at the places where the bodies of the victims had been found. It brought him a thrill of danger and a sense of satisfaction. The first of them had been strangled very near his home on a path which first passed between draggled allotments, then became an alley plunging between the high brown wall of a convent and the lower red brick wall of a school.

Barry took this route to the livelier part of the town, walking rapidly but without fear and pausing at the point – a puddle of darkness between lamps – where the one they called Pat Leston had died. It seemed to him, as he stood there, that the very atmosphere, damp, dismal, and silent, breathed evil and the horror of the act. He appreciated it, inhaled it, and then passed on to seek, on the waste ground, the common, in a deserted back street of condemned houses, those other murder scenes. After the last killing they had closed the underpass, and Barry found to his disappointment that it was still closed.

He had walked a couple of miles and had hardly seen a soul. People stayed at home. There was even some kind of panic, he had noticed, when it got to six and the light was fading and the buses and tube trains were emptying themselves of the last commuters. In pairs they scurried. They left the town as depopulated as if a plague had scoured it.

Entering the high street, walking its length, Barry saw no one, apart from those protected by the metal and glass of motor vehicles, but an old woman hunched on a step. Bundled in dirty clothes, a scarf over her head and a bottle in her hand, she was as safe as he – as far, or farther, from the right category.

But he was still on the watch. Next to viewing the spots where the six had died, he best enjoyed singling out the next victim. No one, for all the boasts of the newspapers and the policemen, knew the type as well as he did. Slight and small-boned, long-legged, sway-backed, with huge eyes, pointed features, and long dark hair. He was almost sure he had selected the Italian one as a potential victim some two weeks before the event, though he could never be certain.

So far today he had seen no one likely, in spite of watching with fascination the exit from the tube on his own way home. But now, as he entered the Red Lion and approached the bar, his eye fell on a candidate who corresponded to the type more completely than anyone he had yet singled out. Excitement stirred in him. But it was unwise, with everyone so alert and nervous, to be caught staring. The barman's eyes were on him. He asked for a half of lager, paid for it, tasted it, and, as the barman returned to rinsing glasses, turned slowly to appreciate to the full that slenderness, that soulful timid look, those big expressive eyes, and that mane of black hair.

But things had changed during the few seconds his back had been turned. Previously he hadn't noticed that there were two people in the room, another as well as the candidate, and now they were sitting together. From intuition, at which Barry fancied himself as adept, he was sure the girl had picked the man up. There was something in the way she spoke as she lifted her full glass which convinced him, something in her look, shy yet provocative.

He heard her say, 'Well, thank you, but I didn't mean to . . .' and her voice trailed away, drowned by the other's brashness.

'Catch my eye? Think nothing of it, love. My pleasure. Your fella one of the unpunctual sort, is he?'

She made no reply. Barry was fascinated, compelled to stare, by the resemblance to Pat Leston, by more than that, by seeing in this face what seemed a quintessence, a gathering together and a concentrating here of every quality variously apparent in each of the six. And what gave it a particular piquancy was to see it side by side with such brutal ugliness. He wondered at the girl's nerve, her daring to make overtures. And now she was making them afresh, actually laying a hand on his sleeve.

'I suppose you've got a date yourself?' she said.

The man laughed. 'Afraid I have, love. I was just whiling away ten minutes.' He started to get up.

'Let me buy you a drink.'

His answer was only another harsh laugh. Without looking at the girl again, he walked away and through the swing doors out into the street. That people could expose themselves to such danger in the present climate of feeling intrigued Barry, his eyes now on the girl who was also leaving the pub. In a few seconds it was deserted, the only clients likely to visit it during that evening all gone.

A strange idea, with all its amazing possibilities, crossed his mind and he stood on the pavement, gazing the length of the High Street. But the girl had crossed the road and was waiting at the bus stop, while the man was only just visible in the distance, turning into the entrance of the underground car park.

Barry banished his idea, ridiculous perhaps and, to him, rather upsetting, and he crossed the road behind the oncoming bus, wondering how to pass the rest of the evening. Review once more those murder scenes, was all that suggested itself to him and then go home.

It must have been the wrong bus for her. She was still waiting. And as Barry approached, she spoke to him, 'I saw you in the pub.'

'Yes,' he said. He never knew how to talk to girls. They intimidated and irritated him, especially when they were taller than he, and most of them were. The little thin ones he despised.

'I thought,' she said hesitantly, 'I thought I was going to have someone to see me home.'

Barry made no reply. She came out of the bus shelter, quite close to him, and he saw that she was much bigger and taller than he had thought at first.

'I must have just missed my bus. There won't be another for ten minutes.' She looked, and then he looked, at the shiny desert of this shopping centre, lighted and glittering and empty, pitted with the dark holes of doorways and passages. 'If you're going my way,' she said, 'I thought maybe . . .'

'I'm going through the path,' he said. Round there that was what everyone called it, the path.

'That'll do me.' She sounded eager and pleading. 'It's a short cut to my place. Is it all right if I walk along with you?'

'Suit yourself,' he said. 'One of them got killed down there. Doesn't that bother you?'

She only shrugged. They began to walk along together up the yellow and white glazed street, not talking, at least a yard apart. It was a chilly damp night, and a gust of wind caught them as, past the shops, they entered the path. The wind blew out the long red silk scarf she wore and she tucked it back inside her coat. Barry never wore a scarf, though most people did at this time of the year. It amused him to notice just how many did, as if they had never taken in the fact that all those six had been strangled with their own scarves.

There were lamps in this part of the path, attached by iron brackets to the red wall and the brown. Her sharp-featured face looked greenish in the light, and gaunt and scared. Suddenly he wasn't intimidated by her any more or afraid to talk to her.

'Most people,' he said, 'wouldn't walk down here at night for a million pounds.'

'You do,' she said. 'You were coming down here alone.'

'And no one gave me a million,' he said cockily. 'Look, that's where the first one died, just round this corner.'

She glanced at the spot expressionlessly and walked on ahead of

405

Barry. He caught up with her. If she hadn't been wearing high heels she wouldn't have been that much taller than he. He pulled himself up to his full height, stretching his spine, as if effort and desire could make him as tall as his cousin Ronnie.

'I'm stronger than I look,' he said. 'A man's always stronger than a woman. It's the muscles.'

He might not have spoken for all the notice she took. The walls ended and gave place to low railings behind which the allotments, scrubby plots of cabbage stumps and waterlogged weeds, stretched away. Beyond them, but a long way off, rose the backs of tall houses hung with wooden balconies and iron staircases. A pale moon had come out and cast over this dismal prospect a thin cold radiance.

'There'll be someone killed here next,' he said. 'It's just the place. No one to see. The killer could get away over the allotments.'

She stopped and faced him. 'Don't you ever think about anything but those murders?'

'Crime interests me. I'd like to know why he does it.' He spoke insinuatingly, his resentment of her driven away by the attention she was at last giving him. 'Why d'you think he does it? It's not for money or sex. What's he got against them?'

'Maybe he hates them.' Her own words seemed to frighten her and, strangely, she pulled off the scarf which the wind had again been flapping, and thrust it into her coat pocket. 'I can understand that.' She looked at him with a mixture of dislike and fear. 'I hate men, so I can understand it,' she said, her voice trembling and shrill. 'Come on, let's walk.'

'No.' Barry put out his hand and touched her arm. His fingers clutched her coat sleeve. 'No, you can't just leave it there. If he hates them, why does he?'

'Perhaps he's been turned down too often,' she said, backing away from him. 'Perhaps a long time ago one of them hurt him. He doesn't want to kill them but he can't help himself.' As she flung his hand off her arm the words came spitting out. 'Or he's just ugly. Or little, like you.'

Barry stood on tip-toe to bring himself to her height. He took a step towards her, his fists up. She backed against the railings and a long shudder went through her. Then she wheeled away and began to run, stumbling because her heels were high. It was those heels or the roughness of the ground or the new darkness as clouds dimmed the moon that brought her down.

Collapsed in a heap, one shoe kicked off, she slowly raised her head and looked up into Barry's eyes. He made no attempt to touch her. She struggled to her feet, wiped her grazed and bleeding hands on the scarf and immediately, without a word, they were locked together in the dark.

Several remarkable features distinguished this murder from the others. There was blood on the victim who had fair hair instead of dark, though otherwise strongly resembling Patrick Leston and Dino Facci. Apparently, since Barry Halford had worn no scarf the murderer's own had been used. But ultimately it was the evidence of a slim dark-haired customer of the Red Lion which led the police to the conclusion that the killer of these seven young men was a woman.

The New Girl Friend

The New Girl Friend

'Y ou know what we did last time?' he said.

She had waited for this for weeks. 'Yes?'

'I wondered if you'd like to do it again.'

She longed to but she didn't want to sound too keen. 'Why not?'

'How about Friday afternoon, then? I've got the day off and Angie always goes to her sister's on Friday.'

'Not *always*, David.' She giggled.

He also laughed a little. 'She will this week. Do you think we could use your car? Angie'll take ours.'

'Of course. I'll come for you about two, shall I?'

'I'll open the garage doors and you can drive straight in. Oh, and Chris, could you fix it to get back a bit later? I'd love it if we could have the whole evening together.'

'I'll try,' she said, and then, 'I'm sure I can fix it. I'll tell Graham I'm going out with my new girl friend.'

He said goodbye and that he would see her on Friday. Christine put the receiver back. She had almost given up expecting a call from him. But there must have been a grain of hope still, for she had never left the receiver off the way she used to.

The last time she had done that was on a Thursday three weeks before, the day she had gone round to Angie's and found David there alone. Christine had got into the habit of taking the phone off the hook during the middle part of the day to avoid getting calls for the Midland Bank. Her number and the Midland Bank's differed by only one digit. Most days she took the receiver off at nine-thirty and put it back at three-thirty. On Thursday afternoons she nearly always went round to see Angie and never bothered to phone first.

Christine knew Angie's husband quite well. If she stayed a bit later on Thursdays she saw him when he came home from work. Sometimes she and Graham and Angie and David went out together as a foursome. She knew that David, like Graham, was a salesman or sales executive, as Graham always described himself, and she guessed from her friend's life style that David was rather more successful at it. She had never found him particularly attractive, for, although he was quite tall, he had something of a girlish look and very fair wavy hair.

Graham was a heavily built, very dark man with a swarthy skin. He had to shave twice a day. Christine had started going out with him when she was fifteen and they had got married on her eighteenth birthday. She had never really known any other men at all intimately and now if she ever found herself alone with a man she felt awkward and apprehensive. The truth was that she was afraid a man might make an advance to her and the thought of that frightened her very much. For a long while she carried a penknife in her handbag in case she should need to defend herself. One evening, after they had been out with a colleague of Graham's and had had a few drinks, she told Graham about this fear of hers.

He said she was silly but he seemed rather pleased.

'When you went off to talk to those people and I was left with John I felt like that. I felt terribly nervous. I didn't know how to talk to him.'

Graham roared with laughter. 'You don't mean you thought old John was going to make a pass at you in the middle of a crowded restaurant?'

'I don't know,' Christine said. 'I never know what they'll do.'

'So long as you're not afraid of what I'll do,' said Graham, beginning to kiss her, 'that's all that matters.' There was no point in telling him now, ten years too late, that she was afraid of what he did and always had been. Of course she had got used to it, she wasn't actually terrified, she was resigned and sometimes even quite cheerful about it. David was the only man she had ever been alone with when it felt all right.

That first time, that Thursday when Angie had gone to her sister's and hadn't been able to get through on the phone and tell Christine not to come, that time it had been fine. And afterwards she had felt happy and carefree, though what had happened with David took on the colouring of a dream next day. It wasn't really believable. Early on he had said: 'Will you tell Angie?'

'Not if you don't want me to.'

'I think it would upset her, Chris. It might even wreck our marriage. You see . . .' He had hesitated. 'You see, that was the first time I – I mean, anyone ever . . .' And he had looked into her eyes. 'Thank God it was you.'

The following Thursday she had gone round to see Angie as usual.

In the meantime there had been no word from David. She stayed late in order to see him, beginning to feel a little sick with apprehension, her heart beating hard when he came in.

He looked quite different from how he had when she had found him sitting at the table reading, the radio on. He was wearing a grey flannel suit and a grey striped tie. When Angie went out of the room and for a minute she was alone with him, she felt a flicker of that old wariness that was the forerunner of her fear. He was getting her a drink. She looked up and met his eyes and it was all right again. He gave her a conspiratorial smile, laying a finger on his lips.

'I'll give you a ring,' he had whispered.

She had to wait two more weeks. During that time she went twice to Angie's and twice Angie came to her. She and Graham and Angie and David went out as a foursome and while Graham was fetching drinks and Angie was in the Ladies, David looked at her and smiled and lightly touched her foot with his foot under the table.

'I'll phone you. I haven't forgotten.'

It was a Wednesday when he finally did phone. Next day Christine told Graham she had made a new friend, a girl she had met at work. She would be going out somewhere with this new friend on Friday and she wouldn't be back till eleven. She was desperately afraid he would want the car – it was *his* car or his firm's – but it so happened he would be in the office that day and would go by train. Telling him these lies didn't make her feel guilty. It wasn't as if this were some sordid affair, it was quite different.

When Friday came she dressed with great care. Normally, to go round to Angie's, she would have worn jeans and a tee shirt with a sweater over it. That was what she had on the first time she found herself alone with David. She put on a skirt and blouse and her black velvet jacket. She took the heated rollers out of her hair and brushed it into curls down on her shoulders. There was never much money to spend on clothes. The mortgage on the house took up a third of what Graham earned and half what she earned at her part-time job. But she could run to a pair of sheer black tights to go with the highest heeled shoes she'd got, her black pumps.

The doors of Angie and David's garage were wide open and their car was gone. Christine turned into their driveway, drove into the garage and closed the doors behind her. A door at the back of the garage led into the yard and garden. The kitchen door was unlocked as it had been that Thursday three weeks before and always was on Thursday afternoons. She opened the door and walked in.

'Is that you, Chris?'

The voice sounded very male. She needed to be reassured by the sight of him. She went into the hall as he came down the stairs.

'You look lovely,' he said.

'So do you.'

He was wearing a suit. It was of navy silk with a pattern of pink and white flowers. The skirt was very short, the jacket clinched into his waist with a wide navy patent belt. The long golden hair fell to his shoulders, he was heavily made-up and this time he had painted his fingernails. He looked far more beautiful than he had that first time.

Then, three weeks before, the sound of her entry drowned in loud music from the radio, she had come upon this girl sitting at the table reading *Vogue*. For a moment she had thought it must be David's sister. She had forgotten Angie had said David was an only child. The girl had long fair hair and was wearing a red summer dress with white spots on it, white sandals and around her neck a string of white beads. When Christine saw that it was not a girl but David himself she didn't know what to do.

He stared at her in silence and without moving and then he switched off the radio. Christine said the silliest and least relevant thing.

'What are you doing home at this time?'

That made him smile. 'I'd finished so I took the rest of the day off. I should have locked the back door. Now you're here you may as well sit down.'

She sat down. She couldn't take her eyes off him. He didn't look like a man dressed up as a girl, he looked like a girl and a much prettier one than she or Angie. 'Does Angie know?'

He shook his head.

'But why do you do it?' she burst out and she looked about the room, Angie's small, rather untidy living room, at the radio, the *Vogue* magazine. 'What do you get out of it?' Something came back to her from an article she had read. 'Did your mother dress you as a girl when you were little?'

'I don't know,' he said. 'Maybe. I don't remember. I don't want to *be* a girl. I just want to dress up as one sometimes.'

The first shock of it was past and she began to feel easier with him. It wasn't as if there was anything grotesque about the way he looked. The very last thing he reminded her of was one of those female

414

impersonators. A curious thought came into her head, that it was *nicer*, somehow more civilized, to be a woman and that if only all men were more like women . . . That was silly, of course, it couldn't be.

'And it's enough for you just to dress up and be here on your own?'

He was silent for a moment. Then, 'Since you ask, what I'd really like would be to go out like this and . . .' He paused, looking at her, 'and be seen by lots of people, that's what I'd like. I've never had the nerve for that.'

The bold idea expressed itself without her having to give it a moment's thought. She wanted to do it. She was beginning to tremble with excitement.

'Let's go out then, you and I. Let's go out now. I'll put my car in your garage and you can get into it so the people next door don't see and then we'll go somewhere. Let's do that, David, shall we?'

She wondered afterwards why she had enjoyed it so much. What had it been, after all, as far as anyone else knew but two girls walking on Hampstead Heath? If Angie had suggested that the two of them do it she would have thought it a poor way of spending the afternoon. But with David . . . She hadn't even minded that of the two of them he was infinitely the better dressed, taller, better-looking, more graceful. She didn't mind now as he came down the stairs and stood in front of her.

'Where shall we go?'

'Not the Heath this time,' he said. 'Let's go shopping.' He bought a blouse in one of the big stores. Christine went into the changing room with him when he tried it on. They walked about in Hyde Park. Later on they had dinner and Christine noted that they were the only two women in the restaurant dining together.

'I'm grateful to you,' David said. He put his hand over hers on the table.

'I enjoy it,' she said. 'It's so – crazy. I really love it. You'd better not do that, had you? There's a man over there giving us a funny look.'

'Women hold hands,' he said.

'Only *those* sort of women. David, we could do this every Friday you don't have to work.'

'Why not?' he said.

There was nothing to feel guilty about. She wasn't harming Angie and she wasn't being disloyal to Graham. All she was doing was going on innocent outings with another girl. Graham wasn't interested in her new friend, he didn't even ask her name. Christine came to long for Fridays, especially for the moment when she let herself into Angie's house and saw David coming down the stairs and for the moment when they stepped out of the car in some public place and the first eyes were turned on him. They went to Holland Park, they went to the zoo, to Kew Gardens. They went to the cinema and a man sitting next to David put his hand on his knee. David loved that, it was a triumph for him, but Christine whispered they must change their seats and they did.

When they parted at the end of an evening he kissed her gently on the lips. He smelled of Alliage or Je Reviens or Opium. During the afternoon they usually went into one of the big stores and sprayed themselves out of the tester bottles.

Angie's mother lived in the north of England. When she had to convalesce after an operation Angie went up there to look after her. She expected to be away two weeks and the second weekend of her absence Graham had to go to Brussels with the sales manager.

'We could go away somewhere for the weekend,' David said.

'Graham's sure to phone,' Christine said.

'One night then. Just for the Saturday night. You can tell him you're going out with your new girl friend and you're going to be late.'

'All right.'

It worried her that she had no nice clothes to wear. David had a small but exquisite wardrobe of suits and dresses, shoes and scarves and beautiful underclothes. He kept them in a cupboard in his office to which only he had a key and he secreted items home and back again in his briefcase. Christine hated the idea of going away for the night in her grey flannel skirt and white silk blouse and that velvet jacket while David wore his Zandra Rhodes dress. In a burst of recklessness she spent all of two weeks' wages on a linen suit.

They went in David's car. He had made the arrangements and Christine had expected they would be going to a motel twenty miles outside London. She hadn't thought it would matter much to David where they went. But he surprised her by his choice of an hotel that was a three-hundred-year-old house on the Suffolk coast.

'If we're going to do it,' he said, 'we may as well do it in style.'

She felt very comfortable with him, very happy. She tried to imagine what it would have felt like going to spend a night in an hotel with a man, a lover. If the person sitting next to her were dressed, not in a black and white printed silk dress and scarlet jacket but in a man's suit with shirt and tie. If the face it gave her so much pleasure to look at were not powdered and rouged and mascara'd but rough and already showing beard growth. She couldn't imagine it. Or, rather, she could only think how in that case she would have jumped out of the car at the first red traffic lights.

They had single rooms next door to each other. The rooms were very small but Christine could see that a double might have been awkward for David who must at some point – though she didn't care to think of this – have to shave and strip down to being what he really was.

He came in and sat on her bed while she unpacked her nightdress and spare pair of shoes.

'This is fun, isn't it?'

She nodded, squinting into the mirror, working on her eyelids with a little brush. David always did his eyes beautifully. She turned round and smiled at him.

'Let's go down and have a drink.'

The dining room, the bar, the lounge were all low-ceilinged timbered rooms with carved wood on the walls David said was called linenfold panelling. There were old maps and pictures of men hunting in gilt frames and copper bowls full of roses. Long windows were thrown open on to a terrace. The sun was still high in the sky and it was very warm. While Christine sat on the terrace in the sunshine David went off to get their drinks. When he came back to their table he had a man with him, a thickset paunchy man of about forty who was carrying a tray with four glasses on it.

'This is Ted,' David said.

'Delighted to meet you,' Ted said. 'I've asked my friend to join us. I hope you don't mind.'

She had to say she didn't. David looked at her and from his look she could tell he had deliberately picked Ted up.

'But why did you?' she said to him afterwards. 'Why did you want to? You told me you didn't really like it when that man put his hand on you in the cinema.'

'That was so physical. This is just a laugh. You don't suppose I'd let them touch me, do you?'

Ted and Peter had the next table to theirs at dinner. Christine was

417

silent and standoffish but David flirted with them. Ted kept leaning across and whispering to him and David giggled and smiled. You could see he was enjoying himself tremendously. Christine knew they would ask her and David to go out with them after dinner and she began to be afraid. Suppose David got carried away by the excitement of it, the 'fun', and went off somewhere with Ted, leaving her and Peter alone together? Peter had a red face and a black moustache and beard and a wart with black hairs growing out of it on his left cheek. She and David were eating steak and the waiter had brought them sharp pointed steak knives. She hadn't used hers. The steak was very tender. When no one was looking she slipped the steak knife into her bag.

Ted and Peter were still drinking coffee and brandies when David got up quite abruptly and said, 'Coming?' to Christine.

'I suppose you've arranged to meet them later?' Christine said as soon as they were out of the dining room.

David looked at her. His scarlet-painted lips parted into a wide smile. He laughed.

'I turned them down.'

'Did you *really*?'

'I could tell you hated the idea. Besides, we want to be alone, don't we? I know I want to be alone with you.'

She nearly shouted his name so that everyone could hear, the relief was so great. She controlled herself but she was trembling. 'Of course I want to be alone with you,' she said.

She put her arm in his. It wasn't uncommon, after all, for girls to walk along with linked arms. Men turned to look at David and one of them whistled. She knew it must be David the whistle was directed at because he looked so beautiful with his long golden hair and high-heeled red sandals. They walked along the sea front, along the little low promenade. It was too warm even at eight-thirty to wear a coat. There were a lot of people about but not crowds for the place was too select to attract crowds. They walked to the end of the pier. They had a drink in the Ship Inn and another in the Fishermen's Arms. A man tried to pick David up in the Fishermen's Arms but this time he was cold and distant.

'I'd like to put my arm round you,' he said as they were walking back, 'but I suppose that wouldn't do, though it is dark.'

'Better not,' said Christine. She said suddenly, 'This has been the best evening of my life.'

He looked at her. 'You really mean that?'

She nodded. 'Absolutely the best.'

They came into the hotel. 'I'm going to get them to send us up a couple of drinks. To my room. Is that OK?'

She sat on the bed. David went into the bathroom. To do his face, she thought, maybe to shave before he let the man with the drinks see him. There was a knock at the door and a waiter came in with a tray on which were two long glasses of something or other with fruit and leaves floating in it, two pink table napkins, two olives on sticks and two peppermint creams wrapped up in green paper.

Christine tasted one of the drinks. She ate an olive. She opened her handbag and took out a mirror and a lipstick and painted her lips. David came out of the bathroom. He had taken off the golden wig and washed his face. He hadn't shaved, there was a pale stubble showing on his chin and cheeks. His legs and feet were bare and he was wearing a very masculine robe made of navy blue towelling. She tried to hide her disappointment.

'You've changed,' she said brightly.

He shrugged. 'There are limits.'

He raised his glass and she raised her glass and he said: 'To us!'

The beginnings of a feeling of panic came over her. Suddenly he was so evidently a man. She edged a little way along the mattress.

'I wish we had the whole weekend.'

She nodded nervously. She was aware her body had started a faint trembling. He had noticed it too. Sometimes before he had noticed how emotion made her tremble.

'Chris,' he said.

She sat passive and afraid.

'I'm not really like a woman, Chris. I just play at that sometimes for fun. You know that, don't you?' The hand that touched her smelt of nail varnish remover. There were hairs on the wrist she had never noticed before. 'I'm falling in love with you,' he said. 'And you feel the same, don't you?'

She couldn't speak. He took her by the shoulders. He brought his mouth up to hers and put his arms round her and began kissing her. His skin felt abrasive and a smell as male as Graham's came off his body. She shook and shuddered. He pushed her down on the bed and his hands began undressing her, his mouth still on hers and his body heavy on top of her.

She felt behind her, put her hand into the open handbag and pulled out the knife. Because she could feel his heart beating steadily against her right breast she knew where to stab and she stabbed again and again. The bright red heart's blood spurted over her clothes and the bed and the two peppermint creams on the tray.

A Dark Blue Perfume

It would be true to say that not a day had passed without his thinking of her. Except for the middle years. There had been other women then to distract him, though no one he cared for enough to make his second wife. But once he was into his fifties the memory of her returned with all its old vividness. He would see other men settling down into middle age, looking towards old age, with loving wives beside them, and he would say to himself, Catherine, Catherine . . .

He had never, since she left him, worked and lived in his native land. He was employed by a company which sent him all over the world. For years he had lived in South America, Africa, the West Indies, coming home only on leave and not always then. He meant to come home when he retired, though, and to this end, on one of those leaves, he had bought himself a house. It was in the city where he and she had been born, but he had chosen a district as far as possible from the one in which she had gone to live with her new husband and a long way from where they had once lived together, for the time when he had bought it was the time when he had begun daily to think of her again.

He retired when he was sixty-five and came home. He flew home and sent the possessions he had accumulated by sea. They included the gun he had acquired forty years before and with which he had intended to shoot himself when things became unendurable. But they had never been quite unendurable even then. Anger against her and hatred for her had sustained him and he had never got so far as even loading the small, unused automatic.

It was winter when he got home, bleak and wet and far colder than he remembered. When the snow came he stayed indoors, keeping warm, seeing no one. There was no one to see, anyway, they had gone away or died.

When his possessions arrived in three trunks – that was all he had amassed in forty years, three trunkfuls of bric-à-brac – he unpacked wonderingly. Only the gun had been put in by him, his servant had packed the rest. Things came to light he had long forgotten he owned, books, curios, and in an envelope he thought he had destroyed in those early days, all his photographs of her.

He sat looking at them one evening in early spring. The woman who came to clean for him had brought him a bowl of blue hyacinths and the air was heavy and languorous with the sweet scent of them. Catherine, Catherine, he said as he looked at the picture of her in their garden, the picture of her at the seaside, her hair blowing. How different his life would have been if she had stayed with him! If he had been a complaisant husband and borne it all and taken it all and forgiven her. But how could he have borne that? How could he have kept her when she was pregnant with another man's child?

The hyacinths made him feel almost faint. He pushed the photographs back into the envelope but he seemed to see her face still through the thick, opaque, brown paper. She had been a bit older than he, she would be nearly seventy now. She would be old, ugly, fat perhaps, arthritic perhaps, those firm cheeks fallen into jowls, those eyes sunk in folds of skin, that white column of a neck become a bundle of strings, that glossy chestnut hair a bush of grey. No man would want her now.

He got up and looked in the mirror over the mantelpiece. He hadn't aged much, hadn't changed much. Everyone said so. Of course it was true that he hadn't lived much, and it was living that aged you. He wasn't bald, he was thinner than he had been at twenty-five, his eyes were still bright and wistful and full of hope. Those four years' seniority she had over him, they would show now if they stood side by side.

She might be dead. He had heard nothing, there had been no news since the granting of the divorce and her marriage to that man. Aldred Sydney. Aldred Sydney might be dead, she might be a widow. He thought of what that name, in any context, had meant to him, how emotive it had been.

'I want you to meet the new general manager, Sydney Robinson.'

'Yes, we're being sent to Australia, Sydney actually.'

'Cameron and Sydney, Surveyors and Valuers. Can I help you?'

For a long time he had trembled when he heard her surname pronounced. He had wondered how it could come so unconcernedly off another's tongue. Aldred Sydney would be no more than seventy, there was no reason to suppose him dead.

'Do you know Aldred and Catherine Sydney? They live at number

22. An elderly couple, yes, that's right. They're so devoted to each other, it's rather sweet . . .'

She wouldn't still live there, not after forty years. He went into the hall and fetched the telephone directory. For a moment or two he sat still, the book lying in his lap, breathing deeply because his heart was beating so fast. Then he opened the directory and turned to the S's. Aldred was such an uncommon name, there was probably only one Aldred Sydney in the country. He couldn't find him there, though there were many A. Sydneys living at addresses which had no meaning for him, no significance. He wondered afterwards why he had bothered to look lower, to let his eyes travel down through the B's and find her name, unmistakably, incontrovertibly, hers. Sydney, Catherine, 22 Aurora Road . . .

She was still there, she still lived there, and the phone was in her name. Aldred Sydney must be dead. He wished he hadn't looked in the phone book. Why had he? He could hardly sleep at all that night and when he awoke from a doze early in the morning, it was with her name on his lips: Catherine, Catherine.

He imagined phoning her.

'Catherine?'

'Yes, speaking. Who's that?'

'Don't you know? Guess. It's a long long time ago, Catherine.'

It was possible in fantasy, not in fact. He wouldn't know her voice now, if he met her in the street he wouldn't know her. At ten o'clock he got his car out and drove northwards, across the river and up through the northern suburbs. Forty years ago the place where she lived had been well outside the great metropolis, separated from it by fields and woods.

He drove through new streets, whole new districts. Without his new map he would have had no idea where he was. The countryside had been pushed away in those four decades. It hovered shyly on the outskirts of the little town that had become a suburb. And here was Aurora Road. He had never been to it before, never seen her house, though on any map he was aware of precisely where the street was, as if its name were printed in red to burn his eyes.

The sight of it at last, actually being there and seeing the house, made his head swim. He closed his eyes and sat there with his head bent over the wheel. Then he turned and looked at the neat, small house. Its paint was new and smart and the fifty-year-old front door had been replaced by a panelled oak one and the square bay by a bow window. But it was a poor, poky house for all that. He sneered a little at dead Aldred Sydney who had done no better than this for his wife.

Suppose he were to go up to the door and ring the bell? But he wouldn't do that, the shock would be too much for her. He, after all, had prepared himself. She had no preparation for confronting that husband, so little changed, of long ago. Once, how he would have savoured the cruelty of it, the revenge! The handsome man, still looking middle aged, a tropical tan on his cheeks, his body flat and straight, and the broken old woman, squat now, grey, withered. He sighed. All desire for a cruel vengeance had left him. He wanted instead to be merciful, to be kind. Wouldn't the kindest thing be to leave her in peace? Leave her to her little house and the simple pursuits of old age.

He started the car again and drove a little way. It surprised him to find that Aurora Road was right on the edge of that retreating countryside, that its tarmac and grey paving stones led into fields. When she was younger she had possibly walked there sometimes, under the trees, along that footpath. He got out of the car and walked along it himself. After a time he saw a train in the distance, appearing and disappearing between green meadows, clumps of trees, clusters of red roofs, and then he came upon a signpost pointing to the railway station. Perhaps she had walked here to meet Aldred Sydney after his day's work.

He sat down on a rustic seat that had been placed at the edge of the path. It was a very pretty place, not spoilt at all, you could hardly see a single house. The grass was a pure, clean green, the hedgerows shimmering white with the tiny flowers of wild plum blossom which had a drier, sharper scent than the hyacinths. For the time of year it was warm and the sun was shining. A bumble bee, relict of the past summer, drifted by. He put his head back on the wooden bar of the seat and fell asleep.

It was an unpleasant dream he had, of those young days of his when he had been little more than a boy but she very much a grown woman. She came to him, as she had come then, and told him baldly, without shame or diffidence, that the child she carried wasn't his. In the dream she laughed at him, though he couldn't remember that she had done that in life, surely not. He jerked awake and for a moment he didn't know where he was. People talking, walking along the path, had roused him. He left the seat and the path and drove home.

All that week he meant to phone her. He longed fiercely to meet her. It was as if he were in love again, so full was he of obsessional yearnings and unsuspected fears and strange whims. One afternoon he told himself he would phone her at exactly four, when it got to four he would count ten and dial her number. But when four came and he had counted ten his arm refused to function and lift the receiver, it was as if his arm were paralysed. What was the matter with him that he couldn't make a phone call to an old woman he had once known?

The next day he drove back to Aurora Road in the late afternoon. There were three elderly women walking along, walking abreast, but not going in the direction of her house, coming away from it. Was one of them she?

In the three faces, one pale and lined, one red and firm, the third waxen, sagging, he looked for the features of his Catherine. He looked for some vestige of her step in the way each walked. One of the women wore a burgundy-coloured coat, and pulled down over her grey hair, a burgundy felt hat, a shapeless pudding of a hat. Catherine had been fond of wine-red. She had worn it to be married in, married to him and perhaps also to Aldred Sydney. But this woman wasn't she, for as they passed him she turned and peered into the car and her eyes met his without a sign of recognition.

After a little while he drove down the street and, leaving the car, walked along the footpath. The petals of the plum blossom lay scattered on the grass and the may was coming into green bud. The sun shone faintly from a white, curdy sky. This time he didn't sit down on the seat but left the path to walk under the trees, for today the grass was dry and springy. In the distance he heard a train.

He was unprepared for so many people coming this way from the station. There must have been a dozen pass in the space of two minutes. He pretended to be walking purposefully, walking for his health perhaps, for what would they think he was doing, there under the trees without a companion, a sketching block or even a dog? The last went by – or he supposed it was the last. And then he heard soft footfalls, the sound light shoes make on a dry, sandy floor.

Afterwards he was to tell himself that he knew her tread. At the time, honestly, he wasn't quite sure, he didn't dare be, he couldn't trust his own memory. And when she appeared it was quite suddenly from where the path emerged from a tunnel of trees. She was walking towards Aurora Road and as she passed she was no more than ten yards from him.

He stood perfectly still, frozen and dumb. He felt that if he moved he might fall down dead. She didn't walk fast but lightly and springily as she had always done, and the years lay on her as lightly and gently as those footfalls of hers lay on the sand. Her hair was grey and her slenderness a little thickened. There was a hint of a double chin and a faint coarsening of those delicate features – but no more than that. If he had remained young, so had she. It was as if youth had been preserved in each of them for this moment.

He wanted to see her eyes, the blue of those hyacinths, but she kept them fixed straight ahead of her, and she had quickly gone out of his sight, lost round a curve in the path. He crept to the seat and sat down. The wonder of it, the astonishment! He had imagined her old and found her young, but she had always surprised him. Her variety, her capacity to astound, were infinite.

She had come off the train with the others. Did she go out to work? At her age? Many did. Why not she? Sydney was dead and had left her, no doubt, ill-provided for. Sydney was dead . . . He thought of courting her again, loving her, forgiving her, wooing her.

'Will you marry me, Catherine?'

'Do you still want me – after everything?'

'Everything was only a rather long bad dream . . .'

She would come and live in his house and sit opposite him in the evenings, she would go on holiday with him, she would be his wife. They would have little jokes for their friends.

'How long have you two been married?'

'It was our second wedding anniversary last week and it will be our forty-fifth next month.'

He wouldn't phone, though. He would sit on this seat at the same time tomorrow and wait for her to pass by and recognize him.

Before he left home he studied the old photographs of himself that were with the old photographs of her. He had been fuller in the face then and he hadn't worn glasses. He put his hand to his high, sloping forehead and wondered why it looked so low in the pictures. Men's fashions didn't change much. The sports jacket he had on today was much like the sports jacket he had worn on his honeymoon.

As he was leaving the house he was assailed by the scent of the hyacinths, past their prime now and giving off a sickly, cloying odour. Dark blue flowers with a dark blue perfume . . . On an impulse he snapped off their heads and threw them into the wastepaper basket.

The day was bright and he slid back the sunshine roof on his car. When he got to Aurora Road, the field and the footpath, he took off his glasses and slipped them into his pocket. He couldn't see very well without them and he stumbled a little as he walked along.

There was no one on the seat. He sat down in the centre of it. He heard the train. Then he saw it, rattling along between the tufty trees and the little choppy red roofs and the squares of green. It was bringing him, he thought, his whole life's happiness. Suppose she didn't always catch that train, though? Or suppose yesterday's appearance had been an isolated happening, not a return from work but from some occasional visit?

He had hardly time to think about it before the commuters began to come, one and one and then two together. It looked as if there wouldn't be as many as there had been yesterday. He waited, holding his hands clasped together, and when she came he scarcely heard her, she walked so softly.

His sight was so poor without his glasses that she appeared to him as in a haze, almost like a spirit woman, a ghost. But it was she, her vigorous movements, her strong athletic walk, unchanged from her girlhood, and unchanged too, the atmosphere of her that he would have known if he had been not short-sighted but totally blind and deaf too.

The trembling which had come upon him again ceased as she approached and he fixed his eyes on her, half-rising from the seat. And now she looked at him also. She was very near and her face flashed suddenly into focus, a face on which he saw blankness, wariness, then slight alarm. But he was sure she recognized him. He tried to speak and his voice croaked out:

'Don't you know me?'

She began walking fast away, she broke into a run. Disbelieving, he stared after her. There was someone else coming along from the station now, a man who walked out of the tree tunnel and caught her up. They both looked back, whispering. It was then that he heard her voice, only a little older, a little harsher, than when they had first met. He got off the seat and walked about among the trees, holding his head in his hands. She had looked at him, she had seemed to know him – and then she hadn't wished to.

When he reached home again he understood what he had never quite faced up to when he first retired, that he had nothing to live for. For the past week he had lived for her and in the hope of having her again. He found his gun, the small unused automatic, and loaded it and put on the safety catch and looked at it. He would write to her and tell her what he had done – by the time she got his letter he would have done it – or, better still, he would see her once, force her to see him, and then he would do it.

427

The next afternoon he drove to her house in Aurora Road. It was nearly half-past five, she would be along at any moment. He sat in the car, feeling the hard bulge of the gun in his pocket. Presently the man who had caught her up the day before came along, but now he was alone, walking the length of Aurora Road and turning down a side street.

She was late. He left the car where it was and set off to find her, for he could no longer bear to sit there, the pain of it, the sick suspense. He kept seeing her face as she had looked at him, with distaste and then with fear.

Another train was jogging between the tree tufts and the little red chevrons, he heard it enter the station. Had the green, the many, varied greens, been as bright as this yesterday? The green of the grass and the new beech leaves and the may buds hurt his eyes. He passed the seat and went on, further than he had ever been before, coming into a darkish grove where the trees arched over the path. Her feet on the sand whispered like doves. He stood still, he waited for her.

She slowed down when she saw him and came on hesitantly, raising one hand to her face. He took a step towards her, saying, 'Please. Please don't go. I want to talk to you so much . . .'

Today he was wearing his glasses, there was no chance of his eyes being deceived. He couldn't be mistaken as to the meaning of her expression. It was compounded of hatred and terror. But this time she couldn't walk on without walking into his arms. She turned to hasten back the way she had come, and as she turned he shot her.

With the first shot he brought her down. He ran up to where she had fallen but he couldn't look at her, he could only see her as very small and very distant through a red haze of revenge. He shot her again and again, and at last the white ringless hand which had come feebly up to shield her face, fell in death.

The gun was empty. There was blood on him that had flown from her. He didn't care about that, he didn't care who saw or knew, so long as he could get home and re-load the gun for himself. It surprised him that he could walk, but he could and quite normally as far as he could tell. He was without feeling now, without pain or fear, and his breathing settled, though his heart still jumped. He gave the body on the ground one last vague look and walked away from it, out of the tree tunnel, on to the path. The sun made bright sheets of light on the grass and long, tapering shadows. He walked along Aurora Road towards the car outside her house.

Her front door opened as he was unlocking the car. An old woman

428

came out. He recognized her as one of those he had seen on his second visit, the one who had been wearing the dark red coat and hat. She came to the gate and looked over it, looked up towards the left a little anxiously, then back and smiled at him. Something in his stare must have made her speak, show politeness to this stranger.

'I was looking for my daughter,' she said. 'She's a bit late today, she's usually on that first train.'

He put his cold hands on the bar of the gate. Her smile faded.

'Catherine,' he said, 'Catherine . . .'

She lifted to him enquiring eyes, blue as the hyacinths he had thrown away.

The Orchard Walls

I have never told anyone about this before.

The worst was long over, of course. Intense shame had faded and the knowledge of having made the greatest possible fool of myself. Forty years and more had done their work there. The feeling I had been left with, that I was precocious in a foul and dirty way, that I was unclean, was washed away. I had done my best never to think about it, to blot it all out, never to permit to ring on my inward ear Mrs Thorn's words:

'How dare you say such a thing! How dare you be so disgusting! At your age, a child, you must be sick in your mind.'

Things would bring it back, the scent of honeysuckle, a brace of bloodied pigeons hanging in a butcher's window, the first cherries of the season. I winced at these things, I grew hot with a shadow of that blush that had set me on fire with shame under the tree, Daniel's hard hand gripping my shoulder, Mrs Thorn trembling with indignant rage. The memory, never completely exorcised, still had the power to punish the adult for the child's mistake.

Until today.

Having one's childhood trauma cured by an analyst must be like this, only a newspaper has cured mine. The newspaper came through my door and told me I hadn't been disgusting or sick in my mind, I had been right. In the broad facts at least I had been right. All day I have been asking myself what I should do, what action, if any, I should take. At last I have been able to think about it all quite calmly, in tranquillity, to think of Ella and Dennis Clifton without growing hot and ashamed, of Mrs Thorn with pity and of that lovely lost place with something like nostalgia.

It was a long time ago. I was fourteen. Is that to be a child? They thought so, I thought so myself at the time. But the truth was I was a child and not a child, at one and the same time a paddler in streams, a climber of trees, an expert at cartwheels – and with an imagination

430

full of romantic love. I was in a stage of transition, a pupa, a chrysalis, I was fourteen.

Bombs were falling on London. I had already once been evacuated with my school and come back again to the suburb we lived in that sometimes seemed safe and sometimes not. My parents were afraid for me and that was why they sent me to Inchfield, to the Thorns. I could see the fear in my mother's eyes and it made me uncomfortable.

'Just till the end of August,' she said, pleading with me. 'It's beautiful there. You could think of it as an extra long summer holiday.'

I remembered Hereford and my previous 'billet', the strange people, the alien food.

'This will be different. Ella is your own aunt.'

She was my mother's sister, her junior by twelve years. There were a brother and sister in between, both living in the north. Ella's husband was a farmer in Suffolk, or had been. He was in the army and his elder brother ran the farm. Later, when Ella was dead and Philip Thorn married again and all I kept of them was that shameful thing I did my best to forget, I discovered that Ella had married Philip when she was seventeen because she was pregnant and in the thirties any alternative to marriage in those circumstances was unthinkable. She had married him and six months later given birth to a dead child. When I went to Inchfield she was still only twenty-five, still childless, living with a brother-in-law and a mother-in-law in the depths of the country, her husband away fighting in North Africa.

I didn't want to go. At fourteen one isn't afraid, one knows one is immortal. After an air raid we used to go about the streets collecting pieces of shrapnel, fragments of shell. The worst thing to me was having to sleep under a Morrison shelter instead of in my bedroom. Having a room of my own again, a place to be private in, was an inducement. I yielded. To this day I don't know if I was invited or if my mother had simply written to say I was coming, that I must come, that they must give me refuge.

It was the second week of June when I went. Daniel Thorn met me at the station at Ipswich. I was wildly romantic, far too romantic, my head full of fantasies and dreams. Knowing I should be met, I expected a pony carriage or even a man on a black stallion leading a chestnut mare for me, though I had never in my life been on a horse. He came in an old Ford van.

We drove to Inchfield through deep green silent lanes – silent, that is, but for the occasional sound of a shot. I thought it must be something to do with the war, without specifying to myself what.

'The war?' said Daniel as if this were something happening ten thousand miles away. He laughed the age-old laugh of the countryman scoring off the townie. 'You'll find no war here. That's some chap out after rabbits.'

Rabbit was what we were to live on, stewed, roasted, in pies, relieved by wood pigeon. It was a change from London sausages but I have never eaten rabbit since, not once. The characteristic smell of it cooking, experienced once in a friend's kitchen, brought me violent nausea. What a devil's menu that would have been for me, stewed rabbit and cherry pie!

The first sight of the farm enchanted me. The place where I lived in Hereford had been a late-Victorian brick cottage, red and raw and ugly as poverty. I had scarcely seen a house like Cherry Tree Farm except on a calendar. It was long and low and thatched and its two great barns were thatched too. The low green hills and the dark clustering woods hung behind it. And scattered all over the wide slopes of grass were the cherry trees, one so close up to the house as to rub its branches against a window pane.

They came out of the front door to meet us, Ella and Mrs Thorn, and Ella gave me a white, rather cold, cheek to kiss. She didn't smile. She looked bored. It was better therefore than I had expected and worse. Ella was worse and Mrs Thorn was better. The place was ten times better, tea was like something I hadn't had since before the war, my bedroom was not only nicer than the Morrison shelter, it was nicer than my bedroom at home. Mrs Thorn took me up there when we had eaten the scones and currant bread and walnut cake.

It was low-ceilinged with the stone-coloured studs showing through the plaster. A patchwork quilt was on the bed and the walls were hung with a paper patterned all over with bunches of cherries. I looked out of the window.

'You can't see the cherry trees from here,' I said. 'Is that why they put cherries on the walls?'

The idea seemed to puzzle her. She was a simple conservative woman. 'I don't know about that. That would be rather whimsical.'

I was at the back of the house. My window overlooked a trim dull garden of rosebeds cut out in segments of a circle. Mrs Thorn's own garden, I was later to learn, and tended by herself.

'Who sleeps in the room with the cherry tree?' I said.

'Your auntie.' Mrs Thorn was always to refer to Ella in this way. She was a stickler for respect. 'That has always been my son Philip's room.'

Always . . . I envied the absent soldier. A tree with branches against one's bedroom window represented to me something down which one could climb and make one's escape, perhaps even without the aid of knotted sheets. I said as much, toning it down for my companion who I guessed would see it in a different light.

'I'm sure he did no such thing,' said Mrs Thorn. 'He wasn't that kind of boy.'

Those words stamped Philip for me as dull. I wondered why Ella had married him. What had she seen in this unromantic chap, five years her senior, who hadn't been the kind of boy to climb down trees out of his bedroom window? Or climb up them, come to that . . .

She was beautiful. For the first Christmas of the war I had been given *Picturegoer Annual* in which was a full-page photograph of Hedy Lamarr. Ella looked just like her. She had the same perfect features, dark hair, other-worldly eyes fixed on far horizons. I can see her now – I can *permit* myself to see her – as she was then, thin, long-legged, in the floral cotton dress with collar and cuffs and narrow belt that would be fashionable again today. Her hair was pinned up in a roll off her forehead, the rest left hanging to her shoulders in loose curls, mouth painted like raspberry jam, eyes as nature made them, large, dark, alight with some emotion I was years from analysing. I think now it was compounded of rebellion and longing and desire.

Sometimes in the early evenings she would disappear upstairs and then Mrs Thorn would say in a respectful voice that she had gone to write to Philip. We used to listen to the wireless. Of course no one knew exactly where Philip was but we all had a good idea he was somehow involved in the attempts to relieve Tobruk. At news times Mrs Thorn became very tense. Once, to my embarrassment, she made a choking sound and left the room, covering her eyes with her hand. Ella switched off the set.

'You ought to be in bed,' she said to me. 'When I was your age I was always in bed by eight.'

I envied and admired her, even though she was never particularly nice to me and seldom spoke except to say I 'ought' to be doing something or other. Did she look at this niece, not much more than ten years younger than herself, and see what she herself had thrown away, a future of hope, a chance of living?

433

I spent very little time with her. It was Mrs Thorn who took me shopping with her to Ipswich, who talked to me while she did the baking, who knitted and taught me to knit. There was no wool to be had so we unpicked old jumpers and washed the wool and carded it and started again. I was with her most of the time. It was either that or being on my own. No doubt there were children of my own age in the village I might have got to know but the village was two miles away. I was allowed to go out for walks but not to ride the only bicycle they had.

'It's too large for you, it's a twenty-eight inch,' Mrs Thorn said. 'Besides, it's got a crossbar.'

I said I could easily swing my leg behind the saddle like a man.

'Not while you're staying with me.'

I didn't understand. 'I wouldn't hurt myself.' I said what I said to my mother. 'I wouldn't come to any harm.'

'It isn't ladylike,' said Mrs Thorn, and that was that.

Those things mattered a lot to her. She stopped me turning cart-wheels on the lawn when Daniel was about, even though I wore shorts. Then she made me wear a skirt. But she was kind, she paid me a lot of attention. If I had had to depend on Ella or the occasional word from Daniel I might have looked forward more eagerly to my parents' fortnightly visits than I did.

After I had been there two or three weeks the cherries began to turn colour. Daniel, coming upon me looking at them, said they were an old variety called Inchfield White Heart.

'There used to be a cherry festival here,' he said. 'The first Sunday after July the twelfth it was. There'd be dancing and a supper, you'd have enjoyed yourself. Still, we never had one last year and we're not this and somehow I don't reckon there'll ever be a cherry festival again what with this old war.'

He was a yellow-haired, red-complexioned Suffolk man, big and thickset. His wide mouth, sickle-shaped, had its corners permanently turned upwards. It wasn't a smile though and he was seldom cheerful. I never heard him laugh. He used to watch people in rather a disconcerting way, Ella especially. And when guests came to the house, Dennis Clifton or Mrs Leithman or some of the farming people they knew, he would sit and watch them, seldom contributing a word.

One evening, when I was coming back from a walk, I saw Ella and Dennis Clifton kissing in the wood.

*

434

Dennis Clifton wasn't a farmer. He had been in the RAF, had been a fighter pilot in the Battle of Britain but had received some sort of head injury, been in hospital and was now on leave at home recuperating. He must have been very young, no more than twenty-two or three. While he was ill his mother, with whom he had lived and who had been a friend of Mrs Thorn's, had died and left him her pretty little Georgian house in Inchfield. He was often at the farm, ostensibly to see his mother's old friend.

After these visits Daniel used to say, 'He'll soon be back in the thick of it,' or 'It won't be long before he's up there in his Spitfire. He can't wait.'

This made me watch him too, looking for signs of impatience to return to the RAF. His hands shook sometimes, they trembled like an old man's. He too was fair-haired and blue-eyed, yet there was all the difference in the world between his appearance and Daniel's. Film stars set my standard of beauty and I thought he looked like Leslie Howard playing Ashley Wilkes. He was tall and thin and sensitive and his eyes were sad. Daniel watched him and Ella sat silent and I read my book while he talked very kindly and encouragingly to Mrs Thorn about her son Philip, about how confident he was Philip would be all right, would survive, and while he talked his eyes grew sadder and more veiled.

No, I have imagined that, not remembered it. It is in the light of what I came to know that I have imagined it. He was simply considerate and kind like the well-brought-up young man he was.

I had been in the river. There was a place about a mile upstream they called the weir where for a few yards the banks were built up with concrete below a shallow fall. A pool about four feet deep had formed there and on hot days I went bathing in it. Mrs Thorn would have stopped me if she had known but she didn't know. She didn't even know I had a bathing costume with me.

The shortest way back was through the wood. I heard a shot and then another from up in the meadows. Daniel was out after pigeons. The wood was dim and cool, full of soft twitterings, feathers rustling against dry leaves. The bluebells were long past but dog's mercury was in flower, a white powdering, and the air was scented with honeysuckle. Another shot came, further off but enough to shatter peace, and there was a rush of wings as pigeons took flight. Through the black trunks of trees and the lacework of their branches I could see the yellow sky and the sun burning in it, still an hour off setting.

Ella was leaning against the trunk of a chestnut, looking up into

435

Dennis Clifton's face. He had his hands pressed against the trunk, on either side of her head. If she had ever been nice to me, if he had ever said more than hallo, I think I might have called out to them. I didn't call and in a moment I realized the last thing they would want was to be seen.

I stayed where I was. I watched them. Oh, I was in no way a voyeur. There was nothing lubricious in it, nothing of curiosity, still less a wish to catch them out. I was overwhelmed rather by the romance of it, ravished by wonder. I watched him kiss her. He took his hands down and put his arms round her and kissed her so that their faces were no longer visible, only his fair head and her dark hair and their locked straining shoulders. I caught my breath and shivered in the warm half-light, in the honeysuckle air.

They left the place before I did, walking slowly away in the direction of the road, arms about each other's waists. In the room at Cherry Tree Farm they still called the parlour Mrs Thorn and Daniel were sitting, listening to the wireless, drinking tea. No more than five minutes afterwards Ella came in. I had seen what I had seen but if I hadn't, wouldn't I still have thought her looks extraordinary, her shining eyes and the flush on her white cheeks, the willow leaf in her hair and the bramble clinging to her skirt?

Daniel looked at her. There was blood in his fingernails, though he had scrubbed his hands. It brought me a flicker of nausea. Ella put her fingers through her hair, plucked out the leaf and went upstairs.

'She is going up to write to Philip,' said Mrs Thorn.

Why wasn't I shocked? Why wasn't I horrified? I was only fourteen and I came from a conventional background. Adultery was something committed by people in the Bible. I suppose I could say I had seen no more than a kiss and adultery didn't enter into it. Yet I knew it did. With no experience, with only the scantiest knowledge, I sensed that this love had its full consummation. I knew Ella was married to a soldier who was away fighting for his country. I even knew that my parents would think behaviour such as hers despicable if not downright wicked. But I cared for none of that. To me it was romance, it was Lancelot and Guinevere, it was a splendid and beautiful adventure that was happening to two handsome young people – as one day it might happen to me.

I was no go-between. For them I scarcely existed. I received no words or smiles, still less messages to be carried. They had the phone, anyway, they had cars. But though I took no part in their love affair and wasn't even with accuracy able to calculate the times when it was conducted, it filled my thoughts. Outwardly I followed the routine of days I had arranged for myself and Mrs Thorn had arranged for me, but my mind was occupied with Dennis and Ella, assessing what meeting places they would use, imagining their conversations – their vows of undying love – and re-creating with cinematic variations that kiss.

My greatest enjoyment, my finest hours of empathy, were when he called. I watched the two of them as intently then as Daniel did. Sometimes I fancied I caught between them a glance of longing and once I actually witnessed something more, an encounter between them in the passage when Ella came from the kitchen with the tea tray and Dennis had gone to fetch something from his car for Mrs Thorn. Unseen by them, I stood in the shadow between the grandfather clock and the foot of the stairs. I heard him whisper:

'Tonight? Same place?'

She nodded, her eyes wide. I saw him put his hand on her shoulder in a slow caress as he went past her.

I slept badly those nights. It had become very hot. Mrs Thorn made sure I was in bed by nine and there was no way of escaping from the house after that without being seen by her. I envied Ella with a tree outside her window down which it would be easy to climb and escape. I imagined going down to the river in the moonlight, walking in the wood, perhaps seeing my lovers in some trysting place. My lovers, whose breathy words and laden glances exalted me and rarefied the overheated air . . .

The cherries were turning pale yellow with a blush coming to their cheeks. It was the first week of July, the week the war came to Inchfield and a German bomber, lost and off course, unloaded a stick of bombs in one of the Thorns' fields.

No one was hurt, though a cow got killed. We went to look at the mess in the meadow, the crater and the uprooted tree. Daniel shook his fist at the sky. The explosions had made a tremendous noise and we were all sensitive after that to any sudden sound. Even the crack of Daniel's shotgun made his mother jump.

The heat had turned sultry and clouds obscured our blue skies, though no rain fell. Mrs Leithman, coming to tea as she usually did once in the week, told us she fancied each roll of thunder was another bomb. We hardly saw Ella, she was always up in her room or out

437

somewhere – out with Dennis, of course. I speculated about them, wove fantasies around them, imagined Philip Thorn killed in battle and thereby setting them free. So innocent was I, living in more innocent or at least more puritanical times, that the possibility of this childless couple being divorced never struck me. Nor did I envisage Dennis and Ella married to each other but only continuing for ever their perilous enchanting idyll. I even found Juliet's lines for them – Juliet who was my own age – and whispered to myself that the orchard walls are high and hard to climb and the place death, considering who thou art . . . Once, late at night when I couldn't sleep and sat in my window, I saw the shadowy figure of Dennis Clifton emerge from the deep darkness at the side of the house and leave by the gate out of the rose garden.

But the destruction of it all and my humiliation were drawing nearer. I had settled down there, I had begun to be happy. The truth is, I suppose, that I identified with Ella and in my complex fantasies it was I, compounded with Juliet, that Dennis met and embraced and touched and loved. My involvement was much deeper than that of an observer.

When it came the shot sounded very near. It woke me up as such a sound might not have done before the bombs. I wondered what prey Daniel could go in search of at this hour, for the darkness was deep, velvety and still. The crack which had split the night and jarred the silence wasn't repeated. I went back to sleep and slept till past dawn.

I got up early as I did most mornings, came downstairs in the quiet of the house, the hush of a fine summer morning, and went outdoors. Mrs Thorn was in the kitchen, frying fat bacon and duck eggs for the men. I didn't know if it was all right for me to do this or if all the cherries were reserved for some mysterious purpose, but as I went towards the gate I reached up and picked a ripe one from a dipping branch. It was the crispest sweetest cherry I have ever tasted, though I must admit I have eaten few since then. I pushed the stone into the earth just inside the gates. Perhaps it germinated and grew. Perhaps quite an old tree that has borne many summer loads of fruit now stands at the entrance to Cherry Tree Farm.

As it happened, of all their big harvest, that was the only cherry I was ever to eat there. Coming back half an hour later, I pushed open the gate and stood for a moment looking at the farmhouse over whose sunny walls and roof the shadows of the trees lay in a slanted leafy pattern. I looked at the big tree, laden with red-gold fruit, that rubbed its branches against Ella's window. In its boughs, halfway up, in a fork a yard or two from the glass, hung the body of a man.

In the hot sunshine I felt icy cold. I remember the feeling to this day, the sensation of being frozen by a cold that came from within while outside me the sun shone and a thrush sang and the swallows dipped in and out under the eaves. My eyes seemed fixed, staring in the hypnosis of shock and fear at the fair-haired dangling man, his head thrown back in the agony of death there outside Ella's bedroom window.

At least I wasn't hysterical. I resolved I must be calm and adult. My teeth were chattering. I walked stiffly into the kitchen and there they all were, round the table, Daniel and the two men and Ella and, at the head of it, Mrs Thorn pouring tea.

I meant to go quietly up to her and whisper it. I couldn't. To get myself there without running, stumbling, shouting, had used up all the control I had. The words rushed out in a loud ragged bray and I remember holding up my hands, my fists clenched.

'Mr Clifton's been shot. He's been shot, he's dead. His body's in the cherry tree outside Ella's window!'

There was silence. But first a clatter as of knives and forks dropped, of cups rattled into saucers, of chairs scraped. Then this utter stricken silence. I have never – not in all the years since then – seen anyone go as white as Ella went. She was as white as paper and her eyes were black holes. A brick colour suffused Daniel's face. He swore. He used words that made me shrink and draw back and shiver and stare from one to the other of the horrible, horrified faces.

Mrs Thorn was the first to speak, her voice cold with anger.

'How dare you say such a thing! How dare you be so disgusting! At your age – you must be sick in your mind.'

Daniel had jumped up. He took me roughly by the arm. But his grasp wasn't firm, the hand was shaking the way Dennis's shook. He manhandled me out there, his mother scuttling behind us. We were still five or six yards from the tree when I saw. The hot blood came into my face and throbbed under my skin. I looked at the cloth face, the yellow wool hair – our own unpicked carded wool – the stuffed sacking body, the cracked boots . . .

Icy with indignation, Mrs Thorn said, 'Haven't you ever seen a scarecrow before?'

I cried out desperately as if, even in the face of this evidence, I could still prove them wrong, 'But scarecrows are in fields!'

'Not in this part of the world.' Daniel's voice was thin and hoarse. He couldn't have looked more gaunt, more shocked, if it had really been Dennis Clifton in that tree. 'In this part of the world we put them in cherry trees. I put it there last night. I put *them* there.' And he pointed at what I had passed but never seen, the man in the tree by the wall, the man in the tree in the middle of the green lawn.

I went back to the house and up to my room and lay on the bed, prone and silent with shame. The next day was Saturday and my parents were coming. They would tell them and I should be taken home in disgrace. In the middle of the day Mrs Thorn came to the door and said to come down to lunch. She was a changed woman, hard and dour. I had never heard the expression 'to draw aside one's skirts' but later on when I did I recognized that this was what she had done to me. Her attitude to me was as if I were some sort of psychopath.

We had lunch alone, only I didn't really have any, I couldn't eat. Just as we were finishing, I pushing aside my laden plate, Daniel came in and sat down and said they had all talked about it and they thought it would be best if I went home with my parents on the following day.

'Of course I shall tell them exactly what you said and what you inferred,' said Mrs Thorn. 'I shall tell them how you insulted your auntie.'

Daniel, who wasn't trembling any more or any redder in the face than usual, considered this for a moment in silence. Then he said unexpectedly – or unexpectedly to me, 'No, we won't, Mother, we won't do that. No point in that. The fewer know the better. You've got to think of Ella's reputation.'

'I won't have her here,' his mother said.

'No, I agree with that. She can tell them she's homesick or I'll say it's too much for you, having her here.'

Ella hid herself away all that day.

'She has her letter to write to Philip,' said Mrs Thorn.

In the morning she was at the table with the others. Daniel made an announcement. He had been down to the village and heard that Dennis Clifton was back in the Air Force, he had rejoined his squadron.

'He'll soon be back in the thick of it,' he said.

Ella sat with bowed head, working with restless fingers a slice of bread into a heap of crumbs. Her face was colourless, lacking her

440

usual make-up. I don't remember ever hearing another word from her.

I packed my things. My parents made no demur about taking me back with them. Starved of love, sickened by the love of others, I clung to my father. The scarecrows grinned at us as we got into the van behind Daniel. I can see them now – I can permit myself to see them now – spreadeagled in the trees, protecting the reddening fruit, so lifelike that even the swallows swooped in wider arcs around them.

In the following spring Ella died giving birth to another dead child. My mother cried, for Ella had been her little sister. But she was shy about giving open expression to her grief. She and my father were anxious to keep from me, or for that matter anyone else, that it was a good fifteen months since Philip Thorn had been home on leave. What became of Daniel and his mother I never knew, I didn't want to know. I couldn't avoid hearing that Philip had married again and his new wife was a niece of Mrs Leithman's.

Only a meticulous reader of newspapers would have spotted the paragraph. I am in the habit of reading every line, with the exception of the sports news, and I spotted this item tucked away between an account of sharp practice in local government and the suicide of a financier. I read it. The years fell away and the facts exonerated me. I knew I must do something, I wondered what, I have been thinking of it all day, but now I know I must tell this story to the coroner. My story, my mistake, Daniel's rage.

An agricultural worker had come upon an unexploded bomb on farm land near Inchfield in Suffolk. It was thought to be one of a stick of bombs dropped there in 1941. Excavations in the area had brought to light a skeleton thought to be that of a young man who had met his death at about the same time. A curious fact was that shotgun pellets had been found in the cavity of the skull.

The orchard walls are high and hard to climb. And the place death considering who thou art, if any of my kinsmen find thee here . . .

441

Hare's House

A murderer had lived in the house, the estate agent told Norman. The murder had in fact been committed there, he said. Norman thought it very open and honest of him.

'The neighbours would have mentioned it if I hadn't,' said the estate agent.

Now Norman understood why the house was going cheap. It was what they called a town house, though Norman didn't know why they did as he had seen plenty like it in the country. There were three floors and an open-tread staircase going up the centre. About fifteen years old, the estate agent said, and for twelve of those no one had lived in it.

'I'm afraid I can't give you any details of the case.'

'I wouldn't want to know,' said Norman. 'I'd rather not know.' He put his head round the door of the downstairs bathroom. He had never thought it possible he might own a house with more than one bathroom. Did he seriously consider owning this one then? The price was so absurdly low! 'What was his name?'

'The murderer? Oh, Hare. Raymond Hare.'

Rather to his relief, Norman couldn't remember any Hare murder case. 'Where is he now?'

'He died in prison. The house belongs to a nephew.'

'I like the house,' Norman said cautiously. 'I'll have to see what my wife says.'

The area his job obliged him to move into was a more prestigious one than where they now lived. A terraced cottage like the ones in Inverness Street was the best he had thought they could run to. He would never find another bargain like this one. If he hadn't been sure Rita would find out about the murder he would have avoided telling her.

'Why is it so cheap?' she said.

He told her.

She was a small thickset woman with brown hair and brown eyes and a rather large pointed face. She had a way of extending her neck and thrusting her face forward. It had once occurred to Norman that she looked like a mole, though moles of course could be attractive creatures. She thrust her head forward now.

'Is there something horrible you're not telling me?'

'I've told you everything I know. I don't know any details.' Norman was a patient and easy-going man, if inclined to be sullen. He was rather good-looking with a boyish open face and brown curly hair. 'We could both go and see it tomorrow.'

Rita would have preferred a terraced cottage in Inverness Street with a big garden and not so many stairs. But Norman had set his heart on the town house and was capable of sulking for months if he didn't get his own way. Besides, there was nothing to *show* Hare had lived there. Rather foolishly perhaps, Rita now thought, she had been expecting bloodstains or even a locked room.

'I've no recollection of this Hare at all, have you?'

'Let's keep it that way,' said Norman. 'You said yourself it's better not to know. I'll make Mr Hare the nephew an offer, shall I?'

The offer was accepted and Norman and Rita moved in at the end of September. The neighbours on one side had lived there eight years and the neighbours on the other six. They had never known Raymond Hare. A family called Lawrence who had lived in their large old house surrounded by garden for more than twenty years must have known him, at least by sight, but Norman and Rita had never spoken to them save to pass the time of day.

They had builders in to paint the house and they had new carpets. There were only two drawbacks and one of those was the stairs. You found yourself always running up and down to fetch things you had forgotten. The other drawback was the bathroom window, or more specifically, the catch on the bathroom window.

Sometimes, especially when Norman was at work and she was alone, Rita would wonder exactly where the murder had taken place. She would stand still, holding her duster, and look about her and think maybe it was in that room or that one or in their bedroom. And then she would go into the bedroom, thrusting her head forward and peering. Her mother used to say she had a 'funny feeling' in the corners of some houses, she said she was psychic. Rita would have liked to have inherited this gift but she had to admit she experienced no funny feelings in any part of this house.

She and Norman never spoke about Raymond Hare. They tended to avoid the very subject of murder. Rita had once enjoyed detective stories but somehow she didn't read them any more. It seemed better not to. Her next-door neighbour Dorothy, the one who had lived there eight years, tried one day to talk to her about the Hare case but Rita said she'd rather not discuss it.

'I quite understand,' Dorothy said. 'I think you're very wise.'

It was a warm house. The central heating was efficient and the windows were double glazed except for the one in the upstairs bathroom. This bathroom had a very high ceiling and the window was about ten feet up. It was in the middle of the house and therefore had no outside wall so the architect had made the roof of the bathroom just above the main roof, thus affording room for a window. It was a nuisance not being able to open it except by means of the pole with the hook on the end of it that stood against the bathroom wall, but the autumn was a dull wet one and the winter cold so for a long time there was no need to open the bathroom window at all.

Norman thought he would have a go at re-tiling the downstairs bathroom himself and went to the library to look for a do-it-yourself decorating manual. The library, a small branch, wasn't far away, being between his house and the tube station. Unable at first to find Skills and Crafts, his eye wandered down through Horticulture, Botany, Biology, General Science, Social Sciences, Crime . . .

Generally speaking, Norman had nothing to do with crime these days. He and Rita had even stopped watching thriller serials on television. His impulse was to turn his eyes sharply away from these accounts of trials and reconstructions of murders and turn them away he did but not before he had caught the name Hare on the spine of one of the books.

Norman turned his back. By a happy chance he was facing the section labelled 'Interior Decoration'. He found the book he wanted. Then he stood holding it and thinking. Should he look again? It might be that the author's name was Hare and had nothing at all to do with his Hare. Norman didn't really believe this. His stomach began to feel queasy and he was conscious of being rather excited too. He turned round and quickly took the book off the shelf. Its title was *Murder in the Sixties*, the author was someone called H. L. Robinson and the cases examined were listed on the jacket: Renzini and Boyce, The Oasthouse Mystery, Hare, The Pop Group Murders.

Norman opened it at random. He found he had opened it in the middle of the Hare case. A page or two further on were two photographs, the top one of a man with a blank characterless face and half-closed eyes, the other of a smiling fair-haired woman. The caption said that above was Raymond Henry Montagu Hare and below Diana Margaret Hare, née Kentwell. Norman closed the book and replaced it on the shelf. His heart was beating curiously hard. When his do-it-yourself book had been stamped he had to stop himself actually running out of the library. What a way to behave! he thought. I must get a grip on myself. Either I am going to put Hare entirely out of my mind and never think of him again or else I am going to act like a rational man, read up the case, make myself conversant with the facts and learn to live with them.

He did neither. He didn't visit the library again. When his book had taught him all it could about tiling he asked Rita to return it for him. He tried to put Hare out of his mind but this was too difficult. Where had he committed the murder was one of the questions he often asked himself and then he began to wonder whom he had killed and by what means. The answers were in a book on a shelf not a quarter of a mile away. Norman had to pass the library on his way to the station each morning and on his way back each night. He took to walking on the other side of the street. Sometimes there came into his mind that remark of Rita's that there might be something horrible he wasn't telling her.

Spring came early and there were some warm days in March. Rita tried to open the bathroom window, using the pole with the hook on the end, but the catch wouldn't budge. When Norman came home she got him to borrow a ladder from Dorothy's husband Roy and climb up and see what was wrong with the catch.

Norman thought Roy gave him rather a funny look when he said what he wanted the ladder for. He hesitated before saying Norman could have it.

'It's quite OK if you'd rather not,' Norman said. 'I expect I can manage with the steps if I can find a foothold somewhere.'

'No, no, you're welcome to the ladder,' said Roy and he showed Norman the bathroom in his own house which was identical with the next-door's except that the window had been changed for a blank sheet of glass with an extractor fan.

'Very nice,' said Norman, 'but just the same I'd rather have a window I can open.'

That brought another funny look from Roy. Norman propped the ladder against the wall and climbed up to the window and saw why it wouldn't open. The two parts of the catch, a vertical bolt and a slot for it to be driven up into, had been wired together. Norman supposed that the builders doing the painting had wired up the window catch, though he couldn't imagine why. He undid the wire, slid down the bolt and let the window fall open to its maximum capacity of about seventy-five degrees.

On 1 April the temperature dropped to just on freezing and it snowed. Rita closed the bathroom window. She took hold of the pole, reached up and inserted the hook in the ring on the bottom of the bolt, lifted the window, closed it, pushed up the bolt into the slot and gave it a twist. When she came out of the bathroom on to the landing she stood looking about her and wondering where Hare had committed the murder. For a moment she fancied she had a funny feeling about that but it passed. Rita went down to the kitchen and made herself a cup of tea. She looked out into the tiny square of garden on to which fluffy snow was falling and melting when it touched the grass. There would have been room in the garden in Inverness Street to plant bulbs, daffodils and narcissi. Rita sighed. She poured out the tea and was stirring sugar into her cup when there came a loud crash from upstairs. Rita nearly jumped out of her skin.

She ran up the two flights of stairs, wondering what on earth had got broken. There was nothing. Nothing was out of place or changed. She had heard of haunted houses where loud crashes were due to poltergeist activity. Her mother had always been able to sense the presence of a poltergeist. She felt afraid and sweat broke out on her rather large pointed face. Then she noticed the bathroom door was closed. Had it been that door closing she had heard? Surely not. Rita opened the bathroom door and saw that the window had fallen open. So that was all it was. She got the pole and inserted the hook in the ring on the bolt, slid the bolt upwards into the slot and gave it a twist.

It had been rather windy but the wind had dropped. Next day the weather began to warm up again. Norman opened the bathroom window and it remained open until rain started. Rita closed it.

'That window's not the problem I thought it might be once you get the hang of using the pole,' said Norman.

He was trying to be cheerful and to act as if nothing had happened. The man called Lawrence who lived opposite had got into conversation with him on his way home. They had found themselves sitting next to each other in the tube train.

'It's good to see someone living in your place at last. An empty house always gets a run-down look.'

Norman just smiled. He had started to feel uneasy.

'My wife knew Mrs Hare quite well, you know.'

'Really?' said Norman.

'A nice woman. There was no reason for what he did as far as anyone could tell. But I imagine you've read it all up and come to terms with it. Well, you'd have to, wouldn't you?'

'Oh, yes,' said Norman.

Because he had his neighbour with him he couldn't cross the street to avoid passing the library. Outside its gates he had an almost intolerable urge to go in and take that book from the shelf. One thing he knew now, whether he wanted to or not, was that it was his wife Hare had murdered.

Some little while after midnight he was awakened by a crash. He sat up in bed.

'What was that?'

'The bathroom window, I expect,' said Rita, half-asleep.

Norman got up. He took the pole, inserted the hook into the ring on the bolt, slid up the bolt and gave it a firm clockwise twist. The rest of the night passed undisturbed. Rita opened the window two or three days later because it had turned warm. She went into their bedroom and changed the sheets and thought, for no reason as far as she could tell, I wonder if it was his wife he murdered? I expect it was his wife. Then she thought how terrible it would be if he had murdered her in bed. Hare's bed must have stood in the same place as their own. It must have because of the position of the electric points. Perhaps he had come home one night and murdered her in bed.

A wind that was more like a gale started to make the house cold. Rita closed the bathroom window. About an hour after Norman got home it blew open with a crash.

'It comes open,' said Norman after he had shut it, 'because when you close it you don't give the bolt a hard enough twist.'

'It comes open because of the wind,' said Rita.

'The wind wouldn't affect it if you shut it properly.' Norman's handsome face wore its petulant look and he sulked rather for the rest of the evening.

Next time the window was opened petals from fruit tree blossom blew in all over the dark blue carpet. Rita closed it an hour or so before Norman came home. Dorothy was downstairs having a cup of tea with her.

447

'I'd have that window wired up if I were you,' said Dorothy, and she added oddly, 'To be on the safe side.'

'It gets so hot in there.'

'Leave it open then and keep the door shut.'

The crash of the window opening awoke Norman at two in the morning. He was furious. He made a lot of noise about closing it in order to wake Rita.

'I told you that window wouldn't come open if you gave the bolt a hard enough twist. That crashing scares the hell out of me. My nerves can't stand it.'

'What's wrong with your nerves?'

Norman didn't answer. 'I don't know why you can't master a simple knack like that.'

'It isn't me, it's the wind.'

'Nonsense. Don't talk such nonsense. There is no wind.'

Rita opened the window in order to practise closing it. She spent about an hour opening and closing the window and giving the bolt a firm clockwise twist. While she was doing this she had a funny feeling. She had the feeling someone was standing behind and watching what she did. Of course there was no one there. Rita meant to leave the window open as it was a dry sunny day but she had closed it for perhaps the tenth time when the phone rang. The window therefore remained closed and Rita forgot about it.

She was pulling up weeds in the tiny strip of front garden when a woman who lived next door to the Lawrences came across the road, rattled a tin at her and asked for a donation for Cancer Research.

'I hope you don't mind my telling you how much I like your bedroom curtains.'

'Thank you very much,' said Rita.

'Mrs Hare had white net. Of course that was a few years back. You don't mind sleeping in that bedroom then? Or do you use one of the back rooms?'

Rita's knees felt weak. She was speechless.

'I suppose it isn't as if he actually did the deed in the bedroom. More just outside on the landing, wasn't it?'

Rita gave her a pound to get rid of her. She went upstairs and stood on the landing and felt very funny indeed. Should she tell Norman? How could she tell him, how could she begin, when they had never once mentioned the subject since they moved in? Norman never thought about it anyway, she was sure of that. She watched him eating his supper as if he hadn't a care in the world. The window

448

crashed open just as he was starting on his pudding. He jumped up with an angry shout.

'You're going to come with me into that bathroom and I'm going to teach you how to shut that window if it's the last thing I do!'

He stood behind her while she took the pole and inserted the hook into the ring on the bolt, pushed the bolt up and gave it a firm twist.

'There, you see, you've turned it the wrong way. I said clockwise. Don't you know what clockwise means?'

Norman opened the window and made Rita close it again. This time she twisted the bolt to the right. The window crashed open before they had reached the foot of the stairs.

'It's not me, you see, it's the wind,' Rita cried.

Norman's voice shook with rage. 'The wind couldn't blow it open if you closed it properly. It doesn't blow it open when I close it.'

'You close it then and see. Go on, you do it.'

Norman closed it. The crash awakened him at three in the morning. He got up, cursing, and went into the bathroom. Rita woke up and jumped out of bed and followed him. Norman came out of the bathroom with the pole in his hand, his face red and his eyes bulging. He shouted at Rita:

'You got up after I was asleep and opened that window and closed it your way, didn't you?'

'I did *what*?'

'Don't deny it. You're trying to drive me mad with that window. You won't get the chance to do it again.'

He raised the pole and brought it down with a crash on the side of Rita's head. She gave a dreadful hoarse cry and put up her hands to try and ward off the rain of blows. Norman struck her five times with the pole and she was lying unconscious on the landing floor before he realized what he was doing. Norman threw the pole down the stairwell, picked Rita up in his arms and phoned for an ambulance.

Rita didn't die. She had a fractured skull and a broken jaw and collarbone but she would survive. When she regained consciousness and could move her jaw again she told the people at the hospital she had got up in the night and fallen over the banisters and all the way down the stairwell in the dark. The curious thing was she seemed to believe this herself.

Alone and remorseful, Norman kept thinking how odd it was there

449

had nearly been a second murder under this roof. He went to the estate agents and told them he wanted to put the house back on the market. Hare's house, he always called it to himself these days, never 'my house' or 'ours'. They looked grave and shook their heads but brightened up when Norman named the very low figure he intended to ask.

Now he was going to be rid of the house Norman began to feel differently about Hare. He wouldn't have minded knowing what Hare had done, the details, the facts. One Saturday afternoon a prospective buyer came, was in raptures over Norman's redecorations and the tiles in the downstairs bathroom, and didn't seem to care at all about Hare. This encouraged Norman and immediately the man had gone he went down the road to the library where he got out *Murder in the Sixties*. He read the account of the case after getting back from visiting Rita in hospital.

Raymond and Diana Hare had been an apparently happy couple. One morning their cleaner arrived to find Mrs Hare beaten to death and lying in her own blood on the top landing outside the bathroom door. Hare had soon confessed. He and his wife had had a midnight dispute over a window that continually came open with a crash and in the heat of anger he had attacked her with a wooden pole. Not a very interesting or memorable murder. Robinson, in his foreword, said he had included it among his four because what linked them all was a common lack of any kind of understandable motive.

But how could I have tried to do the same thing and for the same reason? Norman asked himself. Is Hare's house haunted by an act, by a motiveless urge? Or can it be that the first time I looked into that book I saw and read more than my conscious mind took in but not more than was absorbed by my *unconscious*? A rational man must believe the latter.

He borrowed the ladder from Roy to climb up and once more wire the window catch.

'By the way,' he said. 'I've been meaning to ask you. It's not the same pole, is it?'

'Your one, you mean? The same as Hare's? Oh, no, I don't know what became of that one. In some police museum, I expect. You've got ours. When we had our window done we offered ours to Mr Hare the nephew and he was very glad to accept.'

Norman found a buyer at last. Rita was away convalescing and he was obliged to find a new home for them in her absence. Not that he had much choice, the miserable sum he got for Hare's house. He put a deposit on one of the terraced cottages in Inverness Street, hoping poor Rita wouldn't mind too much.

Bribery and Corruption

Everyone who makes a habit of dining out in London knows that Potters in Marylebone High Street is one of the most expensive of eating places. Nicholas Hawthorne, who usually dined in his rented room or in a steak house, was deceived by the humble-sounding name. When Annabel said, 'Let's go to Potters,' he agreed quite happily.

It was the first time he had taken her out. She was a small pretty girl with very little to say for herself. In her little face her eyes looked huge and appealing – a flying fox face, Nicholas thought. She suggested they take a taxi to Potters 'because it's difficult to find'. Seeing that it was a large building and right in the middle of Marylebone High Street, Nicholas didn't think it would have been more difficult to find on foot than in a taxi but he said nothing.

He was already wondering what this meal was going to cost. Potters was a grand and imposing restaurant. The windows were of that very clear but slightly warped glass that bespeaks age, and the doors of a dark red wood that looked as if it had been polished every day for fifty years. Because the curtains were drawn and the interior not visible, it appeared as if they were approaching some private residence, perhaps a rich man's town house.

Immediately inside the doors was a bar where three couples sat about in black leather chairs. A waiter took Annabel's coat and they were conducted to a table in the restaurant. Nicholas, though young, was perceptive. He had expected Annabel to be made as shy and awkward by this place as he was himself but she seemed to have shed her diffidence with her coat. And when waiters approached with menus and the wine list she said boldly that she would start with a Pernod.

What was it all going to cost? Nicholas looked unhappily at the prices and was thankful he had his newly acquired credit card with him. Live now, pay later – but, oh God, he would still have to pay.

Annabel chose asparagus for her first course and roast grouse for her second. The grouse was the most expensive item on the menu. Nicholas selected vegetable soup and a pork chop. He asked her if she would like red or white wine and she said one bottle wouldn't be enough, would it, so why not have one of each?

She didn't speak at all while they ate. He remembered reading in some poem or other how the poet marvelled of a schoolmaster that one small head could carry all he knew. Nicholas wondered how one small body could carry all Annabel ate. She devoured roast potatoes with her grouse and red cabbage and runner beans, and when she heard the waiter recommending braised artichokes to the people at the next table she said she would have some of those too. He prayed she wouldn't want another course. But that fawning insinuating waiter had to come up with the sweet trolley.

'We have fresh strawberries, madam.'

'In November?' said Annabel, breaking her silence. 'How lovely.'

Naturally she would have them. Drinking the dregs of his wine, Nicholas watched her eat the strawberries and cream and then call for a slice of chocolate roulade. He ordered coffee. Did sir and madam wish for a liqueur? Nicholas shook his head vehemently. Annabel said she would have a green chartreuse. Nicholas knew that this was of all liqueurs the pearl – and necessarily the most expensive.

By now he was so frightened about the bill and so repelled by her concentrated guzzling that he needed briefly to get away from her. It was plain she had come out with him only to stuff and drink herself into a stupor. He excused himself and went off in the direction of the men's room.

In order to reach it he had to pass across one end of the bar. The place was still half-empty but during the past hour – it was now nine o'clock – another couple had come in and were sitting at a table in the centre of the floor. The man was middle-aged with thick silver hair and a lightly tanned taut-skinned face. His right arm was round the shoulder of his companion, a very young, very pretty blonde girl, and he was whispering something in her ear. Nicholas recognized him at once as the chairman of the company for which his own father had been sales manager until two years before when he had been made redundant on some specious pretext. The company was called Sorensen-McGill and the silver-haired man was Julius Sorensen.

With all the fervour of a young man loyal to a beloved parent, Nicholas hated him. But Nicholas was a very young man and it was beyond his strength to cut Sorensen. He muttered a stiff good evening and plunged for the men's room where he turned out his pockets, counted the notes in his wallet and tried to calculate what he already owed to the credit card company. If necessary he would have to borrow from his father, though he would hate to do that, knowing as he did that his father had been living on a reduced income ever since that beast Sorensen fired him. Borrow from his father, try and put off paying the rent for a month if he could, cut down on his smoking, maybe give up altogether . . .

When he came out, feeling almost sick, Sorensen and the girl had moved farther apart from each other. They didn't look at him and Nicholas too looked the other way. Annabel was on her second green chartreuse and gobbling up *petit fours*. He had thought her face was like that of a flying fox and now he remembered that flying fox is only a pretty name for a fruit bat. Eating a marzipan orange, she looked just like a rapacious little fruit bat. And she was very drunk.

'I feel ever so sleepy and strange,' she said. 'Maybe I've got one of those viruses. Could you pay the bill?'

It took Nicholas a long time to catch the waiter's eye. When he did the man merely homed in on them with the coffee pot. Nicholas surprised himself with his own firmness.

'I'd like the bill,' he said in the tone of one who declares to higher authority that he who is about to die salutes thee.

In half a minute the waiter was back. Would Nicholas be so good as to come with him and speak to the maître d'hôtel? Nicholas nodded, dumbfounded. What had happened? What had he done wrong? Annabel was slouching back in her chair, her big eyes half-closed, a trickle of something orange dribbling out of the corner of her mouth. They were going to tell him to remove her, that she had disgraced the place, not to come here again. He followed the waiter, his hands clenched.

A huge man spoke to him, a man with the beak and plumage of a king penguin. 'Your bill has been paid, sir.'

Nicholas stared. 'I don't know what you mean.'

'Your father paid it, sir. Those were my instructions, to tell you your father had settled your bill.'

The relief was tremendous. He seemed to grow tall again and light and free. It was as if someone had made him a present of – well, what would it have been? Sixty pounds? Seventy? And he understood at once. Sorensen had paid his bill and said he was his father. It was a little bit of compensation for what Sorensen had done in dismissing his father. He had paid out sixty pounds to show he meant well, to show that he wanted, in a small way, to make up for injustice.

454

Tall and free and masterful, Nicholas said, 'Call me a cab, please,' and then he went and shook Annabel awake in quite a lordly way.

His euphoria lasted for nearly an hour, long after he had pushed the somnolent Annabel through her own front door, then climbed the stairs up to the furnished room he rented and settled down to the crossword in the evening paper. Things would have turned out very differently if he hadn't started that crossword. 'Twelve across: Bone in mixed byre goes with corruption. (7 letters)' The I and the Y were already in. He got the answer after a few seconds – 'Bribery'. 'Rib' in an anagram of 'byre'. 'Bribery'.

He laid down the paper and looked at the opposite wall. That which goes with corruption. How could he ever have been such a fool, such a naive innocent fool, as to suppose a man like Sorensen cared about injustice or ever gave a thought to wrongful dismissal or even believed for a moment he *could* have been wrong? Of course Sorensen hadn't been trying to make restitution, of course he hadn't paid that bill out of kindness and remorse. He had paid it as a bribe.

He had paid the bribe to shut Nicholas's mouth because he didn't want anyone to know he had been out drinking with a girl, embracing a girl, who wasn't his wife. It was bribery, the bribery that went with corruption.

Once, about three years before, Nicholas had been with his parents to a party Sorensen had given for his staff and Mrs Sorensen had been the hostess. A brown-haired mousey little woman, he remembered her, and all of forty-five which seemed like old age to Nicholas. Sorensen had paid that bill because he didn't want his wife to find out he had a girlfriend young enough to be his daughter.

He had bought him, Nicholas thought, bribed and corrupted him – or tried to. Because he wasn't going to succeed. He needn't think he could kick the Hawthorne family around any more. Once was enough.

It had been nice thinking that he hadn't after all wasted more than half a week's wages on that horrible girl but honour was more important. Honour, surely, meant sacrificing material things for a principle. Nicholas had a bad night because he kept waking up and thinking of all the material things he would have to go short of during the next few weeks on account of his honour. Nevertheless, by the morning his resolve was fixed. Making sure he had his cheque book with him, he went off to work.

Several hours passed before he could get the courage together to

455

phone Sorensen-McGill. What was he going to do if Sorensen refused to see him? If only he had a nice fat bank account with five hundred pounds in it he could make the grand gesture and send Sorensen a blank cheque accompanied by a curt and contemptuous letter.

The telephonist who used to answer in the days when he sometimes phoned his father at work answered now.

'Sorensen-McGill. Can I help you?'

His voice rather hoarse, Nicholas asked if he could have an appointment with Mr Sorensen that day on a matter of urgency. He was put through to Sorensen's secretary. There was a delay. Bells rang and switches clicked. The girl came back to the phone and Nicholas was sure she was going to say no.

'Mr Sorensen asks if one o'clock will suit you?'

In his lunch hour? Of course it would. But what on earth could have induced Sorensen to have sacrificed one of those fat expense account lunches just to see him? Nicholas set off for Berkeley Square, wondering what had made the man so forthcoming. A weak hopeful little voice inside him began once again putting up those arguments which on the previous evening the voice of a common sense had so decisively refuted.

Perhaps Sorensen really meant well and when Nicholas got there would tell him the paying of the bill had been no bribery but a way of making a present to the son of a once-valued employee. The pretty girl could have been Sorensen's daughter. Nicholas had no idea if the man had children. It was possible he had a daughter. No corruption then, no betrayal of his honour, no need to give up cigarettes or abase himself before his landlord.

They knew him at Sorensen-McGill. He had been there with his father and, besides, he looked like his father. The pretty blonde girl hadn't looked in the least like Sorensen. A secretary showed him into the chairman's office. Sorensen was sitting in a yellow leather chair behind a rosewood desk with an inlaid yellow leather top. There were Modigliani-like murals on the wall behind him and on the desk a dark green jade ashtray, stacked with stubs, which the secretary replaced with a clean one of pale green jade.

'Hallo, Nicholas,' said Sorensen. He didn't smile. 'Sit down.'

The only other chair in the room was one of those hi-tech low-slung affairs made of leather hung on a metal frame. Beside it was a black glass coffee table with a black leather padded rim and on the glass lay a magazine open at the centrefold of a nude girl. There are some people who know how to put others at their ease and there are those

456

who know how to put others in difficulties. Nicholas sat down, right down – about three inches from the floor.

Sorensen lit a cigarette. He didn't offer the box. He looked at Nicholas and moved his head slowly from side to side. At last he said:

'I suppose I should have expected this.'

Nicholas opened his mouth to speak but Sorensen held up his hand. 'No, you can have your say in a minute.' His tone became hard and brisk. 'The girl you saw me with last night was someone – not to put too fine a point on it – I picked up in a bar. I have never seen her before, I shall never see her again. She is not, in any sense of the words, a girlfriend or mistress. Wait,' he said as Nicholas again tried to interrupt. 'Let me finish. My wife is not a well woman. Were she to find out where I was last night and whom I was with she would doubtless be very distressed. She would very likely become ill again. I refer, of course, to mental illness, to an emotional sickness, but . . .'

He drew deeply on his cigarette. 'But all this being so and whatever the consequences, I shall not on any account allow myself to be blackmailed. Is that understood? I paid for your dinner last night and that is enough. I do not want my wife told what you saw, but you may tell her and publish it to the world before I pay you another penny.'

At the word blackmail Nicholas's heart had begun to pound. The blood rushed into his face. He had come to vindicate his honour and his motive had been foully misunderstood. In a choked voice he stuttered:

'You've no business – it wasn't – why do you say things like that to me?'

'It's not a nice word, is it? But to call it anything else would merely be semantics. You came, didn't you, to ask for more?'

Nicholas jumped up. 'I came to give you your money back!'

'Aah!' It was a strange sound Sorensen made, old and urbane, cynical yet wondering. He crushed out his cigarette. 'I see. Youth is moralistic. Inexperience is puritanical. You'll tell her anyway because you can't be bought, is that it?'

'No, I can't be bought.' Nicholas was trembling. He put his hands down flat on Sorensen's desk but still they shook. 'I shall never tell anyone what I saw, I promise you that. But I can't let you pay for my dinner – and pretend to be my father!' Tears were pricking the backs of his eyes.

'Oh, sit down, sit down. If you aren't trying to blackmail me and

457

your lips are sealed, what the hell did you come here for? A social call? A man-to-man chat about the ladies you and I took out last night? Your family aren't exactly my favourite companions, you know.'

Nicholas retreated a little. He felt the man's power. It was the power of money and the power that is achieved by always having had money. There was something he hadn't ever before noticed about Sorensen but which he noticed now. Sorensen looked as if he were made of metal, his skin of copper, his hair of silver, his suit of pewter.

And then the mist in Nicholas's eyes stopped him seeing anything but a blur. 'How much was my bill?' he managed to say.

'Oh, for God's sake.'

'How much?'

'Sixty-seven pounds,' said Sorensen, 'give or take a little.' He sounded amused.

To Nicholas it was a small fortune. He got out his cheque book and wrote the cheque to J. Sorensen and passed it across the desk and said, 'There's your money. But you needn't worry. I won't say I saw you. I promise I won't.'

Uttering those words made him feel noble, heroic. The threatening tears receded. Sorensen looked at the cheque and tore it in two.

'You're a very tiresome boy. I don't want you on my premises. Get out.'

Nicholas got out. He walked out of the building with his head in the air. He was still considering sending Sorensen another cheque when, two mornings later, reading his paper in the train, his eye caught the hated name. At first he didn't think the story referred to 'his' Sorensen – and then he knew it did. The headline read: 'Woman Found Dead in Forest. Murder of Tycoon's Wife.'

'The body of a woman,' ran the story beneath,

was found last night in an abandoned car in Hatfield Forest in Hertford-shire. She had been strangled. The woman was today identified as Mrs Winifred Sorensen, 45, of Eaton Place, Belgravia. She was the wife of Julius Sorensen, chairman of Sorensen-McGill, manufacturers of office equipment.

Mrs Sorensen had been staying with her mother, Mrs Mary Clifford, at Mrs Clifford's home in Much Hadham. Mrs Clifford said, 'My daughter had intended to stay with me for a further two days. I was surprised when she said she would drive home to London on Tuesday evening.'

'I was not expecting my wife home on Tuesday,' said Mr Sorensen. 'I had no idea she had left her mother's house until I phoned there yesterday. When I realized she was missing I immediately informed the police.'

Police are treating the case as murder.

That poor woman, thought Nicholas. While she had been driving home to her husband, longing for him probably, needing his company and his comfort, he had been philandering with a girl he had picked up, a girl whose surname he didn't even know. He must now be overcome with remorse. Nicholas hoped it was biting agonized remorse. The contrast was what was so shocking, Sorensen cheek to cheek with that girl, drinking with her, no doubt later sleeping with her; his wife alone, struggling with an attacker in a lonely place in the dark.

Nicholas, of course, wouldn't have been surprised if Sorensen had done it himself. Nothing Sorensen could do would have surprised him. The man was capable of any iniquity. Only this he couldn't have done, which none knew better than Nicholas. So it was a bit of a shock to be accosted by two policemen when he arrived home that evening. They were waiting in a car outside his gate and they got out as he approached.

'Nothing to worry about, Mr Hawthorne,' said the older of them who introduced himself as a Detective Inspector. 'Just a matter of routine. Perhaps you read about the death of Mrs Winifred Sorensen in your paper today?'

'Yes.'

'May we come in?'

They followed him upstairs. What could they want of him? Nicholas sometimes read detective stories and it occurred to him that, knowing perhaps of his tenuous connection with Sorensen-McGill, they would want to ask him questions about Sorensen's character and domestic life. In that case they had come to the right witness.

He could tell them all right. He could tell them why poor Mrs Sorensen, jealous and suspicious as she must have been, had taken it into her head to leave her mother's house two days early and drive home. Because she had intended to catch her husband in the act. And she would have caught him, found him absent or maybe entertaining that girl in their home, only she had never got home. Some maniac had hitched a lift from her first. Oh yes, he'd tell them!

In his room they sat down. They had to sit on the bed for there was only one chair.

459

'It has been established,' said the Inspector, 'that Mrs Sorensen was killed between eight and ten p.m. on Tuesday.'

Nicholas nodded. He could hardly contain his excitement. What a shock it was going to be for them when he told them about this supposedly respectable businessman's private life! A split second later Nicholas was left deflated and staring.

'At nine that evening Mr Julius Sorensen, her husband, was in a restaurant called Potters in Marylebone High Street accompanied by a young lady. He has made a statement to us to that effect.'

Sorensen had told them. He had confessed. The disappointment was acute.

'I believe you were also in the restaurant at that time?' In a small voice Nicholas said, 'Oh yes. Yes, I was.'

'On the following day, Mr Hawthorne, you went to the offices of Sorensen-McGill where a conversation took place between you and Mr Sorensen. Will you tell me what that conversation was about, please?'

'It was about my seeing him in Potters the night before. He wanted me to . . .' Nicholas stopped. He blushed.

'Just a moment, sir. I think I can guess why you're so obviously uneasy about this. If I may say so without giving offence you're a very young man as yet and young people are often a bit confused when it comes to questions of loyalty. Am I right?'

Mystified now, Nicholas nodded.

'Your duty is plain. It's to tell the truth. Will you do that?'

'Yes, of course.'

'Good. Did Mr Sorensen try to bribe you?'

'Yes.' Nicholas took a deep breath. 'I made him a promise.'

'Which must carry no weight, Mr Hawthorne. Let me repeat. Mrs Sorensen was killed between eight and ten. Mr Sorensen has told us he was in Potters at nine, in the bar. The bar staff can't remember him. The surname of the lady he says he was with is unknown to him. According to him you were there and you saw him.' The Inspector glanced at his companion, then back to Nicholas. 'Well, Mr Hawthorne? This is a matter of the utmost seriousness.'

Nicholas understood. Excitement welled in him once more but he didn't show it. They would realize why he hesitated. At last he said:

'I was in Potters from eight till about nine-thirty.' Carefully he kept to the exact truth. 'Mr Sorensen and I discussed my being there and seeing him when I kept my appointment with him in his office on Wednesday and he – he paid the bill for my dinner.'

'I see.' How sharp were the Inspector's eyes! How much he thought he knew of youth and age, wisdom and naivety, innocence and corruption! 'Now then – did you in fact see Mr Sorensen in Potters on Tuesday evening?'

'I can't forget my promise,' said Nicholas.

Of course he couldn't. He had only to keep his promise and the police would charge Sorensen with murder. He looked down. He spoke in a guilty troubled voice.

'I didn't see him. Of course I didn't.'

The Whistler

Jeremy found the key in one of the holiday flats while he was working for Manuel. The flats were being painted throughout in a colour called champagne and so far they hadn't found a machine to do this. Jeremy hoped they wouldn't until the job was done. Manuel was an American citizen though he came from somewhere south of the border – Cuba, Jeremy had always supposed. Jeremy himself came from somewhere a long way north of the border, England in fact, and he had been feeling his way around the United States for a couple of years now, always hoping for his luck to change. The key, he thought, might be a piece of luck.

It was up in a corner of the bedroom windowsill, under the blind. Manuel was in the living room, whistling country music. He whistled all the time he was working, never anything Spanish, always Western or country stuff, and he never played the radio which Jeremy would have preferred. The key had a label tied on its head with a piece of string. On the label an address was written. Jeremy started to say, or thought of saying, 'Hey, Manuel, look at this . . .' and then checked himself. The whistling went on unbroken. Whatever might be on offer at the address on the key label, did he want to have to share it with Manuel? Or, worse, did he want Manuel to take the key off him?

Finding things in the flats wasn't unusual. People were very careless. They rented these flats at Juanillo Beach for a couple of weeks in the high season and went off home to New Jersey or Moscow, Idaho, or wherever it might be, leaving their jewellery behind and their cameras, not to mention such trifles as books and tapes and so on. The company who owned the property were supposed to come in and check before Manuel started but they didn't make much of a job of it. Jeremy had found a roll of banknotes, over eighty dollars, in a kitchen unit, and in a gap between tiled floor and wall, a diamond ring. A jeweller in downtown Miami had given him $250 for the ring and that was probably a fraction of its value. It had been a mistake telling Manuel about it. Manuel hadn't cared about the banknotes but he had jibbed at the ring. It wasn't that he was more honest than the next man, but he had this contract with Juanillo Beach Properties Inc. and he didn't want to lose it. At any rate he had warned Jeremy off helping himself to anything he found in the flats – which was enough in itself to make Jeremy pick up the key and put it in the pocket of his jeans. In the next room the whistling continued, becoming very rollicking and Rocky Mountain.

It was starting to get hot and the air conditioning had broken down. Or Juanillo Beach Properties had taken the fuse out, Jeremy thought. He wouldn't put it past them. By noon it would be up in the nineties. Well, it was for the climate he'd come down here and for the climate he stayed. It is easier to be poor in a warm climate. He thought of England with horror, of being deported and having to go back there as his worst nightmare. It couldn't really be like that, it wasn't, but he remembered his native land as green and cold, full of rich elderly people who had log fires going all the year round, a land of joblessness and privilege where, though he had been born there, he had never felt welcome. Now the blind was up he could see the subtropical garden in which the apartment block was, palms and citrus and Indian paintbrush and oleander and here and there the sliced spear leaves of a banana. Yellow and black striped zebra butterflies flitted among the thick shiny leaves. And the sun blazed from a clear blue sky. It suited him here, or would if he had a bit of money.

In London he had had a very small room, for which he paid £25 a week, and had shared bathroom and kitchen two floors down with four other tenants. Here he had a motel room with bath – well, shower – for less than that. And he didn't need a kitchen because eating out was cheap. But sometimes he thought he'd come to the United States too late to seek his fortune, maybe fifty years too late. That was what Josh who owned the motel said. Josh didn't know he was there illegally of course. Or if he did he didn't say.

After work he and Josh sometimes had a beer together on the porch at the rear of the motel office building. The motel was in a rough area and was pretty shabby but if there was one thing Josh kept in repair it was the screens round that porch. All the mosquitos of the diaspora came down there, Josh said, driven out of more prosperous parts.

Jeremy remembered the address on the key. 'Where's Eleventh Avenue?'

There were two more cans of Coors on the table, sweating icy drops, and a bag of toasted pecans. A little brown lizard ran up the screen on the outside.

'What d'you mean, Eleventh Avenue? Eleventh Avenue where?'

'Miami.'

'There's not so many cities in this country you'll find the avenues numbered. Streets, yes. Why? What d'you ask for?' He didn't wait for an answer. 'Take LA, take Philly – they don't have numbered avenues.'

'New York has.'

'New York's different,' said Josh which was something Americans always said, Jeremy had noticed.

'So how about Miami?'

'Sure Miami's got an Eleventh Avenue. Downtown. There's a street plan in the office.'

Jeremy had a look at it. The address on the key was 1562A Ave. 11. No city, no state. The label was rather smudged and there had been more of the address there, a couple of capital letters, in fact. The second letter was certainly a J or a Y. Y for York? J for Juanillo? He knew without enquiring that there was no First Avenue in Juanillo, let alone Eleventh. Come to that, could he be sure the writer had meant Eleventh Avenue? Ave. 11 was a funny way of putting it, more a European way, except that Europeans don't number their streets much.

It wasn't likely to be Miami. People from Miami wouldn't rent a flat at Juanillo Beach. But he could try. Burglary would be so simple, scarcely dishonest even, when you didn't have to break in. That evening he was going to eat out with Manuel and Lupe in a Thai restaurant out in posh Fort Cayne where Manuel lived. But first he'd make a little trip downtown and try the key on the front door of 1562A Eleventh Avenue.

The place wasn't guarded, all was quiet. He rang the bell, waited, rang again, tried the key. It didn't fit. In the taxi going out to Fort Cayne he thought about what Josh had said about not many American cities having numbered avenues. Of course Josh might be wrong, he had only named three cities . . . Wasn't it more probable anyway that the key opened an apartment in New York? What was Eleventh Avenue, New York, like and how far uptown would 1562A be? If it was 1562 Fifth they were talking about he'd have some idea. He imagined a gorgeous New York apartment full of treasures waiting for someone to walk in and take them. The trouble was that the fare to New York was something around $300 round trip.

464

The restaurant was called the Phumiphol and it was in one of those glossy malls. Jeremy got there first and ordered a vodka on the rocks. Put it on the check, please. It was going to be a bit awkward meeting Lupe again. Nothing he couldn't handle, of course, but he did need that vodka.

Her real name was Guadelupe or Maria del Guadelupe or some such thing and she was an illegal immigrant like him. A small dark beautiful girl with the huge eyes and symmetrical features of those Mexican film stars of thirties Hollywood. She resembled a photograph he had seen of Dolores del Rio. Manuel was going to marry her and she too would become an American, as much a citizen as the President's wife or a Daughter of the American Revolution.

The vodka came and a little dish of something that looked like salted beetles but couldn't be. Jeremy had first met Lupe in Manuel's apartment. Not that she lived there with him. Manuel was very strict and very Spanish about that sort of thing. His affianced wife had to be a virgin and manifestly seen by all the world to be a virgin.

Oddly enough, Lupe had been. Jeremy had never actually come across one before. She lived in a room in a Cuban lady's house and every day she came to clean Manuel's apartment for him and iron his shirts. Manuel put his shirts through the washer himself but Lupe ironed them. Wherever she came from she didn't want to go back there and that, Jeremy had been sure, was why she was waiting on and obeying Manuel in the hope of marrying him. Manuel was an ugly devil, very thin and somehow spiderlike with a pockmarked hatchet face while Jeremy was tall, blond and good-looking which was partly, no doubt, why Lupe had fallen in love with him.

Or whatever you called it. At any rate she hadn't resisted much. Manuel had had to go home because his father was dying. He died before Manuel got there, so he was only away two days but that was enough. Jeremy and Lupe were making love in the apartment at Hacienda Alameda before Manuel got on the plane. Lupe's virginity was a surprise and bit daunting but after the third or fourth time it was all the same as if it had been gone five years.

The trouble was that they couldn't stop and at last Manuel found out. One stupid afternoon when Jeremy had the day off and Lupe was cleaning the apartment they forgot discretion and succumbed. They might so easily have gone to the motel, he thought afterwards. Manuel didn't find them, nothing so crude as that, he found a blond hair and a long chestnut wavy hair on the pillow where only a black-haired man slept.

Jeremy was finishing off his vodka when Manuel and Lupe came in. Manuel looked cheerful and pleased with himself, talking about the holiday he would take away from Florida when the really hot weather started. Make it a honeymoon, was what Jeremy would have said a few months back. They say Alaska's a great place in the summer. Something stopped him saying it now. Manuel hadn't mentioned marriage since that night.

They had some transparent soup with flowers floating in it. A jar of sake and a bottle of Perrier water. Neither Manuel nor Lupe drank much. Then came little pancakes, shredded vegetables, perfumed duck. It was all as if dolls had cooked it. Lupe ate daintily, chewing every mouthful twenty times, keeping her head bent.

'I want to act like a civilized man,' Manuel had said, and pathetically, Jeremy thought, 'Like an American gentleman.' He looked ridiculous when he was unhappy, a black crow with mud on its feathers. 'My ancestors would have killed you and her too.'

Jeremy had cast up his eyes at that. Oh, Christ . . .

'Times have changed. With me it will be as if it had never happened.' Manuel looked at Lupe. 'But it must never happen again.'

'It won't happen again,' said Lupe.

'Of course not.' Jeremy didn't want her any more anyway. All this fuss was enough to put one off more desirable women than Lupe Garcia.

'Then you stay working for me,' Manuel said to Jeremy, 'and bygones shall be bygones.' He smiled. He insisted on shaking Jeremy's hand. Then he went to the kitchen to open a bottle of wine, whistling 'The Tennessee Waltz' as he went. An apposite if tactless choice, Jeremy thought, but perhaps Manuel didn't know the words. Lupe tried to catch his eyes but Jeremy wouldn't look.

That had been two months ago and this was the first time since then that he had seen Lupe. It was archaic the feeling the whole set-up gave him that by that one initial act, let alone the others, he had spoiled her for Manuel, she was damaged goods. She had grown more subdued. She didn't look unhappy. They ate little cakes of dough in syrup sauce.

Manuel had his car, though he lived only round the corner. Jeremy was asked back for coffee. He went to the bathroom and saw unmistakable signs of Lupe's occupancy, a jar of skinfood, an eyeliner, a bottle of the cologne she used. It hadn't taken long for Manuel's

466

principles to break down, Jeremy thought with a quiet laugh to himself.

'Yes, I've moved in,' she said to him.

He looked at her hand and she saw him looking. Not even an engagement ring.

Manuel drove him home. He had just taken delivery of this year's new car. Jeremy often wondered where the money came from. You didn't own a condominium at prestigious Hacienda Alameda and have a new car every year and fly home to see your family every couple of months out of painting ceilings. It was no business of his. He'd be moving on soon anyway. Maybe to California when he could raise the fare.

The coconut palms round Josh's Motel hummed with tree frogs as if they themselves were sensate things, an unbroken droning that twitched at the nerves. They kept Jeremy awake. He could go to New York instead and try out that key. There were two letters on that label after Ave. 11 and one of them could be a Y. Perhaps there were only two cities in the United States with numbered avenues – and perhaps there were dozens.

A couple of days later he and Manuel moved on into the next apartment. It was the same as the one they had finished except that no one had left a key on the window sill. Manuel was whistling away in the next room, a song about the sunflowers of Kansas. He had taken off the fancy pale blue blouson he had been wearing and slung it down over the side of the bath. There was nowhere else to put it. Jeremy felt in the pockets. He had done this before when times were hard and hauled himself fifty bucks. Manuel was too careless about money to notice. The whistling continued, only the tune changing and going south to become 'The Yellow Rose of Texas'. Jeremy pulled out a wad of notes, all of them twenties, a lot of money.

He couldn't just pocket it, that was no good. He looked about him, thinking quickly. The bath plug was the metal kind, operated by a lever underneath the taps but nevertheless removable. Jeremy removed it and carefully poked the roll of notes inside. The roll expanded a little to fit the hole as he had known it would. He put the plug back.

Manuel or he usually went out at lunchtime and fetched back a couple of Whoppers, onion rings and two Cokes. It was Manuel who always paid. Cutting off the whistling, he went to the bathroom for his jacket and the six or seven dollars Jeremy would need at Burger

King. This time he wasn't quite so philosophical about the loss of his money.

'I know you're not accusing me,' Jeremy said. 'I know you wouldn't do that, but for my own sake I'd like to show you.'

He pulled the empty pockets out of his jeans, stripped off his shirt, kicked off his shoes, handed Manuel his own denim jacket with just $8 in the pocket.

'I don't know how much you had on you, Manuel, but you were swinging that thing around when we got in the car at my place. It's a rough old area round Josh's . . .'

'And finding's keepings, eh?' Manuel used a lot of quaint old English expressions that sounded crazy uttered in his Spanish accent. 'There's worse things happen at sea,' he said. 'But you must pay for the lunch.' He laughed and patted Jeremy on the back.

Jeremy hooked the notes out of the plughole before he went home. There were sixteen of them, more than enough to get to New York on. But suppose the place the key opened wasn't in New York? He'd have wasted all that money. It was an expensive looking key, a *classy* key, he thought, shinier, heavier, more trimly cut, than the keys that opened Hacienda Alameda . . .

Manuel went off home the following week and Lupe was alone. There was no way Jeremy was going to get himself involved with her again. He intended to avoid Fort Cayne altogether for the four days Manuel was gone.

She came to him. He was sitting out on the porch with Josh when she drove on to the parking lot in Manuel's new car. There was something uncertain and vulnerable in the way she drove, the way she parked. She had the lowest self-image of anyone Jeremy knew. Because she thought of herself as dirt people treated her like it, though physically she was obsessively clean, had two showers or baths every day. It was Oriental not Latin girls that had been compared to little flowers but Lupe reminded one of a flower, a hibiscus maybe.

'I should be so lucky,' said Josh.

'Help yourself.' Jeremy shrugged. Lupe had opened the screen door and was coming hesitantly up the steps. 'There's a new rule here,' he said to her. 'No members of the opposite sex in guests' rooms after sunset,' and he laughed at his own wit.

Her face grew hot. Josh who usually had a great sense of humour didn't laugh for some reason but asked her to sit down and how about a drink on the house? Lupe said quietly that she'd have a Coke if there was one. Josh brought the Coke and asked where Manuel was. He had once or twice met Manuel.

'San José,' said Lupe.

That did surprise Jeremy. 'His mum lives in California? I never knew that.'

'Not California, Costa Rica,' Josh said. 'Isn't that right? The capital of Costa Rica?'

She nodded. Jeremy barely knew where Costa Rica was and cared less. Josh said he'd never been there but he'd heard it didn't have an army and it was the only real democracy in Central America. Lupe hadn't been there either. Nicaragua was where she came from. They were actually having a conversation. Let's keep it that way, Jeremy thought.

He didn't know if she was devoted to Manuel or only to his money and his citizenship. Whichever it was, she talked about him all the time. He was a devoted son to his mother, he'd bought her a house in the best residential suburb of San José. Lupe had photographs which she proceeded to show them of a bungalow covered in bougainvillea with gilded bars on its windows.

Jeremy looked at the photographs which had been done by a professional whose address was stamped on the back. Ave. 2, it said, San José, Costa Rica.

From a bookshop in downtown Miami he managed to get a street plan of San José. It was a city in which the streets or *calles* were numbered and so were the avenues or *avenidas*. 'Ave.', of course, could be short for *avenida* as well as avenue. A grid-plan city more or less, with the avenues running east to west and the *calles* north to south. At Juanillo Beach Properties they told him that one of the apartments had last been occupied by a couple from Costa Rica. A lot of Costa Ricans came to Florida for a week or a few days. Shopping was cheaper and better here. Electrical goods, for instance, were half the price they were in San José. But no, they couldn't give him the address. If he had found something in the flat let them have it and they'd send it on. Jeremy handed over a couple of rolls of film he'd bought just now at Gray Drug. The Juanillo Beach Properties girl looked at him as if he was out of his mind.

The travel agent he went to could get him a three-day package to San José for a lot less than he'd nicked off Manuel. Manuel was back by now and they were on the last apartment in the block. When

Jeremy said he'd like next week off Manuel didn't put up any objections and seemed interested when he said he was going to New York. He smiled and patted Jeremy's shoulder and said something about the Big Apple and in a funny old-fashioned phrase, not to do anything he, Manuel, wouldn't do. Then he took a clean brush and the bucket of emulsion and went off into the bedroom whistling that song about a boy called Sue.

Jeremy got there in the late afternoon. There were more Costa Ricans than Americans on the flight and when the captain announced they were beginning their descent for San José they all clapped and cheered and drummed their feet. Evidently they were a patriotic lot. A bus the tour company had laid on took him into the city. It was four thousand feet up and cooler than Florida though a lot nearer the equator. There was a view of blue mountains behind coffee plantations and banana groves and the whole was dotted with flame-of-the-forest trees like points of fire. Jeremy had seen a bit of the Third World one way and another and immediately outside the city he expected to see the shantytowns of poverty, the huts made of tin and sacks and plastic bags, the rubbish tips and flies. Poverty didn't bother him, he never thought about it, but here in a kind of subconscious way he expected to see it just as in his native land he expected rain and Tudor mansions, but there was none to be seen. Only neat stucco bungalows and little houses like on an English council estate.

In case the plan had lied it was a comfort to see the *avenidas*. The Hotel Latinoamericana was on Avenida Central and if it wasn't exactly the Hilton it was the best hotel Jeremy had ever stayed in and about five stars up on Josh's. The dark came down at six o'clock. Carmen the tour guide had warned them about pickpockets in the city where thieves abounded. Jeremy thought he would have an early night. San José did anyway, the hotel bar closing at ten sharp.

In the morning he swam in the hotel pool. The water was icy. Outside in the Avenida Central the atmosphere was thick and stinking with petrol fumes. He walked downtown a bit but the pollution which hung as blue smog and obscured the mountains made him cough. Another thing Carmen had said was that if you took a taxi you should settle the fare with the driver first. Jeremy found a taxi and haggled a bit but he had no Spanish and the driver hardly any English and when he had seated himself in the back he was fairly certain he'd be ripped off. The driver was going to take him on a city tour.

First they went to that suburb on the road to Irazu where the finest houses were and the foreign embassies. It wasn't Avenida 11 nor was Manuel's mother's house to be seen. The driver pointed out places of interest that Jeremy wasn't interested in. He showed him the university and the museum of art and then, not far from the children's hospital, Jeremy did see a bungalow very like Manuel's mother's, perhaps indeed the very one, with orange bougainvillea swarming all over it, a golden grille to keep out the burglars and a little white dog peering out of one of the windows. At one point they actually drove along Avenida 11 but nowhere near number 1562. It wasn't far from the Latinoamericana though, he could easily walk there.

After dark? That might be best. Or should he watch the house or flat or whatever it was for the occupants to go out? He remembered that after all he had only two days. He paid the taxi driver – twice, it seemed to him, what they had fixed on – and walked up the Calle Central to Avenida 11. There were two branches of it, the street being broken rather ominously by the Central Prison.

When he found the house he was deeply disappointed. It wasn't even up to the standard of Manuel's mother's place, far below it in fact. He thought of where his parents lived in London, in North Finchley. This bungalow, standing alone on the side of the road, might itself have been in North Finchley but for the two palm trees in front of it and the thorn hedge with red flowers which divided it from the abandoned lot stacked with empty oil drums next door.

Lace curtains, none too clean, hung at all the windows. The paint was faded. It looked unoccupied but he didn't dare try the key. He walked across the oil drum lot and looked round the back. Everything shut up. An empty dog kennel and a broken rusty dog chain.

He found a McDonald's and lunched there. The unaccustomed high altitude was tiring and after a few drinks in the hotel bar he slept. By six-thirty it was quite dark. He walked up the Calle Central on to Avenida 11 and back to the bungalow. It was in darkness, not a light on in the place. The traffic was beginning to thin and with it the smog so that it was possible now to see the stars and a wire-thin curve of moon. He stood on the opposite side of the street and watched the house. For a quarter of an hour he did that. He went round the back across the oil drum lot and looked round the rear. Nothing. No one. Darkness. There were fewer people on the street now. He walked away, as far as the zoo, back again along a nearly deserted street, breathing clean fresh air. The house looked just the same. He took the key out of his pocket, walked up to the front door and inserted it in the lock. The door opened easily.

471

He closed it behind him and stood in the small square hall. The place smelt dusty, stuffy, breath-catching as places do that have been shut up a long time in a warm dry climate. Not only was it unoccupied now, it had been unoccupied for months. A little light came in from the street but not enough. Jeremy switched on his torch. He pushed open a door and found himself in a bedroom, insufferably stuffy, smelling of camphor. By the marks on the walls he could see that pieces of furniture had been removed from it and only the big bed with carved mahogany headboard and white lace cover remained. The bungalow was a sizable house, much bigger than it seemed from outside. There were two more bedrooms, one empty of furniture. Either the traffic on Avenida 11 had ceased or you couldn't hear it in here. He moved through the rooms in dim musty silence, directing the torch beam across walls and floors.

The front room or parlour was also half-furnished. There had been a piano or chest of drawers up against one wall. Shabby wooden-armed chairs stood around. The wallpaper was stained and yellow, imprinted with small paler rectangles where framed photographs had once hung. One still remained, hanging crookedly, a family group.

There was nothing worth taking. The most valuable thing was probably the hand-crocheted lace bed cover which, when he looked at it again, turned out to be scored by the depredations of moths. He returned to the living room. There was a drawer in the table which he didn't expect to contain the family silver or wads of whatever they called their currency, *colones*, but he might as well look. It didn't. He was right. The drawer had two paper table napkins in it and a United States ten cent piece, a dime. Closing the drawer, he raised the beam of the torch and it fell on the single framed photograph. Something made Jeremy look more closely, bringing the light right up to the glass.

He gasped as if a hand had fallen on his shoulder. The picture was of an old wrinkle-faced man and a stout old woman with three young men standing behind them, one of them spidery thin, very dark, sharp-featured. Jeremy looked and shut his eyes and looked again. He thought, I have to get out of here and fast. It may be too late. There may be someone in the house now, he may have been here all the time, one of those brothers . . .

He put out the torch. He listened. There was only the dark dusty silence. He went out into the hall, his heart beating quickly, sweat standing on his forehead. When he opened the front door . . . But he

472

dared not open it. A window? The back way was obviously the worst idea. It was dark, desolate, empty at the rear. Though Avenida 11 seemed deserted the front door was still his best bet. He ought to have a weapon. A poker? It was never cold enough in this country to have a fire. He groped his way into the kitchen, opened the door and yelled aloud, clamping his hand too late over his mouth.

Something tall and thin was standing in an embrasure of the wall between sink and cupboard. He didn't know what he'd imagined but when he shone the torch on it he saw it was a six-foot-tall houseplant in a tub, dried-up, brown, dead. There was a piece of iron pipe with a tap on it lying on the draining board. Jeremy took it with him.

Gripping his weapon in his right hand, he opened the front door with his left. There was no one there, no sound, no still or moving shadow. A car with only side lights on cruised slowly down Avenida 11 and turned into a side street. The ten minutes it took Jeremy to get out of the neighbourhood and find a taxi were some of the worst he had ever spent. He knew one of Manuel's brothers had to be lying in wait for him in a doorway or else following him until he reached a totally dark and secluded part of the road.

The house he had been in had obviously once been the home of Manuel's parents. It was probably now up for sale. Manuel had of course moved his mother somewhere more plush. Jeremy could see it all, how he had been led here, but he didn't let himself think too much about the ins and outs of it until at last a taxi came and he was safely in it. No haggling about fares this time.

Why had Manuel done it? Because Jeremy had stolen $320 from him, no doubt. Anyway, it hadn't come off. Perhaps he had gone to the house in Avenida 11 earlier or later than they'd expected or one of those brothers had got the date wrong. Or it might even be that Manuel's desire to get his own back would be satisfied by Jeremy's disappointment at finding nothing to steal in the house. For Manuel might only be hoaxing him, merely playing a *joke*.

Jeremy felt relieved at this idea. If Manuel's aim had simply been to teach him a lesson – well, that was OK with him. He'd been taught a lesson. If he ever saw another key lying about he'd leave it where it was. But his fear was ebbing with every turn the taxi took to bring him nearer the Latinoamericana. It was all right, he was safe now, he could even see the funny side of it – the irony of getting nothing out of the burgled house but an old iron tap.

At the desk he asked for his key. The reception clerk said Jeremy hadn't handed it in, so Jeremy felt in his pockets but it wasn't there.

He had a hollow feeling first that he had had the key and his pocket had been picked, then that someone must have come into the hotel while he was out and taken the key from the pigeon-hole. It could very easily be done by reaching across the end of the counter while the clerk had his back turned or was attending to another guest.

The clerk found a second key to his room and sent the wizened old bellboy up with him. The door was locked. The bellboy bent over and picked something up from the floor, something that had been half-hidden by the bottom of the door.

'Here is your key, señor.'

Jeremy was beginning to hate the sight of keys. He sent the man away. Was it possible he had dropped the key there himself? As soon as he was inside he knew there was no question of that. The room had been turned upside down. What he had planned to do, he thought, they had done to him. He sat down in the wicker chair and surveyed the mess. His bedding was in a heap, the mattress doubled over and half on the floor. All the drawers in the dressing table-cum-writing desk had been pulled out. He hadn't brought much luggage with him, a zipper bag only, but they had taken everything out of it and strewn the contents, spare pair of jeans, sweat shirt, sponge bag, half-bottle of duty-free Kahlua, across the floor. But nothing had been damaged or destroyed. There was nothing missing – or was there?

An empty envelope lay half under the sweat shirt. Jeremy read what was written on it and remembered. 'Fond thoughts from Lupe.' He had told her that wasn't the way to write it. You should say 'love from' or 'best wishes from'. Inside had been a cassette of Latin-American love songs, awful stuff he'd never even bothered to take out of the zipper bag he'd had with him that weekend at Hacienda Alameda . . .

And obviously he never had taken it out. He had repacked the bag with the cassette – wrapped in red tissue paper, he recalled, sealed in this envelope – still inside. Well, if it was that tape they wanted they were welcome to it. But why should they want it? Jeremy hauled the mattress back on to the bed. He felt horribly uneasy, his hands shook and a muscle twitched in his forehead. He could have done with a drink but the bar closed at ten and it was past that. He pulled the stopper off the Kahlua bottle and then thought: suppose they put something in it?

Had the whole exercise been mounted simply to get back a tape Lupe had given him? No, of course not. It wasn't being done because

474

he'd stolen the $320 either, he saw that now. It was because he'd stolen Lupe. Manuel had probably *meant* him to steal the money, had indeed set it up. It wasn't normal for a man, however well off, to be quite so careless with cash as that or so indifferent to its loss . . .

Jeremy was too frightened now not to drink the Kahlua. It enabled him to get some sleep. First, though, he pulled the heavy writing desk across the door. A sound he thought came from in the room awakened him and he jumped up with a cry, but it wasn't in the room, it was outside in the corridor, the people next door coming in late. A Kahlua hangover began to bash his head. He had no aspirin and dared not leave the room to go and ask for some.

Thank God he was going back to Miami today. He didn't leave the hotel. He breakfasted in the dining room, despite the cost, and sat for the rest of the morning on the leather settee facing reception and reading one of the few books in English the Latinoamericana had, a James M. Cain paperback. Nothing untoward happened. He jumped out of his skin when a voice uttered his name into his ear. It was only Carmen, the tour guide.

'The bus for the international airport is going thirteen hundred hours. Have a nice day!'

Could he go back and work for Manuel again? The chances were Manuel wouldn't say a word, would want bygones to be bygones, in his own phrase. Jeremy thought he'd work for him just long enough to get the fare together for California . . . It was a long three hours before the bus came. He'd finished *The Postman Always Rings Twice* and was reduced to reading travel brochures. He didn't bother with lunch. It was only something else that cost money.

Nobody drummed feet or clapped when the aircraft began its descent for Miami. But Jeremy felt a lightening of his heart. For one thing, Immigration would doubtless allow him a further six months' stay in the United States. His last six months' allowance had long since expired but he'd torn the slip out of his passport and would say it had fallen out and got lost. That was a trick he'd used successfully coming over the border from Mexico once before. Feeling you were legal even for a little while gave you a sense of security.

He walked into Customs. They tended to search young people coming in after a short stay in Central or South America. Josh had told him. So he wasn't concerned when the Customs man took everything out of the zipper bag and only mildly surprised at the close examination his sponge bag was subjected to.

There was a split in the bottom seam. The Customs man put his fingers through, then his whole hand, and drew out from between cover and lining a package wrapped in red tissue paper. The red tissue, which he'd last seen round Lupe's cassette, unfolded to reveal its contents, a fine white crystalline powder.

Jeremy had never seen it before but he knew what it was. He thought briefly of the annual new car, of Hacienda Alameda, and then he thought of himself and how he need not worry about his stay in the United States being curtailed. He would be there a long time.

The Convolvulus Clock

'Is that your own hair, dear?'

Sibyl only laughed. She made a roguish face.

'I didn't think it could be,' said Trixie. 'It looks so thick.'

'A woman came up to me in the street the other day,' said Sibyl, 'and asked me where I had my hair set. I just looked at her. I gave a tiny little tip to my wig like this. You should have seen her face.'

She gave another roar of laughter. Trixie smiled austerely. She had come to stay with Sibyl for a week and this was her first evening. Sibyl had bought a cottage in Devonshire. It was two years since Trixie had seen Sibyl and she could detect signs of deterioration. What a pity that was! Sibyl enquired after the welfare of the friends they had in common. How was Mivvy? Did Trixie see anything of the Fishers? How was Poppy?

'Poppy is beginning to go a bit funny,' said Trixie.

'How do you mean, "funny"?'

'You know. Funny. Not quite *compos mentis* any more.'

Sibyl of all people ought to know what going funny meant, thought Trixie.

'We're none of us getting any younger,' said Sibyl, laughing.

Trixie didn't sleep very well. She got up at five and had her bath so as to leave the bathroom clear for Sibyl. At seven she took Sibyl a cup of tea. She gave a little scream and nearly dropped the tray.

'Oh my conscience! I'm sorry, dear, but I thought that was a squirrel on your chest of drawers. I thought it must have come in through the window.'

'What on earth was that noise in the middle of the night?' When Sibyl wasn't laughing she could be downright peevish. She looked a hundred without her wig. 'It woke me up, I thought the tank was overflowing.'

'The middle of the night! I like that. The sun had been up a good hour, I'm sure. I was just having my bath so as not to be a nuisance.'

They went out in Sibyl's car. They had lunch in Dawlish and tea in Exmouth. The following day they went out early and drove across Dartmoor. When they got back there was a letter on the mat for Trixie from Mivvy, though Trixie had only been away two days. On Friday Sibyl said they would stay at home and have a potter about the village. The church was famous, the Manor House gardens were open to the public and there was an interesting small gallery where an exhibition was on. She started to get the car out but Trixie said why couldn't they walk. It could hardly be more than a mile. Sibyl said it was just under two miles but she agreed to walk if Trixie really wanted to. Her knee hadn't been troubling her quite so much lately.

'The gallery is called Artifacts,' said Sibyl. 'It's run by a very nice young couple.'

'A husband and wife team?' asked Trixie, very modern.

'Jimmy and Judy they're called. I don't think they are actually married.'

'Oh my conscience, Sibyl, how can one be "actually" married? Surely one is either married or not?' Trixie herself had been married once, long ago, for a short time. Sibyl had never been married and neither had Mivvy or Poppy. Trixie thought that might have something to do with their going funny. 'Thankfully, I'm broadminded. I shan't say anything. I think I can see a seat ahead in that bus shelter. Would you like a little sit-down before we go on?'

Sibyl got her breath back and they walked on more slowly. The road passed between high hedges on high banks dense with wild flowers. It crossed a stream by a hump-backed bridge where the clear brown shallow water rippled over a bed of stones. The church appeared with granite nave and tower, standing on an eminence and approached, Sibyl said, by fifty-three steps. Perhaps they should go to Artifacts first?

The gallery was housed in an ancient building with bow windows and a front door set under a Georgian portico. When the door was pushed open a bell tinkled to summon Jimmy or Judy. This morning, however, they needed no summoning for both were in the first room, Judy dusting the dolls' house and Jimmy doing something to the ceiling spotlights. Sibyl introduced Trixie to them and Trixie was very gracious towards Judy, making no difference in her manner than she would have if the young woman had been properly married and worn a wedding ring.

Trixie was agreeably surprised by the objects in the exhibition and by the items Jimmy and Judy had for sale. She had not expected such a high standard. What she admired most particularly were the small pictures of domestic interiors done in embroidery, the patchwork quilts and the blown glass vases in colours of mother-of-pearl and butterfly wings. What she liked best of all and wanted to have was a clock.

There were four of these clocks, all different. The cases were ceramic, plain and smooth or made in a trellis work, glazed in blues and greens, painted with flowers or the moon and stars, each incorporating a gilt-rimmed face and quartz movement. Trixie's favourite was blue with a green trellis over the blue, a convolvulus plant with green leaves and pale pink trumpet flowers climbing the trellis and a gilt rim round the face of the clock which had hands of gilt and blue. The convolvulus reminded her of the pattern on her best china tea service. All the clocks had price cards beside them and red discs stuck to the cards.

'I should like to buy this clock,' Trixie said to Judy.

'I'm terribly sorry but it's sold.'

'Sold?'

'All the clocks were sold at the private view. Roland Elm's work is tremendously popular. He can't make enough of these clocks and he refuses to take orders.'

'I still don't understand why I can't buy this one,' said Trixie. 'This is a shop, isn't it?'

Sibyl had put on her peevish look. 'You can see the red sticker, can't you? You know what that means.'

'I know what it means at the Royal Academy but hardly here surely.'

'I really do wish I could sell it to you,' said Judy, 'but I can't.'

Trixie lifted her shoulders. She was very disappointed and wished she hadn't come. She had been going to buy Sibyl a pear carved from polished pear wood but now she thought better of it. The church also was a let-down, dark, poky and smelling of mould.

'Things have come to a pretty pass when shopkeepers won't sell their goods to you because they're upset by your manner.'

'Judy wasn't upset by your manner,' said Sibyl, puffing. 'It's more than her reputation is worth to sell you something she's already sold.'

'Reputation! I like that.'

'I mean reputation as a gallery owner. Artifacts is quite highly regarded round here.'

'You would have thought she and her — well, partner, would be glad of £62. I don't suppose they have two half-pennies to bless themselves with.'

479

What Sibyl would have thought was never known for she was too out of breath to utter and when they got home had to lie down. Next morning another letter came from Mivvy.

'Nothing to say for herself of course,' said Trixie at breakfast. 'Practically a carbon copy of Thursday's. She's going very funny. Do you know she told me sometimes she writes fifty letters in a week? God bless your pocket, I said. It's fortunate you can afford it.'

They went to Princetown in Sibyl's car and Widecombe-in-the-Moor. Trixie sent postcards to Mivvy, Poppy, the Fishers and the woman who came in to clean and water the plants in the greenhouse. She would have to buy some sort of present for Sibyl before she left. A plant would have done, only Sibyl didn't like gardening. They went to a bird sanctuary and looked at some standing stones of great antiquity. Trixie was going home on Tuesday afternoon. On Tuesday morning another letter arrived from Mivvy all about the Fishers going to see the Queen Mother open a new arts centre in Leighton Buzzard. The Fishers were crazy about the Queen Mother, watched for her engagements in advance and went wherever she went within a radius of 150 miles in order just to catch a glimpse of her. Once they had been at the front of the crowd and the Queen Mother had shaken hands with Dorothy Fisher.

'We're none of us getting any younger,' said Sibyl, giggling.

'Well, my conscience, I know one thing,' said Trixie. 'The days have simply flown past while I've been here.'

'I'm glad you've enjoyed yourself.'

'Oh, I have, dear, only it would please me to see you a little less frail.'

Trixie walked to the village on her own. Since she couldn't think of anything else she was going to have to buy the pear-wood pear for Sibyl. It was a warm sunny morning, one of the best days she'd had, and the front door of Artifacts stood open to the street. The exhibition was still on and the clocks (and their red 'sold' discs) still there. A shaft of sunlight streamed across the patchwork quilts on to the Georgian dolls' house. There was no sign of Jimmy and Judy. The gallery was empty but for herself.

Trixie closed the door and opened it to make the bell ring. She picked up one of the pear-wood pears and held it out in front of her on the palm of her hand. She held it at arm's length the way she did when she had helped herself to an item in the supermarket just so that there couldn't be the slightest question of anyone suspecting her of shoplifting. No one came. Trixie climbed the stairs, holding the pear-wood pear out in front of her and clearing her throat to attract attention. There was no one upstairs. A blue Persian cat lay sleeping on a shelf between a ginger jar and a mug with an owl on it. Trixie descended. She closed the front door and opened it to make the bell ring. Jimmy and Judy must be a heedless pair, she thought. Anyone could walk in here and steal the lot.

Of course she could just take the pear-wood pear and leave a £5 note to pay for it. It cost £4.75. Why should she make Jimmy and Judy a present of 25p just because they were too idle to serve her? Then she remembered that when she had been here with Sibyl a door at the end of the passage had been open and through that door one could see the garden where there was a display of terracotta pots. It was probable Jimmy and Judy were out there, showing the pots to a customer.

Trixie went through the second room and down the passage. The door to the garden was just ajar and she pushed it open. On the lawn, in a cane chair, Judy lay fast asleep. A ledger had fallen off her lap and lay on the grass alongside a heap of books. Guides to the management of tax they were and some which looked like the gallery account books. It reminded Trixie of Poppy who was always falling asleep in the daytime, most embarrassingly sometimes, at the table or even while waiting for a bus. Judy had fallen asleep over her book-keeping. Trixie coughed. She said 'Excuse me' very loudly and repeated it but Judy didn't stir.

What a way to run a business! It would serve them right if someone walked in and cleared their shop. It would teach them a lesson. Trixie pulled the door closed behind her. She found herself tiptoeing as she walked back along the passage and through the second room. In the first room she took the ceramic clock with the convolvulus on it off the shelf and put it into her bag and she took the card too with the red sticker on it so as not to attract attention to the clock's absence. The pear-wood pear she replaced among the other carved fruit.

The street outside seemed deserted. Trixie's heart was beating rather fast. She went across the road into the little newsagent's and gift shop and bought Sibyl a teacloth with a map of Devonshire on it. At the door, as she was coming out again, she saw Jimmy coming along the street towards the gallery with a bag of groceries under one arm and two pints of milk in the other. Trixie stayed where she was until he had gone into Artifacts.

She didn't much fancy the walk back but there was no help for it.

When she got to the bridge over the stream she heard hooves behind her and for a second or two had a feeling she was pursued by men on horseback but it was only a girl who passed her, riding a fat white pony. Sibyl laughed when she saw the teacloth and said it was a funny thing to give someone who *lived* in Devonshire. Trixie felt nervous and couldn't eat her lunch. Jimmy and Judy would have missed the clock by now and the newsagent would have remembered a furtive-looking woman skulking in his doorway and described her to them and soon the police would come. If only Sibyl would hurry with the car! She moved so slowly, time had no meaning for her. At this rate Trixie wouldn't even catch her train at Exeter.

She did catch it – just. Sibyl's car had been followed for several miles of the way by police in a Rover with a blue lamp on top and Trixie's heart had been in her mouth. Why had she done it? What had possessed her to take something she hadn't paid for, she who when shopping in supermarkets held 17p pots of yogurt at arm's length?

Now she was safely in the train rushing towards Paddington she began to see things in a different light. She would have paid for that clock if they had let her. What did they expect if they refused to sell things they had on sale? And what *could* they expect if they went to sleep leaving their shop unattended? For a few moments she had a nasty little qualm that the police might be waiting for her outside her own door but they weren't. Inside all was as it should be, all was as she had left it except that Poppy had put a pint of milk in the fridge and someone had arranged dahlias in a vase – not Poppy, she wouldn't know a dahlia from a runner bean.

That would be just the place for the clock, on the wall bracket where at present stood a photograph of herself and Dorothy Fisher at Broadstairs in 1949. Trixie put the photograph away in a drawer and the clock where the photograph had been. It looked nice. It transformed a rather dull corner of the room. Trixie put one of the cups from her tea service beside it and it was amazing how well they matched.

Mivvy came round first thing in the morning. Before letting her in Trixie quickly snatched the clock off the shelf and thrust it inside the drawer with the photograph. It seemed so *exposed* up there, it seemed to tell its history in every tiny tick.

'How did you find Sibyl?'

Trixie wanted to say, I went in the train to Exeter and got out at the station and there was Sibyl waiting for me in her car . . . Only if you started mocking poor Mivvy where would you end? 'Very frail, dear. I thought she was going a bit funny.'

'I must drop her a line.'

Mivvy always spoke as if her letters held curative properties. Receiving one of them would set you up for the winter. After she had gone Trixie considered replacing the clock on the shelf but thought better of it. Let it stay in the drawer for a bit. She had read of South American millionaires who have Old Masters stolen for them which they can never show but are obliged, for fear of discovery, to keep hidden away for ever in dark vaults.

Just before Christmas a letter came from Sibyl. They always sent each other Christmas letters. As Trixie said, if you can't get around to writing the rest of the year, at least you can at Christmas. Mivvy wrote hundreds. Sibyl didn't mention the theft of the clock or indeed mention the gallery at all. Trixie wondered why not. The clock was still in the drawer. Sometimes she lay awake in the night thinking about it, fancying she could hear its tick through the solid mahogany of the drawer, through the ceiling and the bedroom floorboards.

It was curious how she had taken a dislike to the convolvulus tea service. One day she found herself wrapping it in tissue paper and putting it away in the cupboard under the stairs. She took down all the trellis work round the front door and put up wires for the clematis instead. In March she wrote to Sibyl to enquire if there was a new exhibition on at Artifacts. Sibyl didn't answer for weeks. When she did she told Trixie that months and months back one of those ceramic clocks had been stolen from the gallery and a few days later an embroidered picture had also gone and furniture out of the dolls' house. Hadn't Sibyl mentioned it before? She thought she had but she was getting so forgetful these days.

Trixie took the clock out of the drawer and put it on the shelf. Because she knew she couldn't be found out she began to feel she hadn't done anything wrong. The Fishers were bringing Poppy round for a cup of tea. Trixie started unpacking the convolvulus tea service. She lost her nerve when she heard Gordon Fisher's car door slam and she put the clock away again. If she were caught now she might get blamed for the theft of the picture and the dolls' house furniture as well. They would say she had sold those things and how could she prove she hadn't?

Poppy fell asleep halfway through her second buttered scone.

'She gets funnier every time I see her,' Trixie said. 'Sad, really. Sibyl's breaking up too. She'll forget her own name next. You should

483

see her letters. I'll just show you the last one.' She remembered she couldn't do that, it wouldn't be wise, so she had to pretend she'd mislaid it.

'Will you be going down there again this year, dear?' said Dorothy.

'Oh, I expect so. You know how it is, you get to the stage of thinking it may be the last time.'

Poppy woke up with a snort, said she hadn't been asleep and finished her scone.

Gordon asked Trixie, 'Would you like to come with us and see Her Majesty open the new leisure complex in Rayleigh on Monday?'

Trixie declined. The Fishers went off to do their shopping, leaving Poppy behind. She was asleep again. She slept till six and, waking, asked Trixie if she had put something in her tea. It was most unusual, she said, for her to nod off like that. Trixie walked her back to the bus stop because the traffic whipped along there so fast you had to have your wits about you and drivers didn't respect zebra crossings the way they used to. Trixie marched across on the stripes, confident as a lollipop lady but without the lollipop, taking her life in her hands instead.

She wrote to Sibyl that she would come to Devonshire at the end of July, thinking that while there it might be best to make some excuse to avoid going near Artifacts. The clock was still in the drawer but wrapped up now in a piece of old flannel. Trixie had taken a dislike to seeing the colour of it each time she opened the drawer. She had a summer dress that colour and she wondered why she had ever bought it, it didn't flatter her, whatever it might do for the Queen Mother. Dorothy could have it for her next jumble sale.

Walking back from posting a letter, Mivvy fell over and broke her ankle. It was weeks getting back to normal. Well, you had to face it, it was never going to be *normal*. You wouldn't be exaggerating, Trixie wrote to Sibyl, if you said that obsession of hers for writing letters had crippled her for life. Sibyl wrote back to say she was looking forward to the last week of July and what did Trixie think had happened? They had caught the thief of the pieces from Artifacts trying to sell the picture to a dealer in Plymouth. He had said in court he hadn't taken the clock but you could imagine how much credence the magistrate placed on that!

Trixie unwrapped the clock and put it on the shelf. Next day she got the china out. She wondered why she had been so precipitate in pulling all that trellis off the wall, it looked a lot better than strands of wire on metal hooks. Mivvy came round in a taxi, hobbling up the path on two sticks, refusing the offer of the taxi driver's arm.

'You'll be off to Sibyl's in a day or two, will you, dear?'

Trixie didn't know how many times she had told her not till Monday week. She was waiting for Mivvy to notice the clock but at this rate she was going to have to wait till Christmas.

'What do you think of my clock?'

'What, up there? Isn't that your Wedgwood coffee pot, dear?'

Trixie had to get it down. She thrust it under Mivvy's nose and started explaining what it was.

But Mivvy knew already. 'Of course I know it's a clock, dear. It's not the first time I've seen one of these. Oh my goodness, no. The young man who makes these, he's a friend of my nephew Tony, they were at art school together. Let me see, what's his name? It will come to me in a minute. A tree, isn't it? Oak? Ash? Peter Oak? No, Elm is his name. Something Elm. Roland Elm.'

Trixie said nothing. The glazed surface of the clock felt very cold against the skin of her hands.

'He never makes them to order, you know. He just makes a limited number for a few selected galleries. Tony told me that. Where did you get yours, I wonder?'

Trixie said nothing. There was worse coming and she waited for it.

'Not around here, I'm sure. I know there are only two or three places in the country they go to. It will come to me in a minute. I shall be writing to Tony tomorrow and I'll mention about you having one of Richard's – no, I mean Raymond's, that is, Roland's, clocks. I always write to him on Tuesdays. Tuesday is his day. I'll mention you've got one with bindweed on it. They're all different, you know. He never makes two alike.'

'It's convolvulus, not bindweed,' said Trixie. 'I'd rather you didn't write to Tony about it if you don't mind.'

'Oh, but I'd like to mention it, dear. Why ever not? I won't mention your name if you don't want me to. I'll just say that lady who goes down to stay with Auntie Sibyl in Devonshire.'

Trixie said she would walk with Mivvy up to the High Street. It was hopeless trying to get a taxi outside here. She fetched Mivvy's two sticks.

'You take my arm and I'll hold your other stick.'

The traffic whipped along over the zebra crossing. You were at the mercy of those drivers, Trixie said, it was a matter of waiting till they condescended to stop.

'Don't you set foot on those stripes till they stop,' she said to Mivvy.

Mivvy didn't, so the cars didn't stop. A container lorry, a juggernaut, came thundering along, but a good way off still. Trixie thought it was going much too fast.

'Now if we're quick,' she said. 'Run for it!'

Startled by the urgency in her voice, Mivvy obeyed, or tried to obey as Trixie dropped her arm and gave her a little push forward. The lorry's brakes screamed like people being tortured and Trixie jumped back, screaming herself, covering her face with her hands so as not to see Mivvy under those giant wheels.

Dorothy Fisher said she quite understood Trixie would still want to go to Sibyl's for her holiday. It was the best thing in the world for her, a rest, a complete change, a chance to forget. Trixie went down by train on the day after the funeral. She had the clock in her bag with her, wrapped first in tissue paper and then in her sky-blue dress. The first opportunity that offered itself she would take the clock back to Artifacts and replace it on the shelf she had taken it from. This shouldn't be too difficult. The clock was a dangerous possession, she could see that, like one of those notorious diamonds that carry a curse with them. Pretty though it was, it was an *unlucky* clock that had involved her in trouble from the time she had first taken it.

There was no question of walking to Artifacts this time. Sibyl was too frail for that. She had gone downhill a lot since last year and symptomatic of her deterioration was her exchange of the grey wig for a lilac-blue one. They went in the car though Trixie was by no means sure Sibyl was safe at the wheel.

As soon as they walked into the gallery Trixie saw that she had no hope of replacing the clock without being spotted. There was a desk in the first room now with a plump smiling lady sitting at it who Sibyl said was Judy's mother. Trixie thought that amazing – a mother not minding her daughter cohabiting with a man she wasn't married to. Living with a daughter living in sin, you might put it. Jimmy was in the second room, up on a ladder doing something to the window catch.

'They're having upstairs remodelled,' said Sibyl. 'You can't go up there.' And when Trixie tried to make her way towards the garden door, 'You don't want to be had up for trespassing, do you?' She winked at Judy's mother. 'We're none of us getting any younger when all's said and done, are we?'

They went back to Sibyl's, the clock still in Trixie's bag. It seemed to have grown heavier. She could hear it ticking through the leather and the folds of the sky-blue dress. In the afternoon when Sibyl lay down on the sofa for her rest, the lilac wig stuck on top of a Poole pottery vase, Trixie went out for a walk, taking the clock with her. She came to the hump-backed bridge over the stream where the water was very low, for it had been a dry summer. She unwrapped the clock and dropped it over the low parapet into the water. It cracked but the trellis work and the convolvulus remained intact and the movement continued to move and to tick as well for all Trixie knew. The blue and green, the pink flowers and the gilt, gleamed through the water like some exotic iridescent shell.

Trixie went down the bank. She took off her shoes and waded into the water. It was surprisingly cold. She picked up a large flat stone and beat at the face of the clock with it. She beat with unrestrained fury, gasping and grunting at each blow. The green trellis and the blue sky, the glass face and the pink flowers, all shattered. But they were still there, bright jewel-like shards, for all to see who came this way across the bridge.

Squatting down, Trixie scooped up handfuls of pebbles and buried the pieces of clock under them. With her nails she dug a pit in the bed of the stream and pushed the coloured fragments into it, covering them with pebbles. Her hands were bleeding, her knees were bruised and her dress was wet. In spite of her efforts the bed of the stream was still spread with ceramic chips and broken glass and pieces of gilt metal. Trixie began to sob and crawl from side to side of the stream, ploughing her hands through the blue and green and gold gravel, and it was there that one of Sibyl's neighbours found her as he was driving home over the bridge.

He lifted her up and carried her to his car.

'Tick-tock,' said Trixie. 'Tick-tock. Convolvulus clock.'

Loopy

At the end of the last performance, after the curtain calls, Red Riding Hood put me on a lead and with the rest of the company we went across to the pub. No one had taken make-up off or changed, there was no time for that before The George closed. I remember prancing across the road and growling at someone on a bicycle. They loved me in the pub – well, some of them loved me. Quite a lot were embarrassed. The funny thing was that I should have been embarrassed myself if I had been one of them. I should have ignored *me* and drunk up my drink and left. Except that it is unlikely I would have been in a pub at all. Normally, I never went near such places. But inside the wolf skin it was very different, everything was different in there.

I prowled about for a while, sometimes on all fours, though this is not easy for us who are accustomed to the upright stance, sometimes loping, with my forepaws held close up to my chest. I went up to tables where people were sitting and snuffled my snout at their packets of crisps. If they were smoking I growled and waved my paws in air-clearing gestures. Lots of them were forthcoming, stroking me and making jokes or pretending terror at my red jaws and wicked little eyes. There was even one lady who took hold of my head and laid it in her lap.

Bounding up to the bar to collect my small dry sherry, I heard Bill Harkness (the First Woodcutter) say to Susan Hayes (Red Riding Hood's Mother):

'Old Colin's really come out of his shell tonight.'

And Susan, bless her, said, 'He's a real actor, isn't he?'

I was one of the few members of our company who was. I expect this is always true in amateur dramatics. There are one or two real actors, people who could have made their livings on the stage if it was not so overcrowded a profession, and the rest who just come for the fun of it and the social side. Did I ever consider the stage seriously?

My father had been a civil servant, both my grandfathers in the ICS. As far back as I can remember it was taken for granted I should get my degree and go into the civil service. I never questioned it. If you have a mother like mine, one in a million, more a friend than a parent, you never feel the need to rebel. Besides, Mother gave me all the support I could have wished for in my acting. Acting as a hobby, that is. For instance, though the company made provision for hiring all the more complicated costumes for that year's Christmas pantomime, Mother made the wolf suit for me herself. It was ten times better than anything we could have hired. The head we had to buy but the body and the limbs she made from a long-haired grey fur fabric such as is manufactured for ladies' coats.

Moira used to say I enjoyed acting so much because it enabled me to lose myself and become, for a while, someone else. She said I disliked what I was and looked for ways of escape. A strange way to talk to the man you intend to marry! But before I approach the subject of Moira or, indeed, continue with this account, I should explain what its purpose is. The psychiatrist attached to this place or who visits it (I am not entirely clear which), one Dr Vernon-Peak, has asked me to write down some of my feelings and impressions. That, I said, would only be possible in the context of a narrative. Very well, he said, he had no objection. What will become of it when finished I hardly know. Will it constitute a statement to be used in court? Or will it enter Dr Vernon-Peak's files as another 'case history'? It is all the same to me. I can only tell the truth.

After The George closed, then, we took off our make-up and changed and went our several ways home. Mother was waiting up for me. This was not invariably her habit. If I told her I should be late and to go to bed at her usual time she always did so. But I, quite naturally, was not averse to a welcome when I got home, particularly after a triumph like that one. Besides, I had been looking forward to telling her what an amusing time I had had in the pub.

Our house is late Victorian, double-fronted, of grey limestone, by no means beautiful, but a comfortable well-built place. My grandfather bought it when he retired and came home from India in 1920. Mother was ten at the time, so she has spent most of her life in that house.

Grandfather was quite a famous shot and used to go big game hunting before that kind of thing became, and rightly so, very much frowned upon. The result was that the place was full of 'trophies of the chase'. While Grandfather was alive, and he lived to a great age, we had no choice but to put up with the antlers and tusks that sprouted everywhere out of the walls, the elephant's foot umbrella stand, and the snarling maws of *tigris* and *ursa*. We had to grin and bear it, as Mother, who has a fine turn of wit, used to put it. But when Grandfather was at last gathered to his ancestors, reverently and without the least disrespect to him, we took down all those heads and horns and packed them away in trunks. The fur rugs, however, we did not disturb. These days they are worth a fortune and I always felt that the tiger skins scattered across the hall parquet, the snow leopard draped across the back of the sofa and the bear into whose fur one could bury one's toes before the fire, gave to the place a luxurious look. I took off my shoes, I remember, and snuggled my toes in it that night.

Mother, of course, had been to see the show. She had come on the first night and seen me make my onslaught on Red Riding Hood, an attack so sudden and unexpected that the whole audience had jumped to its feet and gasped. (In our version we did not have the wolf actually devour Red Riding Hood. Unanimously, we agreed this would hardly have been the thing at Christmas.) Mother, however, wanted to see me wearing her creation once more, so I put it on and did some prancing and growling for her benefit. Again I noticed how curiously uninhibited I became once inside the wolf skin. For instance, I bounded up to the snow leopard and began snarling at it. I boxed at its great grey-white face and made playful bites at its ears. Down on all fours I went and pounced on the bear, fighting it, actually forcing its neck within the space of my jaws.

How Mother laughed! She said it was as good as anything in the panto and a good deal better than anything they put on television.

'Animal crackers in my soup,' she said, wiping her eyes. 'There used to be a song that went like that in my youth. How did it go on? Something about lions and tigers loop the loop.'

'Well, *lupus* means a wolf in Latin,' I said.

'And you're certainly loopy! When you put that suit on I shall have to say you're going all loopy again!'

When I put that suit on again. Did I intend to put it on again? I had not really thought about it. Yes, perhaps if I ever went to a fancy-dress party, a remote enough contingency. Yet what a shame it seemed to waste it, to pack it away like Grandfather's tusks and antlers, after all the labour Mother had put into it. That night I hung it up in my wardrobe and I remember how strange I felt when I took it off that second time, more naked than I usually felt without my clothes, almost as if I had taken off my skin.

Life kept to the 'even tenor' of its way. I felt a little flat with no rehearsals to attend and no lines to learn. Christmas came. Traditionally, Mother and I were alone on the Day itself, we would not have had it any other way, but on Boxing Day Moira arrived and Mother invited a couple of neighbours of ours as well. At some stage, I seem to recall, Susan Hayes dropped in with her husband to wish us the 'compliments of the season'.

Moira and I had been engaged for three years. We would have got married some time before, there was no question of our not being able to afford to marry, but a difficulty had arisen over where we should live. I think I may say in all fairness that the difficulty was entirely of Moira's making. No mother could have been more welcoming to a future daughter-in-law than mine. She actually wanted us to live with her at Simla House, she said we must think of it as our home and of her simply as our housekeeper. But Moira wanted us to buy a place of our own, so we had reached a deadlock, an impasse.

It was unfortunate that on that Boxing Day, after the others had gone, Moira brought the subject up again. Her brother (an estate agent) had told her of a bungalow for sale halfway between Simla House and her parents' home and it was what he called 'a real snip'. Fortunately, *I* thought, Mother managed to turn the conversation by telling us about the bungalow she and her parents had lived in in India, with its great colonnaded veranda, its English flower garden and its peepul tree. But Moira interrupted her.

'This is *our* future we're talking about, not your past. I thought Colin and I were getting married.'

Mother was quite alarmed. 'Aren't you? Surely Colin hasn't broken things off?'

'I suppose you don't consider the possibility *I* might break things off?'

Poor Mother could not help smiling at that. She smiled to cover her hurt. Moira could upset her very easily. For some reason this made Moira angry.

'I'm too old and unattractive to have any choice in the matter, is that what you mean?'

'Moira,' I said.

She took no notice. 'You may not realize it,' she said, 'but marrying me will be the making of Colin. It's what he needs to make a man of him.'

It must have slipped out before Mother quite knew what she was saying. She patted Moira's knee. 'I can quite see it may be a tough assignment, dear.'

There was no quarrel. Mother would never have allowed herself to be drawn into that. But Moira became very huffy and said she wanted to go home, so I had to get the car out and take her. All the way to her parents' house I had to listen to a catalogue of her wrongs at my hands and my mother's. By the time we parted I felt dispirited and nervous, I even wondered if I was doing the right thing, contemplating matrimony in the 'sere and yellow leaf' of forty-two.

Mother had cleared the things away and gone to bed. I went into my bedroom and began undressing. Opening the wardrobe to hang up my tweed trousers, I caught sight of the wolf suit and on some impulse I put it on.

Once inside the wolf I felt calmer and, yes, happier. I sat down in an armchair but after a while I found it more comfortable to crouch, then lie stretched out, on the floor. Lying there, basking in the warmth from the gas fire on my belly and paws, I found myself remembering tales of man's affinity with wolves, Romulus and Remus suckled by a she-wolf, the ancient myth of the werewolf, abandoned children reared by wolves even in these modern times. All this seemed to deflect my mind from the discord between Moira and my mother and I was able to go to bed reasonably happily and to sleep well.

Perhaps, then, it will not seem so very strange and wonderful that the next time I felt depressed I put the suit on again. Mother was out, so I was able to have the freedom of the whole house, not just of my room. It was dusk at four but instead of putting the lights on, I prowled about the house in the twilight, sometimes catching sight of my lean grey form in the many large mirrors Mother is so fond of. Because there was so little light and our house is crammed with bulky furniture and knick-knacks, the reflection I saw looked not like a man disguised but like a real wolf that has somehow escaped and strayed into a cluttered Victorian room. Or a werewolf, that animal part of man's personality that detaches itself and wanders free while leaving behind the depleted human shape.

I crept up upon the teakwood carving of the antelope and devoured the little creature before it knew what had attacked it. I resumed my battle with the bear and we struggled in front of the fireplace, locked in a desperate hairy embrace. It was then that I heard Mother let herself in at the back door. Time had passed more quickly than I had thought. I had escaped and whisked my hind paws and tail round the bend in the stairs just before she came into the hall.

Dr Vernon-Peak seems to want to know why I began this at the age of forty-two, or rather, why I had not done it before. I wish I knew. Of course there is the simple solution that I did not have a wolf skin before, but that is not the whole answer. Was it perhaps that until then I did not know what my needs were, though partially I had satisfied them by playing the parts I was given in dramatic productions? There is one other thing. I have told him that I recall, as a very young child, having a close relationship with some large animal, a dog perhaps or a pony, though a search conducted into family history by this same assiduous Vernon-Peak has yielded no evidence that we ever kept a pet. But more of this anon.

Be that as it may, once I had lived inside the wolf, I felt the need to do so more and more. Erect on my hind legs, drawn up to my full height, I do not think I flatter myself unduly when I say I made a fine handsome animal. And having written that, I realize that I have not yet described the wolf suit, taking for granted, I suppose, that those who see this document will also see it. Yet this may not be the case. They have refused to let *me* see it, which makes me wonder if it has been cleaned and made presentable again or if it is still – but, no, there is no point in going into unsavoury details.

I have said that the body and limbs of the suit were made of long-haired grey fur fabric. The stuff of it was coarse, hardly an attractive material for a coat, I should have thought, but very closely similar to a wolf's pelt. Mother made the paws after the fashion of fur gloves but with the padded and stiffened fingers of a pair of leather gloves for the claws. The head we bought from a jokes and games shop. It had tall prick ears, small yellow eyes and a wonderful, half-open mouth, red, voracious-looking and with a double row of white fangs. The opening for me to breathe through was just beneath the lower jaw where the head joined the powerful grey hairy throat.

As the spring came I would sometimes drive out into the country-side, park the car and slip into the skin. It was far from my ambition to be seen by anyone, though. I sought solitude. Whether I should have cared for a 'beastly' companion, that is something else again. At that time I wanted merely to wander in the woods and copses or along a hedgerow in my wolf's persona. And this I did, choosing unfrequented places, avoiding anywhere that I might come in contact with the human race. I am trying, in writing this, to explain how I felt. Principally, I felt *not human*. And to be not human is to be

493

without human responsibilities and human cares. Inside the wolf, I laid aside with my humanity my apprehensiveness about getting married, my apprehensiveness about *not* getting married, my fear of leaving Mother on her own, my justifiable resentment at not getting the leading part in our new production. All this got left behind with the depleted sleeping man I left behind to become a happy mindless wild creature.

Our wedding had once again been postponed. The purchase of the house Moira and I had finally agreed upon fell through at the last moment. I cannot say I was altogether sorry. It was near enough to my home, in the same street in fact as Simla House, but I had begun to wonder how I would feel passing our dear old house every day yet knowing it was not under that familiar roof I should lay my head.

Moira was very upset.

Yet, 'I won't live in the same house as your mother even for three months,' she said in answer to my suggestion. 'That's a certain recipe for disaster.'

'Mother and Daddy lived with Mother's parents for twenty years,' I said.

'Yes, and look at the result.' It was then that she made that remark about my enjoying playing parts because I disliked my real self.

There was nothing more to be said except that we must keep on house-hunting.

'We can still go to Malta, I suppose,' Moira said. 'We don't have to cancel that.'

Perhaps, but it would be no honeymoon. Anticipating the delights of matrimony was something I had not done up till then and had no intention of doing. And I was on my guard when Moira – Mother was out at her bridge evening – insisted on going up to my bedroom with me, ostensibly to check on the shade of the suit I had bought to get married in. She said she wanted to buy me a tie. Once there, she reclined on my bed, cajoling me to come and sit beside her.

I suppose it was because I was feeling depressed that I put on the wolf skin. I took off my jacket, but nothing more of course in front of Moira, stepped into the wolf skin, fastened it up and adjusted the head. She watched me. She had seen me in it before when she came to the pantomime.

'Why have you put that on?'

I said nothing. What could I have said? The usual contentment filled me, though, and I found myself obeying her command, loping across to the bed where she was. It seemed to come naturally to fawn on her, to rub my great prick-eared head against her breast, to enclose her hands with my paws. All kinds of fantasies filled my wolfish mind and they were of an intense piercing sweetness. If we had been on our holiday then, I do not think moral resolutions would have held me back.

But unlike the lady in The George, Moira did not take hold of my head and lay it in her lap. She jumped up and shouted at me to stop this nonsense, stop it at once, she hated it. So I did as I was told, of course I did, and got sadly out of the skin and hung it back in the cupboard. I took Moira home. On our way we called in at her brother's and looked at fresh lists of houses.

It was on one of these that we eventually settled after another month or so of picking and choosing and stalling, and we fixed our wedding for the middle of December. During the summer the company had done *Blithe Spirit* (in which I had the meagre part of Dr Bradman, Bill Harkness being Charles Condomine) and the pantomime this year was Cinderella with Susan Hayes in the name part and me as the Elder of the Ugly Sisters. I had calculated I should be back from my honeymoon just in time.

No doubt I would have been. No doubt I would have married and gone away on my honeymoon and come back to play my comic part had I not agreed to go shopping with Moira on her birthday. What happened that day changed everything.

It was a Thursday evening. The stores in the West End stay open late on Thursdays. We left our offices at five, met by arrangement and together walked up Bond Street. The last thing I had in view was that we should begin bickering again, though we had seemed to do little else lately. It started with my mentioning our honeymoon. We were outside Asprey's, walking along arm in arm. Since our house would not be ready for us to move into till the middle of January, I suggested we should go back for just two weeks to Simla House. We should be going there for Christmas in any case.

'I thought we'd decided to go to an hotel,' Moira said.

'Don't you think that's rather a waste of money?'

'I think,' she said in a grim sort of tone, 'I think it's money we daren't not spend,' and she drew her arm away from mine.

I asked her what on earth she meant.

'Once you get back there with Mummy you'll never move.'

I treated that with the contempt it deserved and said nothing. We walked along in silence. Then Moira began talking in a low monotone, using expressions from paperback psychology which I am glad to say

I have never heard from Dr Vernon-Peak. We crossed the street and entered Selfridge's. Moira was still going on about Oedipus complexes and that nonsense about making a man of me.

'Keep your voice down,' I said. 'Everyone can hear you.'

She shouted at me to shut up, she would say what she pleased. Well, she had repeatedly told me to be a man and to assert myself, so I did just that. I went up to one of the counters, wrote her a cheque for, I must admit, a good deal more than I had originally meant to give her, put it into her hands and walked off, leaving her there.

For a while I felt not displeased with myself but on the way home in the train depression set in. I should have liked to tell Mother about it but Mother would be out, playing bridge. So I had recourse to my other source of comfort, my wolf skin. The phone rang several times while I was gambolling about the rooms but I did not answer it. I knew it was Moira. I was on the floor with Grandfather's stuffed eagle in my paws and my teeth in its neck when Mother walked in.

Bridge had ended early. One of the ladies had been taken ill and rushed to hospital. I had been too intent on my task to see the light come on or hear the door. She stood there in her old fur coat, looking at me. I let the eagle fall, I bowed my head, I wanted to die I was so ashamed and embarrassed. How little I really knew my mother! My dear faithful companion, my only friend! Might I not say, my other self?

She smiled. I could hardly believe it but she was smiling. It was that wonderful, conspiratorial, rather naughty smile of hers. 'Hallo,' she said. 'Are you going all loopy?'

In a moment she was down on her knees beside me, the fur coat enveloping her, and together we worried at the eagle, engaged in battle with the bear, attacked the antelope. Together we bounded into the hall to pounce upon the sleeping tigers. Mother kept laughing (and growling too) saying, what a relief, what a relief! I think we embraced. Next day when I got home she was waiting for me, transformed and ready. She had made herself an animal suit, she must have worked on it all day, out of the snow leopard skin and a length of white fur fabric. I could see her eyes dancing through the gap in its throat.

'You don't know how I've longed to be an animal again,' she said. 'I used to be animals when you were a baby, I was a dog for a long time and then I was a bear, but your father found out and he didn't like it. I had to stop.'

So that was what I dimly remembered. I said she looked like the Queen of the Beasts.

'Do I, Loopy?' she said.

We had a wonderful weekend, Mother and I. Wolf and leopard, we breakfasted together that morning. Then we played. We played all over the house, sometimes fighting, sometimes dancing, hunting of course, carrying off our prey to the lairs we made for ourselves among the furniture. We went out in the car, drove into the country and there in a wood got into our skins and for many happy hours roamed wild among the trees.

There seemed no reason, during those two days, to become human again at all, but on the Tuesday I had a rehearsal, on the Monday morning I had to go off to work. It was coming down to earth, back to what we call reality, with a nasty bang. Still, it had its amusing side too. A lady in the train trod on my toe and I had growled at her before I remembered and turned it into a cough.

All through that weekend neither of us had bothered to answer the phone. In the office I had no choice and it was there that Moira caught me. Marriage had come to seem remote, something grotesque, something that others did, not me. Animals do not marry. But that was not the sort of thing I could say to Moira. I promised to ring her, I said we must meet before the week was out.

I suppose she did tell me she would come over on the Thursday evening and show me what she had bought with the money I had given her. She knew Mother was always out on Thursdays. I suppose Moira did tell me and I failed to take it in. Nothing was important to me but being animals with Mother, Loopy and the Queen of the Beasts.

Each night as soon as I got home we made ourselves ready for our evening's games. How harmless it all was! How innocent! Like the gentle creatures in the dawn of the world before man came. Like the Garden of Eden after Adam and Eve had been sent away.

The lady who had been taken ill at the bridge evening had since died, so this week it was cancelled. But would Mother have gone anyway? Probably not. Our animal capers meant as much to her as they did to me, almost more perhaps, for she had denied herself so long. We were sitting at the dining table, eating our evening meal. Mother had cooked, I recall, a rack of lamb so that we might later gnaw the bones. We never ate it, of course, and I have since wondered what became of it. But we did begin on our soup. The bread was at my end of the table, with the bread board and the long sharp knife.

Moira, when she called and I was alone, was in the habit of letting herself in by the back door. We did not hear her, neither of us heard her, though I do remember Mother's noble head lifted a fraction before Moira came in, her fangs bared and her ears pricked. Moira opened the dining-room door and walked in. I can see her now, the complacent smile on her lips fading and the scream starting to come. She was wearing what must have been my present, a full-length white sheepskin coat.

And then? This is what Dr Vernon-Peak will particularly wish to know but what I cannot clearly remember. I remember that as the door opened I was holding the bread knife in my paws. I think I remember letting out a low growl and poising myself to spring. But what came after?

The last things I can recall before they brought me here are the blood on my fur and the two wild predatory creatures crouched on the floor over the body of the lamb.

Fen Hall

When children paint a picture of a tree they always do the trunk brown. But trees seldom have brown trunks. Birches are silver, beeches pewter colour, planes grey and yellow, walnuts black and the bark of oaks, chestnuts and sycamores green with lichen. Pringle had never noticed any of this until he came to Fen Hall. After that, once his eyes had been opened and he had seen what things were really like, he would have painted trees with bark in different colours but next term he stopped doing art. It was just as well, he had never been very good at it, and perhaps by then he wouldn't have felt like painting trees anyway. Or even looking at them much.

Mr Liddon met them at the station in an old Volvo estate car. They were loaded down with camping gear, the tent and sleeping bags and cooking pots and a Calor gas burner in case it was too windy to keep a fire going. It had been very windy lately, the summer cool and sunless. Mr Liddon was Pringle's father's friend and Pringle had met him once before, years ago when he was a little kid, but still it was up to him to introduce the others. He spoke with wary politeness.

'This is John and this is Roger. They're brothers.'

Pringle didn't say anything about Roger always being called Hodge. He sensed that Mr Liddon wouldn't call him Hodge any more than he would call *him* Pringle. He was right.

'Parents well, are they, Peregrine?'

Pringle said yes. He could see a gleam in John's eye that augured teasing to come. Hodge, who was always thinking of his stomach, said:

'Could we stop on the way, Mr Liddon, and buy some food?'

Mr Liddon cast up his eyes. Pringle could tell he was going to be 'one of those' grown-ups. They all got into the car with their stuff and a mile or so out of town Mr Liddon stopped at a self-service shop. He didn't go inside with them which was just as well. He would only have called what they bought junk food.

Fen Hall turned out to be about seven miles away. They went through a village called Fedgford and a little way beyond it turned down a lane that passed through a wood.

'That's where you'll have your camp,' Mr Liddon said.

Of necessity, because the lane was no more than a rough track, he was driving slowly. He pointed in among the trees. The wood had a mysterious look as if full of secrets. In the aisles between the trees the light was greenish-gold and misty. There was a muted twittering of birds and a cooing of doves. Pringle began to feel excited. It was nicer than he had expected. A little further on the wood petered out into a plantation of tall straight trees with green trunks growing in rows, the ground between them all overgrown with a spiky plant that had a curious prehistoric look to it.

'Those trees are poplars,' Mr Liddon said. You could tell he was a schoolteacher. 'They're grown as a crop.'

This was a novel idea to Pringle. 'What sort of a crop?'

'Twenty-five years after they're planted they're cut down and used for making matchsticks. If they don't fall down first. We had a couple go over in the gales last winter.'

Pringle wasn't listening. He had seen the house. It was like a house in a dream, he thought, though he didn't quite know what he meant by that. Houses he saw in actual dreams were much like his own home or John and Hodge's, suburban Surrey semidetached. This house, when all the trees were left behind and no twig or leaf or festoon of wild clematis obscured it, stood basking in the sunshine with the confidence of something alive, as if secure in its own perfection. Dark mulberry colour, of small Tudor bricks, it had a roof of many irregular planes and gables and a cluster of chimneys like candles. The windows with the sun on them were plates of gold between the mullions. Under the eaves swallows had built their lumpy sagging nests.

'Leave your stuff in the car. I'll be taking you back up to the wood in ten minutes. Just thought you'd like to get your bearings, see where everything is first. There's the outside tap over there which you'll use of course. And you'll find a shovel and an axe in there which I rely on you to replace.'

It was going to be the biggest house Pringle had ever set foot in – not counting places like Hampton Court and Woburn. Fen Hall. It looked and the name sounded like a house in a book, not real at all. The front door was of oak, studded with iron and set back under a porch that was dark and carved with roses. Mr Liddon took them in the back way. He took them into a kitchen that was exactly Pringle's idea of the lowest sort of slum.

He was shocked. At first he couldn't see much because it had been bright outside but he could smell something dank and frowsty. When his vision adjusted he found they were in a huge room or cavern with two small windows and about four hundred square feet of squalor between them. Islanded were a small white electric oven and a small white fridge. The floor was of brick, very uneven, the walls of irregular green-painted peeling plaster with a bubbly kind of growth coming through it. Stacks of dirty dishes filled a stone sink of the kind his mother had bought at a sale and made a cactus garden in. The whole place was grossly untidy with piles of washing lying about. John and Hodge, having taken it all in, were standing there with blank faces and shifting eyes.

Mr Liddon's manner had changed slightly. He no longer kept up the hectoring tone. While explaining to them that this was where they must come if they needed anything, to the back door, he began a kind of ineffectual tidying up, cramming things into the old wooden cupboards, sweeping crumbs off the table and dropping them into the sink. John said:

'Is it all right for us to have a fire?'

'So long as you're careful. Not if the wind gets up again. I don't have to tell you where the wood is, you'll find it lying about.' Mr Liddon opened a door and called, 'Flora!'

A stone-flagged passage could be seen beyond. No one came. Pringle knew Mr Liddon had a wife, though no children. His parents had told him only that Mr and Mrs Liddon had bought a marvellous house in the country a year before and he and a couple of his friends could go and camp in the grounds if they wanted to. Further information he had picked up when they didn't know he was listening. Tony Liddon hadn't had two halfpennies to rub together until his aunt died and left him a bit of money. It couldn't have been much surely. Anyway he had spent it all on Fen Hall, he had always wanted an old place like that. The upkeep was going to be a drain on him and goodness knows how he would manage.

Pringle hadn't been much interested in all this. Now it came back to him. Mr Liddon and his father had been at university together but Mr Liddon hadn't had a wife then. Pringle had never met the wife and nor had his parents. Anyway it was clear they were not to wait for her. They got back into the car and went to find a suitable camping site.

It was a relief when Mr Liddon went away and left them to it. The obvious place to camp was on the high ground in a clearing and to make their fire in a hollow Mr Liddon said was probably a disused gravel pit. The sun was low, making long shafts of light that pierced the groves of birch and crab apple. Mistletoe hung in the oak trees like green bird's nests. It was warm and murmurous with flies. John was adept at putting up the tent and gave them orders.

'Peregrine,' he said. 'Like a sort of mad bird.'

Hodge capered about, his thumbs in his ears and his hands flapping. 'Tweet, tweet, mad bird. His master chains him up like a dog. Tweet, tweet, birdie!'

'I'd rather be a hunting falcon than Roger the lodger the sod,' said Pringle and he shoved Hodge and they both fell over and rolled about grappling on the ground until John kicked them and told them to stop it and give a hand, he couldn't do the lot on his own.

It was good in the camp that night, not windy but still and mild after the bad summer they'd had. They made a fire and cooked tomato soup and fish fingers and ate a whole packet of the biscuits called iced bears. They were in their bags in the tent, John reading the *Observer's Book of Common Insects*, Pringle a thriller set in a Japanese prison camp his parents would have taken away if they'd known about it, and Hodge listening to his radio, when Mr Liddon came up with a torch to check on them.

'Just to see if you're OK. Everything shipshape and Bristol fashion?'

Pringle thought that an odd thing to say considering the mess in his own house. Mr Liddon made a fuss about the candles they had lit and they promised to put them out, though of course they didn't. It was very silent in the night up there in the wood, the deepest silence Pringle had ever known, a quiet that was somehow heavy as if a great dark beast had lain down on the wood and quelled every sound beneath under its dense soft fur. He didn't think of this for very long because he was asleep two minutes after they blew the candles out.

Next morning the weather wasn't so nice. It was dull and cool for August. John saw a Brimstone butterfly which pleased him because the species was getting rarer. They all walked into Fedgford and bought sausages and then found they hadn't a frying pan. Pringle went down to the house on his own to see if he could borrow one.

Unlike most men Mr Liddon would be at home because of the school holidays. Pringle expected to see him working in the garden which even he could see was a mess. But he wasn't anywhere about. Pringle banged on the back door with his fist – there was neither bell

502

nor knocker – but no one came. The door wasn't locked. He wondered if it would be all right to go in and then he went in.

The mess in the kitchen was rather worse. A large white and tabby cat was on the table eating something it probably shouldn't have been eating out of a paper bag. Pringle had a curious feeling that it would somehow be quite permissible for him to go on into the house. Something told him – though it was not a something based on observation or even guesswork – that Mr Liddon wasn't in. He went into the passage he had seen the day before through the open door. This led into a large stone-flagged hall. The place was dark with heavy dark beams going up the walls and across the ceilings and it was cold. It smelled of damp. The smell was like mushrooms that have been left in a paper bag at the back of the fridge and forgotten. Pringle pushed open a likely looking door, some instinct making him give a warning cough.

The room was enormous, its ceiling all carved beams and cobwebs. Even Pringle could see that the few small bits of furniture in it would have been more suitable for the living room of a bungalow. A woman was standing by the tall, diamond-paned, mullioned window, holding something blue and sparkling up to the light. She was strangely dressed in a long skirt, her hair falling loosely down her back, and she stood so still, gazing at the blue object with both arms raised, that for a moment Pringle had an uneasy feeling she wasn't a woman at all but the ghost of a woman. Then she turned round and smiled.

'Hallo,' she said. 'Are you one of our campers?'

She was at least as old as Mr Liddon but her hair hung down like one of the girls' at school. Her face was pale and not pretty yet when she smiled it was a wonderful face. Pringle registered that, staring at her. It was a face of radiant kind sensitivity, though it was to be some years before he could express what he had felt in those terms.

'I'm Pringle,' he said, and because he sensed that she would understand, 'I'm called Peregrine really but I get people to call me Pringle.'

'I don't blame you. I'd do the same in your place.' She had a quiet unaffected voice. 'I'm Flora Liddon. You call me Flora.'

He didn't think he could do that and knew he would end up calling her nothing. 'I came to see if I could borrow a frying pan.'

'Of course you can.' She added, 'If I can find one.' She held the thing in her hand out to him and he saw it was a small glass bottle. 'Do you think it's pretty?'

He looked at it doubtfully. It was just a bottle. On the window sill behind her were more bottles, mostly of clear colourless glass but among them dark green ones with fluted sides.

'There are wonderful things to be found here. You can dig and find rubbish heaps that go back to Elizabethan times. And there was a Roman settlement down by the river. Would you like to see a Roman coin?'

It was black, misshapen, lumpy, with an ugly man's head on it. She showed him a jar of thick bubbly green glass and said it was the best piece of glass she'd found to date. They went out to the kitchen. Finding a frying pan wasn't easy but talking to her was. By the time she had washed up a pan which she had found full of congealed fat he had told her all about the camp and their walk to Fedgford and what the butcher had said:

'I hope you're going to wash yourselves before you cook my nice clean sausages.'

And she told him what a lot needed doing to the house and grounds and how they'd have to do it all themselves because they hadn't much money. She wasn't any good at painting or sewing or gardening or even housework, come to that. Pottering about and looking at things was what she liked.

' "What is this life if, full of care, we have no time to stand and stare?" '

He knew where that came from. W. H. Davies, the Super-tramp. They had done it at school.

'I'd have been a good tramp,' she said. 'It would have suited me.'

The smile irradiated her plain face.

They cooked the sausages for lunch and went on an insect-hunting expedition with John. The dragonflies he had promised them down by the river were not to be seen but he found what he said was a caddis, though it looked like a bit of twig to Pringle. Hodge ate five Mars bars during the course of the afternoon. They came upon the white and tabby cat with a mouse in its jaws. Undeterred by an audience, it bit the mouse in two and the tiny heart rolled out. Hodge said faintly, 'I think I'm going to be sick,' and was. They still resolved to have a cat-watch on the morrow and see how many mice it caught in a day.

By that time the weather was better. The sun didn't shine but it had got warmer again. They found the cat in the poplar plantation, stalking something among the prehistoric weeds John said were called horse tails. The poplars had trunks almost as green as grass and their leafy tops, very high up there in the pale blue sky, made rustling

504

whispering sounds in the breeze. That was when Pringle noticed about tree trunks not being brown. The trunks of the Scotch pines were a clear pinkish-red, as bright as flowers when for a moment the sun shone. He pointed this out to the others but they didn't seem interested.

'You sound like our auntie,' said Hodge. 'She does flower arrangements for the church.'

'And throws up when she sees a bit of blood, I expect,' said Pringle. 'It runs in your family.'

Hodge lunged at him and he tripped Hodge up and they rolled about wrestling among the horse tails. By four in the afternoon the cat had caught six mice. Flora came out and told them the cat's name was Tabby which obscurely pleased Pringle. If she had said Snowflake or Persephone or some other daft name people called animals he would have felt differently about her, though he couldn't possibly have said why. He wouldn't have liked her so much.

A man turned up in a Land-Rover as they were making their way back to camp. He said he had been to the house and knocked but no one seemed to be at home. Would they give Mr or Mrs Liddon a message from him? His name was Porter, Michael Porter, and he was an archaeologist in an amateur sort of way, Mr Liddon knew all about it, and they were digging in the lower meadow and they'd come on a dump of nineteenth-century stuff. He was going to dig deeper, uncover the next layer, so if Mrs Liddon was interested in the top, now was her chance to have a look.

'Can we as well?' said Pringle.

Porter said they were welcome. No one would be working there next day. He had just heard the weather forecast on his car radio and gale-force winds were promised. Was that their camp up there? Make sure the tent was well anchored down, he said, and he drove off up the lane.

Pringle checked the tent. It seemed firm enough. They got into it and fastened the flap but they were afraid to light the candles and had John's storm lantern on instead. The wood was silent no longer. The wind made loud sirenlike howls and a rushing rending sound like canvas being torn. When that happened the tent flapped and bellied like a sail on a ship at sea. Sometimes the wind stopped altogether and there were a few seconds of silence and calm. Then it came back with a rush and a roar. John was reading Frohawk's *Complete Book of British Butterflies*, Pringle the Japanese prison-camp thriller and Hodge was trying to listen to his radio. But it wasn't much use and after a while they put the lantern out and lay in the dark.

About five minutes afterwards there came the strongest gust of wind so far, one of the canvas-tearing gusts but ten times fiercer than the last; and then, from the south of them, down towards the house, a tremendous rending crash.

John said, 'I think we'll have to do something.' His voice was brisk but it wasn't quite steady and Pringle knew he was as scared as they were. 'We'll have to get out of here.'

Pringle put the lantern on again. It was just ten. 'The tent's going to lift off,' said Hodge.

Crawling out of his sleeping bag, Pringle was wondering what they ought to do, if it would be all right, or awful, to go down to the house, when the tent flap was pulled open and Mr Liddon put his head in. He looked cross.

'Come on, the lot of you. You can't stay here. Bring your sleeping bags and we'll find you somewhere in the house for the night.'

A note in his voice made it sound as if the storm were their fault. Pringle found his shoes, stuck his feet into them and rolled up his sleeping bag. John carried the lantern. Mr Liddon shone his own torch to light their way. In the wood there was shelter but none in the lane and the wind buffeted them as they walked. It was all noise, you couldn't see much, but as they passed the plantation Mr Liddon swung the light up and Pringle saw what had made the crash. One of the poplars had gone over and was lying on its side with its roots in the air.

For some reason – perhaps because it was just about on this spot that they had met Michael Porter – John remembered the message. Mr Liddon said OK and thanks. They went into the house through the back door. A tile blew off the roof and crashed on to the path just as the door closed behind them.

There were beds up in the bedrooms but without blankets or sheets on them and the mattresses were damp. Pringle thought them spooky bedrooms, dirty and draped with spiders' webs, and he wasn't sorry they weren't going to sleep there. There was the same smell of old mushrooms and a smell of paint as well where Mr Liddon had started work on a ceiling.

At the end of the passage, looking out of a window, Flora stood in a nightgown with a shawl over it. Pringle, who sometimes read ghost stories, saw her as the Grey Lady of Fen Hall. She was in the dark, the better to see the forked lightning that had begun to leap on the horizon beyond the river.

'I love to watch a storm,' she said, turning and smiling at them.

Mr Liddon had snapped a light on. 'Where are these boys to sleep?'

It was as if it didn't concern her. She wasn't unkind but she wasn't involved either. 'Oh, in the drawing room, I should think.'

'We have seven bedrooms.'

Flora said no more. A long roll of thunder shook the house. Mr Liddon took them downstairs and through the drawing room into a sort of study where they helped him make up beds of cushions on the floor. The wind howled round the house and Pringle heard another tile go. He lay in the dark, listening to the storm. The others were asleep, he could tell by their steady breathing. Inside the bag it was quite warm and he felt snug and safe. After a while he heard Mr Liddon and Flora quarrelling on the other side of the door.

Pringle's parents quarrelled a lot and he hated it, it was the worst thing in the world, though less bad now than when he was younger. He could only just hear Mr Liddon and Flora and only disjointed words, abusive and angry on the man's part, indifferent, amused on the woman's, until one sentence rang out clearly. Her voice was penetrating though it was so quiet:

'We want such different things!'

He wished they would stop. And suddenly they did, with the coming of the rain. The rain came, exploded rather, crashing at the windows and on the old sagging depleted roof. It was strange that a sound like that, a loud constant roar, could send you to sleep . . .

She was in the kitchen when he went out there in the morning. John and Hodge slept on, in spite of the bright watery sunshine that streamed through the dirty diamond window panes. A clean world outside, new-washed. Indoors the same chaos, the kitchen with the same smell of fungus and dirty dishcloths, though the windows were open. Flora sat at the table on which sprawled a welter of plates, indefinable garments, bits of bread and fruit rinds, an open can of cat food. She was drinking coffee and Tabby lay on her lap.

'There's plenty in the pot if you want some.'

She was the first grown-up in whose house he had stayed who didn't ask him how he had slept. Nor was she going to cook breakfast for him. She told him where the eggs were and bread and butter. Pringle remembered he still hadn't returned her frying pan which might be the only one she had.

He made himself a pile of toast and found a jar of marmalade. The grass and the paths, he could see through an open window, were littered with broken bits of twig and leaf. A cock pheasant strutted across the shaggy lawn.

'Did the storm damage a lot of things?' he asked.

'I don't know. Tony got up early to look. There may be more poplars down.'

Pringle ate his toast. The cat had begun to purr in an irregular throbbing way. Her hand kneaded its ears and neck. She spoke, but not perhaps to Pringle or the cat, or for them if they cared to hear.

'So many people are like that. The whole of life is a preparation for life, not living.'

Pringle didn't know what to say. He said nothing. She got up and walked away, still carrying the cat, and then after a while he heard music coming faintly from a distant part of the house.

There were two poplars down in the plantation and each had left a crater four or five feet deep. As they went up the lane to check on their camp, Pringle and John and Hodge had a good look at them, their green trunks laid low, their tangled roots in the air. Apart from everything having got a bit blown about up at the camp and the stuff they had left out soaked through, there was no real damage done. The wood itself had afforded protection to their tent.

It seemed a good time to return the frying pan. After that they would have to walk to Fedgford for some sausages – unless one of the Liddons offered a lift. It was with an eye to this, Pringle had to admit, that he was taking the pan back.

But Mr Liddon, never one to waste time, was already at work in the plantation. He had lugged a chain saw up there and was preparing to cut up the poplars where they lay. When he saw them in the lane he came over.

'How did you sleep?'

Pringle said, 'OK, thanks,' but Hodge, who had been very resentful about not being given a hot drink or something to eat, muttered that he had been too hungry to sleep. Mr Liddon took no notice. He seemed jumpy and nervous. He said to Pringle that if they were going to the house would they tell Mrs Liddon – he never called her Flora to them – that there was what looked like a dump of Victorian glass in the crater where the bigger poplar had stood.

'They must have planted the trees over the top without knowing.'

Pringle looked into the crater and sure enough he could see bits of coloured glass and a bottleneck and a jug or tankard handle protruding from the tumbled soil. He left the others there, fascinated by the chain saw, and went to take the frying pan back. Flora was in the drawing room, playing records of tinkly piano music. She jumped up, quite excited, when he told her about the bottle dump.

They walked back to the plantation together, Tabby following, walking a little way behind them like a dog. Pringle knew he hadn't a hope of getting that lift now. Mr Liddon had already got the crown of the big poplar sawn off. In the short time since the storm its pale silvery-green leaves had begun to wither. John asked if they could have a go with the chain saw but Mr Liddon said not so likely, did they think he was crazy? And if they wanted to get to the butcher before the shop closed for lunch they had better get going now.

Flora, her long skirt hitched up, had clambered down into the crater. If she had stood up in it her head and shoulders, perhaps all of her from the waist up, would have come above its rim, for poplars have shallow roots. But she didn't stand up. She squatted down, using her trowel, extracting small glass objects from the leafmould. The chain saw whined, slicing through the top of the poplar trunk. Pringle, watching with the others, had a feeling something was wrong about the way Mr Liddon was doing it. He didn't know what though. He could only think of a funny film he had once seen in which a man, sitting on a branch, sawed away at the bit between him and the tree trunk, necessarily falling off himself when the branch fell. But Mr Liddon wasn't sitting on anything. He was just sawing up a fallen tree from the crown to the bole. The saw sliced through again, making four short logs now as well as the bole.

'Cut along now, you boys,' he said. 'You don't want to waste the day mooning about here.'

Flora looked up and winked at Pringle. It wasn't unkind, just conspiratorial, and she smiled too, holding up a small glowing red glass bottle for him to see. He and John and Hodge moved slowly off, reluctantly, dawdling because the walk ahead would be boring and long. Through the horse tails, up the bank, looking back when the saw whined again.

But Pringle wasn't actually looking when it happened. None of them was. They had had their final look and had begun to trudge up the lane. The sound made them turn, a kind of swishing lurch and then a heavy plopping, sickening, dull crash. They cried out, all three of them, but no one else did, not Flora or Mr Liddon. Neither of them made a sound.

Mr Liddon was standing with his arms held out, his mouth open and his eyes staring. The pile of logs lay beside him but the tree trunk

509

was gone, sprung back roots and all when the last saw cut went through, tipped the balance and made its base heavier than its top. Pringle put his hand over his mouth and held it there. Hodge, who was nothing more than a fat baby really, had begun to cry. Fearfully, slowly, they converged, all four of them, on the now upright tree under whose roots she lay.

The police came and a farmer and his son and some men from round about. Between them they got the tree over on its side again but by then Flora was dead. Perhaps she died as soon as the bole and the mass of roots hit her. Pringle wasn't there to see. Mr Liddon had put the plantation out of bounds and said they were to stay in camp until someone came to drive them to the station. It was Michael Porter who turned up in the late afternoon and checked they'd got everything packed up and the camp site tidied. He told them Flora was dead. They got to the station in his Land-Rover in time to catch the five-fifteen for London.

On the way to the station he didn't mention the bottle dump he had told them about. Pringle wondered if Mr Liddon had ever said anything to Flora about it. All the way home in the train he kept thinking of something odd. The first time he went up the lane to the camp that morning he was sure there hadn't been any glass in the tree crater. He would have seen the gleam of it and he hadn't. He didn't say anything to John and Hodge, though. What would have been the point?

Three years afterwards Pringle's parents got an invitation to Mr Liddon's wedding. He was marrying the daughter of a wealthy local builder and the reception was to be at Fen Hall, the house in the wood. Pringle didn't go, being too old now to tag about after his parents. He had gone off trees anyway.

Father's Day

Teddy had once read in a story written by a Victorian that a certain character liked 'to have things pleasant about him'. The phrase had stuck in his mind. He too liked to have things pleasant about him.

It was to be hoped that pleasantness would prevail while they were all away on holiday together. Teddy was beginning to be afraid they might get on each other's nerves. Anyway, it would be the last time for years the four of them would be able to go away in October for both Emma and Andrew started school in the spring.

'A pity,' Anne said, 'because May and October are absolutely the best times in the Greek Islands.'

She and Teddy had bought the house with the money Teddy's mother had left him. The previous year they had been there twice and again last May. They hadn't been able to go out in the evenings because they had no babysitter. Having Michael and Linda there would make it possible for each couple to go out every other night.

'If Michael will trust us with his children,' said Teddy.

'He isn't as bad as that.'

'I didn't say he was bad. He's my brother-in-law and I've got to put up with him. He's all right. It's just that he's so nuts about his kids I sometimes wonder how he dares leave them with their own mother when he goes to work.'

He was recalling the time they had all spent at Chichester in July and how the evening had been spoilt by Michael's insisting on phoning the baby-sitter before the play began, during the interval and before they began the drive home. And when he wasn't on the phone or obliged to be silent in the theatre he had talked continually about Andrew and Alison in a fretful way.

'He's under a lot of stress,' Linda had whispered to her sister. 'He's going through a bad patch at work.'

Teddy didn't think it natural for a man to be so involved with his children. He was fond of his own children, of course he was, and anxious enough about them when he had cause, but they were little still and, let's face it, sometimes tiresome and boring. He looked forward to the time when they were older and there could be real companionship. Michael was more like a mother than a father, a mother hen. Teddy, for his sins, had occasionally changed napkins and made up feeds but Michael actually seemed to enjoy doing these things and talking about them afterwards. Teddy hoped he wouldn't be treated to too much Dr Jolly philosophy while on Stamnos.

Just before they went, about a week before, Valerie Wilton's marriage broke up. Valerie had been at school with Anne, though just as much Linda's friend, and had written long letters to both of them, explaining everything and asking for their understanding. She had gone off with a man she met at her Commercial French evening class. Apparently the affair had been going on for a long time but Valerie's husband had known nothing about it and her departure had come to him as a total shock. He came round and poured out his troubles to Anne and drank a lot of scotch and broke down and cried. For all Teddy knew, he did the same at Linda's. Teddy stayed out of it, he didn't want to get involved. Liking to have things pleasant about him, he declined gently but firmly even to discuss it with Anne.

'Linda says it's really upset Michael,' said Anne. 'He identifies with George, you see. He's so emotional.'

'I said I wasn't going to talk about it, darling, and by golly I'm not!'

During the flight Michael had Alison on his lap and Andrew in the seat beside him. Anne remarked in a plaintive way that it was all right for Linda. Teddy saw that Linda slept most of the way. She was a beautiful girl – better-looking than Anne, most people thought, though Teddy didn't – and now that Michael was making more money had bought a lot of new clothes and was having her hair cut in a very stylish way. Teddy, who was quite observant, especially of attractive things, noted that recently she had stopped wearing trousers. He looked appreciatively across the aisle at her long slim legs.

They changed planes at Athens. It was a fine clear day and as the aircraft came in to land you could see the wine jar shape of the island from which it took its name. Stamnos was no more than twenty miles long but the road was poor and rutted, winding up and down over low olive-clad mountains, and it took over an hour for the car to get to Votani at the wine jar's mouth. The driver, a Stamniot, was one of those Greeks who spend their youth in Australia before returning home to start a business on the money they have made. He talked all the way in a harsh clattering Greek-Strine while his radio played bouzouki music and Alison whimpered in Michael's arms. It was hot for the time of year.

Tim, who was a bad traveller, had been carsick twice by the time they reached Votani. The car couldn't go up the narrow flagged street, so they had to get out and carry the baggage, the driver helping with a case in each hand and one on his head. Michael didn't carry a case because he had Andrew on his shoulders and Alison in his arms.

The houses of Votani covered a shallow conical hill so that it looked from a distance like a heap of pastel-coloured pebbles. Close to, the buildings were neat, crowded, interlocking, hung with jasmine and bougainvillea, and the hill itself was surmounted by the ruins, extravagantly picturesque, of a Crusaders' fortress. Teddy and Anne's house was three fishermen's cottages that its previous owner had converted into one. It had a lot of little staircases on account of being built on the steep hillside. From the bedroom where the four children would sleep you could see the eastern walls of the fortress, a dark blue expanse of sea, and smudgy on the horizon, the Turkish coast. The dark came quickly after the sun had gone. Teddy, when abroad, always found that disconcerting after England with its long protracted dusks.

Within an hour of reaching Votani he found himself walking down the main street – a stone-walled defile smelling of jasmine and lit by lamps on iron brackets – towards Agamemnon's Bar. He felt guilty about going out and leaving Anne to put the children to bed. But it had been Anne's suggestion, indeed Anne's insistence, that he should take Michael out for a drink before supper. A whispered colloquy had established they both thought Michael looked 'washed out' (Anne's expression) and 'fed up' (Teddy's) and no wonder, the way he had been attending to Andrew's and Alison's wants all day.

Michael had needed a lot of persuading, had at first been determined to stay and help Linda, and it therefore rather surprised Teddy when he began on a grumbling tirade against women's liberation.

'I sometimes wonder what they mean, they're not "equal",' he said. 'They have the children, don't they? We can't do that. I consider that makes them *superior* rather than inferior.'

'I know I shouldn't like to have a baby,' said Teddy irrelevantly.

'It's because of that,' said Michael as if Teddy hadn't spoken, 'that we need to master them. We have to for our own sakes. Where should we be if they had the babies and the whip hand too?'

Teddy said vaguely that he didn't know about whip hand but someone had said that the hand which rocks the cradle rules the world. By this time they were in Agamemnon's, sitting at a table on the vine-covered terrace. The other customers were all Stamniots, some of whom recognized Teddy and nodded at him and smiled. Most of the tourists had gone by now and all but one of the hotels were closed for the winter. Hedonistic Teddy, wanting to have things pleasant about him, hadn't cared for the turn the conversation was taking. He began telling Michael how amused he and Anne had been when they found that the proprietor of the bar was called after the great hero of classical antiquity and how ironical it had seemed, for this Agamemnon was small and fat. Here he was forced to break off as stout smiling Agamemnon came to take their order.

Michael had no intention of letting him begin once more on the subject of Stamniot names. He spoke in a rapid violent tone, his thin dark face pinched with intensity.

'A man can lose his children any time and through no fault of his own. Have you ever thought of that?'

Teddy looked at him. Notions of kidnapping, of mortal illness, came into his head. 'What do you mean?'

'It could happen to you or me, to any of us. A man can lose his children overnight and he can't do a thing about it. He may be a good faithful husband, a good provider, a devoted father – that won't make a scrap of difference. Look at George Wilton. What did George do wrong? Nothing. But he lost his children just the same. One day they were living with him in his house and the next they were in Gerrards Cross with Valerie and that Commercial French chap and he'll be lucky if he sees them once a fortnight.'

'I see what you're getting at,' said Teddy. 'He couldn't look after them though, could he? He's got to go to work. I mean, I see it's unfair, but you can't take kids away from their mother, can you?'

'Apparently not. But you can take them from their father.'

'I shouldn't worry about one isolated case if I were you,' said Teddy, feeling very uncomfortable. 'You want to forget that sort of thing while you're here. Unwind a bit.'

'An isolated case is just what it isn't. There's someone at work, John Frost, you don't know him. He and his wife split up – at her wish, naturally – and she took their baby with her as a matter of course. And George told me the same thing happened in his brother's marriage a couple of years back. Three children he had, he lived for

514

his children, and now he gets to take them to the zoo every other Saturday.'

'Maybe,' said Teddy who had his moments of shrewdness, 'if he'd lived for his wife a bit more it wouldn't have happened.'

He was glad to be back in the house. In bed that night he told Anne about it. Anne said Michael was an obsessional person. When he'd first met Linda he'd been obsessed by her and now it was Andrew and Alison. He wasn't very nice to Linda these days, she'd noticed, he was always watching her in an unpleasant way. And when Linda had suggested she take the children up to the fortress in the morning if he wanted to go down to the harbour and see the fishing boats come in, he had said:

'No way am I going to allow you up there on your own with my children.'

Later in the week they all went. You had to keep your eye on the children every minute of the time, there were so many places to fall over, fissures in the walls, crumbling corners, holes that opened on to the empty blue air. But the view from the eastern walls, breached in a dozen places, where the crag fell away in an almost vertical sweep to a beach of creamy-silver sand and brown rocks, was the best on Stamnos. You could see the full extent of the bay that was the lip of the wine jar and the sea with its scattering of islands and the low mountains of Turkey behind which, Teddy thought romantically, perhaps lay the Plain of Troy. The turf up here was slippery, dry as clean combed hair. No rain had fallen on Stamnos for five months. The sky was a smooth mauvish-blue, cloudless and clear. Emma and Andrew, the bigger ones, ran about on the slippery turf, enjoying it because it was slippery, falling over and slithering down the slopes.

Teddy had successfully avoided being alone with Michael since their conversation in the bar but later that day Michael caught him. He put it that way to himself but in fact it was more as if, unwittingly, he had caught Michael. He had gone down to the grocery store, had bought the red apples, the feta cheese and the olive oil Anne wanted, and had passed into the inner room which was a secondhand book-store and stuffed full with paperbacks in a variety of European languages discarded by the thousand tourists who had come to Votani that summer. The room was empty but for Michael who was standing in a far corner, having taken down from a shelf a novel whose title was its heroine's name.

'That's a Swedish translation,' said Teddy gently.

'Oh, is it? Yes, I see.'

'The English books are all over here.'

Michael's face looked haggard in the gloom of the shop. He didn't tan easily in spite of being so dark. They came out into the sunlight, Teddy carrying his purchases in the string bag, pausing now and then to look down over a wall or through a gateway. Down there the meadows spread out to the sea, olives with the black nets laid under them to catch the harvest, cypresses thin as thorns. The shepherd's dog was bringing the flock in and the sheep bells made a distant tinkling music. Michael's shadow fell across the sunlit wall.

'I was off in a dream,' said Teddy. 'Beautiful, isn't it? I love it. It makes me quite sad to think we shan't come here in October again for maybe – what? Twelve or fourteen years?'

'I can't say it bothers me to have to make sacrifices for the sake of my children.'

Teddy thought this reproof uncalled for and he would have liked to rejoin with something sharp. But he wasn't very good at innuendo. And in any case before he could come up with anything Michael had begun on quite a different subject.

'The law in Greece has relaxed a lot in the past few years in favour of women – property rights and divorce and so on.'

Teddy said, not without a spark of malice, 'Jolly good, isn't it?'

'Those things are the first cracks in the fabric of a society that lead to its ultimate breakdown.'

'*Our* society hasn't broken down.'

Michael gave a scathing laugh as if at the naivety of this comment. 'Throughout the nineteenth century,' he said in severe lecturing tones, 'and a good deal of this one, if a woman left her husband the children stayed with him as a matter of course. The children were never permitted to be with the guilty party. And there was a time, not so long ago, when a man could use the law to compel his wife to return to him.'

'You wouldn't want that back, would you?'

'I'll tell you something, Teddy. There's a time coming when children won't have fathers – that is, it won't matter who your father is any more. You'll know your mother and that'll be enough. That's the way things are moving, no doubt about it. Now in the Middle Ages men believed that in matters of reproduction the woman was merely the vessel, the man's seed was what made the child. From that we've come full circle, we've come to the nearly total supremacy of women and men like you and me are reduced to – mere temporary agents.'

Teddy said to Anne that night, 'You don't think he's maybe a bit mad, do you? I mean broken down under the strain?'

'He hasn't got any strain here.'

'I'll tell you the other thing I was wondering. Linda's not up to anything, is she? I mean giving some other chap a whirl? Only she's all dressed up these days and she's lost weight. She looks years younger. If she's got someone that would account for poor old Michael, wouldn't it?'

It was their turn to go out in the evening and they were on their way back from the Krini Restaurant, the last one on the island to remain open after the middle of October. The night was starry, the moon three-quarters of a glowing white orb.

'There has to be a reason for him being like that. It's not normal. I don't spend my time worrying you're going to leave me and take the kids.'

'Is that what it is? He's afraid Linda's going to leave him?'

'It must be. He can't be getting in a tizzy over George Wilton's and Somebody Frost's problems.' Sage Teddy nodded his head. 'Human nature isn't like that,' he said. 'Let's go up to the fort, darling. We've never been up there by moonlight.'

They climbed to the top of the hill, Teddy puffing a bit on account of having had rather too much ouzo at the Krini. In summer the summit was floodlit but when the hotels closed the lights also went out. The moonlight was nearly as bright and the turf shone silver between the black shadows made by the broken walls. The Stamniots were desperate for rain now the tourist season was over, for the final boost to swell the olive crop. Teddy went up the one surviving flight of steps into the remains of the one surviving tower. He paused, waiting for Anne. He looked down but he couldn't see her.

'The Aegean's not always calm,' came her voice. 'Down here there's a current tears in and out like a mill race.'

He still couldn't see her, peering out from his look-out post. Then he did – just. She was silhouetted against the purplish starriness.

'Come back!' he shouted. 'You're too near the edge!'

He had made her jump. She turned quickly and at once slipped on the turf, going into a long slide on her back, legs in the air. Teddy ran down the steps. He ran across the turf, nearly falling himself, picked her up and hugged her.

'Suppose you'd fallen the other way?'

The palms of her hands were pitted with grit, in places the skin broken, where she had ineffectually made a grab at the sides of the fissure in the wall. 'I wouldn't have fallen at all if you hadn't shouted at me.'

At home the children were all asleep, Linda in bed but Michael still up. There were two empty wine bottles on the table and three glasses. A man they had met the night before in Agamemnon's had come in to have a drink with them, Michael said. He was German, from Heidelberg, here on his own for a late holiday.

'He was telling us about his divorce. His wife found a younger man with better job prospects who was able to offer Werner's children a swimming pool and riding lessons. Werner tried to kill himself but someone found him in time.'

What a gloomy way to spend an evening, thought Teddy, and was trying to find something cheerful to say when a shrill yell came from the children's room. Teddy couldn't for the life of him have said which one it was but Michael could. He knew his Alison's voice and in he went to comfort her. Teddy made a face at Anne and Anne cast up her eyes. Linda came out of her bedroom in her dressing gown.

'That awful man!' she said. 'Has he gone? He looks like a toad. Why don't we seem to know anyone any more who hasn't got a broken marriage?'

'You know us,' said Teddy.

'Yes, thank God.'

Michael took his children down to the beach most mornings. Teddy took his children to the beach too and would have gone to the bay on the other side of the headland except that Emma and Tim wanted to be with their cousins and Tim started bawling when Teddy demurred. So Teddy had to put up a show of being very pleased and delighted at the sight of Michael. The children were in and out of the pale clear green water. It was still very hot at noon.

'Like August,' said Teddy. 'By golly, it's a scorcher here in August.'

'Heat and cold don't mean all that much to me,' said Michael.

Resisting the temptation to say Bully for you or I should be so lucky or something on those lines, Teddy began to talk of plans for the following day, the hire car to Likythos, the visit to the monastery with the Byzantine relics and to the temple of Apollo. Michael turned on him a face so wretched, so hag-ridden, the eyes positively screwed up with pain, that Teddy who had been disliking and resenting him with schoolboy indignation was moved by pity to the depths of himself. The poor old boy, he thought, the poor devil. What's wrong with him?

'When Andrew and Alison are with me like they are now,' Michael began in a low rapid voice, 'it's not so bad. I always have that feeling, you see, that I could pick them up and run away with them and hide them.' He looked earnestly at Teddy. 'I'm strong, I'm young still. I could easily carry them both long distances. I could hide them. But there isn't anywhere in the civilized world you can hide for long, is there? Still, as I say, it's not so bad when they're with me, when there are just the three of us on our own. It's when I have to go out and leave them with *her*. I can't tell you how I feel going home. All the way in the train and walking up from the station I'm imagining going into that house and not hearing them, just silence and a note on the mantelpiece. I dread going home, I don't mind telling you, Teddy, and yet I long for it. Of course I do. I long to see them and know they're there and still mine. I say to myself, that's another day's reprieve. Sometimes I phone home half a dozen times in the day just to know she hasn't taken them away.'

Teddy was aghast. He didn't know what to say. It was as if the sun had gone in and all was cold and comfortless and hateful. The sea glittered, it looked hard and huge, an enemy.

'It hasn't been so bad while we've been here,' said Michael. 'Oh, I expect I've been a bore for you. I'm sorry about that, Teddy, I know what a misery I am. I keep thinking that when we get home it will all start again.'

'Has Linda then . . . ?' Teddy stammered. 'I mean, Linda isn't . . . ?'

Michael shook his head. 'Not yet, not yet. But she's young too, isn't she? She's attractive. She's got years yet ahead of her – years of torture for me, Teddy, before my kids grow up.'

Anne told Teddy she had spoken to Linda about it. 'She never looks at another man, she wouldn't. She's breaking her heart over Michael. She lost weight and bought those clothes because she felt she'd let herself go after Alison was born and she ought to try and be more attractive for him. This obsession of his is wearing her out. She wants him to see a psychiatrist but he won't.'

'The trouble is,' said Teddy, 'there's a certain amount of truth behind it. There's method in his madness. If Linda met a man she liked and went off with him – I mean, Michael could drive her to it if he went on like this – she *would* take the children and Michael *would* lose them.'

'Not you too!'

'Well, no, because I'm not potty like poor old Michael. I hope I'm a reasonable man. But it does make you think. A woman decides her marriage doesn't work any more and the husband can lose his kids, his home and maybe half his income. I mean if I were twenty-five again and hadn't ever met you I might think twice about getting married, by golly, I might.'

Their last evening it was Anne and Teddy's turn to baby-sit for Michael and Linda. They were dining with Werner at the Hotel Daphne. Linda wore a green silk dress, the colour of shallow sea water.

'More cosy chat about adultery and suicide, I expect,' said Teddy. Liking to have things pleasant about him, he settled himself with a large ouzo on the terrace under the vine. 'I shan't be altogether sorry to get home. And I'll tell you what. We could come at Easter next year, in Emma's school hols.'

'On our own,' said Anne.

Michael came in about ten. He was alone. Teddy saw that the palms of his hands were pitted as if he had held on to the rough surface of something stony. Anne got up.

'Where's Linda?'

He hesitated before replying. A look of cunning of the kind sane people's expressions never show spread over his face. His eyes shifted along the terrace, to the right, to the left. Then he looked at the palm of his right hand and began rubbing it with his thumb.

'At the hotel,' he said. 'With Werner.'

Anne cottoned on before he did, Teddy could see. She took a step towards Michael.

'What on earth do you mean, with Werner?'

'She's left me. She's going home to Germany with him tomorrow.'

'Michael, that just isn't true. She can't stand him, she told me so. She said he was like a toad.'

'Yes, she did,' said Teddy. 'I heard her say that.'

'All right, so she isn't with Werner. Have it your own way. Did the children wake up?'

'Never mind the children, Michael, they're OK. Tell us where Linda is, please. Don't play games.'

He didn't answer. He went back into the house, the bead curtain making a rattling swish as he passed through it. Anne and Teddy looked at each other.

'I'm frightened,' Anne said.

'Yes, so am I, frankly,' said Teddy.

The curtain rattled as Michael came through, carrying his children,

Andrew over his shoulder, Alison in the crook of his arm, both of them more or less asleep.

'I scraped my hands on the stones up there,' he said. 'The turf's as slippery as glass.' He gave Anne and Teddy a great wide empty smile. 'Just wanted to make sure the children were all right, I'll put them back to bed again.' He began to giggle with a kind of triumphant relief. 'I shan't lose them now. She won't take them from me now.'

The Green Road to Quephanda

There used to be, not long ago, a London suburban line railway running up from Finsbury Park to Highgate, and further than that for all I know. They closed it down before I went to live at Highgate and at some point they took up the sleepers and the rails. But the track remains and a very strange and interesting track it is. There are people living in the vicinity of the old line who say they can still hear, at night and when the wind is right, the sound of a train pulling up the slope to Highgate and, before it comes into the old disused station, giving its long, melancholy, hooting call. A ghost train, presumably, on rails that have long been lifted and removed.

But this is not a ghost story. Who could conceive of the ghost, not of a person but of a place, and that place having no existence in the natural world? Who could suppose anything of a supernatural or paranormal kind happening to a man like myself, who am quite unimaginative and not observant at all?

An observant person, for instance, could hardly have lived for three years only two minutes from the old station without knowing of the existence of the line. Day after day, on my way to the Underground, I passed it, glanced down unseeing at the weed-grown platforms, the broken canopies. Where did I suppose those trees were growing, rowans and Spanish chestnuts and limes that drop their sticky black juice, like tar, that waved their branches in a long avenue high up in the air? What did I imagine that occasionally glimpsed valley was, lying between suburban back gardens? You may enter or leave the line at the bridges where there are always places for scrambling up or down, and at some actual steps, much overgrown, and gates or at least gateposts. I had been walking under or over these bridges (according as the streets where I walked passed under or over them) without ever asking myself what those bridges carried or crossed. It never even, I am sorry to say, occurred to me that there were rather a lot of bridges for a part of London where the only railway line, the Underground, ran deep in the bowels of the earth. I didn't think about them. As I walked under one of the brown brick tunnels I didn't look up to question its presence or ever once glance over a parapet. It was Arthur Kestrell who told me about the line, one evening while I was in his house.

Arthur was a novelist. I write 'was', not because he has abandoned his profession for some other, but because he is dead. I am not even sure whether one would call his books novels. They truly belong in that curious category, a fairly popular *genre*, that is an amalgam of science fiction, fairy tale and horror fantasy.

But Arthur, who used the pseudonym Blaise Fastnet, was no Mervyn Peake and no Lovecraft either. Not that I had read any of his books at the time of which I am writing. But Elizabeth, my wife, had. Arthur used sometimes to give us one of them on publication, duly inscribed and handed to us, presented indeed, with the air of something very precious and uniquely desirable being bestowed.

I couldn't bring myself to read them. The titles alone were enough to repel me: *Kallinarth, the Cloudling, The Quest of Kallinarth, Lord of Quephanda, The Grail-Seeker's Guerdon* and so forth. But I used somehow, without actually lying, to give Arthur the impression that I had read his latest, or I think I did. Perhaps, in fact, he saw through this, for he never enquired if I had enjoyed it or had any criticisms to make. Liz said they were 'fun', and sometimes – with kindly intent, I know – would refer to an incident or portion of dialogue in one of the books in Arthur's presence. 'As Kallinarth might have said,' she would say, or 'Weren't those the flowers Kallinarth picked for Valaquen when she woke from her long sleep?' This sort of thing only had the effect of making poor Arthur blush and look embarrassed. I believe that Arthur Kestrell was convinced in his heart that he was writing great literature, never perhaps to be recognized as such in his lifetime but for the appreciation of posterity. Liz, privately to me, used to call him the poor man's Tolkien.

He suffered from periods of black and profound depression. When these came upon him he couldn't write or read or even bring himself to go out on those marathon walks ranging across north London which he dearly loved when he was well. He would shut himself up in his Gothic house in that district where Highgate and Crouch End merge, and there he would hide and suffer and pace the floors, not answering the door, still less the telephone until, after five or six days or more, the mood of wretched despair had passed.

His books were never reviewed in the press. How it comes about that some authors' work never receives the attention of the critics is a mystery, but the implication, of course, is that it is beneath their notice. This ignoring of a new publication, this bland passing over with neither a smile nor a sneer, implies that the author's work is a mere commercially motivated repetition of his last book, a slight variation on a tried and lucrative theme, another stereotyped bubbler in a long line of profitable pot-boilers. Arthur, I believe, took it hard. Not that he told me so. But soon after Liz had scanned the papers for even a solitary line to announce a new Fastnet publication, one of these depressions of his would settle on him and he would go into hiding behind his grey, crenellated walls.

Emerging, he possessed for a while a kind of slow cheerfulness combined with a dogged attitude to life. It was always a pleasure to be with him, if for nothing else than the experience of his powerful and strange imagination whose vividness coloured those books of his, and in conversation gave an exotic slant to the observations he made and the opinions he uttered.

London, he always insisted, was a curious, glamorous and sinister city, hung on slopes and valleys in the north of the world. Did I not understand the charm it held for foreigners who thought of it with wistfulness as a grey Eldorado? I who had been born in it couldn't see its wonders, its contrasts, its wickednesses. In summer Arthur got me to walk with him to Marx's tomb, to the house where Housman wrote *A Shropshire Lad*, to the pond in the Vale of Health where Shelley sailed boats. We walked the Heath and we walked the urban woodlands and then one day, when I complained that there was nowhere left to go, Arthur told me about the track where the railway line had used to be. A long green lane, he said, like a country lane, four and a half miles of it, and smiling in his cautious way, he told me where it went. Over Northwood Road, over Stanhope Road, under Crouch End Hill, over Vicarage Road, under Crouch Hill, under Mount View, over Mount Pleasant Villas, over Stapleton Hall, under Upper Tollington Park, over Oxford Road, under Stroud Green Road, and so to the station at Finsbury Park.

'How do you get on to it?' I said.

'At any of the bridges. Or at Holmesdale Road. You can get on to it from the end of my garden.'

'Right,' I said. 'Let's go. It's a lovely day.'

'There'll be crowds of people on a Saturday,' said Arthur. 'The sun will be bright like fire and there'll be hordes of wild people and their bounding dogs and their children with music machines and tinned drinks.' This was the way Arthur talked, the words juicily or dreamily enunciated. 'You want to go up there when it's quiet, at twilight, at dusk, when the air is lilac and you can smell the bitter scent of the tansy.'

'Tomorrow night then. I'll bring Liz and we'll call for you and you can take us up there.'

But on the following night when we called at Arthur's house and stood under the stone archway of the porch and rang his bell, there was no answer. I stepped back and looked up at the narrow latticed windows, shaped like inverted shields. This was something which, in these circumstances, I had never done before. Arthur's face looked back at me, blurred and made vague by the dark, diamond-paned glass, but unmistakably his small wizened face, pale and with its short, sparse beard. It is a disconcerting thing to be looked at like this by a dear friend who returns your smile and your mouthed greeting with a dead, blank and unrecognizing stare. I suppose I knew then that poor Arthur wasn't quite sane any more. Certainly Liz and I both knew that he had entered one of his depressions and that it was useless to expect him to let us in.

We went off home, abandoning the idea of an exploration of the track that evening. But on the following day, work being rather slack at that time of the year, I found myself leaving the office early and getting out of the tube train at Highgate at half-past four. Liz, I knew, would be out. On an impulse, I crossed the street and turned into Holmesdale Road. Many a time, walking there before, I had noticed what seemed an unexpectedly rural meadow lying to the north of the street, a meadow overshadowed by broad trees, though no more than fifty yards from the roar and stench of the Archway Road. Now I understood what it was. I walked down the slope, turned south-eastwards where the meadow narrowed and came on to a grassy lane.

It was about the width of an English country lane and it was bordered by hedges of buddleia on which peacock and small tortoise-shell butterflies basked. And I might have felt myself truly in the country had it not been for the backs of houses glimpsed all the time between the long leaves and the purple spires of the buddleia bushes. Arthur's lilac hour had not yet come. It was windless sunshine up on the broad green track, the clear, white light of a sun many hours yet from setting. But there was a wonderful warm and rural, or perhaps I should say pastoral, atmosphere about the place. I need Arthur's gift for words and Arthur's imagination to describe it properly and that I don't have. I can only say that there seemed, up there, to be a suspension of time and also of the hurrying, frenzied bustle, the rage to live, that I had just climbed up out of.

I went over the bridge at Northwood Road and over the bridge at Stanhope Road, feeling ashamed of myself for having so often walked unquestioningly *under* them. Soon the line began to descend, to become a valley rather than a causeway, with embankments on either side on which grew small, delicate birch trees and the rosebay willow herb and the giant hogweed. But there were no tansy flowers, as far as I could see. These are bright yellow double daisies borne in clusters on long stems and they have the same sort of smell as chrysanthemums. For all I know, they may be a sort of chrysanthemum or belonging to that family. Anyway, I couldn't see any or any lilac, but perhaps Arthur hadn't meant that and in any case it wouldn't be in bloom in July. I went as far as Crouch End Hill that first time and then I walked home by road. If I've given the impression there were no people on the line, this wasn't so. I passed a couple of women walking a labrador, two boys with bikes and a little girl in school uniform eating a choc ice.

Liz was intrigued to hear where I had been but rather cross that I hadn't waited until she could come too. So that evening, after we had had our meal, we walked along the line the way and the distance I had been earlier and the next night we ventured into the longer section. A tunnel blocked up with barbed wire prevented us from getting quite to the end but we covered nearly all of it and told each other we very likely hadn't missed much by this defeat.

The pastoral atmosphere disappeared after Crouch End Hill. Here there was an old station, the platforms alone still remaining, and under the bridge someone had dumped an old feather mattress – or plucked a dozen geese. The line became a rubbish dump for a hundred yards or so and then widened out into children's playgrounds with murals – and graffiti – on the old brick walls.

Liz looked back at the green valley behind. 'What you gain on the swings,' she said, 'you lose on the roundabouts.' A child in a rope seat swung past us, shrieking, nearly knocking us over.

All the prettiness and the atmosphere I have tried to describe was in that first section, Highgate station to Crouch End Hill. The next time I saw Arthur, when he was back in the world again, I told him we had explored the whole length of the line. He became quite excited.

'Have you now? All of it? It's beautiful, isn't it? Did you see the foxgloves? There must be a mile of foxgloves up there. And the mimosa? You wouldn't suppose mimosa could stand an English winter and I don't know of anywhere else it grows, but it flourishes up there. It's sheltered, you see, sheltered from all the frost and the harsh winds.'

Arthur spoke wistfully as if the frost and harsh winds he referred to were more metaphorical than actual, the coldness of life and fate and time rather than of climate. I didn't argue with him about the mimosa, though I had no doubt at all that he was mistaken. The line up there was exposed, not sheltered, and even if it had been, even if it had been in Cornwall or the warm Scilly Isles, it would still have been too cold for mimosa to survive. Foxgloves were another matter, though I hadn't seen any, only the hogweed with its bracts of dirty white flowers, garlic mustard and marestail, burdock and rosebay, and the pale leathery leaves of the coltsfoot. As the track grew rural again, past Mount View, hawthorn bushes, not mimosa, grew on the embankment slopes.

'It belongs to Haringey Council.' Arthur's voice was always vibrant with expression and now it had become a drawl of scorn and contempt. 'They want to build houses on it. They want to plaster it with a great red sprawl of council houses, a disfiguring red naevus.' Poor Arthur's writing may not have been the effusion of genius he seemed to believe, but he certainly had a gift for the spoken word.

That August his annual novel was due to appear. Liz had been given an advance copy and had duly read it. Very much the same old thing, she said to me: Kallinarth, the hero-king in his realm composed of cloud; Valaquen, the maiden who sleeps, existing only in a dream-life, until all evil has gone out of the world; Xadatel and Finrael, wizard and warrior, heavenly twins. The title this time was *The Fountains of Zond*.

Arthur came to dinner with us soon after Liz had read it, we had three other guests, and while we were having our coffee and brandy I happened to say that I was sorry not to have any Drambuie as I knew he was particularly fond of it.

Liz said, 'We ought to have Xadatel here, Arthur, to magic you some out of the fountains of Zond.'

It was a harmless, even rather sympathetic, remark. It showed she knew Arthur's work and was conversant with the properties of these miraculous fountains which apparently produced nectar, fabulous elixirs or whatever was desired at a word from the wizard. Arthur, however, flushed and looked deeply offended. And afterwards, in the

527

light of what happened, Liz endlessly reproached herself for what she had said.

'How were you to know?' I asked.

'I should have known. I should have understood how serious and intense he was about his work. The fountains produced – well, holy waters, you see, and I talked about it making Drambuie . . . Oh, I know it's absurd, but he *was* absurd, what he wrote meant everything to him. The same passion and inspiration – and muse, if you like, affected Shakespeare and Arthur Kestrell, it's just the end product that's different.'

Arthur, when she had made that remark, had said very stiffly. 'I'm afraid you're not very sensitive to imaginative literature, Elizabeth,' and he left the party early. Liz and I were both rather cross at the time and Liz said she was sure Tolkien wouldn't have minded if someone had made a gentle joke to him about Frodo.

A week or so after this there was a story in the evening paper to the effect that the Minister for the Environment had finally decided to forbid Haringey's plans for putting council housing on the old railway line. The Parkland Walk, as the newspaper called it. Four and a half miles of a disused branch of the London and North-Eastern Railway, was the way it was described, from Finsbury Park to Highgate and at one time serving Alexandra Palace. It was to remain in perpetuity a walking place. The paper mentioned wild life inhabiting the environs of the line, including foxes. Liz and I said we would go up there one evening in the autumn and see if we could see a fox. We never did go, I had reasons for not going near the place, but when we planned it I didn't know I had things to fear.

This was August, the end of August. The weather, with its English vagaries, had suddenly become very cold, more like November with north winds blowing, but in the last days of the month the warmth and the blue skies came back. We had received a formal thank-you note for that dinner from Arthur, a few chilly lines written for politeness' sake, but since then neither sight nor sound of him.

The Fountains of Zond had been published and, as was always the case with Arthur's, or Blaise Fastnet's, books, had been ignored by the critics. I supposed that one of his depressions would have set in, but nevertheless I thought I should attempt to see him and patch up this breach between us. On 1 September, a Saturday, I set off in the afternoon to walk along the old railway line to his house.

I phoned first, but there was no answer. It was a beautiful afternoon and Arthur might well have been sitting in his garden where he couldn't hear the phone. It was the first time I had ever walked to his house by this route, though it was shorter and more direct than by road, and the first time I had been up on the Parkland Walk on a Saturday. I soon saw what he had meant about the crowds who used it at the weekends. There were teenagers with transistors, giggling schoolgirls, gangs of slouching youths, mobs of children, courting couples, middle-aged picnickers. At Northwood Road boys and girls were leaning against the parapet of the bridge, some with guitars, one with a drum, making enough noise for a hundred.

I remember that as I walked along, unable because of the noise and the press of people to appreciate nature or the view, that I turned my thoughts concentratedly on Arthur Kestrell. And I realized quite suddenly that although I thought of him as a close friend and liked him and enjoyed his company, I had never even tried to enter into his feelings or to understand him. If I had not actually laughed at his books, I had treated them in a light-hearted cavalier way, almost with contempt. I hadn't bothered to read a single one of them, a single page of one of them. And it seemed to me, as I strolled along that grassy path towards the Stanhope Road bridge, that it must be a terrible thing to pour all your life and soul and energy and passion into works that are remaindered in the bookshops, ignored by the critics, dismissed by paperback publishers, and taken off library shelves only by those who are attracted by the jackets and are seeking escape.

I resolved there and then to read every one of Arthur's books that we had. I made a kind of vow to myself to show an interest in them to Arthur, to make him discuss them with me. And so fired was I by this resolve that I determined to start at once, the moment I saw Arthur. I would begin by apologizing for Liz and then I would tell him (without revealing, of course, that I had so far read nothing of his) that I intended to make my way carefully through all his books, treating them as an *oeuvre*, beginning with *Kallinarth, the Cloudling* and progressing through all fifteen or however many it was up to *The Fountains of Zond*. He might treat this with sarcasm, I thought, but he wouldn't keep that up when he saw I was sincere. My enthusiasm might do him positive good, it might help cure those terrible depressions which lately had seemed to come more frequently.

Arthur's house stood on this side, the Highgate side, of Crouch End Hill. You couldn't see it from the line, though you could get on to the line from it. This was because the line had by then entered its valley out of which you had to climb into Crescent Road before the

Crouch End Hill bridge. I climbed up and walked back and rang Arthur's bell but got no answer. So I looked up at those Gothic lattices as I had done on the day Liz was with me and though I didn't see Arthur's face this time, I was sure I saw a curtain move. I called up to him, something I had never done before, but I had never felt it mattered before, I had never previously had this sense of urgency and importance in connection with Arthur.

'Let me in, Arthur,' I called to him. 'I want to see you. Don't hide yourself, there's a good chap. This is important.'

There was no sound, no further twitch of curtain. I rang again and banged on the door. The house seemed still and wary, waiting for me to go away.

'All right,' I said through the letterbox. 'Be like that. But I'm coming back. I'll go for a bit of a walk and then I'll come back and I'll expect you to let me in.'

I went back down on to the line, meeting the musicians from Northwood bridge who were marching in the Finsbury Park direction, banging their drum and joined now by two West Indian boys with zithers. A child had been stung by a bee that was on one of the buddleias and an alsatian and a yellow labrador were fighting under the bridge. I began to walk quickly towards Stanhope Road, deciding to ring Arthur as soon as I got home, to keep on ringing until he answered.

Why was I suddenly so determined to see him, to break in on him, to make him know that I understood? I don't know why and I suppose I never will know, but this was all part of it, having some definite connection, I think, with what happened. It was as if, for those moments, perhaps half an hour all told, I became intertwined with Arthur Kestrell, part of his mind almost or he part of mine. He was briefly and for that one time the most important person in my world.

I never saw him again. I didn't go back. Some few yards before the Stanhope bridge, where the line rose once more above the streets, I felt an impulse to look back and see if from there I could see his garden or even see him in his garden. But the hawthorn, small birches, the endless buddleia grew thick here and higher far than a man's height. I crossed to the right hand, or northern, side and pushed aside with my arms the long purple flowers and rough dark leaves, sending up into the air a cloud of black and orange butterflies.

Instead of the gardens and backs of houses which I expected to see, there stretched before me, long and straight and raised like a causeway, a green road turning northwards out of the old line. This debouching occurred, in fact, at my feet. Inadvertently, I had parted the bushes at the very point where a secondary branch left the line, the junction now overgrown with weeds and wild shrubs.

I stood staring at it in wonder. How could it be that I had never noticed it before, that Arthur hadn't mentioned it? Then I remembered that the newspaper story had said something about the line 'serving Alexandra Palace'. I had assumed this meant the line had gone on to Alexandra Palace after Highgate, but perhaps not, definitely not, for here was a branch line, leading northwards, leading straight towards the palace and the park.

I hadn't noticed it, of course, because of the thick barrier of foliage. In winter, when the leaves were gone, it would be apparent for all to see. I decided to walk along it, check that it actually led where I thought it would, and catch a bus from Alexandra Palace home.

The grass underfoot was greener and far less worn than on the main line. This seemed to indicate that fewer people came along here, and I was suddenly aware that I had left the crowds behind. There was no one to be seen, not even in the far distance.

Which was not, in fact, so very far. I was soon wondering how I had got the impression when I first parted those bushes that the branch line was straight and treeless. For tall trees grew on either side of the path, oaks and beeches such as were never seen on the other line, and ahead of me their branches met overhead and their fine frondy twigs interlaced. Around their trunks I at last saw the foxgloves and the tansy Arthur had spoken of, and the further I went the more the air seemed perfumed with the scent of wild flowers.

The green road – I found myself spontaneously and unaccountably calling this branch line the green road – began to take on the aspect of a grove or avenue and to widen. It was growing late in the afternoon and a mist was settling over London as often happens after a warm day in late summer or early autumn. The slate roofs, lying a little beneath me, gleamed dully silver through this sleepy, gold-shot mist. Perhaps, I thought, I should have the good luck to see a fox. But I saw nothing, no living thing, not a soul passed me or overtook me, and when I looked back I could see only the smooth grassy causeway stretching back and back, deserted, still, serene and pastoral, with the mist lying in fine streaks beneath and beside it. No birds sang and no breeze ruffled the feather-light, golden, downy, sweet-scented tufts of the mimosa flowers. For, yes, there was mimosa here. I paused and looked at it and marvelled.

531

It grew on either side of the path as vigorously and luxuriantly as it grows by the Mediterranean, the gentle swaying wattle. Its perfume filled the air, and the perfume of the humbler foxglove and tansy was lost. Did the oaks shelter it from the worst of the frost? Was there by chance some warm spring that flowed under the earth here, in this part of north London where there are many patches of woodland and many green spaces? I picked a tuft of mimosa to take home to Liz, to prove I'd been here and seen it.

I walked for a very long way, it seemed to me, before I finally came into Alexandra Park. I hardly know this park, and apart from passing its gates by car my only experience of it till then had been a visit some years before to take Liz to an exhibition of paintings in the palace. The point in the grounds to which my green road had brought me was somewhere I had never seen before. Nor had I ever previously been aware of this aspect of Alexandra Palace, under whose walls almost the road led. It was more like Versailles than a Victorian greenhouse (which is how I had always thought of the palace) and in the oblong lakes which flanked the flight of steps before me were playing surely a hundred fountains. I looked up this flight of steps and saw pillars and arches, a soaring elevation of towers. It was to here then, I thought, right up under the very walls, that the trains had come. People had used the line to come here for shows, for exhibitions, for concerts. I stepped off on to the stone stairs, descended a dozen of them to ground level and looked out over the park.

London was invisible, swallowed now by the white mist which lay over it like cirrus. The effect was curious, something I had never seen before while standing on solid ground. It was the view you get from an aircraft when it has passed above the clouds and you look down on to the ruffled tops of them. I began to walk down over wide green lawns. Still there were no people, but I had guessed it likely that they locked the gates on pedestrians after a certain hour.

However, when I reached the foot of the hill the iron gates between their Ionic columns were still open. I came out into a street I had never been in before, in a district I didn't know, and there found a taxi which took me home. On the journey I remember thinking to myself that I would ask Arthur about this curious terminus to the branch line and get him to tell me something of the history of all that grandeur of lawns and pillars and ornamental water.

*

I was never to have the opportunity of asking him anything. Arthur's cleaner, letting herself into the Gothic house on Monday morning, found him hanging from one of the beams in his writing room. He had been dead, it was thought, since some time on Saturday afternoon. There was a suicide note, written in Arthur's precise hand and in Arthur's wordy, pedantic fashion: 'Bitter disappointment at my continual failure to reach a sensitive audience or to attract understanding of my writing has led me to put an end to my life. There is no one who will suffer undue distress at my death. Existence has become insupportable and I cannot contemplate further sequences of despair.'

Elizabeth told me that in her opinion it was the only review she had ever known him to have which provoked poor Arthur to kill himself. She had found it in the paper herself on that Saturday afternoon while I was out and had read it with a sick feeling of dread for how Arthur would react. The critic, with perhaps nothing else at that moment to get his teeth into, had torn *The Fountains of Zond* apart and spat out the shreds.

He began by admitting he would not normally have wasted his typewriter ribbon (as he put it) on sci-fi fantasy trash, but he felt the time had come to campaign against the flooding of the fiction market with such stuff. Especially was it necessary in a case like this where a flavour of epic grandeur was given to the action, where there was much so-called 'fine writing' and where heroic motives were attributed to stereotyped or vulgar characters, so that innocent or young readers might be misled into believing that this was 'good' or 'valuable' literature. There was a lot more in the same vein. With exquisite cruelty the reviewer had taken character after character and dissected each, holding the exposed parts up to stinging ridicule. If Arthur had read it, and it seemed likely that he had, it was no wonder he had felt he couldn't bear another hour of existence.

All this deflected my thoughts, of course, away from the green road. I had told Liz about it before we heard of Arthur's death and we had intended to go up there together, yet somehow, after that dreadful discovery in the writing room of the Gothic house, we couldn't bring ourselves to walk so close by his garden or to visit those places where he would have loved to take us. I kept wondering if I had really seen that curtain move when I had knocked at his door or if it had only been a flicker of the sunlight. Had he already been dead by then? Or had he perhaps been contemplating what he was about to do? Just as Liz reproached herself for that remark about the fountains, so I reproached myself for walking away, for not hammering on that door, breaking a window, getting in by some means. Yet, as I said to her, how could anyone have known?

In October I did go up on to the old railway line. Someone we knew living in Milton Park wanted to borrow my electric drill, and I walked over there with it, going down from the Stanhope Road bridge on the southern side. Peter offered to drive me back but it was a warm afternoon, the sun on the point of setting, and I had a fancy to look at the branch line once more, I climbed up on to the bridge and turned eastwards.

For the most part the leaves were still on the bushes and trees, though turning red and gold. I calculated pretty well where the turn-off was and pushed my way through the buddleias. Or I thought I had calculated well, but when I stood on the ridge beyond the hedge all I could see were the gardens of Stanhope Road and Avenue Road. I had come to the wrong place, I thought, it must be further along. But not much further, for very soon what had been a causeway became a valley. My branch line hadn't turned out of that sort of terrain, I hadn't had to climb to reach it.

Had I made a mistake and had it been on the *other* side of the Stanhope Road bridge? I turned back, walking slowly, making sorties through the buddleias to look northwards, but I couldn't anywhere find that turn-off to the branch line. It seemed to me then that, whatever I thought I remembered, I must in fact have climbed up the embankment to reach it and the junction must be far nearer the bridge at Crouch End Hill than I had believed. By then it was getting dark. It was too dark to go back, I should have been able to see nothing.

'We'll find it next week,' I said to Liz.

She gave me a rather strange look. 'I didn't say anything at the time,' she said, 'because we were both so upset over poor Arthur, but I was talking to someone in the Highgate Society and she said there never was a branch line. The line to Alexandra Palace went on beyond Highgate.'

'That's nonsense,' I said. 'I can assure you I walked along it. Don't you remember my telling you at the time?'

'Are you absolutely sure you couldn't have imagined it?'

'*Imagined it?* You know I haven't any imagination.'

Liz laughed. 'You're always saying that but I think you have. You're one of the most imaginative people I ever knew.'

I said impatiently, 'Be that as it may. I walked a good two miles along that line and came out in Alexandra Park, right under the palace, and walked down to Wood Green or Muswell Hill or somewhere and got a cab home. Are you and your Highgate Society friends saying I imagined oak trees and beech trees and mimosa? Look, that'll prove it, I picked a piece of mimosa, I picked it and put it in the pocket of my green jacket.'

'Your green jacket went to the cleaners last month.'

I wasn't prepared to accept that I had imagined or dreamed the green road. But the fact remains that I was never able to find it. Once the leaves were off the trees there was no question of delving about under bushes to hunt for it. The whole northern side of the old railway line lay exposed to the view and the elements and much of its charm was lost. It became what it really always was, nothing more or less than a ridge, a long strip of waste ground running across north London, over Northwood Road, over Stanhope Road, under Crouch End Hill, over Vicarage Road, under Crouch Hill, under Mount View, over Mount Pleasant Villas, over Stapleton Hall, under Upper Tollington Park, over Oxford Road, under Stroud Green Road, and so to the station at Finsbury Park. And nowhere along its length, for I explored every inch, was there a branch line running north to Alexandra Palace.

'You imagined it,' said Liz, 'and the shock of Arthur dying like that made you think it was real.'

'But Arthur wasn't dead then,' I said, 'or I didn't know he was.'

My invention, or whatever it was, of the branch line would have remained one of those mysteries which everyone, I suppose, has in his life, though I can't say I have any others in mine, had it not been for a rather curious and unnerving conversation which took place that winter between Liz and our friends from Milton Park. In spite of my resolutions made on that memorable Saturday afternoon, I had never brought myself to read any of Arthur's books. What now would have been the point? He was no longer there for me to talk to about them. And there was another reason. I felt my memory of him might be spoiled if there was truth in what the critic had said and his novels were full of false heroics and sham fine writing. Better feel with whatever poet it was who wrote:

I wept as I remembered how often you and I
Had tired the sun with talking and sent him down the sky.

Liz, however, had had her interest in *The Chronicles of Kallinarth* revived and had reread every book in the series, passing them on as she finished each to Peter and Jane. That winter afternoon in the living room at Milton Park the three of them were full of it, Kallinarth, cloud country, Valaquen, Xadatel, the lot, and it was they who tired the sun with talking and sent him down the sky. I sat silent, not really listening, not taking part at all, but thinking of Arthur whose house was not far from here and who would have marvelled to hear of this detailed knowledge of his work.

I don't know which word of theirs it was that caught me or what electrifying phrase jolted me out of my reverie so that I leaned forward, intent. Whatever it was, it had sent a little shiver through my body. In that warm room I felt suddenly cold.

'No, it's not in *Kallinarth, the Cloudling,*' Jane was saying. 'It's *The Quest of Kallinarth*. Kallinarth goes out hunting early in the morning and he meets Xadatel and Finrael coming on horseback up the green road to the palace.'

'But that's not the first mention of it. In the first book there's a long description of the avenue where the procession comes up for Kallinarth to be crowned at the fountains of Zond and . . .'

'It's in all the books surely,' interrupted Peter. 'It's his theme, his leitmotiv, that green road with the yellow wattle trees that leads up to the royal palace of Quephanda . . .'

'Are you all right, darling?' Liz said quickly. 'You've gone as white as a ghost.'

'White with boredom,' said Peter. 'It must be terrible for him us talking about this rubbish and he's never even read it.'

'Somehow I feel I know it without reading it,' I managed to say.

They changed the subject. I didn't take much part in that either, I couldn't. I could only think, it's fantastic, it's absurd, I couldn't have got into his mind or he into mine, that couldn't have happened at the point of his death. Yet what else?

And I kept repeating over and over to myself, he reached his audience, he reached his audience at last.

About the Author

Ruth Rendell, "the best mystery writer...anywhere in the English-speaking world" (*Boston Sunday Globe*), is the author of *Talking to Strange Men, Live Flesh, The New Girl Friend, An Unkindness of Ravens, The Tree of Hands, The Killing Doll, Speaker of Mandarin, The Fever Tree and Other Stories of Suspense, Master of the Moor, Death Notes, The Lake of Darkness, From Doon with Death, Sins of the Fathers, Wolf to the Slaughter, The Best Man to Die*, and many other mysteries. She now has five major awards for her work: two Edgars from the Mystery Writers of America for her short stories "The New Girl Friend" and "The Fallen Curtain"; *Current Crime*'s Silver Cup for the best British crime novel of 1975, *Shake Hands Forever*; the Crime Writers' Association's Golden Dagger for 1976's best crime novel, *A Demon in My View*; and the 1980 Arts Council National Book Award in Genre Fiction for *The Lake of Darkness*. Her books have been translated into fourteen languages. Ruth Rendell lives in Polstead, England.